As the full moon ~~...~~ ground almost at Aldric's feet. He flung himself backward without knowing how.

A face appeared above the valley rim, its jaw transmuting to a tapered muzzle even as he watched through shock-dilated eyes. The skull flattened; the ears became triangular, tufted and twitching; dark fur spread like ink across the pallid skin; fangs glimmered moistly as they sprouted from pink gums.

Aldric had never dreamed, even in his darkest nightmare, how intimate and how obscene the lycanthropic metamorphosis could be. . . .

The transformation had almost run its course now—but for just a moment the eyes remained unchanged, staring at him with a horrible pity; then intelligence was overwhelmed by another, more feral impulse.

Hunger . . . a blind, bestial instinct that sent this creature of dark and deadly magic in a howling leap straight for Aldric's throat!

The Book of Years Volume One:

The Horse Lord
The Demon Lord

The Book of Years Volume Two:

The Dragon Lord
The Warlord's Domain

THE BOOK OF YEARS
VOL 1

The Horse Lord
The Demon Lord

PETER MORWOOD

DAW BOOKS, INC.
DONALD A. WOLLHEIM, FOUNDER
375 Hudson Street, New York, NY 10014

ELIZABETH R. WOLLHEIM
SHEILA E. GILBERT
PUBLISHERS
www.dawbooks.com

First Printing, June 2005
1 2 3 4 5 6 7 8 9

DAW TRADEMARK REGISTERED
U.S. PAT. OFF. AND FOREIGN COUNTRIES
—MARCA REGISTRADA
HECHO EN U.S.A.

PRINTED IN THE U.S.A.

The Horse Lord

For my father,
who had to leave early.

With acknowledgment and thanks to:

Alastair Minnis and Diana Wynne Jones;
Charles Redpath and David Lavery;
Rosie Freel and Trish Burns;
and my mother and sister, who put up with it all.

Preface

". . . bye virtue of his lady wyfe.

In this yeare also, being but ye eighth of ERHAL-OVERLORDE his holding of his Seate in ye fortress of Cerdor, was there war and stryfe in ye north kingdomes through ye Malice and foul Usurpations of that Sorcerer since ynamen Kalarr cu Ruruc.

ERHAL-OVERLORDE having setten him forth with an hoste being of soche numberes as fyve thousandes of Horse and of Foote ten thousandes, he did bring defeate to his enemy and ruination utterly by force of armes at Baelen Fyghte.

But in that field did fall and perish ERHAL, most Noble and Gentle of LORDES (this of an Arrow betwixt ye Harness joyntes) and with him dyveres soche Honourable men as ykepen oath even unto Deathe, to ye numberes of seven thousandes both hygh and humble. And of hygh-clan yfallen are . . .

. . . And this is all their names that be yknowen slaine. Now to their sonnes hath ycomen fell Ambition wherebye each hath ycraven landes held of another for his own, and hath ytaken seizen of full many an halle and citadel each from another. Now indeed doth red War make of ALBA his dwelling-place to the dolour and exceeding Heaviness of all honest folke, and noble LORDES do slay those that were their hearth-friendes not four monthes agone.

May-be by HEAVENES grace this lande may be de-

livered from sore Travail, and by ITS Endeless Mercy
the people may be ysafen from blood and pestilence to
live again in Peace . . ."

Ylver Vlethanek an-Caerdur
The Book of Years, Cerdor

Prologue

Boots thudded in rotting vegetation, slapped in patches of slushy snow. As the sound grew, a solitary figure came stumbling through the forest gloom, slumped against a tree and then slid face-downwards into the dirt and wet dead leaves.

The runner was twenty years old and sick with fear. His tunic was open despite the chilly air, and the neck of a once-fine shirt hung loose. Sweat glistened on his face and body, sticking sodden clothing and tails of wet hair to his skin. The boy's chest heaved, veins beat in throat and temples and his whole frame quivered with exertion.

He listened, holding his breath and lying quite still in the clammy ooze of slime where he had fallen. At first there was nothing but the hesitant patter of raindrops and the slamming of his heart. Then he heard it—a soft, ponderous sound not quite drowned by the whisper of wind through autumn-bared branches. As it drew closer he clawed at the tree trunk, struggled upright and then fell back. Though his left shoulder barely touched the unyielding wood, he convulsed and an agonised moan escaped his clenched teeth. Around the arrow jutting obscenely from torn flesh, crusted stains grew slick and oily beneath a film of fresh blood.

The arrow had ceased to pain him hours ago when all feeling had left his arm, and he had almost forgotten its presence. Until now. He had forgotten, too, how long he had been running. There was only the dull realisation that his flight was almost over. Fatigue was spreading a seductive warmth through him like a drug—or a poison.

It invited sleep, stiffening his muscles even as he gulped the air which kept them working.

Lightning flickered, etching the world starkly black and white. Its thunder growled like some vast beast among the trees and nameless things scuttled slavering through his brain, sniffing the air for their quarry's scent. His scent. He fled again through a flurry of rain.

Something struck at his leg and he flinched wildly, almost tumbling headlong before realising it was his longsword. The weapon's straps had slackened, letting it swing free; another minute and it would have been lost. The boy fumbled to run his hand into the complex hilt. He dared not stop, yet his left arm was useless to halt the scabbard's crazy wavering. The blade was only half-drawn when he fell.

The storm was to blame. Great banks of cloud had drifted up in silence, then vented their fury directly over-head. Blinded and deafened, the fugitive did not even see the tree root which jerked both feet from under him. Raising his head painfully, he stared at the thing in his fist. Only a jagged splinter remained in the hilt—the rest of his finely tempered blade was gone. With a sound that was half sob and half curse he flung the remnant away and reeled on.

After another crash of thunder it began to rain in earnest, slashing sheets of water which drummed a knee-high haze from the ground. A tree loomed suddenly from the murk and raked crooked branches across his shoulder. The impact tore a ragged scream from his throat.

Whimpering with pain, he knew that the running had ended. Death hung at his hip; a shortsword for them . . . and a black *tsepan* dirk for himself. Its triple edges would be preferable to being taken back alive.

The boy straightened with an effort, choosing with pathetic pride to be found standing rather than grovelling in the mud. He fell twice, for the ground had been hammered into greasy mud by the downpour, but at last remained steady enough to draw the blade. He glanced down at the dirk, waiting loose in its sheath; there would be no dignity for its use, no ceremony or ancient ritual phrases. Just a hasty inward stab before they could lay hands upon him. But they would be cheated. He almost smiled bitterly at that. And then he waited, while the rain fell steadily. And while nothing else happened.

Even the curses he began to howl were swallowed up by a long rumble of receding thunder. As the courage of desperation ebbed away his shoulders drooped and at last he began to cry, softly, like a child.

Suddenly the boy stopped abruptly and wiped his face with one muddy sleeve. There was a feeling—a tingling deep within his brain—that he knew from previous experience. He was no longer alone. Panic welled up again, and he would have run if only he knew which way was safe.

Then a hand came out of the dark and gripped his injured arm. With a croaking gasp the boy lashed out and staggered away, but made only two swaying strides before his knees gave way and a deeper black than the night closed in around his eyes.

He did not hear the footsteps padding closer until they stopped beside his head . . .

1

Hunter's Moon

Autumn sunshine warmed Gemmel's whitewashed cottage and gilded its thatched roof, making him smile. In the fifty years since he had first come here, he had often compared the modest dwelling unfavourably with his other home under Glaselyu Menethen, the Blue Mountains dimly shading the western horizon. But on days like this such criticism was out of the question.

The locals called him *an-pestrior,* the wizard, and he was content to let them do so. There were no words in the Alban language—or in any other, for that matter— to adequately describe what he really was. Which, when he gave the matter thought, was just as well. Even so, over the past few years he had done little to warrant his title. Gemmel Errekren had retired from active sorcery . . . and he was bored.

One of a long-lived race, during his years of exile he had performed spells, travelled the known lands and some unknown as well, learned the martial arts of half a dozen kingdoms. He *had* . . . and there lay the problem. Everything had been done, was completed, past tense, and now ennui gripped him in soft and cloying paws.

The sun dipped behind a cloud and brought the old man out of his reverie with a yawn. He eyed the changing sky and decided it was time he prepared something to eat . . .

Outside was dark and blurred with rain, a curtain of drops briefly sparkling as they passed through the wash of lamplight from the cottage windows. Inside was snug and smelling of hot food as the master of the house, who could have stopped the storm had he chosen, sat down to his meal.

Gemmel stopped with a mug of ale halfway to his lips. The sound had reached his ears was nothing to do with any storm. It seemed more like the howling of a wolf, he reflected as he finished his drink. Then he set the cup down with a sharp little click and turned to stare out into the night. There were words in this wolf's howl.

The sorcerer's eyes flashed green in the lamp-glow and a smile tugged at the corners of his thin mouth as he stood up. Hung over the fireplace was his *athame,* an iron knife inlaid with silver runes and whetted to a razor edge. It was a weapon potent against any foe, human or . . . otherwise. There were other weapons too, but Gemmel ignored them with an effort. He had made a vow not to use such things without good reason, and even a possible werewolf was not sufficient justification for him to unclip them from their racks. Instead, as he stepped out into the rain-swept night he drew the *athame,* holding it point-up like a practised knife fighter. Which he was.

The howling continued barely long enough for him to guess its source. Then it faded away and the hiss of falling water filled his ears once more. Despite the deluge he moved slowly, ready with the *athame* or matter-ripping spells should anything spring from the darkness. Neither was required. Before long a new sound reached him and Gemmel stopped, eyes narrowing as he listened to the wretched, heartbroken sobbing that had no place here. He hesitated, then sheathed the knife and walked on, peering warily through the gloom.

Then he came upon a vague, ragged figure crying bitterly as the sky opened above him. Moved to pity, Gemmel put out one hand to lead the stranger back to his cottage—and almost lost fingers as a blade hacked feebly at them. The muddy-faced youngster choked and wrenched away, wide-eyed with such terror as the enchanter had seldom seen. Then he tried to run, but after two wobbly paces went down in a heap.

Gemmel blinked, then rubbed his hands together. They felt sticky, and when he glanced down there were dark smears across both palms. With a surge of strength ill-matching his venerable appearance he lifted the slack-limbed body and bore it carefully back to his house. At every stride he felt warm blood soaking through his sleeve.

*

The wizard's guest lay on a hastily cleared table while Gemmel boiled water and rummaged for long-forgotten jars and bottles. Cutting away the boy's clothing, he swore softly when he saw what attempts to free the arrow had done to an originally clean puncture. The old man cursed again, damning the oversight that had left his proper healing materials back under the mountains. Then he shrugged and resigned himself to making the best of what means were at hand.

As he washed after dropping some instruments into the boiling water, a groan made him turn round. The youngster's eyes were open, wide and white in a mask of bloodied mud. "Get out!" he gasped. Weak though it was, his voice had a commanding edge that made Gemmel stare. "I'm being followed! I can't lose them. Get . . . *out,* you fool! Kill me clean . . . then . . . run . . ." The effort cost him dear, for his staring eyes unfocused and rolled shut as his lifted head dropped with an ugly thud to the table. With no reason to disbelieve him, Gemmel moved fast. Seizing a few items, he ran from the house. But not to hide—he was, after all, a wizard.

The rain had stopped as suddenly as it had begun and wind was shredding the remaining clouds. Instinct, mingled perhaps with a forlorn hope, raised the old man's gaze toward the remote glint of stars, searching . . . Then he snorted and marched around the cottage, muttering under his breath. At each compass-point he stopped, bowed, drew a sign in the air and flicked pinches of dust from the leather bags he carried. Both sign and dust glowed blue for an instant afterwards. At the front door he raised one hand and pronounced one of the lesser Charms of Concealment. As the spell took effect a bluish haze shimmered briefly, and though when it faded nothing had apparently changed, Gemmel breathed more easily. Now at least he would have enough time to patch up his visitor so that they could both get well out of the way. But charm or no charm, once inside he bolted the door. Twice.

Before long he had the arrow out, the wound bandaged after a fashion and his blanket-wrapped patient set in a chair by the fire. The wizard poured himself another drink with the feeling that he deserved it. Apart from where Gemmel had been working, the boy's skin and clothes were caked with muck until they were hard to tell apart. Knowing Albans perhaps better than they knew themselves, the sorcerer stoked his bath-house fire and turned the pine tub right-side-up.

When he reentered the front room, his guest's eyelids fluttered up, only to squeeze shut again as pain seared his torn back. Gemmel hastily offered him a wooden beaker. "Drink this," he instructed. "It should ease the effects of my surgery somewhat."

Obediently the young man put back its bitter contents in a single face-twisting gulp, and after a time felt the throbbing dwindle. He nodded gratefully. "Thanks . . . for the surgery as well." His wry little smile went crooked when a determined twinge worked through the drug. "If you will excuse my ill manners, I will not bow just yet."

"I will excuse you until you've rested," said Gemmel considerately.

"And bathed," the Alban put in. "I stink."

Gemmel grinned slightly. "Well, since you mention it . . ." he conceded. "But tell me something, if you would. Who are you?"

Suspicion welled up in the boy's grey-green eyes, turning them cold and flinty. "Who wants to know?" Something in the demand—it was no less—made Gemmel very glad he had thought to set any weapons out of reach.

"I do. The man who took a broken arrow from your back."

"Oh . . . I beg pardon—my rudeness was—"

"Understandable in the circumstances."

Despite the way it obviously hurt him, the boy insisted on making an awkward bow. Gemmel took note, wondering what he was going to hear. It wasn't anything he might have expected.

"Talvalin," the youngster said "*kailin-eir* Aldric." Even though he didn't look the part, Gemmel was convinced. Little things indicated a high rank: the excellent quality of shortsword and dirk; a tunic where heavy embroidery glinted gold wherever mud had dried sufficiently to flake away; something which might be a crest-collar showing now and then as its wearer moved. Only the hair was wrong, hacked crudely short instead of tied in a queue.

"So . . . Aldric-*eir,* you are safe in this house, and my guest. Though I cannot offer food after that drug, there's hot water in the bath-house and a spare bed. Feel free with both."

Aldric's face was puzzled under its mud. "Why are you doing this?" he asked finally.

"I have a kind heart." The wizard grinned toothily. "Go to bed, boy. You'll have more questions in the morning, and by then I shall feel more like answering them." Opening a jar, he mixed its contents with hot water and held up the potion. "This should help you sleep—and ensure some pleasant dreams."

It occurred to Aldric as he clumsily undressed that he had not asked his benefactor's name. Then he dismissed the matter and had as relaxing a bath as possible under the circumstances. Despite the drugs it hurt to move his arm, but actually to be clean again, to wash away the dirt and the sweat and the smell, was worth a few aches. When at last he crept under a thick down quilt, he fell asleep almost at once. Not so the wizard.

Glancing once towards the silent guest room, Gemmel put more logs on the fire and settled back into his cushioned chair. Mixed with the sleeping-draught was a generous pinch of *ymeth,* freezing Aldric's mind for probing by any wizard with the necessary skill. It was simple, fast, proof against lies—and gave both parties a splitting headache.

That was something Gemmel felt he could tolerate. He began to breathe evenly, and after a time his eyes went cold and dead, green crystals reflecting not even the dance of flames. Though the logs burned slowly, they had died under a film of ash before life returned to the old man's face.

By then he had learned all that he wanted to know.

*

There was an art to the use of *ymeth,* requiring great delicacy not to probe deeply and too slowly, yet not so shallowly and fast that facts were lost in the blurred recollections of another's brain. Gemmel was a master of that art.

At first there was only the beat of two hearts in a dark warmth. Then came light and cold and a kaleidoscopic whirl of colours. Faces focused and faded, voices swam together in a confusing babble, there were names meaning nothing and yet significant. Now and then the images of important memories grew clear, like an awareness of reality . . .

Swords glittered in sunlight. A voice issued crisp instructions. Steel grated, its shrillness deadened by the hot, heavy air. Blades met with harsh percussive music, again and again. These were fencing lessons.

Watched with sleepy amusement by his eldest brother Joren, Aldric went through the exercises of *taiken-ulleth,* the art of longsword fighting. It had once been an art in which blade and body, hand and heart and mind and eye all worked as one; but the last true master was more than two centuries in his funeral urn and *taikenin* were now just ordinary swords. Insofar as *taikenin* were ever merely "ordinary."

The boy was fourteen now, and in Joren's opinion very good—though he had not bothered to tell Aldric so, even after ten years' tuition. Praise was something hard-earned and not freely given. Nonetheless . . .

"That's enough for now." Joren waved away the soldier who had partnered Aldric's exercises, acknowledging the man's salute and his brother's bow with the same nod. Then he frowned as Aldric stuck his practice foil into the ground, and kept his stern expression until the blade had been withdrawn and sheathed with proper respect. Custom demanded the honourable treatment of honourable weapons, especially in practice where no true harm was meant.

"Joren," the word came out in a gasp as Aldric sank crosslegged on to the grass, "I would much rather swim. It's too hot for this."

"Later. You've another half-hour to go yet." Joren's

toe nudged lazily at his little brother. "And sit up straighter. Look neat."

In response Aldric flopped back and grinned, untidily comfortable, raking his fingers through the hair which, though short and boy's length as it would remain for six years, still fell into his eyes whenever possible. "When I'm a *kailin-eir* like you I'll be proper and correct, I promise. But while I can relax, I will."

Staring at him doubtfully, Joren touched his own warrior's queue and high-clan earbraids, then shrugged slightly. He had come of age and been made *kailin* only that spring, and in all fairness to the boy there were times when his insistence on propriety bordered on the obsessive. But he had his position to think of, as eldest son and heir to ranks and titles, while Aldric was merely third son and heir to very little.

"All right. No arguments then. But if you cannot look like a gentleman, let's at least see if you can fight like one."

"Difficult, I'd say," cut in a suave voice and Aldric's smile died. There had never been much affection between him and his other brother Baiart, Joren's twin. There was little love between the twins either. Twin, and yet second son—by all of five minutes. That twist of fate had twisted Baiart somewhat, ever since he became old enough to understand it.

"Manners!" reproved Joren in a soft voice which bore the merest hint of menace. Baiart stepped out of shadow into the full wash of sunlight. He was tall, blond and blue-eyed like his twin and four sisters, and though the light flattered his hair it did nothing for his expression. Aldric was the only one of seven children to carry his Elthanek mother's dark hair and grey-green eyes, as if she had given up those as well as her life when he was born. Baiart had always suspected there might be another reason, though he dared not say so. And he hated the child who had usurped Lady Linnoth's place in the family after killing her. His love for his mother had always been more intense than that of the others. Almost too intense for comfort, his or hers. But that also was never spoken of.

"Dear elder brother," he said with a mocking bow,

"I'm sure our little brother can speak for himself." If he had hoped to needle anyone into an unseemly outburst Baiart was disappointed. Then Aldric rose to his feet with feline grace.

"If you want to prove something, dear brother, I suggest you try it now. Here. With these." He extended the foils.

Baiart had spent most of his time at court in Cerdor, returning only at feast-days and when his allowance ran out, as now. Though aware that Aldric had learned *taiken*-play, he still had no idea how skilled the boy had become. Aldric knew of his ignorance; it was one of the reasons he had "allowed" the duel to apparently arrange itself in the first place. Baiart needed a lesson.

A formal Alban duel was totally unlike combat. Since the Clan Wars five hundred years before, when three-quarters of the ancient aristocracy had destroyed one another, it was illegal for *kailinin* to fight to the death except in war and raid—or with permission from their lord. Duelling foils were light, thrusting weapons, tipped with sharp spurs which did nothing worse than draw blood, and the movements were more of dance than duel.

What was fought that day under the shadow of Dunrath-hold's great citadel was no such cautious ritual. Saving only that the blades were blunt, it was the same whirl of cut-and-thrust which had characterised the fierce warrior clans for almost two millennia. Agile and swift, Aldric was able to score two quick points before Baiart grew wise and used his longer arm to keep the boy at a distance. Then he saw an opening for a thrust.

But instead Baiart cut with such force that, blunt sword or not, it would have ripped his brother's face apart had it been successful. Aldric felt the sting of skin peeling off his cheek even as he jerked his head aside. He retreated, shaken not by the insignificant wound but by Baiart's clear intention. And by something he had never met before—the feeling which had made him dodge. He hadn't ducked so fast because of training but because of the unsummoned warning inside his head, without which he would surely have been blinded. Knowledge of that made his temper foul; and Baiart's grin made it fouler yet.

The bigger man saw something in his brother's dark eyes that he did not like, and broke ground hastily. With blood bright across his face and shirt, Aldric shifted *taiken* to both hands and came after him. Joren saw the change of position and realised his pupil was no longer playing. He opened his mouth to shout, then realised that an interruption now could prove deadly—for someone.

When Baiart jabbed, a warning move to keep Aldric away, the other blade beat against his own so viciously that the weapon was almost knocked from his grasp. Aldric grinned the grin of a cat whose mouse is secure under one paw, just before the claws come out. Then he stamped and shouted both at once. This surprised Baiart enough for the boy to advance in a precise, gliding pass, reach out his left hand and wrench his brother's sword away.

His own blade thrust home with unnecessary force on Baiart's chest an instant later. With a painful grunt he held up both empty hands, signalling surrender. Aldric stared at him through slitted, feral eyes. "That, dear brother," he said very softly, "was to win." Touching fingertips to his face, he scowled at the blood on them, then suddenly swung his sword.

The horizontal cut was invisibly fast, savage and perfect. It hit Baiart across the waist, doubling him up; the same blow with a live blade would have sliced him to the spine and everyone present knew it. Except for the ugly sound of retching it was very quiet in the fortress gardens. Joren remembered that Aldric's name was seven centuries old in his mother's line, Elthanek rather than Alban. Every man who had borne it had been a warrior of the old style: a renowned and ruthless slayer.

Aldric slowly regained his breath and eyed Baiart with more sardonic mirth than any fourteen-year-old should have possessed. "But that," he smiled coldly, "was purely personal."

*

Haranil Talvalin was Clan-Lord, master of Dunrath and responsible for the king's peace in the north. Unlike many of his ancestors, who had often to cope with full-scale war, Haranil's foremost worry was cattle-reaving along the Elthanek border, and even that was more an over-rowdy sport than a conflict. There was occasionally much more trouble under his own roof.

Against all the odds, Aldric was growing up. His father's first step was to forbid the boy, on his honour, to fight needlessly. With such a charge laid on him, Aldric obeyed, keeping out of most duels—but not, of course, all. He fought often enough with hot-headed comrades for his skill to become notorious; at last it became difficult for him to find anyone willing to chance even the friendliest contest. Though he never lost his temper or his control, there hung about him an air of restrained violence that was disturbing.

There was one memorable episode in a seedy tavern of Radmur's old town, when somebody had suggested that, since young Aldric had not yet found himself a woman, he probably bedded with his broadsword. Aldric had not drunk enough to find the comment funny, and the escalating argument had broken two heads, several limbs, an uncounted number of ale barrels and had ended with the whole unsavoury den catching fire and toppling sideways into the canal.

He had been seventeen then, at five feet eight inches not very tall for a Talvalin though average for most Albans. Approaching his twentieth birthday, he was broader in chest and narrower in waist—but only an inch taller. That was not good, for the five remaining clans of the old nobility each had their hereditary distinguishing feature, strong enough at least in the male line to survive interclan marriages. Talvalins were invariably tall, blond and blue-eyed—except for Aldric. By the time he neared legal maturity any remarks on this had ceased, though not through fear of Talvalin displeasure even though the clan was notorious for its implacable avenging of insulted honour. Aldric's skill with a blade was reason enough.

He spent the early part of that year with one arm in a sling after falling from a galloping horse in full armour. Even before the arm had knitted he was back in the saddle. *Kailinin* relied on mobility, not brute force, and the subtleties of horsemanship were of paramount importance. Learning to control a mount with knees alone was difficult enough with hands clasped on head. Over jumps it became painful as well.

With work so intense, it was only reasonable that recreation should also take extreme forms. One such was the hunting of wild boar, using a spear from horseback. It was lively, often dangerous and therefore popular with the highborn youngsters; also with those old enough to know better . . .

*

Two riders picked their way carefully down an overgrown bridle-path, arguing as they went. The silence of autumnal woodland was disturbed only by their voices and by the distant belling tones of boar-hounds.

"I tell you he's escaped," drawled Aldric lazily. Joren slapped his saddlebow irritably with one hand and waved the other in a huge sweep which took in most of the forest and came very close to taking off the end of his brother's nose.

"Listen to the hounds! They've got him at bay somewhere!"

"Those yapping puppies would bark at their own shadows; you know that."

"At my age I should know when hounds are giving tongue and when they are not!"

Aldric remained calm with an effort. "And at your age you should know when you're in the wrong," he pointed out. Their wrangle was over a boar which had somehow evaded Joren's favourite thrust, and it was injured pride rather than the loss of his roast pork which made the big man so peevish. Aldric did not much care for pork, which explained his lack of interest. Also he enjoyed gently teasing his brother; it always proved rewarding. All at once the yelping died away and Aldric shot an "I-told-you-so" glance from the corner of one eye before lifting a horn from his belt.

"It's too late to start again," he said. "I'm calling the others in and then we'll go home, eh?" Joren expressed his opinion in several crude syllables and began easing his horse round in the confined space of the path. Suddenly a cry went up away to the left and with it the renewed baying of hounds. Joren saw Aldric's face and laughed aloud, then jabbed heels to his steed's flanks and crashed off through the undergrowth, whooping as he went. Aldric rolled despairing eyes heavenward, then shrugged, put the horn away and followed—rather more cautiously.

The scene was familiar enough; dogs raved in a semi-circle round the base of a tree, while horsemen fussed and fidgeted behind them. Their quarry hunched almost invisible in the shadows between a fork of roots, huge and black with a drool of froth hanging from his champing tusks. The boar regarded them with mad red eyes, secure in his defensive redoubt and quite content to wait for his antagonists to make the first move. His wait proved to be short.

When cries of encouragement failed to move the hounds, one hunter used his spear-butt. The beasts snarled and one twisted to snap at the iron-shod ash wood. Through this opening the boar came charging like a bristled thunderbolt, chopping one of the hounds as he passed before sidestepping a clumsy jab and shooting away with the hunt hot after him. As the bracken gave way to open woodland the speed of the chase increased, heedless of the low branches which scraped an occasional rider from his saddle.

The forest ended abruptly in a smooth valley, dotted with clumps of gorse and carpeted with poppies. The setting sun glared across it, making everyone blink and slow down. All except the boar. Instead of crossing the valley he fled along its rim in an attempt to double back, only to find stragglers emerging from the woods all along his escape route. And still he tried to avoid running in the obvious direction. A thrown spear changed his mind; faced with immediate death or the strange fear welling from the valley, he galloped over the ridge and began to descend the slope.

The hounds' baying stopped in mid-cry, while that of their masters redoubled as horses reared, wild-eyed and whinnying. Neither soft words nor hard blows would induce them to enter the valley. Normally fierce hounds backed off with tails curled to their bellies and hackles bristling. Adding to the hunters' rage was the boar; no longer pursued, he slowed to an insolent amble and then stopped with a piggy sneer seeming to curve his chops.

"What in hell's the matter?" snarled Aldric, his coolness slipping. He thumped his stamping, sidling horse. "Why won't this brute follow that one?"

"Sorcery," said Joren flatly. "And I don't know why it's here," he put in quickly as Aldric's mouth opened for the inevitable question. "This is an ancient part of the forest."

As Joren spoke, his brother looked around with dark un-Talvalin eyes wide with curiosity. That same curiosity had driven him to read many of the writings which lay forgotten in Dunrath's great library, and had given him knowledge beyond that offered by his most liberal-minded tutors. "It was here before the fortress was built," Joren continued, "though mother's people were here even before that. You'd better read the Archive when we get back."

"And leave the boar?" Aldric's imagination landed, returning him to reality. "Not I!" He favoured the beast with a thoughtful glance.

"The horses won't . . ." began Joren, then stopped as Aldric dismounted. "Idiot! We haven't cross-head spears—he'll come right up the shaft to get at you."

"Let him try," grinned Aldric, but the grin was a little thin and stretched. Drawing a heavy falchion from its sheath under one saddleflap, he thumbed the edge, nodded and strapped the weapon to his belt. Joren made a disbelieving noise and then exploded.

"What the hell d'you think you're doing?" he blazed. "You're not impressing anyone . . . ! Light of Heaven, if you get killed what am I to tell father?"

"You'll think of something," mocked Aldric gently.

"I . . . just be careful." Joren playfully ruffled his youngest brother's hair and Aldric flinched away. It was *kailin*-length now, and he was close enough to the *Eskor-rethen* ceremony to resent its being touched by another warrior. No *kailin* put hand to another's queue except to lift his severed head. That was a tradition old enough to be almost law.

Then he regretted the hasty move and smiled crookedly up at Joren. "Me, careful? But surely, aren't I al-

ways?" He hefted his spear, loosened the falchion in its
sheath and walked down towards the boar. The animal
watched him, snapping its tusks nastily as he continued
to advance.

Then it charged.

Aldric dropped to one knee, spear braced, and let the
boar run straight onto its levelled point. As Joren had
said, the creature came on up the shaft as if nothing had
happened, but by that time the boy had let go his spear,
sidestepped quickly and drawn the falchion. Its wide blade
lifted, hovered and whipped down across the boar's thick
neck even as Aldric skidded and fell flat. Even so, he
was in no danger. With its head half off the boar was
down and dead before its slayer could pick himself up.
Aldric shook his head, feeling foolish. There was a lot
of blood and its coppery stink clogged his nostrils, making him sick and giddy. His head buzzed inside and the
walls of his mouth went dry and sour.

Then he shuddered violently and stared about him.
For a few ugly seconds the valley had become a battlefield, the ground scarlet not with poppies but with gore,
strewn with corpses in ancient, ornate armour hacked
and torn with fearful wounds. He rubbed his eyes and
the fit was past. A skylark chirruped faintly high up in
the blue dusk, and things were all so ordinary now that
Aldric thought he had been dreaming. But looking at
the carcass he felt more than willing to leave without it.

He lost his chance when the others came running and
sliding down the slope, bubbling with congratulations
and good-humoured banter. When they started the butch-
ery Aldric retreated hastily. Then a hound whined and
licked his hand. Dogs and horses alike had followed
their masters into the valley as if they had never feared
it. Odd . . . Aldric shook his head again, to clear it of
confusion this time, and looked across to the far slope.
A few hazy mist-patches trailed like forgotten scarves
along the ground, ghostly pale against the shadows.
Remnants of sunset glowed amber behind the trees sil-
houetted blackly on the skyline. Aldric sighed and sat
down.

With a yelp he sprang up again, rubbing an injured

rump. There were no trees nearby, so the offending object could hardly be a root. He kicked at it irritably, but when something shifted under the turf he looked more closely. Then his eyebrows went up and he dug the object free with falchion and fingers. It was a sword-hilt, in the blocky, massive style not made since the Clan Wars so long ago. He had seen one before in Dunrath; horseman's weapons both, as the chained pommels and wrist-bands bore witness. They were constructed so that, if the weapon was knocked from its owner's hand in battle, with the band around his wrist at least his sword was not lost underfoot. There was something strange about this rusty remnant of someone's forgotten battle, something Aldric could not at first pin down. Although the weapon had been lying out under the sky for years uncounted, and was deeply corroded, it was still in passable condition for something which one would have expected to have been entirely eaten away.

Aldric recalled his hallucination, wondering now if it was anything so simple. Before *an Mergh-Arlethen,* the Horse Lords, came out of the sea mist to claim Alba for their own, Cernuek and Elthanek scholars had already been writing history, legend and plain gossip for an age and an age. But some things they had not written. These survived only as tales told in winter by the great log fires, stories for children and the credulous. Or truths no one dared to believe.

A wolf howled balefully among the distant trees and Aldric's fingers clenched the ancient hilt. He scowled, both at the display of nerves and at the beast which should have been miles further north at this time of year. Making a mental note to organise another hunt, he moved the hilt towards one of his hunting-jerkin's deep pockets. Then an odd thing happened: between one heartbeat and the next, he lost all interest in the relic. If it had not been easier to complete the pocketing movement, he would have dropped it back on to the ground, and even so he had forgotten the hilt's existence before it had completely slithered out of sight.

As he mounted up, Aldric's mind wandered down macabre lanes, the back alleys of imagination. He recalled

stories read, overheard or gloatingly told by Baiart when
they were both much younger. Stories of men who, willing or not, became beasts at the full of the moon.

He sat back in the lofty Alban saddle—then shivered
involuntarily. Just visible through the eastern trees was
a disk which shone like a newly minted mark: the full
moon. Wiping chilly moisture from hands and face, Aldric laughed hollowly at having worked himself into such
a state.

Joren, laden with joints of boar, overheard the laugh
and gave him a strange look, but witheld other comment.
Stars had appeared before they were ready to leave, and
as the moon rose further it washed woods and valley
with a frosty sheen. Aldric felt cold, and as the others
rode off he gladly turned his horse to follow. Then he
jerked on the reins and stood up in his stirrups.

A fragment of shadow had detached itself from the
forest and was flitting from one gorse-clump to the next.
Without reason the fine hair on Aldric's arms and neck
stood on end. There was a crossbow hanging in a loop
by his knee, and he reached for the weapon's cool walnut stock as if seeking comfort from its weight. He had
had enough irrationalities for one night; at least the bow
was heavy, solid and real. Spanning and loading it, he
strained his eyes to see what the lean shadow might be.
He thought he knew already.

He was right: a monstrous wolf, its grey coat tipped
silver by the moonlight, came padding up the slope. It
ignored the dark patch where the boar had been cut
up—most unwolflike and suspicious, had Aldric been noticing such things—and made for the small patch of disturbed earth where something had recently been exhumed.
Aldric frowned slightly as a faint memory nagged him
for a moment, but could recall nothing of importance.
Whimpering eagerly the wolf began to dig, carefully at
first and then with increasing frenzy until soil flew in all
directions. Then abruptly it stopped and raised its long
muzzle in a wary sniff.

Downwind, and invisible under the trees, Aldric levelled his bow, hoping the uncertain light would not spoil
his shot. Taking a deep breath he set finger to trigger,
noting absently how the beast's eyes reflected the moon,

glowing like tiny bluish candles. They seemed almost to be watching him; ridiculous of course, or the creature would have run long ago.

Just before he tripped the sear a low, rumbling snarl reached his ears and the wolf crouched, not to flee but to pounce. A beast of that size could have him out of the saddle in two bounds and a snap . . .

"Aldric!" Both boy and wolf started and the crossbow went off, its bolt flinging the animal backwards in a squirming heap. Wood snapped as it bit the missile from a hind leg and rose unsteadily, blazing eyes fixed on Aldric as if etching his shocked face into its memory. Then Joren came trotting up, the younger man glanced towards him and when they both looked back the wolf was gone.

"What's the matter with you?" After hurrying back in case his little brother had fallen foul of roots or hanging branches, Joren was none too pleased to find him shooting at shadows. "Well?"

"Nothing," Aldric replied, far too quickly. "Nothing at all."

Joren eyed him narrowly. "Does 'nothing' usually make you sweat like a wash-house window?" he asked rather more gently. Aldric realised with clammy distaste that his whole body was damp and cold, and he tugged a shirtsleeve away from sticky skin.

"I saw a wolf down there," he explained lamely. Joren blinked.

"Oh, did you? I think I heard one earlier, but . . . Pity you missed it—if it was there at all."

Aldric coloured. "It was! And I didn't miss!"

"Then where's the body?"

"I . . . it ran off when you appeared . . ."

"As I said—pity you missed." There was something in Joren's tone of voice which stopped any further protests. "Now come on home, or you'll catch a chill."

Aldric stared doubtfully across the valley one last time, then shrugged and did as he was told.

2

Rites of Passage, Rites of Blood

On an evening some five weeks later, the great feast-hall at Dunrath was filled with music and ablaze with light made brilliant by the shifting hues of *elyu-dlasen,* the formal Colour-Robes of the Alban clans. It was Aldric's twentieth birthday, his coming of age, and Haranil-*arluth* was making an occasion of it, inviting relatives and friends to the least degree. He was even willing to welcome total strangers.

"My lord?" The *arluth* looked up to where his steward had appeared silently by his chair. The man bowed low. "There is a man at the gatehouse, my lord. He craves shelter."

"So?" Although travellers were unusual at this season, it was equally unusual to be told of their arrival. Normally they were simply admitted with courtesy, since such hospitality was expected by the fortress-lord. Looking uncomfortable, the steward bowed again, twitchily.

"My lord, he will not come in." Haranil raised his brows at that. "You must invite him across the threshold yourself, it seems. He says it is a custom of his country, and only polite that a host should see what guest enters his home."

The lord groaned softly; he was very comfortable where he was, but in such circumstances a refusal was out of the question. Signalling those at his immediate table to remain seated, he rose, shrugged into an over-mantle and strode out. Returning alone some minutes later, he met a quizzical glance from Joren.

"He's changing into more suitable clothing," the *ar-*

luth explained. "A very courteous gentleman—unlike some." His gaze touched an empty chair; Baiart had refused to attend the feast.

When the guest eventually appeared, he proved arresting enough to mute conversation for several seconds. Not that he was impressive in himself, being stocky, round-headed and balding. What little hair he retained over his ears, and the small beard framing his thin lips, was brindled silvery grey like a wolfhound or a wolf. But his clothing was in stark contrast. Over unassuming grey trimmed with silver fur he wore an over-robe of royal quality, ankle-length and pure white lined with azure. Its stiffly embroidered surface rustled when he knelt to give Haranil Talvalin the respect proper to his rank.

"Gracious good my lord," he said, somehow projecting a murmur clearly from the door, "may the warmth of hospitality be always in the hearth of this house." Haranil acknowledged the compliment with a nod and indicated Baiart's empty seat. As the stranger moved to take it he limped, wincing and favouring his left leg before sitting down with an air of relief. Seeing the lord's concern he patted the limb and smiled.

"My horse and I argued with a tree, lord—I lost." Then his smile was replaced by a concerned expression. "But your pardon! Here I sit at your table, nameless." Putting one hand over his heart, he spread the other wide. "Duergar Vathach, an indifferent scholar and historian, very much at your service." His eyes glittered as he smiled again; they were the palest blue Haranil had ever seen, and seldom blinked.

The scholar's slight accent and occasional difficulty with Alban didn't prevent him from talking virtually all the time he was not eating. It would have been most unmannerly had his conversation been boring, but he spoke entertainingly about every subject raised at the lord's high table. Except for one put forward by Aldric.

"Duergar-*an,* did you come south from Datherga?" The pale eyes stared at him, and Aldric noticed how the man's face went cold and sinister when he forgot to smile. Actually, Duergar was trying to decide whether this young man merited a title.

"Sir, you are . . . ?" he ventured cautiously. Aldric inclined his head politely.

"*Kailin-eir* Aldric *un-cseir* Haranil-*arluth* Talvalin. Third son." He rather enjoyed saying that—it was the first time he had chanced giving anyone his full rank and title and it sounded good. Duergar concealed slight surprise, then realised that he was after all seated at the lord's high table.

"No, my lord—I came by Elmisford and Baelen Forest." Aldric leaned forward eagerly.

"Did you see or hear any wolves—wounded, irritable wolves?"

"I confess I did not, my lord. Is it important?"

"I shot one over a month ago; it was never caught. Certain people"—he stared hard at Joren—"would say, and have said, that I missed. At that sort of range I don't miss, so the brute's wounded and dangerous. I want it found before someone gets hurt." He caught an odd expression on the scholar's face and stopped. "You disapprove?"

"Well, yes," Duergar admitted. "You don't know who the wolf might have been." His grin was stillborn as an awkward silence fell on those who had overheard.

"That," said old Lord Dacurre, "is not amusing." Farther down the hall, rowdy normality continued with such gusto that the silence became painful. When Duergar stood up and bowed, very low, someone cleared his throat and began to talk again, the uneasy moment forgotten.

Two retainers set a carved stool on the gallery of the great stairway and the murmur of voices died to an expectant whispering. An old, white-bearded man was helped to his seat and a harp of black wood was put into his hands. He made obeisance towards the high table and spoke in a resonant voice, thick with a Hertan burr.

"Gracious good my lords and ladies fair," he said, "I would have your leave to sing." With equal formality Haranil-*arluth* and Lord Santon's wife granted him that leave, and he sat down with a smile. The old man did not begin at once; he ran one finger across his harp, stroking a rippling chord from the strings. The hall fell silent as he played a liquid melody, long fingers flickering delicately across the instrument. As the old bard plucked the harp's strings, he also began to touch the hearts of his listeners.

He played of sunrise and spring, courage and love and laughter, the sheen of swords and maidens' golden hair; he played of the wind in the trees, the waves on the sea, of luck and the joy of living. Then he began to sing at last, and though older than any in the hall, his voice still filled its every corner with cunning music and subtle words.

He sang the old stories of magic and adventure, when lean firedrakes flicked flaming across the sunlit sky and sorcerers worked their spells by starlight. He sang of battles lost and won and the love of kings' daughters for brave strangers. Archaic names sprinkled his songs like rare jewels, and earlier ages flowed from his music in a golden haze of memories. Long-forgotten voices spoke again through the harper's mouth, captains and kings and beautiful ladies who returned from the dust to live for a space, warmed by the suns of past summers.

The old Hertan struck three crystal notes which shimmered to silence in the vast hall, and bowed his head. There was a pause and then his audience erupted, most un-Alban, into waves of applause. Haranil had the old man brought before his chair, where he filled a guardsman's high-crowned helm with golden deniers and placed it in the harper's hands. Then he unclasped a ring of massy Pryteinek gold from his wrist and snapped it shut about the minstrel's arm. This was something more personal than mere wages and the old man knew it. He traced the deeply-incised crests on the wrist-band and bent his head deeply in gratitude. They were the Talvalin spread eagle, set within the double border of a Clan-Lord; such tokens would greatly increase his fame, for they were never presented lightly.

"*Arr' eth-an,* a question for you," Aldric said quietly, giving the old man his proper title. "Have you heard any tale about Baelen Forest—and a valley filled with dead men's bones?" He was conscious of curious stares, for until now he had made no mention of what he had— or thought he had—seen after the hunt. There had been sparse mention of a battle in earlier Archive volumes, but no details either there or anywhere else in an exhaustively searched library. Although Aldric did not admit it even to himself, the experience had worried him. Thus his willingness to try any other source, and thus his mixed emotions when the harper replied.

"I know that legend, lord. It is called 'The Fall of Kalarr cu Ruruc.' " He paused and studied Aldric with eyes blue as faded cornflowers. "It is not a tale for this occasion. Your pardon, lord, but I will not sing that song tonight." His departure was marked by Haranil-*arluth*'s bow to honour him, an action which by custom the entire hall must copy. It served at least to mask the expression of slight horror which rested briefly on Aldric's face.

Only Duergar noticed it. "An interesting story, lord, even though untrue," he pointed out. Aldric's mouth shaped a silent "Oh?" at him and the historian started to explain. By accident or design his lecture was complex, boring and obscure, so that before long Aldric had stopped paying any attention whatsoever and was regretting he had ever raised the subject.

Kalarr had been a sorcerer in the days before the Clan Wars, when Alba had been divided into petty kingdoms whose rulers paid only lip service to the dominion of their Overlord. It was a situation bubbling with intrigue, as the lesser lords plotted their own advancement. None could say from whence Kalarr cu Ruruc had come; he simply *was*. At first the sorcerer made pretence of aiding the conspirators until such time as he could get them all in one place under his eye. That day came at a feast in his citadel of Ut Ergan, where he slew his allies with fire from the air and seized their lands for his own.

The Overlord, undeceived by soft words, gathered his warriors and rode north to destroy the usurper. Cu Ruruc's army was broken utterly in Baelen Forest and the sorcerer himself was cut down. But the Overlord and many of his nobles were also slain, which by the succession of their ambitious sons led directly to the Clan Wars and all that followed.

Aldric had read these bare bones before, but worse than learning nothing new was the way Duergar talked down to him as if he was a child. At length the rather haughty youngster yawned—a slow, exaggerated and supremely insolent yawn like a cat's. Duergar stopped in mid-sentence. "Do I bore you, dear my lord?" he enquired silkily.

"In a word, yes. I'm twenty years old, man, yet you treat me like an infant. I do not like that." Duergar's smile was beginning to set his teeth on edge, and when the scholar made several benevolent noises as if to a squalling baby, Aldric's temper flared.

"Duergar-*an,* I dislike your manner, your condescension and your smile," he said, and though his voice remained soft and pleasant, thinned lips and narrowed eyes gave ample indication of his feelings. "In short, historian, I dislike you! Good evening." Rising without a bow of courtesy, he stalked away.

Without even blinking Duergar watched him go, then smiled a slow smile to himself and drank more wine with satisfaction.

Aldric was seething inwardly, at himself this time. He had broken one of the many customs surrounding high-clan *kailinin* by showing both boredom and irritation to a guest. It made him look foolish. It made him lose face. It made him damned angry!

He was saved from further brooding by the retainer, who appeared before him with the information that everything was ready for his coming-of-age ceremony. Regaining control of himself, he followed the servant out of the hall to be prepared for the rituals.

*

Kneeling before his father, Aldric bowed until his forehead touched the ground between his hands. It was the only time in his life he would be expected to give First Obeisance to anyone other than royalty, and he took care to do it correctly. Then he sat back on his heels, took the Book of Ancestors from *yscop* Gyreth, bowed to the priest and pressed the ancient holy relic to his brow. From Lord Dacurre's hands he received his father's *taiken,* unsheathed a handspan of blade and touched that cold, keen metal lightly to his lips, careful not so much of the weapon's age as of its edge.

Haranil Talvalin rose from his seat, laid both hands on his son's head and swept up the hair at the back.

Uncut for six months except to keep it neat, it fell at
once into the queue which Haranil secured with a crested
clip. Though some clans required that the full head of
hair be put in queue, this single tail had sufficed for
more than twenty generations of Talvalin warriors.

After that the lord pulled free the long locks Aldric
had kept anchored over and behind his ears, letting them
fall one along each cheek to the jaw-hinge. Then he
stepped back and bowed as one warrior to another. Aldric acknowledged with forehead against hands crossed
on the floor, Second Obeisance, from a *kailin-eir* to his
lord. Then he stood up, bowed as an equal and spoke the
oath which would bind him from this moment onward.

"I am *kailin-eir* Aldric Talvalin," he said in a clear
voice. "Know me, and know I have a Word of Binding.
On it I swear now to keep the laws of Heaven and the
King, that my name and ancestors be not dishonoured.

"I do also swear to keep true the honour of my House
and Clan, even to the ending of my life.

"I lastly swear to be the king's liege man, to live and
die as may best serve him. Under Heaven and upon my
Word, I do truly swear."

Everyone present bowed respectfully when he had
finished speaking. When they straightened, Joren looped
the shoulder-belt of a sword about his brother's neck,
taking care not to touch his hair, then fastened a silver
crest-collar around his throat and made way for Lord
Santon.

Aldric's mouth went a little dry—not because of the
warlord's sinister appearance, his *elyu-dlas* of purple and
dark blue contrasting with the pale skin of all the Santon
clan, but because of the slender rod he bore so carefully
in both hands. Lacquered a hard, intense black, it was
capped at either end with silver. Santon moved his hands
and the rod broke in two, revealing a five-inch triple-
edged stiletto blade, toylike and glittering, sharp as a
needle. An icicle of steel. A *tsepan*.

Now it was a badge of rank and a piece of masculine
jewellery, its materials of the very finest for the sake of
the wearer's honour. But it remained an echo of the
older, harsher codes which once laid down both the liv-

ing and the dying of a warrior. The *tsepan* was for suicide; it had no other purpose.

There had been a time when the reasons for its use were petty: shame that a word could have erased; dishonour; the ultimate emphasis to a protest. And there were reasons still justified now: avoiding capture by an implacable, dishonourable enemy; self-execution as repentance and admission of guilt—an act which also kept forfeit lands from seizure by the crown.

But in war, where common sense prevailed over pride and bloody obsession with honour, the dirk took on another aspect: that of mercy. When a man lay in the dirt split asunder by a *taiken*'s sweeping stroke, it could never be anything but kindness to end his irreparable pain. Though it was never admitted, there was tacit acceptance that each *kailin*'s dirk was carried, at the last, for himself. A man was luckless indeed if in the hour of his hopeless agony there was neither blade nor compassionate hand to make his passage to the darkness quick and clean.

Santon spoke the old phrases in High Alban, the Horse-Lords' priestly tongue, forgotten save in rituals such as this. It was a language rich, rhythmic and musical, but hard and stern as those who had first pronounced it.

"Behold this blade, black and belt-borne," the lord intoned slowly. "Honourable it is, pride-protecting, death without dishonour's darkness. Mark its meaning in your mind with Word of Binding and with blood." From the corner of one eye Aldric saw servants unroll a length of bandage and shivered slightly.

"Word and blood will bind me. I will bear the blade." The young *kailin* held out his open left hand, muscles taut to stop the fingers trembling. Lord Santon laid the *tsepan* on the offered skin and cut once with each edge, marking duty to Heaven, to Crown and to Clan.

White-faced and barely breathing, Aldric watched dark blood welling from the parallel wounds until they were covered with white gauze and a fine linen bandage. He felt very slightly sick. The cuts themselves had hurt little, so keen was the fragile dirk, but now a throbbing crawled hotly up his arm. Clenching his fists he bowed, then retired for a while as was his right.

The ceremony was over and his life for the next few years was laid out in orderly fashion. A youth spent in weapon-training had been to prepare him for this: service in some high lord's garrison before officer rank if he earned it and promotion perhaps to the Guards' cavalry barrack in Cerdor. Not an appealing prospect, but better at least than the other choice of a lord's third son— Aldric had never seen himself as a priest. Grinning at the thought, he gathered himself up and went to find something to drink.

*

Sitting astride his roan gelding at the crest of a small rise, Aldric twisted in the saddle to look back at Dunrath's distant bulk. The donjon of the citadel and the loftier fortress turrets gleamed straw-gold in the sunrise, but the rest was still lost in mist and pre-dawn gloom, with only a few firefly specks to show where people were up and about. Aldric hunched deeper into the fur of his travelling cloak, for autumn was drawing to a close and the days were both short and chilly. The horse stamped and shook its mane; it at least was eager to be off, and with a final glance Aldric settled back and let the beast make its own way down the slope, towards the broad army road that led to Radmur.

*

"Radmur? At this time of year?" Joren had been startled when he first heard Aldric's plan. He had been inclined to treat it as a joke until he realised his young brother was quite serious. Then he began to grow suspicious. "Why, may I ask, are you so set on going?"

"I've told you once—I want to see my friends before winter closes in, because there won't be time come spring before I go to Leyruz." Joren cleared his throat. "To *Lord* Leyruz. Sorry."

"Eight leagues is a fair distance even in summer," muttered Joren dubiously. "You'd not find me doing it."

"But then I'm not you, am I?"

"No, praise Heaven!" The big man's vehemence made Aldric laugh. Joren was right, of course; nobody he knew about was worth a twenty-five-mile social call in the present weather—but it made a good enough excuse . . . Unlocking a chest, Aldric hauled out clothing, then swore softly and began to dump three months' accumulated debris from the pockets of his favourite leather jerkin. Something clanked loudly on the bottom of the trunk and he fished out a decrepit, rusty sword-hilt with a broken chain through its pommel. Flakes of corrosion sprinkled his clean clothes, and he muttered something under his breath. Joren stared out of a window, wondering how his little brother had grown up to be such a wise fool. Collecting rubbish, going visiting in such weather . . . "It wouldn't be a woman, hmm?" he speculated idly.

If he had not been watching the clouds Joren might have wondered about the glance Aldric shot at him. Then the expression vanished as he realised Joren was only joking. He dropped the sword-hilt and resumed his packing with a careful laugh.

"Wrong again. When I find a lady, she'll live a damn sight nearer home!"

*

Now Aldric cantered on, whistling between his teeth. Apart from a peasant or two who gave him "Good day" and respectful bows, the road was deserted and winter unquestionably drawing near. Everything seemed draped in grey—the sky, the hills, the clumps of woodland—and Aldric wondered why he had not stayed at home. Haranil-*arluth* had given him three days—pleasing enough until the old man elaborated. A day to go, a day to stay and a day to return. Aldric had made the mistake of protesting, forgetting he was no longer a child whose whims were humoured. Haranil had simply said, "I am your lord, warrior," and Aldric had wisely argued no further.

The smooth sad wail of a wolf floated down from the woods beyond the ridge, and Aldric resisted the temptation to jam in his heels. He had not forgotten the strange events after the boar-hunt, nor Duergar Vathach's enigmatic remark at the feast. Strange man, he thought idly. Spends all day wandering about the woods, never minds the weather, seldom gets back till after dark. Weird . . . his musing was interrupted by the raindrop which hit him in the eye. With a shower coming on, he shook the gelding to a gallop and reached a way-house just in time to watch the downpour from beside a roaring log fire.

He and the horse were both tired when at last he reined in and looked at the walled city of Radmur. Stiff and saddle-sore, he stood in his stirrups as the beast trotted towards the gates where already lights were glowing yellow, newly lit and smelling of oil and resin. Exchanging a brief greeting with the guards, more polite than usual when they saw his hair, he handed his steed over to one of the city ostlers. As in other Alban cities, horses were forbidden beyond the perimeter roads, and as his aching thighs complained he toyed with the idea of a palanquin or chair. Then he reminded himself that he was still only twenty and not fat, and walked.

Tewal's inn was much as he had last seen it, dim and snug under adzed oak beams. At this time of night it smelt mouthwatering, with various things cooking in the kitchen, and in the common room a fire like a forge and bowls of salted dainties—both deliberate, to encourage thirst and deep drinking. Aldric didn't care about that. Hitching his sword's crossbelt so that the scabbard hung comfortably across his back, he took a handful of beef slivers and began munching. Unmannerly, but then he was hungry.

Tewal himself was not long in appearing, summoned by one of the serving wenches. Short, fat and cheerful, he emerged red-faced from the kitchen where by his smudged nose he had been blowing life into a brazier. "Well now, my lord. I thought I'd seen the last of you till spring," he said, and slapped Aldric on the shoulder, warrior-rank or no. Aldric winced—the little man had big, broad hands—and grinned at him.

"There's no need to sound so disappointed," he said. Tewal tugged his ginger beard and shook his head.

"Oh, no, dear me no, not like that at all, my lord. I was only saying to Egyth, Egyth my dear, I said, that young lord Talvalin—" Aldric held up one hand for silence. Tewal always made him feel out of breath.

"Tewal," he said firmly, "I'm tired and hungry. Feed me and then you can tell me everything you've said to everybody this week. But please, not just now, eh?"

*

The tavern slowly filled with other customers as the evening drew on and Aldric, never fond of crowds, retreated to a quiet corner with his wine and carried on a sporadic conversation with the innkeeper's wife. They had been swapping scraps of gossip for perhaps half an hour when Aldric's flow of speech faltered and an odd expression crossed his face. Not because of the drink—his head was harder than that—but he had the feeling that someone was watching him.

Setting down his tankard, the *kailin* swept a quick glance across the smoky taproom. Merchants with long-stemmed pipes—a curious habit Tewal also affected now—mingled with off-duty guards and their ladies of the moment. Otherwise there was nothing out of the ordinary—until his gaze reached the doorway.

Her name was Ilen; that was all she had admitted and he had not pressed her for more. Their relationship was a complicated one, since she was the lady of a good friend of one of Aldric's good friends and he was reluctant to do anything which would break these long-standing ties. The young man had absolutely no previous experience of women to guide him; Joren had guarded his morals with the same energy as he had taught him to fight, and at the age of twenty Aldric was shy, frustrated, obsessively honourable and nervously virginal. His visit to Radmur was intended to rectify this uncomfortable situation, since at their last meeting—at somebody else's birthday feast—Ilen's friendship had shown signs of becoming something more intimate.

As Ilen crossed the room Aldric half-rose and bowed with as much grace as his apprehension allowed. He was downright scared of doing something which might appear foolish or awkward in the girl's eyes, and was consequently becoming reluctant even to move. Then he did move, very smoothly and with a speed even Joren would have applauded.

Ilen had come too close to the table where three soldiers just off punishment drill were drowning their sorrows, and one had made a grab at her. His fingers had closed around the girl's slender wrist and he was hauling her closer with as much finesse as a fisherman landing herrings. The man's drunkenness was some excuse—but in Aldric's opinion, not much. "Let her alone, friend," he said harshly, tugging the guardsman's shoulder and relying on his rank to gain obedience.

As he sorted out his legs from those of an upturned table and wiped blood from his lip, Aldric realised such reliance had been a little optimistic. Scrambling upright, he intercepted a tray of tankards and helped himself to one, then moved in on the little group of soldiers—rather more carefully this time. They were trying to kiss Ilen and laughing heartily as she tried to flinch away. Aldric's teeth showed briefly and he tapped the nearest man on the back. The soldier swung round, blearily looking for trouble, and found it in the shape of a tankard smacking him very hard under the chin. Not surprisingly he fell down with a crash that took his comrades' table and their drinks down with him.

In the ensuing silence Aldric extended one hand to Ilen. "Let us leave, now," he suggested calmly, and there was a clattering as several of the more timid customers took his advice, just before somebody grabbed his queue from behind with an excessively vicious jerk.

Nobody did that to a *kailin-eir!* Without looking, Aldric slammed elbow backwards at mouth level and felt the crunch of a good square impact shoot down his arm. The "somebody" let go of his hair and tried to yell, a sound muffled by several displaced teeth. It gave Aldric the chance to roll sideways under the shelter of a friendly table, where he could watch the developing fight in relative peace and quiet.

Something heavy hit the ground behind him and he found himself no longer alone. Not that his visitor was anyone he could talk to—the spice seller had been on the wrong end of a bottle, brandy by the smell, and was in no fit state for conversation. Judging by the rising uproar, things were getting out of hand and Aldric guessed that *kailin-eir* or not he had best not be around when the Watch came calling. Radmur's Prefect of Police doubtless remembered the last time well enough.

One of the chairs by his table shot straight up out of sight, followed by loud noises and a rain of splintered wood. Drawing his sword was out of the question, of course; this was only a friendly fight and while brawling was one thing, bladeplay was quite another. As two squealing wenches ran for the door Aldric stood up and followed them, oozing innocence.

This fooled nobody, as three swinging fists made quite clear. By the time he had sorted out that problem—easily enough, since he was sober and his attackers were not—someone else had departed noisily through the window and Aldric hastened his own exit. The sound of breaking glass drew Radmur's City Watch like wasps to syrup, and Tewal's big front window had held enough panes to attract the deafest constable.

Then, despite the risk of being jumped on, he stopped. Ilen had been backed into a corner by her drunken acquaintance of earlier on, and by the look on the man's ugly face he was after more than a kiss this time. There was a small knife in Ilen's hand, but the guard was in no mood to sweet-talk her out of using it. Instead he drew a dagger from his boot and advanced with a nasty grin.

When Aldric shouted he looked round—having learnt nothing from the fate of his colleague—and then lunged. The young *kailin* dodged, grabbed the knife-hand's wrist and used it to hurl the soldier over his shoulder and headlong into a handy pile of chairs. "All a matter of balance," he said dryly, then led Ilen out into the dark, cool peace and quiet of the street.

Opening his mouth to make some comment, Aldric shut it again as his mental alarm sounded for the first time that evening. He spun, one hand flying to his sword-hilt—then lowered it as a halberd prodded his stomach.

"So, my lord Aldric," said the Prefect of Police with a gentle smile. "At least there is nothing in the canal this time. Yet."

*

Heavy flakes of snow wavered to the ground as Aldric galloped fast for Dunrath. The fall had begun just after he left Radmur and was making the paved road treacherous, but he was in no mood for caution. The magistrates had taken two days to decide who was responsible for the riot in Tewal's inn, and though they had finally given Aldric an honourable discharge they had taken too

long over it. The damage was already beyond repair;
it would now seem to Haranil-*arluth* that he had been
deliberately misunderstood. And deliberate disobedience
was one thing the old man had never tolerated. He
would be in just the right frame of mind to hear the
real reason for the delay; Aldric's stomach went cold at
the thought.

He stopped perforce at the way-station, not to feed
himself but to rest his lathered horse before the beast
dropped under him. Not all the stamping up and down
nor the rapping of quirt on boot could hurry the weary
animal's recovery and at last Aldric gave up trying. He
went inside and stared in grim silence at the fire.

Nearer home the sky began to clear and he approached
the fortress in cold, brilliant sunshine. The frosty air was
still and silent, the only sound his steed's hoofs muffled
by the snow. He could see no guards, no sentries . . .
not a soul. The roan passed over the outer drawbridge,
and still no one challenged his presence.

Aldric frowned and scanned the courtyard, then dismounted. Though the stables were empty of grooms
there were horses in the stalls and even his new battle
armour still boxed in one corner, not yet unpacked. Intrigued and by now wary, he moved quietly up into the
citadel itself.

Inside was cold, the gloominess accentuated by the
dust-flecked shafts of light streaming from the western
windows. There was neither movement nor sound save
that made by Aldric himself. He had never seen the long
corridors so still and dark; even late at night there were
usually lamps and servants, but now there was nothing
except the slow eddy of golden specks washed by the
evening light. Aldric shivered and his sword appeared in
one hand almost of its own volition. Very carefully he
eased back one of the great hall's doors and slipped
inside.

The vast chamber was completely deserted; the ashes
of dead fires slumped grey in the hearths and of lamps
and candles only charred wicks remained. Crossing the
hall at a run, Aldric took the stairs four at a time, up
the right fork leading past the galleries, into the donjon

and towards the lord's private apartments. Twice he almost went headlong, for apart from a little light filtering in the passages were in total darkness.

At the foot of the spiral stair leading to his father's tower rooms, he paused to regain his breath and to listen. All the corridors with access to that door had *encanath,* singing floors, uncarpeted loose-laid boards designed to creak at the slightest pressure. Now they were silent; almost as silent as the young warrior who slid upstairs like a stalking cat.

The planks groaned thinly when Aldric set foot to them and he hesitated briefly before continuing to his father's door. Beginning to ease it open, he grimaced— with the floors announcing his every step, further caution seemed superfluous. He threw open the door and went inside.

The sword slid from his slack fingers. A thousand thoughts became one vast silent scream ringing endlessly through the echoing caverns of his mind.

Haranil-*arluth* Talvalin sat in his high-backed chair by the fireplace, with his great *taiken* resting on his knees. His head drooped forward on to his breast and it seemed that the old lord slept. Only the spear which nailed him to his chair destroyed the illusion.

A few feet away Joren and his four sisters lay heaped against the wall, their rich garments glimmering like so many cut flowers in the wan light. The women had each been stabbed once, in the neck from behind, but someone had fought. Blood puddled thickly on the floor, spattered the walls and smeared across ripped fabrics and hacked furniture. Aldric stared for a long time at Joren's face, at the loosely gaping mouth and the obscene emptiness of wide, dead eyes.

Then he began to cry.

When he had recovered from the convulsive sobbing, Aldric pressed his face to the cool wood of the door and tried to comprehend the enormity forced upon him. He had been late. He had promised his father, his lord, that he would return at a certain time and he had broken that promise. Broken his Word. Logic nagged that this was not of his choosing, that he would anyway have done no more than die with the rest. But logic had no place in a *kailin*'s honour-code. Without a Word he would be better dead.

As his arm hung limply by his side something touched it. Aldric glanced down and his scarred left palm seemed to burn with a fresh and freezing pain. The hilt of his *tsepan* glittered coldly at him, and his stomach lurched.

Slowly he drew the thin blade. Its lacquered hilt was chill against his hand, and the hand itself trembled. Staring at the bitter point and cruel edges, he quailed at what was expected of him. To die . . . And for what purpose? It would neither avenge the killings nor mourn them; nor even carry out the funeral rites. But not to do so would dishonour his name throughout eternity.

"No!" The word spat from bloodless lips, chasing the *tsepan* as it flickered across the room to thud into a panel. Thrumming with the impact, its pommel swayed so that the blue-enameled crest—his crest—winked at him like a sardonic eye, mocking his cowardice. Aldric rubbed his throbbing hand, but the pain would not go away. His haunted eyes looked far into the distance, towards the sun hanging low over the Blue Mountains, edging a lapis lazuli sky with gold. A gentle breeze passed through the shattered window, caressing his face and the sweat beading it.

I have lived as well as I may, Aldric thought. I have eaten good food and drunk fine wine, I have had worthy friends. I might have loved . . . I have never slain a man. Why then fear to die? All must go out into the darkness, and only *kailinin* may choose their time of passing. It is an honourable right, that one may leave this melancholy world to return reborn in the great circle.

Quietly he crossed the room and twisted the *tsepan* free, then returned to kneel at his father's feet, laying the dirk before him. Caring nothing for the still-wet blood upon it, he bowed and pressed his brow against the floor. Cold stickiness spread across his skin. The formal phrases for the rite of *tsepanak'ulleth* refused to form in his head and he was ashamed. Quickly he opened tunic and shirt, then reversed the dirk and nuzzled its point into place under his breastbone. The weapon stung.

"My lord father," he whispered at last, "I am dishonoured and full of sorrow. I ask forgiveness and offer my life as recompense."

"Do . . . not!"

The barely audible words shocked Aldric like the stroke of a mace. Blood trickled from where the *tsepan*'s point had broken skin and jabbed deep, but the boy felt nothing. He stared into eyes lit from within by the effort of holding off death by force of will alone.

"You live . . . good. Good . . ." Aldric kept quiet, knowing that Haranil-*arthul* must have had good cause to cling to this half-life so long. "Duergar has done this . . ." the old man gasped hoarsely. "Destroyed us . . ." As Aldric listened, his father choked out the story. It made grim listening. Duergar Vathach had been a familiar figure at all hours of the day or night, and when he appeared just before dawn the doors were opened. But hiding in the shadows had been a gang of hired bravoes who had rushed the sleeping citadel, slaying all who refused to serve their master. Duergar was no scholar, but a necromancer of the Drusalan Empire, aflame with some mad scheme. Clan Talvalin had been convenient hosts, now no longer needed.

"Forget *tsepan*—laws—honour if you must. But live— let the clan survive. It must . . . not die . . . as I die . . . Please . . . my son . . ." Aldric clutched the old man's hand desperately as his father stiffened, dragging in a shuddering breath. That breath came out again in a faint little moan as Haranil, the Clan-Lord Talvalin, in his sixty-sixth year, relaxed in his chair for the last time. Aldric felt the life take its leave, released at last by the stubborn will to brush past like a movement in the air. And then it was over.

Although his face was taut with grief and tears ran down his cheeks, Aldric had no time for mourning; he had much to do. Reaching down, he lifted the *tsepan* and pressed it to his lips.

Then he sliced it deeply across the scars on his left palm, cancelling all other oaths in a scarlet spurt of blood. The pain purged him of confused emotions, and he was able to stare dispassionately at the pulsing cut before putting it to his mouth and swallowing some of the sweet-salt flow. It was warm in his cold throat.

"En mollath venjens warnan," he said harshly. "The curse of vengeance be upon thee, Duergar Vathach my enemy. Thy life will pay the weregild for my father. On my blood I swear it." Gripping his queue in smeared fingers he slashed it off with the dirk, then did the same to each ear-lock and flung all three to the ground. The cropped hair gave him a strange, youthful look belied by his eyes and by the blood oozing down his face. "I renounce my duty," he intoned as each tag of hair came free. "To Heaven if it guard thee; to any king whose laws protect thee; and to my honour lest it make me fear to slay thee—by any means I may." It was a sentence of death for Duergar and maybe for himself as well. He completed the old ritual of the *venjens-eijo,* the avenging exile, by sheathing his dirk and saluting with his sword before returning it to the scabbard across his back.

Then from the corridor outside a singing floor began to squeal.

Only a muscle moved in Aldric's cheek for perhaps three seconds. Then he snatched the heavy *taiken* off his father's lap and shrank into the shadows just before the door opened to admit torchlight and men. Their faces were familiar: men who had called themselves traders, on their way from Datherga to Radmur with a wagonload of swords. So they had claimed. They and others like them had trickled through Dunrath like a rivulet of dirty water—Duergar's raiders. With hindsight it was all so very clear.

Both wore *taipanin*—shortswords—through their belts, and armour of a kind, but the first also had a visored helmet and Aldric coldly marked him down. Such headgear would be useful when he had to walk unnoticed from the citadel. Cocking the *taiken* double-handed behind his head, the boy took a soft step forward.

Even now he was not ready to strike without warning from behind like an assassin—but giving this murderer fair warning was downright stupid. Then his problems vanished as, for some reason, the helmeted man looked around. His head tumbled to the floor wearing the slightly confused expression of a man who literally never knew what had hit him.

Aldric stepped across the corpse, *taiken* already in attack position and concentration focused on the second man who gaped, foolishly forgot his torch was a useful makeshift weapon and dropped it in favour of his sword. The delay was nothing less than fatal.

Something flickered across his body from shoulder to hip and the hand which steadied his scabbard. It was a stroke so old that it came from a time when *taikenin* were curved—but neither time nor straight blades reduced its efficiency. The mercenary stood for a moment, eyes and mouth wide with shock. His left hand dropped from its wrist just an instant before his body split along the huge diagonal cut.

Aldric stared at the exploded corpse for several minutes. After his near suicide and the shock of everything that had followed, he was close to fainting. Only adrenalin had kept him on his feet, and now it ebbed swiftly to leave him nauseous and unsteady. This revelation of his own appalling skill was too much. He had never killed before, and to start like this . . . And why that cut—something out of the distant past? The sour taste of vomit rose in his throat and his head spun. Then, as he had been taught, the *kailin* breathed deeply, pushing the shattered dead from his plane of awareness. They ceased to be sickening, just as they had ceased to be threatening. Regrets, qualms and conscience would remain, but they would no longer interfere with his survival.

He did three things in rapid succession: broke his father's sword against the fireplace and left its shards respectfully at the old man's feet; picked up the soldier's helmet, shook out its ex-owner's head and set it on his own; and set a torch to the place. Noting with grim satisfaction that not even fresh-spilt blood stopped the flame from taking hold, Aldric bowed once to the funeral pyre and walked away.

There were still only one or two people to be seen, and he wondered where they had been earlier on. It was only when Aldric rode out of the stable that he realised with horror that he had seen no other horsemen. The roan gelding seemed to be shouting for attention as he trotted quickly for the drawbridge, but since an alarm gong began to sound as dark smoke billowed from the donjon, nobody showed much interest. It gave him the chance to pause near the winding-gear for the draw-bridge and delicately saw through the ropes holding its counterweight portcullis. There were no guards any-where, although the icy wind slicing in from outside should have told him why.

As the cords began to unravel and snap of their own accord under their burden, he set heels to the horse and went over the bridge as fast as he was able. Even then he felt a sudden upward lurch as a rattling rumble broke out behind him. His mount jumped the last few feet as the drawbridge made a violent, uncontrolled ascent and slammed behind him with a huge hollow bang.

Aldric rode straight for Baelen Forest, though had he known of the guards sheltering from the wind within the gatehouse his course might have been more crooked. Instead it remained as unerring as the arrow which slammed into his left shoulder. The boy might have gasped, even screamed—he could not remember. His only recollection was of the world spinning away down a long polished tube that had utter blackness at the bottom.

*

When he came to his senses there were trees all around him and the horse had slowed to a walk. The high saddle had held him in place, as it was meant to do, despite the way he swayed drunkenly with every step the gelding took. Aldric straightened up as best he could. The wind was still sighing about his ears, and when he looked up past dark branches to the sky he could see stars. There was a vague threat of rain in the air; it was marginally warmer and the snow was turning slushy. At least that would make his tracks harder to follow . . .

Then the trees came to a sudden end and a valley yawned before him. Aldric tensed, knowing this place all too well, but with nowhere else to go he rode out from the tumbled light and shadow on to the upper slope. He glanced back painfully, listening for sounds of pursuit and hearing none. What might have been a fragile laugh formed in his throat, only to die in a gurgle when he saw what hung above the forest behind him.

Away to the north-east, above Dunrath, a bloated spiral cloud was swallowing the sky. Long tendrils stretched towards the forest until it resembled some vast hand extending taloned fingers southward to clutch and rend. A flicker passed through the cloud, throwing its coiling bulk into sharp relief—but no lightning Aldric had ever seen was that vivid, venomous green.

Raw fear welled within the youngster's brain and was not dispelled when he tore his eyes from the convoluted sky. Something was disturbing the snow just by his gelding's hoofs. Then the thing broke surface.

Starting backwards in horror, Aldric yelped and clenched his teeth against the stab of pain his sudden movement brought. Then he stared in disbelief. On the ground was what had once been a hand. It was long dead, rotten leather stretched taut over a claw of old brown bones. But it was moving. The Alban looked away, only to meet the empty eyesockets of a skull heaving itself from the earth. Its jaws worked, dribbling ancient mould across the clean snow, and pulpy white things squirmed in its hollow nostrils.

There was a sonorous droning in the air and a humming more felt than heard. Other shrivelled relics rose out of the past into the nightmare present until the whole valley was bubbling like putrescent broth. A vile stench clogged Aldric's mouth and nose until, despite the scarf around his face, he hung retching over his saddlebow.

The hand he had first seen was thrashing more violently now. It had become fleshy, filling out with muscle even as he watched, and the reek of decay lessened somewhat. Then the hand twisted and clutched his horse's foreleg, sending the animal rearing back with a neigh that was almost a shriek of outrage. Aldric was almost thrown and kept his seat more through adhesive willpower than any real skill. Trying impotently to quiet the shuddering roan, he looked down to see an almost exhumed body drag itself from the crumbling soil, then clung frantically to his saddle as the champing horse finally got the bit between its teeth and took off at full gallop.

Aldric reeled back and hammered the shaft in his back against a saddlebag. Red agony overwhelmed him and his mouth gaped wide, but long before any cry emerged he had slipped into the dark again.

3

Parting the Veil

In the grey light of dawn Aldric regained consciousness to find his left arm cold and stiff, hard to move and painful when he tried. But pain meant life. When he was dead he would no longer feel pain; nor love, nor joy, nor laughter. Though in his present mood he might as well be dead, for he was sure that he would never laugh again in this life. The dead felt nothing—even when they moved, he recalled with a shiver. But he was not dead yet, nor helpless either.

He slid clumsily to the ground, supporting himself with a stirrup when his knees threatened to give way. With only one hand, opening a saddlebag posed problems surmounted only by effort, ingenuity and much use of his teeth. Within was dried meat and wheaten bread for himself, grain and a feeding-bag for the horse, and a bottle of wine. Water he had in plenty from the melting slush around him.

Memory made the boy's appetite slighter than it might have been, and he queasily set the meat aside after a few mouthfuls. Instead he turned his mind to the arrow; it had struck into the muscles by his shoulder blade and only the heavy leather jerkin had saved him from a fatal skewering. Panting for breath, he worked up his good hand far enough to hook two fingers over the shaft, whimpering as the head shifted in living flesh. Blood seeped stickily through his clothes, leaving a smell in the cold air that made the roan gelding stamp nervously. Aldric clenched his teeth and jerked the arrow hard.

It snapped and he fell forward into slush and dead leaves, sobbing. He only regained his feet again because the horse leaned over him, so that he could grip the reins and let the gelding lift him upright. Patting the beast's nose, he buzzed affectionate nonsense into its ears.

In the clear autumn-to-winter sky a black crow drifted endlessly. The bird was still circling overhead more than an hour later, descending in lazy spirals wherever the trees grew thick. Now that pain no longer fogged his mind completely, suspicion found some room again in Aldric's brain. He stopped, listening for any sound of pursuit, but Baelen Forest answered only with the noises of small living things. Then a wolf howled thinly in the distance and the crow cawed. Twice, then twice again. The *kailin* looked up with a strange expression on his face and carefully dismounted.

There was a *telek* bolstered on his saddle, and beside it the crossbow which stayed there all the time. Aldric led the gelding under a tree, forcing deep into the shelter of its needled branches, and saw how the crow swung lower. It was then that he took down the crossbow and painfully cranked it back. Above him he could see the crow straining to sight him, and glared at it. "Stay there, bird," he muttered, "and you'll soon find out what I'm doing."

A bolt ripped up through the screening pine needles and feathers burst from between the crow's wings. Aldric swore softly, but not at his good shot; rather because the bird did not caw as it died—it screamed.

The wolf howled again, an anguished sound like hunger made audible. Aldric mounted again and let the horse move off at an easy jog. Panic tempted him to lash his steed to a gallop—but panic was no longer a luxury he could afford.

*

There were dead leaves and mud plastered on his clothes where he had skidded face-down across the ground. Raising himself painfully on one elbow, Aldric tried to shake the whirling stars from his head. How . . . ? The booming in his skull made it so hard to think . . .

Then he rolled over and swore hopelessly. The horse, the poor faithful horse, the blasted brute that was his only hope of escape lay on its side, flanks heaving. Its eyes were rolling with pain and fear, and the cause was all too plain.

Some small animal had dug itself a burrow, and the horse's leg had gone into it almost to the knee. They had only been trotting, but the gelding's leg had snapped like a stick of celery.

Aldric could do nothing for such a break and only one thing for the horse. Kneeling by its head, he gentled it with soft words and drew the short sword from his belt. When the horse relaxed, trusting him, he drew the blade across its neck and felt like a murderer. He regretted killing the horse more than the two men yesterday. They had been unknown killers; the roan gelding had grown up with him since it was a wobbly-legged foal and he a skinny boy in his teens. What he had just done was like severing a limb; *kailin* and mount were a single unit, and the loss of one diminished the other.

There was nothing on the carcass he needed, not even the crossbow, since his need was now to travel fast and light. Taking only a little food and the water bottle, he began to walk.

*

The wolfs howl was much closer now and what Aldric had thought—hoped—was an echo was without doubt an answer. He started to run. It was late afternoon now and the sky would soon be growing dark. Though the full moon was almost a week past, Aldric was afraid of nightfall. His breath hung in smoky clouds on still air that grew more harshly cold every time he sucked it into his lungs.

Then the snarl came; a harsh ripple of ferocity right at his heels. In a desperate attempt to run faster and look behind him, his legs went out from under him and he finished up in an untidy limb-flailing bundle with his throat well placed for ripping. It remained undamaged and cautiously he raised his head. The undergrowth rustled, then emitted a throaty, malicious chuckle. When nothing else happened Aldric hauled himself up and sidled towards the bracken. Then he whirled and sprinted away.

After that the flight became a nightmare. Things snarled and giggled out of thin air; bushes and gnarled roots took on distorted shapes in the shifting evening light; and still he ran, though now his muscles were dull and his legs as slow to move as if he were wading in honey. Sweat soaked him, running down his face and blinding him to the hooked branches which tore at his back. Times without number he collided with trees or fell headlong, dragging himself on by force of will and little else. His grey-green eyes took on a glazed, dead look ghastly in a living face.

Night rose from the ground like a fog, made darker by the clouds shrouding the sky in grey. A small breeze began to hiss among the branches, carrying a few drops of rain from the iron sky. Thunder rumbled distantly, chasing the flash of its lightning across the heavens. Reeling from tree to tree, Aldric knew his mind and body were failing fast. Then the thunder bellowed in earnest and he took another tumble, snapping his sword as the rain came down in a solid mass. Finally he gave up and stood cursing and crying in a storm that slashed rain against him like a hail of arrows. When a hand clutched the raw agony that had been his shoulder there was a brief, blinding moment of abject fear.

Then the ground came up to meet him and all the lights went out.

*

Aldric struggled awake with a pounding headache, hauled up eyelids made leaden by weariness and drugs and looked around him. He saw low wooden beams, simple sturdy furniture and daylight oozing past painted shutters. None of it meant a thing until he tried sitting up. Then a flare of pain tore through the narcotic haze and his memory returned.

After a few minutes spent gathering his wits, he got out of bed and began to dress. There was no trace of his own clothes, except for the leather jerkin and his weapon-belt, but the strange garments were a reasonable fit and clean besides. He finally squirmed into them, even though the operation was punctuated by oaths and gasps of pain, then slung his belt so that both blades were close at hand. Only then did he open the door.

Gemmel saw him from the corner of one eye, blinking owlishly in the watery sunshine, and glanced up from his book. He started to say something, but the words died on his lips at his first clear view of Aldric's face. Last night it had been concealed by a flaking crust of dirt and gore. Today it was the face of his own dead son.

Closer inspection revealed differences: the Alban was not as tall and his hair was lighter. Where Ernol's eyes had been a clear and honest green like Gemmel's own, this young man's gaze was like a cat's: hooded, cold and unreadable. The eyes were disks of flint sheathed in green glacier ice. But the likeness was still close enough to tighten the old man's throat.

Aldric knew the expression "to see a ghost." That was why he felt uncomfortable about Gemmel's intense stare, and he laid one hand on the reassuring metal of his shortsword's hilt. The old man at once looked disapproving. "You won't need that," he said. Aldric's hand stayed where it was and Gemmel felt a twinge of annoyance; suspicion was one thing but ingratitude was quite another. When he spoke again his voice was crisp and commanding. "Let go of that *taipan* at once!" The finger which stabbed out seemed only an emphatic gesture, but Aldric jerked his hand from the weapon as if it had stung him. Which indeed it had. He eyed the old man and forced himself to relax a little.

"Who are you, anyway?" he asked.

"Gemmel Errekren fits most comfortably on short Alban tongues," was the rather condescending reply. "You can call me that."

"Errekren—Snowbeard—that's no clan-name."

"Since I haven't a clan it should not surprise you," Gemmel returned tartly. "Now hurry up. The spell wears off at sunset."

"Spell . . . ?" Aldric repeated the word as if making sure of it. "Perhaps I should have asked *what* are you? Well?"

"I have already—no, I haven't, have I? Forgetful . . ." He rubbed his cropped beard and smiled faintly. "The villagers call me *pestrior* and *purcanyath;* dialect I know, but you understand the words." Aldric did, and to Gemmel's surprise a thin, humourless smile appeared on his face.

"Wizard and enchanter," the boy muttered half to

himself. "Ironic really, to be hunted by one and rescued
by another. For which I thank you." He bowed as well
as possible. "But this isn't your affair. I'll leave at once."

"You'll stay until I have tended that arm properly,"
snapped Gemmel in a tone brooking no refusal, and met
Aldric stare for stare until the Alban flinched and looked
away. He nodded, half in defeat and half in gratitude.

"As you wish. But only until then. I owe too great a
debt already."

"Debts are for merchants," observed Gemmel. "Put
this on." In the old man's hand was a thing like a long-
dead mouse and Aldric eyed it distastefully.

"Where?" he wanted to know. A shake of finger and
thumb revealed the object to be a false beard. Aldric
fitted the whiskers round an expression of faint disgust
and found, as he had feared, that they itched. Even so,
though he looked unlike anyone with a shred of self-
respect, he also looked nothing like a high-clan *kailin*—
which, he reflected with a gloomy scratch, was the whole
point.

Gemmel had acquired mounts for both of them and
Aldric studied his own steed with some dismay. It was
a stocky, barrel-bellied, shaggy little pony, and not the
sort of horse he had ridden for almost thirteen years. It
also tried to bite him, twice. Gemmel watched the young
man mount the skittish beast without difficulty, even
one-handed, and wondered about the Alban's other and
more sinister skills. Then he shifted in his own saddle—
on a horse much finer than Aldric's, something already
noted with some envy. "Best come on, son." If that
"son" was noticed it passed without comment. "Twenty
riders passed at first light, and it won't take many questions in yonder village to bring them right back here."

"How did they miss this place anyway?" Aldric thought
aloud. The wizard waved one hand in the air.

"A simple spell that stops you seeing in a straight
line." His explanation explained nothing. But as Aldric
rode away he saw—or more correctly, did not see—what
the enchanter meant. Stone and thatch faded from sight
as if around a corner and left an empty space where
grass waved in the wind. He said nothing, being consumed with curiosity while doing his best to seem uncon-

cerned. Gemmel found his facial gymnastics most amusing, but very wisely kept the fact to himself.

Riding as fast as the wizard deemed sensible was still not fast enough for Aldric's liking. He kept thinking of those twenty horsemen. After half an hour of cantering across the moorland, always due west and mostly uphill, the *kailin* reined in and turned his horse around. There had been a tingling across his back for several minutes now and he felt sure he knew the cause. Gemmel watched him and wondered.

On the horizon a thread of black crawled into the sky. "I thought there was somebody behind us," the Alban said quietly. Drawing a long-glass from its case at his belt, Gemmel opened it and peered towards the smoke. Aldric did not understand what he said then, but it sounded nasty. "If they were told about the cottage," he pointed out, "they will know about you as well."

Gemmel ignored him.

*

It took almost a week for the Blue Mountains to change from a saw-edged shadow to the tumbled mass of crags which now reared vast and vaguely menacing almost overhead. Snowflakes whirled from a dirty yellow sky and settled thickly on anything they touched, including the two men carefully walking their horses along the treacherously iced mountain path.

"Almost there, lad," called the taller of the pair, shaking a small avalanche from his hood as he moved. The other looked up without much enthusiasm.

"You said that yesterday, and the day before." Aldric found the weather, his itchy beard—mixed now with real stubble—and Gemmel's unfailing optimism depressing, so that he no longer even tried to produce the right responses to his cheerful conversation. Bored, wet, sore and miserable, he neither expected nor was able to see anything other than rocks, even though Gemmel seemed to think otherwise.

"Up there, by the standing stone," he insisted, and Aldric dutifully strained his eyes through the blurring snow before giving up. Handing over his horse's reins, Gemmel scrambled up to the monolith and laid both hands against its side. Following to give what help he could, Aldric realised that the old man's pressure was barely enough to mark the crust of snow under his fingers. He stopped, threw back his hood for a better view and watched. As if finding the right spot Gemmel pushed once, very hard, and the stone shifted with a grinding clearly audible in the snow-silence.

There was an instant's pause—then twenty feet of the rock-face slid open without a sound. Aldric's eyes dilated, for he had never read or heard of anything like this. The cavern thus revealed was no dank cave, but a smooth, polished tunnel whose walls and ceiling were lined with globes of some crystalline stuff. Dropping lightly to the ground, Gemmel touched his hand to a metal plate set into the stone. Immediately the first few crystals glowed, and as Aldric watched the illumination spread from globe to globe down the tunnel until it was filled with a warm golden light.

When he looked back the horses had vanished and Gemmel was shouldering the few items he carried on his saddle. The *kailin* blinked, but realised that if one lived with an enchanter one must learn to live with enchantments. Well then, now was a good time to start.

At the end of the tunnel of lights there was a spiral stair, made of metal but otherwise identical to those in donjon towers. Its upper end was sealed by a smooth metal slab which hissed aside as Gemmel approached, releasing a harsh glare which made Aldric flinch and shield his eyes. He followed the old man when he judged himself used to the brilliance, and discovered it was virtually the only thing he was used to.

The cave—now that was ordinary: sensible. He could grasp the principles of it, even though it was triangular in section and flooded with light of unreal whiteness which struck sparkling reflections from the burnished machinery recessed into both walls. There was a humming in the air and a slight vibration underfoot as of incalculable power hidden somewhere in the rock below. But it was the yawning vault at one end of the cave which totally defied all comprehension.

The vault was vast: more than big enough to swallow an entire fortress and sufficiently high for the loftiest citadel turret to fit in comfort. More of the glowing crys-

tals shone from its walls, but they cast just enough light
for the colossal size of the place to be marked out in
tiny rows of jewels, being nowhere near bright enough
to actually be of use. All around the entrance, pipes and
conduits emerged from the floor and went snaking off
into the shadows; some were bunches of metallic fila-
ment finer than a cobweb, but one slashed with black
and yellow stripes was as thick as Aldric's waist. A slight,
cold drift of air moved out of the cavern, swirling slightly
as breezes will in such monstrous empty spaces. Except
that this space was far from empty.

There was . . . something . . . crouched squarely in
the middle of the cavern floor, an ill-defined mountain-
ous bulk of dark smooth shapes and glinting edges. It
dwarfed all else both in mass and in the eerie suggestion
of dormant power. On trembling legs Aldric stepped towards it, all his senses tingling—and then Gemmel laid
one hand on his uninjured shoulder and steered him
away without a word of explanation.

Warrior stared at wizard for several minutes before
Aldric spoke. "Meneth Taran," he said very softly. "So
this is the Mother of Storms." Gemmel met the boy's
unwinking agate eyes and nodded. Meneth Taran, Thun-
derpeak, was the heaven-scoring crag where the great
tempest was born in the story. People gave the name
half in fun to Sil'ive, tallest of all the Blue Mountains
and one perpetually wreathed in cloud. Half in fun, but
never completely so, and with the very air thrumming in
his ears Aldric could guess why. Even if he gained no
other knowledge from the old enchanter, he had at least
learned the meaning of awe.

*

By contrast, the living apartments were reassuring in
their air of comfort. Most of the rooms were panelled
in wood like a fortress and for the same reason—to conceal the fact that the walls behind were stone: in this
case half a mile of living mountain rock. Live flames
danced in elegant fireplaces and even Aldric wasted no
time wondering where the smoke went to. With warmth
around him for the first time in six days, his shoulder
was taking precedence over frozen feet and hands. It
throbbed wickedly.

Gemmel noticed the slight wince with which Aldric took a seat by the fire in his study and nodded to himself. "Enough of this," he said with a touch of impatience. "Your arm will heal in time, but it will be time wasted. Shirt off, please." He set down a box of instruments on a handy table and opened the lid. Aldric blinked apprehensively at a row of tiny knives and probes, but made no move to obey.

"I'd much rather have a bath and a shave first," he ventured nervously. Gemmel tutted disapprovingly and shook something from its clear case.

"And I would much rather have that wound dealt with. Now!" He set out two metal bottles, three small pads and a pair of gloves which he removed from their sealed pouch and worked onto his hands. With an uneasy swallow born of memories of having his arm set last spring, Aldric did as he was told. Gemmel peeled away the bandages and selected a knife. "This won't hurt . . ." he said. The *kailin* jumped and yelped, then twisted round to fix him with a baleful glare. "Much," the wizard amended.

He told the truth and within five minutes was packing away his medical kit while Aldric felt with increasing delight for a scar that was no longer there. Gemmel grinned broadly; he had forgotten the great satisfaction that surgeon's work always gave him and was pleased to discover that it had not diminished with the years. Then he returned to more basic matters. "Aldric, do you want something to eat now—or would you rather take that bath you mentioned?"

Aldric was definitely in favour of eating first and said so. Emphatically.

*

Even so, being high-clan Alban and as fastidious as a cat, he went to wash directly after the meal, leaving Gemmel to stare at the fire, drink Hertan grain-spirit and try to shape what he wanted to say to this young man with the unsettlingly familiar face. So alike, and yet so totally different. Though Aldric had begun to smile a little in the past week, there was a freezing menace about him that Ernol had never possessed. The *kailin* was—Gemmel at first rejected the word but found it returning to his mind—frightening. "Frightening," he said aloud, as if hearing the word would change its meaning.

"Who is?" asked Aldric from the door.

He had found a clean white shirt and breeches somewhere and there was a towel in one hand. With his short, wet hair and a face freshly shaven smooth, he looked so young that Gemmel's chosen word seemed more out of place than ever.

"I was thinking," the wizard said. Aldric relaxed in a chair by the fire and picked at a loose thread in the towel.

"So was I." He hesitated, watching unobtrusively through the lashes of half-closed, seemingly sleepy eyes. The fireglow carved deep trenches in Gemmel's face, giving him an eldritch appearance. That strange expression had returned; echoes of recognition and regret, all mingled with a bitter memory of loss. It was enough to make Aldric sure his half-formed guess approached the truth. "You knew someone—a long time ago—who looked like me. Or I like him. And he died. A friend? Maybe a relative . . ." What flickered on the old enchanter's features then had nothing to do with firelight, and with an inward wince of sick embarrassment Aldric bit his tongue before it did more hurt. "I—I'm sorry," he finished lamely.

The sorcerer stared at him, wishing he was more stupid or at least less forthright. More like Ernol. At least the Alban was in his own country; he could never—and Gemmel hoped would never—know what it was like to live down the long years, to walk through a crowded city, to exchange friendly words and yet be alone—always, eternally alone. And now this boy with his dead son's face; surely it was some cruel joke perpetrated by an ironic fate. Gemmel regained his composure with an effort and twisted thin lips into a thin smile. "No matter," he said. "I was miles—years—away." Aldric inclined his head in polite acknowledgment that the subject was now closed.

"You started to say something when we were at table, then decided it was best left till later," he said, "this is 'later.' "

"Very well." Gemmel leaned back and steepled his
fingers, staring intently at their nails for a few seconds.
"Recall your last boar-hunt—in as much detail as you
can, but without speaking." Aldric gazed into the shifting embers of the fire and let his memory work. He sat
like that for some minutes, hardly seeming to breathe,
then straightened and blinked several times.

"Now what?"

"There was a spell on that valley to keep animals out,
as you know. It wasn't to preserve the honoured dead
from scavengers but to prevent anything being killed
there. Blood is the catalyst for many powerful forms of
magic. The wizard who cast that spell must have suspected that the spilling of blood would have some terrible consequence. As you must guess now, he was right.
You can blame Duergar for that."

"Duergar . . . ? But what had he—"

"You have shown yourself to have intelligence, boy.
Use it!" That flash of irritation was a warning which
Aldric judged it wise to heed. He sat up straighter and
prepared to make sensible remarks. Remarks for which
he wasn't asked. "You shot a wolf. Did you really fail
to notice which leg you hit—or which leg Duergar Vathach was limping on . . . ? He's wily, that one; he should
really have taken the shape of a fox, it would have suited
him better."

"You *know* that bastard?" The young *kailin*'s voice
was incredulous.

"We . . . met once. In a professional capacity. I didn't
like him then either. Agents of the Empire always make
my skin crawl."

"What is an Imperial agent doing in Alba, or is that
obvious too?" Aldric bit off the words, hoping Gemmel
would snap at him again and give him a really good
excuse to lose his temper. The boy was seething inside,
as much with a feeling of helplessness as anything else.
At mention of the Drusalan Empire his own hopes and
aspirations began to look very small. Seek to be re-
venged on that mighty realm—as well make war on the
sea for drowning your friend. Gemmel saw his face
change.

"It is obvious, Aldric," the old man said quietly.

"Your family may be only the first to die. When Grand Warlord Etzel turns his mind to conquest, he is as inexorable as the incoming tide." Aldric wondered at the wizard's choice of words, and wondered too whether his own mind was still being read. "But even a spring tide can be stopped, if a hole in the sea-wall is plugged before any water passes through."

"Sifting through your metaphors, then," said Aldric with an acid little smile, "if I succeed in my intention to kill Duergar, and do it soon enough, I'll save Alba from an Imperial invasion?"

"Basically, yes."

"I see." From Aldric's face and tone of voice Gemmel could tell he was not very impressed. "And why would the Imperial Grand Warlord want to invade in the first place? Alba has nothing to do with Imperial policies." Gemmel smiled sardonically at that.

"How little you know of power politics, *kailin-eir* Aldric," he said.

"That was Baiart's field, not . . ." The young man's voice trailed off and his eyes went very distant. "Baiart . . ."

"Forget him for now," Gemmel said impatiently. "What do *you* know of the Empire?"

Aldric shrugged. "It's big . . . The Emperor holds most of the countries across Bian-mor in the palm of his hand. Their borders have expanded almost constantly for almost a century—" Seeing Gemmel shaking his head, he stopped. "What did I get wrong?"

"One thing only. The *Empire* rules across the Narrow Sea—the Emperor is lucky if he can command the running of his Palace. Etzel, like all his predecessors as Grand Warlord, is true master of the Empire. But that may change. Emperor Droek is an old man—old before his time, and that time is running out. I predict—no, not by sorcery—that he'll die in a year or so; even though, for a change, the Warlord does not want this to happen. You see, Droek's eldest son had been trained by Etzel's people to be a good Emperor; weak, fond of pleasure, a puppet whose strings would be pulled by the Warlord. But he fell off his horse six months ago and broke his neck."

"Joren said that somebody helped him on his way. I

thought the Warlord might—but from what you say, I doubt it."

"He probably helped himself, with a bellyful of wine and a headful of smoke. Or his brother could have done it."

"His brother?" Aldric sounded disgusted and Gemmel remembered the closeness of Alban family ties. "Baiart didn't like me, but he wouldn't have— Or I don't think he . . . might well, given the chance," he finished lamely.

"How much better reason with an Empire as your prize, eh? But Ioen is a better man than his brother. Much better—or will be. He's only sixteen. Though since he wasn't brought up in the sort of decadence Etzel provides for his puppets, he's probably more adult now than his dear, late brother ever was." Aldric had been paying attention once his interest was aroused and he could see how things fitted together now.

"So like it or not, the next Emperor won't be just a figurehead. And the Warlord is going to do what he can, while he can, because if the Empire stops expanding by war, there will be no need for a Warlord. And he picked on Alba because—because if the worst happens, he'll have a bolt-hole out of the Emperor's reach. And the fact that he's using a filthy, treacherous, back-stabbing . . ." The boy took a deep breath and calmed down a little. "The very fact that he's using a necromancer as his agent, when all sorcery is forbidden in the Empire, shows how desperate he must be to succeed."

Gemmel applauded, with only the faintest trace of an ironic smile creasing his lean face. "And the fact," he mimicked Aldric's slightly pedantic tones with good-humored mockery, "that Alba's king has condoned acts of piracy against Imperial shipping, has drawn up letters of marque for the commissioning of privateers, already signed and only awaiting issue, and that his High Council has been instrumental in the smuggling of arms and gold to insurrections in the Imperial provinces . . . all these have nothing whatsoever to do with it."

"Ah . . ." breathed Aldric. Then with sudden violence: "How in the name of the Highest Hell did you learn all that?" There was no anger in the outburst—just an extreme curiosity.

"I am a wizard, you know," Gemmel pointed out. "Though friends in high places are also useful. But . . ." He paused, deliberately.

"But *what?*"

"But I think you may have it all wrong." Aldric eyed the enchanter and gave up. Trying to keep track of Gemmel's mental processes was worse than trying to read a book at night, without lights, in a thick fog.

"So what is the solution?" Gemmel stood up and wandered across his study to the big oak desk, returning with a long slender pipe which he proceeded to carefully fill and light. Since it was obvious that he was not going to get an answer until the ritual had been concluded, Aldric also rose and helped himself to the sorcerer's wine.

"Now why would Vathach have been sneaking about the old Baelen battlefield?" Gemmel muttered to himself. Aldric glanced towards the enchanter, drained his goblet and then filled it again in anticipation of more convoluted discussion. Then he spilt about half the contents as Gemmel thumped his chair and barked, "Yes, of course!"

"Of course what?" Aldric shook wine from his fingertips into the fire and finished what was left before it too was spilt. "I grow tired of asking simple-minded questions which you never seem to answer." Raising his eyebrows, Gemmel looked at the young man with new respect. There had been an edge to his last words that was more than mere petulance; he had sounded like someone accustomed to obedience—like a *kailin-eir.*

"The sword-hilt which you found," Gemmel explained, only to be met with a quizzical blankness. Then he recalled how the images in Aldric's mind had faded during the *ymeth*-trance. There had been a charm of forgetfulness cast across the valley—but one cast hastily and without due care, or there would have been no trace of the hilt in Aldric's memory at all. So Duergar had been watching the valley either in the form of a wolf, or with witch-sight from a distance. He had been searching for one particular artifact, had been interrupted by the boarhunt and had seen his trophy unearthed quite by accident. After failing to make Aldric drop the old hilt, he had followed it to Dunrath and laid his plans accordingly. The Talvalins had simply been in the way, and as was the manner of such wizards he had snuffed them out without a thought. That thought might have made him more careful to do a thorough job—and the lack of it, Gemmel realised grimly, could prove the end of his scheme. The old enchanter told Aldric his theory, for once without rhetoric, and waited for a reaction.

"It must be Kalarr cu Ruruc's sword!" the boy said firmly. "I can't think of anything else—especially after Vathach took such pains to bore me out of any curiosity on the subject." Gemmel smiled around his pipe-stem.

"He must have considerable talent to do that," the wizard observed dryly. Getting to his feet, he faced one of the bookcases which ran from floor to ceiling around the walls of his study. "There should be something here to enlighten us on why . . . ah, and indeed there is."

He pulled down a thick leather-bound book and leafed rapidly through its pages, then marked one with his finger. "This is not unlike your clan Archives, Aldric," the old man said. Then his teeth showed in a crooked grin. "Except that no hall-scribe would dare write some of the things this book contains, for fear of his very soul." It was an explanation which did nothing for Aldric's peace of mind. "Now let me see . . ." Gemmel read the page quickly, muttering some of the words under his breath; what Aldric caught of them sounded like an archaic form of Alban, not quite the ancient High Speech of religion and ceremony but certainly closer to it than to the language Aldric spoke. He felt suddenly reluctant to hear whatever it was the sorcerer was reading, and was about to say as much when Gemmel set down the book on his desk and stared hard at him.

"Aldric, would you go now and fetch me your old jerkin?" he said, and his voice was strange. Aldric went at once. When he returned, the sorcerer was toying with the pen he had been using to construct a complex table of words and symbols. He tapped his chin with one finger, then drew a large question mark right in the centre of the page. "Turn out your pockets, please," he told the boy without looking up. This revealed the usual mixture of fluff, small coins, notes on scraps of parchment and threads from a hole in the pocket lining.

Gemmel looked at the unprepossessing rubbish, then lifted one of the broken threads and frowned. The frown deepened when scrutiny revealed the jacket's lining to be still intact. A moment later it was anything but, as he took a knife from the desk and sliced the seams apart. Opening his mouth to protest, Aldric quickly closed it again. Something had fallen from the rent and rolled clattering across Gemmel's desk; as it stopped and fell over sideways, the boy could see quite clearly what it was. The wrist-band of a horseman's sword, with three links of rusty chain remaining of the length which had once threaded through a pommel.

"So then," said Gemmel quietly, "Duergar has the hilt and we the band to it. Which is more important, I wonder?" He made no move to touch the age-corroded bronze, but Aldric did. Save only where the chain had left russet flecks, the band was green with verdigris, covering even the studs decorating its surface. The more Aldric studied it, the less he felt it had anything to do with Kalarr. Plain bronze was too . . . too cheap for the trappings of a master sorcerer. With a disgusted noise he dropped it on the table.

"Deceptive, is it not?" Aldric cocked an eyebrow, not quite understanding Gemmel's comment. "But then, such things were meant to fool more than your uninformed scrutiny." He began scratching the band with his small knife, talking the while. "The outward appearance of any object is seldom an indication of its true worth; an older man may be stronger than a young one; a ring plain and unadorned may have greater value than any set with gems; and a band of rusty bronze with simple ornaments may prove of—ah!" Metal squeaked under stress as Gemmel prised back his blade.

"*Has* proven of greater interest than one made of jewelled gold. Aldric . . . look!" He twisted the knife away and a flickering nimbus of pale blue light sprang up around his hands. The radiance poured from one of the studs on the wrist-band, from which Gemmel had scraped a concealing layer of metal, and which now glowed like a sapphire lit from within by cold, fierce white light. It was altogether beautiful—and at the same time as awesome as the vast dark shape Aldric had half-glimpsed in the cavern.

"This," said Gemmel, holding it up carefully, "is one of the seven spellstones of Echainon. They have been lost for a long time—and now I have one in my hand. But I can guess from this what Duergar has in mind." Gemmel laid down the spellstone and gazed for a while into its throbbing core. "And Aldric, had I the choice, an Imperial invasion would be preferable by far."

*

There was a slab of crystal resting on top of the stone plinth, making it look like a catafalque for the lying-in-state of some great man. A slow dance of green flames surrounded it, burning without heat, without smoke and without fuel.

Duergar dozed before it in a cushioned chair, undisturbed by the shifting light. He was so weary that little could disturb him now; the rituals had lasted four days and their completion had left him with an exhaustion such as he had seldom experienced. Held firmly in one hand was an old sword-hilt, scratched and shiny from a recent, over-vigorous cleaning but the letters on its guard and pommel carefully outlined in fresh black ink. Duergar had read them and others like them from the many grimoires scattered about the room. Intricate symbols covered the floor, some drawn with chalk and others outlined in coloured sand. The square, heavy letters were everywhere. A casual observer would have called them ugly, but even the least of closer glances would have changed the adjective to brutal—sinister—menacing. They were all of this and more besides.

Settling in his chair, Duergar drifted into a deeper sleep. As he slept, he dreamed that the sluggishly fluttering flames swirled upwards into a tapering needle like translucent viridian ice. A globe of amber radiance grew at the heart of the fire until its golden light swallowed every trace of green, and then the honey colour darkened through incandescent scarlet to a smoky crimson. The globe began to spin, attenuating to a spindle of dark red poised atop the catafalque. Then even its sullen glare faded and everything grew dark.

Waking with a nervous jerk from something close to nightmare, Duergar found that his dream had become reality. A solitary candle was the only illumination, barely enough to discern outlines, but even so he could see . . . something . . . standing on the granite plinth. Fear rose within him, for like all sorcerers who meddle in such things he lived in dread of the day when the thing he had summoned up was not that which appeared. Today was that day, for whatever he had expected this tall, rustling object was not in any of the possible shapes his grimoires had described. The candleflame sparkled back at him in a hundred ruby-red reflections, from polished metal, from cut gemstones—from gleaming eyes . . .

The eyes blinked lazily, savouring his terror, and then with a susurrant motion glided closer. Sweat coursed down the necromancer's face and his tongue stuck within a dry mouth as he fought to utter the words of a defensive spell. Then the being stopped abruptly and the glowing eyes glanced down. A vivid white line crossed the floor, blocking its path, before joining another part of the pentacle Duergar had drawn so carefully around the catafalque. There was a soft, venomous hiss of indrawn breath, and the dark outline moved unhurriedly sideways, but always the lines of the pentacle flared before it as if tracking its movements. At last the thing retired to the plinth, and Duergar found he could breathe again without the constriction of fear clenched in iron hoops round his chest.

"Who . . . who are you?" he quavered. There was no reply, and made confident by the power of his restraining-spell Duergar began to grow angry. "I summoned you, I command you!" he snapped in a voice very different from his first thin tones. "Give me your name!"

There was a noise almost like a sigh of boredom, and suddenly all the candles sprang to life revealing a man leaning nonchalantly against the catafalque, smiling, but with a glint in his dark eyes that suggested he was any-

thing but amused. "If you could remove this
obstruction . . ." he said in a deep, urbane voice, gesturing towards the pentacle with a crystal-topped staff. The
unwary could drown in that voice, thought Duergar apprehensively, and made no attempt to do as he was
asked.

"What is your name?" he repeated. The man regarded
Duergar with a trace of contempt from eyes resembling
bottomless pits bored into his sombrely handsome face.
His stare burned into the necromancer as if determined
to read his innermost thoughts, then withdrew, leaving
Duergar with the uneasy feeling of a hand unwrapping
from his throat.

"You summoned me, you command me," the man
echoed Duergar's words with undisguised sarcasm. "Are
you so unsure of yourself that you dare not also name
me? Then I will spare you the trouble." He left the stone
plinth and sauntered with a predator's grace to the edge
of the pentacle which flared with intolerable brilliance
to hold him back.

"I am Kalarr cu Ruruc." He made a complex sign in
the air with his hand; it was one of the sigils which identified him as a true summoning and not some shape-
shifting demon. Almost shaking with relief, Duergar
bowed low, almost but not quite abasing himself.

"Your pardon, my lord, but I was not sure . . . welcome, welcome! Let me open a way through the pentacle
for you."

Kalarr studied him with icy humour. "You bade me
welcome, so there is no need. The ancient binding-spell
still holds good, does it not? Somebody invited *you* in,
eh? Foolish of them." He jabbed the staff at the glowing
line before his feet and it split asunder, leaving his path
clear. "You see . . ." He stepped through, smiling.

Duergar cringed like a dog before a beating, but failed
to sidestep the long-fingered hand which wrapped
around his head. "Don't be concerned," Kalarr reassured him. "I merely want to learn. Although I feel
ymeth takes too long." The sorcerer drew in a deep
breath and tightened his grip.

It was not the grip but a feeling of having his mind
wrenched asunder which sent Duergar reeling backwards

with a harsh scream of agony. Kalarr did not follow him; he flexed his fingers and nodded slowly, then smiled again, like a shark. "And that method doesn't give *me* a headache."

His face was lean and high-cheekboned, with distinguished features framed by dark, grey-flecked hair swept back showing a widow's peak on his lofty brow. The nose was thin, high-bridged, bounded above by the notch of a slight frown and below by a mobile, ruthless mouth and a heavy moustache. It was a face of saturnine humour; of suppressed power; the face of a man who seldom hears refusal of his wishes.

"So you want my aid in wrecking this kingdom of Alba, because you think I would enjoy taking revenge for my defeat . . . ? How very true. But instead of turning it over to your Imperial masters, you would hold it for yourself. Laudable ambition—if you succeed. And since you hold the last thing I touched in life"—Duergar nervously raised the sword-hilt as if it was a protective amulet—"I have no choice but to obey your wishes." Cu Ruruc's smile faded as if the implications of what he had said were sinking in, although if Duergar had seen the sardonic glitter in his eyes when they observed the broken chain, he would not have felt so comfortable. "So be it, then," Kalarr's voice was resigned. "I shall obey."

He turned away and as if for the first time, though he had known it all along, Duergar realised that his . . . guest was dressed entirely in red. He had intended to ask how a summoning came into existence fully clothed in the height of half-millennium-old fashion, but thought better of it. No Alban would ever wear red without some other colour; red and particularly vermeil, that shade of deep scarlet or rich crimson which Kalarr wore with such arrogance, was the single most unlucky colour in the spectrum. It was associated with blood, with misfortune and violent death.

Cu Ruruc and his chosen colour were well matched.

4

Isileth—and Kyrin

Aldric lay back, half-dozing, and let his mind wander over the past three years. It still surprised him that they had passed so quickly and that he was already into the spring of his twenty-fourth year. He felt no different, even though he was: not merely older, but with a thin white scar under his right eye and a mind better versed in certain subjects than an honourable *kailin-eir* would care to own. Gemmel called it "survival."

Gemmel . . . When he first told Aldric how long he was to stay, there had been an undignified scene when the youngster lost his temper. To defer his vengeance for so long was the act of a coward, he had snarled, and whatever else he might he be, Aldric, was no coward. Gemmel had weathered the storm of abuse with a little half-smile on his face, thinking to himself how very fitting was the *kourgath* wildcat on Aldric's crest-collar. His smile was that of a man who knows he will always have the last word in any argument, and this one was no exception.

An *eijo,* an honourless wanderer, had nothing to lose by accepting some tuition in the Art Magic. So Aldric thought when the old enchanter offered, since he had already picked up a few *pesok'n,* as the little spells were called, from old books filched from his father's library. Filched, because Haranil-*arluth* considered sorcery sly, devious and no concern of a warrior. Not that ability with dogs, cats and horses, or finding lost trinkets, was anything more than toy magic for women and children. Aldric came face to face with the real thing that day and saw how much chance his intended revenge would have had against Duergar.

None at all.

A few days later he was calling the old man *altrou*, meaning foster-father. It seemed fitting somehow, and Gemmel's unfeigned pleasure at a title meaning more to him than a lordship had broken down the sometimes formal host-guest attitudes once and for all.

Even so, Aldric should not have laughed aloud when the wizard announced he was a *taiken*-master—for one thing, if it was true his mirth was most unwise. The young man knew, as did every warrior, that there had not been a true master since Baiel Sinun died two hundred years ago, and said so. Gemmel was unruffled and his response took Aldric unawares.

"Sinun was passable," he said blandly. "Not as good as some, but he taught me some moves and I him." Before Aldric could recover sufficiently to start asking questions, Gemmel had found a pair of foils and shown him the truth of his words. The lean old man had taken him off-guard three times within the first four passes, and that was something not even Joren had ever done.

Despite his apparent age—and Aldric had not the nerve to ask what it might be in years—Gemmel's gaunt frame concealed a wiry strength and his hands the kind of skill harpers exaggerated about. Gemmel was not a master—he was a genius, a virtuoso, perhaps the finest swordsman Aldric had ever met, seen or heard of. Without false modesty, the *eijo* knew himself to be good—in latter years he had beaten Joren several times and that needed more than luck—but against Gemmel Errekren he was like a child with a stick trying to harm a battle-harnessed *kailin*.

Whenever Aldric thought about fencing now, he could see the wizard, eyes glittering like emeralds, whirling and stamping like some dementedly graceful dancer. Gemmel, when his wizardly dignity was set aside, was opinionated, excitable, quick to argue and impatient to a fault. *Taiken*-master or not, he had no time for any of the rituals Aldric associated with swordplay. He knew, from the *ymeth*-trance, that the boy could fight and not merely duel—he had done so against Baiart so long ago, after all. So when Aldric took up a stylised guard-position with both hands on his hilt, Gemmel copied him and then shot out a free hand and slapped him across the face.

"Two-handed rubbish!" the old man barked. "Had I a dagger, your throat was cut. Only one hand on the hilt, except when you need both. Secure your index finger—thus—over the quillon. The hilt-loops will guard it."

"What hilt-loops?"

"I know what I'm talking about! These are only foils, remember. Again!" His moustache bristled with the intensity of his passion.

Aldric was slapped frequently during the fencing lessons; his teeth were rattled and more than once his nose was caused to bleed. He bore it as calmly as he could, because he had seen early on what Gemmel-*altrou* was doing—having lost one son already, he was trying to teach another how to stay alive.

There came a day when the boy's cheek was opened by an accidental stroke. It was not a dangerous cut, not even unsightly although he would bear its mark to the day he died. But it meant he was too fast for the wizard to slap any more. As the realisation dawned, a grin twisted the stream of blood on his face into grotesque tributaries. Gemmel grounded his blade and leaned on the pommel, watching as Aldric saluted politely. He had no objection to saluting; as he said, in a real fight only the winner *can* salute.

"You'll have a scar when that heals," he observed. Aldric looked at his right cheek in the polished sword-blade and was forced to agree. "Make sure it's the only one you ever receive in single combat." The old man's voice grew severe. "Being wounded in a melee is excusable; if you heed my teaching at all, being wounded in single combat will be damned careless! Remember that."

This fierce tuition was to continue for three hours a day on six days out of every seven. Aldric did not enjoy it, but he had not expected to do so, even though without a doubt he was improving. When Gemmel lectured him on other subjects while they fought and he could remember the discourse; when he was able to think out the often abstruse questions and answer them—sometimes even correctly; when a sudden flurry of Jouvaine or of Low Drusalan words no longer left him floundering in a morass of bad translation and worse parrying: then he knew within himself that he was growing more skilled.

As Gemmel had so waspishly pointed out, Aldric had intelligence. He had guessed long ago that whatever the sorcerer was planning, it was more than simply helping an *eijo* who happened to look like his son to achieve a difficult task. All the lessons in languages, politics and geography added up to something on a scale Aldric preferred not to think about. Even so, one day soon he was going to ask for a full explanation, and not hints and guesses. One day . . . probably after a meal when he had bolstered his courage with a cup of wine—or perhaps two. Interrogating Gemmel when he did not feel like answering questions was definitely a two-cup enterprise and more probably three. As a smile began to form around his mouth, Aldric fell asleep. For once, he did not dream.

*

"Where can he, be?" Kalarr cu Ruruc's voice was a soft, introspective murmur, but it stung Duergar like the shrillest accusation of guilt. He shrugged and made helpless gestures, but on looking up from the books on which he had been working he found that the other sorcerer was ignoring him. The tall, lean figure was outlined against a window of coloured glass, his red *elyu-dlas* blending eerily into the carmine-tinted sunlight. "Where . . . ?" he breathed again.

Duergar did not know, despite hunting Baelen Forest and beyond for almost two years before abandoning his search. In all that time there had been no trace of Aldric Talvalin after his trail went cold at a strange cottage. It had been magically concealed, an insignificant lesser charm which might well have been cast by the Alban himself—Duergar had seen the little cache of dubious books hidden in the youngster's room—but he privately opined that the boy was long since dead from the arrow he had taken as he fled from Dunrath. Kalarr, however, was not so easily convinced, even though had Aldric been alive no power on earth would have stopped him from coming back in a quest for revenge. There were times when Duergar felt that his . . . colleague . . . was trying to find something other than just the *eijo,* irritation though he might prove. What that something might be, the necromancer did not yet know, although he was trying to find out—without cu Ruruc's knowledge.

Aldric was not his only problem. Locked in his desk were five letters, four of them enciphered but one, the latest, written in dangerously unequivocal plain language—and the language was plain indeed. Warlord Etzel was losing patience with his agent's carefully worded excuses; he wanted action and an end to subtlety. The Alban Royal Council, stated the letter, was blatantly financing an insurrection by two prominent Jouvaine city-states and arms of Pryteinek manufacture had been seized in the province of Tergoves, right at the heart of the Empire. Where was the political instability he had been sent to foster? it demanded. Why had his much-vaunted seizure of a fortress not borne fruit before now? What, snarled the spiky letters, did Duergar Vathach think he was doing?

The Drusalan necromancer was perfectly aware of what he was doing—but by the letter's interrogative tone, nobody else was. Not yet, anyway. Except of course for Kalarr, who seemed to derive cynical amusement from Duergar's intended treachery. As always whenever he thought of things which cu Ruruc found humorous, the necromancer put one hand to the sword-hilt which he wore now like a tau cross, around his neck on a chain. Its cold metal afforded him little comfort, and less when he realised Kalarr had caught the gesture. For some reason his mouth curved slowly into a smile that was thin and yet so heavy with malign significance that it made Duergar's stomach clench like a fist inside him.

Although the necromancer had requested that his companion start something—anything—to justify his rebirth and aid Duergar's mission, Kalarr had . . . not actually refused, but been so evasive that the Drusalan's wishes were never carried out. The ancient charm which imbued cu Ruruc's sword-hilt with power over its previous owner should have allowed Duergar to command, not merely request—but the necromancer was strangely reluctant to test his strength even though at present he was unable to define his reasons. He had not recalled all the spies sent out after Aldric and was certain Kalarr remained unaware of the fact.

Duergar was equally unaware that Kalarr had posted spies of his own, under the same orders: find Aldric Talvalin and bring him, with everything in his possession no matter how insignificant, straight back to Dunrath.

It was the wrist-band from the sword, of course. What Duergar had read from an old grimoire given to him by Etzel was a spell of summoning, where any artifact of a sorcerer's previous existence may be used near the place of his death to restore him whole and entire. There had been a rider to the incantation, stating that if such an artifact were the last thing touched before death, it would grant control to whoever held it. While a skilled sorcerer, Duergar knew nothing of Alban military history—otherwise he would have known that a dying man may drop a sword from his fingers but not the metal band clasped about his wrist. It was the sort of niggling oversight which slew many otherwise careful wizards, and when Kalarr no longer had need to pretend subservience he would make sure it slew another. All he needed was to destroy the wrist-band, render it inaccessible by sealing it within a sphere of magic or sinking it in deep water—or best of all, lay his hands on the Echainon spellstone.

If he did that, it would negate the charm of the wrist-band and bring into his grasp a means of focusing his own considerable power, as he had been able to do so many years before, until that stupid day when fear of loss had made him conceal the spellstone under a sheath of bronze on the band of his war sword. The stone's power had been muted by its metal shroud, but he had never foreseen a time when he would not be granted the few seconds needed to free it—until that last suicidal charge by Clan Talvalin's cavalry which had burst his battle-line heedless of their losses and had swept him dying to the ground. He could not remember the then-*arluth*'s name, but if he closed his eyes he could still recall the man's wide blue eyes, the bloodied teeth bared in a fixed snarl under his sweeping blond moustache, the helm buckled and scored—and the shining *taiken* which had lopped his hand in two through the palm. Kalarr could remember the sword's name: Isileth, it was called, so long, long ago. It had ruined his hand and even as he killed the Talvalin *arluth* with a lethal blast of sorcery the long blade had come whirring back towards his face. There had been a flare of red and black, pain, heat, cold dark silence and the deep fall which never reached bottom . . .

Kalarr drew a shuddering breath and massaged his right hand with his left; the palms of both were damp with sweat. It was fitting that he should now hold the Talvalin citadel, but at the same time terrifying that a Talvalin should hold his spellstone. A Talvalin who in defiance of the *kailin* honour-codes read books of sorcery, who failed to kill himself when it was expected of him—what might such a man not do to achieve the vengeance he had brooded on for three years? If he regained the spellstone Kalarr would be invincible; he would show Duergar, and Rynert of Alba, Emperor Droek and his Warlord, show the Earth and the Sun and the Moon the dark majesty of a true Overlord, for after half a thousand years there would be no wizard with enough schooling in the Old Magics that he knew to defy him, once his spells were amplified through the stone of Echainon.

If he regained the stone . . . Even without it he was a power to be feared, but the spellstone was held by one whom he could not judge by any of the rules with which he was familiar. What if this boy, this Aldric, somehow bent the stone to fulfil his own desires? He could pay an enchanter to use it on his behalf if he had not the skill himself. Any enchanter . . . Kalarr shot a sidelong glance of horrid suspicion at Duergar's bowed head and considered several possibilities—but killing him now would be too soon, for his own deep-laid plans would benefit most from the confusion of an imminent invasion and the Drusalan had not yet sent the proper secret codes. But when he did . . .

A bead of perspiration trickled slowly past Kalarr's

eye, tickling the skin and making him blink. His teeth showed and in a sudden excess of frustration he flung the window wide and roared: "Where are you, Talvalin?" into the afternoon air. Duergar started, but only the hollow echoes of cu Ruruc's voice came distortedly back from the citadel walls. Kalarr bowed his head as the door of the chamber opened, then shifted his sombre gaze as the man in the shadows bowed low.

"Is anything wrong, my lord?" he said humbly. Kalarr's face twisted.

"No!" he barked. "Get out!" The man bowed again as he backed through the door.

"As my lord pleases," said Baiart Talvalin.

*

For the first time in longer than he could remember, Aldric snapped out of sleep with an alarm tocsin's clangour in his mind. Without taking time to think about it, he rolled sideways off the bed with one hand already reaching for the holstered *telek* behind the headboard. It cleared leather as he hit the floor and emitted a small, sinister double click as he wrenched its cocking lever back. The spring-gun had a magazine of eight stubby steel darts, and inside twelve paces would put each one through an unarmoured target just as fast as he could crank them out. It was the favoured weapon for places where a sword had insufficient range but a crossbow or longbow was too powerful—such as bedrooms. Such as now.

"Very impressive," said Gemmel from the doorway. "All I had to do was think hard about attacking you and your sense of danger did the rest."

"That wasn't very clever," Aldric replied severely, disarming the *telek* cautiously—it was all too easy to put a dart through one's own foot. "You've trained me not to ask questions in a situation like that one. If I hadn't remembered where I was . . ." Gemmel was not very concerned and said as much.

"The day you take me off guard when *I* set up the ambush, I'll give up sorcery for keeping chickens," he grinned. Aldric snorted and returned the *telek* to its hiding place.

"Don't be too impressed with this sixth sense of mine, by the way," he pointed out. "I've noticed it doesn't always work."

"Such things seldom do. Don't rely on it, that's all."

"I don't, *altrou.*"

"Wise of you. But enough of this dazzling conversation. It's time you found out what has been going on in the world these past few years, because within the next few days you're going to rejoin it."

"You mean I'm leaving? But . . . why?"

"Strange; I would have thought you much more eager to be away."

"I *am* eager, but . . . well, this is one of the situations where you don't like me not to ask questions. Isn't it . . . ?"

*

". . . and that, I guess, is why Kalarr hasn't given Duergar any assistance so far—and why I think that Duergar himself doesn't want to risk forcing the issue yet. But he isn't a fool; if he hasn't already worked out what the true controlling talisman is, a look at any contemporary sword will show him what it must be. Whether he has any notion about the spellstone I cannot say—but if he does enough research a process of elimination should tell him. I doubt if Kalarr will."

"But *altrou,* you're a wizard." Aldric's finger tapped the table to emphasise his words, making the cabochon stone wobble slightly in its velvet-lined case. Cold azure fire spilled out and made a dancing shadow-show on the young *eijo*'s intense features. "Why not use the stone yourself—let it focus your power instead of his?"

Gemmel smiled wanly and shook his head. "Sorcery isn't as easy as picking up another man's sword," he said. "You could probably use a Jouvaine *estoc,* but a man skilled with it would defeat you easily. With any of the seven spellstones I would be the same; I could control them, but they're not one of my fields of study. An expert could turn them against me without even touching the stones himself. And Kalarr cu Ruruc is an expert."

"So then, what do I do?"

"You find out why I gave you such an elaborate education."

They talked over dinner, or rather Gemmel talked and Aldric listened while he ate. The youngster never bothered to ask where food came from; he simply enjoyed it. This meal was a rich stew of three meats, served peasant-style with fresh vegetables on separate dishes and a little bowl of hot red spicy sauce which by the matching colour of Aldric's face he was using liberally. Without the elaborate high-clan table manners Aldric took care to observe at all times, Gemmel finished in half the time and lit his pipe. Not that he was a gluttonous eater, merely that he saw no reason to use salt only left-handed, in three shakes only and setting down the cellar before another three, knife in right hand only and never lift drink with the left. Aldric did—it was a link with what had once been and he was unwilling to break that link, because there was so little else left to him.

"Since I can't use the spellstone, you must get me something I can make use of. I spent this morning trimming down a list made last week, and you'll be glad to hear you won't have to go as far as I had feared at first. Look . . ." The old man cleared dishes to one side and spread a map on the table. "I marked the locations of various talismans on this, and although the closest is here"—his finger touched a red dot in the central Jouvaine provinces—"that's much too close to the Imperial frontier. The provinces are usually lax in the matter of magic, but right now two city-states are in rebellion and Imperial law is stringently enforced. The fact that you come from the country funding the rebels wouldn't be in your favour, and looking for a sorcerous talisman would virtually guarantee your summary execution. However," and a pleased smirk appeared on Gemmel's face, "this ban on enchantments has rebounded on Warlord Etzel. Duergar Vathach isn't his only agent and a Vreijek overlord caught one inside his city walls. The man was . . . induced to say who sent him, and since he was a wizard of some small cult his confession of Etzel's name has that worthy embroiled in a scandal it will take him some time to live down. I was afraid that if old Droek should die Etzel would have tried to usurp Ioen's authority, but now he won't have enough support to risk the attempt. Indeed, the wonder of it is that he is still in office."

"*Altrou*, why are the Imperial lords so much against magic?" Aldric was genuinely interested, because Alba had no such ban and yet the clan-lords had never bothered to use sorcery. Perhaps the two facts were related.

"Not just the lords, Aldric. The common people have been taught that magic is irreligious and disrespectful to Heaven."

The young Alban instantly noticed what Gemmel had hinted. "So that's the teaching. What's the fact?"

With a little shrug the old enchanter poured himself wine and took a careful sip. "I travelled, before I came to Alba. We travelled—my son and I. For no other reason than to see other countries, other cultures. Curiosity, if you like. We came to a village in Tergoves province which for some reason was being . . . 'disciplined' is the Empire's word. I would have left, for we could do nothing, but Ernol tried to rescue a girl and killed two troopers in the process. We fled. Later that afternoon the soldiers came.

"There was a young man with them, unarmoured but in rich robes. He called Ernol over and looked him up and down, smiling pleasantly. 'Did you kill my soldiers?' he asked. 'Yes,' said Ernol. 'Why did you do that?' Ernol told him. "They are expensive to train—can you repay me?' 'I cannot,' replied Ernol. 'Oh, but you can,' said the young man. And then—then . . .

"He slew my only son.

"I went a little mad. I think I screamed—I know I wept. I saw the young man, smiling, wiping his sword, and he was red: his horse was red; the grass and the sky and the sun were all red with the blood of my son and the hate in my brain. Then I raised my empty hand and spoke the Invocation of Fire.

"He burned. He sat on his tall horse with a smile on his lips and a naked sword in his hand and he flared and died like dry straw in a furnace. It mattered little to me that he was the Grand Warlord's second son, Etzel's uncle, or that my action would make the Empire ban all magic thereafter on pain of death. All that mattered was that I had killed him too quickly. I had not repaid him in full for the death of my own, my only son."

Aldric stared unblinking at Gemmel for a time, then poured wine and drank it, not in a careful sip but in a single long gulp though he hardly felt the liquor's warmth through the icy knot in his stomach. He had only ever seen the gentle, studious side of the man he called *altrou,* and had sometimes wondered whether he knew the true meaning of Aldric's own desire for revenge. It seemed that he did. "Not repaid him in full . . ." echoed again through the *eijo's* mind—it might have been his own voice.

"What am I—" now that was his own voice, raspy and shrill from a mouth the wine had barely moistened. Aldric cleared his throat and tried again. "What am I to look for, then—and where?"

"There is a talisman which I think will answer my needs best. It's called Ykraith—the Dragonwand."

"Dragon . . . ?" Aldric wondered aloud. The word had a Drusalan sound.

"Firedrake," Gemmel translated. "There's a cavern on the island of Techaur. That's where you'll find it."

"Where's Techaur?" asked the Alban, squinting at the map. It was a strange thing, drawn on stiff glass-clear parchment with letters much too small to read unaided. The wizard touched a smudge of islands in the Narrow Sea south of Cerenau. Aldric realised what they were and groaned softly. "Not the Ethailin Myl! They're not called the Thousand Islands for a joke!"

"Even so, they're only five days' sailing from Erdhaven."

"And how many days finding one particular unnamed lump of rock, eh?"

"Less than you might think—there are only so many 'lumps of rock' big enough to contain the size of cavern this is supposed to be. If in doubt, ask one of the local fishermen." Aldric grunted, then found something else to quibble about.

"Look here, isn't Kerys much closer? Two, three day sailing at most. Why don't I—"

"Why don't you look at the rest of the map? There's a lot more riding from here to Kerys than there is to

Erdhaven—and that much more time for you to be spotted by a spy and dealt with before you have the Dragonwand."

"Oh . . ."

"Yes, 'oh.' Now, I think it's high time you had a sword
of your own. Follow me—unless of course you have a
few more objections for me to dispose of." The old
man's voice wasn't unkind, more dryly amused, and
though Aldric could have mentioned pirates, Imperial
Fleet patrol-ships and even water-monsters, he decided
to save his breath and follow.

*

"This is my armoury," said Gemmel, indicating a door
with one hand and fishing in his pocket for keys with
the other. As the door hissed open on well-oiled
hinges, Aldric caught his breath at the glitter from
within. After so long with a wizard, he was prepared
for and accustomed to wonders where he least expected them, but the armory was somewhere he had
long wanted to see. He saw it now, lit by a cool, pale
light pouring from slots in the ceiling, and realised that
he was not completely inured to the marvellous after
all—which he considered privately was just as it
should be.

He spent a long time simply wandering up and down,
looking at things. Though he could not put the sensation
into words, he felt that there was one particular weapon
he should be looking for. The feeling was vague, amorphous, but still strong enough to bring him back to Gemmel empty-handed. The enchanter nodded as if he had
expected something of the sort and took a sheathed
blade from a locked cupboard on the wall. He locked
the door again carefully afterwards, then extended the
weapon to Aldric. "Try this," he said. "I think it will
suit you."

The young *eijo* bowed politely, as was the custom
when receiving the gift of a sword—though in truth it
was just a blade, cased in a black battle scabbard chaped,
clasped and throated with silver. Its tang was shrouded
in a binding of soft leather, with the parts of the proper
hilt in a box which Gemmel set out on the armoury
work-bench—a metal box enamelled in deep blue shot

with silver stars, its edges ornamented with designs of significance. How significant, Aldric was soon to learn. Within, each piece was cradled in its own nest of quilted satin; the metal was black and shiny, not because of lacquer or enamel but because the steel itself was jet black. Even the strips of tooled leather braided crisscross on the long grip were black, relieved only by an underlay of silver wire.

The weapon was a *taiken* of exquisite quality, and with sensuous care Aldric revealed part of the straight blade. By tradition no *taiken* was ever drawn by a new owner for the first time except under the light of Heaven, and he contented himself with a mere handspan of the mirror-burnished metal. It flashed under the harsh artificial lights. Smoky blue-grey lines of incredibly hard steel outlined the cutting edges, shifting in a constant play of reflected shadow as he turned the longsword this way and that. Slightly embarrassed to find his hands trembling, Aldric ran the shining blade home with the gentlest of pressures and unwrapped the leather binding from its tang.

This was the only part of the blade where writing was permitted; any other decoration was limited to stylised or abstract engraving. As they scanned the precise, beautiful uncials, flowing as elegantly as if they were penned and not gouged from the unpolished grey metal, Aldric's eyes narrowed and he glanced at Gemmel for a nod of confirmation before staring more intently at the graceful letters. Both they and the language they constituted were in an old form of the Alban High Speech, so that he had to work at the translation—and even when the meaning was clear, his mind found it hard to accept.

"This can't be true!" he breathed.

"The words are true," intoned Gemmel quietly. "It is fitting that this ancient evil should be matched by this ancient blade."

"Forged was I of iron Heaven-born," Aldric read, half to himself. "Uelan made me. I am Isileth."

The weapon Aldric held was almost two thousand year old, older than the coming of the Horse Lords, and though the hilt had been changed many times as fashion and need dictated, the blade itself had a lineage few clans could match. Clan Talvalin did, on the Elthanek side. Aldric did.

The ribbon of steel was too hard to bend, too flexible to break, and the legends said its edges had only once been honed, and then still wet from the quenching bath. A named blade, its formal title was Isileth; but down the years and in the stories it had become known by a simpler, sinister, more accurate epithet: Widowmaker.

Aldric secured the complex hilt, noting absently the quillons deeply forked for parrying or snapping an opponent's blade, and seeing that there were indeed loops to guard his fingers. He locked the pommel in place, lifted the *taiken,* then knelt and pressed the cool smoothness of its lacquered scabbard to his brow. Gemmel bowed slightly, acknowledging his foster-son's courtesy. There were words to say when accepting such a gift, but Aldric could not remember them—and anyway they were probably insufficient to describe his state of mind. Instead he pulled the scabbard on its shoulder-belt over his head in silence and settled it on his left hip, withdrew the longsword's safety-collar a bare half-inch and then sheathed it with a solid click.

"I'll have your horses and armour ready by tomorrow," said Gemmel, interrupting the *eijo*'s reverie as gently as he could. Aldric came out of his waking dream with a start.

"I'll pack my travelling gear," he said quickly. "There are things I don't want to forget." The enchanter looked at him curiously.

"I don't think there's anything I've overlooked."

Aldric smiled a small, enigmatic smile which told Gemmel nothing. "Probably not . . ." was all the young man said.

*

Aldric limited his selection of clothing to essentials, functional rather than fashionable. Apart from the white of shirts and linen, everything was unrelieved black—and some garments were even more functional than their tailor had originally intended. Upending a boot, the Alban shook three sheathed knives from their place of concealment. Neither his family nor, he guessed, his foster-father would have approved of them, since even *venjens-*

eijin were expected to have a modicum of honesty and carry their weapons in plain view. He intended to do no such thing. One, a balanced throwing-knife, buckled round his calf where it was hidden by the long moccasin boots he favoured. Another was a thin stiletto strapped to his left forearm, hilt foremost under the shirtsleeve. While the third . . .

That was the most dubious of all. It was a T-shaped punch dagger whose scabbard hooked to the loops he had secretly sewn inside all his collars. It was dishonourable, an assassin's weapon—and a possibly-fatal surprise for anyone who thought him unarmed. That, Aldric reflected as he settled the tiny knife against his spine, was justification enough for him. Fitting Isileth carefully to one side of a new double weapon-belt, he bowed very slightly, very privately, before slotting his *tsepan* into place. Then quite quickly he gathered up his clothes and left the room, pausing only once to look back at what had been home for three years. Then he closed the door with a sudden, final movement.

In the armoury he packed his saddlebags and waited for Gemmel. When the old enchanter appeared, he strode without pausing straight for the wall which shot up smoothly into the ceiling at his approach, revealing a dusty flight of stairs lit with the yellow dance of live flames. In the dust were traces of feet coming and going, with the latest so recent that nothing had yet dimmed the shiny stair. Aldric smelt the odours of hay and horses. Beyond a green door was his pack-horse, already partially loaded with cased armour—but the youngster made at once for the stall beside it.

Within was a courser, midnight black and gleaming. It was harnessed in black leather bossed and inlaid with silver, saddled in black leather with tassles of silver-shot blue—the Talvalin colours, but too subtle for the idle glance—and geared with bow and quiver, holstered *telekin* and a cased shield. The beast was Andarran, a purebred stallion of a breed extinct this hundred years or more, and his value was beyond price. "The horse's name is Lyard," he heard Gemmel say as he made his saddlebags fast. Aldric's mind was whirling, despite his efforts to control it. There was an overpowering sensation of having slipped unnoticed into a harper's tale, and reality was something harder to grasp than the horse at his shoulder or the sword at his hip.

He led the war-horse forward and secured the pack-pony's reins to a stirrup leather, then glanced around for the way out. Gemmel noticed his enquiring look and gestured with one hand, at which the back wall of the stable ground ponderously open. A breeze whirled in, bringing with it birdsong and the smell of the open air. Walking beside his charger, Aldric stepped back into a world which should have seemed real—except that he was no longer sure just what was real.

Gemmel watched as the warrior with his son's face reached the saddle in a single easy swing, then stepped out behind him into the watery sunshine. "I'm sorry the weather isn't more pleasant," he said apologetically. Aldric didn't care. He had never really appreciated landscapes before, but this was the first scenery he had laid eyes on in far too long and he drank it in.

"This is gold, this silver," the enchanter said, and held out two leather bags. "Six hundred marks should be enough, I hope. If not, and you hurry, you can earn something at the Erdhaven Spring-Feast. Now remember, don't touch anything but the Dragonwand, no matter how tempting. Watch out for spies—and they won't all be human. Trust nobody, especially after dark."

A tiny smile tugged at the corners of Aldric's mouth; it was typical of the old man to give a lecture when all had been already said. "And Aldric . . ." the words hesitated.

"Yes?"

Gemmel shyly rubbed the toe of his boot into the grass. "I was only going to say, come back safe." Aldric smiled and bowed. With a rush of warmth the wizard realised it was the small, informal nod of son to father.

"I'll do my best. *Tau k'noeth-ei, altrou-ain.*" He twitched the stallion's reins and cantered off into the sunrise. Gemmel watched him go.

"And with you also, Aldric . . . my son." Then he turned away.

When Aldric looked back he saw only the grass—but he waved anyway.

*

Behind a securely locked door, Duergar Vathach read the words on a ragged scrap of parchment for the third time, as if hoping they might have changed their meaning. They had not. There was nobody in the room to see how pale his face had become, nor how his fingers trembled before they clenched into white-knuckled fists that clawed the pendant sword-hilt from around his neck. Links of broken chain scattered across the floor with a multiple laughing tinkle, and then the hilt itself went crashing against a wall.

Cradling his sweat-slick head in both hands, Duergar mumbled incoherently to himself. He had long been troubled by the way cu Ruruc showed neither fear nor respect, but ill-concealed amusement, whenever he saw the talisman that supposedly controlled him. And there was the way he had sent out spies to find and bring him . . . something.

Duergar had not known what cu Ruruc sought until a year ago, when some errand had brought him from Dunrath's great library into the Hall of Archives next to it, a place which housed both writings and objects from past history. There he had seen old *taikenin*, relics of the Clan Wars—and seen too, for the first time, the chains and bands which held each sword securely on its owner's wrist. Bands which would remain in contact with the wearer's cooling flesh long after death-slack fingers had released the finest sword-hilt . . .

It had taken Duergar ten months to confirm his nightmare. Ten months of frantic, furtive searching through every document in a fortress all too well supplied with scribbled scraps of information. He had not known what he was looking for, only that he would know it if he found it. As indeed he did.

The evidence was not dramatic; rather, its insignificance was more redolent of some black joke. A bill. A coppersmith's bill, stuffed out of sight and out of mind in a heap of ledgers, destined to be discarded but instead forgotten until Duergar found it; after an interval of some five hundred years.

". . . *from a* kailin *of Ut Ergan citadel, retainer to* Kalarr-arluth, *two markes of silver for ye ensetting of a* jewel (*this blue and most fair*) *under bronze on his swordes clasp against losing of ye same, it being a lucktoken ygiven of his Lorde* . . ." Any sorcerer of intelligence knew that one of the seven Echainon spellstones had vanished from all wizards' knowledge during or before the Alban Clan Wars—and to Duergar's frantically working mind the words he read had only one possible meaning. He was aware, too, that if Kalarr learned that his secret was discovered he, Duergar, would die. But if he, Duergar, was able to retrieve the wrist-band, then when cu Ruruc made his move the other sorcerer would get the shock of both his lives. And if the Echainon spellstone was still "ensetten under bronze" on the sword clasp, then he would be no longer needed.

But if Kalarr should regain the wrist-band and the stone . . . Duergar's mind quailed at the consequences. It explained many of his suspicions about cu Ruruc, and he had no doubt that his so-called ally was also searching for Aldric Talvalin. Except that if Kalarr felt unable to bring the *kailin* back, then rather than risk the stone falling into someone else's hands he would obliterate everything. Duergar had to reach both it and Aldric first . . .

With the strength of extreme fear he dragged his laden desk aside and began to draw a symbol of great power across the wooden floor . . .

*

In the four days' riding since he had left Gemmel, Aldric had encountered no more than a dozen people—but he had already discovered that his status of *eijo* was accorded more respect than a *kailin* of the same age. Reaction was the same in every case: first a curious glance towards the sound of hoofs, then a narrow-eyed survey of the covered shield, the apparently uncoloured trappings, the *tsepan* from which Aldric had prised his clan crest, the cropped hair and the faintly sinister air lent by his scarred cheek. And then the bow, invariably low, formal—and performed with a timidity the young man at first found rather shocking.

An *eijo,* whether with hair unbound to indicate his lordless state or like Aldric's, cropped to mark an oathtaken purpose, was outside the law and without protection from House or Clan. He had only himself to rely on—which made the *eijo* a menacing individual and one for lonely travellers to be wary of. While Aldric was comfortable in the presence of yeomen and peasants—regardless of whether they were comfortable with him about or not—he avoided large towns and the occasional *kailin* he met on the road. When encounters were unavoidable he matched their bows precisely, neither offering nor expecting much respect. When they were low-clan and inferior, as most were, even that rankled.

It was another fortnight before the huge forest of Guelerd began to darken the horizon ahead of him. The place had a well-deserved reputation as a stronghold for ruffians and bandits despite the efforts of King Rynert's father, and what few steadings Aldric passed were large and well-fortified. Rumour had it that only fools and foreigners rode through Guelerd unescorted; a rumour the young man smiled at, since he had seen no trace of hostility all day. It did not occur to him that a full-armed *eijo* on a warhorse was not the most inviting of prospective victims.

By the time he passed under the eaves of the forest, afternoon was already tilting towards evening. He was grateful for the cool of the slanting shadows and almost wished it would rain a little, enough to settle the dust of the paved military road and wash the dry heat from the air. A pair of rooks hopped out of his path, then returned to whatever they had been squabbling over. A solitary fox eyed him from behind a tree before ambling off about its own affairs. There was a crow cawing lazily somewhere. Aldric yawned and tried to remember what the last yeoman had told him of the forest inns. They locked their doors at nightfall and did not admit guests after dark, that much he did know. A glance at the sky relaxed him; it would be a couple of hours yet before the light failed.

Watching darkness fall from a tavern common-room, Aldric sipped ale and sniffed the savoury aroma of his dinner being prepared. He knew now why he had not encountered any highway robbers on the road; after seeing the tavern's prices, it was clear they had all turned innkeeper. Such places catered for the wealthy mer-

chants who travelled towards Erdhaven port, and charged
accordingly. Even the third son of one of Alba's foremost clan-lords could not have stayed in such a house.
It was wryly amusing therefore that a landless *eijo*, an
enchanter's fosterling, could afford the best room and
pay for it in hard coin.

As he ate Aldric became aware of unease among the
other patrons; though to the innkeeper one man's silver
was as good as another, he, Aldric, was probably not
the sort of guest this place liked to attract. The plump
merchants and their ladies—by the look of them,
"wives" was not the word to use—did not like sharing
their dinnertime with an *eijo*, no matter how young or
well-mannered. Aldric was not concerned—although the
fat woman who was probably the only merchant's wife
in the building annoyed him throughout the meal. Lan-
guishing glances and rogueish winks did not go too well
with a fine venison pasty. With a thin, sardonic smile he
fixed an unwinking stare on the would-be-romantic, toying significantly with his knife all the while.

By the time he had to blink, she and her husband had
hurriedly bustled out. Aldric's smile widened fractionally; there were advantages to being *eijo* after all.

With the heat and the ale and the feeling of being
pleasantly full that gave the whole world a rosy glow,
the young man decided it was time for bed. He rose,
stretched mightily and ambled upstairs to where the
room had been shuttered for the night and two lamps
set out. The bed looked soft and inviting, so much so
that he kicked off his boots and lay down fully dressed,
intending to relax for a while before sleeping properly.

That, at least, was his intention. However, once his
eyelids had closed, it soon became too much effort to
open them again . . .

Merchants who lodged in an inn such as this paid too
highly for their rooms to tolerate nocturnal noises. Floors
were thickly carpeted, locks and hinges oiled and silent.
Thus it was that Aldric slept on peacefully while his
window-shutters were teased open and the window itself
slid back. A thin glow of moonlight flowed in, and with
it a dark outline which drifted like fog across the floor.
The Alban whimpered softly in his sleep and rolled over,

making the stealthy intruder freeze where he stood. Only when the youngster was breathing deeply once more did he continue about his furtive business. The same sharp knife which had forced the shutter-catch now sliced saddlebag straps and the lacings on well-filled moneybags too imprudently displayed earlier in the evening. The thief's gloved fingers checked their contents without chinking a single coin, then transferred them to his own belt-pouch before the man retraced his steps and vanished into the night. Lacking in all manners, he did not even close the shutters behind him.

Aldric's eyes flicked open half an hour later to a room streaked skimmed-milk blue by the moonlight pouring through his open window—a window that had been dark and secured when he fell asleep. And a window through which somebody was quietly entering.

He would have grabbed for *taiken* or *telek,* except that one was on the rack built into one wall for the purpose, and both of the other were still bolstered in the stable . . . Instead he made the small noises of restless sleep and gathered his legs under him, sliding the stiletto from his sleeve. The shadowy figure paused warily, watchfully and then bent over his saddlebags.

One hundred and sixty pounds of irritated *eijo* in the small of the back would inconvenience most people and this burglar was no exception. The pair went down in a tangle of flailing limbs and began an impromptu wrestling match which did nothing for the room's furnishings. What with the uncertain light and the black clothes of both combatants, it was a confused and confusing fight, complicated by the fact that the thief refused to do much except try to escape. Though they were much of a size, Aldric quickly discovered himself to be the stronger of the two. Besides which, there was the stiletto to consider.

A dainty sting under the fellow's masked chin stopped the burglar's wriggling long enough for Aldric to drive one knee down hard, winding his opponent for the second time in a matter of minutes. Taking advantage of the man's helpless gasps for breath to open one of the lamps, Aldric raised it high and wrenched off his victim's mask with the other hand.

Only to discover that *he* was actually *she.* "Good gods!" the Alban exclaimed unoriginally, and then let rip with several more interesting swear-words when the girl jerked both knees up into his side and almost threw him over her head. Had those knees struck their intended target, Aldric would have been in no state to prevent her escape and he knew it. That was why he straddled her and sat down hurriedly with his full weight in the pit of her stomach. Her breath came out in a gasp for the third time, and Aldric used the opportunity to make himself more comfortable—then delicately rested his stiletto point in the hollow of her throat as insurance against further attempts on his . . . person. This gave him the chance to look at his catch more closely:

Fine skin tanned to the colour of honey, electrum-pale blonde hair tied back under a black hood, slightly oblique eyes of a brilliant blue that reminded him of the Echainon spellstone, a full mouth half-open over white teeth. She was beautiful—and at the moment very, very angry. "Get off!" she snapped, and even in only two words Aldric noticed a slight, unplaceable accent. "Alban, take that knife away and get *off!*"

"You're scarcely in a position to make demands," Aldric observed with a smugness he did not really mean. "Now—what did you steal?" The girl spat inaccurately at him. "Listen, you," he rasped, waving the stiletto in front of her eyes, "I'm asking you nicely. The Prefect in Erdhaven won't be so pleasant. *What did you steal?*"

"Nothing," she retorted eventually. "There was no gold in your saddlebag."

"No?" Aldric's voice was sharp with disbelief. "I'm at liberty to search you unless you . . ." He cast a thoughtful gaze over the girl's clothing and realised the threat was useless. Her black garments fitted so closely—apart from where they had burst open in the fight—that anything as big as his moneybags would show quite plainly. There was nothing showing at all. The girl saw his face fall, and rather than trying to escape she smiled amiably.

"Your shutters were open, Alban. I doubt if I'm your first visitor tonight." Aldric cursed foully in three languages. "You shouldn't have taken the best room," she pointed out helpfully. "Nor paid for it in gold coins."

Aldric stared at her and almost reluctantly grinned at the irony of it all.

"But I did," he returned flatly. "And much good it did me." He studied the girl more closely, as if realising again how very pretty she was. "Who are you anyway?"

"Alban, if you're going to talk, I'd rather you sat elsewhere—and removed your hand." With sudden embarrassment Aldric jerked his knife hand from between her breasts, having rested it there quite absently the better to keep his stiletto under her chin. The girl closed her shirt and stared up at him levelly. "The second part, Alban. Find a chair."

"Don't try escaping," he warned. "I wouldn't want to—" he thought of various things he would and would not do, then chose the least offensive. "To miss hearing what you're going to tell me," he finished and stood up. Backing away, he turned quickly and slammed the shutters, but when he looked round the girl had merely risen to a cross-legged seat on the floor. She put her head on one side and fluttered her lashes at him mockingly.

"Convinced of my good intentions, Alban?" Aldric nodded, but slung Widowmaker round his shoulder nonetheless.

"*You* aren't Alban, of course." It wasn't a question—her accent made one unnecessary. The girl untied her hood and let her hair fall free before answering him.

"I am Kyrin," she said at length. "Tehal Kyrin, Harek's daughter, of Tervasdal in Valhol." Aldric was startled; he had expected almost anyone but a Valhollan.

"What in the name of Heaven are you doing here?"

"Trying to collect enough money for passage home again. My uncle's ship was wrecked on your so-well-mapped coastal rocks and no merchant will sail to Valhol without being well paid."

"I'm not surprised," admitted Aldric. Then he grinned maliciously. "But if you'd got to my saddlebags first you could have bought your own vessel. With near enough five hundred marks." Kyrin winced, and said something in her native tongue. It sounded vicious.

"So we're both in the same situation," she muttered despairingly.

"Apparently. And what do *we* do now?" It was "we" already, he noted sourly; need breeds strange bedfellows. His eyes slid sideways at the thought of bed, then blinked and shifted away. Not so hasty—not with a Valhollan, anyway.

"We could rob," suggested Kyrin bluntly.

"No. There are limits even for *eijin*. It would be dishonourable."

"Albans and honour!" the girl flared. "You all think it's your exclusive privilege. Mine was the most honourable of honourless choices—rather a thief than a beggar and a robber than a whore . ." She stared grimly at the big bed. "I am—was—to marry at Spring-Return. It was to bind an alliance of families, so Seorth will have married my sister instead." She shrugged carelessly. "So, and so, and so . . . but if I had earned my money in bed, who would marry me for any decent reason? Eh?"

Aldric said nothing; indeed, Kyrin wondered if he had even been listening, because there was a thoughtful, faraway look about him. Then he grinned at her and clapped his hands briskly so that she jumped.

"Thanks for reminding me," he said cheerfully. "I can earn something at the Erdhaven Spring-Feast—not much, but enough."

"Earn? At a religious celebration?"

"Not religious—holiday. It's a market festival of some sort; I've never been to it, but I know they hold weapon contests, archery, *telek*-shooting, horsemanship—and all with prizes of minted silver."

"What about swordplay?" The girl's sharp eyes had noticed a fine *taiken* racked on the bedroom wall and Aldric's reluctance was plain when he shook his head.

"I daren't try single combat. With people looking for me it's too obvious to risk."

"The people who originally owned that money you lost, honourable *eijo?*"

Aldric didn't react to the jibe except with a mirthless leer. "Actually, no. But if they catch me and you're nearby, you'll wish yourself far, far away."

"I . . . see," muttered Kyrin, glad that she did not. Her father had been right all the time—Albans were crazy and this one was crazier than most. She would be well advised to have nothing to do with him; yet travel with this black-clad loon could prove entertaining and maybe profitable as well. "Why do you need the money anyway?"

"I'm taking a sea voyage for the good of my health. Want to come?"

"Why not? It might be interesting." Kyrin wondered then why the young Alban roared with laughter—honest amusement, without sneer or sarcasm. Then he looked at her, still chuckling.

"Oh, I think you'll find it that. Definitely interesting . . ."

5

Resurrection

Aldric was too polite to ask where Kyrin's handsome grey gelding had come from, and she was not yet so sure of him that she would have answered anyway. Not that her daytime wear invited questions: thigh-boots of soft doeskin over tight, faded blue breeches, a loose white shirt indifferently fastened, a leather jerkin armoured after a fashion with a layer of chain mail and a lady's *cymar*—overmantle—flung over all as if to mark her sex. With the complex hilt of a Jouvaine *estoc* riding at her shoulder and the arm-plates from somebody's battle armour strapped over her sleeves, Tehal Kyrin made a brave show alongside the equally picturesque but rather more sombre Aldric. Neither was the sort of person idly approached by passersby.

There were many such; peasants riding ox-carts or walking in noisy groups, well-heeled merchants in their carriages and those less wealthy jolting in horse-palanquins. Certain elderly *kailinin* cast disapproving looks at the younger set, fantastically tricked out in the latest fashion of the Imperial court, the Jouvaine city-states or wherever else took their current fancy. Aldric was relieved to notice that in this holiday atmosphere his and Kyrin's attire was dismissed as whimsical fancy dress.

As they came closer to Erdhaven, the crowds increased; judicious eavesdropping revealed that this Feast was rumoured to be the best and biggest for some years. For a man intending to lose himself among the press of people, that was good news. Aldric glanced up at the birds circling above the road; they were attracted by scraps of food, occasional spillages of grain—and one of them maybe by himself.

The scream of a gull cut through the other noises and his eyes went narrow and thoughtful. Was he not being a bit unimaginative watching out only for crows when a seagull would look less out of place near the coast? Reining in, he stared at one big yellow-eyed brute which seemed suspiciously disinterested in the scraps lying under its beak.

"What's the matter, Aldric?" Kyrin had seen the worried look on his face before she saw the gull, and when her eye fell on it she snorted dismissively. "Those pirates! Vicious—but no concern of ours."

"Of yours, maybe," he said softly, easing a *telek* from its holster. "For myself, I'm not so sure." He cocked the spring-gun and levelled it, taking care to adopt the proper arm's-length posture for contests of skill; with luck he would appear merely to be putting in a little practice. The *telek* thumped and the gull went down in silence. There was no human shriek of agóny, only the reflex spastic flutter of one wing which soon ceased. Ignoring the ironic applause from other travellers, Aldric racked another dart into the weapon and nudged Lyard slowly forward, eyes and *telek* fixed on the dead bird. Kyrin followed, muttering under her breath in her own language and wondering again why she had bothered to come along with this madman. The *eijo* dismounted, nudged the corpse with a toe, rolled it over, then finally picked it up and tugged his missile free. Throughout all, it remained a seagull.

"If you don't tell me at once what this exhibition is about. Alban, I'll leave you to playact on your own."

Aldric eyed her for a moment, then dropped the carcass and wiped his fingers on the grass. "If I don't, could you really bear to leave without finding out something?" he asked good-humouredly.

"Don't twist words!"

"All right then, I won't. I'll tell you everything—that you need to know, at least—but not here. When we've found a room and a bed——"

"Beds, Alban. I've warned you already."

"Beds, then. Or privacy at least. But Kyrin-*ain,*"—the endearment was not accidental, nor was it just to tease her—"Kyrin-*ain,* I doubt that you'll like what you hear. Playacting has no part in it."

"Whether I like it or not is immaterial. What I do not like is all this secrecy. Why don't you trust me?"

"I do trust you. If I didn't, I . . . I wouldn't have told you my name. That's the truth."

The girl stared at him for a long time without saying anything, then bowed very slightly. "I believe what you say, Aldric-*eijo.* And I'll accept anything else you tell me about this business, however little that may be." Then she glanced towards the road and smiled. "Best be on our way if you want to find somewhere to stay for tonight—your small change won't last until tomorrow otherwise."

As they mounted up and cantered towards Erdhaven, neither saw a black crow fluttering heavily from the lower branches of a tree where it had been perched. Nor did they notice how it wheeled high into the blue spring sky before flapping with uncrowlike speed towards the north-west.

And the citadel of Dunrath.

*

Kyrin's guess was close to the truth; they found it almost impossible to obtain rooms and ended up sharing one in a tavern near the harbour. It was better than Aldric had anticipated, but consequently more expensive than he was prepared for. Even after an hour's haggling his meagre funds had been sorely depleted when at last they went upstairs.

"One bed," said the Valhollan in a toneless voice.

"Well, at least there's a chair and blankets . . ." Aldric disliked the implication.

"I paid for this and I'm sleeping in it," he snapped. Kyrin shrugged, dumping her saddlebags before the fireplace as a footstool.

Aldric's irritation evaporated at once. "Kyrin . . . *Kyrin.*" He met her stare, then gestured at the mattress. "It's easily big enough for half each. To *sleep.* We'll need rest, both of us. I know that you . . . that is . . ." He was getting embarrassed now and angry at himself for being so. Finally he drew a deep breath and released it hissing between clenched teeth, unslung Isileth Widowmaker from her travelling-place at his back and laid the sheathed *taiken* precisely down the centre of the bed. "Half—I promise."

The girl looked at him, head tilted quizzically. "You promise . . . like *that?*" Aldric nodded once, fiercely willing her to accept and not make him look foolish. "Very well. I agree . . . to the arrangement." She almost smiled and kept it to a twitching of her lips; the boy—she was older than he was, almost certainly—could be horribly intense sometimes. "But why that way?"

"It—it seemed right, somehow," Aldric tried to explain awkwardly.

"Sometimes, Alban, I wonder if you're real." There was no mockery in her voice and when Aldric remembered his own feelings about the sword and the horse, he matched the twinkle in her ice-blue eyes with a shy smile of his own. But when Kyrin lifted Widowmaker from the bed only her sex restrained him from harsh words; no warrior ever made so free with another's sword and though physically a woman, the Valhollan's sword made her as much a warrior as any *kailin-eir.*

Perhaps she sensed something or heard his gasp of outrage; whatever the reason, she turned almost hastily and bowed from the waist as she had seen her companion do along the road. Holding out the longsword, one hand already incautiously on the hilt, she asked: "May I draw?" Aldric nodded curtly, realising he could not expect customs and protocol from a foreigner, but acknowledging her untutored courtesy all the same.

Isileth hissed from her scabbard with a whisper as of stroked silk. Without raising her eyes from the cruel beauty of the steel, Kyrin murmured, "Have you used this?" and at once regretted the question, suddenly aware of an aura of cold menace settling over the blade as it slid clear. With a shiver she realised this same intangible grey veil sometimes hung around her companion and wondered, not wanting an answer, which of the two was its true source.

"She has been drawn in the dawn-light, under the eye of Heaven, that she may know me," intoned the *eijo* quietly. "But used—not yet . . ." Kyrin sheathed the *taiken* and laid it down, affecting not to notice the slight, caressing touch of Aldric's hand on hers as he retrieved the weapon and secured it on his hip. "Someone tried to insult me once—said I slept with my sword. I can't imagine what he would say now." His small, crooked smile widened fractionally. "By the way, I'm not utterly penniless. Shall we eat now or later?"

*

"I guessed aright, then," Duergar muttered, his pale eyes fixed on a thin man in black who knelt before him. The man's hood was thrown back, revealing yellowish eyes and dark hair which hung in lank tails from perspiration. Had he been a horse he would have been lathered. Until a few minutes previously he had been a crow; he was still lathered. "You are certain of this?"

"Quite certain, lord," gasped the man. He was having difficulty in getting his breath back and Duergar's impatient questions were not helping. "From what I saw, indeed, had the boy spotted me I would have been"— he essayed a gaptoothed smile—"dead certain, as they say here."

"Spare me your feeble humour, man," returned the necromancer wearily. "I have much to do." He stood up and the changeling lowered his head respectfully. "You may rest; there will be rewards for this day's work. Would that all my servants did so well . . ." He crossed to the door and then glanced back. "Mark you, no word of this to lord Kalarr."

"No word?" Kalarr stood in the doorway as it opened, his teeth bared in a hard, mirthless grin. "Whyever not? I'm most curious." There was a *taiken* in his hand, its point resting on the door-ward's lips. "I learned that one of your changeling-crows had returned. Yet this"—his sword prodded delicately—"denies it." Kalarr's gaze swept the room and settled on the black-clad man, who stared back with fear in his eyes. "It seems he lied."

Dispassionately, without even watching what he was doing, the sorcerer crunched his longsword past lips, teeth and neck deep into the panelled wall, pinning the sentry like some grotesque specimen. As Kalarr released the weapon and sauntered past his victim, the unfortunate man slid forward down its blade until the hilt against his face held him in an eternal half-obeisance above the puddle of his own blood. He took a fearful time to die.

Kalarr paid him no further heed; his concentration was now focused on Duergar to the exclusion of all else. "Enough of this charade!" he hissed as the necromancer groped for the talisman at his neck even though he knew it was useless. "I grow weary of it." He emitted a chuckle like tearing metal and raised one finger of his right hand.

A whirl of yellow fire dissipated barely a handspan from Duergar's face, filling the air with heat and the reek of burning. Kalarr gaped; sooner or later every wizard laid a protective charm on himself and he had failed to consider that his erstwhile ally might have done the same. Such things required additional spells to breach them.

By the time he had repeated a fuller invocation Duergar was ready, made bold by his survival after being taken unawares. The changeling scuttled for shelter as power crackled through the room and then his world dissolved into harsh colours and raw, atonal noise. Under the lash of such ravening energies, even wood and stone flared away in coruscations of disrupted matter.

The magics died abruptly amid sparks and vapour. Nothing moved. Echoes of thunder rolled sonorously towards the mountains, while in the shadow of the citadel donjon, ordinary folk raised their heads from the dirt and looked around in terror. Only the sun shone placidly and unconcerned from a clean blue sky.

Kalarr passed one hand across his face and laughed shakily. "It seems we are well matched," he muttered, then coughed on a wisp of acrid smoke. Shaking with exertion and fright, Duergar sat down on the rippled, spell-warped floor but said nothing. Sweat glistened on his bald pate.

After a glance around, Kalarr chuckled again, and even though it still was not a pleasant sound, this time he seemed genuinely amused. What he had found humorous was the state of the room. It had somewhat . . . changed. Walls sloped giddily out of the vertical, floor and ceiling were corrugated into waves like a petrified ocean. The changeling was a grayish silhouette scorched into the window-frame where a blast of force had snuffed him out of existence. The whole place had a dizzy, nauseating look.

"If neither can defeat the other," he mused, turning back to Duergar, "then the obvious solution is to form a true alliance. There is, however, one problem."

The necromancer looked up at that. "Only one?" he repeated in contemptuous disbelief.

Kalarr smiled blandly at him. "Only one; the source of all others. A lack of mutual trust."

"You try to kill me and then you say I lack trust in your intentions?" Duergar choked on a bitter laugh.

"Certainly you lack manners, Drusalan. Hear me out."

"Then talk." Manners were far from Duergar's mind right now.

"What oath of mine would you accept as a token of good faith?"

The necromancer looked blank; such a question was so improbable that he had never considered his possible answer. Finally he shrugged. "Suggest one yourself."

"I was once *kailin-eir,* as much so as the Talvalin boy, before I learned . . . other skills. That clan—and my other name—is five centuries extinct, but I still have rank, and lord-right over lesser men, and honour when I choose to remember it. Those were never stripped from me." As he spoke Kalarr went to the door, twisted his *taiken* free of the wall and wrenched it from the sentry's face, then cleaned the blade with a silken kerchief.

There was a footfall in the corridor and Kalarr swivelled to see who was there. He smiled thinly, then drove his longsword into the wooden floor where it stuck, quivering. "So you alone have the courage to brave this sorcerer's den, eh? Then come in."

Baiart bowed low as he entered, ignoring the corpse in the doorway. "You are both unharmed . . ." he said without any inflection. Kalarr's smile widened into a cruel grin.

"Such deep concern touches my heart," he purred. "All went as usual in Cerdor?"

"Of course. How else would it go?"

"How indeed . . . Tell me, Baiart-*arluth,* Clan-Lord Talvalin, what great oath would a man take if he desired an enemy to trust him? An enemy, mark you." Baiart stared coldly at the wizard. "I don't mock you now, man—not with my question, at least."

"Do you not? Then surely the sun rose from the north today."

"It may well do so tomorrow," hissed Kalarr, setting his pleasant aspect aside like an actor changing character-masks. A flicker of something distorted the outline of his hand so that it seemed wrapped in flame. A dangerous glint awoke in his dark eyes as they bored into Baiart's face. The man flinched, but refused to look away. "Take care, or you might die before you see such marvels."

"Death no longer frightens me, warlock. Since you wove your spells about me I can wear a *tsepan* without you fretting I might use it. So I must take my ending as a gift; given in hatred, given in rage or given in mercy, my passage to the dark is now the only journey I would welcome."

"Quite so." Kalarr looked him up and down and banished the poised spell from his hand. "Then I may give it you in repayment—sometime. But remember Duergar's special skill, and bear in mind that death here is not an ending, but more often a new beginning to more . . . docile service. What you desire, Talvalin, is not your passage to the dark but your passage through the pyre. And I seldom like to see a funeral."

"It smacks too much of waste," said Duergar pleasantly. Baiart's face had long since drained of colour. "Now answer my lord's question." The necromancer's courage had returned now that Kalarr's attention was directed elsewhere. He could defer to whatever scheme was in cu Ruruc's convoluted brain, at least for the present. What happened later would depend very much on how things developed both here and in the Empire. And on whether Kalarr cu Ruruc proved worthy of trust.

Perhaps the sun would rise in the north after all.

"The oath is made in blood, for reasons you sorcerers well understand," said Baiart. "Like all the High oaths, this one is made with a *tsepan.*"

"Give me yours." Kalarr held out one hand, arrogantly refusing to watch Baiart when the *kailin* drew blade right behind his back. The weapon's blue and silver hilt was placed gently in the middle of his open palm, despite the savage expression which twisted Baiart's face. He had tried, anguished, to stab either himself or his undefended target, and his right hand had refused to obey him. Tears of rage and shame trickled down his cheeks, but Kalarr merely nodded absent thanks. "What now?" he demanded.

"You must cut, once only, from thumb to index finger, joining the Honour-scars. But cut shallowly; a man may need to swear many such oaths in his life—especially a man with many enemies." Kalarr ignored the remark. "Then you must make the mark of your crest in the blood, and the first rune of your name, swear the oath, and wipe all clean with a cloth which must be burnt at once."

"I see," said Kalarr. "And if there are no Honour-scars . . . ?" Baiart gasped in outrage and the wizard laughed at his scandalised expression. "Merely a question, Clan-Lord." He opened his hand to reveal the three parallel white scars, then sliced the *tsepan* across the top of each.

Both Baiart and Duergar were privately surprised to see that the blood running out was red, as red as the sorcerer's robes. Using one fingertip, Kalarr drew the crescent and double curve of his crest, the winged viper, and under it the character "Sre."

"The first rune of *your* name," said Baiart urgently, "or any oath is void." Kalarr gazed at him coldly.

"I know," he said. "Duergar Vathach, give me your hand." The necromancer started to protest, then thought better of it and did as he was asked. "You are no Alban, wrapped around with honourable codes," Kalarr said, "but the Empire has a custom of bloodbonding which you should respect. Bloodbond friendship with me, for peace of mind if nothing else."

Duergar shrugged, then jerked slightly as the *tsepan* nicked his thumb. As the two wounds pressed together he received another surprise—Kalarr's blood was as warm as any other man's, neither too hot nor too cold as the necromancer had speculated it might be.

Normally never at a loss for something to say, whether sharp and cruel or once in a rare while almost poetic, Kalarr stared at the flowing blood and spoke not a word. Then with a touch of his hand he closed both wounds, wiped away marks and errant trickles with a kerchief and exploded the wisp of silk into a flash of fire with a single gesture.

"Now that we are allies, my friend, what were you about when I first came in?" he said to Duergar. The necromancer jerked his head in warning at Baiart and a slow smile creased the skin of Kalarr's face. "Ah . . . I understand perfectly." He turned to the Alban and returned his *tsepan* with a sardonic bow. "Would you care to leave us now, Talvalin-*arluth*?"

Baiart nodded as curtly as he dared and made for the door. Duergar called him back. "Cause some servants to come up for yonder carrion," he ordered, indicating the dead sentry. "He was a strong man and should make a useful addition to the ranks of my *traugarin*." Baiart's mouth twitched but he nodded obediently and went to go out again. Once more he was called back, this time by Kalarr.

"You can go—but if you should care to stay"—the tall sorcerer paid no heed to Duergar's frantic hushing noises—"I can promise that what we have planned should be more than entertaining for you. And your brother Aldric."

Baiart's face stayed immobile, robbing Kalarr of much satisfaction and pleasure. The *kailin* merely shook his head and fled from the room, but the sound of sobbing drifted back from the corridor. Duergar cringed inside himself, and cringed even more when he could no longer hear Baiart's weeping—for the noise of cu Ruruc's laughter.

*

There were tents all around the enormous competition field beyond Erdhaven, and Kyrin sat in one of them with a pile of silver marks in front of her and a sheet of sums on her knee. The money came to almost a hundred marks, but no matter how she added up the columns, her sums totalled nearer five. The girl added them up again, then subtracted two entries and nodded to herself. If she could persuade Aldric to leave the horses here, they would be able to afford one of the ships to whose masters she had spoken. Except that parting the *eijo* from his Andarran charger was not going to be quite as simple as arithmetic suggested.

Hoofs sounded outside the tent and then the flap lifted to admit a figure wearing Great Harness, the full battle armour which Albans called *an-moyya-tsalaer*. Aldric unbuckled the straps of his flaring peaked helm and laid aside the war-mask covering cheeks and chin, then unlaced his mail and leather coif with a sigh of relief. Under the armour his hair was dark and wet.

"You should wear one of those new over-robes," observed Kyrin. "All that black metal must absorb a frightful heat from the sun on a day like this."

"Oddly enough, it doesn't," Aldric said, settling into a chair which creaked protestingly. The armour, from Gemmel's armoury, was remarkably light for Great Harness at fifty pounds, but not to a folding camp-chair. From the helm, mask and coif, through the four-panelled lamellar corslet to the peculiar idea of separate mail sleeves and strapped-on arm-plates—like those Kyrin wore—from neck to knuckles, and the equally strange jazerant scales arranged honeycomb-pattern on leather leggings, Alban armour was unique. Despite its cats'-cradle of laces, straps, buckles, belts and hooks it was eminently practical, for each part could be worn individually as the need arose.

Aldric wore it all, not because he needed protection but because it served to conceal who he was. Besides, wearing *an-tsalaer* for a mounted archery contest was entirely in keeping with the spirit of the Spring-Feast.

"Oh, by the way,"—he pulled out a wallet which had been stuffed for safety behind his weapon-belt—"second prize. One fifty." Kyrin caught the wallet as it sailed through the air and added its contents to the money on the table and to her calculations.

"Better!" she said. "But be careful—too many second prizes and people will start talking just as much as if you were taking firsts." Aldric laughed and poured himself some wine.

"You needn't worry on that account. If young Escuar from Prytenon hadn't been nursing a hangover, I would have been lucky to manage fifth place. How are we doing for money?"

"Well enough, but slowly. Aldric, if we left the horses—"

"We'd never see them again, as I've told you before. I'll try horse-riding or shooting the *telek*—but I will *not* leave Lyard in the hands of some would-be thief."

"You don't trust anybody, do you?"

"Not really. I have been given little reason to do so. But at least we can afford to eat better than we have done during these past few days." He punctuated his change of subject by standing up with that creak of leather and metallic slither to which Kyrin was still unaccustomed. "I, for one, am famished."

During festival time, almost all the prices in Erdhaven tripled; however, there were some taverns too proud of their reputations to indulge in such piracy. They were usually small eating-houses, into the fourth and fifth generation of the host's family—and very few people knew about them. Those who did kept quiet about it and used their chosen eating places purely for epicurean gluttony or a little well-mannered seduction. For reasons Aldric did not question, Kyrin knew the owner of one such carvery—he was later to find it was all quite innocent and a matter of family friendship—and was able to persuade the man to find them a table. Comforted perhaps by Aldric's meticulous courtesy, he did not object to the young man being armoured from the neck down.

The food was even better than Kyrin had promised—and her claims had been so extravagant that Aldric had thought them exaggeration. All the wines were imported—red from the Jouvaine Provinces, white from the Empire—and Aldric was interested in how they had gotten through the various blockades and embargoes which made life so difficult for merchants. Then his steak arrived and he forgot the question. The meat was just as he liked it: seared, but otherwise not so much cooked as well heated, and he sliced into the fragrant almost-raw beef with a delicacy that totally belied the speed with which it was devoured.

"One thing I do intend to try, even if it has some risks involved," the young *eijo* said once the edge was off his hunger, "and that's *yril t'sathorn*—the Messenger's Ride. It's a kind of mock battle; obstacles to jump, targets for sword, spear or bow and a moat you have to swim your horse through. It's from an old story about a courier in the Clan Wars."

Kyrin drank white wine and smiled at him. "It all sounds faintly childish," she said.

"Perhaps; but you're allowed to bet on it all the same."

"Indeed?" Kyrin's eyes lit up; like most Valhollans she was fond of gambling, but being prudent disliked long odds if they could be avoided. "Tell me, Aldric," she crooned at him, filling his wine-cup to the brim, "who do you think will win?"

The Alban sipped his drink with relish and smirked like a cat with cream on its whiskers. "Who else but me?" he answered brightly.

Kyrin rather pointedly drank the rest of the wine herself.

*

Clocks in the town of Erdhaven were chiming for the sixth hour of evening when a man sat down at a bench and put fire to a bowlful of crystals. The stuff, sparkling like crushed diamonds, burst into brief flame and then settled to a slow crawl of sparks. Grey smoke coiled up, not dissipating but hanging at eye level, growing thicker and more opaque with every wisp that joined it. The man lowered his head and began to mutter in a soft monotone.

The cloud began to glow from within and an image formed, moving and distorting as the vapour shifted. Its half-seen mouth formed words. "You are late," said Duergar's voice, thickly warped by sorcery and distance.

"Pardon!" The man abased himself hastily. "I beg pardon!"

"It is of little matter. You have the holiday as your excuse, of course?"

"Yes, lord. I couldn't close my shop at the usual time and—"

"Enough. The article I sent you remains unharmed?" Glancing behind him, the man swallowed and nodded affirmation. "Excellent."

Filling most of the shop which fronted his small bronze-foundry was an equestrian statue, life-size, of a warrior scale-armoured after the style of an Imperial *katafrakt*. A masterpiece of casting, it was exclaimed over by everyone who entered the foundry, but the bronze-smith himself preferred not to go near it. There was an eerie quality about the image; its armour was not a hauberk, what the Alban stories called lizard-mail, but fitted more like a lizard's skin and gave the figure a scaly, reptilian look. The rider leaned back in his saddle, war-mask in hand, and stared into an unknown distance from under the peak of his helm. Goat-horns curved from that headgear and the essential inhumanity of the piece was completed when the face was made visible by the lifted mask. There was no face!

In profile the features were of classic, perfect beauty; from any other angle they became merely geometrical shapes, cold and precise. Shadows suggested a soft round-ness to mouth and brows and chin, but clearer light re-vealed only stark hollows and harsh, flat planes. There was no mouth other than a flaw in the verdigrised metal, no eyes at all. Only a bleak power, like the desire for conquest given palpable form.

Duergar's eyes were closed as if in concentration, but the bronze-founder still felt as if he was being watched—and that by someone without his best interests at heart. Despite the threat of his master's anger, the man rose and backed quietly towards the door.

Then a vast shadow fell across him and he spun, mouth gaping in a shriek which never left his throat.

That throat was clamped shut by the inexorable pressure of a bronze hand as the statue leaned down from its pedestal and clutched him by the neck. "I can give it movement for a little while," came Duergar's voice from behind him. "But it must have a life of its own. Yours will suffice." If there was more, the founder did not hear it.

As the metal *katafrakt* straightened up, the workman's wildly dancing legs left the ground in a hanged-man's jig as he was lifted with no effort at all and held dangling at the end of the creature's arm. The last thing he saw was the flawed mouth cracking into a smile, and then the hand on his neck closed to a clenched fist. Though flesh and sinew gave way like wet paper, there was hardly any blood from the frightful wound and what little spurted from the dead man's nostrils to fall upon the bronze armour was absorbed as if by a sponge. The corpse shrivelled in that icy grip, shrinking and contracting as life was sucked from the deepest marrow of its bones. When at last it was released, it fell not with the sodden thud of a body but with a clattering of dry sticks wrapped in a bag of skin.

The ponderous bulk of horse and rider left their pedestal without a squeal of stressed metal, or indeed any sound other than that of an ordinary *kailin*. Only a certain massive deliberation to every movement betrayed that this *kailin* was far removed from the ordinary. The horse stopped and knelt before the smoke-cloud as the warrior astride its bronze back raised one arm in a salute. His voice was deep, resonant as a flawed bell in an empty place of prayer.

"Command me, Lifegiver, my master."

"First you must be named," said Duergar. It was necessary; even such a creature of sorcery was incomplete without a name—but this was not "man" for its flesh was cold bronze, yet nor was it "statue" for it moved. It was Duergar's servant and more than servant—like an extra limb. "You are as one of my hands," the necromancer pronounced at last. "Your name shall be Esel, which is to say 'sword-hand' in the old tongue."

"It is a good name, my master. What is thy will?"

"My will is in your mind, Esel my servant. Seek Aldric Talvalin on the weapon-field tomorrow. You will know him. Yet do not slay him—in this the weapon that you bear will aid you—unless there is no choice. And if he must be slain, then destroy him and everything he carries. Utterly."

"Thy desire shall be fulfilled in all ways, Lifegiver, my master. Thy enemy is my enemy. My victim is thine."

*

Glancing down at himself, Aldric smiled wryly; *yril t'sathorn* really did seem like an elaborate children's game after all, for though armour and harness remained, most of his weapons had been replaced by wooden ones edged and tipped with dye-soaked wadding. He, Lyard and his opponents all wore white overmantles so that any impacts would show up like ink on paper.

The competitors had received instruction earlier that morning from one of the Prefect's officials, a small man over-full of his own importance. "Each rider will be given a scroll," he had announced fussily, "representing important despatches. This must be carried to the judge who sits on this moated island, representing Torhan-*arluth* in his fortified camp of Gorlahr. In various places there will be targets for spear and bow—the Great-bow only, sirs, since the lesser bow is not historically speaking correct—and five mounted *kailinin* of the Prefect's guard representing—"

"—five men on horseback . . . ?" speculated somebody, provoking laughter. The official reddened, coughed, rustled his notes and then continued in a less patronising manner. "Representing enemy forces," he said emphatically. "There is only one bridge to the island. It is guarded. A rider may, if he wishes, swim the moat. He will not then be attacked by any defender, but may I point out that swimming takes longer than galloping and each rider will have his riding timed by turn of sandglass. That, sirs, is all."

That, thought Aldric, was enough. Personally he considered the best way to stop a courier was to shoot the horse from under him, but that was much too practical for a sport like this. He watched through narrowed eyes as Escuar the Pryteinek galloped out to ride the Courier's Ride.

A hidden target came up on its counterbalanced arm and Escuar, twisting in his saddle, drove an arrow neatly into it. Aldric pursed his lips thoughtfully; the young man's mounted archery was very good, but his swordplay was as wooden as the mock *taiken* he used. The fifth and last of the hidden warriors burst from ambush in a clump of trees where a leaf-strewn net had hidden him, and charged with levelled spear. Escuar half-turned, flinging up his shield—and his attacker threw the lance aside, whipped wooden sword from scabbard-tube to

white-clad thigh in a single move and left a blue blotch
visible all over the field. Somebody not far from Aldric
groaned and swore, making the Alban grin as he recognised the sound of lost money. He wondered whether
Kyrin would be loyally backing him or sensibly doing no
such thing.

"Kourgath-*eijo*," said a voice at his elbow, "you ride
now." One of the Prefect's retainers presented him with
a small scroll. Aldric was tempted to pretend to read the
thing and then destroy it, but fancied that such humour
would not be well received and tucked it into the cuff
of his shooting-glove instead. For a moment he wondered what his odds might be, then as the trumpets
blared he dismissed all other concerns and kicked Lyard
into a gallop.

Two warriors pounced before the big Andarran courser
had got into his stride, and Aldric reacted instinctively
as he had been taught to do—charging the nearer man,
sidestepping Lyard at the last minute with tug of rein
and touch of knee, then lunging past the displaced shield
with his spear. The second warrior, sword-armed, was
"dead" before he closed enough to be dangerous.

Children's game or not, Aldric found his heart was
pounding with the excitement of something that was far
more real than anything done in Dunrath's exercise yard
so long ago. A target reared up and he lowered spear-
point, struck squarely home—and felt his spear disinte-
grate as some small unseen flaw gave way under the
impact.

Cursing under his breath, he threw down the pieces
and swept his longbow from its case, drawing an arrow
from the ornate fan of shafts quivered at his back. He
preferred the handier shortbow to this seven-foot asym-
metrical archaism, finding it clumsy by comparison. Like
its modern counterpart the Great-bow of old Alba was
thumb-drawn—but to well behind the archer's ear—and
its arrows were correspondingly long, heavy and destructive. Aldric loosed one at close range and even over the
noise of galloping in full battle armour heard the
wooden target split from top to bottom . . .

Another target appeared, this time craftily set on his
right. The *eijo* bared his teeth in a hard, appreciative

grin; whoever had built the course knew that no horse-archer could shoot to his nearside. Heeling Lyard briefly away to the left, he launched a shaft backwards over the animal's rump—almost missing altogether in his haste—and then turned back towards the judge's island.

The three remaining *kailinin* were waiting for him at the bridge. Lyard reared as Aldric reined back, eyeing the other riders apprehensively. Without a spear, attacking all three would be a risky undertaking, yet he did not want to waste time swimming his horse across the moat. Deciding at last that boldness would be best, he pulled the peak of his helmet down a little, settled more firmly in the saddle and touched heels to his stallion's flanks, aware that the judge had risen from his canopied seat to get a better view.

But the official was not watching him. Aldric's head jerked round, all plans and strategies forgotten as something surfaced in the moat with a hiss of displaced water.

As an armoured horseman surged towards him through the shallows, he thought for just one instant that it was all part of some trick staged by the Prefect. Then weeds fell from the rider's spearhead to reveal not a dye-pad but a long, sharp blade. This trick, if trick it was, had no part in *yril t'sathorn* . . .

There was time enough for his stomach to turn right over as the lance slashed towards his head, then reflex took over and his shield came up. The impact punched it back against him, rocked him in the saddle—and chilled him with the knowledge that such a blow striking home would drive clear through him, armour or no armour. Throwing aside his useless wooden weapons, Aldric rode with desperate haste towards the judge's escort, the only men in range who wore real swords.

The soldiers broke and scattered as he approached, terrified not of the *eijo* but of that which followed him. Aldric snarled and rode one of them down; before Lyard had skidded to a halt he was on the ground and wrenching the dazed man's broadsword from its scabbard. The weapon was no *taiken*—but it was steel, and that was enough.

Before he could regain his saddle the bronze rider was upon him. Aldric twisted away from the jabbing spear and hacked at its shaft, but almost dropped his sword from stinging fingers as it bounced off solid metal. With obvious intent the *katafrakt* continued his charge at Lyard and Aldric screamed a warning. The battle-trained Andarran knew well enough what was meant by that and galloped out of reach.

In the deathly stillness which had fallen over the crowd, Kyrin's whistle rang out clearly. The black stallion hesitated, ears pricked, recognising the signal but knowing that his master had not given it. Kyrin had to repeat the summons twice before she was obeyed.

Rather than press home his advantage, the scaled horseman descended with a harsh metallic slither from his own steed. The sound had an eerie echo, almost a hollowness, as if there was emptiness within both the reptilian armour and the horse's hide. Aldric swallowed sourness and tried not to think what that might imply.

"I am Esel, o enemy of my master," pronounced the *katafrakt,* his voice so deep that Aldric felt it vibrating in the marrow of his bones. That, too, had an ominous metallic quality which confirmed the Alban's fears. His enemy, no matter what he looked like, was not a man. "Return to me the thing ye stole aforetime, ere I take it from thee." Esel paused, the empty glare of his war mask not wavering from Aldric's face. "Speak thy choice."

The *eijo* cleared his throat, trying to still the tremor lurking there. Gripping his broadsword and settling his shield, he smiled a mirthless smile that did little to conceal his fright. "I r-really think—" he tried again: "I really think you have to take it." His voice sounded insignificant.

"As ye will." The monstrous figure turned towards his horse, standing immobile like something cast from metal, and when he swung back there was a sheathed sword in his hand. "My master desires that ye be brought before him, that he may visit condign punishment upon thee at his pleasure. This shall be. It is my master's bidding."

Kyrin shouldered her way furiously through an audience who stood as if spellbound, trying to reach the spot where Lyard waited patiently. She approached the stallion as warily as her need for haste allowed, knowing how dangerous a war-schooled horse could be. When she vaulted into the charger's saddle Lyard reared, pawing the air and shrilling his anger and excitement; but he did nothing worse, knowing the woman on his back as a companion of his master, as someone who had treated him kindly, and was at least familiar with the strangeness which had frightened him. Kyrin sighed with relief, then dug in her heels and rode full-tilt for Aldric's tent and Widowmaker.

Backing away from Esel's stealthy advance, the *eijo* glanced around. Nobody moved, whether through fear or horror . . . or some more sinister reason. Then the bronze *katafrakt* shook the scabbard from his sword, flicking it at Aldric's head. The Alban almost forgot to duck, such was his shock at seeing what Esel cradled easily in one scaly fist.

It was not steel, nor even bronze, but a shimmering translucent stuff like glass which drew the eyes and held them. Aldric gulped as bile rose in his throat and wrenched his gaze away with an effort, feeling sweat begin to film his skin. For perhaps a second the world had tried to slither out of focus, and he knew another second would have left him helpless. It was more rage and fear than courage which sent a whirring cut at Esel's helm, and it was more luck than judgement that permitted it to strike.

With a snap one of the bronze goat-horns spun away, but Esel ignored what should have stunned him and kept on advancing. He had not parried, nor even tried to, and his shield sat uselessly on his arm as he gripped his great sword like a blacksmith's hammer. Or a bronze-founder's maul.

Then heavy feet approached from Aldric's left as one of his erstwhile opponents came charging in with an axe raised in both hands. Why this man had moved when no one else did, the *eijo* did not know. Not that it was of use. The bronze warrior blocked clumsily, his blade emitting a piercingly-sweet chiming note, and Aldric saw the nacreous shimmer drain from the weapon to leave it clear as ice, almost invisible in the sunlight.

Then it chopped home.

The stricken *kailin* dropped his axe and tottered back

a pace. There was no wound, no blood on the white robe covering his *tsalaer*—but those robes had gone strangely rigid and crackled at each sluggish movement. It was a sound Aldric had heard before. As the warrior fell over stiffly, his face frozen into a pallid mask of shock, Aldric knew what Esel's sword had done even before the wave of icy air billowed over him. The man was frozen in very truth, his body, clothing, armour all frosted over—within half a heartbeat on a hot spring day.

Another great sweep of the sword left a trail of chilly white vapour hanging in the air as Aldric ducked, then straightened and smashed his iron-bound shield rim into the bridge of Esel's nose. It should have blinded the bigger man with pain; but the only blindness was that of a war-mask buckled beyond recovery. Esel made a grinding, impatient noise and tore the mask aside to reveal his non-face.

In the next exchange Aldric lost his sword. Not through clumsiness but because, made brittle by appalling cold, its blade abruptly flew into a score of tinkling shards. With blood streaming down his face from where a splinter had ripped skin, Aldric flung the useless hilt—a hilt which frozen perspiration had almost stuck to his hand—at his enemy before backing out of reach. Esel followed, making no attempt to lengthen his stride. He came on with the calm assurance of an executioner.

Aldric knew now that he could not outlast Duergar's sending, because though he was sodden with sweat, exhausted by the dragging weight of *an-moyya-tsalaer* and growing rapidly unsteady on his feet, Esel's movements were still the same: no slower, no faster, patient and inevitable. Resignation joined fatigue in Aldric's brain, combining into the despair of vast weariness so that he almost knelt and waited for the inevitable. Almost . . . but not quite. He was Alban, *kailin-eir* Talvalin. If this thing was to finish it would be on his own terms. Aldric's hand began to close around his *tsepan*'s hilt.

Hoofbeats and shouting cut through his daze and his unfocused eyes finally settled on the blonde figure riding swiftly closer on a black horse. Perhaps, he thought, perhaps there is another way. He forced himself into a shaky run.

Kyrin slid Isileth Widowmaker from her lacquered scabbard and breathed a soft apology to the *taiken,* then flung it as hard and straight as she was able. The weapon came cartwheeling down and quivered in the turf for barely a second before Aldric's fingers closed around its hilt and he turned to face his tormentor.

He turned almost into a cut across the eyes and though he jerked his head a handsbreadth back, the frigid wind which whipped into his war-mask's trefoil opening left frost rimed thickly on eyebrows and lashes. He had no illusions about crossing swords, even with Widowmaker, and made no attempt to press home an attack. Instead he concentrated on the opening that he wanted . . . needed . . . had to have sooner or later.

Bronze was brittle. That helmet-horn had not been cut but broken off like a dry stick. Given the chance— Aldric threw his shield invitingly away—he would test his theory on the bronze man's armour.

Or his arm. Esel's blow was huge but clumsy and Aldric evaded it with ease even in his weakened state. There was nothing weak about the double-handed cut which came down on Esel's sword-arm. The limb shattered halfway to the elbow.

With a shrill noise barely recognisable as a scream, Esel clutched his stump with the remaining hand. There was no blood and instead of flesh an oily pulp bulged from the ruptured metal. It dripped clear ooze that had a sharply chemical stench, and it pulsed with a slow rhythm which in the severed portion fluttered briefly and then stopped.

Aldric fought the churning in his stomach as he lifted the amputated half-arm and twisted the sword-hilt from its slack grip. He moved forward, stiff-legged both with anger and exhaustion.

"Esel . . ." There was no longer any quaver in his voice, only hatred fired and tempered by the memory of how this—this *thing* had frightened him. "If you ever truly lived, you are truly dead now." Aldric poised the huge sword momentarily, then stabbed it home. The iceblade slid into the bronze *katafrak*'s chest as easily as into a scabbard and there stuck fast. A convulsion wrenched the hilt from Aldric's grip—not that he was reluctant to let it go—and Esel staggered drunkenly towards his horse.

Somehow the bronze warrior crawled into his saddle and sat there, plucking feebly at the sword protruding from a torso already thickly caked with ice. Then his horse jerkily raised one foreleg and stopped in that position. Esel leaned back, stump raised as if to hold his missing war-mask in a hand no longer there, and gazed fixedly into the distance.

Both man and mount slowly overbalanced and fell with a vast splash into the moat. As the mass of metal rolled over and sank, the sword reared into view—and in that instant the whole surface of the moat froze over. Then the hilt slid out of sight, dragged through the crust by the weight of the metal in which it was embedded.

Aldric watched it vanish. There was a full minute of shocked silence before the cheers began, and he turned a face curdled with disgust to watch how armed and armoured men came running up. Now that it was safe! The *eijo*'s stomach heaved and tearing off his helmet he started to vomit.

Kyrin bent over him and gently, with a kerchief wetted through a crack in the ice, she began to clean the flaking blood-streaks from his hair and chalk-white face. Reaction struck and, making a tiny whimpering noise, Aldric wrapped his steel-sheathed arms around her waist and clung on tight. Even through the armour she could feel the waves of shudders racking his body. The girl knelt and cradled his head, murmuring soft comforting sounds until the shaking died away.

She glared as soldiers came clattering towards him— then blinked in shock as they levelled curving halberd blades. Their officer, a slight man whose face was sallow inside his rank-flashed helmet, surveyed her with a cold eye, then studied Aldric's face. The *eijo* licked dry lips and whatever flicker of expression crossed his face made the officer take a long step backwards. "Somebody get his sword," the soldier snapped, angry at being startled by a frightened boy in armour. But the fright had almost gone by now and Aldric was not so immature as he appeared. There was a glitter in his grey-green eyes suggesting that after a sorcery-created monstrosity like Esel, a mere officer of guards would give him little trouble.

After several deep breaths he felt capable of speech and straightened his back unconsciously. "What is going on here?" His voice was soft, controlled once more and deliberately laced with menace.

The officer tried to ignore his tacit threat and levelled one gloved finger at Kyrin. "You," he said, "help him to walk. Guards, watch them. Especially the *eijo*. I wouldn't think of escaping, *an-kourgath*," he finished, bolder once his soldiers had closed in.

"I asked you a question," Aldric said. There were no more threats; he was too weary for playacting an unconvincing role and no longer cared whether or not he was given an answer. But he got one just the same.

"My lord wants you," the officer returned. "Both of you. Now. At once."

6

Contact

Neither Aldric nor Kyrin had any idea of where they might be—there had been curtains tightly fastened over every window of the carriage which had brought them here. At least, the *eijo* reflected grimly as he glanced around their place of confinement, the cage was a gilded one.

Gilded was an understatement, for the place was magnificent. Its walls were panelled in maplewood and carved burr walnut, the inlaid floor was thickly strewn with rugs. Scented oil in lamps of gold and crystal filled the air with fragrance and struck myriad reflections from gems and precious metals. The place should have been coarse and garish; instead it was tasteful, restrained and of such elegance that Kyrin found herself considering every move she made, lest it destroy the room's sense of graceful order.

Aldric felt no such compunction; he was long past being overawed by mere fine furnishings and had been irritated both by apparent arrest and by his own brief, shaming loss of face. Slithering comfortably into a chair—and pointedly ignoring what his *tsalaer* was doing to the polished wood—he tried without success to work out who had captured him. If "captured" was the right word, and he was inclined to doubt it. Despite their brusque early treatment, it seemed now that they were less prisoners than guests—reluctant ones of course, but there had been a lack of threats, of locked doors or anything else suggestive of captivity. Wondering just how far his guesses would be borne out, he rose and walked quietly to the door.

It was indeed unlocked and he eased it back a whisker—then bit on an oath and all but slammed it shut. There was a file of soldiers in the corridor outside, at ease, talking quietly, but all with weapons at their sides. So much, thought Aldric, for another fine idea. Closing the door, he leaned back against it until the latch clicked home.

Both he and the girl had been disarmed—except for his *tsepan,* which was either criminal oversight or a deliberate act in keeping with the strangeness of this strange place. That his own armoured body was a useful weapon he knew already, but bareheaded against a dozen men it was nowhere near enough.

There was a small table near one wall; on it stood flagons, goblets of worked metal and tiny, fragile glasses. The *eijo* filled two of these with a wine which was the brilliant, sinister colour of fresh blood and offered one to Kyrin. No word had passed between them since they had been taken and even now she thanked him only with a nod. Looking at the trembling hand she extended for her wine, and at lips compressed so tightly that they had no colour left, he could guess the reason why: Kyrin was terrified.

Forcing his own lips into a smile, yet knowing it must look more like a grin of rage, Aldric slipped one mailed arm around her. "Drink up," he murmured. "If they'd meant us any harm we'd have found it out by now." That was not necessarily true, he thought sombrely, but kept it from darkening the false and brittle brightness of his voice. Kyrin blinked nervously at him and he heard the crystal clink against her teeth as she gulped down its contents. "Another?" he offered, holding up his own glass. "If it does no other good, it will help you to relax. You're shaking." He tightened his embrace a fraction and leaned towards her face.

"I bid you welcome to my house," purred a voice from just behind them. Aldric controlled himself in time, but Kyrin jumped and failed to stifle her gasp of shock. When they turned around, it was with the slowness of exaggerated calm. The speaker stood in a sweep of darkness just beyond the lamplight; his outline was vague, and only the points of light from jewels and embroidered garments gave them any indication of possible shapes.

"I would offer you refreshment—but it seems no longer necessary," the voice observed rather tartly. There might have been some disapproval in its soft tone; there was certainly a thread of accent which put Aldric on his guard at once. Despite the precision of his Alban words, this man was still more accustomed to the guttural consonants of Drusalan: the Imperial tongue.

"I beg pardon," the young *eijo* responded insincerely. He gestured towards the cups and flagon. "May I pour you some . . ."

"My thanks, but no. I do not drink wine. The sun has not yet set." That last irrelevant statement struck Aldric as odd and he stared at the intruder when at last he deigned to leave his cloak of shadows and walk forward so that they could see him. The man was several inches taller than Aldric, but his height was offset by a burly, powerful frame which reminded the Alban of a bear; a weatherbeaten bear whose dark hair was greying, but a cold-eyed, scar-faced carnivore for all that.

Flicking a glance at the worn hilt of a low-slung sword and the blunt, capable hand resting on its pommel, Aldric inclined his head respectfully. He bowed not merely to the physical strength so apparent here, but to the power of authority which the big man wore like a garment; Aldric had possessed a little of such power himself and knew politeness to be just good sense.

"Might we be offered some explanation for what has been happening today?" Aldric speculated warily. The man stroked his moustache, perhaps to hide a smile, perhaps not.

"Curious," he muttered. "Almost the words *I* was going to use." Then he did smile, if anything so small and fleeting deserved the name. "Explanations will be given and received presently. For now, sit down; be still; make free with the wine—I am assured it is excellent."

Aldric opened his mouth to continue this diplomatic exchange, but was interrupted by four soldiers who stamped in and snapped to attention on either side of

the door. The moustached man drew himself more upright, while his two unwilling guests forgot about making
themselves comfortable and instead waited apprehensively for the next development.

This took the form of a man in a gold-worked purple
over-robe who swept an interested gaze around the
room. In his forties, he was slightly built and wore his
thinning fair hair in the three braids of a high-clan *arluth*. He limped as he entered and the padding of his
under-tunic almost—but not quite—concealed the crooked
tilt of his left shoulder. A golden crest-collar at his throat
bore a pendant rayed-sun centred with a single ruby the
size of a thrush's egg. The eyes in his clean-shaven face
were a clear hazel, like sunlight through water, and tiny
crow's-feet wrinkled the skin around them as he stared
long and hard at the two strangers in this tranquil room.

Aldric did not return the stare as he normally would;
instead he knelt with studied feline grace and touched
brow to floor in First Obeisance. Kyrin copied him,
wanting to ask questions but knowing enough to realise
that this was neither the time nor the place. She had
gleaned one important answer from the *eijo*'s bow alone.

This slender man was Rynert, the king.

"Up, you two," he said, taking a seat and accepting
an offered glass of wine. "Now, Dewan . . . what is all
this? Your report was a trifle . . . garbled, shall we say?
Give me the translation, please."

Dewan . . . The name rang a long-forgotten bell in
Aldric's memory; the name of King Rynert's captain-
of-guards, personal champion, adviser, confidant and
friend. Dewan ar Korentin, late of the province of Vreijaur on the edge of the Empire's influence in Jouvann,
and equally late a much-decorated *Eldheisart*—lord-
commander—of the Bodyguard cavalry in Imperial
Drakkesborg.

Ar Korentin spoke briefly, his accent and mode of
speech clipping the words shorter still. As Aldric listened, he wondered that the king even bothered to hear
such an improbable episode, much less give it any credence. Yet Rynert set down his wineglass and listened
closely, twisting at a signet ring on his little finger, turning it round and round again . . . Then he looked up

and Aldric almost fancied he could see the thoughts
swimming like fish in his lord's translucent eyes.

"*Eijo-an,* you call yourself Kourgath—that's only the
beast on your crest-collar. Tell me your true name."

"I . . . *mathern-an arluth,* lord king, I was once *kailin-
eir* Aldric Talvalin."

There was a hiss of indrawn breath from ar Korentin,
and the faint slither of steel as he half-drew his sword
all but drowned a gasp uttered by one of the soldiers
near the door. "You lying—" started the Vreijek angrily,
then fell silent at a gesture from Rynert.

"Put up your sword, Dewan. There will be time for it
later, if need be. You, *eijo,* why do you claim to be one
of the Talvalins, when everyone knows of the plague in
Dunrath three years ago? And choose your explanation carefully."

"Because the name is mine, *mathern-an.* If 'everyone'
knows of this plague, why would I be so stupid as to use
a dead man's name?"

Rynert's eyebrows lifted; he had expected some intricate excuse, not a blunt admission of guilt. Or was it
guilt . . . ? The warrior's reasoning was sound enough.
"Can you give me any proof?" he demanded. Aldric
shook his head; Gemmel had warned him not to carry
anything which might identify him as other than the *eijo*
he was supposed to be. His foster-father had not foreseen *this.*

"Unfortunate." Rynert's voice was cold and sceptical.
"You almost convinced me for a moment. I fear that
Dewan's inquisitors will have to prise the truth from—"
he broke off as one of his guards stepped forward and
slammed a salute.

"Why do you interrupt the king?" snapped ar Korentin dangerously.

"Proof, captain," muttered the soldier, frightened now
by his own boldness. He pulled off his helmet and
dropped to one knee, revealing a homely, well-battered
face and a spreading broken nose.

"Well?" asked Rynert, curious to know what light a
mere sentry could throw on this situation. Aldric doubted
it would do much good; the man's face meant nothing
to him and he doubted if he would have forgotten such

misshapen features if he had ever set eyes on them before.

"I've seen that one before, sire," the soldier said. "Him in the black armour. Wore his hair properly then and didn't have that cut on his cheek, but it's the same man. I'd swear to it."

Rynert smiled coldly. "You might have to. Where and when did you meet him?"

"Not meet, sire. I saw him in a—with respect, sire—in a tavern brawl I got caught up in. In Radmur, that was, a couple of years back."

"A couple?" broke in ar Korentin. "How many exactly?"

"Well, three, captain. Three last autumn, I think. That was when I got this." He touched his flattened nose. "They said he was just past *Eskorrethen*, but he was a rare fighter for all that. Over a woman, the trouble was, and her somebody else's lady too." Stirring uncomfortably, Aldric felt Kyrin's eyes rest on him like two hot coins laid against his skin. "Then the Prefect took us all under arrest and I got posted to the Guards in Cerdor—to give me a taste of discipline they said."

"Dewan, remind me to write to Uwin at Radmurhold," said King Rynert; though he sounded amused, no humour showed on his face. "He must remember that the Guards cohort isn't somewhere to dump his rubbish . . ."

"Captain . . ." the soldier muttered as reproachfully as he dared.

Dewan's face twitched as he too fought down his amusement. "They aren't always rubbish, King. Mostly—but not always."

"I see," Rynert murmured, looking at the guard. "One last question, soldier. What was this *kailin*'s name?"

"Talvalin, sire. Haranil-*arluth*'s youngest son Aldric. That's the name he gave the Radmur magistrates, anyway."

"Enough. Dismissed!" After the sentry had returned to his place Rynert glanced at his captain. "Promote him, Dewan, and make sure he's paid a bounty for this. He's observant, clever enough"—his voice rose slightly—

"and he stopped a miscarriage of justice. Take a seat, Aldric-*an.* I beg pardon for what might have happened." The *eijo* saluted in acknowledgment, then sat down carefully, thankful to get the weight of his armour off legs which had become very weak in the past few minutes.

At a nod from the king, his guards wheeled and left the room. Ar Korentin poured wine for Kyrin, Aldric and—after a swift look out at the sky—himself. "But you said—" the *eijo* began in surprise, then shrugged and fell silent.

"I do not drink wine? Not on holy days, like Spring-Feast; then it's not permitted until after sunset—but it's quite dark now." He took a trial sip. "And this was worth the wait."

"Aldric-*an,*" said Rynert quietly, "I sent my guards outside so that you could speak freely. I want you to tell me what is happening in my kingdom. Leave nothing out—I have a feeling yours is the only story which has all the details I require."

Aldric nodded, moistened his mouth with a little wine and began.

*

"It's incredible," said Dewan ar Korentin. "I have never in my life heard anything so fantastic—except maybe that you want us to believe it."

Very softly, King Rynert cleared his throat. "*I* believe it, Dewan," he murmured. "If he was lying it would be a credible, well-thought-out lie, the kind of thing you've heard in the law courts before now. Not something like this.

"And don't forget what you saw this afternoon, old friend. How thick was the ice on that moat . . . ?" Dewan inclined his head a little but said nothing. "I wondered a little when I saw your hair, Aldric-*an,*" Rynert continued. "Though I've seen *eijin* before, you're the first *venjens-eijo* I've met in my life. The oath was taken against this—Duergar, you called him—this Imperial necromancer, and no one else?"

"Only against him. Why do you ask, *mathern-an?*"

Rynert hesitated then and looked for confirmation at ar Korentin. The Vreijek nodded slowly. "Better that he hears it from you, King," he said. "For he'll hear it somehow."

A coldness awoke in the pit of Aldric's stomach and sent tendrils burrowing up the marrow of his spine. "Hear what . . . ?"

"Aldric-*an* . . . Aldric Talvalin, your brother Baiart told me none of this."

"My . . . brother? Baiart's alive? *Alive?*" The cold in his belly gave a sluggish heave and sourness fouled his throat. "Is he in Cerdor . . . ?"

There was a pathetic hope in the youngster's voice which made Rynert slow to answer. "No. In Dunrath. As Clan-Lord. I granted him the title myself." Aldric looked away, and the only person who saw his face before he controlled it was Kyrin. She winced visibly. "*Kailin-eir* Aldric," the king continued, his tone growing sharp, "do not assume the worst. He may be under threat—or even a spell, if what you've said of Duergar is even half the truth."

"And if he isn't? What then? The word, lord king, is *traitor!*" Slamming one fist against the wall, Aldric heeded neither the crack of a split panel nor the pain and blood of his own torn knuckles. "That oath . . . I cannot kill my own brother. I don't want to. I will not!"

"You will not," echoed the king. "I forbid it. The law—and the crime it governs—is no longer so black-and-white as that recognised by the old Honour-Codes. Leave Baiart Talvalin to the Council Court and to me. Leave your brother to my laws, Aldric. Remember that. Give him some wine, Dewan—no, better make it something stronger. And call a surgeon for that hand."

*

There was a table of black ebony. On it was a mirror of black obsidian which rested in a frame of red gold. The sorcerer who studied it was robed in scarlet cloth. Kalarr drummed his fingers irritably on the table-top and then dispelled the images drifting deep within the volcanic glass. "We underestimated him," he said bleakly. "That must not happen again. It irritates me."

"It doesn't fill me with delight either," snapped Duergar. Since the destruction of Esel he had been sulking, a condition not improved by the fact that Kalarr found it amusing. "Were those soldiers yours?"

"None of mine in Erdhaven," said cu Ruruc. He pushed himself back from the table and stood up. "The only reason your bronze *traugur* was there was your own suspicious nature. I wonder . . ."

"We don't have time to wonder." Duergar started leafing through a thick book. "He wasn't killed on the spot, so I'm assuming he'll be released."

"And what else are you doing there . . . ?"

The necromancer looked up, then tapped his volume. "I'm going to deal with that whelp once and for all."

Kalarr rolled his eyes upward and clenched both fists and teeth. Then he breathed out slowly. "You had your chance to do so and you failed. This is my turn." He smiled, both at the childishness of it all and at the thought which had just struck him. "You couldn't send a spell after him anyway."

"Why not?"

"Not unless the old limit on the range of spells has been overcome—and I don't think it has. At best you'd raise a storm over Erdhaven; at worst the magic would be overextended and would snap back here. You know what that would do, don't you?" Duergar did. "All you can do is form a plague-sending and that's too slow for this game."

"Game?" shrilled Duergar. "It's a game, is it?"

"Of course—and a most stimulating one. You Imperials treat everything too seriously. What's the boy likely to do now, eh?"

"I have no idea," Duergar retorted pettishly.

"After going to a sea-port; after risking his neck to earn money; and you have no idea . . . Then I suggest you try to find out. Now I, I intend to do something about it—and I intend to watch that something happen."

"At sea?" scoffed the Drusalan necromancer. "And you just after mocking me for forgetting about distance. Do you ever listen to yourself, cu Ruruc?"

"At sea," repeated Kalarr calmly. "With a flying eye." Duergar stopped in mid-laugh and stared at his colleague. *What,* he mouthed, but no sound came out. Kalarr dipped one hand into his belt-pouch and threw something at Duergar, who dodged. The missile did not fall, but fluttered round and round his head on silent wings. When he got a close look he gasped in disgust and regretted ever raising the subject. It was, literally, a flying eye: an eyeball the size of a cat's head, bloodshot across the white with tendrils of muscle from its moth-like wings. It circled him like some repellent insect, then returned to Kalarr's pouch with the same movement as a swallow entering its nest. "I'll send this to Erdhaven at first light tomorrow."

"Why not now, tonight?" Duergar wanted to know.

Kalarr glowered at him, then diluted the look with a sardonic grin. "Owls," he said.

*

King Rynert was not in Erdhaven simply to enjoy the festival; no monarch would let an event which gathered scores of *kailinin* in one place go unobserved. Scattered through the town in disguise and camped plainly outside it after a "training march" was almost a full legion of soldiers. Just in case. And there was a ship to be despatched, its cargo of sufficient importance to require Rynert's personal sendoff. That would have been of great interest to the Empire, had its presence not been concealed better than even the best-disguised soldiers.

The king had not forgotten that young Talvalin had mentioned Kalarr cu Ruruc and though he was courtly, sophisticated and cynical, Rynert had never adopted the disbelief so fashionable among his lords. He had been a sickly child, afflicted with a wasting disease which left him lame and crippled, in a body too frail for a warrior. Instead he had strengthened his mind, reading, absorbing knowledge wherever he could find it, learning both military and political strategy—in short, becoming the kind of king who needed no strong arm to rule well. He knew as much about the theory of magic as any lesser wizard and was aware of the power which practical sorcery brought. Rynert had no desire for that power; it soiled the soul like black pitch and made the thought of cu Ruruc a frightening one.

Dewan had called the place *his* house, even though the king was living there. It was somewhere restful away from court, where private councils could be held and where at present the champion's wife was living. Ar Korentin had deserted from his regiment when the Empire annexed his home province some ten years before, and though a storm of protest in the Senate had revoked the annexation only a short while later, by that time Dewan had neither the need nor the desire to return.

"A ship will be leaving port in two or three days time," said Rynert as he rose to go. The others rose as well, bowing politely. "You two will be on board; the cargo is not so urgent that the shipmaster can't make a small diversion on your behalf. Have your adjutant take over, Dewan—you'll be going with them. Convey my apologies to your wife. Good night." The door clicked shut behind him.

"Well now . . ." Ar Korentin released a held-in breath through his teeth. "Lyseun won't like this—or you, *eijo-an*." Aldric did not trouble to ask why; he guessed that he would find out anyway. "By the way," the Vreijek continued, "how long do you practise *taiken* daily?"

"Two hours—one in the morning, one at—"

"I thought so. To the exclusion of all else. Then I've got two or three days in which to sharpen up your archery. That exhibition today, *kailin* Talvalin, wasn't worth a damn in combat. Now, follow me."

Another bloody expert, Aldric thought bitterly—something I could certainly do without. The champion's wife could equally well have done without Aldric; she did not say so, but her disapproval was plain despite the presence of King Rynert's wife Ewise, just across the gaming-board at which they sat. To Lyseun this young *eijo* in the sinister black harness was just another in the series of armoured young men who came with various reasons to take her husband from her side. Lyseun hated them all, for she could see the day when only the young man would return, making some insincere noise of grief about her husband, and then she would be left all alone. She had begged Dewan to stop taking risks and settle down, so he had eventually learned the practice of Alban law. And now here he was with another ice-eyed warrior at his heels, excuses on his lips and that old, familiar inability to look her in the face.

Neither Aldric nor Kyrin liked that room, even though Lady Ewise was a kind and gentle woman who did her best to make them feel at ease. The air was as taut and tingling as an overstretched harpstring, and just as likely to snap with painful consequences. They were both grateful when a servant offered to show them to their rooms.

*

Charcoal-burners stood at apparent random intervals across the peak of Dunrath-hold's great donjon tower, while Kalarr cu Ruruc joined them together with lines of chalk drawn with the aid of a diagram. When he had finished he stood back with a grunt of satisfaction and surveyed his handiwork. The chalk-marks writhed with such complexity that in places they seemed to sink into the stone floor or vanish up into the night sky. Incense-laden censers fumed above certain angles, bowls of clear water rested on others.

"Now," muttered Kalarr, dusting his hands. He laid a heavy book on a lectern and thumbed through the pages until he found the one he had marked with a strip of ribbon, then read the spell through once in silence, his lips moving as they worked out words more outlandish than usual. At last he cleared his throat and pronounced the Summoning aloud.

The charcoal-burners ignited by themselves with small flurries of sparks, and the water started to steam and bubble. A breeze came whining out of the still, silent night and whipped the incense smoke into grey threads whirling across the floor. They spun together, crossing and recrossing until they had woven a great inverted cone which seemed almost solid in the faint starlight. The air throbbed, fluctuating between cold and sticky heat. A glow sprang into being within the shroud of smoke and the charcoal-burners roared as all their fuel was consumed in a single burst of heat that Duergar felt at the far side of the tower. From within the cone he could hear a sound like something huge, shifting and breathing. Then it split from base to apex, spilling out an amber light which made the stars grow dim.

Kalarr stepped forward with his shadow stretching out

long and black behind him and raised both hands in a
gesture of invitation. He voiced a soft, ululating call and
the being in the cloud emerged.

It hung above the magical symbols on motionless
wings, black scimitars like those of a swift but thirty
yards from tip to tip. The thing's breath moaned through
great vents where the wing-roots joined its bulging triangular body, vents guarded by sweeping arcs which resembled horns and yet, growing from its shoulders, were no
such thing. The head was vaguely like a wasp's both in
shape and in the positioning of two bulbous yellow eyes;
but no wasp ever possessed eyelids, even lids which
closed horizontally. The nightmare was completed by
twenty feet of whiplash tail writhing with boneless flexi-
bility behind it.

"An isghun," breathed Duergar in horror. Kalarr nodded, then spoke to the creature in a rapid monotone of
inhuman syllables. "An isghun," the Drusalan repeated.
"You're insane! You don't know what you're doing . . ."

"I do—and I also know the Masterword which controls these things." Otherwise no man in his right mind
would have gone anywhere near the being, and Duergar
had no intention of approaching it even now.

He shrank back against the cold stones as the isghun
drifted lower. Though he could not hear what reply it
made to Kalarr's words, he felt the air vibrating with the
cadences of its speech and wondered what it might be
saying. The baleful eyes closed to vertical phosphorescent slits and then winked out as their owner slept. Even
then its body did not settle on the floor but remained
suspended, immobile on those rigidly outstretched wings.

"You call this a game?" Duergar demanded after an
apprehensive glance towards the vast, hovering bulk.
"Then, my friend and sworn ally, you'll not face me
across a board. Your play is far too rough."

"Rough? An isghun, rough?" Kalarr spat the words
contemptuously. "If the boy had stayed landbound I'd
have given you cause to think my play was rough—I'd
have summoned up a shri."

"A . . . shri?" Duergar whispered, his face turning the
colour of meal. The necromancer's voice trembled. "You
dare to even think . . . You *are* mad!" .

Kalarr smiled: a slow, infinitely cruel smile. "Perhaps I am, Drusalan. Perhaps I am."

*

Kyrin had watched Aldric's first archery lesson under ar Korentin's tuition for only a few minutes before walking away. She felt genuinely sorry for him as the echoes of Dewan's parade-ground bellow followed her from the butts. When next she saw the young *eijo,* late that evening, he was sour-tempered, sore-fingered and very poor company, although he brightened considerably when she caught his eye with a sympathetic smile—until Dewan's voice cut across the general dinner-table chatter. "You're getting better, Aldric-*an,*" he said kindly enough. "Another full day of shooting and you'll be almost quite good." Though Aldric laughed dutifully, Kyrin could see his heart was not really in it.

The following night he was not at table and Kyrin retired earlier than was usual for her. When she reached her room the windows had been shuttered, the lamps lit and the thick down quilt on her bed turned back. The Valhollan girl smiled: if this was how high-clan Albans lived, she approved wholeheartedly. Kicking off her boots, she dropped them with a muffled double thud onto the thick rug, then poked at the scuffed doeskin with her foot.

"Hardly ladylike," she mused, then lifted the *estoc* from its harness across her back. The sword rattled faintly and she stared at the giltwork on its hilt before tossing the weapon into a corner. "Not ladylike at all," she decided; then her eyes strayed to the wardrobes set into the bedroom walls and speculation gleamed in their blue depths. Five Kyrins blinked at her from under five fringes of tousled pale-blonde hair and wiggled their bare toes in five rugs, all reflected in the mirror-faced doors. She had already looked inside them, of course, but the garments within had been so fine and delicate that she had not dared to touch them.

"And why not?" she said aloud. Sliding one wardrobe open, Kyrin gazed longingly at the peacock fabrics. Silk, satin and velvet rustled seductively as she ran her fingers through them and then pulled one gown free, with a guilty glance at the bedroom door as she did so. It stayed shut, and she slithered hastily out of her everyday clothes before draping herself in the sendal over-robe. It was clinging, soft and heavy, pure snowfall white shot through with rainbow lustres which shimmered as she moved. Kyrin neither knew nor cared that it was meant to be worn over a contrasting mantle, but luxuriated in the sensuous feel of the stuff against her skin, twisting and turning before the mirrors in what was almost a graceful dance.

"You look very well," said Aldric softly. Kyrin spun, one hand flying to cover her mouth. The *eijo* smiled, but remained where he lounged elegantly in the doorway. She recoverd quickly and nodded at his compliment.

"I'd almost forgotten I was a woman," she explained shyly.

"I never have," he replied with the beginnings of gallantry, then shook his head as if to clear it of a momentary dizziness. "Kyrin, what I . . . what I came to tell you was that the ship sails tomorrow. It's one of Rynert's fleet and he says—asked me to tell you—that he'll put another vessel at your disposal if you wish to go home."

"And you want me to go . . . ?"

"Light of Heaven, no! That is . . . it's your choice now. You don't have to keep following me to find your passage back. Unless you want to . . ."

"What do *you* want?" she responded. Aldric blinked rapidly, swallowed down a dry throat and avoided Kyrin's steady gaze. "Tell me, Alban."

He was unprotected; out of armour and not even wearing the sinister black which had been his unfailing custom until now. Instead he was dressed simply in a white shirt nipped at the waist by a belt to hold his *tsepan,* and blue boots and breeches worked with silver along the seams. There was a clean-scrubbed look about his face which, when the scar was not visible and his haunted eyes were shadowed, made him seem almost innocent. The pinkness of his skin did not come from washing, however—more from embarrassment.

"I . . . want you to stay. Not just stay here, but stay close to me. Please . . ." He drew in a deep breath and in that instant Kyrin realised just how very scared he was. Her half-formed smile evaporated in case he thought it mocked him, to be replaced by a solemn expression more in keeping with the moment.

"You aren't real, Aldric. Not enough for this harsh world. Keep it that way if you can," she said, then leaned over and kissed him gently on the mouth.

"Kyrin, I—" he began to say. Then he dismissed the words and put his arms around her. Kyrin's lips parted under his and he felt the intimate touch of her tongue entering his mouth, exploring. Her breath, her hair, her body all smelt bright and sweet, like apples in sunlight, warm and firm and curved. As his head bent forward, mouth opening over the soft hollows of her throat, Aldric closed his arms gently, drawing her tight against his chest and the pounding heart within.

*

They lay silent for a long time, arms entwined, still, peaceful and content merely to be together. Then Aldric rolled slightly and raised his head to look at her, fingertips delicately caressing the curve of one breast. She opened sleepy eyes and watched the silver at his throat glinting in the lamplight. "Did I hurt you?" he whispered hesitantly. Kyrin smiled at his concern, stroking the dark hair on his chest as she might have stroked a cat.

"No. Don't worry. I . . . I wasn't a virgin." She felt his silent laughter against her cheek. "What's so funny?"

"Because I was!"

"You were . . . ?"

"Yes. Thank you." He kissed the palm of her hand; but there was something in his voice she did not care for and she sat up in order to see his eyes. They were hooded, languorous and as she leaned closer something flickered in the jade-green depths. An instant later it was masked by his long lashes, but Kyrin breathed out very slowly through her nose.

"Aldric . . . don't get involved. It won't work." She cupped his face in both hands and kissed him lightly on the forehead, smiling at her own restraint. "You can stop pretending to sleep."

His eyes snapped open. "What won't work?" She could feel the words growling low in his throat.

"Anything between us. Behind that cynical mask you're a romantic, Aldric-*ain*. I'm a realist—and a foreigner."

Kyrin felt a spasm of something—anger perhaps, or awareness of what she meant—tense the *eijo*'s muscles. "You can't fight tradition with a sword."

"Oh no . . . ?"

"No. Because you're an Alban *kailin-eir, ilauem-arluth* Talvalin, heir to lands and ranks and titles."

"What the hell difference does that make?" His voice was quiet, but it thrummed with controlled rage for all its softness.

Kyrin laid one finger across his lips to still whatever outburst was building up behind them. "Enough," she said.

"But your father Harek—you called him *ur'lim*. That means 'lord.' "

"It means 'chieftain,' " Kyrin corrected flatly. "He can reckon his lineage back for six generations. Two hundred years. He's very proud of that. How far does your clan go back, Aldric?" The question seemed artless.

His mouth opened and then closed again over clenched teeth as he realised the true significance of what she had asked him. Six generations—two centuries perhaps. But there had been *yrloethen* Taelvallyn, the brothers Shar and Hachen, with the Horse Lords almost two thousand years ago. More than fifty generations past. His Elthanek ancestors went beyond even that into an age almost impossible to comprehend, where written records mingled with stories and legends until they were no longer told apart. Aldric turned his head away, mind reeling under the weight of uncounted years.

"It goes back . . . far too long," he answered thickly.

"You see. What does a line of six chiefs count for now?"

"It counts. I'd make sure it counts."

"Don't be foolish, Aldric." She lay back and their fingers slid apart. "Hush now. You and I have said enough. Go to sleep."

Although she slept almost at once, Aldric stayed propped on one elbow and wide awake for a long time. The creases of a frown smoothed from his face eventually and a thin, wistful smile took its place. Very, very gently he touched her white-blonde hair, letting each silken strand drift across his honourably scarred left hand. "Perhaps you're right," he murmured, drawing the quilt up and across them both. "And perhaps I am. Perhaps . . ." Curling up close to Kyrin's warm body, he looped one arm tenderly about her waist, then closed his eyes and slept like a child.

*

The vessel, *En Sohra*, was an Elherran gallon, a big, burly ship with galion complicated rigging. Her crew was also Elherran, folk of a trading nation which had so far kept its balance on the tightrope of neutrality, and while they looked askance at Kyrin—disapproving perhaps of her wearing men's clothing—they made no open protest.

The galion was towed early into deep water and was well under way by mid-morning, bowling along down the Narrow Sea before a stiff north-easterly breeze. Though her cargo of roofing-lead ballasted the ship and made her ride low and steady, Aldric was unsure whether he liked sailing very much. Not that he was sick . . . just not terribly interested in food.

The queasiness lasted only for a day or so and once he recovered and learned to cope with the rolling deck, he and Kyrin spent much of their time on the poop, screened from prying eyes by sails and rails and cabin. Dewan, who by his profession noticed things, found the way they were always holding hands rather amusing, in an innocently romantic way—but he remained, for a foreigner, honourably discreet.

For the first two days of open sea they encountered nothing but several fishing dories and the usual circling gulls; but on the third morning breakfast in the great cabin was interrupted by a yell from the lookout, in tones of such urgency that the meal was abandoned without a second thought. With her sail taut and filled by the wind whistling in over her stern rail, the galion was making excellent speed, but breaking the grey horizon on the port quarter was a sail.

"What is it?" Dewan demanded when he reached the poopdeck. Somebody passed him a long-glass and he stared through it long and hard, but no matter how much he hoped the image would change his first impression remained the same. The sail was red.

"Well?" asked Aldric, squinting a little in what promised to be a bright, clear day.

"Red sail," the Vreijek said shortly. "That means the Imperial Fleet."

"There's always the possibility it's just a merchant captain who likes the colour red," suggested Kyrin hopefully.

Dewan favoured her with a withering glance. "Maybe so . . . but given the price of that red dye, I wouldn't bank on it."

Within an hour the other vessel was running slightly astern, close enough for them to see an occasional flash from her deck as someone turned a long-glass on the scudding galion. She was a warship; that much was all too clear. What remained obscure was why, no matter what manoeuvres she executed, only her masthead pennants shifted to match the changing wind; both big sails remained square-set and full.

The Drusalan ship was armoured; sheets of steel covered her upperworks and hull almost to the waterline, and by now even unaided eyes could discern where seven turrets rose from her main deck and her bow. The mainsail was vivid red and displayed the Emperor's silver star-with-streamers, but the black sprit-sail bore a white-outlined four-pointed star: the Grand Warlord's badge. A long ram broke surface now and then, although the ship was no galley; the rakish sides towering above *En Sohra* were smooth, unbroken by ports or oarlocks. Still the galion retained her lead.

Then the impossible happened. Under full sail, with no more room on her yards for even a silken kerchief, the warship accelerated. A white bone of foam surged up between the teeth of her ramming gear and in a matter of minutes she scythed past *En Sohra* in a hiss of broken water. The galion's people could hear a clang of gongs sounding battle-stations and then a voice amplified and distorted by a speaking-trumpet. "This is the Imperial Battleram *Aalkhorst!*" it blared. "Heave to and prepare to be boarded!"

Leaning over the galion's waist-rail, Kyrin glanced up at an outburst of sharp words on the quarterdeck above her. Aldric had given orders to *En Sohra*'s master which the sailor seemed reluctant to obey; then the *eijo* put one hand to his *taiken*'s hilt and the captain hastily did as he was told, addressing a string of Elherran to his helmsman. Kyrin knew only two words: "turn" and "run." Consequently she was one of the few people not taken by surprise when the galion heeled over and away from the battleram. Her clumsy-looking lugsails allowed her to sail closer to the wind than almost any other rig, and by rights the big Imperial ship would now be reduced to sluggish tacking. In theory.

Aalkhorst's steersman had not been watching as closely as he should have been, for the warship stayed on course for almost three ship-lengths—in her case a considerable distance—before anything happened. Then she leaned over in a skidding, gunwale-submerged turn which brought her head straight into wind. There her sails should have gone slack and useless—but after a momentary flap they bellied out, ignoring the wind of the world. Then she came boring in at them, faster even than the first incredible dash which had brought her level. For a terrifying instant the spikes of the black star reared high above *En Sohra*'s stern lanterns, and the ram slopped cold brine across the galion's deck as it lifted on the swell and then came crashing back in a shower of spray.

Sliding back into place on the starboard beam, *Aalkhorst* blanketed the merchantman's sails so that they hung limp and her pace faltered. Two of the armoured cupolas on her portside revolved until their shuttered slots faced *En Sohra*, and then the shutters snapped open. Across the narrow strip of salt water Aldric heard a crackle of orders in the guttural Drusalan speech, just before ar Korentin grabbed his arm and jerked him under cover.

There was a clatter and the deck where he had stood sprouted catapult bolts and splinters of chewed-up planking.

A moment later the galion's master had struck his colours and lowered his useless sails. Part of the battleram's armour opened and a small boat was winched down into the sea. Shortly afterwards four soldiers in the red-and-green of Imperial marines clambered up *En Sohra*'s boarding ladder, with their officer following at a more dignified pace.

He was tall, lean, his eyes startlingly blue in a face

tanned by wind and sun. The man took off his rank-barred helmet and cradled it under one arm, passing a hand over his close-cropped scalp as he studied the damage his salvo had inflicted. Then he called for the captain.

"You disobeyed my direct command," he accused. "Why?"

"I . . . that is, we—" the sailor floundered.

"I ordered it," interrupted Aldric.

The officer's arrogant stare switched to him and one of the man's eyebrows lifted quizzically. "I am *Hautmarin* Doern," he rasped. "Who are you?"

"A . . . mercenary. Between employers—not that it's your affair," the Alban retorted frostily.

Doern laughed at him and swept a pointed gaze over the galion's grimy finery. "Indeed. Not a very successful one, if you have to sail on a tub like this. Why did you run?" He barked the question, hoping to startle an admission from somebody.

"I made some enemies," Aldric drawled smoothly. "Powerful enemies. Using an Imperial warship isn't beyond them. So I took no chances." He turned his back and kicked at a hatch-cover. "But since you're real I suppose you'll want to search the bloody ship, so get on with it. I'll not stand in your way. There's been enough time wasted already."

Kyrin was the only person who saw the glance Dewan exchanged with the galion's master at Aldric's words. With a nasty start she realised there was more to *En Sohra* than either she or the *eijo* had been told. Much more.

Doern missed the by-play, which was just as well. He was studying Aldric as if trying to interpret something from the warrior's expression.

"So," he muttered. "You seem honest enough." He turned to his men, gestured at the hold and issued orders. All four marines went below and by the noise they made carried out a most thorough search. There was a sudden clatter and the enraged neighing of a war-horse; Aldric grinned wickedly at the burst of Drusalan swear-words which followed. Then a marine half-emerged from the deck gratings and said something which brought

Doern across the planks in two noisy strides. When he straightened there was a helmet like his own dangling by its chinstrap from one outstretched hand. "Whose is this?" he demanded in a low, dangerous voice. *"Whose?"*

"Mine," said Dewan.

The *hautmarin* glowered at him. "There is a full harness down there," he grated. "Our cavalry pattern. Where did *you* get it?"

"As standard issue," ar Korentin replied crisply, lapsing into fluent Drusalan, "when I served with the Bodyguard in Drakkesborg." He paused just long enough for his words to sink in, then went for the kill. "Holding *eldheisart* rank."

The pine deck boomed as all five Imperial soldiers crashed to attention. "My apologies, lord-commander," muttered Doern. "You should have made yourself known at once."

Ar Korentin cleared his throat but said nothing, letting them stew for a little by taking a short walk around the deck. The *hautmarin* and his marines stayed where they were, heels together and eyes straight ahead. Thus they missed the small wink which Dewan directed at Aldric and *En Sohra*'s captain.

"*Hautmarin* . . . Doern, wasn't it?" said the Vreijek at length, not looking round. "I didn't . . . make myself known to you at all. There was no Imperial armour aboard this vessel. You encountered nothing out of the ordinary." He strode up to the officer and stared at him. "Do I make myself perfectly clear, *hautmarin?*"

"Sir!" Doern slammed once through the rhythmic sequence of a full salute and then looked through ar Korentin as if he was not there. "Reembark!" he ordered. "There's no contraband here. Good day to you, shipmaster."

"One question only, *hautmarin,*" Dewan said quietly. "Doing . . . what "I do, I hear little news from home. How can your ship sail against the wind?"

Doern glanced sideways. "I shouldn't tell even you, sir, but—call it an exchange of confidences. Grand Warlord Etzel paid a sorcerer to lay enchantment on the *Aalkhorst*—to charm a witch-wind into the sails. We can go where we please. But—but I don't like it, sir; magic's

been proscribed for years and now to make so free with
it . . . Something's wrong."

"*Hautmarin,*" Dewan cautioned, "I didn't hear you
say that. And don't let—" His insincerities broke off as
Kyrin shouted, pointing at the sky. She had whiled away
a conversation which she could not understand by peering through a long-glass at whatever caught her attention. One such distant speck had seemed to be a gull at
first, but closer scrutiny and her own suspicions revealed
it to be nothing of the sort. Crossing the quarterdeck in
two long strides, Aldric seized the glass and raised it to
his eye, then flinched visibly and muttered something
savage under his breath. "What the hell is *that?*" he
heard ar Korentin gasp.

Aldric's mouth was dry and he could taste the acrid
bitterness of fear under his tongue. So soon after Esel,
he thought, and felt an ill-suppressed shiver crawl along
his spine. "I can't give you a name," he answered very
softly, "but I think it's looking for . . ." His voice was
drowned by a thin whistling shriek of exhalation as the
isghun passed high overhead, and *En Sohra*'s deck
blinked dark as vast wings slid across the sun. The spellbeast turned, spiralling on one wingtip with heavy, ominous grace, and came back low and fast.

It skimmed past the galion's portside just above the
waves, the banshee scream of its breath slapping back
from whirling disturbed water in its wake, and for just
an instant Aldric met the demon's eyes. The force of
that unhuman gaze was like a blow and, horribly, there
was recognition in it. Then the isghun was gone, soaring
into the hard blue sky white the storm-wind of its passage flailed across both ships.

Aldric laid one hand to *taiken*-hill, sickly aware of
how small both he and Widowmaker were beside the
monster's bulk. He was conscious too of other things; of
how the hand had trembled before he clenched it tight,
of how wind-blown hair and clothing stuck to skin already chilled by sweat, of how he felt more alone than
ever in his life. And more afraid. Esel had at least been
manlike and familiar, no matter what his shape concealed. But *this* . . .

The *eijo*'s last rational thought was one of disbelief

that anything so big could move so fast, as the isghun swept around and dived like a falcon on a mouse. Then he flung himself clear of the quarterdeck. A shadow flashed across *En Sohra* and there was a rending crash right at his heels which made the galion vibrate from stem to stern. Though he landed heavily and barely kept his balance, Aldric was still able to glance up in time to see what might have been his own fate.

The isghun's tail had whiplashed around the companion-ladder where he had been standing and had wrenched it clean out of the deck without apparent effort. Emitting a deep, disgusted grunt, it let the false catch drop more than three hundred feet in a slow end-over-end tumble until the stairway smashed to matchwood against *Aalkhorst*'s armoured stern.

Aldric could hear the sonorous howl as air pumped through great vents in the creature's wings, driven by rippling contractions of muscle to thrust it forward. Its mode of flight gave his racing mind a clue to what might well prove weakness. If only he was able to—

It broke off its lazy circuit of the ship and plunged straight towards him, body rearing high so that its tail was free to clutch. But the tail did not even come close. Over eager, perhaps impatient, straining to reach its victim, the isghun slammed into *En Sohra*'s mainmast with an impact that sprang timbers all over the merchant vessel and then slewed across the deck fighting to stay airborne. As its hideous head came lurching closer Aldric yelped, rolling aside and upright. Isileth Widowmaker blurred out of her scabbard.

Behind the spellbeast sailors lunged with boarding-pikes, only to be hurled aside by its thrashing tail. An arrow ripped through its wing and acid-smelling fluid spurted out of the wound. More missiles drove into its body, penetrating with an ease that betrayed the monster's fragile flesh, if flesh it was. Suction dragged at Aldric's body as air rushed into the isghun, expanding its body even as he watched; none was released and, guessing what was about to happen, the *eijo* gripped something solid and held on tightly.

Muscles contracted, fleshy valves snapped open and what air the demon had drawn in came shrieking out,

blasting its body upwards and hurling three men over-
board. Aldric, though unsteady on his feet, was not one
of them. He slashed Widowmaker deep into the swollen
belly passing just above his head.

A bellow of agony all but deafened him and the isghun lurched uncontrollably sideways as half its body
underwent a violent deflation. Then it struggled sky-
wards and Aldric cried out in shock, for the demon's
tail had looped around his legs and he went up as well.
Somebody shouted incoherently in panic. Himself? The
brutal grip was crushing both his knees and as he was
jerked upside-down his shoulders crashed first against
the deck and then against *En Sohra*'s sterncastle. It was
impossible to use the *taiken* now, because his legs and
the isghun's tail were so entangled that to cut one would
almost certainly wound the other. Unless . . . Aldric
closed both hands around his longsword's hilt; the loss
of a foot was preferable to what Kalarr and Duergar
had in store for him.

The inverted deck jumped up as he abruptly dropped
towards it, but his only pain was in the skull he cracked
on landing. A length of severed tail uncoiled from his
kicking legs, the vinegary stench of isghun blood was in
his nostrils and it was dripping from Kyrin's sword-blade
as she clattered down the remaining stairway from the
quarterdeck. *If my face is as white as hers . . .* Aldric
thought grimly, somehow dredging up a feeble smile of
thanks. "Where is it now?" he demanded, following
Kyrin as she ran towards the poop. The girl raised her
arm in silence and Aldric knew he had been right about
the isghun's vulnerable spot. Injured and unbalanced, it
could only fly in sluggish oblique swoops while the *Aalkhorst* closed at flank speed with white water boiling from
her prow.

Dewan and *Hautmarin* Doern, bearing crossbows,
were both at the starboard rail, and as Aldric drew level
with him the Imperial officer clenched his fist and muttered *"Now!"* As if in response the warship loosened a
ranging volley; then unleashed a salvo from her forward
batteries that made the isghun shudder in midair. Right
from the start, when only two turrets had been enough
to fill *En Sohra*'s deck with darts, Aldric had suspected

that the battleram was armed with something out of the
ordinary. He was right. Her first three turrets carried
quick-firing catapults both wound and triggered by the
same geared mechanism; they could shoot as fast as
crews could crank them.

With its wings shredded and its body punched full of
gaping holes, the isghun fell towards the waiting sea.
And just before it struck, it vanished—winked out of
existence as if it had never been; although *En Sohra*'s
condition gave the lie to that suggestion. Doern watched
his battleram swing back towards them and drew a long
deep breath before settling his helmet' back in place.
"That was . . . ?"

"Sent by my enemies, *hautmarin,*" Aldric returned unsteadily. He felt very tired. "I told you they were
powerful."

"Quite . . ." The officer cleared his throat and spat
across the rail. "I know now what I dislike about sorcery.
Every hell-damned detail! Good luck to you, mercenary." He swung outboard and down towards his waiting
cutter, then paused and looked back. "I fancy you may
need it."

The witch-wind filled *Aalkhorst*'s sails and with a rustle
of canvas she drew away from the galion before turning
leisurely, a wide, arrogant sweep which flaunted her armoured, destructive might to all aboard the merchantman.
As she swung onto a parallel course the warship's bow
rose and foam creamed from her ram as she came slicing
past. A surge of wash made *En Sohra* roll heavily; then
the battleram was gone, dwindling towards the horizon
at the tip of an arrow-straight wake.

As they began to put their damaged ship to rights, the
Elherran crew avoided Aldric, tacitly blaming him for
what had happened. The young *eijo* did not care. He
slumped down in a quiet corner of the deck, knees drawn
up, head resting on his folded arms, weak and shaking
with reaction. Kyrin sat crosslegged beside him, pol-
ishing her sword. "Aldric-*ain,*" she said, "there's something odd about this ship."

Aldric glanced at her and grimaced slightly. "It's not
the ship," he muttered, reluctant to talk. "And it's not
my business."

"I think it is." She told him briefly of the look she had seen pass between the captain and ar Korentin, and of its circumstances. Aldric realised that the girl was right: this affair had become his business.

Dewan was not disturbed by the interrogation which followed; he was more surprised by the Alban's calm, not knowing that its source was simply weariness. Aldric was too exhausted to be angry. "It isn't that we didn't trust you," ar Korentin told him, "but the fewer who know of this, the better." Aldric settled back into the captain's chair and let the Vreijek talk. "Your ignorance meant that you told Doern the truth—as you knew it. And he was convinced. He didn't really expect to find anything aboard, much less the gold we—"

"Gold . . . ? What gold?" There was an edge to Aldric's voice that Dewan disliked and he chose his words more carefully.

"To finance another thorn in Warlord Etzel's side. Just as he financed Duergar Vathach."

The *eijo* stared at him, his grey-green eyes devoid of all expression. "Ignorance," Aldric repeated, as if tasting the word. A faint smile twitched his mouth. "You are a devious bastard." Dewan acknowledged the compliment with a slight bow.

"One of my varied talents," he retorted blandly.

Down on deck Kyrin listened, appreciating the trick. Then she stiffened and gripped her *estoc*'s hilt more firmly. There was a soft fluttering noise behind her—and its source was moving. The girl half-turned and bared her teeth disgustedly at the ball of jelly hovering on small wings beside the rail. Without thinking she chopped the thing in two and watched the pieces drop into the sea; then, very carefully, began to clean her sword again.

*

Kalarr jerked back from his magic mirror and spat an oath. "Bitch!" he finished with feeling.

"You've lost them now," Duergar pointed out unkindly. "What will you do?"

"We," Kalarr emphasised the plural, "will wait. He'll come back. For you, if nothing else." The Drusalan flinched, but Kalarr still knew he had lost face. Rising suddenly, the sorcerer turned to Baiart who was watching from the shadows by the door. "You said one was the king's man. Do you know what that means?" The clan-lord shook his head. "It means, my friend"—and that word dripped vitriol—"that your brother has been speaking to King Rynert. From now on, you don't go back to Cerdor."

"But—" Baiart started, before he was silenced by a glare from eyes as cold and black as the spaces between the stars.

"You will never leave this citadel again." Kalarr's lips thinned above his teeth. "Not even to go to your own execution. And that, dear Baiart, is final."

7

Lair of Dragons

Lying on his back, Aldric made complicated patterns from the dappled sunlight reflected on to his cabin ceiling by the sea. As *En Sohra* rose on the slow deep-water swell, golden blotches chased one another across the planking and down a panelled wall. He had woken at sunrise with a feeling that the ship was no longer moving, but lying at anchor in calm water. Even so, at such a time of the morning he had no intention of leaving his bed—or rather, bunk. It was uncomfortable, narrow and hard, with sheets of linen cloth instead of the usual quilt, and not really big enough for two to sleep in. All the same, he and Kyrin had managed fairly well.

She was still draped across him, head cuddled against his shoulder so that he felt the warmth of each tiny, purring breath, their limbs all tangled with each other and the sheets. Moving one hand up the smoothness of her back, Aldric twisted to kiss her gently on the cheek. "Mmm . . . ?" Kyrin ventured drowsily, and the young *eijo* felt her eyelashes flutter against his throat. She stirred a little in the crook of his left arm, almost awake now.

"I love you, Kyrin," he whispered, touching her face with his lips. They were words he knew she did not want to hear, but equally he felt they had to be said. The girl breathed in deeply, raised her head and opened her eyes wide, then she thought better of it and half-closed them again. Aldric realised she had not heard him—and with that heavy-lidded sapphire gaze resting on him, he lacked the courage to repeat himself. Coward, he thought.

Or over-gentle gentleman . . . ? "I think we've reached our destination," the Alban ventured in a louder voice.

"Is it morning, or could you put that light out?"

"Morning. Sorry, but I can't do anything about it."

Wriggling experimentally, Kyrin succeeded in working her feet free of the knot of bedclothes and sat up. "You could pull the shutters over," she suggested.

"I could," yawned Aldric, making no attempt to do so. "But since you're now closer to them . . ." Kyrin considered this; then she hit him with a pillow.

Somewhat later, as they dozed in a cooling breeze from the still-unshuttered port, ar Korentin rapped loudly on the door. Being an officer and a gentleman— and no fool—he did not open it, but called, "Breakfast, if you want any," through the timbers. Aldric was fairly sure he heard a muted chuckle as the Vreijek walked away, and tried to calculate just what time it really was. Indecently late even for lovers, he guessed, and with a wry grin swung his feet to the floor.

*

Thanks to the weather they were able to eat on deck under an awning, though Aldric seemed disinterested in his food for once; he spent much of his time leaning over the stern-rail with an untouched cup of something cradled in one hand, staring at the green bulk of Techaur Island. It was certainly worth staring at, especially for someone who had never seen anything bigger than a lake-eyot before. Quite apart from the other things he knew about Techaur, about the Dragonwand . . . and about the dragon.

Most of the island reared sheer out of the water, and there surf crashed ruinously against rocks which jutted from the sea like menacing teeth; but the cove in which the galion lay was protected by cliffs on one side and a sloping headland on the other, with a sweep of gravel beach between. Even so, *En Sohra* tugged now and again at her cable when a current drew oily curves across the surface of the little bay, a shift in the prevailing wind would turn this natural harbour into a scoop for waves which would hurl anything—whether weed, driftwood or ship—in ruin on the fanged rocks. Many of the so-called

Thousand Islands earned their title only at low tide, spending the rest of their time awash; covered by an impenetrable shroud of green from the beach to the slopes of its single small peak, Techaur was not one of them. But a visible, tree-clad island could rip the bottom from a ship as easily as any crusted with barnacles and hidden by the sea.

Aldric had watched his destination since starting his meagre breakfast, and liked it no more at the beginning than when he had finished. "Lower a boat, shipmaster," he heard Dewan say behind him, "and tell off some sailors to come with us."

"I will not," the captain answered. Aldric glanced round, half-expecting something of the sort and the captain saw him turn. "No man of mine would go with you to—to that place," he said, as much to Aldric as to Dewan. "Not for all the gold we carry. It is accursed, a haunt of demons. Ask that one"—his finger jabbed at the *eijo*—"if he feels the evil in the air. Ask him! He knows."

Though he could indeed sense something, probably more than the shipmaster would have believed, he had no intention of admitting it. Not after the isghun. Instead he smiled, appearing cool and unconcerned. "Why then did you bring us here, if Techaur is—" Aldric purred the word viciously, knowing how it would sound, "—haunted?"

The sailor's swarthy features darkened at any imputation of cowardice on his part. "I pilot this ship for your king!" he snapped. "He says, bring these three to Techaur Island. He does *not* say, land there yourself. So we will stay on board."

"Then get someone to row us in," Aldric grated, "and we'll wade ashore. That should keep your crew content." The young Alban was unused to having his orders questioned, especially twice by the same man. He began to lose his temper, and the shipmaster made no attempt to help him keep it.

"We stay on board *En Sohra*," he repeated flatly.

Aldric drew in breath and took a step towards the Elherran with one fist clenched; then Kyrin caught her

lover's half-raised arm and smiled a little when he turned
on her.

"Have you ever rowed a boat?" she enquired pleasantly, refusing to be disturbed by what she saw in Aldric's eyes. The *eijo* shook his head, slowly, clearing the
heat from his brain as much as answering her question.

"Well, I have. So come on."

*

They dragged the little rowboat up the beach and for
safety's sake made its painter fast around a boulder before setting off into the undergrowth. Within half a
dozen strides the sea was lost to sight and almost inaudible through the rustling of leaf-heavy branches and the
crackle of dead wood underfoot. Birds were calling
somewhere.

"Dewan, is this common on islands?" Aldric wanted
to know.

"Depends on the size. I'd say this place is big enough
to weather most storms without being drenched in salt
water, but even so, I see what you mean."

"It's uncanny, that's what you're saying," Kyrin put
in. "Look at those trees; they shouldn't be half that size
and you know it."

Dewan made no reply; there was really nothing more
to say, because all three were fully aware of the strangeness of this island, made eerie by being subtly half-
hidden until they looked for it and then appearing to be
all around them.

Once they startled—and were startled by—a sounder
of wild pigs, not boar but smaller, patterned with brown-
and-buff streaks not altogether unlike common farmyard
swine. Dewan saw a pair of goats which he swore had
ram's horns, and then Kyrin found the tracks of some
animal's feet in soft mud near a stream: feet with paws,
not hoofs, which Aldric recognised at once as the pad-
marks of a *kourgath,* the same wild lynx-cat which he
wore as a crest. Except that this *kourgath* was twice as
big as it should have been, easily able to prey now on
pigs, goats—or indeed, any human unwary enough to let
it get too close. It made them realise that when Aldric
had insisted that all three wear armour, he had not done

so as a joke. Though the hot, still air made them sweat just as much inside their battle harness, its weight no longer seemed an unnecessary burden.

Abruptly the trees thinned out, revealing a sheer crag which peaked almost a hundred feet above them, naked rock as seamed and fissured as pine bark, impossible to climb and, by the flaky look of it, dangerous to stand near.

"Where now?" Dewan asked, leaning back to see where the wall of stone went and then glancing at Aldric for an answer. "Up, down or around?"

"Around," the *eijo* said confidently. "There's a way up somewhere, so we'll go . . . this way." As he walked off, Kyrin looked at Dewan. They both had a fair notion that the young Alban was bluffing, though neither was quite sure to what extent.

"Better get after him," said Kyrin after a moment's pause. "He might—just might—know what he's talking about."

"Care to put some money on that?" grinned Dewan. "Say twenty in gold?"

The Valhollan hesitated, listening to Aldric whistling through his teeth, thought for a moment and then nodded. "Make it in silver," she amended carefully.

"Done! But I'd have thought you more confident than that, my dear."

"I am confident—just not *that* confident, or that wealthy even if I was. And I'm not your dear."

Then, quite suddenly, Aldric's whistling stopped.

When they reached the spot, swords drawn, there was no sign of him at all. No blood, no crushed grass, no trace of a struggle—not even somewhere he might have gone "You don't think—" Kyrin began, then jumped backwards with a cry of fright as something black and gleaming heaved out of the turf almost at her feet. Dewan lunged forward and his heavy sword came down with all the Vreijek's muscle behind the cut. It crashed into Aldric's helmet hard enough to cause a shower of sparks, and the *eijo* vanished again without a sound. Kyrin dropped onto hands and knees and peered into the dark hole from which he had appeared and into which he had abruptly been returned. There was a small, anguished groan from deep inside.

"Aldric . . . are you all right?" The Alban's steel-sheathed fingers reappeared and gripped her wrist less gently than she would have liked. Aldric's face was pale under his dented helmet when it came back into view, and he glared at Dewan in a way the Valhollan girl hoped she would never experience. But then, he had good reason to be angry.

"No, my lady," Aldric said between clenched teeth, "I am not all right. I hurt at both ends, thanks to this bloody overeager fool."

"I nearly split your skull!" barked ar Korentin, hiding his relief with irritation. Aldric stared up at him balefully.

"Must you always state the painfully obvious?" the *eijo* snapped.

"Shut up, the pair of you—this is no place for bickering over accidents." Kyrin's voice cut through their argument and silenced them more through surprise than anything else. "Better!" she said. "Now, what is that hole in the ground anyway?"

"Give me some light and I'll tell you," retorted Aldric, still annoyed and sore. Dewan lit one of the ship's lanterns they had brought, then lowered it into the pit. After only a few minutes Aldric's head reappeared; there was a smile of sorts inside his war-mask. "We go down from here on," he said quietly.

The other lamps were lit, and all three descended out of sight. Nothing moved in the clearing for a while after they had gone, until a small bird landed and began to peck through the soil turned up near the tunnel mouth. Then it looked up, twittered nervously and flew away just as one of the nearby branches rustled, very slightly. Then the branch was slowly pulled aside.

*

Dewan and Kyrin speculated quietly as to who might have made the steps down which they walked. There was no reason to speak in hushed voices, but like a religious house or a funeral crypt, this place discouraged loud talking.

By the sound of ar Korentin's voice, he was feeling uncomfortable, almost frightened, though he concealed it well. Aldric smiled mirthlessly into the darkness; even champions have their weak points, he reflected, not thinking any less of Dewan for proving human after all. Having spent the past three years in just such a subterranean complex, the young *eijo* was more at home than his two companions; even so, after having the sky and sea around him he felt cramped and uneasy, though the passage was unnaturally spacious and dry.

Then he hesitated as a movement of the air stroked his face; it was warm, spicily scented and totally unexpected in a tunnel. Light and shadow danced across the walls as he raised his lantern high. It revealed nothing, but from somewhere impossibly distant he could hear a tinkling like windblown crystal bells, mingled with the sweet chattering clash of finger-cymbals.

"Can you hear it?" whispered Kyrin. Metal scraped as the two men nodded armoured heads. Remote sounds as of flute and strings formed unbidden inside the girl's head, a tenuous thread of melody bringing visions of seductive elegance, of sinuous grace. There was a vague suggestion of amber light rising from far below, growing more clearly defined with every downward step.

"Douse your lanterns," Aldric hissed. As they did so the ruddy glow swelled and brightened much more than the fading lamplight seemed to justify, and they shrank back against the wall, each with a mental image of something searching for them with luminescent fingers. There was a creak of leather and a slithery sound as Aldric released the crossbelt supporting Isileth Widowmaker across his back, letting the *taiken* drop into place on his left hip before moving on down the steps. Though he reached out with every sense, stretching them to their limits, he could detect nothing alarming or hostile; only a barely perceptible feeling of . . . awareness.

Hand on hilt, he eased carefully to the stairway bottom and loosened Widowmaker in her scabbard. The steel-scrape was harsh and jarring against the background of soft musical tones—a stark, unequivocally brutal noise which did much to relieve the curious lassitude which he only noticed as it left him. Then he looked out of the tunnel.

Bales of rich fabric, fine garments, precious metals both raw and exquisitely worked, jewels and crystalline bottles; all were littered carelessly along the walls and around the pillars of a great vaulted hall. Piles of coins formed tempting snowdrifts wherever there was room for them—and there was certainly plenty of room. The whole vast chamber was lit by live flames which spilled from the mouths of dragons carved around each pillar, and by a great orange-red glow which pulsed and shifted at the farther end of the hall. Aldric caught his breath at the unimaginable riches piled here, and at the monstrous magnificence of it all. It was . . . glorious.

"What is this place?" Dewan's voice was gruff and he tried hard to keep it matter-of-fact as befitted a man of his rank and station. Aldric could have told him that rank was no defence against the arrogant splendour of a sorcerous hold like this one, but he could tell just by looking at the Vreijek's face that Dewan had already realised as much.

"This," Aldric said quietly, "is the Cavern of Fire-drakes, the lair of Ykraith, the abode of the dragon." Dewan stared at the younger man, then unaccountably felt himself shiver.

Sight, hearing and smell were all dazed in that hall: by the dance of flame on gold; by thin, eerie chords of music; by rare and costly fragrances. Touch and taste begged to be indulged by an insidious compulsion to run fingers through the precious things, to broach the crystal jars which doubtless each held wines of noble vintage. . . . This was not mere avarice, something which might have been expected, but a headier sensuality which amounted almost to a lust. Hands were already reaching out as Aldric remembered the half-forgotten words he had been sifting for at the back of his mind. Gemmel's words, then just one instruction among many but possessed now with a terrible significance: ". . . remember, don't touch anything but the Dragonwand, no matter how tempting . . ."

Against the humming music, Aldric's best modulated voice would have sounded coarse; his incoherent yell of warning rasped hideously. The others jerked as if stabbed by pins and a frightening blankness slowly vanished from their faces. The *eijo* allowed himself a sigh of relief. "I think I said before, don't touch." He made no attempt to hide the tremor in his voice. "Better not, or else . . ." His helmeted head jerked meaningfully at the gaping jaws of carven dragons and at the fires which fumed in each.

Aldric began the long walk down the cavern all alone, but before he had completed three strides Kyrin had pattered level with him. He made a gesture which if completed might have been one of dismissal; but then smiled and lowered his hand before its movement was two-thirds finished. From where he stood to the throbbing fiery glow was a long and lonely way, and he was grateful for her company.

Dewan ar Korentin watched them both dispassionately, then leaned his weight slightly on to his scabbarded sword as he had learned to do on parade in Drakkesborg years before. He did not relax, despite the comfortable warmth of the great hall; it was not a place in which any sane man could ever relax.

As they walked closer, both Aldric and Kyrin could see how the cavern ended in a lofty plinth, massive and conical, a flight of steps cut into its side and its whole surface scored with runes and signs of power. The hot, misty glow welled from its peak and splashed reflections of flame-coloured light across the ceiling, countering them with deep, dark shadows on the floor. Then Kyrin seized Aldric's mailed arm in total, terrified silence and pointed towards the deepest swathe of gloom with a trembling finger.

The Alban's eyes dilated and heat-born redness ebbed from a face in which the mouth opened but emitted not even an expulsion of breath. He found his feet were rooted to the spot, making flight impossible even if it was not being pushed from his mind by an overwhelming sense of wonder.

It slept in the darkness around the base of the plinth: hunched, huge, lean, undulant and elegant. A firedrake. A dragon. Its wings were folded along its spiked back, its monstrous head rested on slender claws and a coil of armoured tail wrapped across its nose, giving a momentary image of some colossal cat asleep by the hearth. There was no trace of life anywhere about it; no breathing moved its scaled flanks, none of the legendary smoke drifted from its half-hidden nostrils. Aldric was almost disappointed that all seemed dark and still and dead. He took a single quiet cat-step forward.

Then he laughed, briefly and harshly, with more disgust than mirth in his voice. That step had been enough to reveal a platform underneath the firedrake's body, carved from onyx, agate and lapis lazuli, inset with turquoise and gold. No wonder the creature seemed dead. Statues were often like that. It was metallic, all polished steel and beaten copper, a lifelike, life-size conversation piece which was worth a great deal of money and had, with the pillars, given the Cavern of Firedrakes its name. But . . . "It's not real!" There was more than a little indignation in his voice.

"You mean—you wish it *was* . . . ?" Kyrin's voice held simple disbelief.

"I'd half-expected that it would be," the *eijo* responded. "Even so . . ." He was remembering Esel now, and recalling that statues were not always as immobile as they should be. It was several minutes before he risked going any closer to the firedrake and Kyrin stayed where she was.

The creature's body rose to more than twice Aldric's own height and was covered in fine scales like lizardmail—another uncomfortable reminder of Esel—which were complete in every detail. The unknown sculptor who had made the dragon had been a true artist in every way; he had possessed the imagination to create such a fantastic beast and the skill to portray it with such realism that it could almost have been taken from a live subject. Silently saluting its creator's genius, Aldric turned away from the firedrake and walked back towards the stairs.

Gemmel had told him what ritual he would have to follow, but typically had refused to divulge any explanation of the whys and wherefores. In the old enchanter's opinion Aldric's interest in—and aptitude for—the Art Magic was unhealthy and not to be encouraged. Even so, he had had no choice but to teach the young man certain charms for his own protection; this had been done reluctantly, but as was Gemmel's way, when in the end it became essential it was done thoroughly.

"You'll have to stay here, I'm afraid," he told Kyrin, hiding nervousness with flippancy.

"I'm afraid too—so I'd rather come with you."

Aldric tugged off helm and war-mask, coif and wrapping-scarf, then shook his bared head. "You can't. But Spiny-tail over there will keep you company until I come down again."

He gave the helm to Kyrin, who took it with an air of resignation.

"I've told you this before, Aldric," she said. "Please . . . take care."

The *eijo* nodded, without his usual sardonic smile, and kissed her gently. There were no longer any words which needed saying between them; but in that brief, tender touching was much more than speech could ever convey. Then he turned to face the plinth, drawing Widowmaker and his *tsepan,* and went down on one knee with the weapons raised before him.

"I swear now by the Low and by the High and by the Ancient Powers that this thing which I must do is not my wish or will, nor is it by my choosing, and I call upon these Powers to witness that my oath is true. I, *kailin-eir* Aldric of the Alban clan Talvalin do swear it by the name which is my own and by the blade which guards my honour and by the blade which guards my life."

As he rose the young man sheathed both sword and dirk, then went up the stairs slowly and with dignity— even though his impulse was to run, to get this thing over with as quickly as possible.

The tapering plinth lacked a point, as if it had been neatly sliced away. If Aldric had realised how much it now resembled a volcanic cone, he might have had some inkling of what to expect. As it was, the discovery came as a most unpleasant surprise.

Instead of a flat platform at the top there was only a narrow rim, and beyond that a sheer drop into the hot embrace of a pool of molten rock. It was from this magma lake that the red-gold light came throbbing up, and with it came a shrivelling blast of heat which struck the *eijo* like a blow in the face. The air danced and shimmered, making it hard to distinguish outlines even though something rose dark and dense in the very middle of the burning haze.

When at last he saw what it was, his already-churning stomach cramped savagely and then turned right over with pure, undiluted fear. There was a slender column of granite rising from the centre of the seething crater, its uppermost part carved into the likeness of a warrior in antique armour. Its outstretched stone hands bore a darkly glinting staff.

Aldric recognised the Dragonwand at once . . . but the only way to reach it was by a causeway which ran, without parapet or rail, from the topmost step just at his feet straight to the statue's base. This too was stone, polished to a gleaming, treacherous smoothness—and it was less than a foot in width. Even given such narrowness, the twenty paces out and back would normally have been a matter of little account. But not with another twenty paces to consider: the distance straight down, to where bubbles burst with obscenely hungry belches in the liquid rock. While sweat formed and trickled on his shuddering skin, Aldric closed his eyes and expelled horrific images from the conscious part of his mind.

Heat and awestruck terror had dried his mouth so much that his first attempt to speak was little more than a rasping croak. The Alban's eyes opened, narrowed by concentration and against the glare. He worked his jaws briefly to produce a slight moisture around his tongue and rearmost teeth; it was a paltry effort, but enough. When he tried again, his voice was still hoarse but at least audible above the gurgling mutter of the earth's hearth-fires. Without feeling self-conscious Aldric raised one arm towards the statue in a full salute, then kept that arm outstretched, hand open and fingers spread apart.

"*Abath arhan*, Ykraith," he said quietly. "*Echuan aiy'yan elhar, arhlath ech'hil alauin.*" He could hear his own heart beating, the sound of his breath and the rush of blood in his ears—but the soft, eternal magma-roar had fallen silent.

And the heat had died away.

Aldric put one booted foot on to the causeway, paused for a downward glance into the furnace maw and then walked quickly to the statue.

Although its hands were tightly closed around the Dragonwand, when Aldric grasped it the stone fingers suddenly relaxed. So suddenly that he took a staggering pace backwards before recovering his balance with a frantic spinal jerk on the very brink of the pit. Flakes of granite crumbled from the edge beneath his heel and were swallowed up.

Aldric's lips stretched thinly over the clenched teeth bared by his grinning snarl. Firelight tinted their enamel a bloody red. Trembling all over, he returned along the narrow bridge, sank down crosslegged on the safety of the plinth's top step and stared at nothing for a long, long time. His racing heartbeat slowed at last to something almost normal and his sodden clothing dried a little, but only when his breath once more was coming slow and deep did he lower his eyes and focus them on the prize which he had won.

It was the height of a man or the length of a good straight spear, heavy, but balancing well in one or both of his hands. Its shaft, so Gemmel had told him in a rare expansive moment, was of the mineral called adamant: a translucent stuff, glinting greeny-black like obsidian glass but shot through with tiny filaments like spun gold. A dragon with scales of greenish gold wrapped its serpentine coils around the shaft, seeming less an inlay of metal than something which had grown from the surface. The dragon's tail, tipped with blued steel, formed the staffs spiked butt, while a green-gold dragon-head with one sapphire eye capped its other end. The empty eye-socket looked less like a hollow from which the stone had been prised loose, than a cavity waiting to be filled for the first time. A flame-shaped crystal, clear as quartz, writhed from the open mouth. It seemed fragile, but when Aldric idly scraped its point across the step under his knees, the delicate-looking substance gouged the stone like a chisel in soft wood.

His daydream was interrupted by a piercing scream from Kyrin in the hall below. Springing to his feet with dignity thrown aside, Aldric came down the stairs in clat-

tering bounds of four at a time. Even above the noise
of his descent he heard a slithering like a thousand
swords all drawn at once.

The firedrake lived!

Aldric jumped the last short distance to the cavern
floor and landed with a crash of harness, skidded wildly,
steadied himself with the Dragonwand and ran to Kyrin's side.

After that single shocked scream she had reacted
more in the way he had expected, and half-crouched
now in a defensive stance, her *estoc* drawn and poised.
The slender thrusting-sword had always reminded Aldric
of a needle, but against such a being as they faced together, it shrank to the merest pin.

Iron coils slid together with a grating sound as the
dragon stirred. Iron talons stretched out, clicking on the
agate of the platform. An iron eyelid lifted. Aldric
wrenched his own eyes away and made sure Kyrin did
the same—he had not listened to so many old stories
without learning something of the lore concerning firedrakes. One did not meet them stare for stare.

Somehow knowing it was the wisest thing to do, Aldric
raised the Dragonwand in both hands. He was painfully
aware of how it looked—more a twig than a talisman of
power. Then the words came; like those Gemmel had
taught him for the Claiming of Ykraith and in the same
language—but these were not words he had ever been
taught.

"Ymareth!" Scales rang with a steely music and he
felt the vast, brooding presence of the dragon leaning
over him, an unimaginable intelligence considering him,
a shadow like the shadow of death hanging right above
him. "Ymareth," he said again, without the first desperation but with more respect; and then a third time.
"Ymareth . . . *sachaur arrhath ebon Ykraith, aiy'yel echin
arhlathal Gemmel pestreyr.*"

The firedrake's movement ceased and Aldric risked
an upward glance, sliding his wary gaze across its armoured eerily beautiful head but always avoiding those
pupilless glowing amber-green eyes. He wondered about
the old tales, especially those in which a dragon spoke.
It seemed unlikey now that such a thing had ever hap-

pened, faced as he was with the reality of a lipless mouth and thin forked tongue which could never form the sounds of any human language. Yet the firedrake was intelligent—he was sure of that—and had understood whatever he had just said. Which was more than he had done himself.

Then it spoke.

The creature's voice was not loud, but it was huge, rustling metallic hiss like cymbals brushed with wire. Aldric could never have pronounced the sibilants—at least, he realised with a touch of irony, not without a lipless mouth and a thin forked tongue—but their meaning was somehow clear, in an archaic, formal mode which seemed entirely right and proper.

"I give thee greeting," said the dragon. "I am Ymareth. Know me, and know that I am lord. What do ye here in mine abiding-place?"

Aldric knelt, bowing forward to give the courtesy of Second Obeisance that was due to any lord in his own hall, then sat back on his heels, hiding his pounding heart behind a mask of elaborate high-clan politeness. "I ask a favour, Lord Firedrake," he responded.

"Speak, man," it said, "that I may judge."

The *eijo* gathered his courage and lifted the Dragon-wand above his head. "I ask to borrow this talisman, Lord Firedrake."

"Upon what cause?" Ymareth rumbled. Grey smoke curled briefly from its jaws, token that its wakening was complete now, even to its banked and glowing inner fires. "Wherefore desire ye Ykraith only and not the many treasures of mine hoard, Aldric Talvalin?"

A muscle twitched involuntarily in the Alban's face, both at the implications of the smoke and at hearing his name issue from such a throat. Yet the dragon had already given its own name quite freely, proof of a colossal self-assurance which Aldric did not share. Gemmel had told him a little about dragons, a year or so past; it had sounded boring and like a fool he had paid small heed. But one thing he recalled quite clearly. "Firedrakes," the enchanter had said between puffs at his pipe, "are no more wicked than the normal run of people; it's just that their notions of good and evil are . . . well, flexible would describe it best. An over-honest man could be easily deceived—but you, I suspect, would be in little danger." The *eijo* managed a small, sour smile at the memory.

"I have no need of gold, Lord Firedrake," he answered. "But I seek revenge on my enemies, and Ykraith will help me. I ask you for it, and do not touch your treasure, because I am an honest man and not a thief."

Ymareth snorted, so that smoke and a few sparks billowed from its nostrils. Aldric could have sworn the huge old thing was laughing at him and perhaps it was. "O prideful!" hissed the dragon softly. "Do I touch too closely on thy honour? So, and so, and so. Now verily this is true, for were ye not an honest man I should not have spoken, save to taunt thee ere thy most assured death."

Aldric raised his eyes slightly. As if expecting him to do so, the dragon opened its mouth fractionally. There was no more blatant menace in it than in any panting dog, but the action gave a glimpse of nine-inch fangs, of great cheek-teeth big enough to shear an ox in two—and a slight, almost accidental but certainly deliberate exhalation of yellow-white flame. Though he cringed within himself, Aldric did not move. Ymareth seemed impressed, if such a word had any meaning to it.

"Speak and say, what foes do so concern thee, that fear of my wrath does not deter thee?"

"One is the necromancer Duergar Vathach," Aldric replied, "and the other is Kalarr cu Ruruc."

There was a coughing sound within the firedrake's throat and tongues of flame licked from Ymareth's jaws as its ruffed head shook with amusement. Aldric began to choke as smoke enveloped him, and when it cleared he saw through streaming eyes that the dragon was leaning towards him, mouth agape. He felt the wash of a great hot breath and the icy stab of the fear of death.

Ymareth unleashed no blast of fire, and when Aldric opened his eyes again—carefully avoiding those of the firedrake—he found the creature wore a tongue-lolling grin like that of some vast fox.

"I compliment thee on thy choice of enemies, *kailineir* Talvalin, if there was choice at all." The dragon's

voice became quiet and deadly. "Cu Ruruc of Ut Ergan
is a creeping viper and made essay to dominate me many
lives of men ago. He was most wise and cunning, well
versed in words of power, but he knew not that Masterword which has governance of dragonkind. Verily it was
his great good fortune to get from here alive that day."
Aldric heard the susurration of a scaled neck, the bright,
ringing clank of a talon laid on the floor and saw the
shadow of the dragon's head move as it leaned down to
study him more closely. He stared hard at his own
gloved hands and tried to ignore the colossal wedge-
shaped head which hung less than an arm's length from
his own; even then he could feel Ymareth's gaze probing
at him, searching for what a firedrake might term false-
hood.

"I did hear thee speak the words of swearing and of
summoning and of claiming. What of the words to master such as I, *kailin* Talvalin?" The voice reeked of heat,
of the clean stench of fire—and of suspicion.

Aldric felt panic welling up inside him; if Ymareth
thought for one instant that its own mighty person was
in danger, it would obliterate him before he could draw
another breath. He took a desperate chance, bowing
with proper respect for the dragon's power before raising his head to stare not at, but between Ymareth's eyes.
Even then that blank, phosphorescent glare glimpsed
only with the edge of sight was enough to set his senses
swaying. It required an effort of which Aldric had not
known himself capable, not to gape in helpless fascination at the golden orbs and let the peace, the stillness,
the terrible tranquillity of the dragon-spell take him
where it would, even to walking down the firedrake's
throat. He could feel runnels of perspiration tickling his
back and taste salt droplets forming on his upper lip.
The eyes enticed, but Aldric managed to keep his gaze
fixed on Ymareth's crest and let it wander nowhere else.

"Lord Firedrake," he managed at long last, "I have
few words of any power, and none that might impose my
will on you. The strongest word controls myself alone. It
is my Word of Honour, and one I try always to keep—
but it is often far from easy."

The spell was withdrawn so abruptly that Aldric cried

out like a man in pain and fell forward on to his hands, forehead almost touching the ground. "Those who speak with dragonkind make use of twisted talk and riddles," said the great voice. "Always until now. It is passing strange that thee of all men should be forthright. Take Ykraith, *kailin-eir* Talvalin, and may it give thee power to visit vengeance on thine enemies that they may be consumed with the heat thereof and entirely eaten up. But when all is accomplished, I would have thee and none other bring it back."

Aldric bowed gratefully, extending deliberately now to the full obeisance which he had reached only accidentally before. Ymareth seemed to ignore him; it was coiling up again on the platform where he had first seen it, slow and sinister grace in every movement. Then its head swung to regard him once more. "The Charm of Understanding wearies me, and I would sleep the long sleep once again. Ere then I would tell thee that which may prove of some purpose. If perchance ye should *possess* a thing sought after greatly by cu Ruruc, make pretence of its destruction and await what follows . . ."

The *eijo* had no idea how Ymareth had gained such knowledge, but its advice seemed sound enough: if Kalarr thought the spellstone was destroyed, then he would also think himself free of any challenge to his own ability and might . . . just might . . . do something stupid. Unless what the dragon really meant was . . . Aldric's head began to pound, what with the unremitting heat, the air stiff with enchantments, and the strain of talking to an old, wise, crafty and—hide it how he would—frightening firedrake in awesome full maturity. The convoluted workings of sorcery and dragon-minds were enough to give anyone a headache.

Scales clicked and grated as Ymareth settled on the plinth, and its eyelids slid down to shutter the glow of those terrible hypnotic eyes. At his side Aldric could sense Kyrin stirring; despite his warning she—and probably Dewan who had been too far away to hear him—had looked full at the dragon's gaze and had been snared, subject only to the firedrake's will. If it had bidden them walk up to be devoured, they would have done so without resistance. The smoke-plumes drifting from

Ymareth's nostrils ceased as some internal process slaked the fires in its belly. There was a heavy silence.

In the shadows at the entrance of hall, something glinted as it moved.

*

When the dragon fell asleep Kyrin shivered violently, glanced from the corner of one eye at Aldric, then threw her arms around him and clung there tightly. After only a few minutes she released him and backed away, her glazed sleepy look rapidly becoming one of disbelief as the spell faded and understanding took its place. "Aldric-*ain* . . ." She faltered, glanced at Ymareth and then looked him full in the face. "You were talking to . . . that thing . . . as easily as you talk to me. Who are you? *What* are you?"

"I'm Aldric Talvalin and I'm scared." The *eijo* smiled, a sour twist of thinned lips, but he was not being funny. Under his black metal carapace he was trembling with reaction, and there was something with big, soft wings flapping around the pit of his stomach. "Which I expected to be. And I'm still alive, which I didn't expect at all. Speaking to firedrakes is . . ." he laughed weakly, ". . . rather a strain."

Ar Korentin came sprinting up with a clatter of armour, but when they turned to look at him he slackened his headlong pace and approached more sedately, as befitted a captain-of-guards—even a thoroughly shocked one. His eyes rested briefly on Aldric, then slid past him to the dragon. The *eijo* could tell there were many questions dammed up behind Dewan's impassive features; questions which he would be well advised to answer. But not just yet.

"Are you both all right?" was all the Vreijek asked, and Aldric nodded.

"Yourself?" he returned.

"Well enough," said Dewan, shrugging off the languorous heaviness in his limbs as unimportant, and showing some teeth in what should have been a grin but fell rather short of the mark. "Though I have felt better."

"So have I," Aldric conceded. Laying the Dragon-wand carefully by his feet, he wrapped head and chin in the heavy silk scarf he had taken off earlier, then settled the comforting weight of coif, mask and helmet over its padding and laced them in place. As he straightened with Ykraith in both hands, he saw ar Korentin watching him thoughtfully. Aldric's mouth twitched into a little smile. " 'In strange places, when all seems still—look to your armor,' " he quoted. "I've got what I came for. Let us leave."

They walked up the hall together, with that strange attraction of the treasure still tugging at them—but after having seen its guardian, resisting the urge to steal was easy. Even though hidden now by shadows at the far end of the cavern, Ymareth's ominous bulk was an ever-present deterrent.

Perhaps his senses had been dulled by the proximity of the firedrake's spell-binding gaze, perhaps his mental faculties were not operating fully in this place of sorcery. For whatever reason, when two swordsmen sprang at him from the stairs Aldric was taken completely by surprise.

Unbalanced, he could not sidestep the nearest man fast enough, and like most *kailinin* he seldom carried a shield when out of the saddle. But he reacted with the speed of training that had become almost a reflex action, blocking the closer cut with the only thing to hand—the Dragonwand. As the sword came slashing down on to his head he flung Ykraith up, braced like a spearshaft in a wide double grip. Steel and glassy adamant met with a harsh belling clang and sparks flew. Splinters also, as the sword-blade shattered.

Aldric twisted at the waist and lunged towards his second enemy with the long, sharp crystal tip, using only his right hand—lower down the staff—to give a longer reach. It was an old trick of straight-spear fighting.

Like so many old tricks, it worked. Ykraith's crystal flame and its dragonhead slammed into the swordsman's throat just where neck joined collarbone, tore through everything in their path and burst from his spine with sufficient force to nail him to the wall. With his neck uncleanly but completely snapped, the man was dead almost before he knew that something was wrong.

Long before that Aldric had released the Dragonwand. His left hand had already freed Widowmaker's safety-collar from her scabbard's mouth and tilted the longsword's hilt forward. His right hand crossed, gripped and drew.

Dewan had already noticed how fast the young *eijo* could move, but he was two hundred years too young to have seen this form of draw before. And his eyes were hardly fast enough to see it now.

With a bright, brief *sring* Isileth blurred from her scabbard in an arc of light. Dewan heard a noise, a thud blended with a moist, ripping crunch; and then Aldric's arm was fully extended after its horizontal sweep, the longsword gleaming in a hand which had been empty one-eighth of a second before. There was a dark, wet smear on the last six inches of its blade. Aldric whirled the *taiken* up behind his head, left hand joining right prior to a vertical cut. It was not needed.

The Alban's opponent made a wheezing sound, not from his mouth but from his chest, and his eyes glistened white as they rolled up and back. Though the man wore a bullhide jerkin, *taikenin* in hands little stronger than Aldric's had cloven armour. Mere human bodies were no obstacle. Isileth's backhand cut had sliced through breastbone, heart and lungs, and as the man collapsed a bubbling spew of blood erupted from his gaping ribcage. Both legs kicked in random jerks and then, as the body accepted it was dead, they quivered and were still.

From beginning to end the thing had taken seven seconds.

With a slow, sweeping movement, Aldric brought the poised longsword over and down into a posture of readiness and drew in a deep, rather shaky breath. The breath whispered softly out between his parted lips as he relaxed, then stepped back, fastidiously avoiding the mess which oozed across the floor. Light and shadow moved within the trefoil opening of his war-mask as he turned his head away. There were spots and trickles of blood on his face, but no emotion; it was cold, immobile as if graven of grey metal, with a flawed imperfection scarring one cheek under the curved black armour.

Kyrin stared at his dispassionate features and an overwhelming sense of unreality filled her mind. This was not the Aldric she knew, the one who smiled and had gentle hands. This *eijo*'s face was that of a stranger who had felt no tenderness in all his life. Her Aldric would not have . . . Would not have done what he had just done without showing some trace of feeling.

Then she met his eyes and saw the pain in their grey-green depths. Aldric was skilled in the art of *taiken-ulleth* and would kill without hesitation. But not without reason. And not without remorse. Not yet.

Dewan, perhaps unfairly, had seen nothing of that brief, wordless exchange; he was impressed merely by the speed and near-surgical precision of Aldric's fighting style. He was not an Alban. "Who were they?" he wondered, half to himself.

Widowmaker, cleansed and sated, hissed softly like an angry cat as she slid down into her scabbard. She had tasted human blood again, for the first time in three centuries and her thirst was quenched once more. Until the next time. Kyrin remembered all the stories she had heard of Alban named-blades and remembered, too, the sense of icy menace she had felt on the only occasion she had drawn the star-steel sword herself. Then she had been unsure of the feeling's source; now she was quite certain. Yet the *taiken* was not evil in itself, no more than men or dragons were—but it had been forged and named with one purpose in mind, and though she could not blame either Aldric or his blade, it did seem that Isileth Widowmaker fulfilled that purpose all too eagerly.

The young *eijo* jerked Ykraith from the stone wall, lowered his second victim to the ground, then eased the Dragonwand's deadly crystal point out of the corpse's neck and brought it round for cleaning. He blinked; the talisman was unblemished by any trace of blood, as if the fluid had refused to touch its surface. Or had been absorbed.

"I said, who were they?" ar Korentin repeated, more loudly than before.

"Your guess is—" Aldric began; then his eyes narrowed and he jumped almost six feet backwards from the entrance to the stairway, Ykraith tucked spearwise close into his right hip. That sixth sense of his had begun to operate again, like a lantern being unshuttered—and not before time, he thought viciously. It was weak, a premonition, a mental tickle rather than the usual full-throated yell of alarm, but it was undoubtedly there. The scuff of his soft-soled boots and the faint rustle of his armour sounded very loud in the stillness his movement had engendered.

Much louder than the suave voice which drifted down the stairs towards him.

"No need to guess, gentlemen," it purred. "They were once my colleagues. Rash fellows both—if I warned them about startling people once, I warned them a thousand times." The voice took on a world-weary, paternal tone. "And now see where such foolishness has brought them. Most regrettable . . ."

The speaker sauntered into view; he was a tall, thin, wolfish man with an overly-precise moustache which looked as painted as a woman's brows, dark, roguish curls rather at variance with the predatory gleam in his grey eyes and a solitary pearl-drop in the lobe of his right ear. His clothes were equally dashing—black breeches with silver medallions down the outer seams, glossy boots worked with gold around their fringed tops, a fine white shirt and a blue coat over all, worked with more gold and embroidery, caught at the waist by a scarlet sash through which were thrust two curved shortswords and a fancifully carved *telek*. It was this individual's stylish—if eccentric—mode of dress which told Dewan what, if not who, he was.

"Pirate," the Vreijek growled, putting all the distaste a king's officer could summon up into that one word.

A flicker of annoyance crossed the other's saturnine face and his lazy smile became momentarily somewhat stretched. "You're over-blunt, my friend," he reproved. "That is not a word I like. I prefer to regard myself as an adventurous businessman, a dealer in the transfer of expensive commodities." He smiled broadly and snapped his fingers. "Now *these* are pirates."

Feet clattered on the stairs and seven more intruders joined the first. They were a motley group, ill-favoured and villainous; some, in ill-fitting and ragged finery, tried to ape their leader's romantic attire, but without taking his painstaking care succeeded only in looking faintly ridiculous—although neither Aldric nor his companions felt like laughing at the spectacle. The remainder dressed—or to judge by the amount of scarred, weather-beaten flesh on view, did not dress—much as the fancy took them, in leather war-harness and furs, or in grubby jerkins and pieces of cast-off armour. Their threatening growls and curses fell to silence as they saw the heaps of treasure strewn about the Cavern of Firedrakes.

Aldric paid them no heed, apart from the germ of an idea in which Ymareth the dragon played a leading role. His attention was focused on their lord, chieftain, captain or whatever he chose to call himself—and the pirate's attention was focused on Tehal Kyrin. Any Valhollan woman could take care of her own virtue, as the *eijo* knew quite well—Kyrin perhaps better than most—but he was still a *kailin-eir* and honour was still something to be upheld.

"Gentlemen, and of course the lovely lady," the pirate murmured in a caressing voice calculated to provoke, "let me explain this delicate situation. Techaur Island is our . . . cashbox, if you like, where we deposit the profits from our various . . . transactions. In such circumstances you must see that your presence here is less than welcome. Apart, of course, from you, my dear." He bowed elaborately to Kyrin who, Aldric was pleased to see, failed to appreciate his courtesy.

"I am not your dear," she snapped, drawing her *estoc* for emphasis.

"For the moment," returned the buccaneer, not one whit deterred by her rejection. "We'll see what more intimate acquaintance produces. You see, gentlemen, we usually feel obliged to execute trespassers but on this occasion I think a fine would be more rewarding. The girl and twice her weight in gold, in exchange for your lives. Agreed?"

"Not agreed." Aldric drove the Dragonwand into the floor with as much ease as piercing a fresh loaf and left it embedded in the flagstones. "Leave my lady right out of your calculations, *pirate*. Consider: there are three of us, eight of you." He was talking now not to the captain but to his common sailors, those with most to gain and lose from a good bargain or a hard fight.

"The odds are not good—but enough to ensure some-body will not live to enjoy whatever the survivors win. All for a girl. Whereas if your captain leaves his own lechery aside, you'll all get gold enough to buy the favours of twenty first-rank courtesans and never a scratch to show for it. So there's my offer. Gold." Widowmaker sang as she slowly left her scabbard. "Or steel. And a death I'll make as painful as my skill allows. Choose."

As a growling mutter rose behind him, the captain looked narrowly at Aldric, then at Kyrin and ar Korentin. All had now drawn blades and the firelight in the hall reflected from their weapons like molten copper—or fresh blood.

"How much gold?" the man asked, much of his mock-ing good-humour dissipated by the possibility of his own violent death.

"As much gold as each man can carry out unaided in one journey. But I want some word of honour that you won't come back again." Careful, Aldric reminded him-self. If you sound too naïve, they will suspect you're up to something. He deliberately sneered at them. "Assum-ing scum like you use oaths for anything but foul lan-guage, of course. Well?"

"By the sea on which we earn our living, I swear we will not return once we have taken what we can carry," the pirate chief said primly.

Dewan guessed that both men were hiding smiles; the buccaneer for his ambiguous oath, which would change with the tide, and Aldric for his devious trick which seemed to be working well. Ar Korentin did not approve of such a scheme, but the circumstances were desperate enough to require harsh measures.

"And my lady?" the Alban persisted.

"You can keep her. I'll settle for a willing woman."

"But *I* will not!"

The bull-bellow startled everyone and almost precipi-tated the fight which Aldric was trying to avoid. Then he stared at the man who was forcing his way to the front of the buccaneers' ranks.

"I am Khakkhur," the huge figure rumbled. "I want *your* woman, now. And what Khakkhur wants, he takes!" The man was a barbarian from the far north, but totally unlike the fair, ruddy-featured big men Aldric had seen on the docks at Erdhaven. Where they had been stern and grim, Khakkhur's heavy features were set in what looked to be a permanent scowl. A mane of coarse black hair hung to his shoulders and his massive body was clad only in boots, swordbelt and a length of bearskin strapped around his hips as a kind of kilt.

The Northrons at Erdhaven had dressed in much the same way, proud of their sleek muscles and showing them off adorned with gold bands and ornaments of bear-teeth. In Aldric's opinion, Khakkhur would have been wiser covering himself up. The man was overdeveloped to the point of grossness, his biceps as thick as the Alban's thigh, the ponderous muscles of his chest like a woman's breasts.

A barbarian, to Aldric, had been one who neither spoke Alban nor lived in a land with permanent towns. He saw now that there was a third, more bestial type, who had left his tribal customs behind but who called civilised laws weak and in consequence did what he pleased. Even the wolf in the wood obeyed the rules of his pack. But not a wild animal like Khakkhur.

"Give me the girl, little black-beetle," the barbarian growled, and drew a heavy broadsword from its sheath at his belt. "Give her to me, or Khakkhur will crack your shell apart and eat your liver raw."

He probably would at that, Aldric reflected sombrely, then wrinkled his nose as a whiff of unwashed body reached him. Not all the big man's bronze skin came from sun and wind; it seemed he had decided soap and water was a mark of civilised decadence, along with manners, morals and the rest. Then the young *eijo*'s teeth showed in an ugly grin. Shell—Light of Heaven, of course! Bare muscles were just meat, no matter how powerful, and Isileth Widowmaker was the ultimate carving-knife. "Captain," he advised, "call your henchman off if he's of any value."

"I cannot do that, my friend," said the pirate with totally false regret. One fewer opponent would bring the odds even more into his favour. "My promise concerned gold. Killing is something else entirely."

Aldric looked at the massive blade in the barbarian's

fist and swallowed hard despite his own confidence. His *tsalaer* was full battle armour, but it wouldn't keep such a weapon out without being so heavy he would be unable to move. Long ago the *kailinin* had struck a balance in their armour: thick enough to turn chance arrows or glancing blows, but light enough to give them speed to dodge anything more deliberate. *Tsalaerin* were not impenetrable and Aldric's mind's eye had seen—was still seeing with hideous clarity—what that huge sword would do to him if it struck home squarely. So keep out of its way, he thought, and roll with what you cannot avoid in time. Duck and sidestep, then cut straight.

The slightly stylised look of *taiken*-fighting had a purpose; it demanded accuracy, not brute force, aiming as it did for the vulnerable points of a fully armoured warrior. Khakkhur had no armour whatsoever, but his unknown strength and skill were as much a threat as any hidden blade might be.

"If you want my lady, you barbaric ox," said Aldric pleasantly, "you will have to come and take her."

Steel rang as the blades met in a tentative probing of defences, then parted with a little slither. Khakkhur chopped suddenly at Aldric's eyes but the Alban sidestepped like the beat of a swallow's wing, just enough to avoid the blow with deft, disdainful ease. He did not parry. There was contempt in the movement, and it looked to Kyrin as if the barbarian should have died at once.

Without knowing how fast his opponent could recover, Aldric was not going for a quick kill—that was the way to risk his own death. Instead he watched even as he jerked aside.

Khakkhur's muscles tensed and he grunted slightly as his sword came out of its swoop. One of Aldric's questions had its answer: the barbarian could swing his weapon with ease, heavy though it was beside an ordinary blade—but sheer momentum made it hard to stop if his weighty stroke should miss and against someone skilled in the disciplines of *taiken-ulleth*, this would usually happen.

The pirate cut back-handed at thigh and was blocked,

both swords ringing like bells and his own, deflected, throwing up sparks as its point gouged the floor. The blades met again with a double clash and a sound like monstrous shears, sprang apart and clanged back. Aldric thrust and was parried by the heavier blade, spun and cut, was blocked and darted away.

There was a pause when the scuff of feet and the panting of breath were the loudest sounds in the whole of the cavern, as both men glided along the perimeter of a circle only they could see. The barbarian was good, tutored in the violent school of experience where failure meant death, but Aldric's tuition, even if not so fatal towards error, had been every bit as rough.

Then a cut went home.

Aldric whirled across the floor and crashed into a pillar, slid down it into a crumpled, untidy heap of black metal and lay very still.

Kyrin bit her knuckle until the blood flowed. She did not cry; she simply did not believe what she had seen. Aldric had said once, in a gloomy moment, that there would be someone, somewhere, stronger or better or faster than he was, and that on the day they met he would go out into the darkness. Now it seemed this had happened.

Dewan seized her by the shoulder and pulled her round to guard his back, knowing that when their surprise had worn off the pirates would surely attack. He was right.

"I think my promise is null and void, don't you?" said their captain cheerfully. He gestured with both hands. "Kill the man, but keep the woman for later."

"Not—so—hasty—friend . . ." Aldric gasped hoarsely. He dragged himself upright with the aid of the firedrake carved around the pillar, then leaned against it and fought for breath.

"You are *dead!*" choked Khakkhur, his face going as pale as his grimy skin allowed.

Aldric coughed on a laugh. "Not quite. I merely look . . . and feel . . . that way." Straightening up, he dragged air into his lungs as the crushed sensation in his solar plexus faded to a queasy throbbing, and almost managed to conceal a slight wince when at last he got all his breath back where it should have been. "I don't wear all . . . this metal . . . without good reason."

Khakkhur's superstitious awe died away as he realised he was not facing a living dead thing, one of the *traugarin* of Alban legend, and he shambled forward to finish what he had started. The barbarian was not to know that an *eijo*—and especially this *eijo*—was far more dangerous than any *traugur* in a story. Isileth was not fiction; she was hard, razor-edged fact.

Aldric did not wait for his enemy to attack. Instead he came to meet him behind a low, vicious lunge which made the pirate parry wildly. Their blades crashed together half a dozen times with blinding speed, near-invisible blurs of steel with enough power to sever heads and arms and legs if they ever had a chance to strike their target. The hall echoed like a bell-tower. Then Khakkhur saw an opening and slashed double-handed at the Alban's neck.

Ducking under that wild swing, Aldric thrust his *taiken* out and through the barbarian's nearest bicep, then sliced sideways and peeled the muscle off its bone with obscene ease. The man screamed harshly and made a frantic attempt to hold his arm together, then shrieked on an impossibly high note for such a bass voice when the young *eijo* laid a forehand drawing cut across the corded sinews of his exposed belly. Mighty muscles—but only so much meat. They parted and everything spilled out in a foetid gush.

Khakkhur folded over the stench of his own ruptured intestines, and with a graceful sliding half-turn Aldric took up position at his side. Isileth swept up in both the Alban's hands, paused momentarily and came whirring down.

"Hai!"

As if propelled by its own long spurt of blood, the barbarian's head flew out of sight, while his body flopped like a puppet with its strings abruptly severed. It gave a single tremor and lay still.

Setting his foot between the corpse's shoulders, Aldric surveyed the buccaneers with all the arrogance at his command. There was blood on his face, running sluggishly from one nostril in a darkly crimson stream. The unblemished glint of his *tsalaer* covered what he guessed to be at least one cracked rib, and it hurt to breathe. Even so, he tried to hide the jabs of pain in case it gave some pirate bold ideas. Better that they think him made of iron, even if he had to drive his nails clear through his palms to convince them fully.

"Are there any more like this one?" he snarled. Nobody spoke. "Very wise. Then we'll be going, captain. Don't try to follow."

As they retreated up the stairs, Aldric leaning on the Dragonwand and trying not to show it, all three kept their swords drawn in case of treachery. There was none—three bloodstained bundles were sufficient warning. Only the pirate captain took a step forward, his eyes fixed on Aldric until the Alban was lost to view. "I'll remember you, swordsman!" he yelled at the darkness.

"Probably for the remainder of your life," somebody replied. The pirate wondered what that meant. He did not see Aldric look back, good sense wrestling with honour-inspired guilt over the cunning trap he had laid. The young man was having second thoughts. Dewan sensed his change of mood, perhaps from some slight hesitation half-glimpsed in the glow from the hall below them, and grabbed one armoured shoulder before the *eijo* could do anything stupid. Such as shout a warning. He regretted his own comment which had caused this change of heart; one did not mock those condemned to death.

Then one of the pirates must have run his fingers through the treasure, for there was that musical chiming sound unique to minted gold and a burst of raucous laughter. Both noises then stopped abruptly and a vast steely grinding took their place.

Ymareth, Lord of the Cavern of Firedrakes, was awake once more.

Perhaps some trace of the charm of understanding remained with him even out of the dragon's gaze, for Aldric found that he still understood the hissing speech which filled the silent cavern. As its meaning penetrated his brain, he cringed inside his armour and began to back away.

"Hear me," said the huge, ominous voice. "Hear my will. Thee shall do only as I bid thee do. So. Forward all, one step. And again. Now. Tall man, thee alone will come a little closer . . ."

Aldric's mailed hands flew to his ears, but could not reach inside his helm sufficiently to block the nauseating sounds which floated up the tunnel after him. Overwhelmed with revulsion and shame he sank on to the steps, racked by shudders which made his teeth chatter like those of a man with the ague. When Kyrin put one arm around him and helped him to his feet, warrior or not he came very close to breaking down. Dewan retired a tactful distance.

"Only a barbarian would not care," the girl said; then, after a glance at the unmoved Vreijek, added, "or a professional. You are neither. But what you did was necessary."

Aldric's face went cold and bitter. "How much will that excuse away, do you think, before the world dissolves in fire? And some power calls *that* necessary?"

Kyrin stared at him for a long time, then shrugged expressively. "Who can say? I hardly think it matters now, do you? Lean on me a little, Aldric-*ain,* and we shall all get out of here."

8

Desires and Excuses

En Sohra's master had never laid much claim to being very brave, but he was a skilled and crafty seaman. After momentary panic when he discovered that he sailed the same stretch of ocean as a shipload of pirates, he did not waste time in tacking laboriously out to open water. Instead he put off the galion's longboat, secured with a towing-line to *En Sohra*'s bows, and filled it with irritated sailors before ordering them to "Row!"

There was a brisk south wind beyond the lee of Tech-aur Island, and after little more than two hours under full sail their anchorage had slipped away below the horizon. There had been no pursuit, but as the afternoon turned into evening a new problem appeared as the wind grew ever stronger. By nightfall the ship's full sail had been stripped to a single topgallant on otherwise bare masts, and still she heeled ponderously as each comber smashed against her side.

At least the bullion in her hold made good ballast; though after every lurch the Elherran captain strained his ears to catch the first rumble of his cargo coming adrift. Not that he expected this to happen, having supervised the loading himself, but ignoring such a possibility would have been foolish in the extreme.

The storm began to die as swiftly as it had risen and stars appeared through rents in the flying clouds. Such sudden gales were common in Alban waters around spring and autumn and the captain had experienced them before; however, familiarity had not increased his liking for them. The sea took longer to calm down than the wind, and as *En Sohra* settled into an evil corkscrewing motion her master glanced towards the master-cabin and wondered how his passengers were faring. One of them, besides being wounded, had already looked sick when he came on board; the captain preferred not to contemplate how he must be feeling now.

*

Aldric felt sore.

Ignoring a constant and rather monotonous stream of abuse which flowed about his uncaring ears, Dewan probed the Alban's wounded side as gently as he could. The galion's irregular pitch-and-roll—something impossible to balance against—meant that this was not really very gently at all, as a gasp and a series of quite original oaths seemed to prove. Finally he straightened and cleaned his hands on a wet towel, since water poured into basins spilled over almost at once in such a sea.

Aldric whimpered softly, unclenching fists and teeth. "You are not much of a doctor," he managed at last.

"I only know some rudimentary field medicine, so what do you expect, comfort?" the Vreijek retorted waspishly. "Not that you're much of a patient. It's a mercy I won't have to nurse you back to health."

"Meaning what—and can I put my shirt on again?"

"Meaning there's less wrong with you than you think or I feared—and no, you can't; I have to bandage that mess first."

"That mess," as Dewan accurately described it, was the bloody purple welt where Khakkhur's sword had landed. It ran across the *eijo's* ribs from left armpit to mid-chest and, though there were no bones broken underneath it, there was plenty of *tsalaer*-patterned broken skin above. After ar Korentin's peeling away of armour and clothing, even without his subsequent accidentally-rough handling, it was bleeding quite impressively.

The Vreijek knew that Aldric would lose more blood from a clumsily-pulled tooth, but he knew also that the young warrior was suffering from shock as much as anything else. There was no doubt that the injury was painful, but when he started to think about such things Aldric would realise that had he not been already twisting aside he would have been split open like a lobster, armour or not. That was rough comfort, of a kind.

Ar Korentin, of course, had been punctured, slashed and dented many times in his career and regarded Aldric's wound as slight. He had said so to Kyrin, only to be informed that some people would call a severed limb a flesh wound and that if he could find nothing more constructive to say, would he please shut up or get out or preferably both. Tehal Kyrin, Dewan had thought both then and afterward, was quite a woman—even if not quite a lady.

"Your problem," he continued sagely but unsympathetically, "is that on top of everything else you're a dismal sailor."

Aldric went slightly pale at the recollection of being sick that last time, long after his stomach had emptied; his side had felt as if it was tearing away from his body. "You don't have to remind me," he snapped. Then hiccupped and groped miserably for a bucket. The pain of Dewan's surgery had diverted his mind and stomach for a while, but now *En Sohra*'s heaving was making him heave again in sympathy.

"I think if you could try to eat something you'd feel much better," Dewan pointed out. The *eijo* doubled over his bucket and retched dryly, wincing as he did so. "At least if you had something to bring up, it wouldn't hurt so much."

"Dewan . . ." Aldric paused, then spat. "Dewan, for a King's Champion, you make a first-class bastard."

The door opened and Kyrin came in with an armful of bandages and several bottles balanced atop the heap. "Feeling better?" she asked pleasantly, then saw the bucket between Aldric's knees. "Oh . . . Probably not. Still, the gale has blown itself out and those waves are getting smaller at long last."

"I'm glad to hear it," Dewan grinned, "and Aldric's *very* glad to hear it."

The Alban laughed without much humour. It hurt.

"Most amusing. Kyrin can put these bandages on—so you go below and make sure the horses are all right. Dewan . . . at once, if you please. Out."

With a mocking little bow, ar Korentin left.

Aldric sat quite still until the door was firmly closed, then got to his feet and locked it. As he gazed curiously at Kyrin, the girl looked away. "What's wrong with you, Kyrin-*ain*?" he wanted to know.

"I'm just tired, that's all."

"You must be . . . that's a very lame excuse. Now Dewan's gone, we can talk quite freely. So why won't you?"

"Lift your arm and let me at that wound," she said briskly, picking up a roll of bandage to avoid both his question and his eyes. Aldric sighed, then submitted to her ministrations with as much good grace as he could muster. He knew that anything but the most banal conversation would be impossible now, just so long as Kyrin had some other activity to hide behind.

By the time she had finished the young Alban's torso was wrapped from neck to navel in strips of linen drawn so tightly that they made it hard to breathe. Even so, this did not stop him trying again to get an answer. "Kyrin—what's the matter?" His voice, perhaps unconsciously, took on a sharper edge.

At that point the Valhollan took his breath away—and effectively stopped his questions—by sprinkling what felt like molten lead from a small bottle over his dressings. "Twice-distilled grain spirit," she said by way of explanation. This was not what he wanted to know, but it did at least tell him why his ribs had just caught fire.

"You said once—" Kyrin began, her back towards him. She hesitated, set the bottle down and absently caught its sideways slither when the ship rolled. Then she turned and the words came pouring out.

"You said once that you'd tell me whatever I needed to know, however little that might be, but you've somehow told me hardly anything. Even when you were talking to your king, half of what you said was masked by hints and vagueness. I thought that this was a simple thing, a bloodfeud; I thought I knew what you were doing, and why you had to do it.

"I'm Valhollan. Tehal *ur'lim* Harek's daughter. I don't usually need to talk like this. But now . . . Aldric, I'm not sure of anything anymore."

The *eijo* was silent, eyes hooded by his long lashes so that the thoughts which drifted through them were unreadable. Aldric was aware that what the girl said was true. He explained events quite clearly up to when he met Gemmel, but after that became reserved and taciturn. No, he corrected himself sharply: the word is secretive.

Of course there were obvious aspects to his situation. *Venjens-eijin* were permitted, indeed expected, to use any means which would further the completion of their oath. But they were not supposed to employ sorcery with anything like the freedom Aldric had already used, much less to the degree which he intended.

The fewer people who were aware of that, the better for his reputation.

He had caught something in King Rynert's voice which seemed to imply that he, Aldric, was likely to be the next Talvalin clan-lord. Kyrin had noticed it too; she had actually called him *ilauem-arluth* on one occasion. Now while an *eijo* could take certain liberties with the honour he had deliberately set aside, it was always with the view that he should never do anything which would shame his clan if and when he rejoined it as a *kailin*. Any high-clan *arluth* displaying Aldric's fondness for the Art Magic could well find himself under uncomfortably close scrutiny from both Cerdor and his peers. It was a delicate, devious business, doing what was required by Gemmel while appearing to do what was expected by tradition and the Honour-Codes.

As far as Ykraith the Dragonwand was concerned, Aldric had taken a deep breath and had half-lied about why he was fetching it from Techaur. The excuse sounded convincing—that he had foolishly offered anything in repayment to the old sorcerer who had healed him, and that when told to bring back the talisman he had been honour-bound to do so. Dewan had looked sceptical then and still seemed more than a little dubious now.

"If I remember rightly, Kyrin, you said you would accept whatever I chose to tell."

"But you've told me nothing."

"I made no promises one way or the other."

"Then what . . . ?"

"I think that after all you've been through, you have

the right to hear a little about what's going on. More at
least than ar Korentin; I wouldn't consider giving him
too many details."

"Why?"

"Because I don't trust him."

"Don't trust your own King's Champion? Then who
can you trust?"

"Kyrin-*ain*, it's because of what Dewan is that I cannot trust him with the whole truth. He's a crown
officer—what I have in mind goes against everything he
represents, and I don't know that he would act sensibly.
Or rather, with my best interests at heart. The law can
be very inflexible sometimes."

"And what about me?"

"You don't have the authority to have me jailed or
worse without trial." Aldric smiled thinly. "Help me
here, will you?" There was a fresh shirt in the loose-cut
Alban style laid out over a chair, and with Kyrin's assistance he managed to wriggle into it with a minimum of
discomfort and close it in front with his weapon-belt.
"When I've put on something warm we'll go up on deck
to talk—it attacts less attention than staying behind a
locked door."

"You are so suspicious . . ."

"Call it cautious." He put out one hand and touched
her gently under one ear with his fingertips. "I'm a man
with a blade at his neck, Kyrin-*ain*. In such a circumstance, can you blame me for avoiding sudden movements?" The Alban donned an overmantle and unlocked
the door, then bowed as deeply—and as sardonically—
as his wounded side permitted. "I know it is not good
manners, lady, but I will follow. If there's anyone standing about doing nothing, let me know. Anyone at all."
He allowed himself what was almost a mischievous grin.
"Apart from what I have already said about not wanting
Dewan to know, I think I owe him something for being
so quiet about this thing's cargo. Eh?"

*

Kyrin stared out over the dark water for a long time
when Aldric had finished speaking. There was a slender
waning moon hanging near the horizon, and stars glittered in a sky which seemed to have been washed clean

and clear by the tempest. There was still something of a choppy sea, and the occasional glimmer of a white-capped wave slid past *En Sohra*'s hull. Finally Aldric broke the silence.

"You see now why I wasn't making free with that sort of information," he said quietly.

"Oh, indeed." Kyrin's voice sounded as if she had to summon up the words from a great distance. "I see a great many things now that I was unsure about before." She moved a little closer and the *eijo* slipped his arms about her waist, "I'm cold, Aldric. The whole world's becoming cold, and harsh, and brutal." The girl turned away from the sea and embraced him tightly. "It's growing so very, very dark. Where will the light come from, when the darkness covers everything?"

"From the sun, as it always has," Aldric replied, and kissed her. He draped a fold of the long overmantle across her shoulders and they watched the moon set, Kyrin with her head snuggled back against his neck and the body-heated silver of his crest-collar pressing warmly on her cheek. There was no passion in the contact; only a tender caring which Kyrin recognised reluctantly as the love she did not want. She shivered and Aldric held her closer. "You are cold," he muttered. "Better go below and get some rest."

"What about you?"

"I'll stay here for a while. I doubt if I could sleep anyway."

Kyrin glanced at him; his words had lacked all inflection, as if he was thinking about something else long ago and far away. "There's something troubling you," she said, not asking but telling. "What is it?"

"I was remembering. Right now, that's not a good thing to do."

"Because of those pirates? Aldric, I mean no insult to ar Korentin, but if it hadn't been for you—*you*—we would all be in pieces now. Or worse."

"The men I cut down don't concern me. Much . . . They had an even chance to do the same to me. Even though that brings my tally up to six—and I'm not yet twenty-four."

"Those swine deserved to die." Kyrin's voice was flat and vicious.

"Perhaps. But honourable death by the *taiken* is a part of my heritage. A firedrake is not. That was too deliberate, too well-thought-out for me to feel any pride in my cunning. Your lover's not a warrior any more, Kyrin-*ain*. He's just a calculating killer—a deathbringer. That's a fine, dramatic title, but it makes me feel dirty. I wish there had been some other way."

"There wasn't. Forget it. If the tables were turned, would your death be preying on Khakkhur's mind? I doubt it very much." Kyrin pulled free of the clinging mantle and walked away, then glanced back at him. "My father's a bigger, fiercer man than you, Aldric, but he told me once that nobody should laugh if they don't know how to cry. Think about that."

The *eijo* did, for a long time.

*

Kyrin was scarcely undressed and into her bunk before the expected knock came at her cabin door. Pulling the sheets modestly high, she said: "Come in."

Dewan ar Korentin slipped inside, closed the door behind him and sat down with the muted rustling click of a man wearing armour under his outer clothing. Mail-rings sparkled momentarily at his collar. Kyrin looked, listened and raised one eyebrow, but the Vreijek paid no attention. Instead he removed the stopper from a wine-jar, filled two cups and offered one to the girl before taking a thoughtful sip himself.

"Well? What did he tell you?"

Kyrin tasted her wine before replying. "Little enough. The Dragonwand staff is, as he said before, a gift for Gemmel-*altrou*."

"His foster-father. And a wizard."

"So it seems."

"That young man asks a lot of questions, or simply stands quiet and listens—but have you ever noticed how seldom he volunteers any answers?"

"Of course I have. It doesn't match the rest of his character—about which, I would remind you, Lord-Commander ar Korentin, I know much more than you do."

"I wasn't about to question that fact, my dear."

"I told you I'm not . . . but let it pass. This time."

"So then, his secrecy seems to you more like an assumed habit; one he has acquired from somebody. The wizard, maybe?"

"Maybe. Some more wine, please."

The Vreijek poured a second cupful for them both, then rose and walked quietly to the cabin door as footsteps approached down the passageway outside. They passed and receded and Dewan smiled to himself before returning to sit—this time on the foot of Kyrin's bunk. She jerked her own feet aside just in time.

"Aldric . . ." mused Dewan softly, then shook his head. "No, not yet. Much as I'd like to, I cannot trust him until I'm sure." Kyrin tried without success to stifle a snort of ironic laughter. "And what do you find so funny?"

"Just a coincidence, that's all." She did not elaborate further.

"Indeed? Kyrin, be careful. Don't let your emotions into any relationship with him. You're only an observer, after all."

"Just because you persuaded the king to grant me use of a ship doesn't give you permission to take liberties with my private life, ar Korentin."

"In exchange for which you agreed to help me keep an eye on him."

"That was only to prove what I thought—your suspicions were groundless."

"It depends rather on whose viewpoint you take, Kyrin-*ain*. Oh yes, I've heard that lover's endearment before. I warned you not to get involved too deeply—it affects your judgement."

"Is that jealousy I hear . . . ?"

"There are high-clan *arluthen* who would be very dubious about how nonchalant he is where magic is concerned—"

"And others who would wonder at how friendly you seem to be with an Imperial ship-captain of the Warlord's faction. To say nothing of what your dear, so-possessive wife would say if I told her—"

"—What? There's nothing to tell!"

"You're a man, I'm a woman. I've seen you watching me. Oh, there's no harm in looking, but if I gave you the chance to do more you'd take it, wouldn't you? Lyseun would think so. All I need to do is substitute your name for Aldric's and you wouldn't be done explaining this side of the grave."

"Now let's not be foolish . . ."

"Get off my bed!"

"You are in love with him, aren't you?"

"No, I'm not."

"What?" Dewan got off the bunk as if he had been kicked. "But I thought . . ."

"Quite clearly, you did not." Kyrin favoured Dewan with the sort of smile he had not received from anyone since he was about ten years old; a smile which said "amusing simpleton, aren't you!" with altogether too much clarity. The Valhollan girl had regained some of her good humour now, thanks to the way she had succeeded in bringing ar Korentin down to a more manageable size. With the threat of his wife suspended like a battleaxe over his head, he was less inclined to bluster and hide behind his rank.

"Then what exactly *is* the situation?" He asked the question rather than demanded it.

"I'm four years older than Aldric. I like the boy—he deserves that much—but for several reasons I cannot and do not love him. Nor does he love me, though he thinks he does. Infatuation describes it better. Dewan, he was a virgin before we met."

Ar Korentin blinked, started to laugh and then thought better of it. "I was thinking such a claim would be easy to make and hard to disprove," he explained. "But he would have no reason to lie. And I remember his brother Joren. He was a very moral gentleman, one of the old type you seldom meet nowadays. I think Aldric told you the truth . . ."

"And I'm sure he did. I won't see him hurt, King's Champion; not simply because you're suspicious of the way he behaves. So long as we understand each other, Dewan, your wife will hear nothing but good about you. You do see what I mean, don't you?"

"In every detail, lady. But remember what I told you and discourage Aldric from any romantic thoughts he might be entertaining. You'll be going home within the month, and . . . well, he is a Talvalin, after all. Very shrewd, very clever—and very dangerous."

"I said I did not want him hurt. Especially by me. I'll manage somehow."

"I hope so, Kyrin. For both our sakes."

The Valhollan stared at him as he gathered up wine, cups and the cloak he had used to cover them, then smiled carefully. "I didn't have the pleasure of meeting Joren Talvalin, but I can tell you this, distrustful Captain-of-Guards ar Korentin,"—she pronounced the title as if it was some obscure and subtle insult—"his brother is as much an honourable gentleman as Joren ever could have been."

"That's as may be—but Joren had the devil's own temper when he thought he had good cause. Remember that when you start explaining things to Aldric—and choose your words with care. Good night, lady."

The door closed behind him with a solid, final click.

*

Kyrin awoke to the sound of more clicks. She rubbed the sleep from her eyes and opened the shutters on her cabin's port, blinking as the newly-risen sun shone full into her face. As she washed and dressed the sharp, brittle clacking noise continued intermittently, although she was sure that nothing was wrong with *En Sohra*; the galion was sailing easily through a gentle deep-sea swell, and the creak of structure and cordage sounded as it should.

Tying back her long hair with a ribbon, Kyrin walked up the companionway and on to the ship's main deck, thinking deeply. There was a familiar quality to the clicking, an irregular rhythm reminiscent of something other than wood. Awareness came an instant before sight.

The sound was that of a duel.

Aldric and Dewan faced each other across the deck, both unarmoured but carrying long staves of polished oak. Kyrin recognised the weapons as *taidyin*—staff-swords—which were usually rolled in a bundle among Aldric's gear, hardwood foils with which he practised daily before exercising with Isileth's live blade. He had never used them against an opponent until now, something which the girl found suspicious in itself. What if he had overheard last night's conversation? Or only a part of it? What if . . . ?

Her thoughts were interrupted by a stinging crack as Dewan blocked a vicious cut at his leg. Aldric darted past him, half-spinning to slice again at the Vreijek's face and Kyrin winced as the *taidyin* crashed together; there was an awful ferocity in that assault, more than seemed justified by a mere training routine. Ar Korentin assumed a defensive attitude and Aldric glided sideways, analysing his opponent's stance before launching another attack.

"Stop this, both of you!" shrieked Kyrin in a mixture of rage and fright. "Stop it at once!" The duellists moved apart, Aldric lowering his *taidyo* to regard her with open astonishment while Dewan, realising at once what she thought had caused the fight, favoured her with a wicked smile.

"What's wrong with you?" Aldric snapped. He had just succeeded in getting ar Korentin where he wanted him and considered the intrusion ill-timed to say the least. "You've seen me practising before, haven't you?" he demanded irritably, then winced a little and pressed one hand to his side.

Kyrin noticed the movement and allowed herself a frown. "I didn't think you were . . . that is, I didn't think you would be training this morning."

"Not without good reason, my dear?" purred Dewan. The Valhollan's frown deepened and Dewan's grin became if anything wider still.

"The reason, Kyrin-*ain,* is just that I don't want this to stiffen up," said Aldric quietly. He tugged up his shirt. "See—no bleeding. The skin's just badly grazed, but all that bruising is going to ache if the muscles are not kept working." He paused, considering, then smiled crookedly. "Not that it doesn't ache whatever the hell I do . . ."

"I thought last night you wouldn't be moving for a couple of days," Kyrin pointed out, tucking the shirt carefully back through his belt.

"Last night somebody had just drenched a raw wound with neat grain spirit!"

"Oh . . . Well, at least it seems to have done some good."

"Some . . . but that wasn't the only thing to make me feel better. You did. You helped me get some sleep. Thank you."

"Then let me help again. Put those sticks aside; rest; take some food."

"Not just yet. There was someone long ago—I've forgotten his name—who claimed there are two sorts of people, the quick and the dead. He was wrong. There are three: the quick, the dead—and the very, very lucky." He grinned and touched his bandaged side. "Like me."

Kyrin smiled a wan little smile and stepped back to watch the next exchange. They were using two *taidyin* each this time, in the *dyutayn* or two-blade style of fighting. It was a complex blend of sidesteps and gliding turns, spinning displacements of the body and circular cuts with the swords.

Aldric was sensible enough to avoid the more vigorous waist-twisting moves, but taking such care slowed him down more than either he or Dewan realised until it was far too late. Halfway through the horizontal double-cut called "interlaced windmill," ar Korentin found that Aldric was a foot closer than he should have been.

His discovery and the crisp snap as his backhand cut struck the young Alban's ribs were almost simultaneous. Aldric cried out and dropped both swords. Oak clattered on pine as they fell to *En Sohra*'s deck. The *eijo*'s face had gone stark white; as white as the shirt now disfigured by a wet, dark-red blotch spreading all over its left side. Aldric put the flat of one hand to where he hurt, trying not to breathe. "You said there were no ribs broken," he said thickly, trying to sound dryly amused. Something like a piece of splintered wood pressed into his palm through the shirt and his senses swam. "I think . . . there's definitely one . . . gone . . . now. . . ." He swayed, feeling giddy, then with no other warning than a little sigh followed his swords to the deck. Soft-edged dark outlines crossed the blue sky above him, bent over him, lifted him gently. The galion was pitching alarmingly and it was getting very dark . . .

"This time he's staying in bed if I have to tie him down," said a voice, half-angry and half-concerned.

"Don't be so drastic," said a second voice. "I doubt if he'll want to move about much anyway."

"You thought that last night too, didn't you?"

"I was wrong; I'm sorry."

"Still, forget the ropes. This ship's medicine-chest holds enough soporific drugs to make him sleep for a week. Satisfied?"

"Where did you learn how to use things like that?"

"Misuse them, my dear. The Imperial Court in Drakkesborg opened my eyes to a lot of . . ."

Aldric did not learn what Dewan had found out in Drakkesborg. The words he heard slurred into a buzzing noise and thence to a silence as absolute as the blackness clouding his vision beyond his leaden eyelids.

*

Aldric's eyelids snapped back and he was awake at once, with no intervening period of drowsiness. He stared straight ahead, not daring to look right or left in case it brought back the dark. There was a flat surface above him, dark planks criss-crossed by adzed red-oak beams. A ceiling . . . ? Not the honey-coloured pine of his cabin, though, and his bed had a proper quilt now, not those foolish sheets. Rain pattered gently on the small panes of a draped window. There was somebody else nearby; he could hear the rustle of a book's pages being turned.

With teeth clenched against any pain which might accompany the movement, Aldric sat up. There was nothing wrong at all; he might as well be waking from a refreshing night's sleep. And there were no bandages either . . .

"Good morning, Aldric," said a familiar voice.

The *eijo*'s head jerked round. *"Altrou!"* he gasped in disbelief. Gemmel nodded, smiling, and after marking his place set down the book and closed it. "But how did you get here? And where is here anyway?"

"Just as before—questions, always questions. I should have expected it and let someone else wait for you to wake up. Still . . ." The enchanter got to his feet, crossed to the window and opened its curtains. "I came here with your king—having rightly assumed after that episode at Erdhaven Festival that he'd appreciate a word with me—" the old man chuckled; "which he did to the tune of three hours' talking without a rest. And this is the port of Kerys, in Cerenau."

"What happened to me, *altrou?*"

"From what I gather, you were being stupid again," the wizard said without rancour. "Trying *dyutayn* with any sort of injury is foolish enough, but with a damaged side of all things, it plumbs the depths of utter idiocy. Fairly typical behaviour, really. Ar Korentin— who knows more than seems quite proper about drugs— kept you asleep until the ship docked, knowing that there would be better doctors ashore. He was right. I was here."

"And you healed me?"

"Of course. A simple enough process with the right equipment—which I had the good sense not to leave behind on this occasion. Now, what about the Dragonwand? I gather you had some small difficulty from various sources."

"Your understatements are showing, *altrou,*" Aldric grinned. "Yes, we did have some trouble—though none of it was connected with *them.*" Gemmel nodded, knowing quite well who *they* were. "I can't understand why, because they found me easily enough in Erdhaven."

"Don't look for reasons—just consider yourself lucky. By the way . . . how do you find talking to firedrakes?"

Aldric made a face. "Hard—very hard. They don't have much in the way of small talk. I'm glad you taught me what you did, because Ymareth doesn't seem like a being that would listen to excuses."

"It isn't. Where is Ykraith now?"

"I gave it to Dewan—he has a sheaf of javelins on his saddle, and the Dragonwand's hidden amongst them. How are the horses, by the way?"

"Quite healthy. Lyard's probably a better sailor than you, by all accounts."

"Not very difficult. Gemmel . . . I'm always asking questions and now I've got two more. Important ones. What does the Dragonwand do? And how do you plan to use it? I'd like a proper answer to each, please."

Gemmel combed his beard with his fingers, neatening

it, then stood up and bowed with mock-politeness. "Of course, my lord," he said. "But not at once, my lord—because I'm telling King Rynert and part of his High Council almost exactly what you want to know, and if you're at the meeting you will find out. Of course, since you're still in bed . . ."

"Not for long. I shall want a bath and something to eat before . . . what time is it, anyway?"

"Dawn, on a wet, windy, thoroughly miserable midsummer day. Well, it's not actually midsummer, but the alliteration pleases me."

"Oh Heaven," Aldric moaned in feigned horror, "what you do to our language is probably illegal."

"Come on, Bladebearer Deathbringer—Rynert expressed a particular desire to see you, and if he doesn't you will be in more hot water than your bath can hold. But afterwards you and I shall have a private little talk concerning the spellstone of Echainon. Good morning once again." He turned and left the room.

"What was that you called me?" Aldric asked an instant too late. Then he shrugged, yawned, stretched and slithered out of bed, shivering in the unaccustomed cold air. As the young man wriggled hastily into a robe he glanced out of the window at the wet rooftops, grimacing as a gust of wind slapped raindrops against the glass. "Fine summer weather," he muttered, and turned away.

He did not notice the crow huddling for shelter under the eaves of an opposite house, even when the bird's head lifted with a jerk as he appeared at the window. Its beady eyes fastened on his face, and its pickaxe beak opened to utter a croak of surprise even as it shuffled further into the shadows. Once Aldric had gone, the crow gurgled to itself in a most uncrowlike fashion and performed a triumphant little dance on the narrow ledge. Then it launched itself into the rain-slashed air on wide black wings and glided silently off across Kerys, heading north-north-west for Dunrath six hundred miles away.

As the crow flies.

*

Lord Endwar *ilauem-arluth* Santon reined in his charger atop the same ridge where Aldric had once sat and, like the younger man before him, gazed at the brooding might of Dunrath-hold. There was an army camped before the fortress, six thousand men in a ring of steel through which nothing passed unchallenged. Santon dismounted and went to sit on a camp-stool under the shade of his blue and purple standards with their white lettering. Not that he needed shade, even though the sun shone brightly from a cloudless sky; there was no warmth from it at all and the wind which tugged the snapping banners overhead was icy cold.

Endwar-*arluth* took off his helmet and scowled. It had taken eight days' hard marching to bring his legion up from Erdhaven; two hundred-odd miles, and somewhere along the road they had passed from one season to another, leaving the Spring Festival far, far behind. Santon had seen with his own eyes a brief but unmistakable scudding of snowflakes across the open moorland. Snow—and summer air like the breath of an underground crypt. He shivered with more than the cold.

Dunrath had been grey when last he saw it, blue-grey stone from the Blue Mountains under a blue-grey autumn sky as he rode to young Aldric's *Eskorrethen* ceremony. Now, perhaps by some trick of the light, the fortress was red. Red with the rustling vermeil silk of Kalarr cu Ruruc's war-flags hoisted over every wall, and red too as if every stone, every tower and every turret had been dipped in some great pool of blood. The crimson hue shifted and changed like the folds of a shaken cloth and only one thing remained constant: the ominous, glistening scarlet of the citadel's donjon, which drew and held the gaze with an awful fascination. It reminded Santon of an Imperial prison he had once seen in the city of Egisburg, the sinister Red Tower whose gates had never yet released a living prisoner.

The lord drank wine offered him by an armed retainer and wondered how long it would be before King Rynert and the other legions joined his leaguer. The men he commanded here were not—save for two thousand foot—regular troops, but levied vassals, *kailinin* of lesser clans who owed him service for their lands and those warriors of his household who had come with him to Erdhaven. Four thousands of foot and two of horse—not enough to take the fortress by either siege or storm, but quite sufficient to bottle up its occupants behind the high, strong walls and put all thought of open battle from their minds.

Dunrath was widely regarded as the mightiest fortress in all Alba; true, it was not so large as Leyruz-*arluth*'s citadel at Datherga, nor as modern and complex as Santon's own hold of Segelin, which he called a "castle" after the Drusalan word—but Dunrath had never fallen to any foe in war. It had changed hands twice during the Clan Wars, leaving and returning to Talvalin possession within the space of two months, but both occasions had been by treachery. And now it had been taken by treachery again. Santon drained his cup and rose, glaring towards the blood-red tower. Why was it so cold? he wondered silently, rapping his commander's baton against one armoured leg. What purpose did it serve? And was the answer one a wise man would want to hear . . . ?

*

After a leisurely bath and a meal which by its size deserved a better title than merely breakfast, Aldric walked back to his room to collect his weapons and put on the only formal *elyu-dlas* he owned. Custom and protocol required that he wear only a *taipan* shortsword with the Colour-Robe, but in the circumstances he felt a *taiken* of Widowmaker's lineage would make an acceptable substitute.

It would have to serve.

The building, indeed the whole town, seemed aswarm with *kailinin,* lesser lords and legion officers, and Aldric had bowed or saluted more often since leaving his bed an hour before than he had done during the previous fortnight. He had also been the source of considerable speculation—the anomaly of a young, short-haired *venjens-eijo* in combat leathers, who yet wore a high-clan crest-collar at his throat and the colours of Talvalin on his *tsepan,* had caused more than one dignified head to swivel in a most undignified manner.

Then Aldric turned a corner and stopped with one eyebrow arching quizzically. Tehal Kyrin was standing a little way from his bedroom door, holding a letter in the fingertips of one hand as if it was a noxious insect, with a distracted expression on her face and her lower lip nipped between her teeth. When she saw the Alban she started slightly, made as if to say something and then instead twisted the letter into an untidy cylinder which she pushed through her belt.

"You look rather better than when I last saw you," she said, venturing a smile which fell rather short of the mark. Aldric failed to notice anything wrong even when he tried to embrace her and found her slipping nervously aside.

"It's surprising what hot food, hot water and a sharp razor can do," he grinned. "Have you eaten yet?" She nodded, toying with the rolled-up letter, and seemed once again on the point of telling him something important when he continued talking. "It looks as if I'm finally going to get some answers out of Gemmel about the Dragonwand. Usually he listens politely to every question you ask and then equally politely avoids giving a reply."

"Sounds familiar," the girl murmured. Aldric let her comment pass.

"He called me Bladebearer Deathbringer. Why? I don't like the title."

"You'll have to get used to it. *En Sohra*'s gone, but her crew did a lot of talking during the few hours they spent in harbour. You're quite a hero."

"Hero!" Aldric laughed without much humour. "I've heard some unlikely things in my life, but that really—" He stopped and reached out one hand to the girl's face, turning it towards the wan daylight from the window at the end of the corridor. "Why are you crying, Kyrin . . . ?"

She pulled away from him, wiping her face with the back of one hand, and with the other drew the letter from her belt and pushed it at him. Aldric unrolled the parchment and scanned it quickly, his gaze flicking once or twice from the writing to her face and back again. Then he took several deep breaths before trusting himself to speak.

"The characters are Alban—but the language is Valhollan, yes?" Kyrin nodded her head sadly. "And this name, Sijord—"

"Seorth," she corrected.

"Seorth, then. That's the man who was to marry you?" Another nod. "I can't read this, but let me guess; Seorth has come looking for you, am I right? And you will go with him, of course." This was not really a question, more a statement.

Kyrin studied her lover's face for a long time before she replied, gently touching the white scar under his eye with her fingertips.

"Yes, I will, as I think you expected all along. I've tried to tell you often enough . . . But it's not a duty—I do have the right to choose—"

"And you choose the man you've known for longer than two weeks. I can't blame you." The look in his dark eyes said differently and Kyrin knew it.

"You put a great deal of living into those two weeks, Aldric," she said. "I've come to know you very well and like you very much—but I have loved Seorth since I was little more than a child, and from this it seems he loves me too. That's why I'm going. Believe me, Aldric-*ain*, you will understand . . . eventually."

"Will I? Tell me why?" He fought to keep the harshness from his voice, knowing that to be *kailin-eir* was of necessity to accept ill-fortune with the same courteous equanimity as the most splendid victory.

"You should know." Kyrin's voice was very soft. "You've come to terms with a greater loss than my going away."

"I . . . I had no choice then. I have now—and the power to alter it. You said yourself I was heir to lands and ranks and titles. So . . . What I want, I take, and no man—or woman—can gainsay me." The girl stared at him in disbelief, then stepped over to his bedroom door and threw it open. One corner of her mouth tugged down as she tried to summon up contempt and failed. "You're crying again," he said, not caring that the words came out like the crack of a whip.

Kyrin flinched as if he had indeed lashed her across the face, and still the tears welled silently from her eyes even when she scrubbed at them with her knuckles in a gesture almost violent enough to bruise the sockets. There were no sobs, and when she spoke her voice was without a tremor though it was faint and desolate. "Yes, I'm crying. Crying for you—for whatever spark within you that must have died last night. Because you aren't the man I knew any more. I'm crying for you, Aldric. Because someone must." She entered the room and returned seconds later with Widowmaker in her hands. "Here, *kailin-eir* Aldric *ilauem-arluth* Talvalin. Wait for Seorth and my father. Justify your token's name and kill them both, then take me to your bed by force. Because you're not a naked barbarian makes all the difference to rape and murder . . ." She flung the longsword at him.

Aldric caught the weapon without thinking, his gaze fixed on the girl's face which still held more of sorrow than of rage. Hard to hurt an enemy, he thought sombrely, easier to hurt a friend—and easiest of all to break a lover's heart. Perhaps it was as well, to make their parting easier. Then his fingers clenched spasmodically around the *taiken*'s hilt. He wanted to shout, to rave, to smash things, to . . . Yes, to kill . . . something, anything, himself. To behave as not even the lowliest of lordless *eijin* should behave.

Then it was as if a sheet of ice closed over the anger boiling in his brain, and he became abruptly calm again. Why so angry? he asked himself. Especially with Kyrin, who had done nothing except react the way any right-minded woman would to his vile temper and grossly dishonourable suggestion. The whole foul episode was his own fault and no one else's. His thoughts touched briefly on the *tsepan* pushed with meticulous nonchalance through his belt, then dismissed it with a mental shrug. Why bother, when at any time within the next three weeks he could be flung into the Void. If he survived beyond that, perhaps his formal suicide might recompense many people for many things, but first and foremost were Kalarr and Duergar. Their deaths, whether formal or otherwise, were long overdue.

Aldric went down on both knees and laid the *taiken* at Kyrin's feet, then bent forward and pressed his brow to the cool, lacquered scabbard. "Tehal Kyrin-*an*," he whispered huskily. "Lady, forgive the words I spoke in anger."

She knelt too, so that their faces were once more level;

so that she could watch his eyes and see if they truly
mirrored what he said, or gave the lie to his courteous
phrases. What she saw was an expression disturbingly
like that he had worn after learning of his brother's apparent treason, except that this time it was directed at
himself. It was shocked, haunted, unwilling to believe
how easily mere words had soured their relationship. A
face which should have wept, but where any tears had
frozen in eyes like obsidian, or flint, or jade. The same
bone-chilling grey-green as a winter sea. A widowmaker's eyes.

"I am truly sorry, Kyrin."

"I believe you."

He bowed forward slightly, as much to hide his face
as to acknowledge her acceptance of his apology. Kyrin
hesitated, then leaned towards him and touched her lips
against each eyelid, then to forehead and mouth. The
movement was less a kiss than a valediction, and Aldric
knew it.

"Go now, Kyrin-*ain*," he muttered. "All the words
were said long ago."

She rose and walked away, then stopped and took a
few steps back towards him. "I cannot just leave like
this," she said firmly. "Aldric-*eir,* the quarrel's already
been forgotten. You acted honourably towards me at all
times, and I shall tell Seorth of it. Any house of ours is
yours, Alban, fire and food and safety if you ever need
it. I promise." Kyrin bowed slightly, the way she had
seen Aldric do so many times. "Go with God, Aldric—
and may Heaven grant you long life."

"Long life is often no great gift," Aldric murmured,
"and can sometimes be a curse." He thought for a moment, staring into space with narrowed, frosty eyes, then
half-smiled and said:

> " 'What is life, except
> Excuse for death, or death but
> An escape from life?' "

"Recall my name with kindness, lady, now and then."
As she left him kneeling there, a black figure with a

black *taiken* before him, Kyrin thought about his poem and as she did she shuddered.

*

From the balcony of Dunrath's donjon Lord Santon's legion resembled a child's toy soldiers, set out in little blocks of men around the fortress walls just out of arrow-shot. Duergar Vathach leaned on a parapet and surveyed them dispassionately, aware of the impasse which had caused the siege. With another thousand picked troopers of Grand Warlord Etzel's guard he could pulverise the small Alban host, while without them he merely stood up here and wished. Fabric rustled behind him and he turned as Kalarr cu Ruruc stepped out on to the balcony, wind whipping at his forbidding vermeil robes.

"Have they altered their disposition?" he demanded.

"Not since dawn. Why? What difference would it make?"

"Enough to annoy me greatly. I've spent the night preparing a spell based on the siege positions they assumed when they arrived last night, and while it's effective it's also inflexible. What about the *traugarin?*"

"The putrefaction stopped once the air cooled—it has not returned."

"Good. One disadvantage about using corpses as soldiers, little necromancer, is that you can resurrect the bodies, but you have to keep fending off the natural processes which follow death. Awkward if you don't want your army rotting away before you can put them to use."

"But having set the Charm of Undeath on them, I have to keep them in that state. The spell will not affect a cadaver more than once."

"Isn't life awkward for the workaday wizard," Kalarr observed drily. "Why you didn't think of weather-magic before, I cannot imagine. After all, even the Drusalan Empire must know that killed meat keeps better when it's cold."

"I don't like nature-magic; it's slow, clumsy, crude—and hard to control safely."

" 'Like!' " scoffed cu Ruruc. " 'Safe!' Those are not words a true sorcerer should have in his vocabulary."

Duergar sensibly did not argue with him and the issue
was tacitly dropped. "It seems," Kalarr continued, "that
yonder lord has sent me his defiance." He grinned with
sinister relish as he used the old term. "Therefore I feel
justified in giving him a demonstration of the power
which he has challenged—making sure, of course, that
enough are left alive for the warning to be noted."
Though his lean face remained devoid of all expression,
there was an ugly purr of eagerness in his voice as it
shaped the prolix phrases.

Duergar looked at Santon's army, the scales of their
tsalaerin twinkling in the chilly sunlight, then turned to
his companion. "What do you intend?" he ventured
carefully, knowing from previous experience that with
this mood of fierce exuberance on him, it was unsafe to
be near Kalarr.

"Once, long ago," cu Ruruc said, "someone called me
the slayer of hosts. It is time, I think, to reaffirm that
title. There's a spell known to few sorcerers and seldom
written in grimoires. I know that spell, and have spent
the night preparing it. Now it merely needs priming and
direction before I can unleash it."

"But . . ." Duergar began, reluctant to raise an objection, yet knowing it had to be done, "but surely they
have some protection—otherwise they wouldn't have
dared to come so close."

Kalarr allowed himself to smile with a slow, evil un-
veiling of his teeth. But he was not angry, merely
amused. "You're very sharp today, my friend," he observed. "Such a theory crossed my mind earlier this
morning, so I tested it. Lesser enchantments only, mere
probes, extinguishing fires and the like—but nothing so
dramatic that it might remind them they're besieging a
sorcerer's fortress. They'll learn that soon enough.

"That army's as helpless as a tethered goat, thanks to
its commander's pride. I know these high-clan *kailinin-
eir,* though they ignored me until I persuaded them
otherwise. A haughty, stubborn breed, who can't see farther than their long patrician noses. Magic's something
from a story to them, and wizards are less than dirt."

"Not to all of them." Neither sorcerer had heard Baiart emerge on to the balcony behind them until he

spoke. "My brother understands you well, cu Ruruc. That's why he's going to kill you."

The wizards glanced at Baiart, then at each other. Kalarr's nostrils twitched and Duergar broke into a high-pitched bray of laughter. "Your brother," spluttered the Drusalan necromancer when he had regained a little composure, "is still floating about on the high seas, prey to everything we choose to throw at him."

"My brother," corrected Baiart with a hint of his old suavity, "passed from your reach when that flying eye was destroyed. I was there. I saw it happen and heard how you reacted. You don't even know where he is anymore, much less have any power to harm him."

Kalarr's saturnine face darkened. "Maybe so, Talvalin," he hissed. "But if you stay here a little longer, you will get some inkling of what awaits bold clan-lord Aldric"—he sneered the words—"if he has the courage to come back."

"You're scared of him, aren't you?" Baiart jeered. "He killed the monsters that you sent to get him and now he's escaped you. And you're afraid!"

"If death is what you want . . ." Duergar snarled, lifting his open hand only to have it seized by Kalarr and forcibly lowered again.

"Then it's the last thing that we'll give you," cu Ruruc finished. "However much you may deserve it—or desire it."

9

Bladebearer

When Aldric eventually stood up, after several minutes of utter stillness, he walked quietly into his room and began to don his armour, dismissing the servant who would have helped him so that he could concentrate completely on the task and so prevent his mind from dwelling on . . . other things. *An-moyya-tsalaer* was difficult to put on without assistance; its complicated design required each part to be fitted in a certain sequence, although once that sequence had been mastered an agile warrior could scramble into his battle harness with remarkable speed.

Aldric could do so in a matter of minutes, but on this occasion he moved slowly and methodically, letting himself become totally absorbed by the precise, almost ritual care needed when a man sheathed himself entirely in metal but wished to remain flexible enough to move. The *elyu-dlas* and its matching wing-shouldered overmantle were both padded to mute the rustling scrape of lamellar armour, and both were marked with the spread-eagle crest of clan Talvalin embroidered in silver on dark blue. Once he had put on both these and arranged the high collars properly, Aldric changed Widowmaker's braided combat hilt for a ceremonial grip of etched silver which someone, probably Gemmel, had left on the low bedside table, and slung the sword horizontally so that hilt and scabbard protruded through the slits cut in his robe for that purpose. In what amounted to court dress, the wearing of *taikenin* slung *eijo*-style across one's back was definitely not encouraged.

Belting his Colour-Robe with a sash through which

he slipped his *tsepan,* Aldric picked up his helmet and, methodical care now set aside, hurried to the council room. From what he had seen of the building, it was constructed in the usual fashion of Alban town houses: the bath-house and the eating-hall had been in the usual places and he guessed the meeting-chamber would be too. On that assumption he felt able to take a shortcut through one of the upper galleries.

Someone had laid down thick mats of woven straw to protect the fine wood floors from many feet in military boots. Since Aldric was wearing his own long, soft-soled moccasins he made virtually no noise as he hastily strode along the corridors. Had he given the matter any thought, he might have realised that walking so quietly through a houseful of high-ranking lords could lead to his being somewhere he was neither expected, wanted nor supposed to be. He gave such a possibility no consideration at all until he crossed a high balcony and by then it was too late.

There was a clear view through its carved screen into a narrow hall well-lit by several tall windows, and from the corner of his eye he caught a glimpse of something which made him pause for a closer look. Glancing down without thought for the consequences of his action, Aldric went suddenly pale and stifled a gasp as he flattened against the wall.

There were three men in a tableau below him: King Rynert sat at one end of the hall, a fully-armoured Dewan ar Korentin stood in the centre with his arms folded so that his drawn sword rested threateningly on his left shoulder, and a third figure knelt politely on one knee in the dark area between two windows. Not that he needed to take such trouble, for he was dressed from head to foot in black with only his eyes and a thin stripe of face visible. In the shadows he was almost invisible. He had no obvious weapons, but the mere reputation of the *tulathin* was reason enough for ar Korentin's caution. Sudden violence and a *taulath* went hand-in-hand.

Aldric could hear the soft murmur of voices, but not enough to make sense of their conversation. He did not really want to know anything about it, and indeed wished most heartily that he had gone another way. It was too late now to creep away; getting in unnoticed had probably used up all his luck for the day on that score at least. Why King Rynert was having any dealings at all with a *taulath*—a shadow-thief—was beyond Aldric's comprehension. *Eijin* were men who, willingly or not, had lost their honour. *Tulathin* did not know the meaning of the word. They were mercenaries; spies, kidnappers, assassins . . . any task at all was performed without question, just so long as their price was met.

There was the muffled chink of a moneybag and then the *taulath* was gone as if he had never been—like a shadow banished by sunlight. Aldric breathed a little more easily, but his heart did not begin to slow down until Dewan and the king had also left the hall. When they did his mouth stretched into something which did not really succeed in being even the wryest of smiles, and he became uncomfortably aware of the light film of sweat which covered his skin.

Today was a day for shocks, it seemed.

*

Lord Santon studied Dunrath from his position on the ridge. For an hour now the uppermost part of the donjon had been veiled by a strange azure mist. There was a dull, sonorous humming in the air, like the sound made by a swarm of bees but deeper, as much felt through the ground a heard in the air. Santon did not like it. Trying to push the mystery from his mind until he was more able to give an answer to it, he opened a chart and tried to concentrate on the lists of figures set out neatly beneath each diagram.

He had barely begun to read when someone shouted.

Endwar-*arluth* Santon wasted no time in idle questions—he knew instinctively where to look. Dunrath's citadel was now wholly shrouded in a globe of coiling blue vapour lit from within by a pale glow. Now and then streaks of brilliant white light spat like shooting-stars from the cloud, dragging long bright tails through the air behind them as they curved down to splash in frosty extinction on the ground before the fortress. The dull hum became more intense, a harsh drone which set the teeth on edge and ground into men's skulls like a rusty drill-bit. It became steadily colder.

Santon stared at his own breath drifting smokily in front of him and then at the perimeter wall of Dunrath's outermost defensive ring. The reddish stone was inches deep in sparkling white crystals, as if snow had fallen and mingled with powdered diamonds as it fell. He swore in disbelief and stooped to lift his helmet, then yelped, swore again more viciously and sucked at fingertips which had left their skin on the icy metal. There were four little blots of tissue on the helmet's neck-guard and even as Endwar looked at them they became hard and bluish-white, like the flesh of a man with frostbite.

The entire fortress was lost now in a blinding, frigid light, and long filaments of bitterly cold energy came whispering through the ranks of his army. "Sound the retreat!" snarled Santon, trying to smother the fear in his voice with an overlay of anger. The nearest trumpeter set his instrument to his lips, then released his breath not in the ordered signal but in a cry of pain as the bronze mouthpiece froze against him. Blood trickled from both lips after he finally wrenched the thing away, ran down his chin but, instead of dripping there, it congealed in crackling cherry-red icicles.

The orderly regimental blocks bulged, heaved and broke as the men in those formations began to run, screaming as they flung away shields, helmets and weapons which had become too painfully cold to touch. Their cries mingled with the wind which rose from a sullen moan through a howl to a shrieking gale, tearing flags from their poles in long shreds of fabric; pavilions and bivouac tents in tatters from the ground and breath from the lungs of men too stabbed by the gelid spears of a blast from between the stars to fight against it.

When he looked down at his armour to find it cased in white rime, and at the faces of his generals made old by frost lying thick on beards and brows, Endwar Clan-Lord Santon knew himself to have been defeated without a blow being struck. Then, with shocking suddenness, the gale died in mid-howl. As one man the officers on the ridge looked towards Dunrath. Some swore. Others prayed. At least one that Santon could see fumbled his *tsepan* from his belt with his hand leaving much of its skin on the weapon's scabbard, and in a fit of despair or impotent rage stabbed himself through the great vessels of the throat. Though his blood spurted steaming from the wound, it had frozen before it could splash on the ground and fell instead as crystals, like rubies crushed in a mortar.

Santon sympathised with the man: at least his death had been an honourable one and not of some wizard's choosing. He was only surprised that the sight of the fortress had not broken other men's minds or driven them to suicide.

Shimmering patterns of force crawled over the massive structure, making it seem imbued with some ghastly form of life. Crystalline rings of energy pulsed heavily above the donjon, stacked like a child's quoits, their shifting, brilliant colours impossible to watch but impossible to ignore, the thick droning pouring from them in waves of raw atonal noise. They hung there, brooding, vast, ominously waiting.

For what . . . ?

*

Aldric paused briefly outside the council chamber to get his breath back while the two guards flanking the double door watched him with tolerant sympathy. "Not to worry, *arluthan*," said one, trying to combine respect with friendliness, "*mathern-eir* Rynert had not really called the conference to order before he was called away. Nobody will notice you being just a little late."

"Is it war, sir, do you think?" asked the other cautiously. Aldric grinned crookedly at the soldier, who stiffened to attention at being directly noticed.

"If I hadn't been late," he observed drily, "I would probably know myself."

The first sentry smiled at his companion's discomfiture, then saluted and opened the door for Aldric. The chamber inside was laid out like most Alban meeting-halls: a row of low chairs along the farthest wall for any high-clan *kailinin-eir* who might be present, a more imposing seat set at right-angles for the king—something always done whether or not the monarch was there—and lesser stools—little more than elevated cushions—set in lines for everyone else. As an *eijo*, Aldric expected to sit on one of these and had in fact taken his place when a retainer in the king's colours ushered him to one of the high-clan chairs. His surprise was made complete when everyone, most of the military and political figureheads in Alba, gave him a low, formal obeisance as they would to any other high-clan *arluth*.

To hide his slight embarrassment, Aldric took exaggerated care over setting Isileth Widowmaker on her stand to the left of his seat, once a retainer had brought one appropriate to the formal, near-vertical mounting of ceremonial *taikenin*, also a small padded mat for the young man's helmet. He was not made any more comfortable by the realisation that he was the only person present not carrying a *taipan*, and that with his short hair and Widowmaker rearing like a striking snake near his shoulder he was the object of scrutiny by everyone in the room.

Then the doors were flung wide open and King Rynert came in, flanked by soldiers and preceded by ar Korentin with his scabbarded sword held free of his belt in one hand, ready for instant defence of his lord. The Vreijek took up position at the right of Rynert's high seat and grounded his blade with a single precise clank. As if at this signal, the room was filled with a metallic susurration as every man present made First Obeisance. Rynert bowed from the waist in acknowledgment and sat down, waited for the warriors to resume their places and then deliberately smiled to signal an end to extreme formality.

"Gentlemen," he said, "I have just received two communications of great interest to us all. First—" he held out one hand and Dewan set a slip of paper in it, "—news from abroad. Two days ago, in the Pleasure Palace at Kalitzim. Emperor Droek joined his far from illustrious ancestors."

Nobody actually cheered—that would have been gravely impolite—but a distinct ripple of shock, relief and pleasure ran through the chamber. Everyone knew what Droek's death meant even before Rynert went on to explain.

"Though I have no confirmation here," the king continued when his audience had settled themselves, "I feel it is safe to assume that we no longer need concern ourselves with possible Imperial interference in the current crisis. Warlord Etzel, General Goth and Prince Ioen have enough problems of their own, I very much hope." There was a little burst of laughter at that. "It seems he was found dead in bed—whose bed, is not made clear." More laughter, the mirth of men suddenly freed from the threat of full-scale war. One man, however, did not laugh.

Aldric was remembering a black-clad *taulath* neither long ago nor far away, and the sound of money changing hands. Something twisted inside him like a knife and he found it very hard to keep contempt from his face when he looked at Rynert the King.

"My second communication is more local," Rynert went on. "Lord Santon has taken six thousand men north and this"—another fragile strip was put into his outstretched hand—"carried by a pigeon which arrived less than an hour ago, confirms that the fortress of Dunrath is now invested and under seige. I intend to—"

Rynert's intention went unheard, for at that moment a tall, lean figure rose from the rearmost row of the low-clan seats and strode forward. Several warriors sprang to their feet, snatching up shortswords to defend the king, and Dewan's long, heavy sword came out of its scabbard with a long, sinister hiss. Aldric too was on his feet, Widowmaker loose in her sheath just in case, but there was no real need.

Gemmel had the sense to stop well out of danger. He regarded the king with cold emerald eyes and then sketched a bow which was the merest token of respect and verged very close on the insolent. Rynert glared at him, ignoring the old man's lack of manners out of consideration for his age but not through any fear of his powers. Rynert of Alba was not the strongest of men in body, but he was afraid of nothing he had yet met in his life.

"You had best intend, king," said Gemmel quietly, "to have a funeral service said for those six thousand men. They will be dead before the sun sets tonight."

In the absolute silence which followed his words, the click as Aldric sheathed his *taiken* was deafeningly loud. It was a measure of the enchanter's imposing presence that not one eye turned from him to look towards the source of the sound.

"What do you mean, Gemmel-*an* Errekren?" Rynert demanded.

"I mean, king, that Lord Santon has gone up against an enemy from whom he has no protection." Gemmel slapped the Dragonwand angrily. "I would not have put Aldric-*an* Talvalin to the trouble and risk of fetching me this talisman if it hadn't been of vital importance. Kalarr cu Ruruc, king, is more powerful than you can possibly imagine—and he has a grudge against you, against every man here, against the whole of Alba, which is five hundred years old. Never think that during that time he has learnt mercy or forgiveness."

"What, then, should we do, *pestreyr-an?*" asked old Lord Dacurre.

"March north at once. This time I—and Ykraith the Dragonwand—will be with you, to turn aside any spells the sorcerers in Dunrath might hurl."

"Can you do nothing for Endwar Santon? He is the husband of my second daughter . . ."

"Lord Dacurre, spells are limited by distance, just like everything else. With my power channelled through it, Ykraith can form a shielding dome perhaps a mile across, but that will decrease as I tire—and I will. Before then I hope your soldiers will have done something useful. But as for Lord Santon—I very much fear that he and all his men are beyond my or indeed any aid."

*

The sky above Dunrath was alive with swirling patterns of power which formed and broke endlessly like visions from a drug-dream given shape and substance. There was no wind and the collective breaths of men and horses formed a fog above and around them, muting outlines but not the eldritch colours of Kalarr cu Ruruc's sorcery.

Then the waiting ended.

The rings of energy held in check for half an hour above the citadel contracted once and then exploded outwards, fragmenting into needles of blazing white light which slashed through battle armour as if the metal scales were so much sodden paper, punching men to the ground with the shock of their impact or striking them dead on their feet. One such bolt sighed over Santon's shoulder and struck his trumpeter full in the chest, burst into a flare of splinters with a brittle cracking noise and enveloped the young man in a cloud of misty pale-blue radiance. The warrior gasped, spun half round on sagging knees and fell on to his face.

Santon leaned down to turn over the already rigid body and gasped in horror as three of the fingers snapped off in his hand. The boy's once-handsome face was now that of a corpse six weeks dead: leathery skin the colour of lead was stretched tightly over his bones, leaving his nose shrivelled into suppurating pits. His lips were drawn back clear of gums where the teeth, cased in frozen saliva, gaped in a rictus of terminal agony, and though his eyes had shrunk into their sockets they still held an expression of utter disbelief.

Death had been quick—but it had obviously been neither clean nor painless.

As if in a snowstorm, the air was full of streaks of white as the darts of sorcerous power went scything through Lord Santon's host, reaping men like ripe corn. Some errant thought in the *arluth*'s mind insisted that all this was wrong, that the slaughter of a legion should be noisier, more indicative of effort and not this near-silent erasure as if a scholar were cancelling out rough diagrams on a slate. But there was only the thin, protracted hissing as the bright streaks of energy slid through the air and the intermittent crackle as they struck home.

Quite suddenly it was over.

Dunrath was once more blue-grey stone, without any trace of alien lights or colours and only the flapping scarlet banners to indicate that the Talvalins were not in possession of their ancestral hold. The drifts of hoarfrost had vanished from its walls and a gentle breeze had scoured away the skeins of mist.

Endwar Santon's army had likewise ceased to exist. Instead there were twisted, discoloured corpses scattered over the ground as far as the eye could see. There, in a pair of dense wedges, lay the two thousand regular troops who had died in their places to a man. Straggled further away were men who had broken near the end, and almost out of sight lay the levied vassals who had been the first to run. There were perhaps a hundred men left alive out of the six thousand—and one of them was Santon.

He had stood very straight and waited for the blast of magic which would strike him down, but even when a virtual blizzard of the things had straddled his position on the ridge and smashed his staff officers into so much frozen meat, he had been unharmed. Such a thing was not accidental; Santon had already guessed as much and his suspicion was confirmed as a great voice boomed out from the sombre fortress.

"Commander!" it blared. "Commander, I know that you can hear me! I know you are alive, commander. I intended that you should be. Go back to your King Rynert, commander, and tell him of the fate which befalls any who would oppose me. And commander, I thank you for the chance to exercise my skills once again. Quite apart from the reinforcements which you have given me. Get you to your king with all despatch, my lord—you may not die till then!"

*

"That was quite a performance you put on back there," said Aldric, pouring himself a strong drink. Gemmel, intent on lighting his pipe, said nothing. "I mean," the *eijo* continued, aware that he was babbling and equally aware of the nervous tension which made him do so, "if you'd been on the stage you would have got a standing ovation at the very least for the sheer intensity of that opening speech."

The wizard stared at his foster-son through a veil of fragrant smoke, wondering just how much Aldric was covering up and how much he actually knew. "Intensity, yes . . ." he murmured. "Knowing that one's words are true does give their delivery a certain weight."

"Santon's dead then—you're certain of that?" Aldric spoke in much more sombre vein; he had not liked the saturnine lord, but had respected him as a proud, honourable, worthy gentleman of a kind nowadays growing rare.

"Probably so—or as good as dead anyway. We'll know

soon enough, I fear. But Aldric, put other people aside for the moment. You heard me explain at some length about the Dragonwand's properties and I presume you've been talking to King Rynert for the past half-hour . . ."

"Talking isn't the way I'd put it," Aldric said, with a small shiver of recollection. "There are things I did not want him to know—my use of magic, for one—but the way he can twist words around so that answering one question leaves you open for three more . . . Gemmel-*artrou*, I tell you without shame he had me scared once or twice. Rynert's worse than ar Korentin at that lawyer's crooked questioning style—and Dewan's bad enough, before Heaven."

"It's all in the degree of practice," Gemmel said drily.

"They've both had far too much of that and most of it on me."

"If you've quite finished . . ."

"Sorry! Yes, I have. Say your piece."

"Thank you. Now you'd better know at once that I was lying about Ykraith's protective powers."

"What?"

"It's a weapon first and foremost—an offensive weapon. Like a sword; you can parry with one, but its prime function is to cut and thrust. Any protection which the army receives will come from my own personal force and from this." Gemmel took a small box from his belt-pouch and set it on the table before lifting off the lid. The blue aura of the Echainon spellstone pulsed out and over the table, giving as always the impression that it must leave a stain, so intense was its brilliant azure colouration. "I haven't the time to explain why just now, but because Kalarr cu Ruruc once used this himself a simple charm will be enough to cause it to absorb any sorcery he invokes—without the usual drain on my physical and psychic strength. Duergar doesn't really concern me; I've studied his methods and it seems he's a necromancer, one skilled at giving life to dead things—and not necessarily corpses, as that bronze monstrosity in Erdhaven proved. As far as really dangerous weapon-magic is concerned, say the Invocation of Fire or the

High Accelerator, he cannot be considered a serious threat.''

"But why lie about it?"

"Aldric, think of the military mind. If any of those legion lords knew this was a weapon they'd insist on using it their way and that would be fatal.''

"Then why—''

"I had to say something other than: 'Unfortunately, king, my personal strategy is going to leave you virtually unshielded for a while. Bad luck.' Rather than let that happen, Rynert would lock me up and throw away the key.''

"Personal strategy . . . ?" Aldric wondered shrewdly. "I have the feeling that includes me.''

"It does. There are certain rules which must be obeyed in this sort of business—and of course it's your duty and no one else's to kill Duergar Vathach. Correct, *venjens-eijo!*''

"Correct.''

"Then we understand one another. You'll need me to prevent Kalarr from turning you to a small smear of crisped fat—''

"You have such a way with words, you know . . .''

"—and in that time the army will be without protection, other than the few charms I shall be able to lay on it before we go.''

"Go? Where?''

"Use your brains, boy. Where else but Dunrath? I'm quite sure there's another way in, apart from the front gate. Mmm?''

"What if there isn't?" hedged Aldric.

"Then I have ways and means of circumventing that difficulty if such should arise. But I feel certain that it won't.''

"Exactly what will you say to King Rynert if anything goes wrong?''

"There are plenty of plausible explanations—perhaps his men went beyond the limits of my spell or something like that. But if anything goes really badly wrong, then making excuses will be the least of our problems. Assuming we or the king are even alive to worry about them.''

"Sometimes, *altrou-ain,* you say the most reassuring things. Just like Ymareth—now there was another . . . oh dear God in Heaven!"

"Aldric—what's the matter?" Gemmel leaned forward urgently because the young *eijo* had gone suddenly, shockingly white. "Are you ill, son?"

"No . . . No, I'm all right." Aldric smiled weakly. "Just bloody stupid."

"Don't take names to yourself without reason," reproved the sorcerer.

"Oh, I've reason enough," the *eijo* muttered. "You might think anything to do with a full-grown firedrake would stick in my mind, but I'd almost forgotten what Ymareth told me. Destroy any talisman of Kalarr's that you hold, it said, and make sure he knows it—then await events. Ymareth's words."

"You forgot that . . . ?" Gemmel stared so hard that at last Aldric was forced to look away. Only then did he nod, once and hastily. "Then you *are* stupid! Listen: if I destroy the spellband, not only will it remove any threat which Duergar might hold over Kalarr—so that once they know it, their alliance will fall apart—but cu Ruruc will think I've failed to recognise the Echainon stone. The kind of mistake a petty wizard might make. So *he* might make a mistake of his own like leaving the security of his fortress—"

"My fortress, please."

"His stolen fortress to defeat Rynert in open battle. That's how he was destroyed last time, so such sweet revenge should be most enticing."

"Well, then," Aldric finished his wine and stood up, "let's do it. Have you noticed any crows about Kerys?"

"A few. Foolish; gulls would be much less obvious round a sea-port."

"Not very imaginative, are they? Come on, *altrou.*"

*

The regiments were already forming up as Aldric and Gemmel sauntered innocently through the streets of Kerys, both quite aware of the black bird which kept pace with them along the rooftops. Gemmel had slipped away briefly and had returned with a sapphire in his hand. Aldric had not asked where the gem had come from, but a word from Gemmel made it glow until now it was a convincing imitation of the Echainon spellstone. The wrist-band was tucked into his belt.

"Carefully now," he said in a voice so soft that Aldric barely heard him. "If our spy guesses that all this is for his benefit, we'll have wasted our time."

"And started cu Ruruc wondering about just why we found it necessary to go through such an elaborate deception . . ."

"Precisely so."

They were looking for some deserted courtyard which would be concealed from ordinary spies, but not from the changeling hopping cautiously in their wake. Though Aldric stopped now and then to glance about suspiciously, he always moved slowly enough for the crow to hide from view. It was more difficult than he had thought to make such a pretence seem convincing. Then Gemmel grabbed his arm and jerked him out of sight.

"In there!" the enchanter hissed in his ear and gave him a firm push between the shoulders. At the end of a narrow, sour-smelling alley Aldric found himself in an old stable, its roof collapsed and open to the sky. Something moved furtively between the broken rafters and the young *eijo* gave a small, grim smile. Gemmel appeared beside him, looking about with every sign of satisfaction. "This will do," he said, and laid the spellband down on a heap of rotting straw. Above their heads, the crow almost fell into the stable as it tried to see what the sorcerer was doing.

Using a piece of wood, Gemmel drew complicated patterns on the dank floor; only he knew they were meaningless, but they looked significant and that was enough. He mumbled nonsense under his breath and accompanied the sounds with imposing gestures. The overall impression was of a fussy, inexperienced conjuror faced for once with an important spell, and Aldric was forced to hide another smile behind his hand.

Steam billowed from the damp straw as the bronze ring began to glow; then its metal ran like wax, exposing the glow of the false spellstone for a few vital seconds before the whole thing was swallowed in a white flash of heat. Only ash and a few spark-pitted cinders remained behind.

"So much for Duergar and Kalarr," Gemmel announced confidently. Something rustled overhead—not the crow, which Aldric had been surreptitiously watching, but a large brown rat. Gemmel glanced up, catching his companion's nod of approval before shouting: "What? A spy!" and pointing his finger at the rodent.

There was a hazy flicker in the dim light and a crack like the lash of a whip. The rat squealed shrilly and its body exploded, throwing bones and internal organs all over the stable as if shot from a *telek*. Though Aldric had been expecting something of the sort, the speed and violence of Gemmel's reaction made him jump. Even so, he missed neither the crow's hasty tumble out of sight nor the rapid clatter of wings as it made a hurried exit.

"I think he's convinced we meant business," he said, forcing a laugh as he glanced towards the messily-deceased rat. "What was that trick anyway?"

"A lesser form of the High Accelerator," Gemmel replied, massaging the pins-and-needles it had caused in his hand.

"Why lesser?"

"Because I saw no need to flatten the stable, that's why."

"Could you have done that?"

"Could you stop asking questions for a while?" the wizard returned testily. His index finger, which had directed the spell, felt as always as if he had hit it with a hammer. Then he relented. "Yes, quite easily. The High Accelerator is a fierce magic, you know; it can make a man's eyeballs jump out through the back of his skull, or push his skull out of his head. Hurling down a wall isn't difficult. Satisfied?"

"For the time being . . ."

*

"He destroyed it?" Kalarr repeated softly. "Are you quite sure?"

One of the thin, yellow-eyed changelings nodded emphatically. "I saw it done, lord—and barely escaped with my life."

"So . . ." The sorcerer stood up and crossed to a window, from which he stared down at where Duergar worked his necromancy on the wreckage of Endwar Santon's legion. Since the great spell two days before, Kalarr had felt drained, exhausted—but now his weariness was replaced by a fierce exultation. "Losing the stone is unfortunate," he mused, then chuckled. It was an ugly sound. "But not so great a loss to me as the wristband is to you, Drusalan."

Swivelling, he fixed both spies with a baleful glare. "Duergar Vathach must not hear of this matter," he growled, and an ominous note in his voice made the changelings quake. Both knew the easiest way in which he could ensure their silence. Then he smiled cruelly. "Good! I see you understand me. Then remember. Now, get out!"

The spies needed no second bidding; they scuttled frantically away with cu Ruruc's harsh laughter in their ears. He settled back in his chair once they had gone and began to plan his strategy, wanting the Albans crushed and under his domination but strangely unsure how to go about it. Now that the old Emperor was dead any aid from that quarter was unlikely—Grand Warlord Etzel was too busy jockeying for real power to be concerned with abstract notions of foreign conquest.

While Kalarr intended to enjoy Duergar's death in the fullness of time, he realised now that the time would have to be deferred. He had nothing like the Drusalan's skill in the art of necromancy, and it was that art which had created and maintained the *traugur* host which garrisoned Dunrath.

Using the same type of huge spell which had annihilated Santon's army was physically impossible; Kalarr knew that it would be more than a month before he could take the physical strain of the High Magic again without hideous deformity. Besides, he knew that a military victory would entice certain ambitious lesser lords to side with him, since they would not be smirching their honour by aiding a wizard, merely a skilful general. Kalarr sneered to himself; he cared nothing for what they thought, but knew that certain proprieties had to be observed. It had been just the same before . . . the last time. Men remained human and never learned the lessons of their own past.

And defeating Rynert in battle would be such a deliciously ironic vengeance that he could scarcely be expected to forego the opportunity . . . Kalarr opened out Lord Santon's battle orders and began to study them with care.

*

Both the great army roads which criss-crossed Alba and the legions which marched along them had been created by Rynert's great-grandfather in the early days of the Imperial threat. Neither had yet been used against the enemy which had caused their birth, but had frequently seen service against Elthanek border reavers and recalcitrant lesser lords who fancied a return to the old independent days before the Clan Wars. The six legions had become little more than a huge police force with a kingdom to patrol, but that state of affairs was changing with every mile they marched further north and every man knew it, whether he was a peasant's son who had joined the Standards because he expected no inheritance or the lordliest high-clan *kailin-eir* resplendent in the plumes and crests of a commander.

Many small villages had grown up near the highways in order to benefit from the travellers and merchants passing to and fro. Most had inns and lodging-houses to make such people stay longer and market places for the buying and selling of their goods. Aldric sat bareheaded in Lyard's saddle at the centre of one such market place. The village around it might have been home to perhaps three hundred people. Once. Not now.

It had been reduced to a jumble of soot-smeared stones and shattered timbers. Greasy black smoke curled up from the wreckage, bringing with it the thick stench of charred meat. The reek was unmistakable. It was the cloying, heavy smell of houses which had burned with people still inside.

Not all had burned. There were a few corpses, two days dead and already bloating, sprawled among the rubble. The sickly-sweet odour of their corruption pricked at the young warrior's nostrils despite the scarf he wrapped around his face. It was horrible, and pathetic in its horror. Hooves had ploughed up the little gardens, pounding flowers and vegetables alike into pulp and shredded fibres. Lyard, battle-schooled, remained quite still, but schooling or not the big horse's laid-back ears signalled his unease. Aldric leaned forward to pat the Andarran charger's neck, then stopped with the movement unfinished as he saw the doll.

It was a simple thing of stitched cloth, with a long rip across its painted face, its yellow woollen hair stiff and dark with dried blood. Part of a child's hand still gripped one ribboned braid. There was nothing else.

Aldric stared at it with his fists clenching until the knuckles gleamed white through his skin, as hate and helpless rage boiled up inside him. More than he had suffered loss at the hands of his enemies, he knew that—but the extent of that loss was only now beginning to sink home. He stroked Isileth Widowmaker as if the longsword was a hawk needing to be gentled, wondering if death by *taiken* was what he really wanted to visit on Duergar and on Kalarr. He knew now why his ancestors had sometimes reacted as they did—there had been one rebel fourteen generations ago who had taken three weeks to die; he had been a destroyer of innocent villagers as well. War was for warriors—any man who visited its horrors on the helpless deserved whatever ingenuities the dark and secret places of the mind could conceive.

Then he heard the hoofbeats and looked up. King Rynert and Dewan ar Korentin were picking their way through the devastation and both, Aldric could see, felt the same way about it as he did. As they drew closer he saluted and asked simply: "Why?"

It was Dewan who answered. Once an Imperial officer, he had seen such things before he knew the twisted reasoning behind them. "To discourage us," he said bleakly. "It must have been Duergar Vathach's suggestion. This is a Drusalan tactic—it's supposed to take the heart from an advancing army when they see their enemies care nothing for human life."

"In the Empire, maybe." Aldric's voice was flinty. "This is Alba."

"I've lived here long enough to know it," Dewan returned. "All this will be repaid with interest, never fear."

He watched the young man and said nothing more, knowing that however sincere he was, his words sounded like the most insipid platitudes.

"Leave this place, *kailin-eir*," Rynert advised gently. "Brooding about it will do no good."

"As you wish, Lord King." Aldric saluted again, bowed carefully and then rode Lyard towards the roads, towards the army—anywhere, so long as it was away from the village and its dead.

Rynert watched him go, then looked across at Dewan. "A young man who lives his life most intensely, I think," he said. "And he feels the loss of the girl, despite what you told me. You were wrong there, Dewan my friend."

"I did not use the word infatuation, king. She did. But perhaps we were both wrong."

"What's your opinion of him?"

Dewan considered briefly. "Whoever chose the *kourgath*-cat for his crest knew what they were doing." Rynert raised one quizzical eyebrow but let Dewan continue without interruption. "He's arrogant, more self-sufficient than I think he knows himself. He's very intelligent, well-educated in . . . in a most interesting variety of subjects. He's foul-tempered when the mood's on him, dangerous, sometimes ruthless, sometimes pitiless—"

"But not all the time, Dewan. Not now, at least."

"I noticed that. He's a strange one. My wife likes him though, whatever Tehal Kyrin was telling her. Lyseun does not usually approve of people who take me away from her, as you well know. But he can be friendly when he wants to be, I suppose . . ."

"You sound almost jealous, captain."

"I don't suffer from it, king."

"Would you trust him now?"

"With my life."

"And with your wife . . . ?" The king was mocking gently, as he sometimes did with people close enough to be almost family. Dewan and his lady were part of that very small, very select group, which was why the Vreijek felt able to grin broadly.

"I'm not a jealous, possessive husband, king. It would depend entirely on what Lyseun said. But yes, I'd trust

young Aldric with her. He's an honourable gentleman."
Dewan's face went suddenly very serious. "That's what
makes him so dangerous."

"I'll bear that in mind. Now, Baiart: if he's taken alive,
he is *not* to be permitted *tsepanak'ulleth*. I intend to
execute him."

Dewan was momentarily aghast, and seemed to find
difficulty in closing his mouth. "You intend—then you'll
seize the Talvalin lands by forfeiture? But Aldric . . ."

"I don't need the lands for myself; but they will be
useful as something to give or withhold. When I return
them—which I'm not obliged to do—my magnanimity
will perhaps engender a little gratitude in that young
man. It won't hurt him to feel something more human
than duty and respect."

"If he doesn't feel it, king, somebody else will definitely be hurt. I admire your cleverness, but in this case
I wish my formal objections to the scheme placed on
record. Young Talvalin's already quite human enough to
resent such a . . . such a trick if he ever finds out about
it. Rynert . . . be careful."

"I will be." The king let Dewan's use of his name go
by without any comment. "But at least it will remind
him that he can't gain everything by his own efforts. I
prefer such a clan-lord to be under obligation to me."

"As you wish. I still—"

Ar Korentin broke off as three horsemen in the orange plumes of couriers came clattering towards them.
All had the look of men who had ridden hard and fast,
but even so the most senior of the messengers leapt from
his skidding steed before the beast had halted and went
down on one knee while the others dismounted in more
restrained fashion.

"Sire," the man announced breathlessly, "we have
found Lord Santon!"

*

Endwar Santon told his tale to a ring of grim-faced, silent men, and if they looked like mourners at a funeral
he looked like the corpse. His armour and weapons were
gone; he had been wandering for more than a week,
eating what little he could scavenge—and with Duergar's

raiders out that was little indeed—while he made his unsteady way south to the road where some friend would eventually pass. And there he had waited.

Even at a forced march, the king's host could not cover six hundred miles in less than three weeks. Santon had been a fortnight without food or shelter before the first outriders came sweeping up ahead of the army; a fortnight of brooding and of black despair, of days darkened by his memories and of nights made bright with the flames of burning cottages.

Rynert's army was now less than four days' march from Dunrath, but their strength of some fourteen thousand was no longer enough to obliterate cu Ruruc's forces—not since these had been reinforced by some six thousand additional men. Only Gemmel gained some small, grim satisfaction from what Kalarr had done; he knew that there was no longer any risk of some awesome spell devastating the entire host while he was unable to protect it. There would be small magics, inevitably, but they would do no more damage than spears and arrows could. Step by step, Duergar and Kalarr were moving up to lay their heads on the block—and neither of them knew it, he was sure.

"He said I could not die until I spoke to you, Lord King," Santon said with difficulty. "I do not know if he mocked me, or laid a charm on me—without a *tsepan* I could not find out . . ." He croaked a low, ugly laugh. "I even threw my sword away, so that I could not fall on it as they did in ancient times. I wanted to die, but I had to tell you everything myself. Now I have done so." Santon laid down the cup of fortified wine someone had given him, uncoiled from his sitting position on the ground and knelt in First Obeisance. "And now I can die, if you will permit me, Lord King."

Rynert hesitated; he had been expecting such a request and trying to work out a polite means of refusing it ever since the messenger had first spoken half an hour before. Then he realised there was only one response after all, and nodded his assent.

The preparations were swiftly completed; a modicum of privacy was granted by making screens from the great clan war-banners, and Santon was left alone with one of the priests who always accompanied the legions. Aldric and several of the other younger lords stood around in a sort of horrified fascination, though few of them knew that Aldric himself had been within a *tsepan*'s length of the same situation. Then King Rynert beckoned to him and Aldric felt his mouth go dry.

"I would ask you to act as Endwar's second, Aldric-*an*," the king said in a low, private voice, "but since he was your father's friend it would be unseemly. Dewan is acting for him instead. Might I ask that he be allowed to use your sword?"

Aldric thought sombrely that Widowmaker was once again justifying her name, but he nodded consent and unhooked the sheathed blade from her slings. Dewan approached, wearing a formal overmantle marked with the crests of his rank, and accepted the *taiken* with a deep, courteous bow before securing it to his belt. Then he backed away three paces, his face an emotionless mask, and bowed again respectfully before turning to vanish behind the makeshift screens. Rynert watched the Vreijek go, then looked at Aldric. "Do you wish to witness this?" he asked.

The young *eijo* hesitated, then forced a small, ironic smile onto his lips. "I don't *wish* to, Lord King," he confessed. "But Endwar Santon was my father's friend and a hearth-companion of clan Talvalin. My absence would dishonour us all. I will be a witness."

*

After it was over, everything went very still for a moment; then the witnesses bowed in unison, rose and departed without a backward glance. All except Aldric. He waited quietly for the various rituals which had to be completed before Dewan could return his sword, then strapped the *taiken* back in place, secretly grateful that she had not been needed after all. Like much else in his life, Lord Santon had required no one's help to leave it. Aldric gazed at the huddled form covered now with a scarlet cloth, then turned to Dewan. "What will they do with him?" he asked. "There's not enough wood to give him a proper funeral."

"There is. You're forgetting that we carry fuel for the cook-fires—but I for one will eat my food cold if I must, to do him honour." Dewan rubbed his hands together; he was not Alban, had not been brought up with *tsepanak'ulleth* and found that the rite disturbed him. "Such courage deserves more than just a hole in the ground."

"I wonder will Baiart be as brave?" Aldric murmured, thinking aloud rather than asking a question. Dewan realised that just in time to stop the words which crowded on his tongue.

"I . . . wonder indeed," he said very softly.

10

Deathbringer

"**L**ord King, I have been trying to speak to you these three days past!" King or no king, Gemmel made no effort to keep the acerbity from his voice, though fortunately for him Rynert was more disposed to amusement than anger.

"I have been somewhat busy, Gemmel-*an*. An army to command, a kingdom to rule at second hand—little things I know, but time-consuming." The enchanter simmered gently, trying hard to keep his temper in check, until Rynert decided that enough was enough and became businesslike. "What do you want, anyway?"

"This concerns your battle strategy, Lord King."

Rynert lifted his eyebrows; there were some things which he considered unwarranted interference and this was one of them. "Oh. So you're a military commander on top of all else?" he said sarcastically. "Imperial service, no doubt?"

"I am an enchanter, Lord King."

"At least we have that clear. So what business is it of yours what strategy I adopt, eh?"

"Because of what you will be fighting. *Traugarin,* Lord King—not men." Rynert said nothing, and Gemmel interpreted this—correctly—as permission to continue. "You're not dealing with an Imperial Lord-General, but with a necromancer whose army has been dead for a long time. Some were resurrected from the old Baelen battlefield, others from the destruction of Lord Santon's legion. The numbers are equal on both sides, so far as I can judge—except that Kalarr's men cannot be killed. Yours can."

"That had not occurred to me, wizard," the king said softly after a pause.

Gemmel smiled slightly. "Precisely why I raised the question in the first place," he purred with some small satisfaction in his voice.

"So Duergar must be killed before his spell is broken. Is that it?"

Better, mused the old man to himself; you are actually starting to think things out for yourself again. Aloud he said: "Aldric Talvalin is oathbound to perform that act. I'll ensure that he survives to do it."

"And what about my army? You told the council that you would protect it. Are you failing in your promise?"

What *promise* did I give? Gemmel almost snapped, but spoke differently. "Of course not, Lord King. I can lay enough protective charms over the host to turn most spells—"

"Most?" Rynert's voice was suddenly sharp and suspicious.

"The spells I cannot turn are those of the High Magic, such as the charm used against Lord Santon. Like necromancy, those must be stifled at source—but I shouldn't worry overmuch. Cu Ruruc is hardly strong enough to use them yet—not without causing himself the most appalling damage."

"I know that much." Rynert was not merely bluffing to save a little face, he knew all about the merciless rules of high sorcery, and about the warping pressures they put on mind and body—which was why the most powerful wizards were never shrivelled ancients but men who might well pass for warriors.

"Also," Gemmel put in silkily, "cu Ruruc wouldn't want to defeat you by any other means than combat if it can be managed. He'll get more Alban allies that way."

By the expression on Rynert's face this also was something he had not considered. "There are *kailinin* whom I asked to join the hosting, both at Erdhaven and since; men who made excuses though they promised support later . . ."

"Watch them, Lord King."

"Oh, I will . . . Damn it, wizard, will you stop meddling in affairs of state!"

"I beg pardon."

The apology did not sound especially sincere, but Rynert was in no mood to press for more. "Then what is it you wish me to do, Lord General Gemmel?" he asked, only half jesting with the title. "Run away? Because we're less than a day from Dunrath."

"No. Not run, anyway." Gemmel stopped perforce as cavalry clattered past the king's pavilion, drowning his words for a few seconds.

Rynert got to his feet and looked out through the tent's door-flap. "Dawn patrol," he observed absently. "Riding point for the column. We'll be moving soon." Picking up his leather leggings he began to buckle them on himself, deciding in view of Gemmel's conversation not to summon any servants until he had to do so. "Well, man, carry on."

"As I said, don't run—but don't meet cu Ruruc head-on either. Skirmish. Duck and weave and sidestep. You know now that a set-piece battle is out of the question, so break your troops into small formations, units of two hundred at most, and disperse them. Your purpose should be to keep the enemy busy—because you can't destroy him. And the busier you keep Kalarr, the better chance Aldric and I will have of slipping unnoticed into Dunrath."

Rynert grunted; it might have been an opinion, or just the effort of tightening a buckle behind his knee. Then he straightened up and gazed at the enchanter. "What's to stop cu Ruruc dealing with each small unit one at a time?" he asked purely as a matter of form, since it was fairly certain Gemmel would already have an answer.

He had, of course. "Two things: first, I'm going to destroy the spies which have been keeping us under constant surveillance, and second, I'll lay a fog over the army before the spies can be replaced. That way—to be quite brutal about it—you'll lose two hundred men at most in any one engagement."

"It is brutal. But also good sense. When will you deal with the spies?"

Gemmel twirled the Dragonwand in a spear-fighter's flourish which made King Rynert smile a little. "Your host is preparing to break camp, so they'll be watching. Now seems as good a time as any."

Rynert shrugged into his plate-and-meshmail sleeves and followed the enchanter outside, tightening their lacings as he went. The king could not have said whether he worked at the armour with the intention of making it comfortable, or merely because he had no desire to seem interested in the practice of magic, despite being in fact interested to the point of fascination. Gemmel was muttering something under his breath and Rynert moved a little closer in order to answer him—then realised with a slight start that the old man was actually addressing the Dragonwand.

"*Abath arhan,* Ykraith," he murmured. "*Acchuad eiya ilearath dua'hr.*" There was a deep, melodious thrumming sound, like an echo of the bass register on a zither, and a translucent shimmer enveloped the crystal in the carven firedrake's mouth. Rynert felt its pressure just as he would have felt the heat from an uncovered brazier, and was conscious of a great stillness settling over the camp. All that moved were the crows which spiralled lazily high above. Gemmel favoured them with a poisonous smile and raised the Dragonwand above his head; everyone who saw him do so instinctively ducked. The enchanter's smile grew more cheerful. "There's nothing to worry about," he called.

Then he spoke a single harsh phrase which unleashed the spellstave's leashed-in force. It lit the cold blue sky with a blizzard of orange sparks, which burst in a great expanding hemisphere from the Dragonwand's crystal tip and lashed with blinding speed across the camp, piercing each changeling-crow as if on a thousand red-hot skewers. The birds spewed smoke and singeing feathers, then tumbled from the sky to leave it cleaner than it was.

"Nothing at all," Gemmel corrected primly, "unless you are a crow!"

*

Kalarr cu Ruruc stared at his magic mirror, drumming armoured fingers on the black ebony of his table's top. The obsidian glass obdurately refused to show him anything but his own darkened reflection. He strode across the chamber floor and back again, noisy in his carapace of scarlet-lacquered steel. There was still no image in the volcanic scry-glass even when he touched it and let some of his own inner power flow through its substance. Finally he swore viciously and smashed the thing to fragments with a single blow of his clenched fist.

Duergar looked round with a jerk at the sound of shattering. "That won't help," he said reprovingly. The window behind him showed greyness and the drifting skeins of fog which had grown thicker in the past half-hour. "Not even your flying eye could see through that murk."

"I know that well enough!" cu Ruruc snarled. "But it should at least show me what it cannot see through. Something's wrong with it. Something's hurt it."

"Then make another," said the necromancer simply.

"I have already told you that I can't," Kalarr grated through clenched teeth, leaning forward pugnaciously with his fists on the table. "There is a limit to that kind of shaping-spell. It's a penalty for the thing's usefulness."

"Usefulness?" Duergar laughed nastily. "What use have we made of it? Now my changelings—"

"Yes, your changelings! When did one of them last report, eh? Not since just after dawn, and now it's almost noon."

"Can't you dispell the mist?" Duergar asked, sidestepping further argument on the spy subject. Kalarr straightened with a gusty exhalation of breath.

"No I can't! As I've already told you!"

"You didn't," Duergar insisted, seemingly determined to annoy. Kalarr refused to react, merely smiling like a shark at his companion.

"All right, perhaps I didn't," he conceded. "I've more to do than remember every word spoken. But clearing away that spell-born fog is beyond my powers at present. You know what the attempt would do to me. Unless that's what you want, of course . . . ?"

"I could try to summon up a witch-wind," suggested Duergar evasively.

"No. Put all your power into keeping the *traugarin* strong. They must not die until I've finished with them—and with the Albans."

Kalarr picked up a helmet and left the chamber, clattering down the spiral stairs with Duergar at his heels.

There were none of the usual guards, either living or *traugur* undead; cu Ruruc had stripped Dunrath of men so that this time there would be no doubt of the outcome of the battle. He intended nothing less than the obliteration of King Rynert's host. Striding down the corridor, he reached the donjon's double doors and flung them open with a crash.

The noise was echoed by the stamp of feet as the army outside slammed to attention. Soldiers choked the courtyard, overflowing through its gates in rank upon rank until they were lost to sight in the swirling mist. Vermeil banners hung above them, marked with cu Ruruc's winged-viper crest, rippling sluggishly in the cold grey air.

There was a burst of cheering from his cavalry, human mercenaries since *traugarin* made useless horsemen, but heavy silence from the rest of his army even when he swung gracefully into his horse's saddle and raised one hand in salute. Kalarr grinned unpleasantly and passed the thin chains of the flail he carried as a baton through his fingers. "That's what I miss about commanding corpses," he remarked drily to Duergar. "The affection troops have for their general. These seem—"

"Lifeless?" the necromancer suggested.

"Ha . . ." Kalarr's gaze swept the courtyard and settled on Baiart, who had appeared at the foot of the stairs and now leaned heavily against the stone balustrade with a winecup in one hand and a brandy-bottle in the other. Baiart Talvalin was very drunk, and consequently very bold. "Hail to the mighty general," he slurred, and then looked pointedly from Kalarr to Duergar and back again. "Who . . . else . . . do you plan to kill today?"

The Drusalan necromancer's head jerked round to stare at him, then much more slowly turned to face Kalarr. That sorcerer's features remained expressionless while he lowered his helmet into place and laced its warmask snugly. It was probably all the unrelieved red armour which made his cheeks seem flushed with rage, because he was smiling most benevolently as he walked his big roan charger across to Baiart and stroked the drunk man's face almost caressingly with the flail's dangling chains. Baiart flinched and shivered at the contact.

"You, perhaps," cu Ruruc purred. His commander's crest nodded above him as he leaned closer and laid the flail-haft along Baiart's nose, between his eyes. "If you're very, very lucky . . ."

*

Gemmel leaned his weight on the Dragonwand and released a long breath which smoked away from his mouth into the fog he had created. Though the air was wintery, he was bathed in sweat from the concentrated effort it had required. "That should hold for long enough," he decided aloud. "I've done everything I can."

"Such as what?" Aldric was sitting in Lyard's saddle some distance away; both were in full lamellar battle armour and the young man was additionally equipped with shield and slender lance. Though the effect was probably unconscious, Gemmel felt that his foster-son was far more dangerous than any of the just-completed spells. Menace hung about him like the fog.

"I've screened the army against death from a distance—Kalarr probably cannot cast such spells yet, but it's best to be cautious where that one is concerned. And I made sure that this fog won't lift until I do it myself, barring accidents of course."

"Accidents . . . ?" Aldric echoed warily, leading the wizard's mount across to him.

"Unforeseen eventualities, then," Gemmel expanded unhelpfully. He slapped the Dragonwand as a man might slap the neck of a favourite horse. "I should be drained of strength," he said thoughtfully, "but thanks to this I'm not even tired." He wiped one hand across his forehead and grimaced at the streaks of moisture gleaming on his palm. "Well, not very."

The old enchanter took a box from his belt-pouch and flicked back the lid, turning the mist briefly blue as the radiance of the Echainon spellstone spilled from its confinement. Then it dimmed, as if the stone itself understood the need for secrecy, and everything returned once more to muted shades of grey. Gemmel smiled thinly and set it into the place where Aldric had long expected the stone to go: the vacant eyesocket of Ykraith's dragon-head. Though he did no more than push it firmly

home, the spellstone locked there as securely as if it had
been set by a master jeweller.

"That should stop cu Ruruc causing any trouble,"
Gemmel muttered. A trumpet yelped and he was forced
to leap aside as a small troop of horsemen came thun-
dering out of the fog, pennons fluttering in the wind of
their speed. Then he laughed. "Of course, he may have
more than our whereabouts to concern—"

"*Altrou,* mount up! Move it!" Aldric's yell was not in
the tone of voice which suffered questions and Gemmel
obeyed instinctively, vaulting into his saddle more nim-
bly than seemed reasonable in a man of his years. He
had barely slid the Dragonwand into a scabbard meant
for javelins when four of the riders came back.

Aldric met them head-on, transfixing the nearest with
his lance so that man and weapon tumbled to the ground
together. A sword shrieked on his helmet as he rode
through the others, bludgeoning one of them off his
horse with the iron-rimmed shield as he passed.

Lyard wheeled under the pressures of heel and rein
as Isileth Widowmaker came hissing hungrily from her
scabbard. Gemmel was lost somewhere in the fog and
Aldric hoped the old man was all right—then, as another
horseman came boring in with a flanged mace in one
hand, he stopped worrying about other people and became totally concerned with himself.

The mace-head boomed against his shield, driving it
back against his body, and then rose to swing downwards
at his head. Widowmaker licked out, sank half her length
into the exposed armpit and wrenched free with a sucking noise. The mace flew out of sight and its owner
sagged forward, coughing a fan of blood across his
horse's neck before sliding from the saddle.

Aldric grunted thickly as a blow across his armoured
shoulders drove the breath out of his lungs. He lurched,
recovered, warded off another stroke with his hastily-
uplifted shield and kicked Lyard into motion, cursing the
stupidity which had allowed this man to close. Then the
mace—another mace, dammit!—smashed against the plates
of his left bicep and that whole arm went numb and
useless, the shield slipping from limp fingers.

Aldric said something savage—against himself for not

keeping the shield-strap round his neck—and met the man in a brief, vicious hacking match where his skill at *taiken-ulleth* gave him all the advantages. It ended abruptly as Widowmaker sheared away both the mace and the hand which held it, then opened the rider's unprotected throat with an adroit backhanded sweep.

The Alban wheeled his mount again just as the man whom he had clubbed down with his shield came lunging with a shortsword towards Lyard's head. That was a mistake; with an outraged squeal the stallion reared and slashed out with one steelshod hoof, smearing the attacker's features into oozing scarlet pulp. Aldric gentled the stamping, snorting Andarran courser, trying hard to get his breath and at the same time restore feeling to his bruised left arm. Gemmel walked his own horse closer, looking not too carefully at the carnage—nor very hard at Aldric either, for the moment. The old man had never watched a *kailin*'s training put to use before, and even from the vague and hazy images which he had seen through drifting fog, he was sure he had no inclination to see it done again.

Aldric stared at his expression of controlled disgust for a few seconds, then smiled sardonically. "Yes. It's rather different from mere practice, isn't it, *altrou-ain?*" he said. Without too much mockery.

"How did you know that they were enemies?" was all Gemmel felt inclined to ask at the moment. Aldric dismounted and recovered his shield—the lance had broken—then wiped Widowmaker carefully and slid her away.

"I saw their armour. It isn't any Alban pattern that I know of, so I was warned. When they attacked us I was sure." He mounted, with a thoughtful look visible within the trefoil opening of his war-mask. "If Kalarr has hired mercenary horsemen, then some of his footsoldiers might be hired as well . . ." he speculated to himself, wondering where the thought might lead. More trumpets shrilled, some distant but one or two too close for comfort, and he put the undeveloped notion from his mind. "Forget it. We'd better go—I don't know what that troop was doing here, and I'd rather not stay to find out. Follow me, *altrou*. Quietly."

"Do you know where you're making for in this fog?" Gemmel sounded dubious.

"I think so." Aldric grinned, almost, but not quite, with honest amusement. "I hope so. You'd better hope so too."

*

On a clear, bright day the citadel of Dunrath-hold could just be seen from where King Rynert set his standards on the crest of Embeyan Ridge, but on this particular mid-morning there was nothing but a wall of grey vapour into which his soldiers faded like figures in a dream. Despite Gemmel's advice he was reluctant to deploy his forces in such small units as the wizard had suggested: instead he had resorted to a troop formation culled from the battle manuals every Alban general carried on campaign, a flexible disposition of mutually supporting staggered regiments known as a "dragon's head" on the forward slope of the ridge. Whether it would be successful was another matter, because although the regular foot soldiers could be relied on to obey their orders with precision, aristocratic *kailinin* and their household warriors would tend to go their own way—which, since nobody could see more than fifty yards in any direction, was something Rynert doubted would be the right way so far as he was concerned.

There had been a brief skirmish with the enemy cavalry an hour before; scouts, maybe a tentative probing of his defences—perhaps even those village-burning raiders. Either way they had been repulsed with heavy losses. But they had been human, not *traugarin*—men able to think for themselves rather than automatons. Rynert wondered if there were more, guessing in the affirmative and not liking his conclusions. Such men where they were not expected could prove a danger out of all proportion to their numbers . . .

The legions rattled and clinked as buckles were drawn tight, swords eased in scabbards and helmets pulled down just that little further. Then the noises stopped and the silence returned, a vast oppressive stillness which proved just as frightening as the more normal sound of an enemy host taking up position.

Not that such a sound had been heard on Alban soil for long enough . . .

Rynert suddenly shuddered, just once but so violently that it made his armour rattle. He frowned, wondering why . . . and then stripped off a gauntlet, licked one fingertip and held it up. The frown deepened to a scowl and a soft, venomous oath hissed past his clenched teeth. A wind was rising. It was little more than a movement in the air, but already the threads of mist had ceased their sluggish weaving and were drifting determinedly with the breeze.

Growing thinner even as he watched.

*

"The fog's begun to blow away!" snapped Aldric, swinging round on Gemmel. "You told me that it wouldn't! What the hell is going on?"

Gemmel had half-expected such an outburst, so when it came it did not cause him much concern. "Wind," he replied coldly. "An ordinary thrice-damned wind. About the only thing I didn't cast securing-spells against."

"Why not?"

"Have you any conception of the sort of power required to hold this fragile stuff in place?" Gemmel flared. "I doubt it! So don't ask bloody stupid questions!"

"But . . ." An icy emerald-green glare from under the wizard's eyebrows made Aldric hesitate, if only for a second. "But isn't this Kalarr's work?"

"Of course not! He'd rip himself to tatters with the strain of any such attempt. And before you ask, no! Duergar's maintaining the *traugur*-charm, so it's not his doing either. This is just a breeze."

"Just a breeze." Aldric allowed himself a hollow, heavily sarcastic laugh. "So there'll be a battle anyway, despite all the plotting."

"There'll be a bloody massacre if Rynert doesn't follow my instructions. Not that we'll be here to watch it if we're not under cover by the time this clears completely."

"That would never do, now would it." Heeling Lyard to a canter, Aldric vanished momentarily and was smil-

ing bleakly when he trotted back. "But you don't have
to worry on that score. Over here, *altrou*. Quickly!"

Gemmel did not move, but watched Aldric through
narrowed, thoughtful eyes until the *eijo*'s gaze refused
to meet his own. "What score are you worrying on?" he
wondered softly. "The men you killed?"

The black helmet nodded, once, then turned so that
the expression within its mask was unreadable. "Yes. A
little. There was no difficulty, no risk to me. I was better
armoured, better armed . . . It was like killing children."

"Children don't carry maces, Aldric. They don't try
to break your bones. Put it out of your mind, boy."

"Easily said," muttered Aldric. His *tsalaer* creaked as
he drew in a slow, deep breath, rising in his stirrups to
stretch like a cat. "Yes . . . easily said. Follow me."

A clump of trees congealed from out of the fog and
Aldric rode straight into their shadow, Gemmel at his
heels. One coppice looked very much like another to the
enchanter, and he wondered what made this one different. Aldric told him briefly: seen from north or south
the tree-trunks formed a cursive "tau" for Talvalin,
while the east-west outline was the uncial "hai" for *hala-
than,* the old name for a bird shown spread-winged on
a crest. Such as clan Talvalin's eagle. Despite his tension
Gemmel chuckled at the simplicity and deviousness of
it all.

"What is this anyway?" he wanted to know as Aldric
tethered Lyard to a branch. "Dunrath's back door?"

"Sort of. More a last-ditch exit, though. In the bad
old days just after the Clan Wars, if there was any sort
of risk a servant would bring horses to this area—not
straight to the trees, obviously, but close enough. If he
had to escape from his own fortress, a clan-lord and his
family could meet here—or if necessary come up—" he
leaned inside a hollow stump and pulled something with
all his strength, "here!" The whole stump shifted sideways, revealing the mouth of a tunnel dropping into
darkness. "Most fortresses as old as Dunrath are riddled
with such passages," the *eijo* continued, "but they usually have just one like this—leading beyond the outer
walls."

"Who told you about it?"

"My father, years ago. It's known only to the *cseirin*-born—the lord's immediate family."

"Then won't Baiart have known about it—and betrayed it?"

"Yes—and I hope, no. None of the retainers or vassals knew of it, so those two swine can have had no suspicion of its existence. And Baiart may have kept it secret in the hope of making his escape some day."

"May have . . . ? That's flimsy, Aldric. Almost reckless."

Clambering down, Aldric felt about with his feet for the steps he half-remembered, then nodded grimly. "I know that. But there's one way to be sure, and I'm prepared to risk it. Are you?" He descended out of sight with a scrape and rustle of black steel, leaving Gemmel alone with the disinterested horses.

The old enchanter looked around, hoping perhaps for inspiration, but saw only that the mist was growing uncomfortably thin. Pushing the Dragonwand's inflexible length through his belt like some oversized sword, he swung his lanky frame over and down. "I'm right behind you," he called, then grinned briefly to himself. "As if there was another choice."

*

By the sun, a straw-pale disc in a chilly azure sky, it was almost noon. Rynert sat uneasily on a camp-stool, baton in hand, and watched the flags and banners round him ripple in that accursed wind. At least now his fighting—or rather, his evading—would be that of a sighted rather than a blind man.

His troops looked neat even though they had been permitted to stand down for their midday meal; this did not reassure the king much, since by all accounts Lord Santon's legion had been equally neat—before the catastrophe.

Dewan ar Korentin, looking odd in his close-fitting Imperial helmet beside so many in the peaked and flaring Alban headgear, stood a little farther down the slope, tapping his own commander's baton against one knee in a nervous, jerky rhythm. The uneventful waiting was beginning to erode even his iron nerves, and Rynert wanted to get up, talk to the Vreijek—do anything to silence the annoyingly irregular tap-tap-tap.

Then it stopped. More than one of the officers on the ridge turned to stare at the sudden silence, heard the distant, hollow muttering which had caused it and shifted their gaze to the ridge north of Embeyan. Dewan cleared his throat and pointed with his baton, a long, slow arc which took in the entire horizon. "Gentlemen, to your places," he said quietly. "Here they come."

Helmets twinkled in the sunlight all along the crest of that far ridge, becoming a line of men who advanced at a measured pace to the sound of drums until the skyline was clear, and then stopped. Another rank of soldiers followed. Then another, and another, and another, until the ridge was black with men. A trumpet blew, its notes thinned by distance, and the line contracted, splitting into wedges faced with overlapping scarlet shields and bristling with spears. Wedges which came trundling ponderously down on to Radmur Plain.

The Alban horns and drums were signalling now, and couriers were galloping down from the generals on the ridge. Each regiment shifted into more open order as the enemy approached, ready to repel attacks from horsemen they could kill or to avoid the *traugarin* they could not.

With the advantage of height, Rynert could see cu Ruruc's host take up their own formation and grinned harshly with reluctant admiration. What he could clearly see as a wide-flanked "swallowtail" encirclement would from a lower vantage-point—such as that of a regimental commander—appear to be the classic "spearhead" of a frontal assault. As simple and as deadly as a stab in the back, thought Rynert. Quite in keeping with Kalarr's reputation. It seems he has guessed I will not meet him unless he forces me to do so.

Drums thudded among the distant wedges and a solitary horn wailed dismally. The red shields began to lumber forward, slowly but inexorably drawing closer. Ar Korentin, mounted now, waved his baton towards Lord Dacurre's cavalry, unleashing them against cu Ruruc's horsemen. It would give the haughty, hard-to-control *kailinin* a chance to do something useful, whereas the likelihood of their doing something stupid increased the longer they were held in check.

Arrows flickered between the riders as they closed with one another, then the Albans returned bows to cases and twirled out their long spears in the same movement, hefted shields high and ploughed into the enemy with a great howling crash. Men were unseated or skewered on both sides in that first shock, and suddenly the two galloping ranks had passed through one another with the trumpets on both sides already screaming recall.

Rynert watched, trying to remain dispassionate as a general should be but aware of a racing pulse and sweaty hands. Other commanders gave way to their excitement with shouts and waving of batons, leaping from their seats for a better view or hammering iron-clad fists on armoured knees. The king extended his own baton, signalling his foot-regiments to fall back and concentrating on their disciplined manoeuvres in an effort to push the drama of the cavalry duel to the back of his mind. Then he heard somebody swear harshly and looked up, not believing what he had heard. Although it was true.

A troop of Kalarr's horsemen came jinking wildly towards Embeyan Ridge with Dacurre's crack household troops hard after them, bows drawn and shooting as they rode. The *kailinin* were clearing saddles at almost a hundred yards and yet still were not gaining enough.

Because these mercenaries were coming for the king.

*

A glow of fox-fire hung around Ykraith's uplifted point, mingling with the shimmer of the Echainon stone to give enough light to see by—if only just. "I'd like to see a little better myself," Gemmel replied in answer to Aldric's complaint, "but I keep thinking of others who might then see *us* as well."

Aldric did not argue further; the silent darkness had begun to play tricks on him, producing footsteps from inside his head and shapes which turned out to be no more than the witch-light reflecting off pieces of quartz, drops of water and even once from the tips of his own eyelashes. He had been along this tunnel only once before, and that was fourteen years ago. In consequence his memories were hazy, and what he did recall reminded him inevitably of the Cavern of Firedrakes. That in itself was enough to make him feel uneasy.

The passage turned a sharp corner and they stopped suddenly, their way blocked by a wall of dry-laid stone, "Your move, I think," said Gemmel and held the Dragonwand aloft, letting his power flow into it until the fox-fire swelled and grew, driving back the shadows so that Aldric could see whatever it was he had to do. "Where does this open on to, by the way?" the wizard put in quickly. "If it's somewhere that might now be the guardroom, I'd like to hear about it rather than find out."

Aldric showed his teeth in a sour smile. "No need to worry over that, at least," he said, and pushed one of the stones back into the wall. Muffled rattling told where counterweights were drawing down long-unused chains, and a doorway ground slowly open. Aldric permitted himself a sigh of relief. "It would have been my luck for the thing to have rusted to pieces," he muttered, and made for the doorway. Then he laughed throatily, stepped to one side and bowed low in a bitter mockery of manners. "I bid you welcome to my house, Gemmel-*altrou*," he said, and waved the old enchanter through the door.

The chamber beyond was vast, lined with old supply-bins and thick with long undisturbed dust. Cobwebs draped their grey shrouds over everything, and there was a musty odour of decay. Gemmel's witch-light showed traces of footprints; they were faint, but still indicated where one large and one small pair of feet had gone out and back in again. Aldric stared at them. "My feet, years ago . . . and my father's." He cleared his throat and walked quickly away, as if to leave his memory behind. Heavy grey clouds rose in his wake and settled again without a sound, already blurring the old footprints and the new.

There was another door at the end of the chamber, which opened with only a slight creak from its hinges. Hesitating on the threshold, Aldric nodded slightly and made a curious little gesture with his right arm that Gemmel did not understand until he was inside.

Then he too made the small salute of respect which honoured generations of Talvalin dead. The crypt was filled with blocks of stone, some elaborately carved, others merely polished and inscribed. More recent burial markers were smaller, upright columns containing not coffins but the ashes of cremation, and he caught up with Aldric beside one such, knowing from the stela's shape that the cinerary urn it held was that of a woman, and guessing without being told whose was the frail-featured pretty face etched into its surface.

"My mother," Aldric said, not looking up. There was a barely discernible catch in his voice. "She died when I was born. My father's place should be at her side . . . except—" The words faltered and his eyes glistened, blinking rapidly in the soft, pale fox-fire. Then Gemmel actually saw the glisten of one emotion become the hard and gemlike glitter of another. "But that's why I've come back."

*

Rynert stared incredulously as the enemy riders came surging up the slope towards him, feeling like someone taking refuge from the spring tide atop a sandhill. This was ridiculous: such suicide charges went out with formal challenges, single combats and the taking of heads. While he did not relish death, Rynert would have accepted being out-thought and out-fought, by a better general—but he seethed with indignation at the prospect of being cut down by a . . . a bloody anachronism. He remained seated, but set down his baton and put that hand to his *taiken*'s hilt. Although the blade remained undrawn.

It was not necessary. Dewan's personal troops, the Bodyguard cavalry, formed a solid wall of men some twenty feet in front of the king, knee-to-knee and four ranks deep in the Imperial manner. They poured down on Kalarr's men with the irresistible shock of a flash flood, breaking what little formation remained and sweeping them away in a swirling mellay. Which pounded them out of existence.

Rynert forced himself to ignore what was happening in order to issue more commands to his infantry, grouping some to draw a charge, scattering others away from

the sluggish futile assaults of heavy *traugur* wedges. The
Deathless Ones would roll right over any men they came
to grips with—but had found the Alban soldiers quite
impossible to catch.

Dewan trotted up, dismounted, saluted and bowed.
Rynert looked at him, at what he carried, and asked
himself what was happening to the modern warfare he
was waging. Ar Korentin went down on one knee and
laid a severed head at the king's feet. "Their captain,
king," he said. "There were no other illustrious person-
ages in that attack." Rynert scratched his nose with the
end of his baton, wondering if he was involved in a
dream or perhaps some overly-elaborate joke. He stared
at the head. Yes, its hair had been combed before pre-
sentation, as the old books said it should be. Illustrious
personage, thought Rynert with a small tremor at the
outdated mode of address, if this is a joke I cannot see
how you can possibly find it funny.

"Very well done, Captain ar Korentin. My congratulations on your war-skill." He had to force the words out
past the questions clustered on his tongue. Then yelling
resounded from the plain and he turned hastily from
unreality to fact, grateful for a genuine excuse to do so.
Beside him Dewan rose to see what was happening, and
Rynert heard him curse savagely between clenched
teeth. The king felt near to rage himself.

There had been at least one wedge of human foot
soldiers among cu Ruruc's host, and they had indeed
been thinking for themselves. Clad like the rest of the
wizard's army, they had moved at the typical slow pace
of the *traugarin* around them until they were close
enough to one of the Alban regiments, and had then
charged home with unavoidable un*traugur*like speed.
That regiment was now locked in combat, unable to ma-
noeuvre, while on either side real, deadly corpse-troops
wheeled and came marching in like so many wasps to
a honeypot.

Worst of all, instead of leaving the solitary regiment
to its inevitable fate as Rynert had commanded,
someone—the king suspected young Lord Andvar, who
had objected with great vehemence to such a ruthless

attitude—had sent four more regiments jogging down the slope as reinforcements.

Reinforcing a broken tide-wall with a bucket of wet mud, Rynert thought viciously. He glanced up at the cluster of vermeil banners along the distant ridge. This is just what you've been waiting for, isn't it? he demanded silently. From the distant yelp of trumpets and the waving signal flags, cu Ruruc's answer was a stark and simple *yes*.

*

"You see, Lord," the mercenary captain told Kalarr. "It is much more difficult to hold an army back than to send it forward." He could almost feel the glow of satisfaction welling from the scarlet-armoured figure at his side.

Cu Ruruc's steel-sheathed fingers opened wide like a clutching metal talon, then closed slowly to a fist. "I have you, King of Alba," he hissed. "I have you now!" Rising in his stirrups, he made a great sweep through the air with his flail. Drums rolled and all across the plain his uncommitted wedges broke, reforming in a crescent which moved forward to outflank the Alban host, to buckle its formations and encircle it. Before annihilation.

"Good," Kalarr purred softly as he watched. "Very, very good. Now, my dear captain . . ."

"Sir?" The mercenary stiffened in his saddle.

"These are your final orders. I need no prisoners, since all who fought here are my enemies—so kill them. Kill them all!"

*

"Where is everyone?" Aldric whispered. "No guards, no retainers, no servants. Nothing."

"All gone to the battle," Gemmel replied just as quietly. "Cu Ruruc has stripped the fortress. He wants to make absolutely sure this time."

"He should have made absolutely sure that nobody would be creeping about behind him . . ." Aldric lowered Widowmaker from across his back and made her scabbard secure or his weaponbelt. "But where's Duergar?"

"Somewhere with a lot of floor-space. He's keeping

thousands of *traugarin* on their feet—that means he'll
need room for a gigantic conjuration circle."

"Then I know exactly where to find him. In the feast-
hall. Follow me." Aldric made off at a quick, stealthy
pace, flitting through the dim, familiar galleries in his
black armour like some ominous shadow from the citadel's past.

Gemmel followed, not too closely, for his sorcery-
honed senses had already warned him about the brooding
violence which hung about the *eijo* now. The enchanter's
fondness for his foster-son was tempered by a wary respect for Aldric's well-schooled viciousness, and he had
no desire to be within the arc of Isileth's blade should
the *taiken* suddenly be unsheathed.

Gemmel remembered thinking the young man was
frightening when they had first met. Now he was sure
of it.

Aldric stopped at the foot of a flight of stairs and
nodded towards the door at the top. "There's the hall,"
he murmured. Then his helmeted head jerked slightly.
"Can you sense anything?"

"No," said Gemmel softly. All I sense is the leashed
ferocity which you wear like a garment, my son, the
wizard thought to himself, but aloud he said: "Why, is
anything wrong?"

Aldric's frown was lost among the shadows shifting
within his war-mask. "I thought I felt, heard, saw . . .
something." Gemmel heard him suck in breath between
clenched teeth. "No matter. Come on."

He was half-way up the stairs when a *traugur* lurched
at him from a side-passage. Aldric jumped back with his
nose wrinkling at the thing's faint charnel stench—and
then gagged with disbelief and horror. It was inevitable
that such a thing might happen, but anticipation was no
defence against the queasy shock of recognising bloated,
undead features.

He had known this man long ago in Radmur; a
trooper in the City Watch and a drinking companion
who had often talked of joining the army in order to
look fine in plumes and metal. He must have done so—
joined Lord Santon's legion—and come to this.

There was rage in the sweeping stroke which Aldric

put through the *traugur*'s chest; rage, and great pity. Isileth Widowmaker clove the rotten flesh like cheese, releasing slimy foulness and a dreadful reek, but the corpse
refused to fall and instead chopped Aldric with its own
big axe. The *eijo*'s stomach heaved with the stink that
filled his nostrils, but he ducked the axe-blow and cut
through the creature's nearest knee, toppling it with a
sodden thump. Even then it tried repeatedly to rise,
while loops of wet intestine bulged greasily through the
hole torn in its body.

Aldric was almost sick at the sight and smell and
sound of it all. He waved Widowmaker at Gemmel, who
was standing near the bottom of the stairs, and snarled,
"Finish it, for pity's sake!" in a voice made thick and
hoarse with revulsion.

"Duergar might sense it if I—"

"Don't argue with me, *altrou!* Do it!"

Gemmel sighed and shrugged, then reached out with
the Dragonwand and, muttering something under his
breath, pressed its crystal point against the *traugur*'s
neck. It flinched back from the contact, twitched once
and flopped head-downwards, already beginning to sag
as its flesh commenced a dissolution which sorcery had
held at bay for almost a month. The enchanter fastidiously stepped across the wide dark stream of fluids trickling down the stairway and drew level with Aldric,
noting how white the young man's face had gone against
the black armour which framed it. The Alban said nothing, but turned quickly and all but sprinted up towards
the door.

For just an instant Gemmel thought that he had put all
sense aside and was going to burst into the hall, but then
the *eijo* stopped, listened and very gently eased the door
back just enough to let him through. Gingerly the wizard followed.

Inside was dark, the daylight kept at bay by curtains
over every window, and the air was heavy with the smell
of incense. It tingled with enchantments, a crawling shud-
dersome sensation which raised the hairs on Aldric's
neck and at the same time made him start to sweat.
There was the sound of chanting from the lord's dais at
the far end of the hall, one sonorous phrase punctuated

by the striking of a gong. After a brief glare of greenish light and a pause in which the threads of scented smoke grew thicker, the chant began again and the gong chimed its single note.

Gemmel recognised the spell; he had broken it not two minutes past, back there on the slimed and stinking stairs. It was a spell which held charmed undeath in *traugarin,* keeping their cold flesh from corruption, and it was a spell which would fade entirely if Aldric's mission was successful. If . . .

Duergar's unmistakable silhouette was plainly outlined by the glow of a charcoal brazier. Short, bald—and a perfect target. Aldric's left hand dropped towards his hip, then clenched in a spasm of black rage as he remembered that he carried neither bow nor *telekin.* All were still cased or bolstered in their places around Lyard's saddle—and might as well be on the far side of the moon for all the good they could do him.

Sliding along the shadows which connected each tall pillar to its neighbour, Aldric drew slowly closer until a single leap would bring him within lunging range of Duergar's back. This was one instance where he had no scruples about a thrust between an unsuspecting victim's shoulders . . . The necromancer had noticed nothing amiss; still chanting, he walked slowly to one side of the dais and returned with a slim rod, using it now to strike the gong, now to sketch an outline in the air. Aldric's hackles rose, but he tensed, moving a little clear of the sheltering pillar to be ready for the instant Duergar turned away.

The necromancer turned—then kept on turning, right around, his left hand thrusting out and the syllables of the High Accelerator tumbling from his lips.

Already gathered to spring forward, Aldric threw himself wildly down and sideways as the destructive shock whipcracked through where he had stood and punched a gaping tear right through the wall. Duergar looked down at the sprawling armoured body and began to laugh.

"You should not have destroyed one of my children, Talvalin," the wizard grinned. "Like any good parent I knew at once something was wrong." The *eijo* said nothing, trying to anticipate which way to roll if he was to avoid the inevitable second blast of power that would otherwise smash him to a pulp.

Something flared like midsummer lightning and a monstrous detonation shattered every window in the hall. Burn-stench swamped the sickly incense odour and when Aldric raised his face from the floor he saw a smoking gash ripped across the dais. It looked as if the very basalt had charred like dry wood.

"Why not test your skill on mine?" Gemmel's hard-edged voice was an arrogant challenge, a verbal slap in Duergar's face, and the Drusalan reacted accordingly with a throwing movement of one hand. Something invisible tugged at the curtains and the door against which Gemmel had been leaning exploded into kindling. "Impressive," the old enchanter observed sardonically from some feet beyond the target. "But slow. Very, *very* slow."

Duergar snarled wordlessly and levelled his wand. The end of it glowed orange-red like the mouth of a furnace. Then the thing belched death.

Gemmel replied with the Dragonwand and the smoky air of the hall was suddenly laced with streaks of flaring light and heat. Pillars erupted fire-cored smoke, fabrics flashed to crumbling ash. All was searing flame and noise and colour.

Aldric pressed flat and shut his eyes.

*

"If Aldric and the old man are going to do anything they had better do it soon," Dewan muttered to the king as he stared at the encircling shields. Rynert mumbled something under his breath. "What I wouldn't give for a clear charge across the plain," the Vreijek went on. "I'd scour that far ridge clean of Kalarr and—"

"Dewan, old friend, stop dreaming." Rynert's face was grim. "We're finished, and you know it. If the fog hadn't blown away . . . if Andvar hadn't broken ranks . . . if—"

"*If* you give up now, you might as well use your *tsepan,* king. And you're too modern in your outlook for such foolishness. We'll not be beaten until cu Ruruc can ride across this slope without fearing for his dirty life. And he can't do that just yet."

The ranks contracted a little more, swords and spears flickering about the iron-rimmed shields. Arrows slashed spasmodically through the air, and Kalarr's host drew their noose another notch tighter. More of the king's men died.

Rynert settled his own shield on his arm, then drew his *taiken* and made to throw the scabbard away. Instead, with a wry grin, he set it carefully across his camp-stool. "I'll collect this later," he told Dewan. "I wouldn't want the lacquer to get chipped . . ."

*

The mercenary captain's smile evaporated as he turned to look for more approval on Kalarr cu Ruruc's face. His master's features were pale and pinched like someone sick or starving and the sorcerer's mouth moved soundlessly. "My lord . . . ?" the mercenary ventured. "My lord, are you well?"

Kalarr jerked like a man awakening from nightmare and stared at the soldier with wide, wild eyes. "Something's wrong," he breathed. "I can feel it. Finish them off! Hurry!" His voice rose to a scream of fury. "I won't lose this time! Not again! I *won't!*"

Trumpets shrilled and war-drums thundered while messengers galloped across the plain with orders to hasten the killing. Kalarr watched them—at least his eyes followed them, though by their glazed dullness they seemed to see other things and other places. Then he reeled in the saddle, recovered himself and twisted round to glare towards Dunrath. "Talvalin . . ." he hissed. "So there you are! Trying to cheat me . . ." An imperceptible shiver passed through the *traugarin* and they seemed to falter momentarily. "No . . ." cu Ruruc moaned, swaying as his charger fretted.

"My lord!" The mercenary captain grabbed his arm, thinking the sorcerer about to fall, then flinched back from the snarl of feral rage which bared his master's teeth. "My lord," the man yelled hoarsely, "what in hell's the matter?"

Kalarr ignored him. He rode unsteadily to the crest of the ridge and stared at the distant spike-edged shadow of the fortress. "The chant," he mumbled. "Continue the chant. The charm is failing, damn you! Ignore Talvalin . . .

Duergar, you are betraying me . . ." Kalarr's roan stallion reared and squealed as its rider sawed savagely on the reins, filled with a sudden need to hurt. "Renew my host, you Drusalan bastard!" he shrieked, and rode like a storm for the citadel.

*

Aldric lifted his head in the sudden shocking silence and looked from side to side before he dared stand up. Duergar stood on the dais, Gemmel in the centre of the floor. Neither moved, but both had their open hands raised before them and the *eijo* could see a dancing, shimmering haze in the air. He did not need to be told that the first man to weaken would die in that same instant.

Then Gemmel spoke. His voice was weak, almost inaudible through the high, eldritch howl of power, but Aldric heard him clearly enough. "This is . . . your fight now," he gasped. "Take Ykraith . . . use it. Knowledge . . . will come . . ."

Aldric started to protest, then looked more closely at the old man's face; thin, drawn, streaked and mottled with blood from a score of splinter-cuts, it pleaded mutely with him to do as he was told. Without any questions—just for once.

Aldric did, and as he scooped the Dragonwand from the ground where it had fallen all other enchantment seemed to stop. Duergar was able to extend his hand and pronounce the Invocation of Fire, but Aldric made an instinctive parrying gesture with Ykraith and the billow of flame splashed impotently against an invisible shield yards short of where he stood.

"Duergar . . ." the Alban said gently.

The necromancer cringed as if he had been threatened with a whip, then lowered his arms resignedly to his sides. "Aldric . . ." he replied, and licked his lips. The *eijo* stared at him through slitted, vengeful eyes and raised the Dragonwand above his head in both hands as if it was a *taiken*, then swung the talisman down in a great slow curve until its crystal flame was levelled at the Drusalan's chest.

"I bring you a gift." Aldric's voice was flat and dispassionate. "Something you have cheated and defied for far

too long. I bring you death." He uttered no word of
power to give life to Ykraith—but the talisman took his
hate and focused it until it became a dazzling pulse of
force which hummed across the hall to enfold Duergar
Vathach in its white-hot embrace.

"No!" he wailed. "You cannot do this to me . . . !"
And then the energy enveloped him. His skin split and
blackened, peeled away until the bones showed through,
and his charring skull gaped its jaws in a soundless shriek
of anguish while a tongue of living flame licked past his
calcined teeth.

The fierce glare dimmed and faded into nothing. A
twisted, flaking charcoal thing lay shrivelled in a puddle
of its own still-molten grease. It was no bigger than a
doll, and it sizzled faintly, sounding and smelling like
meat too long in the pan. Duergar . . .

Aldric took a deep breath, flinching from the horribly
savoury odour which clogged his nostrils as he did so.
The Dragonwand dropped with a clatter to the floor. He
felt drained, sick and unspeakably fouled by what he
had done. The taste of revenge had been sweeter by far
in the anticipation than in the event. He wondered if it
was always so.

*

Radmur Plain was heavy with the silence and the stench
of death. Rynert's legions were still drawn up in a tight
mass at the top of Embeyan Hill, because to move from
their positions would have meant walking ankle-deep in
the morass of deliquescent corpses which Kalarr's army
had become between one swordstroke and the next.
Dewan ar Korentin tied a cloth around the gash in his left
arm, then secured another over his mouth and nose.

"I thought something like this might happen, king,"
he said. "Kill their master and the puppets die."

"He did it then." Rynert fingered his nose tenderly,
wondering if it was broken or not. The last few minutes
of the battle had been a savage brawl very different from
the dignified and elegant combats outlined in his war-
manuals. "Something about this whole business stinks,
Dewan—and I don't mean just because of that filth
out there."

"You're being suspicious again, king. Aldric-*arluth*

took an oath to destroy the necromancer and he has succeeded. That's all."

"Perhaps . . ." If Rynert noticed the use of Aldric's proper title, he gave no sign of having done so. "But I think we should get to Dunrath as quickly as we can. Kalarr's gone, and he's heading for the fortress. I'm sure of it." A retainer brought up the king's horse and Rynert climbed into his saddle. "Don't forget what I said about Baiart Talvalin, either."

Dewan nodded, then issued rapid orders about disposal of the carrion which fouled the hilltop; wood from Baelen Forest and oil from Dunrath featured largely in his instructions, to prevent some other necromancer at some other time from finding the same supply of raw material as Duergar had done. "If old Overlord Erhal had done this in the first place—" he began to say, then fell silent. "But he was killed, of course."

"So were many people," Rynert said. "It's a hazard of life."

*

"Aldric . . . ?" The voice was not Gemmel's and, coming from behind him as it did, made the *eijo* whip Isileth from her scabbard as he turned. "Go right ahead," said the man in the doorway. "I would welcome your edge."

"Baiart . . ." Aldric breathed, and lowered his *taiken's* point to the floor. To his own secret shame, he did not yet feel inclined to sheathe it. "Baiart—before Heaven, *why?*" The word came out sounding like a whimper of pain.

Baiart walked forward and smiled grimly in the smoke-diluted sunlight coming from the shattered windows. "Why indeed? To tell you properly would take me far too long, little brother. But . . . I wanted to live, Aldric. They caught me when I came back from Cerdor that first time; gave me the choice of life as their figurehead or . . . Or undeath as one of Duergar's creatures. I chose life. Existence, rather. I've been dead for years, except that Kalarr never chose to confirm it. He even laid a charm on me so that I could not use my *tsepan*. I was not even able to kill myself, Aldric. He took away the only privilege that I had left . . ."

Widowmaker's blade gleamed as Aldric returned her

to the scabbard at his hip; then he saw the longing in his brother's eyes and shuddered.

"Aldric,"—and this time the voice was Gemmel's—"he has the right to die by his own hand. You know that."

The *eijo* blinked and shook his head. "No . . . I won't. I *cannot*. Not my own brother."

"You don't have to. Give Baiart your *tsepan*—or would you rather watch his execution?"

"His *what!* He's *kailin-eir,* and entitled to—"

"To do something you won't allow, Aldric," Baiart pleaded. "Please . . ."

The younger man had no memory afterwards of handing either the dirk to Baiart or his longsword to Gemmel. But he must have done both, for the old enchanter came back moments later with both weapons in his hands. "It's over, Aldric," he said gently. "And Widowmaker's still clean," he added when the *eijo* seemed reluctant to touch her braided hilt.

"Can I see him, *altrou* . . . ?"

"I don't think—" Gemmel began, then reconsidered. "Very well. If you wish. There can be no harm in it."

Baiart had been covered to the chin in one of the few wall-hangings to survive the sorcerous combat of . . . was it really only ten minutes before? The dead man's eyes were closed, his limbs had been straightened and his face had relaxed from whatever pains had twisted it, into something very close to peace. Aldric gazed down at his brother and knew himself to be alone at last. Utterly, irrevocably alone. The thought no longer frightened him as once it had done. Stooping, he lifted one corner of the tapestry and laid it over Baiart's face—lightly, as if trying not to waken him.

"Is everyone in this damned fortress dead or deaf?" snapped an irritated voice. Gemmel and Aldric jerked round to face this new intrusion, though neither was really sure what to expect. The speaker was a tall man, in full battle armour covered by a leather *cymar;* his helmet had been pushed back and its war-mask hung from loosened laces at his neck, revealing a heavily moustached, sweaty face: the face of a man who has been hurrying. A light flail was tucked through his belt and a *taiken* was slung across his back—which meant that something was missing, if only Aldric could remember what . . .

"Who are you, *kailin?*" the *eijo* demanded. "And where do you come from?"

"I am a courier," the warrior responded shortly, "and I come from the battlefield. Rynert has the victory, and cu Ruruc is dead." He smiled at that.

His news gave Aldric little satisfaction. The manner of Duergar's passing had made him sick of slaughter, and with Baiart's suicide following so soon after, it was little wonder that the young man's mind was dull and introspective.

"This place is—or was—Duergar Vathach's citadel," the courier stated. Steel rang ominously as he drew the flail clear of his belt and looped its strap round his left wrist. "So where is he?"

"Dead!" retorted Aldric. "I killed him. As I promised." He felt Gemmel tap his heel surreptitiously with the Dragonwand and made a tiny gesture of acknowledgment with one hand, knowing what was troubling the old enchanter. It was worrying him as well; things were falling rather too neatly into place, and the alarms were screeching in his mind. As they had been from the moment he first saw this man. A small superstitious shiver crawled up the *eijo's* spine as he realised that under his blue leather over-robe the courier wore vermeil-lacquered armour. All the associations of that colour fought for prominence in his racing brain, each one uncomfortably close to the reality he faced.

No horseman could have covered the distance between Radmur Plain and Dunrath if he had left when the battle had been won. Even riding his mount into the ground, this warrior had to have left—Aldric calculated hastily—at least ten minutes before he could be sure which way the battle was going. And why was he wearing that flail instead of an honest *tsepan* . . . ? The *eijo* felt sure he could put a name to their visitor now.

"You must be Talvalin," the man said as he walked slowly up the hall, glancing from side to side at the extensive and still-smoking damage. There was a well concealed ugly edge in his voice which provoked a nervous whisper of warning from Gemmel. Aldric ignored it, but braced his feet a little wider and waited for events to develop, flicking wary glances towards the flail swinging lazily from the "courier's" wrist. "I've heard about you, *ilauem-arluth,*" he continued as he stopped two arms'-lengths away and bowed fractionally.

By rights the use of his full and proper title should have drawn a much lower bow from Aldric, but nobody except Gemmel knew the rank was his. Apart, that is, from someone who guessed the significance of the honourably laid-out body on the floor. Someone like the scarlet-armoured *kailin* facing him.

Someone like cu Ruruc.

"I have wanted to meet you for a very long time, Lord Aldric. To give you my commiserations; to give you my compliments; and to give you—*this!*"

Though he had anticipated such a move, the flail slashing at his face almost took Aldric by surprise. Almost ... but not quite. In his eagerness Kalarr had misjudged his distance and had come too close.

Instead of ducking away from or under the stroke, Aldric threw his full armoured weight inside its arc, smashing one shoulder against cu Ruruc's belly. All breath went out of the sorcerer's lungs in a single throaty grunt and he staggered backwards, dodging the fingers which jabbed towards his eyes by pure luck and with mere inches to spare. Even then Aldric's hand flattened out and its steel-sheathed edge slammed solidly below cu Ruruc's ear, where the flexible mail-and-leather coif was no protection against percussive blows.

Kalarr was dazed and horrified. Grappling in armour was a skill he had disdained as being beneath his dignity, and the discovery that Aldric had no such dainty notions was a painful one. No man wearing *an-moyya-tsalaer* ever fought barehanded—its weight alone made the metal harness into an impressive bludgeon, and when its plates and scales were coupled to techniques such as the *eijo* was employing, even a clenched fist became as lethal as a mace or blunted axe.

The wizard struck out once more with his flail, in an effort to make his adversary back off rather than do damage, and Aldric blocked it by catching the weapon's chains on his left arm—his shield having been lost when Duergar first attacked him. With that shield, or with any other weapon, the parry would have worked, but not with this one. The chains slapped hard against his vambraced forearm, curled round it and sent their spiked and weighted tips lashing on towards his face. Had those chains been two links longer the Alban would have lost his sight, but he escaped with bloody grazes as they got just inside his war-mask and no further.

As he flinched aside, Aldric clamped his fist shut on the two chains which had wrapped around his palm and heaved with all his strength. The weapon's haft wrenched from Kalarr's grip, hesitated as its leather wrist-strap took the strain for almost two seconds before snapping, and then whirled with a clatter over the *eijo*'s head and out of sight.

"Now, Aldric!" barked Gemmel. "Draw now and finish him!"

"Let be, *altrou,*" Aldric replied quietly. "Everything in good time."

The softness in his foster-son's voice made Gemmel's skin crawl as his sorcery-trained senses read below the voice to what had caused it. What he saw there chilled him and made him take several long, slow steps backward, away from the spot where the inevitable clash would take place. And well away from Isileth Widow-maker, whose hunger had become as tangible as heat or cold. "Not too far!" It was more an order than a request, and Gemmel halted in his tracks. "Watch this one for magic," Aldric continued, "and if he tries to cast a spell, you can obliterate him with my blessing. But otherwise, keep out of it."

Kalarr's eyes narrowed, wondering if this was all just hollow bravado . . . or something more. Then his thin lips writhed into a grin and he swept his *taiken* from the scabbard high across his back. "I need no spells, Talvalin," he said, and laughed. It sounded slightly forced.

"Considering your past performance, you need something, *pestreyr,*" the *eijo* observed. "Feel free to try."

The sorcerer flicked a glance at Gemmel, who smiled

pleasantly back at him. "Don't interfere with this, old man," cu Ruruc growled threateningly. The enchanter shook his head.

"I wouldn't dream of doing so. But I hope that you know how to use your sword."

"Know how . . . ?" Kalarr's voice was incredulous. "I've forgotten more about the *taiken* than this whelp could know. He's dead, old man. And so are you."

"I doubt that very much." returned Gemmel calmly. "For two reasons. I have the Echainon spellstone"—cu Ruruc's slitted eyes dilated as they fell upon the glowing jewel—"and have you looked at Aldric's *taiken*? I don't think you have, somehow. Not carefully enough."

Aldric unhooked the longsword's scabbard from his weaponbelt and pulled its shoulderstrap across so that the sheath rose slantwise to his back, well clear of his legs. He was conscious that Kalarr was staring dubiously at him, and the knowledge provoked a thin and mirthless smile within the shadows of his war-mask. Then he gripped the long hilt rearing like an adder by his head, twisted it to loose the locking-collar and drew.

The faint slither of steel as Isileth slid free of her lacquered sheath was by far the loudest sound in the hall. Louder than the beat of Aldric's heart, louder than the blood whose rushing filled his ears. And far, far louder than the tiny indrawn gasp as cu Ruruc saw what Gemmel meant at last.

"Isileth . . ." he whispered, feeling an old, long-forgotten pain begin to burn the knuckles of his sword-hand.

"Isileth," echoed Aldric. He said nothing more. The time for words was past. Instead, moving with as much care as if under instruction from his swordmaster, he assumed the ready posture of high guard centre and waited for Kalarr to make his move.

After pulling down his helmet and lacing its war-mask tightly into place, the sorcerer adopted a counter-position and slowly circled his opponent. Then he screamed hoarsely as he sprang and cut.

The blades met in a series of blurred strokes before they shrilled apart as both men glided backwards, each analysing the other's fighting style. They met again, more cautiously now, a tentative stroking of steel on steel before the single explosive clangour of cut, parry and stop-thrust which drew threads of glistening scarlet from Aldric's left wrist. Kalarr was good. Very good. But the *eijo* could still use his injured hand, so he was not quite good enough . . .

Or so Aldric hoped. The initial flare of agony had faded from the wound, leaving in its wake a sullen throb of pain which indicated no real harm was done. Though when he took up the waiting attitude of low guard left, it was imperfect, suggesting that there was a weakness in his bloodied wrist. A lesser swordsman than Kalarr would not have seen the error, and a better one would never have been drawn by the potential trap. Cu Ruruc fell between the two.

Darting forward two quick paces, he slashed viciously towards the proffered opening—only to find that opening no longer there and Widowmaker stabbing at his throat. With neither time nor room in which to dodge, he charged right on to the waiting point and jolted to a stop as it took him squarely underneath the chin. Clawing at the blade, Kalarr went lurching sideways as it withdrew.

Then he regained his balance and lunged in turn, so fast and so ferociously that Aldric did not block the stroke in time. Gritting his teeth against the wave of black and crimson anguish threatening to swamp his senses, the *eijo* jerked himself away from Kalarr's sword. It had jabbed between the joints of his *tsalaer* and gouged a long groove in his hipbone. Had it not skidded there, he knew the blade would have transfixed him—small comfort in that knowledge, true, but comfort of a kind. He was not dead yet, at least . . .

As for cu Ruruc's mangled throat, Aldric could see it closing up before his eyes, ripped flesh running like hot wax until in seconds there was only the torn coif to show a thrust had ever been received. Some healing-spell at work, he guessed: made by Kalarr himself. Did you really expect a sorcerer to rely on armour by itself? Not in your heart, no. So start to think, man! Quickly!

Kalarr laughed harshly at the shock on Aldric's pain-blanched face, then pressed home his attack. More blood

spurted onto the black-lacquered armour and smeared
the tiled floor underfoot. It came from small cuts,
wounds without importance in themselves—but the very
fact that Aldric suffered them was like a premonition of
the end.

It seemed to Gemmel that his foster-son was fighting
in a dream, his reactions automatic and often far too
slow. Spells began to fight for precedence within the old
enchanter's mind, but none were selective enough; all
required at least some space between the duellists if both
were not to share the same fate. Then abruptly Gemmel
realised what it was he had to do. "Ykraith, Aldric!" he
yelled above the clamour. "Use the Dragonwand!"

Aldric twitched as if he had been stung, and the fog
of pain cleared somewhat from his eyes. That was the
knowledge he had been seeking, the reason why his
mind had not been on the fight. Breaking ground, he
enveloped yet another thrust in a sweeping circular
parry, trapped cu Ruruc's blade in Widowmaker's deep,
forked quillons and twisted it from the sorcerer's hand.
He sent the weapon skidding out of reach with a kick
from one booted foot, then as Kalarr dived after his
taiken, Aldric ran the other way. "Here, *altrou!*" he
cried. "Throw it!"

The Dragonwand flashed across the hall as Gemmel
hurled it like a javelin, but it landed in the palm of
Aldric's hand more like a falcon settling on a trusted
perch. If he had expected his several wounds to heal at
once, the *eijo* was mistaken—but if he had expected Kalarr to be dismayed, his wish was more than granted. As
the Alban swivelled on one heel and lashed out with the
talisman, cu Ruruc flung himself out of its path so hastily
that he almost fell.

"Now, warlock . . . shall we try again?" gasped Aldric,
levelling Ykraith's carved dragon-head at Kalarr's face.
"With the odds not quite so stacked against me this
time, eh?" He assumed a *dyutayn* position, handling the
Dragonwand as he would a second *taiken.* "Well, come
on, you scarlet bastard," the *eijo* hissed, teeth bared in
a tight-lipped feline snarl. "Or must I go after you?
Come on!"

Kalarr whirled his sword down in a blow to shatter

armour and go cleaving on through flesh and bone, but the great cut never landed. Aldric sidestepped, warding off the blow with Isileth as he began a gliding turn. Both blades met amid a shower of sparks and a steely screech before Kalarr came charging past, carried by the momentum of his fully-harnessed body.

Ignoring what it did to his torn hip, Aldric slewed his upper body round and stabbed out with Ykraith. Its crystal flame drove between cu Ruruc's shoulders, punching through lamellar scales as if they were thick parchment, and the Echainon stone flared so blue and vivid that for just an instant it cast shadows. Then its light went out.

Cu Ruruc chuckled thickly as he reached behind him to pluck the Dragonwand out of his flesh as if it was the sting of some small, irritating insect. There was no blood either on its point or on his back.

Aldric said something under his breath as the sorcerer turned once more to face him, this time with both sword and talisman outstretched. When he saw the young man's startled, disappointed face, cu Ruruc laughed aloud.

He was still laughing when Widowmaker scythed down onto his helmet, splitting its vermeil metal and the coif beneath, silencing his laughter, dazing him. Echoes of the impact rang down the pillared hall. Kalarr reeled, and the weapons slithered from his nerveless fingers to clash against the floor. A thin, bright crimson trickle wandered down his face, as if the battered helmet bled.

Aldric looked at the blood, the pallid skin, the dark, unfocused eyes, and drew a long breath deep into his lungs. His armoured fingers clenched the braided leather of Isileth's long hilt, double-handed, tighter, tighter, the blade beginning to tremble as his energy came boiling up as it had done against Duergar. Except that this way was the *kailin*'s way, *taiken-ulleth*, and clean.

"No . . . my son . . . !" The *eijo* winced as a daggerlike feeling of memory and loss bored into him, and stared again at Kalarr's face. It was . . . changing. Shifting even as he watched to a blue-eyed, white-bearded, lovingly remembered outline. A face that had been dust and ashes these four long years, and yet . . . Something hot and painful swelled up in the Alban's chest; his throat

grew dry and choked so that the name he spoke was
just a muted whisper.

"Haranil-*arluth* . . . ?" Aldric whispered, wanting to
believe. "Oh, father . . ." The wise, dignified face smiled
benignly from inside its vermeil war-mask, then the figure leaned forward slightly to lift something from the
floor. There was a faint sound of steel.

And the charm broke. Haranil's face crumpled, became again cu Ruruc's visage grinning past an upraised
longsword—and collapsed again into a smear of oozing
ruptured tissue. Kalarr's spell had not been illusion but
true Shaping, an enchantment of High Magic that his
weakened body was unable to maintain. And for which
he paid the price.

Widowmaker blurred out in a single thrust that had
four years of grief and hatred riding on her blade.
"Hai!" Aldric shouted as the *taiken* hammered home,
an unstructured, formless cry that unleashed power from
deep inside him to drive the longsword half her length
in armoured bone and muscle.

Isileth burst between the *tsalaer*'s lacquered scales,
snapped two ribs below and sliced the vessels leading
from the wizard's heart, then slowly, slowly twisted one
half-turn before she wrenched free. This time blood
spewed from the wound as if from any ordinary man
and spattered on the floor with a sound like rain, laying
ruby droplets over Baiart's shrouded face and on the
once-more softly glowing stone of Echainon. Aldric
backed away, his features immobile, wondering why he
had not taken off the suppurating head. To leave it on
was to invite a dying curse . . . although cu Ruruc should
have been beyond the power of speech.

Yet he was not. Slumping to his knees, Kalarr stared
upwards at his slayer's face, lips fumbling to shape the
words that refused to come. "It seems that . . . all
along . . . I have underestimated you, Talvalin," he
croaked at last. His mouth twisted briefly as a spasm of
pain ripped through him; then it relaxed and even tried
to form a smile. "Sh-should have known . . . a better k-
killer than myself." He coughed and pink froth dribbled
down his chin. "Foolish, I . . . I'll not make . . . that m-
mistake . . . ah—! again . . ."

The smile remained fixed as all life left his face, and he slumped forward into a final First Obeisance at Aldric's feet. The *venjens-eijo* stared down at the corpse for several seconds, oblivious to the gore that puddled boot-sole deep. His oath was fulfilled, his vengeance now complete. Was it sweet? Aldric did not know; all he could taste was blood and fear and sourness in his gullet. With a single double-handed sweep he lopped off Kalarr's once handsome head, but did not bend to pick it up. The thing repelled him.

Uttering a small sound lost between a snarl and a half-stifled sob, he kicked the grisly trophy out of sight.

*

"He is dead, Lord King. By his own choice and his own hand in the rite of *tsepanak'ulleth.* I . . . did not witness it."

"I see." Rynert looked beyond Aldric's respectfully bowed head and caught Dewan watching them both with an odd expression on his face. Almost like a smile. "You knew," the king continued, "that such a suicide would forestall my seizing Clan Talvalin's lands? *If* I intended such a step."

Aldric looked up, and all the stiff-lipped pride of sixty generations was frozen on his face. The grey-green eyes remained unreadable. "Of course I knew it, *mathern-an.* If I said otherwise I would be a liar or a fool. But my concern was first and foremost with my brother's honour. Believe me or not, as you will."

"I believe you, Aldric-*arluth.*" Rynert used that title quite deliberately, watching for a reaction. It was not what he had expected.

"I would . . . would plead exception from the title for a while yet, Lord King," the young man ventured softly. "I was never trained for it and . . . *Mathern-an arluth,* this citadel holds memories for me; too many for my peace of mind. In a year, maybe. Or two. Appoint a castellan to hold this place for me—until I come back."

"Come back from where, my lord? Valhol, perhaps?"

"I think not, Lord King. The memories are there as well, you see."

"Then if you should venture to the Empire—"

"*Mathern-an,* why should I do that?" Something in his

tone of voice suggested Aldric's question was not as
naïve as he made it sound, and Rynert let a faint smile
cross his face.

"As a favour to your . . . to a valuable, high-ranking
friend, shall we say?"

"Why not? I may well visit the Drusalan Empire after
all. Sometime or other."

"When . . . *If* you do, then convey, ah, certain messages of some delicacy to my allies there. Prokrator
Bruda and—"

"Lord General Goth?"

"Quite so. You know what the situation of the Empire
is; those two want no more wars of conquest and especially no invasion of this realm. They need my personal
assurances that I believe them. You, Lord Aldric, are of
sufficient rank to carry such assurances. Certain codes
and phrases will be implanted *here*"—Rynert almost, but
not quite, touched his fingertips to Aldric's head—
"where they will be forgotten by yourself until Goth and
Bruda speak words which will release them. Only then
will you remember. Do you understand me?"

Aldric understood—and did not like it very much. "Is
that all?" he asked, a little sharply. Rynert smiled again,
without amusement now, and shook his head.

"Not quite. If there is any favour you—and Isileth—
can do to further prove my friendship, then I expect it
to be done. Purely as a token of good will, you
understand?"

"I probably do . . ." Aldric fitted a sardonic, careless
grin on to a face which did not want to carry it; then he
rose, bowed as a clan-lord and walked swiftly from the
room. He was uncertain which would have been more
hazardous, his acceptance or a blunt refusal. Somehow
he fancied the refusal would have made him feel more
comfortable . . . Then he shrugged. The thing was done,
one way or another.

*

It was chilly in the courtyard; the sun had not yet risen
and there were threads of mist hanging in the air. Aldric
swung into his saddle and with a packhorse in tow, rode
out of Dunrath and cantered east to join the Radmur

road. From the ramparts of the donjon, three people watched him go.

"Hold this place till I come back," King Rynert muttered, somewhat dubiously. "Now that we've let him go, will he come back at all?"

The rider and the sun crested the eastern slope together, so that he was lost in a glare of white light and golden vapour. Gemmel leaned against the battlements and watched, even though there was nothing he could see. The enchanter made no reply to Rynert's question. He might not even have heard it. Within the fortress walls, a bell signalled the coming of dawn.

"He will," said ar Korentin firmly. "Duergar and cu Ruruc learnt that much, to their cost. Aldric Talvalin always comes back. When it suits him, and in his own good time."

Warmed by the sun, the mist thinned from the empty ridge, then faded and was gone.

The Demon Lord

For Sandra
who knows why

Preface

"... and did take enseizen of Dunrath-fortress, where was yslayen HARANIL, most Honourable of LORDES, and with him nygh-all of clan TALVALIN ...

... which Exile was of four yeares. Upon his returning to Dunrath in company with RYNERT-KING and an hoste both of Horse and Foote, LORDE ALDRIC did by dyveres secret ways make essay to come unto ye citadel thereof, wherein was ye Necromancer Duergar Vathach. And there by poweres enstryven of that good Enchanter Gemmel, the same that did give him comfort in tyme of sore Distress, LORDE ALDRIC did bring Deathe most well-deserved to his foe and thus ykepen oath unto his Father HARANIL. And by HEAVENES grace (it is said) he did vanquish Kalarr cu Ruruc, who first fell and was yslayen at Baelen Fyghte but was restored unto lyfe for endoen of great Evill to this lande of ALBA ...

Yet took LORDE ALDRIC no delight in Victory, enhaven rather exceeding Sadness that all folke of his Blood were no more, and to ye KING made declaration of soche sorrowful Memories as were in Dunrath. Now to the wonderment and great Amaze of all then setten him forth into ye Empyre of Drusul to find forgetfulness.

But some privy to ye KINGES counsels noise abroad that this LORDE was bidden thence for his own Honoures sake ..."

Ylver Vlethanek an-Caerdur
The Book of Years, Cerdor

Peter Morwood

What is life, except
Excuse for death, or death but
An escape from life?

kailin-eir Aldric-*erhan*,
ilauem-arluth Talvalin

Prologue

The forest was titanic, stretching from the Vreijek border to the eastern edge of sight in a single unbroken sweep of trees. By its size alone it defied belief, but enforced that same belief with its own vast reality. The forest was not a part of the Imperial province known to men as the Jevaiden—it *was* the province. And yet few people lived there, for all its lush, abundant growth. The forest did not invite guests. It was too . . . strange. A thin fringe of humanity dwelt along its edges and some scattered villages had boldly sprouted up a small way within it. But nothing more. Except—on this day—for two impudent, intrusive specks.

Although it was no more than early evening and near midsummer, the forest was already growing dark. Thick, rain-swollen clouds had overlaid the sky with grey, choking all heat and light from an invisible sun. Within the shadow of the trees, where a tang of pine resin scented the air, it was cold and very still.

Until the stillness was shattered by a crash and clatter as horses moved swiftly through the undergrowth, bursting at a gallop from the bracken into a clearing where they skidded to a snorting, stamping halt.

There were three horses—one of them a pack-pony—and two riders. One of the men wore the greens and russets of a forester, and his high-coloured face was crossed by the crescent sweep of a heavy moustache. It was a cheery face, the land where smiles would be frequent, but he was not smiling now. "Satisfied?" he demanded, out of breath and irritable. "Content we've shaken them—if they were ever there at all . . . ?"

His companion did not reply. Ominous in stark, unrelieved black, looking on his sable horse like a part of the oncoming night, he gestured for silence with a gloved right hand and then rose in his stirrups, head cocked to listen for sounds in the forest that were not sounds *of* the forest.

There was nothing—until a crow cawed mocking comment of his unvoiced thoughts and spread dark wings in clattering flight from a branch above him. Its glide across the clearing ended suddenly and violently, when the horseman jerked a weapon from its saddle holster, tracked the bird for a moment and transfixed its body with a dart. He had half-expected the crow to change when his missile struck, and change it did—from a living creature to a bundle of black feathers flung carelessly against a tree trunk near the ground. The smack of its impact was an ugly thing to hear. One leg kicked, then relaxed . . . It did not move again.

"Lady Mother Tesh! It was only a crow, Aldric! Only a crow . . . !"

"I can see that now." Aldric Talvalin's voice was quiet and controlled. "But I do not like crows." Any further criticism was hushed by the *telek* still gripped casually in his ringed left hand. And by his eyes.

They were grey-green, those eyes. Feline. And they betrayed nothing of the thoughts behind them. If a man's eyes were the windows to his soul, as some philosophers maintained, then these windows had been locked and shuttered long ago. They were set in a face whose youth—he was not yet twenty-four—was masked by a studied veneer of weary cynicism . . . A mask which he could hide behind. Its skin was tanned, clean-shaven, but marred—or maybe enhanced in the eyes of some—by the inch-long scar scratched white along its right cheekbone.

"And, friend Youenn," he continued in the same soft voice, "I told you before. Within the Empire, I am no longer Aldric. Remember it!"

He was no longer so many things, for all that they had been regained with a deal of blood; some of that he had spilled with his sword, but some he had spilled from his veins . . . Aldric could still feel the echoes of pain deep inside him, from hurts to both body and spirit. *Ilauem-arluth* Talvalin. He had been clan-lord for so short a time it seemed only a dream. Unreal; like the others, those he drowned with wine to let him sleep. Lord of a clan which no longer existed and master of a citadel whose every stone reminded him of things he would rather forget. And which he would have forgotten, given time. Except that he had not been given time. Not now that he was here, to retain what he had regained by proof of his allegiance. By proof he could be trusted . . . By obeying his lord the king.

By killing a man he had never even met . . .

Aldric could feel moisture on the palms of both his hands as he returned the *telek* to its holster, and the knowledge of it shamed him. Yet he could not help it, for he loathed this place. He had realised that from the first moment he set eyes on its green sprawl beyond the town of Ternon. He loathed its silence, its claustrophobic gloom—and most of all he loathed the memories which it brought flooding back.

Once, in a forest much like this, he had been hunted. Harried through the trees like an animal, for sport. The terror of that time had been avenged a thousandfold, and he himself had never hunted since—but the memories remained, festering in the secret places of his mind like wounds that would not heal.

"I tell you," Youenn Sicard insisted, "so few people travel this part of the Jevaiden that almost any track is secret until you've travelled it yourself!"

"Almost," returned Aldric flatly, "is not enough. We were being followed." He seemed to dare the Vreijek to deny it. "And I'm still not sure . . ." His voice trailed off and a frown drew his brows together as he twisted in his saddle, one hand already reaching for the nearest holstered *telek*.

Then he kicked one foot from its stirrup and fell sideways, *kailin*-style, as something flickered through the space where he had been with an insect-whirr that ended with a noise like a nail driving home as it slammed deep into a tree.

Time seemed to run slow, each second minutes long. Aldric had sensed the arrow before he heard it, had not

seen it at all and had scarcely managed to avoid its flight.
The soft black leather of his sleeve parted in a straight
slit as clean as the stroke of a razor, the bicep beneath
marked with a matching pallid pink scrape where a strip
of skin had been planed away; for one long heartbeat it
seemed harmless, like the scratch left by a thorn. And
then it split wide open and his blood came pulsing out.

"Down!" the Alban screamed, pain edging the urgency in his voice as the wound began to hurt with all
the focused fury of a white-hot wire threaded into the
torn muscle. That pain, and the appalling shock of feeling his own flesh sliced open, could freeze a man for
long enough to die. It could also freeze an unhurt man
who had not seen such injuries before—and Youenn
gaped in startled disbelief, uncomprehending and un-
moving for that killing instant whilst his horse began to
jib as blood-reek filled its nostrils.

Two more arrows followed the first: humming-bulb
arrows, signalling devices used now for another purpose—
to frighten horses. Their shaped heads shrilled an atonal
ululation which horrified the Vreijek's untrained steed
and it reared as the missiles shrieked to either side,
squealing and fighting the air so that Youenn could do
nothing more than grip reins, mane and saddle in a frantic bid to keep his seat.

There was a crashing in the undergrowth at the far
end of the clearing and four horsemen rode clear of the
ferns and brambles. Aldric caught an inverted glimpse
of them under the arch of his own mount's neck:
bandits—or men dressed as bandits for some purpose of
their own, for no thieves that he knew of would ride
in military skirmishing formation with Drusalan guard
hounds at their heels. Ignoring the throb which now
stabbed clear from fingertips to shoulder of his left arm,
he swung upright—then saw three bows loosed and
ducked flat as the arrows wailed above him.

The sound which followed tore through that summer
evening like a thunderclap, penetrating with a dreadful
familiarity even the uproar caused by dogs and horses,
hoarsely yelling men and the hammer of Aldric's own
heart. It was a thudding slap, three impacts following so
closely on each other as to seem just one, and the Alban

knew what he would see when, regardless of the threat from other arrows, he glanced back.

Youenn Sicard clawed at a chest which sprouted feathers from a morass of bloody cloth. The shafts which Aldric had so cleverly avoided . . . At such close range they had driven fletching-deep to skewer everything in their path, and as the Vreijek sagged forward Aldric could see plainly where his back was quilled like that of a porcupine. Except that these barbed quills had pierced him through.

"No . . ." the Alban whispered, his voice thick with that awful helplessness he knew so very well. Youenn's glazing eyes met his with a puzzled question in them, and the Vreijek's mouth stammered open in an attempt to speak it. *Why me . . . ?* he tried to say.

But only blood came out.

The eyes dulled and rolled back in their sockets as the feeble glimmer of life-light drained out of them, and Youenn Sicard pitched headlong to the ground.

"No!" Aldric repeated uselessly. He had seen death too often not to recognise its presence now. Then something snapped within him and his lips drew from clenched teeth. If death was present, let it at least feed full . . .

Slamming heels against his courser's flanks, pack-horse perforce in tow, he charged headlong towards his enemies. Had they known Albans they might have expected such a reaction, but their ignorance took all four men off-guard.

Longsword drawn and in both hands as he passed between the foremost pair of horsemen, Aldric cut right and left in a single whirring figure-eight which emptied both saddles and left a glistening trail of scarlet globules on the air. Each time the sword-blade jolted home he felt the warmth of blood from his own wound splattering against his face.

As the remaining riders flinched away in horror, his black war-horse stumbled for an instant when its hooves crunched down on something softly yielding, then recovered as the screeching hound was pulped beneath steel shoes.

A single hasty arrow wavered after Aldric as he

plunged into the forest; it missed and went rattling harm-
lessly out of sight among the branches. One of the
horsemen nocked another shaft to his bowstring and
rode a few wary yards along the Alban's trail, which was
clear, distinct and would be easy to follow. The man
paused at that. Perhaps too easy . . . He glanced back
at his companion and saw a negative jerk of the head.
Both knew that if they pursued their intended victim
there was every chance that they might catch him. And
they loved life too much for that. With luck the forest
might succeed where they had failed—but there would
be no more pursuit.

Gasping, breathless and sweaty with pain and shock,
Aldric slackened his wild pace at last. The real wonder
about the past five minutes was that no low branch had
hacked him from his saddle . . . Memories, he thought
with a blurred mind—running like a madman through
the woods with an arrow-damaged arm. The longsword
was still clutched in his left hand, blade and fist and arm
all dark and crusting with the mingling of blood that
filmed them. He could hear nothing behind him—
nothing to either side—nothing ahead of him. Aldric
grinned a hard, cold grin without a trace of humour in
it. He had lost them. Then he looked back, remembering
Youenn, and the grin went sour and crooked. Not only
because the Vreijek guide was dead; but because without
Youenn Sicard, Aldric had lost himself as well . . .

1

Wolfsbane

There was a mist that silent morning. It shifted like a living thing in the darkness before dawn, insinuating pale tendrils between the trees with an icy intimacy. Sluggish coils eddied away as Evthan eased from the high bracken, then flowed back to wrap his buckskinned legs in a clammy embrace. The hunter shivered slightly as he knelt to study the vapour-shrouded ground; then his eyes narrowed and he paused, listening.

Somewhere in the gloom a bird twittered and burst into song. Evthan's eyebrows drew together at this ill-timed intrusion—thick brows, which met above his hawk nose even without the frown to join them. He was the best hunter and tracker in the Jevaiden, commanding high fees from the noblemen who came here in late summer seeking game; men said that the lanky Jouvaine could even think like a beast. Right now his thoughts were centred on what he had seen in the damp turf. Nocking an arrow to his bow, he slipped back into cover more quietly than he had emerged. Evthan was not afraid . . . not yet. Just very cautious.

There was a clearing ahead, edged by a stream running down from the edge of the Jevaiden plateau; he knew it well as a place to find deer, where they might come to drink. At first it seemed empty, and then the hunter realised that he faced a wall of fog. Even nearby trees were vague and uncertain through the milky translucence, and he was uncomfortably aware that in the denser patches anything at all could lie unseen. Even the Beast.

His mouth twisted, sneering at the half-formed hope.

It could not be his luck to have that target here today; as it had not been his luck this month or more. That was why Darath had sent him out. To find help. Another hunter. Someone who could kill the Beast. The headman did not know how he had wounded Evthan's pride with that command. Or perhaps he did . . .

The hunter's hands began to tremble. Darath's family had not been spared a visit from the Beast . . .

Evthan remained hidden in the undergrowth while the eastern sky brightened towards sunrise. A faint breeze thinned the fog. That small movement of the air brought a prickling of woodsmoke to the hunter's nostrils and his brooding was abruptly set aside. His thumb hooked more tightly around the bowstring as silhouettes emerged in the clearing, soft unreal forms still half-veiled by the mist. Evthan's held-in breath hissed smokily between his teeth. Tethered to the roots of a long-fallen tree, a pack-horse and a sleek black courser unconcernedly cropped the grass.

Standing near the same tree was a young man dressed in leather and fine mail. As Evthan watched curiously, the stranger secured a bandage around his left arm and flexed the limb experimentally, then nodded in satisfaction and began to buckle on more metal: scaled leggings, sleeves of mail and black polished plate, a cuirass laced with white and dark blue silk. He drew the last strap tight, picked up a sword which leaned against the tree trunk, then faced the dawn and knelt, laying the long sheathed blade across his armoured thighs.

Sitting straight-backed on his heels, the young man gazed full at the newly-risen sun for several minutes, heedless of its glare or of the drifting skeins of mist. They had become a haze of glowing gold, and he was himself outlined in countless points of light from the lacquered scales of his lamellar harness. These rustled faintly as he bowed low from the waist, and their leather strappings creaked a little as he glanced towards the trees. Then he shrugged and rose with easy grace to tend his horses.

Aldric had suspected for some time that all was not quite as it should be. More than ever now, he trusted such warnings when they pushed into his mind. The watcher, whoever he might be, had not used his advantage of surprise; if he was an enemy, that mistake would be fatal. Literally. But if he was a friend . . . ? Aldric dismissed the notion. He had no friends in the Jevaiden—or anywhere else in the Drusalan Empire, for that matter. Not since Youenn Sicard had been killed by the "bandits" whose motives the Alban was now sure had not included simple robbery. Especially when their victims likely carried—he grimaced sourly at his saddlebags— nothing but the Empire's worthless silver coins. Once five hundred florins would have made him a wealthy man . . . but not now. That was what sickened him about his guide's death; if, despite all appearances to the contrary, the attackers *had* been merely thieves, then the little Vreijek had died for nothing.

But that was why the half-seen shadow in the forest made him so nervous; there was no longer any honestly dishonest reason for an ambush—only intrigue and assassination. And counter-assassination, said a still small voice in the silence at the back of his mind. It was as if someone knew what King Rynert had commanded him to do, for all the elaborate secrecy surrounding it . . .

Aldric felt a bead of apprehensive sweat crawl from his hairline, and knew that beneath the armour his back was growing moist and sticky. The arrow wound in his left arm began to sting as salty perspiration bit at it like acid, and acting calmly required a conscious effort. Even then there was nothing calm about the memories of events two months past which tumbled through his skull . . .

*

"*Mathern-an arluth,* lord king, I have just regained this fortress—and now you tell me I must leave again. I have the right to know your reason for such a command." There was, perhaps, more outraged protest in Aldric's voice than proper courtesy permitted used toward the king, but Rynert let it pass. They were alone in the great hall of Dunrath-hold, in the donjon at the citadel's very heart, and the king's footsteps were echoing in the emptiness as he paced to and fro.

"Aldric-*an*," he said, his soft words barely carrying to the younger man's ears, "the only reason that I am

obliged to give is that I am your lord . . ." Several silent
seconds passed while Aldric digested this unpalatable
fact and his consequent emotions ran the gamut from
anger to resignation. For what Rynert said was no more
than the truth, "there is another way of viewing this, of
course," Rynert continued. "Despite your youth you are
still a high-clan lord—and *ilauem-arluth* Talvalin deserves at least the privilege of respect due his rank."

"I thank you for it, *mathern-an,*" Aldric responded,
carefully neutral, inclining his head in acknowledgement.
There was nothing that a glance could read from the
thoughts which drifted in the hazel depths of Rynert's
eyes, and simple caution forbade staring.

"You know of course what is said in the Empire about
the warriors of Alba, my lord?" asked Rynert suddenly.
Aldric did not—he shrugged and shook his head to
prove it. "They simplify—" the king hesitated, correcting
himself, "—they oversimplify the Honour-codes: all the
rules of duty and obligation which make us what we are.
They say: if his lord commands a *kailin* to kill, he kills;
and if he is commanded to die, he dies."

Aldric considered the stark statement for a few seconds. Then he shrugged again. "Stripped to the bones,
Lord King, but accurate enough."

"Then you accept this, Aldric-*an?* You accept this
bare simplicity of *kill* and *die?*"

Uneasy now, not liking the trend of conversation, Aldric nodded once. "I have seen both sides; I can do
nothing save accept it. Lord Santon and . . . And my
own brother . . ." The recollection hurt like an open
wound and his voice faltered into silence.

"Their honour commanded them to die and they
died," said Rynert. "The oath made to your father commanded you to kill." He paused in his incessant pacing
and gazed at the wall, looking beyond it to the battlefield
of Radmur Plain and the great mass pyres which still
smouldered there, streaking the sky with smoke. "And
you fulfilled your oath. Oh, yes. No man can deny it—
least of all Kalarr." His voice hardened. "And Duergar.
After the way you dealt with him . . ."

So that was it, thought Aldric grimly. Use of sorcery.

A clan-lord might well be expected—or indeed ordered—to perform *tsepanak'ulleth* for so flouting the cold laws of the Honour-codes. Santon had. Baiart had. Was it Rynert's intention that he should follow them along the same self-made road into the Void? "What is your word, *mathern-an?*" he said aloud to break the silence and the gathering tension. "Die . . . ?"

"Kill."

It gave Aldric little comfort. "Do I know the name?" he asked, and within him was a sickness, a rising terror that the answer would be *yes*.

"I doubt it. Crisen, the son of Geruath Segharlin. An Imperial Overlord. The father is an ally, the son . . . not. It is time that the account was settled. With finality. I trust Lord Crisen considers the gold he stole is worth its price."

"Gold . . . ?" echoed Aldric. Rynert missed the subtle nuances of that single word, missed too the flicker of disgust on Aldric's face as the younger man realised he was being commanded to kill a stranger for the sake of money, when bare minutes earlier he had been steeling himself against the thought of his own suicide for such an intangible thing as honour. He would have done that . . . but he was less sure about this. Something would have to be said, even though he did not now how to begin to say it. "I . . . I am *kailin-eir* again, *Lord King*"—Rynert's head jerked round sharply at the betraying stammer—"and you yourself said that I am *ilauem-arluth* Talvalin. But I cannot—"

"Cannot what?"

"Cannot . . ." and then the words came out in a rush, ". . . cannot be your executioner or your assassin. Not for gold. That would make me no more than a—" Aldric bit his tongue before it could betray him.

Less than four weeks past, he had been accidental witness to an exchange which neither he nor any other man apart from Rynert's bodyguard, Dewan ar Korentin, was meant to see. His king, his honourable lord, had given money to a masked and black-clad *taulath* mercenary. Within half an hour this same king had informed his War Council that the Drusalan Emperor was

dead. Perhaps the two events were mere coincidence—
or perhaps not. Aldric had kept silent and had drawn
his own conclusions.

He knew very little about *tulathin*—shadow-thieves, as
they were called on the rare occasions when decent men
spoke of them—but he knew enough. They had no honour. Only a love of gold which bought them. Gold hired
their unique talents of subtlety and secrecy and ruthless
violence for whatever task that ambition, politics or simple hatred might require fulfilled. A *taulath* would spy
on, steal, kidnap or kill anything or anybody for anyone
who could pay the price.

A king could pay it easily . . .

Keeping such thoughts from his face and eyes with an
effort, Aldric said softly, "That would make me no more
than a man without honour." And let Rynert take what
he would from the toneless voice.

"Your honour, my lord Aldric," snapped the king,
"requires obedience above all else. Obedience to duty,
to obligation—to me! So obey!"

It was not the reaction which the younger man had
expected. *"Mathern-an,"* he protested miserably, "why
choose *me* to be a murderer?"

Rynert stopped pacing at last. He turned to face his
unruly vassal and jabbed an accusing thumb at him.
"You speak as though you had never killed before. I
choose you because I choose you!" Then his taut,
almost-angry face relaxed and he flung both arms wide
in a helpless gesture. "And I choose you because I
must."

The king stalked to a chair, sat down heavily and
leaned back, steepling his interlaced fingers and staring
at them through hooded eyes before touching their tips
thoughtfully to his mouth. One booted foot hooked another chair and dragged it closer. "Aldric-*an,* sit down,"
he said. "You and I must talk."

Aldric hesitated a moment, then did as he was told,
perching uneasily on the very edge of the seat in a nervous fashion that ill-suited the third most powerful lord
in the realm.

Rynert gazed at him, noting stance, posture, carefully
neutral expression and involuntary betrayals such as di-

lated pupils and bloodless lips. "Aldric Bladebearer Deathbringer," muttered the king. "You have something of a reputation already, my lord. A reputation for strangeness, too; one that borders almost on eccentricity. You are . . . unusual. And you dismay people."

"People?" Aldric wondered, as suspiciously as he dared.

"My other lords. The way in which you recovered this fortress and fulfilled the oath made to your father was unconventional. You have—and now I merely report what I have been told—an unsettling, un-Talvalin, un-Alban aptitude for sorcery and no compunction about using it. Furthermore, you are a wizard's fosterling"— Aldric's eyebrows drew together and his mouth opened—"which is *not* meant as an insult, so think before you say something you may regret . . ." Aldric subsided. "But it means that this past four years you have lacked the support and the protection of your clan. You have learned to think for yourself, and the uncharitable see a young lord who appears to owe nothing to his king—no obligation, no duty and perhaps no loyalty."

Aldric nodded. Rynert's statements were logical and reasoned, beyond argument. "But why choose me for this . . . assassination?" he repeated.

"Because you have a better chance of success than any other man in my realm." The king said it flatly, without the warmth which would have made his words a patronising compliment. He merely spoke what he saw as a fact. "Those very reasons which require me to choose you, also incline me to choose you. My lord, your behaviour is not that of a *kailin,* or a clan-lord. But you are a man who holds to his Word of Binding, once that word is given—even if it is not a word strictly based in what my lord Dacurre regards as Honour . . ." Rynert allowed himself a smile at that: Lord Dacurre, Elthanek master of Datherga, eighty years old and inflexibly opinionated, was a by-word in his own lifetime for blinkered conservatism.

"And *mathern-an*—what if I refuse?"

The king's smile vanished. "Then you would forfeit"— he glanced around the hall, and by implication at the fortress and the wide lands which surrounded it—

"everything. For the sake of the men who died here, keeping faith. If you cannot be seen as equally loyal, you cannot be seen to rule."

Aldric shrugged expressively, but did not speak. There was nothing more to say.

It was Rynert who suggested the high-minded and blatantly selfish reason which Aldric put forward for leaving. That reason—that the atmosphere of the citadel upset him—was greeted with dismay and even anger but with little real surprise from those who knew the young lord. Or thought they knew him . . . After all he had survived in his long vendetta to regain the place, it might seem improbable that he would put it behind him: unlikely at best, false and a cover for something else at worst. It was strange.

But as Rynert said, Aldric himself was strange. And now he was the king's messenger, for good or ill. And an assassin, or a landless exile. The choice was his . . .

*

After working his fingers into mailed gloves and settling a helmet on his head, the warrior swung unhurriedly into his charger's saddle and nudged the animal with booted heels. As he rode past with his pony in tow, Evthan crouched out of sight and remained so until the beat of hoofs faded to silence. Then he straightened and scratched his head in confusion, for there were many questions in what he had just seen, but not a single answer.

Then behind him, someone politely coughed.

Aldric stood there, longsword drawn. Its point glittered barely a handspan from the hunter's throat, looking very bright and unsettlingly sharp. Evthan could see what might have been a smile, but the warrior's face was shadowed by his flaring peaked helm and by the warmask over cheeks and chin. Not that such a smile was reassuring—rather the reverse, for when the hunter dropped his bow in token of surrender, the sword rested its tip in the soft spot where Evthan's collarbones met and used this convenient hollow to push him backwards. Its blade was sharp indeed, for a thin trickle of blood began to ooze down his chest even though there was hardly any pressure after the initial prod. The wound

was not really painful, but the situation lacked dignity—
Evthan stood a good head taller than his captor and
could have knocked him flying with one hand. Except
that now this did not seem a sensible idea. Instead he
backed up as required, carefully and very, very slowly.

When they stopped the armoured man took a long
step sideways, out of Evthan's reach but not beyond the
measure of his longsword's sweep. A sword which now
hung indolently from one hand in a display of nonchalance which fooled nobody and was not intended to. Aldric had seen the rage well up in his prisoner's eyes and
though the man seemed to control it, did not intend to
offer him a chance to let it loose.

"What are you doing here?" He spoke in carefully
correct Drusalan, but did not trouble to conceal his accent. A little controlled confusion was never out of
place, just so long as he controlled it . . .

Evthan frowned, both at the question and at the voice
which uttered it. "I am forest warden," he retorted
sharply. "I should ask the questions."

"You . . . ?" Aldric rested his *taiken* in the crook of
one arm; its blade grated against the mail-rings of his
sleeve and its edges gleamed a tacit threat. He looked
from the comfortably nestling longsword to Evthan's
angry face and smiled a thin smile. "I think not. Now,
once again, who sent you?"

"Sent me? Nobody sent me—unless you mean my village headman."

"And what would he send you to find?"

Evthan's lips compressed and at first he said nothing.
Then, in a voice thickened by shame, he muttered: "Another hunter."

"A better hunter, maybe," observed Aldric, "than one
who lets an armoured man walk up behind him?" He
had selected the barb with care, and saw the Jouvaine's
facial muscles twitch as it struck home. Either the man
was a consummate actor, or he was what he claimed to
be. Relaxing slightly, he even spared a fraction of a second to regret the accuracy of the guess; but at least he
knew that the man's hostility was not just for him. "Another hunter," the Alban mused, half to himself. "To
hunt what?" There was no reply and he stared hard at

the other man, guessing again. "A wolf, perhaps?" he ventured softly.

Evthan flinched, as if expecting such free use of the word to summon its owner from the forest. "Not a wolf," he whispered. "*The* Wolf. The Beast!"

A moment's silence followed this enigmatic statement, broken by the steely slithering as Aldric ran his *taiken* back into its scabbard. So they need a hunter, he thought. And I need somewhere to hide in case there are more . . . bandits in the forest. The longsword's blade clicked home as he stared Evthan in the eye. "I can't just call you forest warden, man," he said, speaking Jouvaine now with a crooked grin to take the bite out of his words. "Say your name."

"I am Evthan Wolfsbane, *hlensyarl*," returned the hunter. He did not smile. "I am warden here for Geruath of Seghar, and in his name I greet you."

He might have thought the change of Aldric's expression came from being called *outlander*—the word was Drusalan and insulting—but he would have been more worried had he known the true reason for the bloodless compression of the warrior's lips.

Lord's-man, the Alban thought. Haughty, and proud of his rank. He let the subtle insult pass unnoticed for the sake of peace, being more concerned by the coincidence—if it was merely that—of meeting such a man as Evthan. Yet he sensed the hunter wanted him kept at a distance, almost as if the man was afraid of knowing him—or indeed of being known—any better. Aldric was not overly surprised, since he had been speaking the Empire's language. He knew the reputation of the Empire and that of its swordsmen; while Evthan continued to think he might be one of them, he might well think that Aldric would be worse than any wolf. Even this Beast he seemed to fear so much.

"I thank you, Evthan Wolfsbane, forest warden of the Jevaiden." Aldric bowed courteously, judging the inclination of his head to a nicety. "I am . . ." he hesitated, considering: ". . . Kourgath-*eijo,* late of Alba." Which was not strictly true, something made quite clear by his delicate pause. He explained no further.

Evthan had not expected him to.

"Tell me about this wolf of yours," the Alban commanded, settling catlike onto a tree trunk seat. His horses, summoned by a whistle, now stood in the clearing as if nothing untoward had happened—though both stared distrustfully at Evthan and would not come too close.

"The Beast," began the hunter, sitting down cross-legged and comfortable as he would at a council fire, "came to this forest at the end of the winter. Four moons past. He preys on more than Valden—my village—because there are many holdings in the Jevaiden, and for weeks we hear only the small wolves. But what man cares for them? Yelpers at night, runners after sheep. They are nothing. And we forget. Not the Beast, but his speed, his silence, and above all his cunning. All these are so much more than those of any other wolf . . . And then he returns." He fell silent.

Quietly Aldric took off mask and helmet, unlaced the mail and leather coif beneath and slipped it from his head. In token of trust.

"There was a meeting of elders at this new moon," Evthan said eventually. "They came from all the villages. It is now known that since he came among us the Beast has taken thirty people for his food."

"Thirty . . . ?" Aldric echoed softly, not believing. Not wanting to.

"Among them were my wife and little daughter."

"*Mollath Fowl,*" the Alban breathed, his oath seeming half a prayer. "I am sorry." Even as the words left his mouth he knew they sounded hollow. He had sensed a tingling of tension since riding into the forest country five days before, and had thought it a reaction to his own narrow escape, or maybe the proximity of the Empire. Now he knew differently. But so many deaths, and the killer still at large in this land famous for its huntsmen . . . ?

Might not—the thought arose unsummoned—might not this Beast be more than it seemed? He wondered that Evthan had not voiced the same suspicion, for the hunter was no fool. But he was superstitious: he had feared to name the Beast aloud, because to speak of evil was to risk inviting it. And once invited . . . Aldric knew

the consequences of an unwise invitation all too well.
And if Evthan shied away from saying "wolf," then he
would never dare to name—the Alban found his own
mind unwilling to complete the word—whatever horror
roamed the forest after dark.

"So brave, this Beast of ours," he heard the hunter
mutter bitterly. "Women, old folk and children. Never
a full-grown man to make him earn his meat."

"Not brave." Aldric's voice was flat and toneless.
"Clever. Too clever." He tightened girths, set boot to
stirrup and mounted, then swung in his saddle to stare
down at the Jouvaine. "I think it's time this . . . wolf
was dead."

Evthan bowed, accepting the unspoken offer. He had
seen something bleak in the young man's grey-green
eyes which had turned them cold and hard, like jade
encased in ice. They made him shudder.

After a time Aldric glanced down again. Evthan was
striding tirelessly beside the black Andarran charger,
matching Lyard's haughty pace with ease; but he had
the look of someone in a daydream—that was more than
half a nightmare . . . *Why?* Aldric wondered to himself.
He saw a sheen of perspiration forming on the Jouvaine's long-jawed face—much more than the mild day
justified—and was uncertain whether he should interfere,
or wait and hope to learn something. Then as thatched
roofs appeared between the leaf-thick branches, he
found an excuse to speak. "There's your village, hunter,"
he said, watching Evthan closely. "A bowshot yonder."

The Jouvaine blinked, seeming to return from a place
that was far beyond the forest, and drew in a trembling
breath. He recovered his composure with an effort and
met Aldric's unwinking gaze with another. "Best I lead
the way, Kourgath. Since the . . . the Empire's troubles
we—"

"Are not over-fond of armoured riders? Yes. So I can
believe." Reining in, he dismounted and unhooked his
sword, hanging it from the saddle near his lesser bow.
"Walk on. I'll be behind you."

The rest—that this was where he would prefer to
stay—he left unsaid.

*

Valden was tiny, a cluster of lime-washed cottages huddled in a clearing hacked out of the living forest. The newly-built stockade which ringed it kept the trees at bay but gave the place a grimly claustrophobic air, that of a fortress under siege. Aldric could almost smell the fear. He guessed that many shared his feelings as to the nature of the Beast, but not one dared to voice the thought. People stopped the tasks they listlessly performed and watched with dull-eyed resignation as he entered the stockade. They had lost faith in their hunter long ago and were fast losing hope; they might have left the village had the forest not surrounded it, but they did nothing now. Except await the Beast.

He understood the hunter better now, realising the cause of his black mood. Valden's despair was an infection which needed cautery to cure it. Destruction to bring healing . . . The destruction of the Beast.

After what Evthan had told him, Aldric was surprised to find two women in the hunter's house. "Aline, my sister," the Jouvaine explained, "and Gueynor, my niece." That would be the girl who backed nervously into the shadows as Evthan brought his guest indoors. "I hoped I would return with . . . company, so I asked them to prepare a meal. It will be better than my poor efforts."

Aldric was grateful and said so—not only for the food, but for the chance to shed the lacquered second skin of steel whose weight he could endure but not ignore. Typically Alban, he insisted on taking some time to wash and change before the meal, and used some of the privacy thus afforded to rearrange the contents of his saddlebags. He distrusted everyone on principle, and while Imperial florins might not be worth much, such a quantity as he possessed could well prove cause for comment. And there were other things which he preferred that no one saw at all.

When they had eaten, Evthan pushed back his chair from the table and coaxed life into a long-stemmed pipe with a taper from the fire. Everything was so comfortable and—and ordinary, Aldric thought—that he could have forgotten the atmosphere outside quite easily had it not been for Gueynor. Cradling his wine-cup, he shot a speculative glance towards her. She had stayed, seemingly fascinated, but at the same time he had seldom seen a girl more clearly terrified. Why, he could only guess: fear of the Beast, of himself . . . or her uncle, maybe? Did Evthan lash out at the remnants of his family when the helplessness became too much for him to bear? Or was she frightened *for* him, for his loss of reputation, for what a stranger's presence and success might do to the little self-esteem that he had left? Aldric did not know.

What he did know was that her high-boned cheeks and braided pale-blonde hair were achingly familiar. There had been no women in his life since he left Alba, although more than one had caught his eye; but Gueynor was somehow . . . different. She wore the usual loose blouse and skirt, tight boots and bodice, all embroidered and quite plainly her best clothes. That too was strange. Their eyes met and he smiled.

At that instant a deep, sonorous wail rose and fell out among the trees. Gueynor gasped, her gaze tearing away from Aldric towards her uncle's face as if expecting to see—or startled not to see—some sort of reaction. The hunter was very calm; he breathed out fragrant smoke and looked at the girl, then briefly towards Aldric. "The Beast," he said, "is in our woods again."

The Alban rose, set down his cup—noting sourly that his hand transferred a tremor to the surface of the wine—and crossed slowly to the open window. Everything was very still. No birds sang, not even a breeze moved the air. The world seemed shocked to silence by that dreadful, melancholy sound. And inevitably the unbidden images coiled out of his subconscious, souring the wine-taste underneath his tongue. He had not drunk quite enough to drown them . . .

It was a dream. And within the dream was nightmare. Snow falling, drifting, a white shroud across a leaden winter landscape. Out of that stillness, the sound of tears and a buzz of glutted flies . . . The smell of spice and incense and of huge red roses . . . Flame, and candlelight, and the distant mournful howling of a wolf beneath a silver full-blown moon. Pain, and the gaudy splattering of blood across cracked milk-white marble . . .

Turning, Aldric leaned against the wall and stared at Evthan. "Are you quite sure that thing's a wolf?" he demanded bluntly. It was perhaps an effect of the light, or of his black clothing—or of some thought passing through his mind—but for a moment the Alban's face had blanched: not to a natural pallor, but as stark as salt. Then Evthan blinked and Aldric moved and the image, like those which had created it, was gone.

"I told you before," the hunter said quietly. "Not a wolf. *The* Wolf." He drew again on his pipe while Aldric lifted his discarded wine-cup and studied the contents, realising how very much like blood was the dark wine. Then he sat down and for a moment closed his eyes, trying to clear his mind, to impose some order on the thousand thoughts which tumbled through it.

"But what," he asked eventually, "does your Overlord say about all this? And what has he done?" He waited for an answer, but heard not even an indrawn breath.

There was still no answer to his question when his eyes opened, and he looked from side to side with a carefully-schooled expression of mild curiosity which would never have deceived anyone who knew him at all well. However, neither Jouvaine knew him even slightly . . .

"Has anything been done by Geruath at all?" he asked again. Gueynor glanced at her uncle, and from the corner of one lash-hooded eye Aldric caught a glimpse of Evthan's answering nod. What that meant, he was unsure—but the very fact that he permitted her to speak, and that she required permission in the first place, was interesting. If "interesting" was the word he wanted, which he doubted very much.

"The Overlord's son—Crisen—sent messengers once," she said, very firmly as if daring him to deny it. "They were asking about . . ." Gueynor met the Alban's intent stare and her voice faltered and then tailed off, once more becoming nervous and uncertain. "They asked all of us about . . . about . . ."

"About *what*?" Aldric prompted. There was no answer. "You tell me, Evthan," he asked over his shoulder without turning round.

"She doesn't know."

"Obviously. That was why I asked you." His abrupt-

ness was deliberate; Evthan was proud and if insulted
might well lose his temper, forgetting whatever mask of
innocence or ignorance he was hiding behind.

In the event, however, Aldric was to be disappointed.

"They asked about the Beast," Evthan said flatly, and
instead of becoming loudly angry he grew stiff-necked
and haughty. "May I remind you, *hlens'l,* that you are
guest in this my house, and—"

A strange attitude for a peasant to adopt, thought Aldric sardonically. "And I intend to help you hunt this
Beast!" he snapped. "But before then I deserve to know
about it! I think I have that right, at least! *Estai
tel'hlaur,* Evthan?"

The hunter looked abashed. Proud he might be, but
he was embarrassed and ashamed by his outburst. "I do
not deny it, Kourgath. Your pardon."

Aldric nodded cold acknowledgement and drained his
wine-cup down to the bitter dregs, then clicked it firmly
back on to the table.

"I want," he said, "to see your blacksmith."

"I'll take you to him, Kourgath." Gueynor was on
her feet at once without noticing how, for a heartbeat's
duration, Aldric had failed to respond to his assumed
name.

Evthan, saying nothing, waved them both from the
room. Gueynor led the way, not trying to talk. The man
who had smiled at her had seemed younger than the
not-quite-twenty-four he claimed, but now with face taut
and humourless he looked much older, disturbingly solemn and in no mood for idle chatter.

*

The smith showed Aldric where everything was in his
small, well-appointed forge, then found himself dismissed by a curt nod. Gueynor remained behind, watching with unsettling attentiveness. Aldric was certain he
had let slip nothing that was not already suspected, but
even so her interest disturbed him. "Doesn't anyone in
Valden own a hunting dog?" he asked.

The girl twitched, apparently emerging from some
very private inner world to which she had retreated.
"Laine bought two," she replied. "After the Beast came.
But he uses them to catch deer."

"They'll do." Aldric jerked his head towards the door. "Go speak to him. And better take your uncle. This—Laine, was it?—might not want to put his hounds at risk." Gueynor hesitated. "All right, then leave your uncle out of it. But go!" She went.

And directly she was gone he pulled the bag of newly-minted florins from inside his jerkin, shook a dozen into a crucible and pushed them deep into the fire. Working hastily, he pumped the bellows until sparks whirled up and the charcoal panted from dull red to a blaze of yellow.

Aldric was sweating, and not just with the heat. He dare not be caught, not now he had begun to melt the silver coins. His ideas, theories, suspicions were made plain there in the fire—and, moreover, what he meant to do about them. The less was known about that, the better; because he was scared of what might happen in this damned strange place with its damned peculiar people. They might panic . . . and in that panic, somebody would die.

A glance from the doorway told him no one was about so, slipping out, he headed at a run towards the stable where his gear was stowed. There were arrows underneath one arm when he came back—and nocks, beeswax and untrimmed fletchings in the other hand to answer awkward questions.

Born into one of Alba's oldest high-clan houses, he had been educated as well as any and better than most; though the Art Magic was neither approved of by clan-lords nor taught to their children—as well as knowledge about subjects that were far from wholesome. No matter that he had heard the howl at midday in bright sunshine, the moon tomorrow night was full—and he was far too cynical to trust what legends claimed were the limitations of a werewolf.

Then he stopped, with a freezing sensation knotting his stomach. Someone—or something—was moving in the smithy. Reversing one of the arrows and holding it like a dagger, Aldric drifted noiselessly through the door and then sideways, away from the betraying brightness at his back.

Gueynor had not heard him come in—probably she would not have done so had he kicked the door wide open. But she turned anyway, very slowly, and when he saw her face he lowered the arrow.

"Why did you come back?" The rasp in his voice was born of tension, no more. "There's nothing here to interest you," he added when she remained silent. It was then he saw what dangled from her fingers: his money-bag.

"Coins," the girl said dully. "Silver coins. And others melting." Her eyes swept his face, then slid down to the arrow. "So you—you *do* think that . . ." She took several gasping little breaths, fuelling the scream he sensed was building up inside her. "I—I thought . . . I hoped . . . but then . . ." Her voice was getting shrill. "You don't just think! You *know!* Or else you wouldn't—" Her hand jerked convulsively, fingers clawing at her face, and florins chimed across the floor. "It's true, isn't it? You know, and it's . . . it's—"

"A precaution, nothing more!" He cut into her hysteria with an iron-edged snap that was the vocal equivalent of a slap in the face. The scream died still-born and a tiny, desolate whimpering was all that escaped her lips; when Aldric put his arms around the girl he felt her shiver at the touch. "Gueynor," he said more softly, "I have been wrong before."

"But what if you're right? It means that the Beast is—might be . . ." She began to cry.

Aldric winced inwardly. He knew what she meant. Werewolves had no choice in the matter of their changing, and no control over their bestial counterparts. They were victims, just as much as those they killed—and they might not even know about the change . . .

Just what had Gueynor and Evthan been concealing from him? Why did Crisen Geruath want to know about the Beast and then do nothing? What was happening here? And how much had Rynert known of it when he selected Aldric as his emissary?

"I don't want you to fret," he murmured, cupping her chin with one hand and wiping away her tears with the other. "Or to tell any one else about this. Please. Because I could be wrong. And probably am." Very gently he kissed her cheek, smiling thinly at the chaste gesture, and just for a moment with the touch of her skin still warm on his lips was tempted to do more. She was so very like Kyrin . . .

Aldric shivered slightly, realising what it was about the girl that had attracted and intrigued him. It was a bittersweet memory which the Alban had tried to dismiss and did not like to dwell on. And yet that . . . difference . . . remained. He frowned and backed away, shaking his head as if waking from some convoluted dream, then with a courteous little bow ushered the puzzled Gueynor out. And locked the door behind her.

There were silver coins and steel-tipped arrows on the floor. Aldric stared at and through them, then squared his shoulders and turned towards the forge. There was still work to do.

*

Evthan was standing outside the smithy when the Alban finally emerged. Both men looked at one another silently, neither wanting to be the first to speak. Then the hunter cleared his throat. "I spoke to Gueynor," he began.

Aldric watched him but offered no response.

"She saw how you looked at her, and—and thought to pay you for the Beast's life. We can't do so in coin . . . But you—you . . ."

"Threw her out? Nothing so violent, I hope. I had my reasons."

"You are . . . strange." It was not an insult. "And you acted honourably with my niece." Evthan hesitated, searching for the right words. "If—if the worst should happen, I would not have you sent into the Darkness by our rites without someone to name you truly. For the comfort of your spirit. And Kourgath is not your true name, my friend. I—I beg pardon if I offend."

"You do not." So you know a little Alban, Aldric guessed. *An-kourgath* was the little forest lynx-cat he wore as a crest on his collar—it was not a proper name, only a nickname and that rarely. And what else do you know that I have yet to find out . . . ? He gave the man a formal bow of courtesy, no irony or sarcasm in the graceful movement or on his face. "My name is safe enough with you, I fancy, Evthan Wolfsbane."

"Do not, if—" Evthan started to say, but Aldric hushed him with a gesture and a crooked smile. Six days ago—Compassion of God, so long already?—had things gone otherwise his only funeral rites would have been those of the kites and the ravens. Like Youenn Sicard . . .

"Somebody should have my name," the Alban said. "If only to remember me. I am Aldric Talvalin. I was *kailin-eir, ilauem-arluth*—a warrior of noble birth and a lord in my own right. Once. Now . . . now I am *eijo*, landless, lordless, a wanderer on the roads of the world." Again the sour smile twisted his lips, and the darkness was on him again as it had not been since the humming-bulb arrows came warbling in and hammered Youenn dead from his saddle to the dirt . . . "Can you blame me if I seek some peace in anonymity now and then?"

Evthan drew his own conclusions from the young man's sombre words. "You were involved in the fighting that we heard of?" he asked. Aldric nodded—it was true enough. "And you left Alba as a consequence?"

"Persons of rank and power suggested it."

"A mercenary." Evthan seemed content now. "Some have already guessed as much. But we protect our friends, Kourgath. You are safe in Valden."

What about in the woods? thought Aldric. Aloud he said merely, "I thank you for that," then pushed the arrows he was carrying into his belt. Without his hand around them the gleaming heads were plain to see—and plainly not just steel.

Evthan gestured at them, and the Alban saw how the hunter's blue eyes narrowed to conceal the fear which flickered through their depths. Gueynor had kept her secret, as he had asked, and now his own stupidity had revealed it. His oath was no less venomous for being silently directed at himself.

"Those are . . . interesting," Evthan muttered. "No one else suspects the Beast might be . . . not just a wolf."

Liar, Aldric said inwardly. Apart from himself there was Gueynor, Evthan and Crisen Geruath—and what had provoked interest from that quarter anyway? The other two had good reason to know, and to be afraid of what they knew, but Crisen was the Overlord's son: he should have had no curiosity at all about the doings of peasants. And instead he had sent messengers asking about the Beast. . .

Unanswerable questions of his own flashed through Aldric's mind and he glanced northward, in the direction where he had been told the Geruath hold of Seghar lay. "I told Gueynor that these are only a precaution," he said quietly, then drew in a long deep breath and looked up at the sky. "Time we began. Get the dogs—I'll see to my own gear." He watched the Jouvaine's back as Evthan walked away, and twitched one shoulder in a little shrug. Any hunt today or tonight would be a waste of time, at least for the quarry he hoped to flush. But tomorrow could prove another matter. Especially after moonrise.

*

His arming-leathers were sturdy enough for hunting, but despite that it was only after long deliberation that he set aside his battle armour, knowing that the *tsalaer* was far too heavy. Even so he detached both armoured sleeves from the cuirass and strapped them on beneath his jerkin, just in case. With rather more regret—and the courtesy which she deserved—he unhooked Isileth Widowmaker from his weapon-belt and set the *taiken* in her accustomed place on his saddle. He had come to regard the ancient longsword as a luck-piece, and disliked being separated from her by more than the length of his arm, but he knew she wasn't practical for hunting. Hunting animals, at least.

The *tsepan* dirk remained, of course. That was a matter of self-respect; a *kailin* could leave off rank, and family, and name—but never the suicide blade which preserved his honour.

Aldric decided on the shorter of his two war-bows, it being more easily managed among the trees than the seven-foot-long assymetrical Great bow, and belted the weapon's case around his waist before sliding the silver-headed arrows in beside it. In addition to the special arrows he picked out half-a-dozen more with bowelraker tips, heavy flesh-tearing shafts which were meant to stop anything unarmoured dead—or shockingly maimed—in its tracks. And he removed one of the two holstered *telekin* which hung to either side of his saddle.

Like Widowmaker, the spring-gun was not a hunter's weapon, but it had distinct advantages over a sword—principally that of range. This one could project its steel darts with fair accuracy and considerable force for some twelve paces—almost forty feet—and could do so as fast as Aldric could crank its cocking-lever and squeeze the trigger. Adjusting the holster's straps and laces until it hung snugly against the left side of his chest, he drew out the *telek* and turned it over in his hands. It was a beautiful thing, if a weapon could properly be called so; its stock was not the usual walnut, but lustrous maple wood carved and shaped to fit his hand so that aiming was as natural as pointing a finger. Unlike the *telekin* he was accustomed to, with their clumsy box magazines, this had an eight-chambered rotary cylinder which—most modern—turned on a ratchet as the weapon's heavy drive-spring was racked back so that cocking and reloading were completed in one swift movement.

He broke the *telek*'s action, swung magazine and barrel downwards and checked the sear and trigger-clips before emptying the polished cylinder of half its darts. After a swift over-shoulder glance towards the closed door at his back, he withdrew their replacements from his belt-pouch. Like the arrows cased beside his bow, they too were tipped with silver. Evthan might have seen the arrows, but no one, he was sure, had seen the darts—and he intended to keep it that way. Sliding each one into its respective chamber, he rotated the cylinder once more and then snapped it shut, engaging the safety-slide with a push of his thumb.

Behind him, the stable door creaked open and Aldric turned with shocking speed, the *telek* rising to shooting position almost of its own volition. Gueynor stood framed in the doorway, gilded by the sunlight at her back, wide eyes fixed on the unwavering muzzle which hung bare inches from her face. There was a wicker basket in her hands. Aldric watched her but said nothing as he returned the spring-gun to its holster, observing even as he did so that she had shown no fear. Surprise,

certainly—the *telek* had thrust out at the end of his arm
like the head of a striking snake—but not even a tremor
of fright. And he wondered how much of her hysteria
in the forge had been a skilful act . . . He was curious
to hear what reason she had found to bring her back—
and glad within himself that there was any cause at all.

"I thought . . . my aunt asked me to bring you these.
She said they might be of some use."

He took the proffered basket and glanced inside; it
was full of small sealed jars and bunches of herbs.

"Provisions for the hunt?" he hazarded uncertainly.

The girl shook her head, but did not elaborate. Aldric
set out two or three of the stoneware pots, noticing how
their stoppers were tied down, sealed with wax into
which a character of the Drusalan language had been
scored. He could speak it but not read it, so the lettering
made little sense. Nor did the dried pieces of vegetation
help at first, even though he recognized some of them: a
stalk of withered foxglove, two roots and the cowled dark
flower of monkshood, a handful of dwale berries . . .

Dwale . . . ? Aldric realised suddenly what was in the
basket. *"Awos arl'ih Dew!"* he muttered, setting it down
very carefully. "Poison! Enough poison, I think, to kill
this entire village a score of times. Yes?"

"Yes," Gueynor echoed, her voice toneless.

"But why?"

"My aunt said they might be useful," she reiterated.

"Your aunt . . . but not yourself? Never mind? I'll
find some use for them, one way or another."

Gueynor nodded, gazed at him for a few seconds without expression and then backed away, closing the door
behind her. Aldric stared at the blank wooden surface
without really seeing it and tried to make some sense
out of the brief exchange. Poison was of no use against
a werewolf: did the girl's sinister gift mean that she had
guessed much less than he suspected, or had it another
meaning altogether? That difference between Gueynor
and the other peasants he had met still nagged at him.
There was a *wrongness* somewhere, if he could only define it . . .

Aldric found himself reluctant to touch the jars now
that he knew what they contained; he had the *kailin-*

eir's deeply ingrained detestation of poison in any form, and especially as a weapon. Its use, cowardly and secret, went against all the honour-codes. But still . . .

The wax seal cracked across and across as he ran his thumbnail under it, releasing a faint sour odour that prickled unpleasantly in his nostrils. From the bunch of dried herbs fastened to it by a length of cord, Aldric guessed that this jar held a distillate of monkshood. His lips drew back very slightly from his teeth in a smile that had no humour in it; in Elthan and Prytenon this same root was called wolfsbane. The irony was appropriate, and appreciated.

He drew out the *telek* holstered at his side, broke it, and systematically packed in the interstices of each openwork steel point with gummy black toxin, taking extreme care not to scratch or prick his skin in doing so. Then he grimaced, shrugged slightly and did the same for the four darts tipped with silver. Perhaps if one did not work, the other would.

And if neither did—goodnight, my lord.

2

Lord of the Mound

It was warm in the forest, and very still; no breeze blew to cool the heavy air. Under the spreading canopy of branches sunlight became a green, translucent glow, filtering through layered leaves until the tall trunks looked like sunken pillars in some drowned and long-forgotten hall. Though occasionally a bird sang, the liquid notes were oddly flat and lifeless and soon died in the oppressive silence. Aldric's moccasin boots hissed softly through the grass and bracken, while Evthan the hunter made no sound at all.

That there were no dogs had been a source of some slight friction between the two men. Laine had refused to let his precious pets be subjected to the lurking dangers of the woods, and Evthan had not pressed him over-hard. Aldric might have done so but for lack of time—and a feeling that Evthan's reluctance could well prove significant.

He paused, uncased his heavy composite bow and nocked an arrow to the string. His fingers were clumsy, and when he saw Evthan was watching he restrained a scowl—he would have preferred the Jouvaine not to see that momentary fumble. The latest bird to risk a chirrup faltered and went quiet, and as each leaden minute trickled by it seemed the forest held its breath.

As the sun slid down the western sky the air grew cool; light dimmed and shadows lengthened. Aldric's nerves were stretched by waiting, watching, listening for the movement which would betray . . . whatever made it. Evthan, by contrast, appeared relaxed; there seemed to be no alertness in him, and he was silent apparently only through long habit. This struck Aldric as peculiar; the hunter was not behaving as might be expected.

"Which way now?" the Alban asked. His voice was startlingly loud, an alien and unwelcome sound.

Evthan looked about him, then raised an arm to point north-east.

"Into the Deepwood," he replied, and walked on without waiting for a response.

There was none; Aldric was slightly puzzled by the Jouvaine's form of speech, using a noun instead of an adjective as if he meant a place rather than just thicker woods. That did nothing to relieve Aldric's tension; instead it made him feel worse, for now the scrutiny of every tiny forest creature was acting on his senses, making him jumpy, causing him to start at nothing more than a stoat or a squirrel—above all making him mentally exhausted, less attentive and more careless.

Aldric had no need to ask when they had reached what Evthan called the Deepwood; it was only too obvious why it had been given the name, which was singularly well-deserved. The woodland near Valden had been, he realised, cleared of undergrowth for the hunting pleasure of the Overlord and his noble guests; it was virtually parkland—like an open meadow compared with the thick, claustrophobic tangle of brush, brambles and dark, sinister evergreens. After half an hour Aldric's eyes yearned for the sight of a beech-tree or an oak, anything to relieve the sombre monotony of the pines— living, dying or dead, but all upright in one another's close-meshed needled embrace.

They were old, as old as anything that he had ever seen. There was a monstrous, brooding stillness in the Deepwood, a darkness and a sense of such vast antiquity that even he, high-clan Alban, *cseirin*-born, brought up with a history of nigh on sixty generations, felt insignificant and an intruder on the peace of long, slow ages.

"Evthan," he said, his voice hushed as if he feared to wake whatever ancient presence slumbered here in the warm, close confines, "turn about. Go back to the village. Now." He was not commanding any more.

Evthan looked at him with what might have become a smile tugging at the corners of his thin mouth. But the smile—if such it was—did not extend beyond that twitch of muscles; instead he nodded, turned in his tracks and moved back the way he had come. Aldric stood quite still with only his dark, gloom-dilated eyes following the hunter, and felt the blood of shame burn in his face. He had come so very close to pleading, and not even because of honest fear which anyone might feel—even *kailinin-eir*. Oh, no. He was just nervous, that was all, aware that he was a trespasser in this quiet place; out of his depth in a hostile environment where he was neither welcome nor had any right to be. Or was it more than that . . . ? He almost called Evthan back, to insist that they continue; then glanced over his shoulder at the dim encroachment of dusk and walked quickly after the Jouvaine. But not *too* quickly.

He was whistling a soft, sad little tune as he drew level with Evthan, and the hunter gave him another of those half-amused looks, sidelong, without turning his head. He said nothing. Above their heads, far beyond the confines of the Jevaiden Deepwood, the sky became a smoky blue-grey which dissolved to saffron as it swept down to the horizon and the last faint residue of sunset. That cool amber light beyond the trees transformed them into hard-edged silhouettes, every branch, every twig, every leaf and needle etched precise and black against the afterglow. Aldric glanced from side to side as his world grew dark . . . and ceased to be the world he knew at all.

Unconsciously he lengthened his stride to keep up with the hunter; it was difficult to match long legs that could keep pace with a war-horse. All around him were small sounds as the night-forest came to life: tiny creaks and twitterings, an occasional snap and rustle of minute movement. Little noises, usual in the evening, and undisturbed by the Alban's own muted musical contribution. Then his whistle faltered, began again uncertainly and trailed away in a scatter of unconnected notes. An eerie tingling sensation crawled over the skin of neck and arms like the half-forgotten memory of a shiver. But he knew instinctively what it was . . . and why it was.

Someone—or some *thing*—was close behind him.

Aldric stopped, holding his breath to hear more

clearly while his grey-green eyes, narrowed now and wary, raked the undergrowth. There was nothing but a slither of fern-fronds and then silence, so that it seemed he had heard only the echoes of his own passage through the bracken. Except that this "echo" came from maybe thirty feet off to his right. And why had everything else gone quiet . . . ?

He knew the answer to his own unspoken question almost at once; because the lurking presence was still out there, invisible in the thick vegetation, studying him, assessing him with interest and curiosity but no malice . . . for the present. It had stopped whenever he had stopped, which made him reluctant to move again for fear of what might follow.

"Evthan," he said quietly. There was no reply. His head snapped round and with an ugly tremor of shock the young Alban found he was alone. Or, more accurately, was not alone at all. That awareness was driven home with dreadful emphasis by the soft crunching as something huge moved purposefully closer. A metallic tang beneath his tongue soured Aldric's dry mouth, and one hand flicked up to the *telek* holstered under his left arm. It cleared leather with a harsh scrape that normally would have angered him but this time could no be loud enough, then click-clicked sharply as he wrenched back on the cocking lever.

The slow movement in the forest ceased at once.

Aldric could feel the clammy embrace of sweat-saturated cloth against his skin, and the all-too-familiar queasiness in his stomach. Fighting a desire to turn and run, he reversed along the narrow track which was all that Evthan had left him to ease his route through the Deepwood. There was no sound of pursuit. Then all at once he noticed something which, however briefly, took his mind away from whatever he had faced down in the forest. The polished metal of the *telek* was glinting in the moonlight.

Moonlight . . . ?

Aldric's head jerked back, his gaze shooting up between the tree trunks to what little of the sky was visible between their lowering columns, and if he had been uneasy before it was as nothing to how he felt when he saw the moon. It perched like some obscenely bloated fruit on the extremity of a branch, shining ever more brilliantly as dusk crawled into night.

Regardless now of what might—indeed, certainly would—hear him, Aldric yelled, "Evthan! *Evthaaan!*" at the top of his voice. In his heart the last thing that he expected was an answer.

"What's wrong, man?" The hunter seemed to coalesce from a jumble of shadows and Aldric almost jumped out of his skin, then sagged with a relief that he made no attempt to conceal, trying to get his breath back and thankful that the darkness could not betray how much he was shaking. Evthan Wolfbane was not a fool, whatever else the Alban suspected he might be; after a single glance at his companion's shocked, white face he jerked an arrow from the quiver at his back and set it to his longbow's string. "Or should I say, what's out there?"

Aldric managed a false, inadequate laugh. "The Beast, maybe. Or a bear. Or a rabbit. Or something out of my own head. Dear God in Heaven, Evthan, I didn't want to wait and see!"

The hunter's teeth gleamed as he smiled reassuringly. "I don't blame you," he said. "The Deepwood after dark is no place for a novice hunter, especially one who is . . ." he altered a word on the very tip of his tongue, ". . . ill at ease in thick forest. As you are. Yes?"

The forced bravado drained from Aldric's face and in the moonlight only shame remained. "You mean frightened, don't you?" His voice was a low, grim monotone. "Scared out of my wits!"

Evthan shook his head. "I do not. Every man has his own special fear: close confinement; open space; a high place. I have that fear—I can climb a tree at need, but in truth would rather not. So with you and the forest. But I am no more ashamed of my fear than I am of having blue eyes when my father's were brown."

Aldric's own eyes widened fractionally—what had made the Jouvaine shape his words like that? There was no way in the world that he could know . . . was there? The *cseirin*-born—the lord's immediate family—of Alba's ancient high clans all shared hereditary features as distinctive as their crests, and the marks of clan Talvalin were height, fair hair and blue eyes. It was ironic therefore that the last clan-lord of all should have none of these things, and this had rankled deep down for a long time now. He made a wordless noise in reply to Evthan's philosophising, and noted coldly that this peasant hunter was once more proving to be more than he appeared.

How much more would doubtless be revealed, for Aldric as he grew calmer had made one observation which left him far from comfortable in Evthan's presence after dark: the moon was not yet full. He had known as much in the light of day, but his assurance had been badly shaken by the apparently complete silver disk peering at him through the trees. Looking again without the magnification of fear, it plainly lacked the merest nail-paring along the rim. Which meant that tomorrow night was still to come. The night of the full moon, and the night of the summer solstice. Aldric slid his *telek* back into its holster, but was not inclined to buckle down the peacestrap which normally secured it there. Not yet.

So far as the Alban could tell, Evthan's route out of the Deepwood was much more direct than that which he had followed on the way in. Why that should be, Aldric did not know—unless maybe it was out of consideration for himself. And if that was the case, then he was not sure that he wished to be patronised to that extent. He was still trying to phrase a reply which would not insult a gesture offered in honest kindness when he became aware of two things: one was that Evthan had become almost as nervous as he himself had been a half-hour earlier, and the other was that even in the shadow-streaked uncertain light, he could see that they were walking along a path. It was narrow, true, twisting and uneven, flanked closely on either side by trees, but still a path. In the Deepwood . . . ?

And then he saw the clearing.

It glistened under the moon like a pool of quicksilver, and at its centre was a solitary tree. Not growing; once it might have been an oak—or an ash or an elm—but now it was unrecognisable, centuries dead, a split and blasted monument to the fury of some long-forgotten storm. Grateful for an open space at last, Aldric paused to rest his Deepwood-wearied eyes on it. Perhaps five-score yards from where he stood, the forest began again as if the hands of men had never interrupted it. For this was no natural clearing; northward, beyond the shattered tree, was the remnant of a mound ringed by standing stones. The place exuded a sense of profound age, for the megaliths were everywhere: some upright; some leaning crazily askew; others lintelled, one laid across two others like colossal doorways into nowhere; a few fallen and half-hidden in the grass.

His brain aswirl with images that made his scalp prickle, Aldric took a cautious step towards the ruined mound. He had seen things like this before, for his own long-dead bloodkin—*an Mergh-Arlethen,* the Horse Lords—slept in such mounds scattered throughout the southern part of Alba. Their great barrows were not round like this had been, but long, reminiscent of the ships which had brought them and their tall steeds across the deep sea, and they dotted Cerenau and Prytenon up past Andor and Segelin to the very eaves of the forest of Guelerd. In his homeland they were untouched, undisturbed, honoured as much for their many years as for what they were.

But here, on the fringes of the Empire . . . This mound was already open to the sky and Aldric knew what to expect: the tomb torn apart by disrespectful hands, its burial chamber violated in search of any treasures buried with the dead, the poor old bones scattered and their long rest disturbed. To any Alban such thoughts were repellent, and especially to *ilauem-arluth* Talvalin whose reverence for his ancestors came close to worship now that they were all he had. Yet some strange, sad curiosity compelled him to look closer, almost as if he might make some amends for the rude treatment meted out by others.

Then Evthan's hand closed on Aldric's left bicep, holding him back—and in that grip discovering the meshed mail and splinted steel beneath the Alban's leather sleeve. If the revelation startled him he gave no apparent sign, but met the younger man's eyes without blinking as Aldric's head swung round in annoyance. "Do not go into . . . that place," he said, his voice low and intense.

"Why not?" The annoyance did not colour the flat way in which Aldric asked his question, and that in itself was faintly ominous, as if something was being held in check—something which might be unleashed if the reply proved unsatisfactory.

"Because . . . Because it was once a holy circle of the Flint Men, where they worshipped gods who were before the Gods."

Religion, thought Aldric, and almost smiled. Never debate a man's religion, politics or taste in women.

But then Evthan muttered, "Would that it still was, instead of being . . ." and let his words tail off in a way that Aldric did not like. Maybe it was more than just religion after all.

"Instead of being what, Evthan?" he prompted.

"Instead of being what it is now! Unhallowed and evil! Keep away from the ring of stones, Kourgath. Avoid it, as everyone else does."

"All the more reason for me to look, then. I sense nothing evil about either the ring or the mound—and the dead have never done the living harm." Even as the words left his mouth he knew that they had been spoken impulsively, and were a lie; for he remembered the *traugarin* raised out of death by Duergar the necromancer, and Kalarr cu Ruruc who had first died before the Clan Wars five centuries ago . . . "At least, the peaceful dead," he amended quietly.

"But why should the lord beneath the hill be at peace?" Evthan argued with inexorable logic. "His great sleep ended when *they* broke open his tomb."

"*They* . . . ?" The single soft word did not invite excuses. "Explain to me—who are *they?*"

Evthan hesitated, then shrugged. Aldric caught the little movement. "Do you not know—or not wish to tell me?"

"I know," the hunter answered.

"And, I think, so do I. Lord Crisen. The name which appears too many times without an adequate reason for it."

"He, and his father. Lord Geruath searched for ancient weapons—he collects them in his tower at Seghar as another man might gather works of art. But the other—"

"Lord Crisen."

"—Sought other things."

"And did he find them?"

Evthan's teeth showed in a hard, tight smile. "Now, Kourgath—Aldric—how much would you expect a mere hunter to know of the private doings of his Overlord?" It was a roundabout way of saying that he would hear nothing more, and like it or not, the Alban accepted it without protest.

"I should like to meet your Overlord—and his son," was all he said.

"And I should like to be there to see that meeting," returned Evthan.

"Perhaps you will. But for now I'll be content to see this holy place—which may no longer be holy, but certainly grows more interesting by the moment."

"But I told you—" Evthan started to protest.

"Nothing but a superstition which convinces me of nothing. But I'll give the mound-king your respects if I should chance to meet him." The hunter flinched at that and Aldric saw him flinch. Was it because of his own casual, thoughtless remark . . . or for some other reason? Soon, he promised inwardly, soon all the questions will be answered.

He walked slowly out across the moonlit clearing, towards the mound—and from the shadows he was watched by unseen eyes.

*

Things hidden by the long grass gave way beneath his soft-soled boots with sharp, dry cracking sounds. They were not twigs, not branches. Aldric knew what they were and twice he stopped, knelt, and lifted them into the thin wash of silvery light to see the objects better. It was something he would not have done in daylight, for this was viper country if ever he had seen it—on a hot day the big lethal snakes would have been out everywhere, basking. In the cool of the night they were all gone, leaving him alone to impudently fumble with old sacrificial bones. He found their very age a reassurance, and on both occasions that he took a closer look the remnants proved to be those of animals—sheep, maybe, or goats.

But then something crunched under his heel and skidded slightly in a manner so uniquely nasty, and so unlike any sensation which had gone before, that for several seconds curiosity and distaste were evenly matched. Curiosity, inevitably, won—and Aldric was to regret that it had done so.

For what he picked up was a human hand. The phalanges were shattered—that had been the crunch which he had felt as much as heard, like treading barefoot on a snail—and its pulpy, putrefying flesh had burst and smeared under his weight. It had lain on the ground for a month or more, and he was thankful that his own hands were gloved as a foul ooze soiled the black leather covering them and a thick reek of rottenness wafted past his nostrils, offending the clean air of evening. But it was neither of these far-too-familiar horrors which brought his stomach to the brink of nausea, nor was it the griping pain of that incipient retch which stung his eyes to tears.

It was realisation that this hand had been a child's.

He was already drawing breath to summon Evthan when he remembered what the man had told him at their first meeting, and the recollection shut his mouth with an audible click of clenching teeth. The most cruel thing in all the world would be to let the Jouvaine hunter see what he had found, because he guessed that this pathetic remnant was a leaving of the Beast. Perhaps all that remained of Evthan's daughter . . . Aldric hoped not. He gently laid down the fragment and, with an effort, kept any hint of revulsion from the way he wiped his fingers clean. Then he drew his *tsepan* from its lacquered sheath and used the needle point to scratch out a little grave. In other circumstances he would have muttered an apology for dishonouring the dirk with such a menial task, but not now. The needs of simple decency were worthy of an honourable weapon.

After he had finished and pressed the acid soil back into place, Aldric remained on his knees, head bowed and eyes tight shut as he tried to force himself back to calmness. Instead of the detached regret he might have expected, he was filed with such a rage as he would never have imagined possible over the death of some unknown foreign peasant's unknown child. Its intensity made his whole body tremble, so that frosty reflections danced along his *tsepan*'s blade. For once Crisen Geruath and the inner turmoil of his own honour ceased to be important. If by razing the Jevaiden down to bare black rock he could have been assured of the obliteration of the Beast, he would have fired the forest without a second thought.

As that first spasm of impotent fury faded to a leashed-in killing mood—something infinitely more dangerous— Aldric realised bitterly why Evthan was subject to such strange fits of brooding. If he, outlander, *hlensyarl,* could be so overwhelmed by grief and anger at the evidence of a single slaying, then what state must the Jouvaine's mind be in now that thirty people, many of them known to him, had been ripped apart and eaten? And how many of that thirty had walked all unaware into the jaws of the Beast because they trusted the protection of a man they called the finest hunter in the province . . . ?

There was a film of icy perspiration on the Alban's face as he rose, and a little twitch of terror in the way he slid the *tsepan* out of sight. In Evthan's place he would have been expected to use the wicked blade as it was meant to be used, and be grateful for the privilege of an honourable end. Except for one thing: in this situation not even the most sincerely contrite ritual suicide would help either the dead or those still living. It would help only the Beast. Aldric bared his teeth viciously.

And then, because there was nothing of any immediacy to be done, he clamped down on his feelings and pushed them to the back of his mind. Not that they ceased to have substance—no man's willpower was so powerful—but distanced from his conscious self, they would no longer affect his actions unless he desired it.

Or events required it.

He continued his walk towards the mound, concentrating on it, forcing himself to be calm by letting the tranquil images of antiquity cool what still seethed in his brain. Aldric paused, rested one hand against the rough surface of a fallen sarsen and looked back towards Evthan. The hunter was barely visible; indeed, he seemed to be backing apprehensively away from the clearing, from the mound, from the moonlight and into the comfortable darkness under the trees. Aldric shivered at that, finding the massive trunks and their ink-thick blots of shadow far from comforting. Even in such a place as this, he preferred to have the sky above his head. With that unspoken preference in mind, he appreciated the rich irony of his next three steps, which brought him under the great stones of the burial chamber and into a confined space of dark and silence.

*

That the dome would be so complete as to exclude all light was a possibility which had not occurred to him. Expecting cracks and crevices—perhaps even the gaping access hole left by whatever grave-robbers the Overlord had employed—he was surprised, unsettled and more than a little shocked by just how black inside the cist really was. Un-light pressed all around him like the intangible folds of some heavy cloth, and even though the pupils of his grey-green eyes expanded to enormous proportions in their quest for a glimmer of useful luminescence the involuntary effort was entirely wasted.

Aldric reached out warily until his outstretched fingers touched the great blocks of the dry-laid chamber wall, and only then moved cautiously forward, trusting to luck and any irregularities in the stones for a warning of the floor abruptly sloping down beneath him. Then he stopped again, muttering a soft, annoyed oath at himself, and reached into the pouch pendant from his belt. In it was a tinderbox and a thick candle of best-quality white beeswax, something he always carried but never had use for—and consequently forgot about, most of the time . . .

Half-closing his light-sensitive eyes to guard them from its flash of sparks, Aldric tripped the spring of the tinder box. Then *tsked* in annoyance and did it again, twice, before the fluffed linen wisps caught fire sufficiently for him to ignite the candle's triple-thickness braided wick. Unused, it smouldered furiously for a few seconds until a blue-cored yellow bud swelled from the stem of the wick, blossoming rapidly into a tall, saffron flame-flower. Only when he was assured that it would not go out, and had fixed its brass shield-ring to catch any potential drips, did Aldric look about him. And when he did, it was enough to make him catch his breath in wonderment.

The roof of the hollow hill hung grey and huge an arm's length above his head. He had not known what to expect, for every mound that he had seen before had been intact, the secrets of construction hidden under high-heaped soil and green grass. Aldric knew that each had at least one chamber in its heart, where the dead were laid, but how those chambers were formed had been a mystery to him until now.

That grey roof was a single colossal slab balanced with ponderous delicacy on three tapering pillars, and only the strength born of great grief or great piety could have raised such a structure. Even though it had stood thus for maybe forty centuries, its presence looming over him sent a shudder fluttering through the marrow of his bones. If something—anything at all—made the capstone fall, then he, like the owner of the tomb, would be nothing but a memory.

Shadows crawled out of the crevices between the stones as he raised the candle for a better look. There was a strangeness to the barrow, something so obvious that for a few moments it escaped him. Then awareness dawned. The place was clean . . . There was no earth trodden between the slabs of the floor, no trace of debris either from the breaking of the mound or from the forest outside, whose dry, dead vegetation would percolate inside with every gust of wind. Instead the cist seemed to have been swept and dusted—recently, at that. As he stalked warily towards where the old chieftain lay, Aldric wondered who in the Jevaiden could be so contemptuous of local legends as not only to enter a place commonly avoided—except by cynical, inquisitive Albans—but to tidy it besides. The original occupant could hardly be in a fit state to appreciate such a gesture. Could he . . . ?

Other chambers opened off the main crypt; store-rooms for the possessions necessary for status and comfort in the Afterworld, Aldric guessed. He did not trouble to investigate them, sure that his predecessors here would have cleaned them out just as thoroughly as they had the main tomb—and in the same sense of the word. Even so, it was hard to ignore the yawning entrances, for they made him uneasy. Almost as if something foul might creep from them the moment his back was turned . . . A foolish notion, of course—he was the only living thing in this place, and moreover he was armed.

Aldric shifted the candle from right hand to left, the better to loosen his *telek* in its holster, and found that he disliked what that shift had done to the way in which the shadows moved. Disliked it most intensely. The *telek* slipped free without a sound, his thumb releasing its safety-slide as the weapon's weight was cradled by the heel of his hand. Nothing moved now but the play of light and darkness at the corners of his nervous eyes. But Aldric turned and kept on turning with his bootheel as a pivot, tracking his line of sight with the springgun's muzzle as he raised the candle higher.

And cast light across the lord beneath the hill.

Even though he had expected something of the kind, he found the corpse disturbing, although its appearance was not as unpleasant as he had been prepared for. The old chieftain had been too long dead for stink and putrefaction.

His very frame had crumpled underneath the weight of years, contracting in upon itself until it had become mere sticks and leather; no more frightening than firewood.

The ceremonial trappings of the aftermath of death held no terrors for an Alban *kailin-eir* of high-clan birth, because such a man was aware that he, however exalted he might be, would eventually come to this. More aware, indeed, than most; the *cseirin*-born were early introduced to what would be their ultimate destiny. Aldric could remember, when he was five years old, being taken by his father Haranil to the vaults beneath Dunrath-hold, not to see the crypt but quite specifically to be shown his own funeral column, with its vacant, patient, niche awaiting the day when an urn of ashes would be set in it. Aldric's ashes. His name and rank and date of

birth were recorded on the polished basalt in vertical
lines of elegant cursive characters, but the last line ended
abruptly, incomplete. It required another date to give
the carved inscription perfect symmetry . . . Even at the
age of five, the experience had been sobering.

Detecting an old smell in the air now, compounded of
more than mustiness and candle-smoke, Aldric glanced
sidelong at the withered corpse with one eyebrow raised,
then shook his head. The thought had been an idle one,
for there was nothing of decay about this odour; it was
sweet, but not with the sickliness of corruption. Rather,
it was more like perfume . . . He walked closer, then
remembered his manners and inclined his head politely,
the still-drawn *telek* glinting in the candle-light as his
right arm made the small, graceful gesture of respect to
the dead. This was someone's ancestor, and if the dead
man was held in such regard as would raise this tomb
around him, then courtesy would not be misplaced.

He met the dark gaze of the skull's empty orbits without blinking, but did not mirror its taut and mirthless
grin. "Bones, and rags, and dust," Aldric said softly.
"Our way is better, lord of the mound. Fire is clean."
The skin around his mouth scored chevrons of shadow
into itself as his teeth showed momentarily in the candle's flame. Praise be to Heaven, he thought, that in
wisdom death is at the end of life and not at the
beginning . . .

Then thought stopped.

There was colour amid the ivory and brown of the
thin hands, piously folded on the dead man's breast, and
that colour was the source of the elusive fragrance.
Roses were twined between the bony fingers—three
bloated, baleful roses that were so darkly crimson they
seemed almost black, their great petals velvet and luxuri-
ant, their scent far heavier than any he had smelt before.
Rich as incense, almost overpowering; like the drug
ymeth, the dreamsmoke of Imperial decadence, and yet
somehow less wholesome still.

The dream . . . And within that dream, nightmare . . .
Aldric was aware that his hands were trembling—not
much, but enough to send a spiral of black smoke from
the candle wick as it guttered under molten wax. He

wished too late that he had told everything to Gemmel when he had the chance, and not hidden behind false, drink-born bravado; at least he might know by now what all this meant . . . !

Yet there was probably a reasoned and logical explanation for the presence of the flowers. Maybe Geruath the Overlord had discovered this dead man to be long-forgotten blood kin, and the roses were an apology of sorts for the indignities to which his tomb had been subjected. Yes . . . that was probably the solution. Aldric was half ashamed of his own reactions, and at the same time knew quite well that he was trying to fool himself. There was nothing reasoned or logical about what was going on in the Jevaiden, in Valden—or in this tomb.

He walked slowly around the bier, looking down at the shrivelled corpse, and wondered who this man had been . . . what he had been . . . what he had done to make his people grant him so imposing a burial; and it was at the far side of the rough cafafalque that he discovered the crypt was not entirely empty after all.

His boot pressed down on something which crackled loudly in the silence, and Aldric felt his mouth go dry. The "thing" was a sheet of parchment, its edges dry and crumbling, and as he gazed at it he was overwhelmed by an ugly sense of déjà-vu. Coincidence could not be strained so far . . . The last time he had found an object lost by others, so many, many deaths had followed. Deaths, and horrors, and the extinction of his clan. He almost used his boot to scrape the page to tatters against the floor.

But he was Aldric Talvalin, as much prey to the vice of foolish, fatal curiosity as any proverb-maker's cat— and he read it first, setting the candle on one corner of the dead chief's bier and holstering his *telek* before he picked up the page in apprehensive fingers. It was a poem of some sort, written with a pen in the crabbed letters of formal Jouvaine script, and he could read that language; indeed, any lettered man could read it, for High Jouvaine was the tongue of learning, a lingua franca understood—in varying degrees—by scholars all over the world. Even the Albans conceded that. He scanned the lines twice—once for the translation and once for the sense—then abruptly ripped the brittle sheet across and across, crumpled the remnants between his palms and dropped them back onto the stones of the floor with finality.

"And what would you have done with it?" he asked the chieftain idly, with false amusement in his voice. "Kept the thing? Not knowing what I know!" The skull's grin did not alter in response and its empty sockets continued to gaze at the entrance of the burial chamber as if watching something living eyes could not see. Talking to a corpse, Aldric thought—are you going mad? He stared down for several seconds at the pieces of parchment by his feet, unsettled by the memory of what he had read and trying to forget it. He had thought the thing was *an-pesoek,* some little charm like the two or three he knew, but *pesok'n* had not such an ominous sound to them . . .

> *The setting sun grows dim*
> *And night surrounds me.*
> *There are no stars.*
> *The Darkness has devoured them*
> *With its black mouth.*
> *Issaqua sings the song of desolation*
> *And I know that I am lost*
> *And none can help me now . . .*

A tiny voice seemed to be whispering the words inside his head, over and over again, their rhythms weaving circles round his brain and making sense that was no sense at all. Aldric's lips compressed to a bloodless line as he shrugged, seeming to dismiss the whole thing from his mind . . . except that it was not so simple as the shrug suggested.

He dusted flakes of parchment from his hands and reached out to pluck a rose from between the corpse's claws; then gasped and jerked back his fingers. There was as much shock as pain in his small, muted cry, for although he had barely touched it the fiercely spined blossom had thrust a thorn straight through his glove and into the pad of his thumb. Almost as if it had struck at him like an adder. A single ruby bead of blood welled out of the skin-tight black leather, momentarily rivaling the colour of the flower's petals before it became a sluggish drop which fell onto the chieftain's brow and trickled down between his empty eyes.

Aldric teased his trophy free with much more care this time and raised it to his nostrils. There was no need to inhale; the breath of its overblown perfume flowed into his lungs like a thick stream of hot honey, making his senses swim as if with vertigo. It was not a natural scent . . . not here, not now—not at all. Too rich . . .

Then the blood so recently tapped by the rose he held froze in his veins as something moved behind him. It was only a tiny scuff of noise, but it was *here,* in a place where no such noise should be unless *he* made it. And he had not . . . The pounding of his heart fluttered in the Alban's throat, constricting it, and the rose fell from his slack fingers as he became as immobile as was the dead lord—or as he had been.

Aldric did not want to turn around, but when at last he did, twisting at the waist, his right hand snapped the *telek* from its holster up into an arm-stretched formal shooting posture aimed point-blank at . . .

Nothing. The lord of the mound lay as he had lain through all the long years since his kinfolk built the cist around him, a solitary gleaming gem of Aldric's blood upon his forehead like a mark of rank. There was no longer any sound, but in the entrance to the crypt there was a glitter that had not been there before. The glint that comes when flame reflects from polished steel.

"Evthan . . . ?" Aldric's arid mouth had difficulty in articulating the word for his tongue clung to his palate. "Evthan—what are you doing, man? Come into the light where I can see you!"

At first there was no reply—and then with a clatter of footsteps four men burst into the burial chamber. They were dressed as soldiers, lord's retainers, in quilted body armour and round helmets, and all four carried shortswords drawn and ready. There were no shouts of warning, no commands for him to drop his weapons— simply a concerted charge to kill. He had no sword, his cased bow was useless at such close quarters and these men—probably local peasants who wore their newly elevated status in their scabbards—appeared not to know what an Alban *telek* was, much less what it could do. Aldric educated them.

He could not understand why his warning sixth-sense had not put him on his guard before now; it happened sometimes, that was all. There was more of a defensive reflex action than either fear or anger in the way he reacted, shooting the foremost soldier in the chest without an instant's hesitation. A crossbow would have punched the fellow backwards off his feet, but the dart's strike full in the solar plexus was even more dramatic for being unexpected: sudden, massive nerve-shock collapsed the man's legs under him so totally that he went down in his tracks.

After that first shot Aldric's arm swung up and back with a smooth, precise, blurred speed betraying hours of practice with the weapon. His left hand gripped the cocking lever and jerked it back in a continuation of the same movement, so that the *telek* was reloaded and presented in what seemed an eyeblink. It was *t'lek'ak*, not one of the formalised actions but a bravo's trick and consequently frowned upon—but combined with the modern mechanisms built into his paired *telekin*, it could be appallingly effective.

The second of the four leapt over his comrade's body, raising his sword to chop at Aldric's head. He was so close when the Alban triggered his second dart that the man almost struck his face against the *telek*'s muzzle. Almost, but not quite—with an ugly, sodden sound the missile burst the soldier's left eyeball and passed through its socket into the brain. His head jerked back as if kicked beneath the chin and he was dead before his legs gave way. He fell and his sword fell with him. No matter that its wielder was a corpse—the blade was sharp and aimed at Aldric's skull. Flinging himself aside with barely room to do so, the Alban slammed against the crypt wall with a bone-jarring thud and a screech of stressed metal as his jerkin sleeve shredded between the lacquered mail inside it and the stone which raked his arm from wrist to shoulder. Pain lanced through him to his very teeth, and a flood of moist warmth spread towards his elbow as the half-healed wound in his left bicep split wide open for the second time within a week. Numbness flowed into the outraged muscle as blood leaked out, and after a few seconds began to dribble from his fingertips. In the heavy silence that ensued, it made the sound of rain.

Aldric was not overly surprised when all movement ceased; such intervals were common in a killing fight, and the two quick deaths he had inflicted would give pause to any but the most hardened warrior, let alone these yokels who in all likelihood had never lifted blade in anger against someone who could match them stroke for stroke. God, but his arm hurt . . . !

Then something did surprise him. One of the corpses moved.

He took three quick steps backwards, aware that the two remaining soldiers had also retreated. But surely I took him through the heart! a voice inside his head protested. As the man rolled into an untidy, half-seated slump with his head resting against the chieftain's bier, Aldric realised he had done nothing of the sort. Deceived by the meagre light of his own solitary candle and by the speed of the attack, he had shot too low. The quilted armour had resisted penetration by the dart, absorbing its force sufficiently at least to save the retainer's life; but the impact of a puncture wound full on a nerve-centre had felled him as effectively as a punch to that same spot. Even now the man was shaky and found it hard to make his legs obey him, though his first tentative attempts to move had dislodged the missile from its shallow gouge below his breastbone. Aldric decided he was not a threat—for the moment. He had briefly considered finishing what he had started, there and then, but the killing of a helpless man in cold blood was not part of the *kailin*-codes; nor was it a part of Aldric Talvalin, save as a most reluctant act of mercy.

Yet he was still outnumbered two to one. By peasants, though—he could take them both one-handed if he had to. A grating twinge down the innermost core of his left arm brought sweat out on his skin and reminded him sharply that he no longer had a choice in the matter. If he took them, it would *have* to be one-handed . . . One of the pair shifted his feet, the scruff of leather on stone very loud, and Aldric's eyes focused on the man at once. Tall and thin, with a lean face, deepset eyes and a small, mean mouth, he had the face of a weasel. The mouth opened a fraction, showing teeth. *"Venya'va doss moy!"* he snapped at his companion, waving the other man back.

"Keel, asen sla—" The protest was silenced by another abrupt gesture and a quiet, ugly chuckle. Aldric recognised the language, even understood it sketchily—and it was not Jouvaine but a Drusalan dialect from the Central Provinces. That told him two things: the men he faced were not locals but imported mercenaries—and he was fortunate still to be alive. Sheer chance had enabled him to reduce the odds so early in the fight, and now that surprise had worn off he was in grave peril. The soldier he faced now was probably more dangerous than all the others put together; he had that unmistakable confidence in his own ability and the way he held his sword bespoke a knowledge of its proper use. Certainly better than that of his erstwhile comrades, and probably better than Aldric as well.

The Alban's skills were with *taiken* and *taipan*, lance and *telek*, horse and bow, but use of this Drusalan shortsword seemed likely more akin to dagger-play. At close quarters on badly lit unfamiliar ground, that could be more deadly than any other fighting art. And other than his *tsepan*, he had no blade at all . . .

Had he not been so unsure of the *telek*, Aldric guessed that the man called Keel would already have made his move, based on a suspicion that the weapon was discharged and harmless. But after seeing two men shot down in what must have appeared a single instant, mere suspicion was not enough. He needed certainty. Aldric knew what was passing through the soldier's mind; and knew, too, where one of the discarded shortswords lay. A swift glance to confirm it . . . then a quick jerk back of the *telek* to feint the movement of reloading.

He was aware of what would happen, but the speed of Keel's reaction took him by surprise. His glance had not gone unnoticed and had confirmed in his opponent's mind the half-formed notion that he faced an empty

weapon. But Keel was not merely skilled—he had all
the craftiness learnt in eight years spent fighting other
people's wars, and he waited, waited, waited those long
seconds until, inevitably, he was invited to attack.

And then, already poised, he came lunging in far
faster than Aldric had expected. The Alban's neat sidestep turned instead into a wild wrenching of his body
clear of the stabbing point, and did not—quite—make
it . . . !

Keel felt the slight jarring in his fingers as the blade
sliced home—and the shattering jolt against his wrist as
something clubbed down on it. He too threw himself
aside for fear of worse, rebounded from the massive
stones of the cist and lashed out to make an end.

Aldric was not there.

Fire scored his side where the sword had parted jerkin, shirt and the topmost layer of his skin, but it faded
almost at once. Keel's edge had opened a few dozen
capillaries and given him a hellish fright, nothing more.
He cursed himself even as he swung the *telek* against
the soldier's arm in an automatic parry that was one full
half-second too late to be of use, knowing that he had
committed the cardinal sin of underestimating an enemy.
Once . . . but not twice!

The thoughts tumbled through his mind as he flung
aside the spring-gun and dived at full stretch for the fallen
sword, agony searing his left arm as he hit the ground and
closed the fingers of that hand around the weapon's hilt,
rolling both to break the impact of the fall and to bring
him clear of Keel. Sinews cracked as he fought the momentum of his own weight, shifting the direction of that roll
a few degrees from left to right split-seconds before the
mercenary's blade gouged sparks and splinters from the
wall—just at the place where Aldric should have
been . . .

The weasel-faced retainer was good. Very good! But
the sword he had acquired with so much pain and effort
was a crude thing, little more than a pointed cleaver
with a single razor edge, no guard and less balance. Aldric weighed it in his hand, thought of Widowmaker's
excellence and snarled softly.

"You are clever," Keel observed, using Jouvaine now.

"But not so clever, or you would have kept clear of this place. Lord Crisen does not like intruders."

"Talk on, man," Aldric returned bleakly, wondering meanwhile what in the name of nine Hells Evthan could be doing all this time. "I have fought a few like you. Talkers. None were a threat. And none talk now—" a mirthless smile slid deliberately across his face,"—save to the worms." He spoke in court Drusalan, making full use of its insulting arrogance and implications of superiority, but allowed his own Elthanek burr to colour the words. He was rewarded by the expression of mingled anger and confusion which suffused Keel's face; it hinted at a wavering of concentration which in its turn boded ill for Keel.

They circled the bier slowly, warily, boots sliding across the floor, and at long last a tiny feeling of awareness tickled at the back of Aldric's mind as if his whole body was emerging from a trance. The smell of candle-smoke and roses blended with the more immediate odours of blood and sweat; he could feel the pounding of his heartbeat, the contained panting of his and Keel's breath, the groans of the wounded man on the floor. In the darkness of the burial chamber there was little to see but the shift of monstrous shadows across monstrous stones, separated by the ultimate, ominous glitter of sharp steel. The soldier in the doorway was not a danger yet; only watchful, set there to prevent his escape and nothing more. Killing was to be Keel's pleasure—and it would be a pleasure, for he could almost taste the man's eagerness to inflict pain, like thick bitter cream smeared on his tongue. Keel had a need to hurt, as others needed fire, or bread, or honour . . .

Their swords met with a harsh clank, the blades too short for a true, shrill clash of steel, and the sound which they emitted seemed somehow more brutal, more threatening even than the icy music of *taikenin* which could cleave a man in half from crown to crotch. The exchange lasted bare seconds before both broke ground and retired: a testing of wrists, no more, and singularly useless when both weapons were designed for stabbing.

"You have some skill," hissed the Drusalan, his point weaving slowly to and fro like the head of a snake.

"That is good. I might be entertained this evening after all."

Aldric ignored him and restrained his own anger at what the mercenary was, at what he represented. Anger was not the way to win this fight. Calmness . . . Tranquillity . . . *Taipan-ulleth*. He adopted a deceptively relaxed stance, sword raised unhurriedly but not high enough to be a threat, and waited.

Keel was more confused than ever. He was accustomed to opponents who came after him, drawn on by taunting and insults, stabbing and slicing until they ran on to his ready sword. Not men who stood still, expressionless and almost unprepared for any sort of defensive move should he lunge home. Not men who were without fear, or anger, or . . . who *smiled* at him . . . ?

For Aldric did smile, not with cynicism that Keel could understand, but openly, honestly and gently, as if to a friend, or an honoured guest. "Tell me, lord's man," he murmured, "here in the Deepwood, do you not fear the Beast?"

"The moon—" Keel caught his tongue. Then he understood, or thought he understood, and grinned a nasty weasel's grin. "We need fear nothing!" There was too much confidence in his declaration, Aldric thought quietly. Four men might have no fear, but two? One, alone?

"Tell me more about the moon," he invited. Keel was silent, "Is that why Lord Crisen sent you here so late at night? Or were you sent to fetch him this?" His foot scraped once, destructively, across already-shredded parchment, and as Keel recognised what it had been his eyes went wide with horror. "You were late," Aldric reminded him. "Now what will Crisen say?" There was no reply. "I think that you at last fear something, Keel. I suggest you fear me, too—and this forest most of all."

With all the impact of a perfect cue, a wolf howled and the echoes throbbed and faded within the barrow. Aldric had heard that same sound not twelve hours ago, and it had been startling enough by daylight. Now, at night, in an ancient crypt filled with shadows and the ill-matched reek of blood and roses, the awful savage sadness of the cry appalled him.

In any other place Keel would not even have flinched, because he was familiar with all the noises of the woodland and especially with this one. But the eerie atmosphere beneath the hollow hill had been eroding his once-iron nerves these past few minutes, and despite the years of ingrained training he responded like any ordinary man—and turned his head a fraction.

The tiny movement was enough.

Three heartbeats later he was slumped against the wall and sliding down it as his legs gave way, his muscles growing slack and his chest awash with blood and pain where Aldric's blade had thrust beneath the ribs and up to pierce a lung. Pink froth welled out of Keel's mouth and nose, and his hands tried feebly to plug the rent through which his life leaked out. The Alban stepped back, point lowered, and watched dispassionately with the knowledge that this bitter victory came not from his skill but through luck—and by the intervention of the Beast. There was no feeling of satisfaction or triumph—only slight disgust at his own aptitude for slaughter. And thinking of the Beast, where in all this while was Evthan . . . ?

The mercenary coughed twice, painfully, and a third attempt to clear the fluid from his lungs drowned in a vile wet bubbling that went on and on until at last he shuddered and was still. Aldric stared at nothing and wiped one hand across his face, not caring that each finger left a glistening smear of crimson in its wake, then lifted his gaze towards the last of the retainers, hoping that the man was gone. But he was still there, standing in the doorway with the lines of shock engraved by shadows on his face.

"You too?" asked the Alban wearily. He knew the answer. Another death added to his score, or news of what had happened here would reach Lord Crisen's ears before the night was out; and he had few illusions of its consequence for the villagers of Valden who had sheltered him. The *telek*, he thought, not wanting more blood spattered over him than there was already. The weapon lay on the floor within easy reach, half-cocked, half-loaded, half-prepared to—No, not that—to shoot another dart.

Killing is always simpler at a distance; cheaper to pay the cost of death when you cannot see in detail how very high it is. How much easier would it be if one's victims were so far away that they ceased to be people and were reduced to numbers on a tally of the dead . . . ? So might the world die, consumed by fire while its leaders calculated how much loss each could accept before defeat or victory. So might Valden be destroyed—although more intimately, by the vengeful whim of he who was son of the Overlord.

Aldric snatched up the spring-gun and levelled it—but hesitated when he realised the soldier had not moved. The man's arms hung by his sides, his head was turned away and he was simply waiting for what he knew to be inevitable. His terror was a palpable thing, and the Alban felt a sickness churning in his stomach. The *telek*-muzzle wavered, and in vain Aldric tried to summon images of what men like this would do to Valden—and to Gueynor—when Crisen turned them loose. He could not justify what he had to do . . . Not unless the man attacked him or tried to run—or did anything that might give him reason to complete that pressure on the trigger . . .

"Come on," he snarled between his teeth. "The odds are even now. Rush me!"

Now is that not the worst of all? said a small, stern voice inside his head. It sounded just like Gemmel. *If you must kill, then kill. But whatever you do, waste no time trying to persuade yourself that what you do is right!*

Aldric whimpered softly, like a hurt child. And squeezed the trigger.

*

The running footsteps dwindled, replaced after a few moments by the rapid, fading beat of hoofs. They had horses! Of course they would have horses. It is a long march down from Seghar, by all accounts. Will they march or come on horseback when Crisen sends them to obliterate the village because of what I did—and could not do . . . ?

Very slowly Aldric lowered his *telek,* looking at it and smiling a small, wan smile. What he had not done . . . ! He had not shot the soldier—because he had not fully cocked the weapon. Perhaps it was an accident, perhaps unconsciously deliberate. Either way, it no longer mattered. Three deaths in one night were enough for any man. Although the killing might be over, the dying was not finished, for the first man he had shot was irrevocably doomed. Aldric had not forgotten the poison on each dart's sharp point. At least the wolfsbane would send an easier, a kinder death than some of the other venoms which he might have used—if any death before its time could be called kind.

Stripping off his right-hand glove, he knelt and pressed his fingers to the soldier's neck. The man's skin was cold, and clammy with perspiration; senses numbed and body paralysed, he did not react to Aldric's presence save with an upward rolling of his eyes. The pulse was slow beneath the Alban's touch, irregular and weak; like the uneven, shallow breathing, soon to stop. There was nothing he could do. Nothing anyone could do, not now. Except . . . reaching up toward the chieftain's bier, Aldric moved his candle closer. At least the lord's-man would not die in the dark. But the gasps for breath had stopped before he set the candle down.

Aldric's eyes closed for several minutes; then he straightened and decided it was time to leave this place. On a whim, he bent and lifted the red rose which had lain undisturbed throughout the fighting. Its fragrance was as potent as before, still with that slight voluptuous suggestion about it. But at least it did not stink of fresh-spilled blood. Then, just as he had touched the soldier, he reached out with those same fingertips and laid them lightly on the chieftain's dry, brown skull. The contact was cool, with the slight leather slickness of an old book-binding.

"Lord of the mound," said Aldric. It sounded like a salutation. "Did they leave your hawks and hounds and horses here, and the chosen of your warriors to guard your goods and ease your loneliness in the long night of the grave? Maybe. You will have more company from this night on."

He had hoped for magic, or an answer to the many riddles which troubled him; and had found only pain and the echoes of nightmare, and death. With a small, slight bow, he turned and walked away.

3

A Sense of Trust Betrayed

The reflex jerk of one slim leg awoke her, wrenched sweating and wild-eyed out of a dreadful dream of endless falling. There was no warm interval of drowsiness: one minute she was deep in restless sleep, the next shocked wide awake by her own spasmodic movement. Through a crack where the bedroom shutters failed to meet across one window, the moon shone into her eyes, and for an instant the young woman thought that she had somehow lost all of one day and night—then realised with a relief concealed by the darkness that its disc was not just yet at full.

She was Sedna ar Gethin, the present consort of Lord Crisen Geruath and, some said, a sorceress of great—though undefined—ability. Not that any who lived in Seghar town beneath the shadow of their Overlord's lowering citadel were rash enough to use that word, or indeed any of its variants: an over-forthright merchant from Tergoves had been torn by horses in the public square merely for hazarding such a speculation aloud. Yet when regarded in the light of what the Empire's law demanded as the punishment for sorcerers, Crisen's swift and ferocious reprisal became if no less excessive, then at least more understandable. Though men of power and privilege in Drusul and the other Imperial provinces ringing Drakkesborg could do much as they pleased, protected by what they were or who they knew, the same did not apply to petty noblemen out on the Jevaiden plateau. Especially those who were determined to avoid attention if they could—and it was a measure of how such things were measured in the Empire now, that an execution without trial was no longer cause for comment.

Sedna curled her legs beneath her and sat up, knowing that sleep would prove elusive for a while—and, remembering a little of her dream, was glad of it. The plump, down-stuffed quilt slipped from her shoulders and permitted the night air to take liberties with her naked upper body. She shivered, and not just from cold: the sensation had been uncomfortably like . . . an experience earlier that night. Moving carefully for fear of waking Crisen she began to snuggle lower, but the Overlord's son, disturbed by the intrusion of a cool draught, muttered something to his pillow and rolled over, clawing still more of the quilt from Sedna's limbs. She glared at him, momentarily debated what to do while her skin grew rapidly colder, then came to a decision and swung both legs out of bed as she reached for her discarded robe. This was of cream silk patterned with sunflowers, and lined with a costly apricot satin whose weight made it cling to the curves of her body as if both fabric and flesh were oiled—but more important still, that heavy lining made it warm.

She was not so much slim as slender, almost thin, with all the implied plainness which that word suggested. But "almost" only, for Sedna was not thin and not plain, not even merely pretty: she was beautiful, possessed of the translucent fragility of an exquisite porcelain figurine for all that she was taller than most men. Her straight black hair added to her height; no blade had touched it since her birth and now, worn as she preferred it in the courtly, simple high-clan Alban style of a single switch— tied back with a thumb-thick silken cord—it flowed in a glossy raven sheet the full length of her spine and beyond. Its darkness, and the deep brown of her long-lashed eyes, accentuated the soft pastels of a face which had never tanned, even when as a peasant's child she had played out of doors all day. Not that she seemed much more than a child now, for all her willowy elegance—at the age of twenty-two, she had the unblemished features of a sixteen-year-old nun. But Sedna ar Gethin was neither nun nor innocent; she was Vreijek, a sorceress, and a long way from home.

The thick, unpleasant smells of burnt *ymeth* and stale wine lingered in the bedroom; Sedna wrinkled her nose distastefully and wished herself more than ever back in Vreijaur—or indeed anywhere that was far from here and now. She looked down at the muffled bulk of Crisen's sleeping body, staring in a dispassionate way which she knew would have annoyed him intensely had he been awake and aware of it.

He was not a bad man, she thought, at least no more man most in his situation; ambitious of course, but then so many were. *She* was ambitious—that was why she was here. But she felt sure that there was no real evil in him, unlike some of the men she had encountered in this same fortress during recent months. Lord-Commander Voord for one, who slept in a guest-room in the same wing of the citadel, not sufficiently far away from the Vreijek's peace of mind. Or, she reflected, more likely did not sleep but sat bolt upright in a high-backed chair with his unblinking pale eyes fixed on nothing, no more needing to close them than an adder. Because there was something undeniably reptilian about him, something cold and patient. Sedna was unaware why so young a man should warrant such high rank, and had no desire to find out. She guessed that ignorance of Voord's doings was an advantage, when one had to speak to him—an ordeal which she had so far kept to an absolute minimum. The man frightened her.

Wrapping the lined robe close about her and tying it in place, Sedna walked towards the casement and swung one shutter wide. Now that there was no longer such strong contrast between out-of-bed and in, the night air was refreshing rather than chilly and she drew it deep into her lungs as a man might breathe in the fragrant smoke from his pipe. The dream still troubled her, for there was more behind it than a simple nightmare—of that she was quite certain. Suddenly she was afraid of the moonlit darkness. One finger stretched out towards an oil-lamp, and there was a small, sharp crack as its wick ignited when she pronounced the Invocation of Fire. Sedna was a sorceress indeed, and one who was considerably skilled in the Art Magic; her nonchalant lighting of the lamp demonstrated as much by her control of that one spell. A less capable wizard could quite easily have set the entire table aflame . . .

She set herself to concentrated thought, knowing that she was not given to precognition or to visions yet aware that such, in this instance, was the case. There had been death in her dream, the violent ending of more than one life—but where, and why should it concern her? Then her gaze turned on Crisen with the beginnings of a horrid certainty, as she felt sure that this affair would prove to concern him most of all. Sedna could not have given any reason why, even to herself—but nonetheless she *knew*.

He had always shown a little inquisitive interest in her magics—only so much as any man might have in something of importance to a lover but of no account to himself—and had used his rank and status as a shield to guard her from the consequences of her studies. Yet on more than one occasion past she had discovered that her books had been disturbed. There was no reason for complaint at that; none were damaged and mere curiosity was again accountable. But now with her suspicions aroused, Sedna began to see connections which earlier had not been apparent. How many other times had all been tidied carefully, so that she was unaware of them . . . ?

Her well-thumbed copy of *The Grey Book of Sanglenn* had been withdrawn from its case, read and replaced with its place-tag moved from "Herblore"—a most appropriate subject here in the forest country—to "Shapeshifting," an art in which she had no interest whatsoever. More ominously her rarest and most expensive grimoire—a hand-bound, handwritten Jouvaine translation of the proscribed Vlechan work *Enciervanul Doamnisoar*—On the Summoning of Demons—had been moved fractionally and one hasp of the reputedly woman's-hide cover was not quite snapped shut. Sedna had noticed that intrusion straight away, for she had bought the volume at a high price when the opportunity had arisen and since that time had not opened it except to ascertain that all its pages were in place. It was a book for owning, not for use—and it was certainly not for idle browsing by the uninitiated.

Now the realisation that someone—perhaps Crisen, perhaps not—had looked between its covers unsettled her, where before it had merely irritated her. The phrase "forbidden knowledge" was one greatly over-used by the ignorant, but in the case of *Enciervanul*'s contents it was no more than the truth. There were stories and unsubstantiated rumours of what had befallen the translator, one year and a day after the completion of his self-appointed task. At least, Sedna hoped that they were only stories . . .

She knew what she would have to do, for her own peace of mind, and though she would far rather have waited until daylight it would have to be done at once. Pushing her feet into soft slippers, she slid the bedroom door aside just enough to let her out, then with a glance back towards the still-sleeping Crisen, Sedna squeezed through the crack and pulled it shut behind her.

Three seconds passed. Then Crisen Geruath sat up.

*

The Overlord's son had granted his lady two rooms for her own private use; one was a library and the other a great cellar underneath the oldest part of Seghar citadel, where she could perform such spells as she desired without causing untoward disturbance—or attracting unwelcome curiosity. It was in that chamber that she occasionally made entertaining magics for Crisen's amusement: conjuring minor elemental spirits, like those which caused the blossoming of great red summer roses four months ago at the waning of winter, when snow outside still clothed the Jevaiden in white drifts six feet deep.

Once, and once only—for she detested the dark necromantic art—Sedna had called up the spirit of one of Crisen's ancestors. Crisen had not been pleased, for all that he had insisted she perform the sorcery; just as many men are angered when a careful scholar reveals their line to have sprung from less exalted stock than they had hoped or led others to believe. It had been thus in this instance; Sedna's spell had revealed beyond all doubt that her lover and his father were descended from a bastard line. Such a secret was probably common enough among the new aristrocracy, elevated through

their friendship and support for the Grand Warlords—
although the fact that something was common did not
help to make it palatable. The old nobility regarded ille-
gitimacies as mere human failings—within reason, of
course—strengthened as they were by generations of
lordship. Only families such as Crisen's felt it necessary
to be over-sensitive about the misbehaviour of men and
women long since dead—as if it did anything to alter
history . . .

Sedna occasionally wondered what lords had preceded
the Geruaths here—although she knew without being
told who they had supported—the wrong side! That was
why they no longer ruled and why Overlord Gueruath
did. The Vreijek sorceress was either not brave enough
or, more practically, insufficiently foolhardy to ask what
had become of them. But she could guess, and she was
becoming increasingly aware that she had been terribly
blind, terribly mistaken about Crisen's harmlessness. He
might not have the aura of sophisticated pleasure in cruelty that Lord-Commander Voord wore like a cloak, but
Crisen Geruath could be dangerous enough. His ambition would make sure of that. And when his sense of
rank and importance—greater even than his father's—
was either threatened or belittled, then the Three Gods
guard those who opposed him! For no man living under
Heaven could.

As she padded swiftly and in silence through the darkened corridors of the citadel, Sedna considered her own
unspoken words. Some of them brought a wry smile to
her face: to swear by or to call upon the triune gods was
tantamount to suicide in this place, being a confession
of the Tesh heresy which carried a sentence of immediate death by fire. It was, she thought, a flaw typical of
the Drusalan Empire that, not content with all their
other problems, its rulers should seek to influence what
people believed, what gods they prayed to, what After-
lives they went to when they died. As if one life was
not trouble enough! She was not overly religious; few
sorcerers were—indeed, few sorcerers could be, knowing
what they did about the nature of things. But unwarranted intrusion into spiritual matters angered her more
than most of the Empire's petty interferences. Rumour

had it that some of the more radical Drusalan priests were demanding that all adherents of the Teshirin sect be declared anathemate; if such a demand were to be granted by the Senate, the Imperial legions would have a mandate to go with fire and sword from one end of Vreijaur to the other, killing one in every three of the population. Which had a certain macabre aptness, in the circumstances . . .

The Albans were much wiser, thought Sedna idly. They revered their ancestors because of what they were—a part of each clan's history—rather than because of what they had been or what they had or had not done, and they prayed to the power of a single God manifested in the sun that they called the Light of Heaven. It was strange that such a people, bound around with oaths and honour-codes which sometimes seemed more than half in love with death, should pay so much respect to a symbol of life. Or maybe not so strange, at that.

There were few sounds within that wing of Seghar's citadel so late at night. No sentries patrolled—they were retainers, after all, servants more than soldiers except in time of war; the only truly military force for twenty miles—Voord's personal guard—was barracked on the other side of the sprawling antique fortress. But although the halls and corridors were quiet it was a mistake on Sedna's part to assume she was alone, and more unwise still to allow her concentration to wander into a debate on religious intolerance. For she was wrong in her assumption. Twice over.

The Vreijek sorceress padded rapidly across the open space of one last gallery and stopped outside her library door, now—and only now—glancing warily from side to side before withdrawing its key from the cache which she had secretly constructed underneath one glazed tile of the elaborately mosaiced floor. She fitted it, turned it with only the faintest of heavy clicks from the mechanism and pushed; the well-greased door swung silently open to admit her, and in equal silence Sedna locked it from within and drew a heavy curtain across so that no escape of light along its edges could betray her presence here. Only then did she exert her powers sufficiently to

conjure flame into the lamps and candles. All of them—
for Sedna was growing to hate the very thought of shadows. They caught with a sequential crackling like dry
reeds flung onto a fire, their scented oils and waxes filling the room with pleasant blended perfumes and a wash
of golden light.

It was, as might have been expected, a room devoted
to books. In the provinces a library could mean three or
four handwritten volumes and a dozen or so of print-set
works—maybe a score of books in all. But this library
was on such a scale as to seem improbable outside one
of the great Imperial cities, being not merely devoted to
but full of books. They ran on rows of shelves from wall
to wall and floor to ceiling: an emperor's ransom in
paper, parchment and painted silk, tooled-leather tomes
and fragile scrolls in lacquer cases, books common,
books rare and books priceless, all jostling for prominence. Almost all had come from the famous shop at
the Sign of Four Cranes in Ternon, and did not need to
be kept under lock and key except for their value to any
discerning thief, should one be bold enough to rob the
Overlord's fortress.

But some few had come from other sources, and these
were locked away from prying eyes in the one object
which spoiled an otherwise lovely room. At first glance
the place looked scholarly, somewhere philosophers
could comfortably debate an obscure point of dogma
over a dish of honeyed fruit and a glass or three of dark
red Jouvaine wine. Two incongruities gave the lie to that
gentle image; one was a casket made of dully-gleaming
blued steel and the other, an enormous velvet curtain
stretching half the length of the end wall. Ignoring that
curtain for the present, Sedna walked to the metal
case—almost as tall as herself, its surface etched with
delicate, minutely detailed and gruesomely active
figures—and stared at it while she gathered up the courage needed to look inside.

Its key went everywhere with her built into a massive
ring which dominated the centre knuckles of her slim
left hand. The key and the casket which it fitted had
been brought at her own considerable expense from the
foundries of Egisburg, and had been installed here quite

openly. Her excuse both then and now was safety and nothing more; it was, she considered, a reasonable reason for locking any door, and Crisen at least did not question it. Also, and more importantly to Sedna's mind, she possessed the only key. Unsnapping a jewelled catch which released its elaborate wards from the body of the ring, she inserted that only key into the lock and twisted: once, twice, and the iron door opened.

Had Sedna been a little more observant she might have noticed the miniscule scratches round the keyhole's outer rim, and also might have discovered a thin film of grease within it, the metal-flecked residue of which glistened faintly on the key as she withdrew it. But she was not . . . and she did not.

For at that point she hesitated, and strangely so; all her preceding actions had been swift and sure, not considered by first or second thoughts. Yet now something prevented her from reaching into the casket. Fear, perhaps, or merely apprehension—an unwillingness to discover at last what it was that had brought her here.

Steeling herself, Sedna put both hands inside and withdrew the bulk of *Enciervanul Doamnisoar,* momentarily repelled as always by the smooth, sleek contact of its flawless leather cover, knowing as she did what that leather was supposed to be: the skin of a virgin girl, probably of the same peasant stock as Sedna was herself, her back flayed with flint while she still lived and then tanned to the softness of a lady's glove as binding for this most terrible of grimoires.

"Probably pigskin," Sedna muttered to herself as she laid the book down on a lectern. She said something of the sort on every occasion when she had cause to touch the awesome volume, although Father and Mother and Maiden all witness how few those occasions had been; and despite that reassuring scepticism she still had to resist a wish to wipe some unseen residue of suffering from her hands. It was several minutes before she could force herself to unsnap the three bronze hasps which held the covers shut, and longer still before she opened them.

When at last she did so, she found with a little thrill of horror that no searching through its pages would be necessary. The book was accomplishing that all by itself. Logic stated that this was because—like all such thick-spined hand-bindings—there was a tendency to fall open at some weak point in its structure. But logic had no room for argument where magic was concerned . . . The leaves flicked past, making a tiny sound like mice behind wainscoting, and gradually slowed as if some unseen scholar neared the place he sought. Then they stopped.

And Sedna bit back on a wail of fear.

Unseen behind her, two pairs of eyes watched curiously through spyports all but hidden behind a carefully arranged half-row of scrolls . . .

*

Aldric emerged slowly from the barrow, noting with a faint, disinterested surprise that the shadows thrown by the surrounding trees had barely encroached upon the clearing from the places where he had last observed them. This meant that he had been within the mound for less than a quarter-hour—yet it had seemed much more. Strange indeed . . .

A human figure, no more than a vague outline of black against the silvered grass, was watching him from beneath the lightning-blasted tree. Though he could not see the eyes, he could sense them on him and sense too something else: annoyance . . . ? disbelief . . . ? perhaps relief . . . ? Aldric could not tell. His hand moved almost of its own volition to the holstered *telek;* but he had already recognised the silhouette of Evthan's lanky frame and forced himself not merely to relax, but even to wear a thin smile on a face which it did not fit. False bravado, he thought grimly, was coming to be a habit and a bad one at that. A poor, playacting affectation. The smile dissolved as if it had never been.

As he drew closer, he could make out details—and these did not accord with the image he had formed inside his head of what he might expect to see. Angered that no alarm and no aid had come from outside when he needed it, during the past few minutes he had conjured reasons enough out of his imagination. Consequently he more than half expected to find Evthan dead or injured—even to meet him emerging from wherever he had hidden from a superior number of armed men.

Even this last, a demonstration of caution to the point of cowardice, would not have irritated the Alban— Evthan was a hunter rather than a warrior—or at least, not as much as what he actually found: a man unhurt, unruffled and not even out of breath. There was no trace at all of Evthan's involvement in a scuffle; even his bow was unstrung and his quiver laced shut. Like the bubbles in a pot of boiling water, Aldric felt fury begin to swell up inside him, rising to the surface so that he was hard put to control his features long enough to hear the Jouvaine's explanation. Which, from Evthan's first words, did not exist in any recognisable form.

"One got away," the hunter said.

Even in the pallid moonlight Aldric's face flushed visibly red with rage, and the only sense the he could utter was: "*What* did you say . . . ?"

"One of them escaped," Evthan repeated, either unaware of or unconcerned by the effect his words were having. "I assume the other three are dead?"

"You *assume* . . ." A more choleric man than Aldric would have spluttered then, or shouted, but instead he spoke in a soft, low, freezing voice which at long last told Evthan that all was not as he thought it should be. "And you did nothing." The accusation was unmistakable. "You saw them, you clearly counted them and yet you did nothing. Why, for God's sweet sake?"

"Because I thought I heard something." Even as he spoke both men knew how feeble any excuse must sound aloud. And both were quite correct . . . "You heard it yourself," Evthan elaborated. "You must have done. A wolf howled."

"A wolf howled . . ." Aldric echoed, and his disbelieving tone was an unpleasant thing to hear. "I know a wolf howled. But I also know how long those soldiers were in the tomb before I heard it . . . so credit me with some intelligence at least! I ask again, one last time: you chose to give me neither help nor warning. Why not?"

"Aldric, I tell you—" Evthan tried to say, but he was cut short by a glare and by a gesture of one blood-encrusted hand. That the movement hurt did nothing to improve the Alban's temper.

"You tell me *nothing!* All through this hunt, you have

told me nothing. Since we met, you have told me nothing!'' That was not quite true, and Evthan knew it—but he was not so rash as to point out the error. "Back to Valden, forest warden, Geruath's retainer!''

So *that* was what was wrong, the hunter realised, and it sent a shiver of unease crawling down his backbone. He looked at his companion's face, and did not like what he saw there even though he recognised it easily enough. That same sick, raging helplessness had burned behind his own eyes too many times for him to mistake it now.

"I have finished speaking, Wolfsbane." Aldric's cold voice cut into the Jouvaine's thoughts. "Walk. In front of me, and slowly." Many things that he might say came to Evthan's mind in a single instant, but he rejected each and every one of them with just one weary shrug.

Aldric watched him walk away and fell into step not too far yet not too close behind. If the hunter had glanced back at that moment, he would have seen the Alban ease his bow out of its case and fit a carefully selected arrow to the string. The missile's flared and wicked barbs flashed once in the broken moonlight; not steel but silver, and rather less than razor sharp—but at such a range as this an untipped shaft alone would be enough to kill . . . If such a need arose.

Though he could give no proof of his suspicions, Aldric was filled with an overwhelming sense of being used—that he was a dupe, a catspaw, an unwitting pawn in someone else's game. Crisen Geruath's, maybe—or even *mathern-an* Rynert's. Or General Goth's, or Prokrator Bruda's . . . There were too many players, and evidently insufficient pieces to go round . . .

He had nothing more to say to Evthan; no questions left to ask, even had he hoped for some half-truthful answers. Because he knew already who the soldiers served—the one called Keel had told him as much—and even why they had come to the old barrow after dark, though that was heavily padded out by guesswork and his own memories. Memories . . . ? If only he could forget . . . !

> *Issaqua comes to find me*
> *To take my life and soul.*

For I am lost
And none can help me now.
Issaqua sings the song of desolation
And fills the world with Darkness.
Bringing fear and madness.
Despair and death to all.

As shreds of cloud slid slowly in to mask the moon, Aldric found the fine hairs on his skin prickle at his clothing as if he was cold. Except that he was not cold— or if he was, the weather had nothing to do with it.

*

The gates of the village were shut and barred when they reached them, and Evthan had to shout at the top of his voice several times before someone inside opened up. It was probably, he explained, because the villagers were all asleep by now. Aldric stared at him but said nothing, long past the need to make small talk. He guessed the hunter was probably right but both guess and explanation were completely wrong, as became clear once they were within the palisade.

Instead of darkness there was light. An extravagance of lamps and torches and candles hung outside each house; and most of all around the home of headman Darath. Aldric half-heard Evthan mutter, "A council meeting? Now . . . ?" but paid no attention as he pushed past the Jouvaine and stepped inside the headman's house. Maybe half a dozen of those sitting nearest the door looked up as he came in, but the rest were more concerned with their own affairs, an attitude which told him how important those affairs must be. There were no questions about his success—or otherwise—in hunting, no interest at all in the fact that he was smeared and spotted with dry blood and—most curiously—no invitation, polite or otherwise, for him to leave, even though he had expected something of the sort.

Sensing Evthan at his back, Aldric moved to one side, leaned against the wall and listened to a debate which judging both by volume and by passionate gesticulation had been going on for quite some time. Though for the most part they used the Jouvaine language that he knew, there were still enough dialect words flung to and fro across the table for the Alban to need all his concentration if he was to make sense of what they said.

And what they were discussing, if the uproar could be dignified by such a word, was a suggestion that the village be abandoned. Reasons good and bad, for and against, were expounded loudly and at length; but it all boiled down to the same thing—the Beast, and the Beast alone, was the source of all the forest's troubles. Aldric turned his head, caught Evthan's eye and raised one doubting eyebrow. *Oh indeed,* he thought; *how little they know.*

One man, a grizzled elder, got to his feet and rapped the table. It was a measure of the respect he commanded that the shouting and argument died away almost at once.

"Say what you will about how long your families have lived here; all of us know what is wrong now and why we can live here no longer. This three months past we have put no silver in the coffers of Valden, though we have taken out as much as—more than—ever we do in Spring. I have looked at the money-chests, and they are *empty.* Nothing remains. Soon we will begin to starve. All this, because six men must do the work of one, for fear of the Beast."

There was an undertone of condemnation in his voice which provoked a rippling of murmurs—but significantly, nothing loud enough to be distinguished from the buzz of sound nor sufficiently clear for any source to be identified. Aldric too was tempted to point out that men, above all, seemed in no danger from the Beast—had not Evthan told him so, in as many words?—but he kept the comment to himself. Justified or not, it was not his place to say so, especially when he had other words for the assembled villagers to hear.

His clenched right fist boomed against the wall, and now not half-a-dozen but every head in the place turned as if on a single neck to stare at him. Already, like some defensive mechanism, he was smiling that thin, sardonic smile which was becoming far too much at home on his face.

"You will eventually choose to do whatever you think is best, of course," he said, in a tone suggesting that their choice of "best" would not be his at all. "But I would advise you not to waste much time on your deliberations."

"How came you bloodied, sir?" The formal phrasing came from Darath himself; unmistakably the headman, he sat at the head of the table, farthest in the room from Aldric and his high-backed chair was carved more richly than any other in the room. More richly, thought the Alban, than a peasant should be sitting on—and the carvings were not folk-art, trees and flowers and animals, but armed warriors and stylised crest-beasts. Another question added to the many . . . Darath himself was greying, dignified, his face half-hidden by the sweep of a steel-hued moustache. Peasant or not, Aldric straightened from his slouch and bowed before replying.

"That, sir, is the point of my advice," he answered. "In the forest I had cause to kill tonight. Three mercenary soldiers in the service of your Overlord." Aldric heard the collective gasp of horror but his gaze did not break contact with the headman's eyes. Even at that distance he saw a dilation of the pupils. "This," he raised his left hand in its clotted web of red-black trickles, "is my own blood, while this—" the gloved right hand came up, its smooth black leather roughened by unpleasantly coagulated spatterings, "—is from the veins of a Drusalan man called Keel."

"You have slain Keel . . . ?" Darath's voice was neutral now and Aldric could read nothing into it or from it. He nodded, once.

"In a fight, face to face."

"Then, honoured sir," and the warmth in Darath's voice was unmistakable, "you have rid the Jevaiden of an evil greater than the Beast. At least it has excuses for its beastly nature—Keel had not."

"Listen to me, headman!" Aldric cut through a rising undercurrent of jubilation. After what they had discussed tonight, and evidently all but decided, any small triumph would be a cause for celebration. Let them celebrate then—but only with full awareness of the whole story. *"Darath!"* Sudden silence—it was unlikely that anyone had pronounced a headman's name like that in his own house since Valden village was chopped from

the trees. "Let me finish, will you?" the Alban snapped.
"I killed three. There were four. One escaped. Even now
he's probably telling Geruath and Crisen everything that
happened . . . and he'll mention that before they attacked me I spoke Evthan's name aloud. How long will
it be before more soldiers raid this village, looking for
him, for me—for anyone who gave me food, gave me
water, gave me even a friendly word? Eh?"

"How . . ." Darath's voice cracked and he was forced
to try again. "How, if you were able to kill three, did
you let one get away?" There was a pathetic desperation
in the way he asked the question and for just a moment
Aldric wished that he had a better answer. But he had
not.

"Ask Evthan all about it," he said grimly, inclining
his head into another slight bow of departure. "I am
going to my bed."

                              *

Even though that bed was in Evthan's own house, the
hunter did not follow to let him in. Aldric was not surprised, for after that enigmatic parting shot the council
would hardly let him leave without some sort of explanation. Yet when he reached the house its door was already unlocked, held only by the hasp.

Gueynor was inside, sitting on a low stool near the
fire. She glanced up as he entered but said only, "Good
evening, *hlensyarl*," before returning her attention to the
pot which was creating such a savoury smell as it simmered above a bed of raked red coals.

Aldric nodded to her with equal curtness as he took
a seat. "Good evening to you too, woman of the house,"
he said, and the way in which he spoke was neither
complimentary nor particularly humorous. Seeing her
had reawakened his own dull feeling of self-loathing,
such as any *kailin-eir* would feel after using poisoned
weapons against men. It was a vague brooding sensation,
not directed at anyone specifically, but Gueynor was
here now and she had offered him the venoms in the
first place, so . . .

She lifted a lid, stirred, tasted, stirred again and replaced the lid before looking at him for any length of

time. "You had no success in your hunting, then?" It was more an observation than a question.

"No," the Alban returned laconically.

"But there is always tomorrow." Aldric stared at her but said nothing, trying to sift the many meanings from that simple sentence. A red-glazed flask of wine: and a cup made from the same material sat on a table near him, and he poured himself a brimming measure, draining more than half of it before he trusted his own brain and tongue sufficiently to speak. There was also a slight hope that it would numb the steadily increasing throb of his left arm, which from the disgusting wet squelch of his shirt-sleeve was still leaking stealthily. "Tomorrow night," he said quietly and carefully, "is both full moon and summer solstice."

If Gueynor read more than the obvious from his soft words, her firelit face showed no sign of it. Instead she merely shrugged and said, "The full moon should give good light to hunt by."

So we understand one another at long last. Aldric favoured her with a smile which put a more than reasonable number of his teeth on show: a wolfish smile. She did not match it, even mockingly, but looked away instead and prodded with a poker at the coals as if they had suddenly become her enemy and the flat-tipped bar of iron a sword. The Alban emptied another cup of wine in silence. Then a third. He could feel his senses start to swim as the alcohol entered his blood, and was glad of it—there were many reasons why he wanted to be drunk tonight. He poured again, and over the rim of that half-finished measure stared at Gueynor through hooded eyes. "What brings you here after midnight anyway?"

The girl regarded him through wide blue eyes that were full of innocence. "To feed you, why else?" she replied.

Aldric smirked again, a deliberately nasty expression that was harsh and humourless. "I can think of several reasons," he purred. The challenge hung unanswered on the air, and he adopted another method of inquiry. "That stuff you keep stirring—what is it?"

His abruptness seemed to have awakened an answering chord in Gueynor, for she retorted, "Stew," and left it at that.

Aldric repeated himself. "What is it?"

She told him, at some length, then stared and said acidly, "Why? What else do you want in it?"

Again the wolfish smile. "And will you tell me how it's prepared, if I ask further?" he wondered aloud. "For instance, when do you add something from your aunt's basketful of potions? Before or after the salt?" It was unjust to say such things and, worse, he knew the injustice of it. But he was frightened, sickened, in considerable pain and above all tired of being someone else's plaything.

Gueynor did not raise her voice in protest at his unspoken accusation, nor was she even irritated by his petulant righteousness at condemning the poisons she had only offered—but which he had used. "They were given you to kill the Beast," was all she said. "I neither know nor want to know what else you used them for. I only know what they were meant to kill."

The young Alban set down his wine-cup and leaned towards her. "Tell me, Gueynor," and now his voice was flat and neutral, "do you really think that poison will affect the thing which roams the woods at night? For I do not."

"I merely hope."

"Hope . . . ?" said Aldric sombrely. "I think that hope is worth next to nothing where the Beast is concerned."

"Then you are convinced?"

"Convinced enough. As much, as least; as any man need be—lacking absolute proof."

Part of a thick log, burned through, slumped in the fire and gave birth to a cloud of whirling sparks. Flames sprung up with a crackle and as quickly died away. Aldric felt the sudden splash of heat against his face and pulled back with a gasp, but Gueynor did not move even though she sat much closer to the fire than he did.

"You'll burn up if you stay there, girl! Take my hand."

She looked at the outstretched glove in ill-concealed horror, seeing for the first time the caked blood and involuntarily shrinking away from the grisly sight. Then

Gueynor's gaze went to the Alban's left hand, as if expecting it to be proffered instead, and saw there still more clotted gore. "You didn't tell me you were hurt," she said, and somehow managed to make it sound as if he was to blame.

There was only one response to such an approach and despite the cliché Aldric used it: "You didn't ask." Had he been a little more sober he would not have said it; had he been more sober and more in control of himself, he would not have said most of the things spoken that night. Easier recall an arrow than a thoughtless word . . .

"Let me see that." Gueynor was on her feet at once, entirely businesslike, all their verbal hacking of the past few minutes set aside. "Take off your jerkin, and your shirt."

Aldric hesitated, shifting uneasily; the girl smiled at what seemed to be embarrassed modesty and reached out to tug gently at his clothes. "I—I would sooner have a bath first," the Alban said, twitching back the half-inch necessary to avoid her fingers. What he would sooner do was discard the armoured sleeves he wore; Evthan knew of them already, quite by chance, and that was one person too many. And the thing he wanted from his saddlebags was an item he most definitely wished kept secret. Gueynor's solicitude was proving awkward. "It doesn't matter if there isn't any hot water—cold will do."

"I'll be washing your whole arm," Gueynor persisted, "not just around the wound. If it's still bleeding you'll have merely wasted time."

Her reasoning was eminently practical and forced Aldric to abandon practicalities as, mind racing, he pressed two fingers against his jerkin sleeve. No blood had yet seeped through the leather—all had been channelled down his arm along the inner surface, after soaking through his shirt and the padded lining of his armour—but even that light touch left a pair of soggy indentations and produced an ugly sucking sound.

Gueynor's face took on an expression of distaste. "You see?" he said. "This will likely make a mess no matter what I do, or when—but I must strip to the skin and wash. Now I . . . killed tonight."

As was becoming habitual with him, Aldric left his

statement uncompleted for the girl to draw her own conclusions. Gueynor did not disappoint him—indeed, she
employed the very word he wanted her to use.

"Unclean?"

He nodded, saying nothing more aloud and thus man-
aging to imply reluctance to discuss the situation further.
It was all nonsense, at least for an orthodox Alban, no
matter how devout—which Aldric certainly was not—for
such things had no part in their religious observances.
Yet it was easy to connect their well-known fondness
for bathing with a requirement to be ritually cleansed
of blood.

Gueynor moved aside, her face clouding with concern
at her apparent indiscretion in mentioning the matter.
Her discomfort, indeed, was communicating itself so
strongly to him that he regretted using such an excuse
at all, lest in every truth some blasphemy pollute him.
When that uneasy notion joined the thoughts already in
his mind, he was repelled. But something would have to
be done to the torn arm, and quickly . . .

Almost unconsciously his right hand traced a pious gesture between lips and brow, blessing himself against ill-
luck or worse, and he murmured, "Avert, amen." Then
blinked; those words had not been spoken since his childhood, and never even then with such honest sincerity. *Why
use them now . . . ?* he wondered nervously, and left the
house more quickly than he had intended.

*

Opening a pannier of his pack-saddle, Aldric rummaged
carefully for several seconds before withdrawing the object he had come for. Gemmel's parting gift . . . At first
sight it appeared to be a piece of jewellery, an armlet
made of silvered steel whose gemstone was protected by
a bag of soft white leather. The Alban stared at it in
silence, then drew in a deep breath and secured its triple
loops about his left wrist, settling the covered jewel comfortably in the hollow of his palm above the four pale
criss-cross lines of his Honour-scars. He flexed his fingers, closing them into a fist; and when he opened them
again, undid the lace and pulled the buckskin pouch
away.

Lambent azure brilliance pulsed from the crystal the

pouch had contained, rising to a tapering blue flame three feet in height before it died down to a pulsing glow that lapped and coiled about his hand like burning brandy. Yet there was no heat emanating from it. None at all.

The spellstone of Echainon . . . One of seven lost to the Wise for many hundred years, this one had been found by Aldric, accidentally, on the battlefield of Baelen Fight. The aftermath of that discovery was something that the Alban had no wish to recall. It was a potent talisman of great antiquity, imbued with such power that even Gemmel did not know its limitations; yet the old enchanter had entrusted him with this awesome thing . . . The responsibility scared him. What scared him more was Gemmel's certainty that he shared some affinity with the crystal, because the last man of whom that was claimed had been Kalarr cu Ruruc. Heedless of Aldric's protests, he had removed it from its setting on Ykraith the Dragonwand and placed it on this bracelet as a luck-piece for his foster son.

"It is not a weapon, Aldric," the old man had told him firmly. "Not like the Dragonwand, at least, although you can use it as such. But I can trust you to treat it honourably, as I could trust few others in this realm. Take it, with my blessing."

"How can I use it?" Aldric had protested. "I don't know how! I'm not a wizard!"

"You *will* know, when you have to. As it will know you." Aldric had not liked the thought of being recognised by a piece of enchanted glass and had said so. "Remember the Claiming of Ykraith," was Gemmel's only further comment; he had not been drawn again.

No matter what he had been told, Aldric knew the spellstone was dishonourable, unAlban, unTalvalin before God! But he had accepted it and carried it—and taken great care not to use it. Until now, and only through necessity. His gloved right hand groped unseeing for his *tsepan* and tugged the still-sheathed dirk out of his weapon-belt. Its massive pommel glittered in the crystal's light like a chunk of ice; pure silver, and anathema to evil magic. Not caring what might happen, he touched it firmly to the spellstone and closed his eyes.

Then opened them again, his breathing coming rather

easier already. There had been no adverse reaction—
indeed, no reaction at all. The stone's cold fire throbbed
now in time with the beating of his heart; it was a part
of him, its energies an extension of his own will. Aldric
sank down crosslegged in the straw of the stable floor,
his back braced by the wall, and set his *tsepan* back in
its accustomed place before raising the talisman level
with his eyes.

"*Abath arhan,*" he said softly, not fully comprehend-
ing where the words came from. "*Alh'noen ecchaur i
aiyya.*" There was a faint humming and he felt the Echainon stone grow warm against his skin, its sapphire nimbus flinging out tendrils of smoky light that poured like
mist between his outstretched fingers.

He was no longer frightened of this sorcery, because
he was no longer ignorant of what to do. Relaxed in
mind and body, he pressed the palms of both his hands
together, fingers interlaced as if in prayer or supplication, and bowed his head until his knuckles touched
his forehead.

And after that, nothing . . .

*

So tired . . . Aldric opened leaden eyelids and rolled his
head back on a neck whose muscles seemed incapable
of supporting any weight. Tired . . .

There was no light in the stable; he had brought no
candle, risking neither fire nor discovery, and the dilute
trickling of moonbeams through almost unseen cracks
did not count as illumination. No light . . . ? Spreading
his clasped hands, Aldric looked down at the spellstone.
It was quite clear now, and magnified the lines and
creases of his palm beneath it as a lens might do; except
that, deep in its very core, there was a tiny fluttering of
blue-white fire. Other than the faint crawl of minute
flames there was nothing to betray the crystal as anything but a fine, first-water diamond cut without facets.

And other than the draining weariness which he had
expected after Gemmel's warning, there was nothing but
wet blood to betray that Aldric had been wounded. Inside the sleeve his arm might show a scar, but it would
be that of a wound completely healed and healthy. The
stone had taken energy from his own body and focused

it, greatly enhanced, on the injured tissues of that same body, accelerating the healing process. A useful magic indeed; but the strength it had withdrawn left him utterly fatigued.

"Sorcery," Gemmel had told him often, "is not free, as the air is free. It has a price which must be paid. Sometimes that price is higher than might be expected—but not even the mightiest wizards can evade it."

Aldric was paying his price now.

He dragged himself upright with an effort that brought sweat to his skin, and leaned panting against the stable wall for many minutes before he dared to take the steps which would bring him to his saddlebags. Aldric had heard of people so exhausted that they fell asleep on their feet, and had never believed the stories . . . Not until this minute. Vaguely he wondered if using the talisman as a weapon would kill him before it killed his enemies . . . then his outstretched fingertips hit the saddle-rack with a jarring impact that shocked him painfully awake. Moving as fast as he was able, Aldric stripped the spellstone's metal framework from his wrist and pushed it deep into the pannier, tugged a few pieces of clothing down to hide it and fumbled the straps back into their buckles.

Only when everything was as he had found it did he stagger to the door and out into the moonlit night. The charm of healing had not taken long—he could tell that from the still-liquid blood on his left arm—but even so it would be better if he was in the bath-house when anyone came looking for him. As they inevitably would.

*

The copper boiler evidently backed onto the cooking-fire of Evthan's house, for it was brimful of scalding water when Aldric looked inside. "Civilised, at least," he muttered, and used most of it to fill the bath-tub—but before he climbed in and inevitably fell asleep he squirmed free of his sticky armour and rinsed it carefully. If there was an unseen crack somewhere in the lacquer proofing, salt blood would etch rust into the metal underneath as quickly as immersion in the sea, corroding it until one day the mail would give beneath a blow . . .

His precautions explained the odd smell of hot oiled metal which pervaded the steamy atmosphere of the bath-house; but it still puzzled Gueynor when she entered unannounced, bearing ointments, bandages—and more ominously, a small brazier of glowing coals with a broad knife thrust into it.

Aldric opened heavy, red-rimmed eyes, gazed at it and had no delusions about why he slithered down into the tub. "You don't believe in knocking, then?" he wondered in a weak attempt at humour.

"No—should I?" There might have been genuine surprise in Gueynor's voice, but the Alban somehow doubted it. Setting her burden on a bench, she spread her skirts and sank down on both knees, drawing the single oil-lamp closer to avoid the splashes on the floor. Aldric watched her kneel with a degree of curiosity; he had seen court ladies perform that self-same action with less grace and elegance. Then he forgot about the things he had or had not seen when she took his left arm in a gentle grasp and drew it closer to examine the ripped bicep.

An instant later she dropped the limb as if it had burned her and her eyes, staring into his, were suddenly the only coloured thing in a shock-bleached face. "Lady Mother Tesh protect me," she whispered, drawing a protective ward-mark between them. *"What happened to your arm?"*

Aldric's own dark agate eyes did not waver. "It healed, as you can see," he said, and flexed the muscle for her inspection. A narrow, slighty uneven line ran white as chalk across the tanned skin; it was not scar tissue, merely a mark such as a brush might leave—but nowhere near as natural.

"What kind of man are you, *hlensyarl?* An enchanter?"

Aldric shook his head. "A man, like other men. Perhaps a little better educated in strange subjects than most, I grant you. But nothing more."

"What do you know of Sedna?" The question was strange; it confused him, and on his tired face the confusion showed. "Sedna ar Gethin," Gueynor added by way of expansion, "Lord Crisen's mist—Consort."

The name told Aldric little but the woman's origin: Vreijaur, to the west of here. And . . . No, impossible . . . ! Dewan ar Korentin's birthplace! He damned the weariness that clogged his mind, because he should have picked up that particular connection straight away. Dewan ar Korentin, presently the champion, confidant and friend of King Rynert—but ten years an *eldheisart* in the Imperial Bodyguard at Drakkesborg!

Not that he suspected the Vreijek of turning traitor, or of betraying him; after what the Empire had done to make him desert a favoured and highly-decorated post, Dewan was most unlikely to offer any aid to *that* source. But Aldric knew a little of how ar Korentin's mind worked and that nothing, no matter how convoluted, was beyond him. A sudden vivid memory struck him: he was sitting in the captain's chair of the galion *En Sohra*, absorbing the knowledge that Dewan had used his ignorant—and therefore unfeigned—innocence to fool the commander of an Imperial battleram. Having considered ar Korentin's explanation for some time, he had finally said: "You are a devious bastard!" He had meant what he said, everyone who heard him knew it. And Dewan had smiled, and bowed, quite happy with the compliment . . .

"Give me a towel, Gueynor, please," said Aldric, just as the girl thought he was drifting back to sleep. "And would you turn your back . . . ?"

Even through her shock, Gueynor had to stifle an automatic smile at his request. Most of the men that she had known in her young life were not exactly overnice . . . Water sloshed in the tub and spattered noisily across the tiled floor, then she heard the slap of bare feet and the scrubbing of the towel being put to use. It was thrown aside when she chanced a rapid overshoulder glance—but by that time Aldric had resumed his leather breeches and was having some small difficulty with their calf-laces.

Gueynor analyzed what she could see of the young Alban's body, and if her scrutiny was a little less dispassionate than a doctor's might have been she concealed it well. He was muscled like an athlete, well-defined but lithe, and there were several traces of past injuries sketched lightly on his skin; yet none could properly be termed scars, apart from that beneath the right eye. All the rest had that strange chalked-on look, as if a damp cloth might wipe them away—and as if the wounds had been repaired by something other than the passage of time.

"Now," he said, straightening, "what about Sedna?" And yawned hugely.

"Never mind questions now," Gueynor replied, even though she had a great many of her own. "You should be in bed. You look," her hand reached out and touched his scarred cheek just below the drooping eyelid, "as if you haven't slept in days."

"But . . ." Gueynor's hand touched his mouth, silencing him.

"Hush! In some ways you may no longer need my help, but in others I can still prove useful." She smiled, but without coquetry.

Aldric blinked and sifted what she said. Despite the content of her words the girl was not playing the seductress; she was genuinely concerned for his health. Why that should be so important, he did not know—unless her reason was tomorrow's hunt. . . But surely Dewan would have told him . . . ? Irrelevancies blurred together in his brain and the room began to swim. He staggered slightly, and might have fallen had not Gueynor caught one outflung arm and helped him regain his balance.

"Bed, Kourgath!" she insisted. "Better lie down—next time I might not be able to hold you." She wondered briefly if he had been drugged, for though he had drunk heavily and rapidly after coming into the house, Gueynor felt sure that three-and-a-half cups would not be enough to get this man into such a state.

It was all very, very strange . . .

4

Shoot Silver at the Moon

... I know that I am lost, and none can help me now ...
Night surrounds me ... I am lost ... None can help
me ... Lost ... Help me ... help me ... help me ...
help me help me *help me HELP*—

"NO!"

And he was awake.

Aldric lay flat on his back, shuddering all over. Even
though he was far too familiar with nightmares, that had
been the worst of all: the kind of dream which would
make him too afraid to ever sleep again, if he could
recall its details afterwards. But it was gone now, vanished like mist in the morning, and only the cold sweat
of fear remained.

The wan light of pre-dawn trickled through his bolted
bedroom shutters, making vague shapes of the furniture.
Familiar shapes, and comforting. Aldric rolled over in
the narrow bed, hoping to find more peaceful sleep—
and instead encountered warm, smooth flesh.

He sat bolt upright, drowsy eyelids snapped wide
open, and thought for just a moment when he saw the
tumbled blonde hair on his pillow that he was dreaming
again, and much more pleasantly this time. "Kyrin ... ?"

Gueynor.

The Jouvaine girl looked up at him and smiled shyly.
"You are embarrassed," she said. "I'm sorry. I should
have woken earlier and left you alone."

"Embarrassed ... ? Not at ... Not very." He raked
hair out of his eyes and knuckled at their sockets. "But
I thought—"

"Kyrin?" Gueynor, he thought, was most perceptive

for so early in the morning. Too perceptive for his liking. He nodded, only once and curtly.

"A lady I . . . once knew." Aldric breathed deeply, and changed the subject. "What happened?"

"Last night—or rather, earlier this morning? You slept. Even standing, on your way here from the bath-house. I have never seen a man so tired. It was . . . not a natural weariness. Do you . . ." She hesitated uncertainly, searching for words.

"Just say it."

"Do you use *ymeth*?"

"Dreamsmoke . . . ?" Aldric stared at her a moment and began to chuckle to himself. Not loudly, but with a quiet, honest amusement she had not seen from him before. "No, lady, not I. Indeed, I don't take any sort of smoke at all. Perhaps . . ." The laughter faltered and was gone. "Perhaps I should; I might sleep soundly every night."

"Not last night," murmured Gueynor. "You cried out. I held you close and kissed your lips, and you were still again. But you did not wake . . ."

"I . . . have bad dreams. Of death, and loss, and darkness. Of my father. I held his hand in mine and I could only watch. All the time and money spent to make me skilled in bringing death, yet I was incapable of bringing him one moment more of life . . . He bade me live, to avenge him. I took that great oath, I set aside my honour and I swore that I would keep faith. But he was already dead . . ."

Aldric's grey-green eyes were cold and distant, bright with unshed tears, and Gueynor shivered as she tried to imagine the mind controlling them. It was as if he read her thoughts.

"Not mad, Gueynor," he whispered, half to himself. "I think too much about the past, that's all. A common Alban vice. But no, not mad."

His left hand, with the heavy gold ring on its third finger, stroked down the line of Gueynor's jaw until it cupped her chin. She could feel the warm metal press against her as his grip closed. Its pressure was neither rough nor painful—but it was inescapable. For just an instant the girl started like a frightened animal, and then she relaxed. Completely. Her behaviour puzzled Aldric, so that the notch of a slight frown inscribed itself between his brows. Although he had often heard of people resigning themselves to the inevitable, this was the first time he had ever seen it happen and the experience was not particularly pleasant. Yet another question, he thought despairingly.

"Since we seem for once to be exchanging intimacies, my lady,"—and there was no sarcasm in his employment of the title—"I grow curious about what secrets you might choose to tell me."

The mere prospect of answering his questions seemed to frighten her, as it invariably did; the Alban suspected that physical assault would affect her less than a verbal interrogation. But why . . . ?

"What do you want to know . . . ?" Gueynor faltered timidly.

Match one question with another . . . What *don't* I want to know? "Tell me . . ." Aldric paused a moment, marshalling his thoughts into some semblance of order. The task rapidly assumed monumental proportions and he shrugged, abandoning the attempt. "Tell me everything," he concluded bluntly. "From the beginning."

Whether or not the girl would do it was another matter. In the event he was to be surprised . . . by many things.

"I have lived here since I was a child," Gueynor began, and if Aldric felt any lack of patience that she should begin by stating the obvious, it did not show on his face. Because just then a tiny, disapproving voice inside his skull said: Hold your tongue, just once! There is no such thing as what you think is obvious! The voice was unmistakably Gemmel's.

Get out of my head . . . ! Aldric caught the words before they reached his lips, and those same lips twisted in a sheepish smile. *It's private—isn't it?* he finished, plaintively inaudible. There was no reply.

"My uncle Evthan," Gueynor was saying when the Alban refocused his attention, "has always been like a father to me; he took my real father's place early in my life, when my parents were . . . When they died."

This was all familiar ground to Aldric. Too familiar by far. "But surely his sister Aline is your—"

"Aunt. My adoptive mother, yes—but my aunt for all that."

"Oh . . ." Evthan had never actually said that his sister and his niece were mother and daughter; Aldric had merely assumed it. And had been wrong, as was not uncommon.

"My mother was called Sula; she was the youngest of the family and a most kind and gentle lady. That was why my father loved her as he did. Not for her rank and lands and titles, for she had none; and despite her beliefs, which were not his. He loved her for herself alone."

The Alban knew now why so many things about Gueynor and her uncle had been out of character for their chosen roles: the obstacles between her father and her mother were painfully familiar ones. But he had to hear the girl say it for herself. "Who was your father, lady?" he prompted quietly. "What was his name?"

"My father was . . . My true father was Erwan Evenou, the last Droganel Overlord of Seghar. Before the Geruaths came."

Aldric released a long sigh of understanding which was also an unconsciously held-in breath. "Ah . . . So! Many thing are becoming clear." He asked no more prompting questions, knowing that with this first hurdle crossed, Gueynor would find the talking—and the remembering— easier.

"Lord Erwan was already married when he met my mother by the river, one warm day in spring. His wife had been chosen for him, to bring an alliance, gold and land to Seghar. You know the custom?"

"I know it."

"He was young, your age or a little more; my mother, Sula, was not yet twenty. He was the Overlord of Seghar and she a peasant; he could have lain with her there and then or taken her to the citadel. He was the Overlord— he had the right. But he was also a courtly gentleman. Instead of violence and rape, he climbed from his tall horse and spoke softly to my mother, and paid her compliments as he would a high-born lady, and with his own hands gathered flowers for her along the river's edge."

Aldric wondered if that was what had really happened

or merely what Gueynor had been told—and immediately regretted his own cynicism. The thing was not impossible; many haughty lords were often romantics at heart. Kyrin had once told him that he himself . . . His mind veered from the memory. Did such long-past facts really matter to anyone but Gueynor anyway? No . . .

"The law allows a man of rank to take formal consorts in addition to his wife, and my father wanted to take my mother into his household respectably and openly. He petitioned his father, High Lord Evenou, at the Emperor's Summer Palace in Kalitzim; my mother told me that he rode there himself, wearing the overmantle of the Falcon couriers so that he could use the post-roads. When I was born the next spring, I was his daughter in all but rights of succession, and I lived in Seghar until I was eight years old."

Gueynor's narrative stopped and Aldric's eyes flicked to her face. The girl was lying on her back with the coverlet pulled up to her throat, and she had been talking into the air as if making a speech—her phrases correct and slightly stilted, her manner evidently unfamiliar. If she had spoken to him like that earlier, her pretence of being a peasant would have caused him even more confusion, and some slight amusement as well. It was plain now—with benefit of hindsight—that she had never really been other than what she was: the much-loved bastard of a lord who in all probability showed her more affection than to his legitimate children, because she was much more than the evidence of duty done to family and politics. Which was a dangerous attitude—alike for him, the child and her mother. Aldric had encountered extremes of jealousy more than once . . .

Gueynor's lips were pressed tightly together in an attempt to still their quivering, and there was a glisten of unshed tears in her wide-open eyes. The Alban could guess why, for he also had memories like that. Out of consideration and a degree of fellow-feeling, he kept his own mouth shut and waited until the girl regained her self-control. It did not take long—there was considerable strength of character beneath that pretty blonde exterior.

"I was happy for those eight years. My mother and my father were happy too. Then everything went wrong."

Aldric nodded; he had expected to hear those words
sooner or later, because the whole situation reeked of
vulnerability. What had happened, and what he was
about to hear, was preordained: as inevitable in its way
as the final scenes of a classic tragedy. All he had to
know was the how and why of it.

"Lord Erwan's wife died in childbed and the infant
died with her. There was no difficulty about inheritance:
he had two sons and another daughter besides myself.
But he decided that now he could, and would, marry my
mother: elevate her, give her rank and style and title
before the law as well as before the Gods."

Gueynor laughed, a hoarse little sound, and pushed
the heel of one hand against her forehead. "The
Gods . . . Yes, that was the trouble. I know nothing
about your Alban beliefs, Kourgath, but here in the Jevaiden and in Vreijaur we have a different faith from the
Imperial lands. In Drusul, Vlech, Tergoves, the Emperor
is held to be a god, descended in direct line from the
Father of Fires. *Ya an-Sherban bystrei, vodyaj cho'da
tlei.* Hah!" She made a spitting noise. " 'Revere all those
of the Sherban dynasty, for their words are the words
of Heaven.' " So they say. It is even written on their
banners . . . And yet how much reverence have the
Grand Warlords shown their Emperors, eh?

"This would be of little account if the Senate had not
ruled that all lords owing fealty to the Empire should
worship as Sherbanul. Also their immediate families."

"Including wives . . . ?"

"Especially wives—or husbands. If they are of a different faith they must reject it, publicly, before the provincial exark. When my mother Sula refused to renounce
the Three Gods, my father Erwan broke with all prece-
dent and adopted the Teshirin holiness. They were married by those rites. It would have been better by far if
he had set aside the lordship first, rather than attempt
to hold it as what the Drusalans are pleased to call a
Tesh heretic.

"The soldiers came, as he thought they would—but
not to depose him, as he had expected. To do that, first
he would have been granted an opportunity to speak
before the Senate and to have been punished by their

ruling. Instead—'' She broke off, but when Aldric rolled over slightly, expecting tears, he saw instead such a cold hatred as he had never witnessed on any woman's face— not even on Lyseun's, and before Heaven ar Korentin's wife had made her dislike of him all too plain.

"The soldiers killed him?" Though the phrasing was a question, Aldric knew quite well that it was the truth. Gueynor quibbled only with his choice of words.

"They *murdered* him. They cut him down in his own High Hall, and they claimed he had been beguiled and tainted beyond redemption even by the Lord Politark at Drakkesborg. They claimed, too, that my mother had enchanted him—that she was a sorceress. And the punishment for sorcery is . . . is—"

"Is better left unmentioned." Aldric knew what the penalty entailed; Gemmel had told him once and had not needed to repeat it. Use was made of slow fires, blades, hot brine and molten lead in a fashion only a sick mind could have created. If that had been done to Gueynor's mother . . . He felt nauseated, his imagination briefly touching on—and then crushing out of existence—vile images which had no place in his brain.

"They killed his whole family. My family. I escaped because Evthan was there that day. He was chief forester to the Overlord, and not just because of Sula; he always merited such titles. When he took me out, past the soldiers, he told any who asked that I was his daughter and that we had come to see the great town of Seghar. Two of them tried to stop us, but I remember their officer— he was very tall, with a black beard—commanded them to let us through. He said, 'If any of my children were in this place, I'd want them out before they saw what we have to do! Get out, you, and quickly,'—this to my uncle—'and don't come back until things settle down!' "

Gueynor's eyes closed and she lay still and silent for so long that it appeared she was asleep. Then she murmured: "Since that day I've lived in Valden. I've learned to be a peasant, as best I can, and to accept my place. You learn a lot in ten years. But I haven't learned how to forget. Or forgive. Oh, you can't understand what it feels like to have everything snatched violently from you!"

Oh, can't I . . . ? thought Aldric. *Maybe one day I'll tell you. Or maybe not.*

"Seghar has been ruled by a succession of soldiers—*eldheisartin, hautheisartin,* high ranks but not so high that they suffer from delusions of grandeur. Two years ago the Geruaths arrived. Father and son, each as . . . peculiar . . . as the other. They make a fine pair. It was Lord Geruath who arranged for my father's murder. I learned this from . . . from sources who know. Yet he bided his time for eight years until he was invited to the Lordship by his patron Etzel. As a reward for continuing support."

"Etzel? Grand Warlord Etzel . . . ?" Aldric had been told that Geruath sided with the Emperor, and had been assured that the Overlord of Seghar was an Alban ally, a means to contact Goth and Bruda. But now . . .

"Of course the Warlord. Who else?" Gueynor, brooding on what might have been, was becoming haughty and impatient. There was something else in her voice as well, something which Aldric recognised but could not place. "My uncle Evthan went to Geruath and humbly requested his place as forester, claiming no more loyalty to my father than to any man who could no longer pay him for his duties. That amused our loving lord, for he's a man like that himself. But one day my uncle will be able to entice Lord Geruath into the Deepwood. Alone. And I'll be waiting for him. I'll teach him the cost of Seghar. It will be the last lesson he'll ever learn . . ."

Aldric knew now what he had detected in her voice—the vocal equivalent of that hate he had seen so briefly on her face. Its venom forced him to repress a shiver: a low, ugly snarl, there was yet no way he could condemn it or its sentiments. He had felt the same way, done the same things, directed the same long-brooded hate at Duergar and Kalarr. Indeed, the loathing which had festered inside him for four years had been so powerful that the talisman Ykraith had focused it, directed it as a pulse of fiery energy and used it to roast Duergar Vathach where he stood. And Gueynor had been anticipating vengeance for ten years . . .

Her mood was past now, but he knew that he would never look at this girl in quite the same way again.

"I wonder if Geruath suspects something?" she muttered to herself, ignoring the Alban as if he was not there, "He hasn't come out of the citadel in months. Except that time they dug up the old mound—and then he and Crisen were surrounded by soldiers. Mercenaries. Why mercenaries . . . ? Don't they trust—"

"What about mercenaries?" Aldric had a certain interest in hired troops after his encounter the previous night.

"There are few Jouvaines in the garrison at Seghar now. Most of them are just retainers—servants and the like—while the rest are Drusalan or Tergovan. Filth! A troop came here four months ago, just at the end of winter. They were riding through to Seghar, nothing more—they hadn't even been taken on by the Overlord when it happened. Which was just as well."

"When *what* happened?" It was apparently Aldric's expected role to utter link questions which would bridge Gueynor's thoughtful pauses; he felt like an unimportant actor in a stage play, one of Osmar's complicated dramas with a deal of talk but little action.

"One of them was a man who called himself Keel." She missed the expression which flicked like the shadow of a bird's wing across Aldric's face. "He offered me silver if I would . . . would go with him into the woods. What he asked . . . He wanted me to . . . It wasn't just soldier's talk, Kourgath—not ordinary lewdness. What he suggested was foul . . . Beastly. My uncle Evthan heard him say it and spilled him from his horse into the mud; he would have done much more if they hadn't both been held.

"Keel wasn't a lord's-man, not yet, so he could do nothing himself. But he took my uncle with him to Seghar and reported what had happened. Not to Geruath, but to Crisen. I don't know why. Crisen ruled that it would be unjust to kill a man of proven loyalty for being as loyal to his own family, and he let my uncle live. But he said that he would not tolerate such disrespect towards his intended retainers, and commanded that it be punished. I don't know what else they did to him, but I do know that they beat my uncle—with riding-quirts and stock-whips from the cattle yard. They beat him and beat him until there was no skin left on his back, and then they rubbed him with salt and flung him into an ox-cart to come home as best he could. He couldn't stand when he came to Valden, he could only crawl on his knees and elbows like an animal.

"And he had barely left his bed when the Beast came . . ." Gueynor stared blankly at the ceiling, remembering. "Kourgath," she said, "my uncle Evthan isn't the man I thought I knew. Not now. Not any more. Maybe it was the beating—or fretting about the Beast, or . . . what happened to his wife and daughter. She was four—did you know that? Four years old . . . I don't know . . ." At last her voice began to tremble. "I don't want to know . . ."

Aldric's mouth quirked, as if some unpleasant taste had flooded it: the rank, bitter flavour of petty oppressions, of casual cruelties. This was a dirty business, and it was growing dirtier by the minute. Inexorably he was becoming involved in more than just the hunting of the Beast. Or King Rynert's murderous political necessities. At least now he had a reason for involvement, regardless of how petty that reason might appear. But was it reason enough to kill . . . ?

No longer restrained by pride and a need to speak, Gueynor was crying openly now: deep, racking sobs that shook her whole body as she lay curled up tightly in the bed like a hurt child, and though Aldric could not begin to guess for whom or what she wept—there were so very many reasons—he was glad to see the tears. She had held back far too much emotion this past while, and such a release could do nothing but good. Words from his past came to him, in a woman's voice accented by the cold and distant north. "Nobody should laugh if they don't know how to cry. Think about that." He had done, and often. Now he put his arms around the girl and held her close until the fit of weeping spent itself.

Then he kissed her tenderly and held her closer still. The embrace changed from comforting to loving as naturally—it seemed to him both then and later—as the rising of the sun outside their window; as if, after the experience of blood and death which they had shared in memory and reality, they needed to share something of life. The two bodies moved together underneath the furs and covers of the big old bed with a slow passion that was less than love and yet much more than merely urgent lust. For the duration of a single heartbeat in that half-lit shuttered room, another face impinged on Aldric's vision. Kyrin . . .

And then was gone.

Only afterwards, when they lay quietly in a warm knot of entwined limbs and soft, quick breathing did the Alban become stingingly aware that Gueynor's nails had drawn blood from his back—not with the clawing of eagerness, but more in reluctance to ever let him go and thus return to the real world outside the house, the room, the bed, where men hurt one another to prove who was superior and a wolf ran in the woods.

His head was cradled in the angle of her neck and shoulder, his left arm curled around her waist below the ribs; dark, tousled hair tickled Gueynor's nose until she shifted slightly, and that small movement was enough to send him sliding face-foremost into the pillows. "I wanted to be the one who paid you for the killing of the Beast," she whispered, almost to herself.

"Nobody had to pay me." The voice was slightly, comically muffled and despite the implied mild criticism in his words, Gueynor found that she was smiling. "Because . . ." he rolled lazily into a more audible position, "I'm doing this for my own reasons now. Because I want to."

The Jouvaine girl traced patterns on his chest with one long finger. "So did I," she said.

"But it isn't dead yet," Aldric reminded her.

"Yet," she repeated. "It will be, soon." Her finger moved up to his throat and touched the silver torque encircling it. The contact was not a caress, not quite. "And then . . . ?"

"Afterwards is afterwards," he murmured enigmatically, his face schooled to neutral wariness. "And it's like another place. Best wait until we get there."

Gueynor nodded as though she understood his meaning, although she was none too sure that she did. Kissing the palm of her own right hand, she pressed it lightly once against his forehead and once against his mouth, echoing the blessing she had seen him use. "Avert all evil, amen," the girl said in a hasty voice which did not trust itself to lengthy speeches; and slipping out of the bed, she gathered up her clothing and hurried from the room.

*

Aldric glanced up towards the sky; it was a clear clean blue flecked with long white clouds very high up, and the sun's disc was barely two handspans over the horizon. It would be a long day; longer still when what he awaited was the night—and the rising of the moon. He had dressed carefully in the clothes and equipment from the previous day, some of it still slightly damp from washing: a clean white shirt from his pack; combat leathers and jerkin with the rips of injury closed with tiny, careful stitches by some woman of the village—or maybe Gueynor herself; the armoured sleeves, concealed still although they were an open secret now; *telek,* short-bow, *tsepan* on his belt. But no poison on the weapons. Not this time. If death was waiting in the forest, it would be the clean death of steel.

Or of silver.

When he left the house that morning, Aldric had deliberately sought out Laine in order to borrow his dogs, remembering how Evthan had put less effort into his own attempt than he might have done. He found a paunchy, fat-faced man whose attitude and air of self-satisfaction angered him at once. After five minutes' venomously whispered conversation he left, knowing there would no longer be objections voiced about his use of the hounds—or indeed about anything he might have demanded from Laine's house. Aldric seldom troubled to make threats, but when he did they were extremely effective . . .

He felt prepared for anything—apart from his first sight of the two beasts he had taken so much trouble to acquire. They were not hunting-dogs at all, but leggy, leering black-and-tan Drusalan guard hounds, creatures with an evil reputation. Aldric's recent acquaintance with them went beyond mere reputation, and he suspected that these brutes were easily as dangerous as anything they might be used to hunt.

Perspiring at the safe end of the leashes, Laine suggested that he give the hounds his scent. Stiff-legged with apprehension and in a mood that was more inclined to give them an arrow apiece—or maybe two—he approached gingerly and held out one hand for the dogs to sniff. Though from their expressions neither would have wagged a tail even had they possessed such an ornament, the animals stopped growling and left the hand still on his wrist. That, he guessed uneasily, would have to be presumed a sign of friendship.

As Evthan wrapped both leashes around his fist, Aldric glanced up and saw Gueynor. Hovering on the edge of the small crowd which had gathered to see them off, she was staring at her uncle most intently as if to fix his features in her mind. There were too many people about for the private words he might have said to her, so instead he made a small half-bow in her direction and hoped that she would understand . . . something at least. An odd expression crossed her face before she turned and walked away.

Evthan touched him lightly on the shoulder and led the way towards the woods. The Alban glanced after him but stood a moment, undecided, confused by the emotion he had seen; then followed slowly, frowning as he tried to identify it. He realised only some hours later that what he had seen was pity.

But by then it was too late.

*

They walked all day. Walked and stopped: to look for tracks; to listen for faint, furtive movement in the underbrush; to allow the dogs to cast about for scent. And all day they saw, heard and smelled nothing. The refreshing clarity of early morning was quite gone now, if it had ever penetrated this far amongst the trees. The air was warm and close, sticky with the threat of rain . . . Breathless. It sucked the moisture out of Aldric's skin to soak into his clothing, and left his mouth tasting dry and acrid; he took frequent gulps from the flask slung at his hip even though every mouthful of its contents—a sour, milky stuff—twisted his face in disgust. All that could be said for the liquid was that it was fairly cool—and even that halfhearted approbation had ceased to apply by noon.

As he had done before, Aldric set an arrow to his

bow. More than once he found himself toying with the
goose-feather fletching, or hooking the thumb of his
shooting-glove over the string in preparation for nothing
at all . . . Each time he jerked one shoulder in an artificial shrug or compressed his lips in a false smile, and
returned the missile to bow-case or quiver. Only to do
much the same thing all over again within a quarter-
hour or so.

As afternoon crawled towards evening the scraps of
sky which they could see beyond the tree-tops clouded
over until no blue was left: only a featureless expanse
of grey sliding from one horizon to the other, tugged
and driven by a distant wind that neither man could feel
or hear. What light there was became dull, with a smoky,
dirty-yellowness about it that seemed to stain whatever
it touched.

"We may as well turn back," Evthan observed, stabbing his toe at the ground. "There's nothing for the dogs
to work on here, and if it starts to rain there'll be no
scent anywhere at all."

Aldric nodded in agreement. He had been waiting to
hear something of the sort for almost an hour now. "As
you wish." His head jerked towards the panting hounds.
"But let me get a step or so ahead of that pair—I don't
think they like me, and I know I don't like them."

As Evthan stepped aside to let him through, the
Alban noticed again—though he had known it since they
left Valden—that the hunter was no longer wearing his
customary buckskins. Instead he was clad in close-fitting
garments of so dark a grey that they were almost black,
and a sleeveless vest, a *coyac,* made entirely of black fur
of such thickness that it caused the lanky Jouvaine to
seem stooped and hunch-shouldered. Wolf-fur, Aldric
guessed, and wondered not for the first time what significance the jacket had apart from being a good-luck
token.

Once again he slid out an arrow, twisting it around
and around between his fingers before nocking it to the
shortbow's string. He looked down introspectively at the
bright steel barb and wondered, glancing backwards,
whether he should . . .

Then in one blurred fluid motion he swung around

and drew and loosed—at Evthan's head. The shaft slashed past so closely that it scored the hunter's jaw, but the incoherent curses spilling from his mouth were drowned out by a yelp of pain.

And Evthan found the Beast behind him.

It was huge and grey, its pelt blotched with blood around the arrow driven deep into its shoulder. Ivory glistened in a wet pink maw and its eyes were embers burning through his own. Then it was gone and the dogs were after it.

"I—I had to take the chance!" Aldric's voice was taut, stammering with shock. "It just . . . appeared. Out of nowhere, right at your back. And it had you, but—"

"But?" Evthan touched the oozing graze across his face and winced.

"But it hesitated! It *waited*. Why . . . ?"

"Indecision," declared the hunter firmly. "If I had been alone, or you . . ." He left the thought unfinished. "But I wasn't, which was why it paused. Then you shot it. With . . . with silver?" His fingers stroked the graze again.

"No. Just steel. Come on and—"

The harsh girning of a fight rang through the woods and scared birds clattered skyward. The frenzied snarling reached a crescendo, changed abruptly to a frantic screech, shot up to a squeal which did not finish and left only echoes hanging on the air. Both men exchanged grim glances and began to run, each hoping to be the first to see the mangled carcass of the Beast—for, outweighed and outnumbered, there could only be one outcome.

That at least was the theory. In practice it proved rather different. The only corpse in sight was one of the Drusalan hounds, lying dreadfully torn amid the bulging coils of its own entrails. Of the other dog, and of the wolf, there was no sign.

Stooping, Aldric lifted something from the spattered grass. It was his arrow—smeared with gore, but then little in the area was not—and it bore no mark of teeth to show how it had been withdrawn. Silently the Alban wiped it on the turf and returned it to his quiver, then carefully chose another—one with a silver head.

The spoor was plain enough: wet red spots dappled the grass in a line leading away from the direction in which they had come. Evthan's eyes read more detail: how the grass-blades were bent by a dragging leg, the distance between each drop which indicated speed, their size which revealed the volume of flow—even, despite the swiftly fading light, how the colour of the blood betrayed the nature of the wound. But he needed no such woodcraft to discern the most important fact.

The Beast was running straight for Valden. And once there . . . If it got inside the palisade the wolf would slaughter like a fox loose in a hen-house.

With such a picture vivid in his mind, Aldric too was running when something barely glimpsed made him flinch aside. He heard a hollow rat-trap clack as teeth met on the spot where his left leg had been, and then his balance went and the ground rose up to meet him. His bow went flying. He rolled hard, knowing what had almost happened, and slammed one knee into the turf to lever himself half-upright, looking around for Evthan and the bow. There was no trace of the Jouvaine hunter.

But straddling the weapon was the grey bulk of the Beast.

He could hear its rumbling growl from where he knelt, could see a ragged gleam of fangs—and could taste the copper sourness of fear on the walls of his mouth. He cursed himself for not bringing his sword, staring at the wolf as if his unwinking gaze alone might force it to retreat, knowing how desperate the Beast must be to break its own unwritten rule and attack men . . .

Aldric wrenched his *tsepan* from its scabbard. Before the dirk was halfway drawn he went crashing back as the wolf—its weight equal to his own—hit him square in the chest, its jaws gaping wide above his throat. They remained gaping in the rictus of death as Evthan pulled the Beast of the Jevaiden aside and twisted his arrow from its skull. The animal had died in mid-leap; and as that fact sank in the hunter squatted by its corpse and ran disbelieving hands through the glossy fur, not even noticing when Aldric scrambled shakily to his feet. Then Evthan noticed something which made him beckon the Alban closer.

"Look here," he said softly, one finger tracing the pale hairs which marked the line of an old scar. "When this was new he couldn't catch his proper prey, and found our women and children easier game. He's our Beast after all."

"Yours, anyway." Aldric looked sidelong at him, then full at the scar. It was such an insignificant little thing that he wondered . . . "Clever," he murmured in that same ambiguous tone. "Very clever." Lifting the wolf's head by its thick-furred scruff, he stared for a long time into the glazing yellow eyes. A pink tongue lolled from the slack jaws. Was this the unseen presence which had watched and stalked him in the Deepwood? As big a wolf as he had ever seen.

Evthan glanced at his companion; the Alban seemed to be waiting for . . . something, but at last he lowered the Beast's head back to the grass with what might have been a small sigh of relief. "But just an ordinary wolf for all that." Aldric tipped back his own head and drew a long breath of the evening air. High above him a star blinked through a tear in the fabric of the overcast, cold and clear and immeasurably distant in the dusk. There was no sign of the moon. Yet . . . His mind returned to closer matters. "Evthan?" The hunter glanced up from an already half-flayed kill. "One dog is dead. Where's the other?"

"I haven't a notion." Evthan's voice was carefree; the Beast was dead and he had killed it—that was all that mattered. Then he set aside his knife and looked directly at Aldric. "How long will you stay here now?"

There was an odd edge to his voice which the Alban did not recognise, although he thought he did and shaped his reply accordingly. "Tomorrow morning, probably no later. There's no reason to remain longer any more." He saw relief in Evthan's eyes and smiled inwardly; the man was already jealous of his new-found status as Saviour of the Jevaiden, and did not want to share it with anyone— least of all *hlensyarlen.* "I had," Aldric concluded, picking his words with care, "little to do with the success of this hunt anyway."

Hearing a rustle of bracken from lower down the slope, where he had almost fallen over, he peered cautiously over the edge—at that point it was sheer—and saw Gueynor forcing a way through the tangled brambles. A mixture of emotions tugged at the Alban's mouth as he backed out of sight.

"Who's that?" Evthan had a vile-looking inside-out wolfskin over his shoulder when he walked across to follow the line of Aldric's stare. Colour drained from his face with shocking suddenness as he recognised his niece. "No, Gueynor," he whispered. "I told you not to follow me—I told you to stay inside—I *told* you to avoid the woods tonight . . ."

"Why tonight?" snapped Aldric, suspicions welling up inside him again. He stopped, his grey-green eyes becoming guarded at what they saw. "Evthan, what happened to your face . . ." At the edge of his vision a shadow drifted from behind a tree. "Look *out!*" he yelled as the shadow coalesced into the second Drusalan hound. Evthan twisted as it leapt straight for him, misled maybe by the smells of blood and wolf which hung about him. He teetered for an instant on the brink, and then toppled backwards into the gloom-filled valley just as the hound came thudding down on to the spot where he had stood.

Crouching low, the dog seemed undecided whether to follow its prey into the bracken-noisy darkness; then it turned to glare at Aldric through crazy red eyes and he knew that it had made its choice. Lips curled back from sharp white teeth as the creature began a monstrous snarl—and in that second of delay the Alban loosed a heavy broadhead point-blank through its chest. At such close range the arrow punched nock-deep: fletching, shaft, crest and all ploughing home to stagger the dog backwards with its impact. The wild eyes dulled like wax-choked candles and it was dead even before its legs gave way.

Aldric rubbed a hand across his clammy forehead and listened to the hammer of his heart, wondering dully why the hound had gone for Evthan rather than himself, the stranger.

There was no longer any movement among the brambles, and that puzzled him; he knew it was not so overgrown down there that it could hold two adults fast, and with a slight frown creasing his brows he walked past the dead dog and knelt carefully. Perhaps someone had been hurt in Evthan's clumsy fall . . . Above his head the full moon slid free of cloud to cast a pale, cold gleam across the forest, and Aldric shivered without knowing why. There was a whimpering below him and an indrawn breath which might have been a sob. "Gueynor . . . ?" he asked, uneasy at having to speak. "What's wrong?"

The howl erupted from the ground almost at his feet and he flung himself backwards without knowing how, only the frantic speed with which he selected and nocked another arrow saving the reaction from being entirely fearful. The silver barb glinted like a shard of sharpened ice.

A face appeared above the valley rim, its jaw transmuting to a tapered muzzle even as he watched through shock-dilated eyes. The skull flattened; the ears became triangular, tufted and twitching; dark fur spread like ink across the pallid skin; fangs glimmered moistly as they sprouted from pink gums.

Why doesn't it run? screamed a voice that was no voice in Aldric's brain. *Why won't it hide? Why is it letting me witness this?* He had never dreamed, even in his darkest nightmare, how intimate and how obscene the lycanthropic metamorphosis could be . . .

The transformation had almost run its course now—but for just a moment the blue, blue eyes remained unchanged, staring at him with a horrible and almost tearful pity. Pity . . . The implications of that look made his guts turn over; then the intelligence was overwhelmed by another, more feral impulse.

Hunger . . . The eyes shone green now, phosphorescent jewels in the moonlight.

As the brute sprang on to level ground, Aldric could see that all of its humanity was gone and only beast remained. Black pelt frosted by the moon, it was all lithe, swift wolf as it stalked clear of the hazard of the drop; only a slight, a ghastly uncertainty of the forelegs betrayed a memory of walking upright. It raised its shaggy head, howling bale-fully towards the glowing sky.

And Aldric shot his silver arrow deep into its throat.

The werewolf lurched but did not fall. Instead it stared at him, an impossible saw-fanged grin stretching the corners of its mouth as the arrow trembled, withdrew of its own accord and dropped to the grass. No blood stained the silver barb—and there was no wound.

The second howl was made, more eerie still by an under-tone of laughter thrumming through it, and Aldric forgot his peril sufficiently to lower the useless bow, gaping in disbelief. What he had just seen was contrary to everything . . .

Then realisation chilled him with the fear of his own death.

His silver arrowheads were useless! He had made them from Drusalan florins that he was aware had lost their value, but had not considered why until this instant. The Imperial economy was rotten and its coinage utterly de-based. He knew now what that meant: silver coins—with no real silver in them!

With a snarl like rending metal the wolf sprang and slammed him to the ground, jaws snapping for the great veins in his neck. Then it uttered an appalling shriek of anguish and leapt away, shaking its head like a dog singed at the fire.

Aldric guessed the cause at once. Like all high-clan Al-bans he wore a crest-collar, and his torque was solid silver. Now if it had been twisted gold, like some he had seen . . . He shuddered and pushed the thought aside, rolled to his feet and drew his *tsepan* dirk. It was no fighting weapon—the blade was delicate, meant only for the single stab of formal suicide—but its blade did not concern him.

His clan colours were blue and white, his personal colour black: so the *tsepan*'s three-edged blade was smoke-blue steel, its sheath and grip of rare lacquered ebony. And its pommel was of unalloyed silver.

The werewolf lunged again, low now for the belly. More prepared this time, Aldric drove his mailed left arm be-tween its jaws with a thud that jarred him to the spine. Huge carnassials crushed down on the steel beneath his sleeve, but the plates of the vambrace held despite the awesome pressure and when the Alban twisted, lithe and savage as any wolf, he felt at least one of the great conical canine teeth snap off.

Unable to bite, barely capable of breathing and panicked by this turning of the tables, the beast whined nasally and tried to break away. With his knees clamped round its narrow ribcage and his trapped arm trapping it in turn,

Aldric smashed his *tsepan*'s pommel down between the werewolf's ears.

Its thick skull shattered like an eggshell and the creature kicked just once. Then it relaxed without a sound. Aldric crouched above it, trembling all over, and only when his limbs had steadied did he inch out his arm past the vicious fangs. He knew what a werewolf's bite would do . . . and only one knew better. That one lay at his feet with a caved-in head.

As the processes of life ran down, the outstretched corpse began a gradual change. Aldric backed away and averted his eyes; right now he felt neither physically nor mentally capable of experiencing the slow revelation of whoever he had killed. Too many memories were jumbled in his mind; words and images were taking on a terrible significance when recalled with hindsight: strange, half-glimpsed expressions; odd behaviour; a peculiar choice of phrase . . .

If he suffered the curse of changing, would he know? the Alban wondered. And if he knew—his eyes went to the *tsepan* still clutched tightly in one clotted hand—would he have the courage to do what had to be done?

Aldric did not know the answer. He had stared into the eyes of the werewolf and had seen there a reflection of himself. They were kindred spirits: killers both. The thought frightened him. He was aware that he had not killed every beast in the Jevaiden woods, but at least had come to terms with one: the Beast asleep within himself which slew men with a sword. He hoped that understanding it would be enough. And in the knowledge of that understanding he turned, already sure who he would see.

Evthan of Valden lay on the moonlit grass, face-downwards in a puddle of his own blood. When Aldric very gently rolled him over, he saw that the hunter's face displayed no pain—nor indeed any mark from Aldric's steel-tipped arrow; that had been completely healed before the change had come upon him, and had not gone unnoticed though little good had come from the Alban's observation of it. There was only peace and the merest shadow of a tiny, grateful smile . . .

Aldric saw it and felt a wave of sadness sweep over him.

"This was your intention all along," he murmured sobrely. "To find another hunter . . . who would do what you could not. And while the Beast lived you were hidden. Who would have dreamed of two wolves in one forest, both eating men but one real and one . . . Poor man! Did you ever dare to wonder which of them took your wife and daughter . . . ?"

A shadow fell across him and his head jerked up. Gueynor's face was lost in darkness, but he could feel her gaze bore through him. Feeling awkward, he stood up and waved a hand at Evthan's body. "I . . . I'm sorry." Oh God, how insincere that sounded . . . "Your uncle was—"

"I know. I saw. But he still remains my mother's elder brother." There was no emotion in her voice as she held out a kerchief. "Clean your hands and help me move him. No one else must know." They shifted the corpse to lie in accordance with the story Aldric prepared for the elders of Valden: that Evthan had saved him by shooting the Beast but that, in its final throes, the wolf had flung him against the root which had dashed out his brains. The tale was hastily contrived, but better at least than the truth.

Afterwards, with the villagers almost upon them— doubtless attracted by the sound of fighting almost on their doorstep—Aldric tried again to speak. "He saved my life." One of Evthan's arrows lay beside the flayed body of the Beast.

Gueynor looked, the tear-tracks down her cheeks turned silver by the moonlight. "And mine," she whispered. "When—when the change began, I was beside him. But he went for you, and let you see quite clearly what he was. Although you don't see, even yet. Look at him, Alban! Something does not accord with all the lore you so obviously know. Look at him . . ."

Aldric turned his head and stared. The hunter's body was sprawled where they had set it, at the foot of a tree, and his long limbs hung loose in that unconnected way all dead things had. The beautiful deep fur of his *coyac* glistened dully on one shoulder, where it was soaked with drying blood that would turn the fine pelt harsh and spiky. The *coyac*—which he had been wearing all the time.

"*Domne diu . . .*" Aldric breathed. "He was fully

dressed!" And he spoke that obvious fact as if it was remarkable.

Which it was, for all the books and old tales said the same thing; that before a man becomes a werewolf he must strip stark naked, right to the skin, bared of even rings or chains or any sort of jewel. For lycanthropy, they said, is skin-changing, whether it be to wolf or any other animal. While this was . . .

"Shifting. Shape-shifting, before Heaven! Sorcery." Aldric had seen the like before; Duergar Vathach had prowled Baelen Wood beyond Dunrath in the shape of a wolf, and he had changed men into crows to act as his spies. "Did Crisen do this to him?" Gueynor nodded. "Just because he struck an insolent soldier who wasn't even in the Overlord's service . . ."

"My uncle let you see him, Kourgath, so that you would know what you had to do. Because he hoped . . ." Gueynor raised her head to look him in the eyes and the full moon was mirrored in her own. That pale light had washed all colour from his face and transformed it to a mask of metal, eyed with grey-green flints and with its shadows deeply etched. A slayer's face. "No, not hoped," the girl said finally. "Knew. He knew that you would kill him."

Aldric sighed and it was as if the mask had never been. He felt tired, and sick, and old as Death. *"Ai, gev'n-au tsepanak'ulleth,"* he muttered grimly to himself, and then to Gueynor: "He used me as his *tsepan*—as his release from life. I've performed an honourable, charitable act." He glanced up towards the mocking moon. "So what makes me feel so filthy . . . ?"

5

Reflections in a Clouded Glass

That same full moon hung in the sky at midnight, its pale face licked by tongues of drifting cloud; but not a glimmer pierced the heavy velvet curtains which covered Sedna's windows. Her only illumination was the wan yellow glow of six black corpse-fat candles, each one man-high and thicker than a strong wrist. They stank.

As her slender white-robed form moved through the incense-spicy air, smoke curled from many censers to billow in the sorceress' wake. Patterns of power writhed across the dark red floor under her bare feet, and for many minutes Sedna compared each symbol and inscription with its original in the vellum pages of an ancient grimoire. Finally she cleared her throat and began to read aloud in a rapid monotone, tracing each sentence with a grisly little gold-tipped wand made from the spine of a kitten.

"There had best be purpose to this playacting," said someone well beyond the pools of candle-light, "for I am wearied of it." Without inflection, irritation or impatience, the words were still heavy with an assurance born of rank and power. Metal scraped as one of the soldiers who enforced that power shifted uneasily. "And do not think this waste of time impresses me," the icy voice continued. "You are far from indispensable. There are other warlocks—most of them a deal more skilled than you."

Sedna paused in her reading and dared to look reproachful, but the only response was a dry, artificial chuckle which nevertheless served to make the Vreijek marginally bolder. "More skilled perhaps, *Eldheisart*

Voord," she replied, shaking back strands of hair from her face and giving the man his proper title, "but certainly no faster. This ritual—my playacting, as you are pleased to call it—is a requirement of the spell. And of safety: mine, yours . . . everyone here." That nervous rustle of armour was repeated, and a wintry smile thinned her full lips as she returned to the incantation.

"Your safety maybe, spellmaker!" snapped Voord, angered by her impudence. "Not mine! Tonight's performance is for Lord Crisen alone."

Sedna's head jerked round, eyes widening, and for an instant stark fear edged her voice before she controlled it, betraying the raw nerve that Voord's words had touched. "Not tonight of all nights!" she gasped, then collected herself and continued more calmly, as if the outburst had never taken place. "This is full moon at the summer solstice. I cannot—I *dare* not make magic of any sort at such a time. Tell him, Crisen—make him understand . . ."

Voord already understood a great many things, among them her significant omission of the underlord's title, although he chose not to pass comment on that . . . yet. And he was far more aware of what had frightened the woman—the witch, he corrected himself—than she imagined. On this night, of all nights in the year save its dark twin at midwinter, enchantments would work only crookedly if at all and would be made doubly treacherous by the lowering presence of the swollen moon. It influenced the tides and the ravings of madmen; it made dogs howl and . . . created other things that also howled at night. Despite himself Voord had to repress a slight shiver. A summoning such as that which Sedna was preparing might fail completely, despite the care with which she drew her circles and her pentad sigils. But under the triple influence of midnight, moon and solstice the charm would more likely warp as it took effect, calling up something totally unexpected and consequently unaffected by the highly specific wards and holding patterns that were effective against one entity but not another. Although that was a piece of knowledge which Voord's cold mind had already filed away as being useful . . .

"She is correct," Crisen said over the *eldheisart*'s shoulder, and by the warmth of his tone favoured her with an indulgent smile. "All this is for tomorrow. We have been most careful since—"

"The last time your amateur conjuring went wrong," Voord finished for him brutally. "In my homeland of Vlech there is a proverb: 'The wise man sheathes his knife before he cuts himself, not after.' A shape-shifting was it not?"

"How did you . . ."

"How do I ever . . . ?" mocked Voord. "There are ways of learning everything, sooner or later. Instead of a changeling you created a werewolf, and then tried to hide your blunder by acquiring yet another wolf and training it to devour only women and children. That was not particularly clever, was it? Especially since between the two of them they have slaughtered some thirty of your forest-dwelling peasants."

"And what's a peasant more or less?"

"In such numbers, cause for unnecessary speculation at a time when—" Voord began, but was interrupted when Sedna's quiet voice cut firmly through his own.

"*I* am a peasant, Crisen," she said.

"You are what I choose to tell the world you are," he retorted, much too quickly. Voord glanced at his companion, and it was as well that his expression was lost in the shadows.

"A private word," he whispered, tugging Crisen's sleeve between finger and thumb in an exaggeratedly fastidious manner. Leading the other man out of the chamber, he stared at him in silence for so long that Crisen became uncomfortable—precisely the *eldheisart*'s intention—and then tapped him sharply on the chest. "Your priorities," he stated flatly, "appear somewhat confused."

They were of an age—late twenties—and similar in height, but there any resemblance ended. Crisen's waist was thick from too much good living, his face heavy-featured and florid even in the sickly-blue moonlight which streamed into the corridor, and his black hair was cut in what had been the height of fashion at the Imperial court some three months past. Voord, by contrast, was whiplash thin in both face and body, pale of skin and flaxen of severely scraped-back hair. There was a disdainful twist to his razor-cut mouth which he made no attempt to conceal.

"Whatever do you mean by that?" Crisen tried to bluster, but found it difficult to do so effectively in such a low-pitched conversation.

"You know quite well . . . my lord." The honorific title came out like an insult. "Tell me—how much do you skim off the Alban stipend to your father? Thirty per cent? Forty?" Crisen cleared his throat apprehensively. "Not more surely . . . ? How much more?"

"Last time," the Jouvaine nobleman confessed after a lengthy pause, "I had to take twelve to the score."

"*Had* to . . ."

"Sedna—that is, *I* needed money urgently!"

"Gaming debts, no doubt," soothed Voord. Then he assumed an air of theatrical incredulity, that of a man doubting the evidence of his own ears. "But does this mean that you subtracted sixty per cent of the gold your father should have received . . . and Lord Geruath did not notice?"

"My father," there was lip-curling venom in the way Crisen sneered the word, "has his own interests."

"As have I—and, it seems, have you . . ."

"He thinks himself clever because he has deceived the Albans into paying for precisely nothing—they still believe he supports Ioen and Goth."

"Oh. Is that why they sent an envoy in near-secrecy to find out *precisely*," he threw back Crisen's word with relish, "how King Rynert's gold is being used?" The Vlechan glanced back into the chamber where Sedna read and chanted, and that look spoke several eloquent phrases. "Or misused. I suggest that you would be advised to spend more on your mercenary cadre and less on your . . . amusements." Crisen stared at him but said nothing. "They seem overly distracting."

"For all the Albans' secrecy, you found out," Crisen flattered blatantly, trying to evade the issue, but Voord was having none of it.

"Of course I found out," he snapped, omitting to say just how.

"And I sent a troop directly you warned me. They were disguised as . . ." The underlord's voice trailed to silence as he saw the expression which had settled on Voord's face.

"As bandits," the *eldheisart* concluded dryly. "Very theatrical. And very useless! They still botched the mission!"

"They killed the Vreijek." Crisen's protest was feeble.

"But they were not sent after the Vreijek, were they?" Voord pointed out with heavy emphasis. "And I specifically forbade killing. It is difficult to get answers out of a corpse even after prolonged interrogation." He was quite plainly not making a joke. "Was that your intention, or your hope . . . ?" The Vlechan paused just long enough for his implied accusation to sink home, but not long enough for Crisen to formulate a coherent excuse. "Because, my lord, it is *only* difficult. Not impossible. Not for me . . ." The smile which accompanied his words was an unpleasant thing to see and Crisen flinched. "Now, thanks to the bungling of your . . . bandits . . . the Alban has not merely eluded us but vanished completely. Yes. Quite! And he was no ordinary courier . . . ?"

"Why? What was he?"

"That," snarled Voord with a sudden burst of anger, "ceased to be your concern when your men lost him! If it was ever your concern at all!" He grew quieter, more introspective, and his cold brain began to calculate with less emotion than an abacus. "Your father remains ignorant of all this, I take it? And I do mean all . . ." Crisen nodded dumbly. "So. Then something may yet be salvaged, if I—" He broke off what was plainly a train of thought and stared at Crisen out of pale eyes. "As for you, leave me. Go get drunk, or get some sleep—but get away from here and give me peace!"

Unaccustomed to abrupt dismissal in his father's house, Crisen made no move and was plainly gathering enough nerve to assert himself. Voord took away his chance to even try with a single snap of the fingers which summoned his honour guard from where they had stood in silence ten paces down the corridor, and once the mailed troopers were at his side Crisen Geruath felt it wise to hold his tongue while they waited patiently for instructions.

"Tagen, Garet, esvoda moy," said Voord, deliberately employing the Vlechan dialect which he already knew Crisen could not understand. *"Inak Kryssn ya vaj, dar boedd'cha. Najin los doestal Najin. Slijei?"* The armoured men saluted with a precise double click and flanked Crisen more closely then he liked. "Your escort," Voord said flatly, "will see

you safe and uninterrupted to your room. Good night, my lord."

When he could no longer hear the cadenced footsteps, Voord opened the door of Sedna's chamber a finger's width. As he watched, she completed the patterning of a diagram with carefully poured white powder, each line stark against the red-dyed wood of the floor, and once again stood back to check what she had done against the grimoire, balanced now on a spindly lectern. The *eldheisart*'s gaze scanned what she had drawn, rested briefly and almost with regret on the outline of her body where the candleglow beyond it made translucent mist of her thin robe, and settled at last on the key of the heavy door, resting within easy reach on its usual small shelf. Lifting it down, Voord turned it over in his hands once or twice, then looked again towards the Vreijek woman. "Such a waste . . ." The words were barely audible even to himself. "If you had been less inquisitive, then perhaps . . ." The dreamy glaze behind his eyes froze over so that they became two chips of ice. "But not now, my dear. You know too much. I'm sorry." He closed the door and locked it. From the outside.

*

Although he would never admit it, Lord-Commander Voord was frightened. The sensation was unfamiliar, and made worse by its very novelty; usually he had no reason to be afraid of anyone or anything—indeed, was more likely to be the cause of fear in others—but tonight he faced the realisation that events which he had once controlled were overtaking him. That, too, was unsettlingly novel.

"Damn her!" the *eldheisart* spat softly. "Damn him! Damn them all to the black Pit!" He was not a man given to profanity, for he seldom needed it; but he often made promises and his voice had a horrid edging of sincerity about it now. Not a threat; rather an intimation of things to come.

Four of Crisen Geruath's retainers, acting on his orders, had gone into the Deepwood on a certain errand late last night. Three of the horses had returned so far, but not a man of the four. Nor the item whose retrieval he had specifically entrusted to their ferret-featured leader, Keel. He should have given early consideration to his own words about the poor quality of the Overlord's hired troops, and instead sent a squad of his own guards. Hindsight, thought Voord with the bitterness experienced by many in such circumstances, was a truly remarkable thing.

"Damned Jouvaines," he said aloud with the beginnings of fury, aware that his oaths were becoming as repetitive as those of any common soldier. "Damn Crisen!"

There was an air of gloomy self-satisfaction in the knowledge that the underlord was going to do that to himself quite literally, sooner or later. Few men meddled with sorcery in the slapdash manner that Crisen did, and lived long to talk about it. Madness . . . Which was a Geruath family trait, evidently, for the old man was hardly what Voord considered sane. Such insanity in the Overlord did not concern him overmuch—a man could be stark raving mad and rule the Empire like that without creating comment; indeed it had already happened once or twice—but when that same madness impinged on Lord-Commander Voord's precisely set-out schemes, then somebody would suffer. And his name would not be Voord . . .

If Crisen had not been so clumsy about the completion of his peculiar experiments with that huntsman, the Vlechan felt sure that his own more esoteric researches in the small, select part of Sedna's library would have gone unnoticed long enough for discovery to be unimportant. He did not, of course, blame himself for matching clumsiness with carelessness. That was not Voord's way.

At least the Jouvaine had possessed sufficient wit to waken him when Sedna transformed her suspicions into action. The woman knew something of what had been going on behind her back—behind the backs of everyone in Seghar—of that Voord was certain. He had known it for at least three days now; had been more certain of a wrongness in her attitude than even the witch herself. A man grew knowledgeable after supervising lengthy interrogations, learning to spot the signs of deception and concealment. She had spoken barely at all that whole day, and what little she had said had been bright with a false, brittle gaiety which betrayed her as surely as a signed and witnessed confession.

He and Crisen had watched her through the concealed peepholes which he had personally made not long after effecting Sedna's introduction to the underlord and thence to the citadel. That match-making had been a masterful stroke, he congratulated himself again. A pity that, having brought such a loving—and useful—couple together, he would now have to be the agent of their parting. Permanently. "Ah well, the sages say that nothing lasts forever." The echoes of his own brief, ugly chuckle startled him in the quiet, moonlit corridors and he fell silent reflecting uneasily on what he was about to do.

Voord reached the door of Sedna's library all too quickly. Anticipation was sending shudders down his limbs and the anticipation was not of pleasure. Without pausing he bent down and, after two mistakes, found the tile beneath which Sedna hid her key. He had observed her opening the door just once, but once had been enough. Since then, the *eldheisart* had entered when it pleased him, and so far had escaped detection. After tonight, it would no longer matter . . .

The library was pitch-black inside, darker even than the incense-and-manfat-reeking cellar where he had left the Vreijek witch. Voord fumbled for his tinderbox, not wishing to enter that black embrace unprepared. He struck flint and steel together, and despite his vaunted self-control drew an apprehensive breath as the swift flash of sparks was caught and returned to his dilated eyes by polished metal, glass and fine gold leaf. To his guilty, nervous mind each small reflection seemed to be the accusing, unwinking gaze of creatures waiting in the shadows. He laughed once, harshly, to show them how little he was afraid, and heard instead the dry cough of an ancient, dying man. After that, Voord did not laugh again.

Like Sedna before him, he only felt at ease once every lamp and candle had been lit. If he left any dark places the tiny bright-eyed things would surely hide there, watching him—and Voord wanted no witnesses at all. There was another, more practical reason for him to flood the room with light: its presence, he had read, would serve as an additional protection against . . . It. As Voord touched fire to the last lamp he wished that there were more.

He dragged rugs and furniture aside to make a clear space

on the floor, and with a chunk of natural chalk from his belt-pouch—itself painted with words of ritual significance—began to draw a complicated series of linked symbols. They meshed together, one into another, forming a protective pattern as close-knit as any coat of mail: not a summoning, but a guarding circle, intended to keep him safe. Any sorcerer looking at its interwoven curves and angles would have known at once what entity it was meant to guard against; and having recognised, would then have prudently fled . . .

Only when the circle was complete did Voord cross to the locked steel cabinet. He withdrew a slender metal probe from a hidden pocket—hidden because the probe's shape broadcast its function to any world-wise eyes that might see it—and with a twist used it to operate the lock's tumblers. It had taken him almost half an hour and three different lockpicks, the first time. Now . . . it was as if he owned a key.

Voord's nostrils twitched; he had smelled old books before and knew their distinctive mingling of leather, dust and age, but there was a different tang in the odour which billowed out of the casket at him—a musky, sour-sweet acid sharpness that reminded him of . . . Heat rose in his face as he blushed scarlet. "It isn't possible . . ." the *eldheisart* breathed, knowing even as he uttered the denial that it was possible, for the scent was unmistakable now. Lust; arousal; passion . . . Sex.

When he laid hands to the cover of *Enciervanul Doamnisoar* he discovered—though he had already half-guessed it—where that scent originated; but the shocking revelation which accompanied the discovery was enough for him almost to drop the book.

For it was warm!

The grimoire pulsed, as vibrant with obscene eagerness as any bitch in heat. Voord's courage almost failed him, and he had to make an effort of will before his fingers would close with sufficient pressure to lift the ghastly volume from its shelf. As he took its weight the book seemed to squirm fractionally, rubbing its leather-bound spine against the soft skin of his palms in a mock-erotic travesty of the way a woman he remembered fondly had moved beneath his touch. He knew, without requiring any proof, that all the stories he had heard about the making of this vile thing's cover were nothing but the truth, and felt the burning bile in his throat as his stomach turned over. Irrationally, the Vlechan wondered if he would ever feel completely clean again . . .

Had it continued to throb and writhe when he stepped inside the boundaries of his spell-circle, Lord-Commander Voord might well have flung down the volume and abandoned his purpose. But it stopped, as he had hoped it might—suddenly and with finality, lying inert on his cringing skin as any ordinary book might do. Voord's wavering determination returned with a rush of relief which seemed to him almost as audible as the gasp of pent-up breath released from between his clenched teeth.

Setting down the grimoire on a complex triple whorl of thin chalk lines which acted as a focus for the circle's power, he straightened up and squared his shoulders as he had not done since the last time he was on parade in Drakkesborg. With brisk parade-ground strides he walked to the end wall of the library and threw back the curtain which shrouded it from floor to ceiling. There was more force in the sideways jerk of his left arm than he had perhaps intended, and certainly more weight in the thick velvet than he recalled—both factors combined to send folds of the heavy fabric careering along their rail with a hiss and a staccato clash of bronze rings. Voord started at the unexpected burst of noise above his head and then took a rapid pace back—but his backward step had less to do with any noise than with his reaction to what the curtain had concealed.

He had seen it before, of course: when he had first invaded Sedna's private domain, he had explored each nook and cranny with the care and thoroughness born of long training in such matters, and had guessed the function of the thing behind the curtain directly he discovered it. "A mirror of seeing," he had heard it called in another place and another time, but the one referred to then was nothing like this.

On that first occasion the entire wall-space behind the curtain had been composed of a single monstrous sheet of some dark, shining substance—black mica, perhaps, or quartz, or obsidian sheared so thin that its pigmentation merely tinted the reflected image of whoever looked into its surface.

Except that there had been no reflection whatsoever . . . And there was no reflection now, despite the fact that the mirror's surface was no longer dark but as polished, smooth and flawless as a bowl of quicksilver. It should have reflected something, logic dictated that much at least, but instead it merely stood there and defied all logic by its refusal to flow in a liquid stream across the library floor. Voord stared at it, and as he stared a series of slow, concentric ripples began to spread out from the centre of the mirror, as if it was a glassy, undisturbed pond and his intent gaze the stone carelessly dropped into it.

With the hackles rising on his close-cropped neck, *Eldheisart* Voord stalked rapidly to the insubstantial security of his spell-circle, and only when he stood once more within its boundaries did he dare to breathe a little easier. With great care that the chalk-marks were not disturbed or, infinitely worse, erased, he sank down crosslegged and shifted his weight until he was as comfortable as he could expect to be on the hard floor. Such a desire for comfort was more important than it seemed; from previous experience the Vlechan knew that he had to attain a degree of physical ease if he was to enter the light trance through which his barely-trained mind could summon the intensity of purpose which sorcery required of him.

Gathering that concentration as a man might form a snowball, Voord projected a pulse of mental force at the huge mirror. For an instant nothing happened—and then more ripples raced across its surface, faster now and much more violent, strange in their utter silence. He could hear only the muffled drumbeat that was his own heart; all other sounds were muted. It was as if he had breathed warm air on an opaque, frost-sheathed window so that he could peer inside; as they crossed the mirror's once-glistening surface, the ripples drew a swirling greyness in their wake, each one less dense than its predecessor until at last the wall appeared transparent. A window into nowhere.

An image formed, condensing from nothingness as clouds are born from unseen vapours, and it was an image Voord knew well for it had been the focus of his thoughts these many minutes past. Sedna's chamber of enchantments . . .

Initially a miniature scene viewed from far away, it grew and expanded as the sourceless rippling had done until it filled the mirror, filled the wall, filled Voord's vision with a shifting, living picture. As he had hoped but never dared believe aloud, the mirror of seeing gave him disembodied access to a place that was not only many paces distant but enshrouded by many thicknesses of stone. And it was not a picture from the past, drawn from the Vlechan's memories, but from the present; yet more eerie even than the successful magic was his awareness that his viewpoint was exactly that which he had occupied a quarter-hour before. Sedna padded to and fro, drawing, checking, chanting; she had almost completed her work of preparation, and soon would go to the door that he had locked . . . Despite the trance which dulled his outer senses, a great shudder racked his limbs and Voord knew that he was still afraid. But not remorseful. A thin, cruel smile twisted at the corners of his mouth—afraid he might be, but not so afraid as the witch would be . . .

Voord withdrew further into himself and it was with the fumbling movements of a sleepwalker that he reached down to the book laid on the floor before him. His heavy-lidded eyes had rolled back in their sockets until only two moist crescents of veined white remained, and it was impossible that he could see to read; yet he opened the grimoire and leafed through its pages with a swiftness and a surety which belied his self-imposed blindness. He did not know, as Sedna had discovered, that a book whose very name was *On the Summoning of Demons* might not need the aid of human hands to find its proper place . . .

The rustling of pages ceased and Voord put down the volume. "Hearken unto me, all ye who dwell beyond the portals of the world," he intoned in a flat, dead voice totally unlike his own. "I would name those that have no name. I would look upon those that have no form known unto men. In token of good faith and as a sign of my most earnest wishes, I make now this blood-offering to thee."

Reaching to his pouch once more, Voord withdrew a leaf-shaped sliver of flint; its blue and cream edges were

scalloped and serrated, flaked until they were as thin
and sharp as any razor. He knew well that the ancient
powers on which he called would not look kindly on an
offering made to them with cold iron. Setting the stone
knife to his left hand, he drew a diagonal line across
the palm. Nothing happened. Sharp though it was—and
Voord had tested it that very evening on a piece of
leather—the flint skidded across his skin and left only a
faint indentation to mark its passage. His eyes opened,
stared at the pink groove which faded even as he
watched and dulled with the nauseous anticipation of
agony. Pain suffered suddenly in the heat of combat was
one thing, but this brutal premeditation was quite another. It was not beyond the powers of the Void to blunt
his blade as a test of his strength of purpose, and if they
had taken sufficient notice of him to create such a test,
then it was already too late to refuse.

Gritting his teeth, the Vlechan cut again with as much
strength as he dared employ, and cried out in a thin,
nasal whine like a hurt dog as the flint gouged into his
flesh. Frantic to be done with this self-inflicted torment,
Voord leaned still harder—and suddenly the stone blade
was sharp again, shearing deeper than he had intended
until it crunched jarringly into the mosaic of bones that
made up the structure of his hand. He shrieked then,
the sound filled with as much surprise as anguish, and
collapsed forward over the mangled, spurting mass of
flesh. Blood spewed inexorably from the ragged wound,
sufficient to satisfy any summoned spirit, and even as his
mind teetered near a swoon Voord knew why the ancient powers were sometimes called "the Cruel Ones."
They feasted on pain, on wounds to the spirit as much
as on flesh and blood, and they had a sardonic sense of
humour indeed if they could force a torturer to torture
himself for their sakes.

The hand was irreparably crippled, dislocated bone
and severed tendons already drawing the fingers into
that crooked claw he knew so well from the interrogations he had supervised. It throbbed and burned as if he
had dipped it into molten lead. It hurt so *much* . . .
Voord rocked back and forth, cradling his mutilated limb
close to his chest as if it was a child, sobbing with the

shock of what he had done to himself. All the words of
ritual were quite forgotten; there was no longer any
room for such coherent thought in his reeling brain. But
no matter how much he now regretted it, the sacrifice
had been made.

And accepted.

Between one jolting heartbeat and the next, the silence of past midnight was fragmented by a tearing crash
of thunder which boomed and rumbled massively across
the heavens until the very dust-motes drifting in the air
vibrated with its echoes. Yet there was no cloud of such
necessary magnitude remaining in the moonlit sky, and
since late that afternoon there had been no rain nor even
the brief flickering of summer lightning which needs no
storm to give it birth. There was no reason for the thunder whatsoever. As if, even calm and detached, the
Vlechan's mind could have convinced him that mere
weather was its cause at all . . .

The library grew cold, then colder still until Voord's
breath smoked white around his face and coils of steam
rose from the blood which pulsed sluggishly past the
shattered fingers and the whole. But with that grinding
chill came a surcease of pain and an end to bleeding;
the flesh of Voord's left hand was pallid now, blue about
the nails, bloodless and dead—as if, from wrist to fingertips, it had been drained dry. The *eldheisart*'s taut body
sagged; with nothing for his will to fight against, he was
sure that he would faint.

He did not. Unconsciousness eluded him as surely as
the ability to tear his eyes free of the mirror of seeing.
He stared at it like a bird at a snake, trapped and fascinated, unable even to blink; and in a time that no beginning and would never have an end, he learned what it
meant when mortals called upon the Old Ones . . .

*

Sedna heard nothing of the thunder. She completed a
final—the final—diagram, bowed politely and weighed
the relative merits of tidying up against those of going
to bed at once. She was tired. Then she coughed, and
as tears stung her eyes realised there was a third alternative: something to drink. Her throat felt harsh and dry,
an acrid taste lay on her tongue; both results of the bitter

aromatic smoke which filled the room, and of chanting
seemingly interminable formulae in a hoarse contrabasso
scarcely suited to a woman's vocal organs. So much trouble over a small spell, she thought wryly, and pressed
both hands hard into the small of her back in the vain
hope that it would somehow ease the aches of repeated stooping.

Wine . . . Cool white wine from the southland to re-
fresh and soothe her mouth, relax her muscles, calm her
nerves—perhaps even give her sufficient courage to challenge Crisen Geruath, if she drank enough of it. But not
Eldheisart Voord. Never Voord. No wine in all the
world, no beer, no ale, no ardent spirits could make her
brave enough for that . . .

There was always wine in this cellar; before she came
to Seghar it had been filled with kegs and barrels, stoneware flasks of fine imported vintages and leather bottles
of the dry, rough local red. Now, depending on her
mood, there might be a silver pitcher and two goblets,
or a simple jug and cups of red-ware. Sedna knew she
drank too much and had been drinking more these few
days past: since Voord and his soldiers came, she realised, as if the knowledge was new to her. Fear did it.
No, not fear . . . apprehension. Crisen was a stranger to
her when the Vlechan was about, and she muttered brief
thanks that his visits to Seghar were always short and
infrequent.

On this night there was an elegant carafe three-
quarters full of straw-pale wine, and two stemmed
glasses; all were in the simple, understated Alban style,
made from blown crystal and consequently rare and
costly. Splashing wine into one of the glasses, Sedna
drank it rapidly and took a deep breath to help the
fumes mount quickly to her head. More glasses followed
the first until she observed with some surprise that she
had almost emptied the carafe without really intending
to. "So . . . ?" she muttered in response to a pang of
self-criticism, and already her voice was growing blurred.

Sedna could see now, with the clarity of sudden drunkenness, what she would have to do for her safety's sake.
Self-respect, peace of mind, honour—if witches were
permitted that aristocratic foible—would go by the

board, but at least she might sleep sound at night. She would leave. Leave Crisen, leave Seghar, leave all the Jouvaine provinces far behind her and go home, back to Vreijaur where men and women indulged honest, normal vices and where the animals which roamed the woods were only that and not . . . Not more than they seemed.

"Leave all this luxury?" Sedna asked herself as light was caught and refracted in the facets of her crystal cup. "Why not?" she answered. "You can live without it. You did before." She refused to voice the thought which had flashed meteorically across the conscious surface of her mind: that if she stayed here much longer, she might not live at all.

"Crisen can make his own magic," she said as decisively as she could—*Father, Mother, Maiden, I am truly drunk tonight!*—and even as she said it found herself wondering why Crisen had asked her to prepare a summoning-spell. The last time she had done that he had learned unwanted things about his ancestry, so why again . . . ?

The wine turned to hot acid in her stomach. A stark-edged shadow—*her* shadow—was smeared as black and dense as pitch across the floor and up the wall before her. And shadows were created by . . .

Light! Greenish radiance danced at Sedna's back, above the centre of the circle drawn with such care on the crimson floor. Perspiration broke out all over her body, gluing the thin robe to her skin as it soaked up the moisture, and slowly, with an awful reluctance, she turned around.

The crystal goblet in her hand exploded into shards as the hand clenched to a fist, and though splinters drove deep she felt nothing. No pain, at least. Only terror . . .

The spell-circle was occupied. Compressed into a towering unstable column by the restrictive limit of the holding-pattern was a thing that—mercifully—she had never seen before in all her life. But she had looked between the woman's-leather covers of *Enciervanul Doamnisoar* not twenty hours before, and the memory of what she had seen—and *not* seen where it should be—still burned like a dark hot cinder in the shuttered places of her brain. Though this . . . this Thing had neither definite shape nor constant colour, she knew what It was, well enough at least to put a name to It. *Ythek'ter auythyu an-shri.* Warden of Gateways, Guardian of the portals which lie between men and the Outer Dark. The Herald of the Ancient Ones. Ythek Shri.

"Who has called thee now?" Sedna managed the question only after three attempts, knowing that all such entities were bound by certain rules and one such was the answering of questions. There was no immediate response and in that brief time she suddenly didn't want to hear Ythek's reply. She wanted rid of It. At once!

"You came in obedience," she said firmly, fighting down the quaver in her voice because she knew that no such obedience was owed to her. "Depart in obedience. Return to your proper place. Go back to the Void. I, Sedna ar Gethin, command it!" Immediately the words were out she knew that she had made a mistake: she had made the demon a free gift of her name. Swallowing bitterness, she recited a charm of dismissal and made the swift gesture which sealed it, watching as the shadowy mass shifted a little, bulging and contracting, swirling in and out of itself like ink poured into water. But it did not fade, did not vanish . . . Did not alter at all.

Sedna repeated the charm again and again, stammering in her haste as she varied the rhythm and order of its phrases. Still they had no effect. Blinking sweat out of her eyes, she walked as steadily as she was able towards the lectern where she had left her grimoire. Opening the weighty volume, she leafed quickly through its pages, trying all the time to remain calm, to avoid panic, and yet feeling the desire to run begin to tremble in the sinews of her legs. *Do not run!* Never run, never show fear . . . not even when dread has turned the marrow of your bones to meal . . .

The whole cellar vibrated slightly, as if a deep-sea swell had rolled beneath the floor, and became cold. It was not the sharp, exhilarating chill of a bright day in winter, but a heavy rigor like the inside of a long-forgotten tomb; the kind of cold which penetrated flesh and blood and marrow until they would never feel warm and alive again. Sedna's damp robe frosted over, white rime on white silk, until it became so stiff that each fold crackled as she moved. She felt, too, a sense of malice emanating from the core of the slowly twisting pillar of darkness. Muted tones of dull green, grey and sullen blue slithered across its convoluted surface, and with the malevolence came a low, moaning wind. Sparks whipped from the smouldering incense and the candle-flames fluttered wildly; fingers of moving air lashed the sorceress's face with strands of her own hair.

Refusing to be distracted, she found her page at last and laid one slim finger on the spell, an exorcism held to be effective against all demons. The words were archaic, difficult and complex in their nuances of meaning, and Sedna muttered them under her breath before daring to speak the incantation aloud. Ythek Shri congealed from an amorphous cloud to something more clearly defined and in doing so gave her a brief, appalling hint of what its true shape might be.

Otherwise her great spell had no effect.

Again panic bubbled up inside her; gripping her entrails in an icy clutch that made breathing difficult and full of effort. With a shocking oath she flung the useless spellbook at the circle and its occupant. As Sedna might have guessed, her curse did nothing. But the book produced results, although they were not such results as she would have wished . . .

Fifteen pounds of leather and parchment hurled with the strength of fear and hatred struck and toppled one of the tall bronze censers, so that not only the grimoire but a spray of perfumed charcoal went flying to the floor. One alone might have been insufficient; both together were more than enough to disrupt the patterns of the circle's double rim.

The wind gusted to a screeching gale and as suddenly fell away into silence. Only a single candle remained alight, its unsteady flame doing eldritch things to the many shadows which now crowded into the cellar. Sedna wasted no time in staring. With hands that shook she ripped the tops from jars and drew protective signs around herself in coloured dust, joining them into a broad, unbroken ring of power. Again there came that lurching sensation of an ocean wave surging under the floor. Red-stained boards rose and fell like the deck of a ship, sending a rack of bottles crashing into ruin, and Sedna stared fearfully towards the dark column, knowing It to be the source. The cloudy mass no longer swirled, but hung immobile as a rag suspended from the ceiling. It exuded an air of patience—and there was movement near its base.

The solitary candle showed no detail and only the vaguest of impressions, its feeble light falling into the darkness that absorbed it as a sponge drinks water, but there was enough for Sedna to realise what was happening. And when she did, the horror of that instant brought vomit spewing from her throat. Whatever was confined by the holding-pattern was spreading the scattered ashes, using them to erase the lines of force which penned it in. Enlarging the breach which *she* had made.

Something gross and glistening bulged from the blackness, paused, then with a mucous sucking sound forced itself a little farther out. Nothing was visible except the candle-flame's reflection on moist and moving surfaces. Its distorted yellow gleam shifted in another long, slow heave as the shape slid inexorably from its confinement.

Sedna wiped her mouth and cursed herself for not running when first she had the chance. It was too late now. Talons extended across the floor, clicked, flexed and gouged deep in search of anchorage, sinking effortlessly through floor-timbers into the solid stone beneath. Within her circle the Vreijek sorceress cringed. Home seemed very far away now.

The ponderous mass that was Ythek *an-shri* came loose in three rippling contractions, swayed on slender limbs and rose upright in utter silence. There was a slight, harsh scraping as a length of spike-tipped tail coiled heavily around the demon herald's claws. Then there was silence once more. The silence of the grave.

Scarcely daring to breathe, Sedna studied the entity for a long time. She had the impression that it was exhausted by the effort of dragging itself into the world of men; that it suffered the exertions of mother, midwife and child simultaneously. Perhaps it was asleep . . . perhaps the very air was proving poisonous. A muscle in her thigh jerked and quivered in protest at her lack of movement. Wincing, she massaged the cramped limb and measured her distance to the door, remembering the heavy lock that would surely be strong enough to hold it shut while she fled. Sedna decided not to waste time warning the citadel's household; if the demon was secured there would be no need, and if it broke out— the thought was callous but accurate—they would know without requiring her to tell them. If only she had known the thing would take so long escaping . . . If only her blind rage and terror had not breached the circle in the first place . . .

If only.

Taking infinite care not to disturb her own circle's fragile outline, she stepped across it with both eyes fixed on the irregular blot of blackness. Nothing happened: there was no snarl, no sudden murderous burst of life. It remained as deathly still as any lizard on a stone.

Sedna took another step towards the door. Then a third. They were long strides, as quiet as her bare feet could make them, and each one took her closer to escape.

But further from the circle.

A fourth step. There were, she judged, four more to take before she reached the door. Halfway . . . She glanced to where the demon crouched like some gigantic upright insect. Fearfully thin attenuated limbs were wrapped around its hunched body, and there was not even the rhythmic movement of breathing to show that it lived. If it did . . .

Five steps from the circle, three from the door.

Another nervous glance, this time back over her shoulder. The demon squatted in the shadows of its own making, a grotesque gargoyle shape, placid and still. New perspiration soaked into the silken robe, thawing the crust of frost so that the garment clung close as a second skin to Sedna's trembling body.

Six steps and two.

There was an awful eagerness in the long, bubbling hiss when at last it came. Sedna hesitated for the barest instant as her heart seemed to stop, then flung herself towards the door and heaved at it with all her strength. The feeling of betrayal when she found it locked was a physical hurt, swamping even terror for the moment that it lasted. She should have—indeed, *had* expected something such as this, but against all hope had thought that she was wrong. Wrong to have believed other than treachery and death was possible in Seghar . . .

There was no time now for regret; no time either for subtlety of finesse. With a mental wrench that caused her actual pain, Sedna dredged the words and patterns of the High Accelerator from her subconscious and flung the fierce spell at the lock. The whole door jolted on its hinges as lock, hasp and part of the jamb were hammered loose in a twisted mass of metal and fell clattering into the corridor outside. The demon had scarcely moved, was surely still sufficiently far away for her to run . . . With trembling hands that were already sore and bruised by the transmission of the spell, Sedna clutched at the weakened door and dragged it wide enough for her to—

—Spin half around and almost fall as something unseen blurred past her head to jerk the door from her enfeebled grasp and slam it shut with awful finality. The reverberations of its closing faded down the corridor, mocking her imprisonment with their escape. An enormous talon at the end of an impossibly long, sinewy limb had lashed over Sedna's shoulder with piledriver force to end her hopes of freedom. And of life. A little to one side and that frightful appendage could have smeared her frail human body across unyielding stone as she might squash a bug. But it had not—and the implications of that merciless compassion were far worse than any sudden death she could imagine.

With a rending of fibres the great crooked claw pried one another loose, each of the three digits flexing independently like the legs of a spider. Once free they reached for Sedna's face with all the delicacy of a lover's caress.

The woman whimpered softly and shrank away, her own hands raised in a useless gesture of supplication. Another spell would prolong the inevitable, no more. It would not avert it. Would not save her. Nothing would. She was lost and none could help her now . . .

The enamel-glossy black triangle that was the being's

eyeless, armoured head dipped closer, as if to study her. Four shearlike mandibles which ended that head slid open with a metallic sound like scissors, and an errant flicker of the candle revealed a vile array of spiked and bladed teeth. They champed together, glistening, as Ythek Shri grinned down at her from its full fifteen feet of height.

And Sedna screamed. Just once. She had no time for more before the demon plucked her from the floor to be Its plaything for a little while, and while it toyed with her the sounds she made could scarcely be described as anything so structured as a scream. Those dreadful noises continued for a long time, but never quite drowned out the splatter of spilling blood and the snap of bones, or the horrid, sodden rip as flesh gave way. At last the demon tired of its torn and broken doll, and secured the still feebly-squirming bundle of tatters while its razor-bladed mandibles gaped wider.

And shut in three protracted, hideously juicy crunches.

Shadows flickered frenziedly across the walls and ceiling as Sedna's legs danced ten feet from the ground. Then they kicked spasmodically, and apart from reflex shudders dangled still and dead at last. Only liquid droplets moved now, dribbling from the demon's meat-clogged maw. One sparkled ruby-red as it descended.

The solitary candle hissed, and choked on blood, and died . . .

*

Fog boiled across the surface of the mirror, so that Voord could see no more—as if he had not seen enough already. Like his hand, the Vlechan's face was almost drained of colour—almost, but not quite. There remained the unmistakable blanched greenness of nausea suppressed by pride alone. To vomit would be to show weakness. In his time as an inquisitor *Eldheisart* Voord had authorised, had supervised, had personally inflicted equally ingenious torments. So why retch at this . . . ?

He had absorbed each image shown him by the mirror with a cold, almost a clinically professional interest; aware with every mutilation that an unseen brooding presence was watching him, noting his reactions, assessing his worthiness for its aid. He had felt shock, disgust, the ever-present crawling fear—but had neither felt nor shown the slightest pang of pity or remorse.

And yet, though he had watched everything, he had still seen less than Sedna. His eyes were not eyes, and his knowledge of sorcery was sparse. Where he had beheld only a monster formed, it seemed, from armoured darkness, she had known exactly what the calling of *anshri* entailed. Like all demons, Ythek Shri had many names, many titles, born of the awe and terror It commanded by its very presence: Warden of Gateways, Devourer in the Dark . . . but most appropriate, and most explanatory to those who knew its meaning, was simply Herald. It was a herald, in very truth, an emissary, an ambassador between the world of men and the planes of the Abyss; and its function, its purpose, its self-appointed, chosen duty was to encourage human wizards in their reverence and summoning of the Ancient. The Demon Lords. To call on Ythek Shri, whether by accident or design, was no end in itself, although it had been so to Sedna ar Gethin. It was a beginning.

Of all this, and of much, much more, *Eldheisart* Voord remained in comfortable ignorance. The only mouth which could have told him, warned him of what he had done, was shredded, half-digested tissue now. It was ignorance, combined with his own lack of patience and the undertow of fear which he would not admit—overshadowed maybe by some other influence—which caused him to forget the ending of his conjuration. The Pronouncement of Dismissal. For no such Pronouncement was made. An envoy had been summoned, without reason for that summoning, and a Gate was open. Both the envoy and the Gate remained—and both were an invitation.

Slowly the grey surface of the mirror began to swirl in upon itself, heavy spirals of movement like stirred water. Slowly at first, but with ever-increasing speed, it became a whirling, dizzying, slick-sided funnel pouring into nothingness. Voord reeled as he stared down its throat, and vertigo tugged hypnotically at him. Had he been standing he might have taken the few unsteady steps required to tumble and be lost, but kneeling—

though his brain spun giddily in time with the vortex and he slumped forward—he caught his weight on outflung, outspread hands. Pain seared him as the ruined palm slapped hard against the floor. Blood flowed again and the spiralling continued ever faster. A whirlpool of mist. A maelstrom that threatened to suck away his very soul.

But he would not, could not be enticed, and with juddering abruptness the spinning of the vortex stopped. With a sound like the breaking of the world, the mirror of seeing cracked from side to side and its surface turned jet black. Crouched helplessly on hands and knees, Voord raised his head enough to see; and he saw darkness, seeping like smoke from the fissure in the mirror's substance. It did not dissipate, as true smoke or true vapour would have done, but became thicker, denser, heavier—as if it was taking physical form. As Sedna had done before him, Voord wondered momentarily what that form would be. But he wondered only for an instant, then apprehensive curiosity gave way to undiluted, abject terror. He sprang to his feet and fled.

6

Demon Queller

Aldric spent a sleepless night in Evthan's house, having made it brutally plain to the rejoicing villagers that he found no cause for celebration in that evening's work. Though Gueynor stayed with him, he did no more than stare into the fire as he held her hand in a grip which seemed his only link to life and sanity. It was as he had said: granting the needful gift of death was no more to an Alban *kailin-eir* than simple decency, like his burial of that pitiful morsel of humanity in the clearing by the mound. It was never a deed done lightly, for no matter what opinions were voiced, no matter what emotion was displayed or hidden, the taking of life left scars upon the life of he who took it, regardless of any just cause. Aldric had killed before, so many times. Yet this killing had somehow soiled him as no other had; as if he had administered a punishment where none was called for. Would it be so with Crisen? he wondered. If the king's command to kill him was not just, but Aldric carried it out through obedience, would that obedience wipe clean his own guilt in the matter . . . ! He was *ilauem-arluth, kailin, eijo,* swordsman, slayer—but he was neither an assassin nor an executioner.

Yet worst of all was the unshakable feeling that he had killed the wrong man. All the responsibility rested on Crisen Geruath's noble shoulders, for Aldric's mind, concentrated by his brooding, had sifted what he knew of the Overlords at Seghar again and again until he almost sickened of it. Round, and round, and round . . .

What had been done to Evthan had not been punishment for striking Keel; that had been the reason given, not the reason for it. Even the ferocious beating he had suffered was meant only to conceal traces of—what was that Vreijek name?—ar Keth . . . no, ar Gethin's shape-shifting sorcery. Aldric wanted words with her. Soon. And with Crisen. And the Overlord himself. As clan-lord and as king's confidant, the Alban realised now, he had certain responsibilities, ignore them or avoid them how he would. He could travel carelessly for just so long, pretending to himself that his sworn word had no imme-diacy to it, and then his duties would overtake him one way or another. As they had done now. Better by far if he turned and met them willingly.

But he was alone, and it was the Geruaths who ruled this province. There was nothing to prevent them dispos-ing of what they might regard as no more than a nui-sance. He recalled the "bandits" who had killed Youenn Sicard. Somebody had already tried such a disposal once . . . It would be best if he sent some kind of mes-sage back to Alba: a form of insurance, perhaps, which would provoke thought and make hasty violence less ap-pealing. Or merely a way to achieve vengeance from beyond the grave . . .

It would have to be committed to the keeping of someone he could trust implicitly, and under Heaven there were few enough of those. Now that Evthan was dead . . .

Gueynor. She had been sitting on her customary cush-ioned stool all night, drawn close beside his chair at the hearthfire of the house, and now she was huddled in uncomfortable sleep with her head resting on the Al-ban's knee. She had walked beside him to the door of Evthan's home, straight-backed and dignified, but once that door had locked behind her and no one else could see, the girl had broken down and cried bitterly for her dead uncle; indeed, had cried herself at last to sleep. It had pained him that he was helpless to comfort her, but he knew that any words he might speak were already redundant, and had kept silent. It would be better for her if she left this place, for whatever reason—Aldric knew only too well how memories refused to heal when they were continually refreshed by association with sur-roundings and places and faces . . . Oh yes, he knew.

But he was puzzled; why had there been no soldiers in the village, looking for him? Twenty-four hours had passed now, plenty of time for the man who had escaped to reach Seghar and make his report, more than enough time for a troop of cavalry to have been detached from the garrison and sent in haste to Valden.

Unless . . . A slow smile of relief spread over Aldric's face as what had been an idle notion—almost dismissed as too unlikely—became more and more probable each time that he reviewed it. The last mercenary had been a young man, very young—and so very, very frightened. Might he . . . ! Why not? When he fled from what must have seemed his own inevitable death, he could easily have kept on running, away from the mound in the forest and out of the Jevaiden, back to whatever farmstead in the Inner Empire he had come from. It was the only possible reason for there being no reaction from the citadel, for neither of the Geruaths seemed men who would indulge in the subtle, cruel game of cat-and-mouse. Where they were concerned, reprisals were invariably immediate. And severe. Aldric was unable to get the image of that Tergovan merchant out of his head: A man pulled apart by horses—for saying something which the lord's son didn't like . . . ! What would be done to a foreigner who killed the Overlord's retainers? Aldric had no idea, and for once had no desire to broaden his education. But it would certainly be imaginative, elaborate— and extremely painful.

Yes . . . it would be best if he sent a letter to Dewan ar Korentin. Gueynor could take it to the coast—at least his Drusalan florins were acceptable that far—and could see it safe aboard an Elherran merchantman. By the time she returned he would have . . . His flow of ideas stalled for lack of information. Would have done something positive, anyway.

First and foremost, he would see the Vreijek sorceress . . .

*

Aldric watched as night crawled slowly towards a cold, wet, miserable dawn that would never have a sunrise, and reached down to gently shake Gueynor out of sleep. She was confused at first, stiff and sore from her uncomfortable posture, and her eyes were still red-rimmed from too many tears. "Morning," the Alban explained. Gueynor glanced at the wan grey light beyond the shutters and closed her eyes again. "Just like any other day."

"Like any other day," she echoed. "Except that today they put my uncle in the earth." Aldric's face did not change. It wore the same hooded, inward-looking, thoughtful expression as when she awoke; except that now it was a shield to hide behind. "I thought I would feel different."

"Nothing changes in a night. Not love, not grief—not hate. I know . . ." He rose silently and left her; to wash, to shave and then to dress himself in the few formal clothes he carried in his saddlebags—the blue and silver *elyu-dlas* of clan Talvalin and a *cymar* of warrior's style, wide-shouldered and marked with crests, all worn over full black battle armour.

And then they buried Evthan Wolfsbane, wearing his old hunting buckskins and with the Beast's pelt for a pillow. There was no coffin, no shroud, no winding-sheet; instead his grave was floored and lined with newly sawn pinewood so that a faint scent of resin hung in the damp air. It was raining slightly, a weeping drizzle from a dull, lead-coloured sky. Gueynor and her mother—Aldric's mind found it hard to make the necessary transition of title to "aunt"—stood together at the graveside with the rest of Aline's family. Tactfully, the Alban stood a little apart, water gathering in great crystal beads on his garb of steel and leather, but making dark blotches where it soaked into the fabric of his over-robe. He watched sombrely as Evthan's body was lowered into the ground, the sight making him uncomfortable; burial like this was an alien concept to one brought up with the swift, bright ending of cremation, and when two villagers lifted spades he inclined his head a fraction, just enough to hide them with the drip-rimmed peak of his helmet, trying not to think of the dank, enveloping darkness and of the worms that would . . .

"Avert," he muttered hastily and was ashamed. From somewhere in the woods beyond the village palisade came the howling of a wolf, small, ordinary and of no account. As that mournful sound slid down the scale to silence it was punctuated by the moist slithering of shovelled soil. Aldric raised one mailed arm, half in salute and half in farewell, and walked slowly from the funeral.

Darath the headman stood between him and the houses. Aldric was reluctant to be disturbed—the gloomy day and its grim events had struck a sympathetic chord within him—but the Jouvaine's courteous bow, so profound it almost mimicked an Alban Low Obeisance, obliged him to at least give the man a hearing. Darath carried something in his arms, swaddled like an infant in many layers of cloth, and the sight of it sent an uneasy shiver along Aldric's steel-sheathed limbs even before the parcel was unwrapped.

It was a gift. Evthan's wolfskin *coyac* had been washed clean of blood, then dried and brushed until the lustrous sheen of its dark fur was quite restored. "Honoured sir," Darath said, and the apprehension in his tone suggested that he had misread the glint in Aldric's war-mask-shadowed eyes, "we would give you silver if we had it—but you know how poor the folk of Valden are. We can only offer food and a warm place to sleep for as long as you require it, and—and this, on this day, as a keepsake. To remind you of a man who would have been your friend, had he survived. He would have wished it so."

The voice was no longer that of a village headman, just an old man who was afraid his offer was inadequate; not knowing all the facts, he had seen dissatisfaction and greed where there was only sorrow. And reluctance.

"What made you think that I would want this?" the Alban wondered softly.

"It is black, honoured sir. I hoped that it would please you." The *coyac* was not black any more; like all else exposed to the fine, drifting mist of rain, the long guard hairs of its pelt were frosted now with moisture. That translucent film of silver did little to allay Aldric's doubts when the garment was offered to him. He stared at it, and then at Darath. The headman bowed again, timidly, his mouth stretched by a nervously ingratiating smile, terrified lest he give offence to a known manslayer.

Aldric was not offended, only a little hurt, but aware he was to blame for his own reputation. Bowing in response, he accepted the gift. After all, together with his board and lodging it was no more than any other payment for a service rendered—no matter how reluctantly.

*

Despite whatever private reservations he might have had, Aldric's acceptance of the *coyac* carried infinitely fewer complications than did Gueynor's reaction to his plan. For she refused it outright.

"I will not be sent away—and I will not be treated as a child!" If her voice had been shrill and petulant the Alban might have known how to deal with it; certainly he would have been more inclined to argue. But it was quiet, controlled, firm and decisive. He could well believe her father had been Overlord in Seghar.

"Not even for your own safety's sake?" he asked.

"My safety . . . ! My safety is hardly at risk. I have killed no one." She considered that statement. "Yet."

"What about the village?"

"Valden is in no danger. When was it—the night before last? And yet, no soldiers. I should have thought the Overlord would have sent his men here long ago, if he knew what you had done. *If.* Therefore . . ."

"It seems he doesn't know." Aldric was unable to suppress the undertone of sardonic amusement running through his voice. The girl had a quick brain—he already knew that—and was therefore someone to be watched. As much, at least, as she was evidently watching him. There was also a singlemindedness about her which he found . . . interesting. All the weeping for her uncle had been done last night; now that he was buried, no more would help—so there would be no more. Now she was concentrating on another matter: Geruath the Overlord, and her revenge on him. The Alban wondered if he had displayed a similar intensity when his thoughts were filled with Duergar and Kalarr. What plans had she already made that he did not know about—and where did he fit into them . . . ?

"What do you intend?" An idle ear would have detected only idle curiosity, with no real interest at all. And anyone who knew Aldric Talvalin would have become immediately most suspicious . . .

"To come with you."

If her reply surprised him, no sign showed and he care-

fully adjusted part of his armour-lacing before bothering
to react. Aldric had guessed something like this would happen, and the last thing he wanted was company—he would
have enough difficulty protecting himself without looking after a girl who, no matter where she had been born,
had spent the past ten years as a peasant in a peasant
village. At least Tehal Kyrin could look after herself . . .

"Oh, indeed. Where had you in mind?"

"Seghar. Where else? That's the next place you'll be
going, Kourgath. You have some interest or other in the
Geruaths. I can tell."

"And I concede the point. But why take you—
someone will know your face, surely?"

"No, I doubt that. I haven't been within the walls in
two years now. And I'm Evthan the hunter's niece: a
peasant, nothing more. Hardly worth noticing." The bitterness in her voice was undisguised now—a raw, ugly
sound which Aldric did not like to hear. Such a festering
preoccupation with rank could prove very, very
dangerous . . .

"You insult yourself. You insult me. And you insult
the intelligence and eyesight of every male past pu-
berty!" The irritable snap of each word negated any
flattery they carried. "I don't care about what you are,
or what you think you should be—looking as you do
now, you'll be both noticed and remembered."

"Don't patronise me, Alban . . ."

"Patronise . . . ! I tell you nothing but the truth." *If
you intend to follow me into the citadel,* he continued
inwardly, *I shall expect you to be of some use. And
reliable. But without attracting everyone's attention.*
Aloud he said, "How well do you know the place?"

"Well enough." She stared at him, into his eyes and
through them as if reading the workings of the mind
beyond. "I'll be of use, don't worry about that."

Aldric could only grin wryly, as any man might whose
secrets are not quite so secret as he might have hoped.
"Even so," his hand reached out to touch her pale
blonde hair, "I think it would be better if you were . . .
someone else. There might be too many memories
aroused by the sight of Evthan's niece in the company
of an armed stranger. I don't know what that soldier did

when he ran away from me. I've guessed, of course—but only guessed. I know he's still alive, somewhere. And if that somewhere is Seghar, and he identifies me, you'll be implicated too. You, and this whole village, will be guilty in the eyes of the Overlord. As I told Darath, I was a fool; I made them a present of Evthan's name. And how many Evthans are there in the Jevaiden . . . ?"

Although the question was rhetorical, Gueynor shrugged her shoulders grimly. "Not enough," she answered. "Not enough by far."

"You see? And you are his niece. This," he stroked her hair again, a gentle caress with the palm of his right hand, "is what people remember of you after other details fade. So what can you dye it with?"

"Dye it?" Gueynor jerked away from his touch as if each finger glowed red-hot. "Are you seriously considering disguises . . . !"

"Quite seriously. Someone has already tried to kill me. They killed my travelling companion instead. Both occurrences are fair justification for me to become very serious indeed, since I do not intend to offer them—or him—a second chance. And I think a mercenary should look the part—" As the drily flippant words left his mouth Aldric's teeth closed with a distinctly audible click, but not quite fast enough to catch them. "Damn," he said softly after a moment's consideration. "I talk too much."

"But you are . . ." Gueynor began to surprise. Then, as he had expected, she stopped and stared. The tensed muscles at the corners of his jaw and the hot anger in his eyes told their own tale. "You are not—and never have been, Aldric Talvalin."

He might have said "Who?" and tried to brazen out the error, but in a strange way he was glad she knew. Aldric had felt increasingly deceitful, an uncomfortable sensation where lovers were concerned, even such casual bedmates as he and Gueynor; but having told one person in the Jevaiden already, he had decided after thought that one was enough. Evthan must have told the girl; maybe in the knowledge of his own impending death, or because he thought that they might kill each other. The reason was hardly important now.

"Gueynor-*an*," the Alban said, using a courteous form to emphasise his words, "I am only who and what I say I am. Nothing more and nothing less. I trust you to make appropriate responses—for both our sakes."

"Aldric-*ain*,"—Gueynor knew enough Alban, it seemed, to use the affectionate, if her pronunciation was correct— "you can trust me with your life, as my uncle trusted you with his."

Aldric looked carefully at her, not particularly sure how to take what she had said. He dismissed its several meanings with a faint, unfinished smile. "Disguises," he said thoughtfully. "Nothing elaborate. Just sufficient to deceive. Long ago I was told that the first element of disguise is to conceal the obvious. Your hair, my scar." He tapped his own right cheekbone, just below the eye. "And I'll become a little darker, too."

"What do you plan about the scar?" Scepticism aside, Gueynor was interested.

"Cover it. An eyepatch should do. Mercenaries collect such things almost as part of their wages. But more important, it will be something to remember: a convenient hook for inconvenient memories to catch on . . . They will remember a black-haired, one-eyed man and his buxom brown-haired lady. No more than that."

"Buxom . . . ?" repeated Gueynor suspiciously.

"Padding! Remove it, remove the patch, wash our hair and faces and we shall be two different people." Gueynor could see that enthusiasm was possibly an Alban failing rather than a strength and said so.

"I think you're mad!"

"Possibly. But it's an entertaining sort of madness, don't you think?"

"It could see us both dead."

"So could walking barefaced into Seghar citadel—and much more quickly."

There was no arguing with that point of view, and Gueynor did not even try.

*

Aldric gazed at his reflection in the disc of polished bronze which had done Evthan duty as a mirror. The face which stared back at him was familiar, but it was not the Aldric Talvalin that he knew. It skin was swarthy now, rattier than tanned; the result of carefully applied berry-juice, mixed with oil to make it waterproof. It smelt a little strange . . . His hair was almost black after a wash with the same stuff, without the telltale fair streaks which were a legacy of his father's family, and was crossed by the dramatic stripe of the patch which covered his right eye and the scar beneath it. Aldric reached out and turned the mirror slightly, his remaining eye narrowing thoughtfully at what he saw. The accumulated alterations, each small in itself, together produced an image which he disliked even though it was what he had hoped for: ruthless, brutal, cold—nobody would ask the owner of that face too many searching questions. And nobody would trust him at all . . .

Other than those few details, he had changed nothing; not even his nationality. Anyone hearing of an Alban mercenary within the walls of Seghar would almost certainly try to see this newcomer at once and, having seen him, not recognise the man they sought and leave him alone. He hoped. At least they would be unsure of his identity. He hoped . . . Aldric grinned viciously at himself, a humourless white gleam of teeth against the olive complexion, and guessed that if his mind worked on that track for long enough he would finish by avoiding the citadel entirely. At least there was no need to adopt a different voice; feigned accents were all very well in their proper place, but that place was not the fortress of a provincial Overlord.

Gueynor's transformation to a mercenary's lady took her almost two hours, and even then it was quicker than Aldric had expected. Although she still regarded his scheme, with a degree of scorn, as an elaborate children's game of dressing-up enhanced by adult reasoning, she had done her best. Her blonde hair now had the rich russet hue of fox-fur, its braids wrapped close around her head instead of hanging loose as was customary for unmarried Jouvaine women. Their lashes shadowed by kohl on both upper lids and lower, the girl's blue eyes were startling in their sapphire brilliance as they stared at Aldric, daring him to utter any comment about her omission of the suggested padding. Wisely, he said not a word. She was dressed in wide-legged, baggy trousers tucked into short boots, a high-necked tunic, and a knee-length hooded riding coat of plainly Pryteinek cut which even bore some Segelin clan-crests worked in contrasting colours along its hem. The colours had little enough to contrast with—fawn and green and brown for the most part. Retiring, self-effacing shades.

The Alban quirked his solitary eyebrow at the coat and wondered how such a garment came to be in this small Jouvaine village. The folk of Prytenon were not renowned travellers, especially in the Empire. Strange indeed . . . Gueynor remained—indeed could never have concealed—the fine-featured, pretty girl whom he had met two days ago—but she was no longer the same girl, either outside or in. It was, considered Aldric, just as well.

"Henna is permanent," he criticised gently, looking at her hair.

"I know. So this isn't henna. It should wash out when it has to."

Aldric smiled a little. "Very well," he said. "I bow to your superior knowledge," and suited the action to the word; not with the elegant inclination of his upper body that she had seen once or twice before, but with a sweeping, insolent bend low over one extended leg, accompanied by extravagant flourishes of his right hand. Gueynor might have been tempted to laugh at such theatricality, but the slight scraping of his longsword and the sinister regard of that dark, one-eyed face dissuaded her.

"You look . . . evil," she whispered.

"Good!" He straightened, brushed his clothing into line with both hands and stalked once around the girl, looking thoughtfully at her and at the long coat. "I won't ask where this came from; I'm not that much interested. But just to satisfy my own curiosity, tell me—can you ride a horse?"

There was an awkward little pause in which Aldric was able to answer his own question, before Gueynor finally admitted in a small voice, "No, I can't."

"I didn't think so." Aldric let the matter drop, for he had no intention of riding very far or very fast anyway. But he hoped that his intention would not be altered by events . . .

*

There was no rain when they rode out of Valden. It was still a little before noon, something which surprised the Alban until he recalled that this was midsummer day, *an Haf Golowan,* the longest day of the year. Last night had been the shortest night . . . except that it had seemed years long to him. He had been awake at dawn; Evthan had been buried in the early morning, at sun-up if the sun had been visible through the featureless overcast. And now they were leaving. Aldric shook his head wearily; it seemed wrong, hurried—what had happened here should have taken longer than two days, had a little more dignity about it. He turned the headshake into a shrug that stated plainly there was nothing to be done. Because it was true.

Gueynor sat his pack-pony's back better than he had anticipated; indeed, there had been moments when he had experienced more difficulty. To give her a mount had entailed a redistribution of saddlebags; Lyard resented being employed as a baggage horse, and the resentment of an Andarran stallion was not easily ignored. At least the big courser had settled now, making his disapproval plain with resigned snorts and blowings-out of his lips. But he had learned not to try any more lively demonstrations . . .

Except for Darath the headman, none of the villagers watched them go. It was as if Valden wanted to forget them both—or at least to forget Aldric—as quickly as possible. Only Evthan had ever really made him welcome and now that he was dead, the Alban could not blame the others. Even the most wooden-headed peasant, seeing that both he and Gueynor had deliberately changed their appearance, would guess that something was far from right and equally, that the less known about it the better. So be it, then. Aldric did not care—not so that anyone could see, anyway.

Out of consideration for Gueynor's inexperience, he held to a soft pace that was little more than an amble, glancing over every now and then to see how she fared. He had improvised a bridle, but her saddle was no more than a folded blanket—without girth, stirrups or pommel. Accustomed for years to the hip-hugging embrace

of a high-peaked war saddle, Aldric himself would have
felt uneasy riding bareback. Gueynor's seat was rigid and
inflexible, her backbone like a poker and probably trans-
mitting every jolt unmercifully; her knees were clamped to
the pony's well-upholstered ribs like pincers—but she
looked well enough, considering . . .

They spoke seldom, each wrapped in private thoughts,
although the Alban occasionally raised a suspicious gaze
towards the sky. He was familiar with this changeable
summer weather and had no wish to be soaked; quite
apart from the discomfort, he doubted that the dye of
their disguises could survive a thorough wetting.

At least his worries were proved groundless. The remaining clouds thinned rapidly and then cleared, until
even in the shadow of trees it was hot. The afternoon
sun blazed overhead and mere branches offered little
shelter to travellers on the narrow forest trails. Wisps of
vapour curled like fragile skeins of cobweb from the
damp undergrowth, and the warm air grew close and
sticky. There was no wind.

"How far to Seghar anyway?" Aldric's voice was quiet,
influenced perhaps by the vast humid stillness that surrounded them. Even the horses' hoofs no longer seemed
to fall so heavily, and he was reminded inescapably of
that first day's hunting. And of all that had followed it.

"One day's walk from Valden," Gueynor replied at
last. "On horseback, maybe a little less."

"At this speed? No less, and probably more. Though
we might get there before full dark." A thought struck
him as he spoke the words—visions of being locked out
during some sort of curfew went floating through his
mind. "If we don't, will they let us in . . . ?"

Gueynor, unhelpfully, didn't know.

Aldric kicked both his moccasin-booted feet free of
the stirrup irons and let them dangle as he stretched
backwards as far as the tall, curved cantle would allow.
"Then we'll stop for a while. If the guards let us in, we'll
get in, and if not it's already too late to hurry." He was
philosphical, resigned, his tone suggesting that he didn't
care one way or the other.

There had been a stream running close beside the
bridle-path for maybe half a mile now, tumbling down

over half-seen granite crags as it flowed from the higher reaches of the Jevaiden plateau, and once in a while it formed wide pools alive with golden light and bronze-green shadowy depths. The twinkling of a thousand sun-shot ripples looked cool and inviting to the Alban's eye; he was hot and he was sleepy. Hungry, too. After last night's waking vigil nothing seemed to be urgent any more. Nothing at all . . .

*

In the first half-hour since the path beneath his pony's hoofs had dried out enough to give off dust again, the fat man's carefully dressed hair and beard had turned to grayish rattails. The round-bellied, short-legged beast was refusing to hurry through such heat, and being of similar proportions himself, its rider could only sympathise. Under richly embroidered garments his skin was gritty, and his nose was acutely aware of how much he was sweating. He and the little horse both . . . except that *it* was not required to impress people, and could not even begin to try. Tugging sticky silk out of his armpits in some distaste, he eyed the nearest pool and decided that, regardless of how cold the water might be—and probably was—a bath and a change of clothing was long overdue.

Dismounting from the relieved pony, he hobbled its forelegs and removed saddle and saddlebags before leaving it to graze while he washed. The water was as shockingly cold as he had feared, and he adopted his usual technique for such an eventuality. Employed, for obvious reasons, only when he was alone, it consisted of a long run-up, a leap accompanied by a yell of anticipation and an explosive backside-foremost landing in the deepest part of the pool. A column of foam-streaked water rose and fell, but the pony, who had seen and heard it all before, merely blew disapprovingly before continuing to eat.

Although a clump of bushes upstream jerked abruptly, as if shocked out of a deep and comfortable sleep . . .

Sitting in the shallows with his legs stuck straight out before him, the man scrubbed himself all over with clean gravel from the riverbed until he glowed with cleanliness and friction, then rinsed it off by swimming splashily across the pool. Like many fat men he·was a good swimmer, buoyant and therefore confident in water, and once the initial chill became merely refreshing he floated on his back and watched the dragonflies as they flicked and hovered briskly over him. For all his idleness his mind was working rapidly; not thinking about anything new, merely reiterating what had passed through it so many times before. *I shouldn't have accepted this commission—it's probably a dangerous one and I'm getting too old for that.* He wondered how long his unenthusiastic search would have to go on before he could justifiably abandon it and go home . . .

There was a quick buzz near his head which ended in an incisive splash, and the dragonflies scattered. "Fish?" he speculated aloud, surprised that his own presence wasn't a deterrent. "Or maybe a diving bird?" Yet the same reason for doubt held true. Intrigued, the fat man rolled over and ducked his face beneath the water to see what *had* made the noise. He saw—and tried to gasp, instead inhaled a lot of river with a gurgling belch and submerged for several choking seconds before he broke surface, sputtering.

There was no fish, no bird. Just a long, slender arrow turning slowly as it drifted tail-first upwards, wreathed in a cloud of tiny, self-made bubbles. The sharp steel head whose weight pulled it from the horizontal glinted ominously under water as it rotated, as coldly malevolent as the eye of any predatory fish and much more immediately threatening.

As he coughed and tried to drag air back into his flooded lungs, the fat man raked wet hair from his eyes as if that would help him to discover who was shooting. It did not. All he could see was forest: either the pillared tree trunks or an impenetrable tangle of undergrowth. But someone could evidently see him . . . The impression was reinforced when a voice said, "Get out, come here—" and when he began to wade towards the shore, added "—and bring my arrow with you."

Despite the risk of another, impatience-provoked shaft, he took a few minutes to wrap himself modestly in a large towel before following that emotionless voice to its source. The fat man was trying hard not to think about what had just happened, for either it was an example of skilled archery or the bowman had intended to kill him and had missed. Neither alternative was appealing . . .

He was startled again only seconds later, this time by an extremely large black horse which appeared without warning from behind a tree. The animal was not hobbled—he could see as much from the way it moved—and it watched him for a moment or two before wandering back into the shade with a snort capable of several interpretations.

The archer, and by inference the horse's owner, was lounging under an oak tree, his booted feet crossed atop a pile of saddlery and gear. There was a young woman seated with equal comfort by the bowman's side, although her back was tensed and her face uncertain. There was no such unease about her companion—or it was concealed with consummate skill behind a palpable aura of restrained menace. The shadows cast by low, leaf-heavy branches effectively masked his features, and it seemed unlikely that they fell just-so by accident rather than design. There was a book set upside-down on the grass to keep its place while its reader folded his arms and dozed, or embraced his lady—or shot at unsuspecting swimmers with the great war bow resting negligently across his thighs.

At first sight everything appeared most casual, almost disorderly; but a second glance revealed purpose behind the chaotic scatter, based on access to the quite unreasonable quantity of weapons this couple carried with them. Besides the longbow in plain view there was a second, much shorter, cased and hanging from the saddle-footstool, with filled quivers for each; and there was a pair of *telekin* neatly holstered either side of the pommel, a dirk at the man's belt and a longsword propped within easy reach.

Hilt and harness, boots, bow and breeches were all stark black, and there was a black wolfskin rolled into a cushion between the stranger's head and the tree trunk against which he reclined. His shirt was white, open to the waist and with its sleeves rolled up; there was a bracer strapped to one brown forearm and a thumb-ringed shooting-glove on the other hand. Silver glittered in the hollow of his throat, a thick torque with a pendant talisman of some kind, and at sight of that metal the fat man relaxed visibly.

"What did I do that you find calming?" The voice still used Drusalan, but now, closer, there was an undertone of some out-of-place accent.

"Silver," the fat man replied with a nod towards it, privately surprised that his voice was so steady. "At least you're not—" a quick, rather insincere grin as if to prove he spoke in jest "—not some forest demon."

At his words the girl sat more upright still, making a soft sound of surprise. "A strange thing for any man to say, Kourgath," she murmured, and the suspicion in her tone was intended to be heard.

Too late now to abandon any commission . . . thought the fat man apprehensively, looking at the bow, the *telekin* and the longsword and begining to fear for his safety. And for his dignity: the towel around his ample waist was working loose. He tugged at it, grateful for something to do with hands that threatened to tremble at any moment, and when he looked up found himself being studied by a single grey-green eye in a much younger face than he had expected to see. Clean-shaven and very brown, there was the stark diagonal of a patch across brow, right eye and cheekbone. As he returned stare for stare with the advantage of two eyes on his side, he saw the archer's gloved right hand come up to ease his patch a little lower as if hiding something.

The implied recent mutilation made him wince a little; that, and the bowman's youth, would make him sensitive and determined to prove something—anything—to a world which might consider him incomplete. It would make him as deadly as a coiled adder. And yet there was something about him which sounded a near-forgotten chord of memory . . . His hair . . . ? It was cut short, yet not close-cropped like that of the Imperial military—but it was black. The memory hovered an instant, and was gone.

The single eye blinked lazily, like a cat's. "No demon, eh? Some would argue. I am *eijo*. And what are you, besides a man of Cerenau?" Those last words were in pure Alban, coloured by that Elthanek burr which had been so hard to reconcile with the Drusalan language, and the fat man blinked.

"Is my accent so obvious?" he said, and laughed— hollowly, and forcing it just a little. *An* eijo, *before Heaven. . . . That explains the hair.* But it did not— quite—explain that tiny, nagging memory. He hid a grimace with a broad, false smile.

"Are you a priest," the girl wondered innocently, and now he wondered how much of that wide-eyed curiosity was no more than an act, "that your first words are concerned with demons?"

"Not a priest," he replied with as much hauteur as a stealthily slipping towel would permit. "I am Marek Endain, demon queller. *The* demon queller." His bow was jerky, laced with a faintly aggressive politeness.

The *eijo* replied with a perfunctory salute and grinned, yet despite its brevity that flash of teeth disarmed the situation. "Demon queller indeed," he murmured softly, half to himself and half to the girl. There might have been awe or respect in his voice, but somehow Marek was inclined to doubt it. "Kourgath, *eijo* of Alba, traveller and mercenary." He cleared his throat, gently mocking Marek's insistent emphasis. "Just *a* mercenary. And my lady: Gueynor of . . ."

"No fixed abode," suggested the demon queller generously.

"Ternon, originally," Gueynor finished for him. "Some years back."

Not too many, thought Marek, looking at her; babes in arms don't leave home alone. I wonder do your parents know about . . . His eyes slid momentarily to the *eijo*'s face. Probably not. Already over the worst of his fright—and despite appearances, Marek Endain did not frighten easily—he was beginning to guess why this young couple were so jumpy and suspicious. The lad in his middle twenties, the girl not twenty yet—well-spoken, both of them. A mercenary and, he guessed, a wealthy merchant's daughter, and not forcibly abducted either by the look of her. Both expecting and fearing pursuit. It was like a story . . . Marek felt warmly sentimental, remembering an occasion when he too had been young.

"Your secrets are safe with me," he announced impulsively, hitching his towel to a new anchorage higher up the majestic curve of his belly. Kourgath and Gueynor looked at him, both wearing the same startled expression, then at each other. They smiled.

And the towel abruptly slipped. Kourgath added to Marek's embarrassment by laughing aloud as the Cernuan grabbed wildly, while Gueynor put one hand in front of her mouth and blushed becomingly. The demon queller was beyond blushing. When the Jevaiden plateau obstinately refused to open up and swallow him he straightened his back and, carefully avoiding anyone's direct gaze, muttered, "If . . . if you don't mind, I'll dress now."

"I don't mind at all," the *eijo* returned with a sardonic grin, "and neither does my lady. In fact we would consider it a wise decision. Very wise indeed."

*

"Do you think that we can trust him?" Gueynor asked softly when the Cernuan had walked away.

Aldric gazed after him and nodded. "Yes, I think so. In any event, we have to—unless you prefer the alternative . . . ?"

"I told you before—I won't agree to murder!"

"Except," Aldric's voice was nasty, "for the Geruaths. So call this self-defence . . ."

"Why? Because it sounds better?"

"If he's dangerous there won't be any choice in the matter."

"Thanks to you!" Gueynor was still angered by what she deemed an ill-considered action on Aldric's part, and with Marek out of earshot was certainly not reluctant to let him know it. "If you hadn't been so hasty he would have passed us by!"

"I . . . doubt it." There was little else that he could say as a reply to her accusation, and no way now that he could start to explain about his sixth-sense feelings or make her understand why he had been certain that Marek's intended route would have brought the demon queller and his pony right on top of them. Knowing that, it had been no more than good tactics to make the first move; he had gained the advantage of surprise and, it seemed now, perhaps, an unsuspecting ally as well.

"Did you see his face?" he murmured thoughtfully, remembering Marek's expression.

"What about his face?"

"I suspect he thinks we've run away together." Gueynor snorted. "No, it's true." He explained briefly what he had read on the Cernuan's bearded features, and the girl examined his reasoning in silence for a moment before she pursed her lips and nodded.

"You might be right," she conceded reluctantly, not sounding particularly convinced. "But what difference does that make?"

"It means that he's formed his own opinions—and they'll be more credible to his mind than anything I might try to feed him. He's forgiven me for that arrow already—at least, he didn't mention it—and I doubt now that he would betray us to anyone, even accidentally. Marek thinks he knows who would be looking for us, and why. He's a romantic at heart, I think—or would like to be."

"You think!"

"I think. No more than that. But I'd still go bond for his silence."

Gueynor stared at Aldric, then very gently reached out to adjust the black patch over his eye. He had raised it to shoot, muttering something about not judging the distance accurately otherwise, had not replaced it snugly enough and had been twitching at it ever since, as if it itched. She patted his cheek afterwards. "Don't go bond for anything," she advised, and the waspishness had left her voice. "You might forfeit more than money."

What then? the Alban thought. Life? Honour . . . ! No, not honour. That was long since lost. Once again he had maneuvered an innocent stranger into accepting him as something he was not, employing deception with a practised ease. It was a dishonourable thing for any Alban warrior to do, and for a clan-lord should have been unthinkable. It had been unthinkable for him, but in a subtly different way—he had not thought about it at all. Maybe if Marek had been from somewhere else

it would not have mattered, would not have had him
thinking like this—but he was Cernuan. South Alban—
though if he was like the other Cernuans Aldric had met
he would not appreciate such a misnomer—and a fellow-
countryman in this foreign province. Maybe he was a
little mad after all, if to be mad meant to no longer care
about losing his own self-respect . . .

Was that why he had helped Evthan in his hunt for
the Beast? And why he now hoped to help Gueynor?
Because he was trying to recover something, to prove
something to the world and to himself . . . ? Prove that
he could have saved his father's life and his own honour
if he had come home in time. And would he always have
to prove it by killing and deceit, down all the days of a
life that seemed sometimes already far too long?

Aldric's mouth opened, but no words emerged and it
closed again with a snap of teeth that Gueynor could
hear. Instead he got to his feet, almost flinging himself
upright and away from the comfort of her hand, her
presence, her sympathy. He seized the black wolfskin
coyac and drew it on over his shirt, hesitating a moment
as he felt its weight settle on his shoulders, then moved
away to stare unseeing down towards the uncomplicated
pool while he tried to come to terms with the complications inside his own head.

When Marek returned he was wearing a splendid
cymar of scarlet patterned with whorls of gold and black;
two stoppered wine-jars were secured between the fingers of his left hand and three beechwood drinking
bowls in the right. His arrival on Aldric's blind side went
unnoticed, but still he glanced warily towards Gueynor,
suspecting that his previous appearance had precipitated
some sort of argument. Only when she patted the ground
where her companion had been sitting and smiled shyly
at him was the Cernuan reassured. Whatever their dis-
pute, he guessed that a little red Elherran wine would
be appreciated. By himself, if no one else!

Aldric heard the distinctive sound of a withdrawing
cork, but ignored it. In his present mood the last thing
he intended was to start drinking, because he knew from
past experience where it would lead. He had been down
that road once before, with less reason than now, and

once was enough. So . . . no wine. With his resolution settled, he counted his breaths for a few moments more and turned round.

Gueynor and Marek were deep in an animated conversation about anything and everything—except, the Alban reckoned cynically, *eijin* who shot at perfect strangers in the middle of their ablutions—while the demon queller organised his mane of long hair into a neat queue. Now he looked considerably more elegant and capable than the dripping, towel-wrapped figure who had stood before them not so long ago. A receding hair-line only served to accentuate his lofty, intelligent brow, framed by the silvered chestnut of hair and full beard. Taller than Aldric, he was a fat man—and yet less fat than he appeared. Most of his surplus weight was carried in his belly—as splendid in its own way as the *cymar* which covered it, but a neatly organised affair as bellies went—while the rest of him was stocky rather than plump. There was real strength hiding in those thick limbs, but seen with the eye and mind of one newly come to recognise deception, Aldric suspected that the Cernuan deliberately chose the image of a middle-aged fat man over-fond of food and drink. He was probably nothing of the sort . . .

"Apart from the obvious," Gueynor wanted to know, "what does a demon queller actually do?" Marek finished forking his beard and drew breath to expound theory and practice.

Even one-eyed and introspective, Aldric recognised the symptoms. "Briefly, of course," he interposed. The demon queller released his gathered breath and with a sharp gasp that sounded slightly outraged; nobody had ever asked him to edit his customary long-winded introduction before, neither was he at all sure that he wanted to, or even could. "Leave out everything which merely *sounds* important," the Alban recommended drily. "That should help." His sombre face had not altered as he spoke, and it was impossible for Marek to say whether or not he was joking. Probably not.

"You might say that I cure wizards' mistakes," he said at length, addressing himself primarily—and pointedly—to Gueynor. "It only needs one error in a ritual—an inaccurately drawn symbol, a broken line—for all hell to break loose. Often literally."

"You see?" said Aldric, baiting gently. "That didn't hurt, did it?" Then he put the question which had been nagging him ever since he first heard Marek's accent: "What brings a Cernuan to the Jevaiden woods? Isn't it rather far to travel?"

"No more than for an Alban *eijo*," Aldric's lips pulled back from his teeth at that, and he nodded to acknowledge a fair hit. "I was visiting a Jouvaine lady associate"—Gueynor stifled a laugh—"and she mentioned something about a wolf. Or a werewolf. Here in the plateau Deepwood." The laughter stopped as if severed by a knife.

"This isn't the Deepwood," Gueynor said softly.

"No matter. I've heard nothing anyway. Probably just peasant exaggeration."

"Not exaggeration. Oh, no." Aldric's gloved right hand stroked the soft fur of the *coyac,* leather and fur, black on black. "There was a werewolf. And a real wolf. Both dead now." The odd expression on his face unsettled Marek slightly, as did the gleam of unshed tears in the Jouvaine girl's blue eyes. This, he realised, was a sensitive subject. "I," finished Kourgath in a whisper, "helped."

There was a brief, uncomfortable silence until Gueynor swallowed carefully and spoke again. "So what now for you? Back to your . . . associate?"

"No need. There was a full moon last night. It influences more than . . . Well, somebody, somewhere will need my services, as likely here as anywhere else."

Aldric frowned. "You seem very sure."

The Cernuan waved one hand in the air, indicating vaguely eastward. "I am sure, Kourgath. We're not so very far from the Imperial frontier. Sorcery is strictly banned within the Drusalan Empire, but now and again those edicts are ignored by men with enough power to do so."

"Such as Grand Warlord Etzel." Aldric regretted the words even as they left his mouth, for they brought a suspicious look to Marek's face and were obviously not such common knowledge as the Alban had supposed.

"At least, so I've heard," he finished lamely, cursing himself.

"You must have listened to some interesting conversations recently," the Cernuan mused, but to Aldric's relief did not pursue the matter further—although he stared for several minutes at the Alban, who found it politic to evade the demon queller's gaze by developing a sudden interest in the lacing of his boots. "As a consequence," he continued eventually, "these Jouvaine border provinces are a haven and a home for a great many enchanters, whose skills are for hire to anyone with the necessary considerable wealth."

"Such as Lord Crisen Geruath?" Gueynor asked. Aldric wished that she would learn to listen in silence, just once, and let him ask the prompting questions, but it was too late now. Far too late.

"Lord Crisen . . . ?" echoed Marek.

"The lord's son at Seghar. His father is Overlord here."

"I didn't know that," marvelled the demon queller. "Tell me, why do you mention his name?"

Shut up! SHUT UP! screamed Aldric inwardly. *You don't live here! You come from Ternon! You don't know any of this!*

"Because his mistress . . ." It appeared that a little of Aldric's desperate silent pleading had reached her at last, because she faltered momentarily; and when she continued it was with a flash of inspired brilliance. "I should have said that this is gossip from the last village we passed through. I wouldn't give it too much credence. Valden, wasn't it?"

"Valden, yes." Aldric could not understand why his voice was steady and not a tremulous croak. "Gossip or not, tell him about the Vreijek woman."

"Lord Crisen's mistress—he calls her a consort!—is supposedly a witch. They say she makes all manner of spells to entertain him. Or rather, they said, to give him . . . pleasure."

"They say . . . Who are 'they'?"

"Oh, everybody." Gueynor was adopting a brightness that grew more artificial with every second. "Absolutely all the people—"

Don't overdo it . . . "Are in terror of their opinions being overheard," Aldric interrupted crisply. "It's the sort of thing they would love to talk about, but dare not. Only the women—" he shot a warning glare at Gueynor—"can't keep from prattling to save their lives. Or anybody else's. There was a merchant who—"

"I heard about him." Marek's tone was disinterested now; he would hear nothing new from this pair. In which he was wrong, for had he not looked away from Aldric he might have seen the Alban's solitary pupil contract as it stared at him.

"Then," he purred silkily, "if you knew about him you must know why it happened." He knelt, settling his heels beneath him. "May I share your wine?" he asked.

Marek nodded hospitably, leaned forward and filled another bowl. It was casually lifted, apparently sipped, and just as casually set down again. Untasted. Aldric did not drink with those he distrusted.

Gold blazed briefly in the afternoon sunshine as his left hand came up to rub wearily at the back of his neck. "And if you know why it happened," he continued, "you must also know already what Gueynor had just told you." His gloved right hand made an elegant, eye-catching gesture towards the girl, and Marek's eyes were caught for maybe half a heartbeat, following it. "So why ask again?"

Abruptly there was steel jutting like a serpent's tongue from between the fingers of Aldric's clenched left fist, its glint a grutal contrast to the soft golden glow of the signet ring beside it as the small blade licked towards Marek's face.

"Aldric, *no!*" Gueynor's gasp was not loud, but it was sibilant with shock and carried all too well.

The punch-dirk stopped just underneath the Cernuan's chin and made a warning upward jerk that stung him and drew blood. "Fool!" said Aldric. His voice, his face, his whole being had gone cold, bleak, deadly . . . and no one could be sure to whom he spoke. To Marek, for asking too much; to Gueynor, for saying too much; even to himself, for thinking too much and letting matters run out of control until they came to this . . . For he would have to kill now, in cold blood, like it or loathe it. The demon queller knew his name. Not the full name, but enough of it to betray him. Too much of it. His fingers tightened sweatily around the tiny dagger's hilt as he steeled himself to push it home.

Marek saw death looking at him; but he saw more now than a one-eyed mercenary. He saw Deathbringer. "Aldric . . . ?" He had to force the words past palsied lips, out of a mouth restricted in its movement by the blade beneath it. But he had to say something—anything—and quickly . . . "Aldric-*erhan* . . . ? *You . . . ?*"

The Alban flinched, not as if he had heard a familiar name but as if he had been struck in the face. A muscle twitched, once, at the corner of his mouth. "Silence," he grated. . . . Must have time to think, to understand . . . "Another word without permission and I cut your throat."

The demon-queller's mouth pressed shut, a bloodless slit in a face the colour of old cream.

"Gueynor, sit *down!*" Aldric's one-eyed gaze had not moved away from Marek and the girl was on his blind side anyway, but— She sat. "Better." The knife stung again, a reminder, before drawing back in a leisurely fashion. Like the paw of a cat. "Now, Marek Endain, demon queller . . . talk."

"Ar Korentin sent me. He told me where to find you. Your foster-father showed me how."

"Ar Korentin," Aldric breathed softly, plainly stunned by the news. "And Gemmel-*altrou* . . ." He seemed to gather himself together, as any man will when coming to terms with an unexpected shock. "So. Easy to say." His attention settled back on to Marek, intense as the grip of a falcon's talons. "Proof. And quickly!"

Heedless of the demand for speed, the demon queller's hand moved with the sluggishness of spilled honey as it reached inside his robe, and both eyes remained fixed apprehensively on the still-bared blade. The tiny strip of parchment he withdrew looked absurd in his big hand, and would have been less out of place around a pigeon's leg. There were minute words written on it in black ink. "Will this do?" he asked.

Aldric scanned it, brow drawn downwards in a frown;

the characters were in cipher, formed with a brush—but it was a cipher that he knew. "You could have killed the real courier and stolen this," the Alban murmured, intentionally loud enough for Marek to hear him.

"I could have—but I did not." The demon queller glared, and his voice grew harsher: knife or no knife, threat or no threat, his patience was running out. "Nor could I have stolen knowledge from within a man's head—for now I say to you the word *suharr'n,* and the word *hlaichad,* and I make in your sight the pattern called *Kuhr-ijn*—thus! And what do you say now, Aldric-*eir* Talvalin?"

Aldric said nothing whatever. His backbone stiffened and his eye glazed, his grey-green iris becoming as lifeless as a sliver of unpolished jade. Gueynor gasped and pushed the knuckles of one hand against her teeth.

"What have you done to him?" she whispered, not knowing whether to be frightened of losing her protector or relieved that the poised violence of the past moments had abated somewhat.

"I? Nothing at all. This was done to him before he left . . ." Marek paused and looked narrowly at the girl. "It was done with his full consent, anyway. I have merely closed the circle slightly before its proper time. And I should have done so at once, rather than"—he gingerly touched the still-oozing nick in this throat—"taking any risks. I knew what he was and should have expected such a reaction. He is very frightened . . ."

"Aldric is . . . ?"

"Terrified. But more terrified of showing it. *Kailinin* are all alike that way, I think. A little crazy." The Alban had not moved, had not blinked, had barely breathed; certainly he could hear nothing of what was being said less than an arm's length away from him. "We'll take this foolish patch off first, so that I can be absolutely sure . . . Yes! That scar. Not much, but distinctive enough to the right—or wrong—people."

Gueynor sensed that the Cernuan was talking as much to himself as for her benefit, but did not interrupt him by so much as a sudden move. She guessed that he trusted her—otherwise she too would have been struck still as stone. The girl didn't like to look at Aldric; it was somehow shocking that one so active could be immobilised by two words and a gesture. Despite Marek's reassurance she doubted that Aldric would have submitted to whatever spell was on him now, no matter who had placed it there.

Marek shaped another complex, writhing symbol in front of the Alban's unseeing face, and this time it was not invisible. A faint tracery of blue fire, almost transparent in the sunlight, hung a moment before dissipating like woodsmoke.

The ugly, mindless glaze drained out of Aldric's eyes and an intelligence returned; but it was not the same intelligence that Gueynor knew, with which she had shared her bed and body. Except for their unaltered colour, these were the eyes of a stranger. Thoughts seemed to swim in them like tiny, wise fish.

Quite suddenly he spoke, forming each word carefully as if considering it before allowing it to become audible. "By this man, my honoured lord and trusted messenger, I do send greetings unto the most high and worthy Goth, Lord Gener—"

"My lord, be still!" said Marek, and though he was both loud and hasty he was also courteous, his tone that of request rather than command. The Alban closed his mouth and his unTalvalin eyes, seeming to fall into a natural sleep. Marek watched him for a moment, then passed the back of one hand across his own forehead, smiling sourly. "I doubt I should have heard that, my lord," he muttered, "so the words are forgotten already." His head turned a fraction towards Gueynor. "By both of us."

She nodded dully in agreement, not wanting to remember either the words or the voice which had spoken them. For it had not been Aldric's voice at all . . .

"Know me, Aldric-*eir*," the demon queller said. "I am a friend, sent by friends to help you." He spoke in a slow, hypnotic monotone, so that Gueynor could not be sure if he uttered persuasive lies or stated truth. She was almost past caring. "*Sachaur arrhathak eban, Aldric. Yman Gemmel; yman Dewan; yman Rynert-mathern aiy'yel echin arhlathall'n.*"

Aldric's eyelids snapped back so abruptly that the

demon queller started; he knew that the younger man should have been incapable of movement. But he too grew motionless when the Alban's own voice whispered, "I am lost . . ." before trailing into silence.

"Where—" The word cracked in his gullet and Marek coughed to clear his throat of the fear-born constriction blocking it. Fear not this time for himself but for Aldric, that in his attempt to reach whatever secrets lay buried in the younger man's subconscious memory he had severed that most delicate and vulnerable of connections, the binding of soul to body. He had read of such a thing and long ago had witnessed it: only once, but the image had so seared itself into the demon queller's brain that he shuddered at the thought that he himself might cause it. Not death, not undeath . . . unlife. Existence. As mud exists . . .

"There are no stars . . ." again that almost inaudible cobweb-fragile thread of sound. "Night surrounds . . . no stars . . . devoured. None can help me now . . ."

The blood in Marek's veins turned to ice-water. He had heard something akin to this said before, read it often, but had never believed it any more than other overly dramatic metaphors. Until now. Nothing else could explain why his limbs trembled and his hands grew pallid and clammy cold. The loss of one man's soul dwindled into insignificance compared with the potential enormity at which Aldric's dreary words were hinting. If they were only hints . . . Marek dared not leap ahead beyond what he had listened to already, for that way lay unspeakable things. He could only wait . . .

He waited—but not long. Aldric's voice was already losing its coherence; his words faltered more often now, stumbling over one another and no longer making sense. The name "Kyrin" meant nothing to the Cernuan, seen though at the sound of it Gueynor turned her head away. Deep, regular breathing, that of heavy slumber, was increasingly replacing the disturbing broken phrases and at last Marek was able to relax. He was overwrought, that was all. Too many things had happened to him in too short a time, without sufficient rest in compensation. There was a small thud as the push-knife fell from relaxing fingers on to the grass at Aldric's side, and his spine lost its rigidity so that his head lolled heavily forward.

"Waken him . . . please!" No matter what he had said, or how much the words had hurt her, it hurt Gueynor more to see him like this. It was wrong for him to be reeling like the lowest drunkard—lacking any quality of dignity.

"A moment more," said Marek. "His mind is still disordered; I rummaged through it somewhat thoroughly, I fear."

The Alban seemed to crumple in on himself, falling limply forward so that the side of his face struck against a tree root with an unpleasant, solid impact. "You bastard!" Gueynor hissed. Before Marek had begun to move—if indeed he intended to do so, or was merely gratified to see a tree do what he would like to have done in recompense for the dagger-notch beneath his chin—the girl was on her knees by Aldric's side, rolling him carefully on to his back so that she could cradle the lividly bruised head in her lap. Blood welled from broken skin in a line from eyesocket to ear, staining her riding-coat and trousers.

Aldric's eyes were almost shut, but not quite. Had she looked down, rather than glowering towards Marek, Gueynor might have seen a faint glitter half-shrouded by his lashes. Whether he was stunned, or spell-dazed still, or feigning either of the two, not even Aldric knew for certain; the only certainty at present was a rush of hot, loud pain which ebbed and flowed inside his ringing skull. He could smell roses . . . great, dark, fanged roses armed with jagged thorns. One still rested in his saddle-bag. Dead now, crushed and bruised as his face . . .

"Honour," he said thickly, "is satisfied."

"How so?" Marek leaned forward, curious now.

"Your neck—my face." Gueynor blinked, wondering how he had known so clearly what she was thinking, but Marek's expression did not change.

"I beg pardon," the Alban said. "Both for what I did and . . . And almost did."

Marek Endain laughed at that. Dryly, from a throat disinclined to humour but amused nonetheless. "Beg no forgiveness of me, Aldric-*eir*," he replied. "Dewan ar

Korentin should beg forgiveness of us both; his mind engineered this confusion." The demon queller reached down, plucked grass blades and twisted them between his fingers. "Do you . . . After all this, do you still want my company? Or my help?"

Gueynor's fingertips prodded Aldric's shoulder blade: trying to attract his attention, trying to will him to refuse. Politely, angrily, rudely—any way at all. Just so long as he said "No."

The Alban ignored her as best he could. He thought about Sedna, and guessed that Marek's knowledge would prove useful when he was speaking to the Vreijek sorceress. "Do you still offer them?" he asked, propping himself on one elbow to read what he could from the Cernuan's face. It was little enough . . .

Marek's mind was turning over what he had heard by accident; not King Rynert's message to Lord General Goth, for politics held no interest at all, but the words which had followed—and which had so horrified him. They could not have been spoken by accident. No delirium, no dream whether born of drink or drugs or sorcery could create those phrases out of nothing. Marek recognised them as disjointed fragments of a warning, and the very recollection chilled him. He knew too what they warned against. He was a demon queller . . .

"I do offer them." Perhaps there was too much force in the way he spoke, but it was of no account. "Without reservation."

"Then I accept." Aldric smiled fractionally. "We could be friends, you and I. So tell me, 'friend,' how well do you know Seghar . . . ?"

7

Citadel

The shadows of dusk were lengthening in Seghar town as they approached it from the south at a leisurely walk. Lamps and ornate flambeaux had been lit at intervals along the outer wall, and their topaz jewels did something to offset an all-too-plain dilapidation. But not enough. The place was as Marek Endain had described it—except that the seedy reality was worse.

Reining Lyard to a halt, Aldric glanced over his left shoulder to see Gueynor's reaction. It was as he had expected: shock, disbelief, finally outrage that a place which she remembered as elegant and find should have been reduced to what they saw now. Then the taut, indignant lines of her face softened . . . relaxed . . . and collapsed. Inevitably there were tears.

"Stop that!" the Alban snapped, "or you'll smear your—" His voice was sharp, yet not so brutal as the words suggested; but he closed his teeth on the stupid heartless phrase before it was completed, knowing even as he did so that Gueynor would not have heard him anyway. Had Seghar been his home, or had Dunrath been altered as this place was from her ten-year-old memory of it, he too would have cried.

It was old. That was excusable, for Dunrath was also old, but Seghar displayed not the time-mellowed dignity of age—only its decrepitude. Stonework had crumbled, or been broken and removed for paving-rubble, and in those few places where repairs had been attempted they were haphazard, incomplete and altogether ugly. More depressing still were the pathetic echoes of long-faded grandeur, scattered like discarded rags among the buildings of the fortress proper: overgrown pleasances and wood-choked parterres, untended drives of fruit trees which had degenerated into tangled, dying vegetation.

And all of it not so much because of apathy as through a policy of planned, deliberate neglect. The ruins of their formal gardens were all that remained of past overlords, but even at this distance Aldric could detect a faint, heavy scent of roses on the evening air—that cloying perfume which he was coming to associate more and more with the name of Seghar.

"Cowards . . ." Gueynor whispered brokenly. "They did not dare destroy what my father made of Seghar—but they let it fall into this . . ."

Aldric met Marek Endain's level gaze over the girl's drooping head and shrugged one shoulder. The Geruaths were evidently capable of far greater subtlety than he had given either of them credit for. Whose idea had this been? he wondered grimly. Geruath himself . . . or Crisen?

"Carefully, my lady," Aldric muttered in a warning undertone. A few armed retainers were mingling with the travellers as they drew closer to the town—there had been a midsummer fair of some sort if their gaudy dress was anything to go by—and it would be wise to avoid attracting untoward attention by either strange behaviour or incautious observations. The reporting of words was commonplace in Seghar, he suspected, once again recalling the fate of that Tergovan merchant, and no lord—even one so lacking in pride as Geruath appeared to be—would like to hear his demesne receive some of the descriptions which were forming inside Aldric's head. Out on the Jevaiden plateau this fortress might be the centre of affairs—elsewhere it would be either a slum or an abandoned derelict.

The inner citadel was primitive, no more than a fortified manor house which had sprouted bartizans and turrets in a jarring, unmatched variety of architectural styles. Lacking great areas of paint and the heavy plaster which usually smoothed raw stone, it was in a sorry state, seeming to cringe into the landscape rather than stand out proudly as donjons were supposed to do. Except, incongruously, for a solitary wooden tower which was of a form so archaic that Aldric had not seen one in reality before—only in the illuminations to old Archive volumes.

And yet it had been built recently, from clean new timber . . . The Alban studied it as he rode closer, but was no wiser as to its function by the time he reached the town wall's southern gate—the Summergate, it was called—even though there was an elusive recollection drifting in the inaccessible reaches at the back of his mind . . .

"You there, stand fast!" Aldric was jerked back to reality by the harsh command; he was unused, even as an *eijo*, to being addressed in such a tone, and it took maybe half a breath for him to remember that he was a mercenary and by that token anybody's potential servant . . . Not that he would have made objection in any case: the *kortagor* who had spoken was flanked by two gisarm-bearing lord's-men and though the heavy weapons were carried at rest they still inspired a degree of immediate respect.

He was a tall man, this officer, with a spade beard jutting pugnaciously from between the cheekplates of his helmet, and he was pointing straight at Aldric with the blackthorn baton that was his mark of rank. "Yes, you!" he repeated in answer to a look of inquiry. The Alban twitched Lyard's reins, stopping the big Andarran courser an easy spear's-length from where the *kortagor* stood, and gave the man a crisp, neutral salute before swinging out of his high saddle. It was always best, whether or not one was playing a part, to avoid annoying those with the power to make life unpleasant . . .

Which was why, instead of voicing one of the several irascible responses which sprang into his mind—and which would have been entirely in character—a precisely calculated interval after his bootsoles hit the pavement, Aldric bowed. Not low, but low enough, the depth exactly gauged to convey respect without servility. The kind of finely tuned politeness at which Albans excelled.

He remained quite still as the officer walked slowly round him, inspecting him as he would a soldier on parade—which, given his chosen role, was close enough to the truth. The man was plainly unsure of what he saw, confused by the mixture of signals which he was reading—signals which sometimes agreed and sometimes contradicted.

Kortagor Jervan had become a good judge of men during twenty years with the Imperial military, and it was not chance which had brought him to this particular gate. He made it his business personally to inspect every stranger who entered Seghar and remained for longer than his own arbitrary limit of two days, but on certain occasions, when his outriders reported anyone or anything of special note, the inspection took place at once. Jervan's assessments were seldom wrong—but he did not like to be unsure, especially where it concerned one man bringing a small arsenal of lethal weapons into the town where he was garrison commander and directly responsible for peace and order.

As if conscious of his gaze, the horseman's hand came up to tug at the patch he wore. Jervan had seen such a movement before. Men were often painfully embarrassed by disfigurement, especially when—like this one—they were young. It was a younger face than the *kortagor* was accustomed to meeting in mercenaries, if such he was, and yet more secretive and shuttered than it had any right to be. There was a hard, careless set to the features, but that was probably an act meant to impress, no more. But there was something about him, something which did not fit—as if he was more accustomed to giving than receiving orders. As if he was accustomed to respect . . .

"Alban," Jervan observed quietly, reaching out with his baton as if to touch the dirk pushed through the rider's belt. The baton hovered, gestured towards the sword-hilt which rose like a scorpion's tail above his right shoulder, again stopping before any insulting contact was made, then grounded its metal-shod tip with a hard, bright clank on the paving stones between Jervan's feet.

Aldric was suddenly, irrelevantly reminded of the last time he had heard such a sound; it had been the clashing of a firedrake's talons against an onyx floor, many miles from here . . .

"Alban," he echoed, even though no question had been asked. "Once, but no more. Now I am less than nothing." He closed his mouth against further elaboration, knowing with his increased experience of the deceiver's art that saying too much was worse than saying nothing at all.

Jervan studied this enigma. There was no insult in the soft-spoken words—or if there was, it was so veiled that the *kortagor* chose not to waste time searching for it. He was a strict man, as his rank required, but a fairminded one as his own decency dictated; if One-eye wanted to enter the Overlord's service, then it was the Overlord who would command him to go or stay. His garrison commander need not interfere until after that decision had been made.

"His name is Kourgath."

The officer's head snapped round, his beard seeming almost to bristle with annoyance at this interruption. A fat man sat on a fat pony and smiled pleasantly at him. "And who the hell," rasped Jervan, "might *you* be?"

"I," the fat man returned, "am Marek Endain, demon queller. Kourgath is my traveling companion and for the present my bodyguard. Yours is a dangerous province, *Kortagor . . .* ?"

"Jervan," said Jervan. "Garrison commander of Seghar."

"Then hail, Jervan." Marek chuckled richly and made an expansive salute that looked more like a benediction.

"What about the woman? Can she speak for herself—or do you do her talking as well?" There was only the faintest trace of sarcasm in the *kortagor*'s voice, but more than a little amusement.

Aldric had seen the look of horror which had flashed across Gueynor's face directly her eyes fell on Jervan. He did not know the cause, only that something would have to be said before the soldier noticed too and his allayed suspicions were once more aroused. "Her name is Aline," he said, pitching his voice loud enough for the girl to hear and trusting she would take the hint.

Jervan's head turned back towards him and he regretted saying anything to draw this man's attention. There was a half-humorous glint in the *kortagor*'s dark eyes, a toleration of interference—up to a point. That point, thought Aldric, has been reached . . .

This time when the blackthorn stick jabbed out at him it did not stop short. The impact on his chest was hardly more solid than that of a pointing finger, but it carried a deal more emphasis than any finger ever could. "Let the lady speak for herself, Alban," Jervan reproved. "If I want your contribution, I shall ask for it. Until then—forgive my vulgarity but—shut up!"

Aldric nodded curtly, and shut up.

"Now, my dear . . ." Aldric would have felt far happier if Jervan's approach had not smacked so much of Dewan ar Korentin at his most suave. "Tell me about yourself."

Gueynor's usual response to such a question—to any question—was to freeze like a rabbit confronted by a stoat. Instead she collected her wits and smiled prettily at the officer. "Aline, sir. My husband used to have a shop in Ternon. We sold such pretty things there: silks and fine lace, velvets—"

"I think I might know the place," purred Jervan. His words jolted both Aldric and Gueynor, but for entirely different reasons. Now the Alban regarded him with a more basic emotion than mere wary suspicion, even though he would not have admitted feeling jealous. Not even to himself . . .

The girl recovered—and covered—well; certainly better than Aldric had expected, although he knew now that there was more to Gueynor than met the eye. Just like her uncle . . . "I doubt you would, commander," she replied, becoming a little sad. "Not this two years past, anyway. I married young, you see . . ."

"And you still are young," Jervan put in gallantly.

"And I was widowed young. There was an accident. My husband . . . a horse took fright and bolted . . ." She looked away as if controlling tears, turning back with a tired expression and a little sigh that told of many things. "I could not maintain the shop alone, or buy anything to sell; at the last I could not afford rent and food together. So I left and now . . ."—she stared over Jervan's head at Aldric, then closed her eyes—"now I travel and I . . . I form association with whoever pays me for my . . . company."

The performance was masterly: understated, elegant, it imitated reality to perfection and provoked sympathy rather than suspicion. *Kortagor* Jervan gazed at her in pity. "There will be no such accidents in this town, lady," he assured her. "Except at livery, horses are not permitted beyond the inner walls."

Aldric was not prepared to let him take full credit for that. "An Alban custom, *Kortagor?*" he asked softly, daring the soldier to deny it. Jervan did not.

"I also travel, Kourgath-*an*," he replied, "although less than I would like. That custom struck me. As did others." What those were he did not say, but it was quite certain that he knew the meaning of Aldric's short-cropped hair. "Marek Endain, a word with you. In private."

The Cernuan dismounted, following Jervan into the shadows of the gate-house and out of earshot. Aldric could guess what that private word involved: himself, as much as was known of his history, and whatever other details the garrison commander of Seghar might find interesting. He had told Marek much the same story as to Evthan—about fighting on the wrong side in Alba that spring, and being forced to leave—with a warning that the tale should not be embellished. Simplicity was safer . . . and easier to remember.

He nodded courteously to the lord's-men, who had not escorted their commander as he had hoped they might—when Jervan said "in private," he evidently meant it—and moved a cautious step or two in Gueynor's direction. When they made no move to obstruct him he walked rapidly to where she sat atop his pack-pony, ashen-faced and looking as if she was going to be sick. Anyone else would have attributed her reaction to the unpleasant memories she had recalled, but Aldric knew differently. The girl was sick indeed—sick with fright. Her hand, when he grasped it, was trembling so much that he could feel it flutter, like a little bird, through the leather of his glove, and the skin of her cheek was cold with more than the onset of evening.

"What's the matter?" he murmured into her ear, trying to appear as if he was comforting her. "What scared you?"

"J—Jervan . . ."

"Jervan . . . ? Light of Heaven, woman, why? He's the nearest thing to a human being I've ever met in Imperial harness." Which observation carried less weight than at first appeared, since Aldric had encountered one ship-commander and an *eldheisart* of the Bodyguard cavalry—though ar Korentin's desertion tended to disqualify him from inclusion. Such a sampling did not entitle Aldric to make sweeping statements about anything, but it was not Jervan's behaviour which had upset her . . .

"I know him, Aldric—"

"Kourgath!"

"But I *know* him! He's the man who let me leave. With Evthan. When the soldiers came to Seghar. It's the same man, I tell you! Tall, with a black beard . . ."

"Are you sure?" Gueynor at least was convinced, and whether or not she was right seemed likely to attract the *kortagor*'s interest by her attitude alone.

"Certain! I know him . . . !"

"So you keep saying. But does he know you?" One open hand pressed to her lips created a welcome silence. "Because I doubt it. Listen, Gueynor, listen to me! He was a grown man then and can't have changed much since. That's why you recognise him. But you were a child and now you're a woman. Calm down; don't worry about it." Aldric wished that he could feel as confident as he sounded.

The garrison commander's private word must have developed into a full-scale private conversation, for it was a nerve-racking twenty minutes before the two dark outlines reemerged from the Summergate. It was more night than evening now, that period of unlight where the sun has gone but its afterglow still means that lamps are useless. "You will stay," came Jervan's voice, "at the Inn of Restful Sleep, where I can find you. Nowhere else. One of my men will guide you there."

"Why nowhere else?" Aldric wanted to know. "So that you don't need to waste time if you decide to arrest us?"

"Hold your tongue, man!" Marek snapped irritably. "Unless you think that you can find another job before the night's out . . . ?" Aldric subsided, saying nothing more, and Marek glanced towards Jervan with a few words that made the soldier laugh. "To answer you, Kourgath—as you would have found out anyway, without this . . . unpleasantness—it's because the Overlord may want to speak to me. Note that! To *me*. Not to you."

It was the most reassuring rebuke that Aldric had ever heard.

*

The summons came sooner than anyone had expected, for they had been in the tavern's pleasant common-room less than half an hour when the door slid aside and a crest-coated retainer came in. Asking for the demon queller, in Lord Crisen's name. And at once.

Marek nodded to the messenger and continued to eat. This retainer was maybe fifteen years old and commanded rather less respect than *Kortagor* Jervan's empty boots. "At once, sir," the youth repeated nervously. "My lord was most insistent on that point."

"While I am most insistent that I complete my supper," the Cernuan replied, gesturing at the cluttered table to show how little had been touched. "I have attended similar meetings in the past, and apart from insubstantial dainties they never include much to eat. Although," he added considerately, "the wine is usually excellent."

"In Lord Crisen's name . . . ? Why he, and not his father?" Despite his lazy voice, there was more than idle curiosity in Aldric's question. Especially knowing what he did about Crisen Geruath's consort.

"I am Lord Crisen's servant, sir," the boy replied. "He sent me, so what I do is in his name; but I feel sure that the Overlord—"

"Of course." Aldric was just as certain that the Overlord had not agreed, or did not know—or whatever affirmation the retainer might have been about to make.

"What about us?" Gueynor asked uncertainly. Despite having recovered from her initial shock, she was still apprehensive—and had begun to doubt her own wis-

dom in following Aldric to Seghar. "Do we stay here
or . . . ?"

"Well," demanded the Cernuan through a mouthful
of chicken, "what about them? Are my companions
included?"

"No, sir. My lord asked only for the demon queller
Marek. No other names were mentioned."

"You realise that they'll eat all the food? Probably
drink up the wine as well. And you know who paid for
all of it, don't you . . . ?"

"Sir, *please* . . ."

Marek looked at the young man, who was virtually
dancing on the spot with impatience, and grunted mo-
rosely in agreement. "All right." Lifting a chop between
finger and thumb, he stripped the meat in two bites and
washed it down with a long, long draught of wine; then
he wiped his mouth and fingers, belched his appreciation
for the innkeeper's benefit and was ready.

Aldric watched him critically, wondering how much of
this act was playing a chosen role and how much was
really Marek. It had occurred to him that the demon
queller might not be pretending after all . . . "You'll
be safe enough without a bodyguard tonight anyway,"
he said.

"I should think—"

"But you have a guard anyway, sir," the retainer interrupted, eager to say something pleasing at long last.
"They're waiting for you outside. My lord sent four soldiers as an escort for your honour's sake—to show
your importance."

"Ah," said Marek thoughtfully. "That was very . . ."
he searched for a word which would not betray his real
feelings on the matter, ". . . very considerate of him.
Yes. Considerate. Very . . ."

*

Despite his fears, whether real or feigned, most of the
food and drink was still on the table when Marek returned from the citadel and he set to hungrily. Aldric,
however—almost alone in the common-room and the
only person still awake—had clearly lost his appetite.
Unaccustomed to the potent Elherran sweet-wine which
she had been drinking in such careless quantities,

Gueynor snored gently on a settle near the fire, wrapped in a blanket and with Aldric's wolfskin *coyac* cushioning her head.

The Alban had realised that he would be unable to relax directly Marek left . . . Unless, of course, he followed Gueynor's example. He had not. Nor did the thoughts which drifted to and fro within his mind help relaxation much; there was such a thing as having read too many subjects in too little detail. He knew enough for his subconscious to work overtime, but insufficient to calm it . . .

Aldric was a typical *kailin* and a typical younger son of his generation—even though he preferred not to think that way; an inveterate scribbler of drawings, of snatches of poetry or song, of scraps of gossip or indeed anything which later might prove of interest. Although he had had small chance to indulge such inclinations in recent months, they remained: a learning that was lightly, negligently, even cynically worn, many accomplishments which could be drawn upon at need—no matter that few were studied in great depth. Just as a cat, no matter how well-fed or pampered, knows how to, can, and will catch mice—but only when it wants to, because it no longer has to.

Leaning back in a chair, one booted foot propped on a stool, he scratched idle sketches with a scrap of charcoal and appeared at ease but Marek, glancing at him, knew otherwise. He stared over the young man's shoulder at the face taking shape on his sheet of rough paper—the face of a girl, blonde-haired, high-cheekboned, pretty; a study in light and shadow where shadow predominated, her gaze turned away into darkness. There was a faint resemblance to Gueynor, but it was plainly not a portrait of the Jouvaine; the differences were far more plain and yet more subtle than a simple change of hair colour . . . "From imagination, Kourgath? Or from memory?"

Aldric started slightly, his head jerking round. The eyepatch had been pushed up into a black band across his brows, and a half-smile scored its chevron at one side of his mouth as he looked back at the drawing, tilting it quizzically. "Both, I think. It's sometimes so hard to be sure." With sudden violence he crushed the paper in his fist and flung it accurately clear across the room into the fire. "But mostly memory. One best forgotten."

His chair scraped back as he stood up, fastidiously dusting charcoal from his fingertips. "Well, what was said by their Lordships?"

Marek glanced warily about the room before risking a reply, and when he did it was evasive. "Have you seen to the horses yet—or do you trust the ostler with your black Andarran?"

"Now that you mention it, no. I trust myself with Lyard. No one else." Aldric lifted an apple from the fruit-dish, studied it a moment and polished it briskly on his sleeve, then pulled his patch back into place. "A walk in the evening air," he suggested, "to aid your digestion?" Marek smiled thinly and nodded.

"Why not . . . ?"

* * *

After they had left the lamps and firelight of the commonroom a prudent distance behind, Aldric removed the cloth patch covering his right eye and slipped it down around his neck like a narrow scarf. "Better," he muttered softly. Unhooking Widowmaker's shoulder-strap, he allowed the longsword to slide into her accustomed place at his left hip before hooking the lacquered scabbard to his weapon-belt. A small push of the thumb released her locking-collar.

Marek watched these preparations dubiously. "Are you expecting trouble?" he asked. Aldric flicked up his apple and caught it neatly, grinning a little.

"Not at present. But just in case . . ."—an inch of *taiken*-blade glinted as it was withdrawn and then returned in lazy threat—"I like to feel ready."

A bonfire was smouldering at one end of the stable-yard, its surface acrawl with the red rats'-eyes of sparks as blue, sharp-smelling smoke trickled up into the night. There was the distant rhythmic swishing of a broom on cobblestones and the clank of a bucket's handle. Someone was whistling tunelessly. All very ordinary, thought Aldric as he pushed the half-door open and stepped lightly inside. One glance at the dim, low-beamed interior confirmed a notion which he had entertained all evening: whatever else it might be, the Inn of Restful

Sleep was no ordinary tavern. Not with its stables laid out as recommended by the Cavalry Manual! The place was a convenient, innocent-seeming guest-house for interesting visitors to Seghar—and was no doubt staffed by members of the garrison. No wonder Jervan had insisted that they stay here.

Even so, Aldric could not complain about the accommodation provided for his horses. He glanced with a critical eye along the line of stalls; solidly built of biscuit-coloured ashlar stone, they were well-drained, well ventilated but nonetheless snug. There were no draughts; a deal of care had evidently gone into getting *that* just right, the Alban mused. And they were clean, remarkably so; no stale reek of dung in this stable—only the warm and somehow friendly odour of the horses mingled pleasantly with a fragrance of fresh hay and straw and the incisive granary scent of oats. The grooms had been at work with brushes, mops and water as if they had anticipated an inspection. And perhaps they had; Aldric knew a little of how the military mind worked.

Bedding rustled as Lyard, sensing a familiar presence, shifted in his box. Walking across, Aldric looked with approval at the stallion; he had been combed and brushed and virtually polished by some stableman who knew good horseflesh and how to bring up the best points of a fine animal, until his coat shone with the midnight lustre of crushed coal. The Andarran whickered softly, regarding Aldric with eyes and ears and flaring nostrils until he click-clicked tongue against back teeth and extended the apple he had brought. Lyard nudged his hand, snuffled at the proffered fruit and crunched it up with relish, frothing pale green around the lips as he did so.

"Four-legged eating machine," Aldric observed in a dispassionate voice; but he patted the big courser's whiskered, apple-sweet muzzle with more affection than his words suggested. "You have something to tell?" he asked in exactly the same tone, speaking Alban now.

"I couldn't before," Marek replied. "You've seen the stables now. You know why."

"*Care of the Horse in Peace and War.* Yes. I read it a long time ago."

"And one can never know who might be listening."

Aldric nodded, went quietly to the wooden frame which supported his tack and untied laces, loosened buckles, threw back the flap of one very particular saddlebag. Reaching deep inside, he took out something which he tucked away swiftly in the front of his jerkin. Marek, watching, caught a momentary glimpse of steel and silver, of intricate patterns formed from metal, of white leather shrouding something from his sight. And then the object was gone. The demon queller knew better than to ask an *eijo* questions—particularly this *eijo*. "Listening—or looking," he amended.

Aldric allowed himself a thin smile but gave no explanation for his actions. They were, he considered, hardly the Cernuan's affair.

"Aldric." At the sound of his real name the Alban's head jerked up minutely before turning with studied, casual inquiry towards Marek. There was anger in his eyes. "Tomorrow morning we are to be given quarters in the citadel." Aldric said nothing. "There has been an accident." Still Aldric said nothing. "Sedna is dead."

Aldric remained silent; but even in the dim light of the stables Marek Endain saw the blood drain from his companion's face until the only colour that remained there was the juice which stained his skin. "When?" His voice was flat and revealed nothing. "And how?"

"There was an accident. Last night. When the moon was full. She was preparing a conjuration and . . . something went wrong."

"How?" Aldric repeated in the same unreal voice. Suspicions were seething inside his head like maggots in dead meat. "What happened to her?"

The demon queller stared at him, mouth twitching behind the full beard as if possessed of its own life. "All right. All right . . . The something that went wrong pulled her apart. And ate the pieces . . . I know. I saw."

"What was it, this something?" Aldric persisted. "An animal? A werebeast?"

"It was a demon! A demon, damn you! And I don't know what sort of demon, before you ask me . . . But it was strong. Strong enough to wrench a human body into chunks the way you would joint a chicken!"

"I," Aldric observed, concealing his own shock behind a callously prim veneer, "have rather better table manners than that."

And Marek hit him. Not a slap of indignation at his attitude, but a full-blooded cuff that caught the younger man unawares and almost rocked him off his feet. The print of the demon queller's palm and fingers flared scarlet across Aldric's pale face from ear to chin, its outline warping as his features twisted in a silent snarl of insulted fury. He had staggered with the impact of the blow, his shoulders hammering against the door of Lyard's stall with a boom that sent the high-strung beast skittering backwards in a thumping of straw-muffled hooves, and had slithered down the planks a handspan before his knees locked to push him upright. And when he straightened there was a dagger in his hand.

The Cernuan had not seen it drawn, had no idea where it had been concealed and did not care. " 'We could be friends, you and I,' " he spat, bitterly hurling Aldric's own words back at him. "I doubt that!"

It was as if he had emptied icy water over his companion's head. A hot mist seemed to clear from inside the Alban's wide, dark eyes and they looked down at the knife as if he held some noxious reptile in his hand. "I might have killed you," Aldric whispered and the horror in his voice was real.

"You might have tried," Marek grated. But deep inside he knew that Aldric spoke the truth. Had he drawn sword instead of dagger—and Marek had seen how fast some Albans could clear steel from scabbard—the *eijo* would have cut him down in a continuation of the drawing stroke. It would have been an instinctive reaction, he would not have truly meant to do it; but at that stage motive or the lack of it would no longer have concerned his target . . . The Cernuan felt his legs grow slightly shaky.

"You struck me." Aldric touched the livid mark, not accusing, just stating the literally painfully obvious. "You are Cernuan. You should know. *Kailinin* are not struck. Not even by their lords. *Never.* I might have killed you . . ."

It was very clear that he was thinking as Marek had

done: about the *taiken,* about the blinding speed with
which he could draw it. About what the consequences
of such reflex retaliation might some day be . . .

He shuddered inwardly and slipped the knife back
into its sheath within his boot. "I regret that. All of it.
But . . . I doubt that what happened was an accident.
And that disturbs me."

"Sedna . . . ?"

"I think that she was killed to keep her quiet."

"But . . . but why?"

"Because of me. Because of what I am. What I really
am, not what I pretend to be." Briefly he explained
ideas, theories and wild surmises, elaborating points
which earlier he had skimmed over or omitted altogether.

"And where does the girl—Gueynor, or Aline, or
whatever she calls herself—come into all this?"

Aldric shook his head. "She does not. That matter is
quite separate—and private. Between us—"

" 'And none of your business, Cernuan,' " Marek
mocked.

"At least you're getting back your sense of humour."

"If I didn't laugh—"

"You'd cry . . . ?"

"I would probably go mad." There was such sincerity
in the demon queller's words that Aldric subsided again.
He turned away and fussed with Lyard for a while, gen-
tling him with a buzz of nonsense that required no
thought on his part. "I'm glad," he muttered finally,
without looking around, "that Geruath wants you to destroy this . . . whatever it is." Aldric patted Lyard's velvet nose and glanced at Marek: "I hadn't given him so
much sense . . ." That swift glance caught an expression
on the Cernuan's face which had no right to be there,
and Aldric's eyes narrowed. *"Doesn't he?"* As the Alban's mind raced ahead of his tongue the last words
came out like the crack of a whip.

"Well . . ." Marek stared at the stable floor, pushed
a single stray wisp of hay back and forth, back and forth
with the toe of his boot, and completely failed to meet
the *eijo*'s gaze. "Not—not quite destroy . . ."

"Then what in the nine hot Hells *does* he want?" For

the horse's sake Aldric held his impatient shout in check, but it required a conscious effort on his part to do so and apprehensive anger thrummed behind the words. He was afraid that he already knew the answer.

And he was right.

"They both want it captured. Tamed. Quelled . . . Broken to their will"—he gazed at Lyard—"as one might break a horse. They think I can control it."

"But you can't, can you?" Marek shook his head. "Then don't you think you ought to tell them so—or are you so keen to end up as leftovers?"

This time the demon queller ignored his verbal brutality. What Lord Geruath wants, he usually—no, invariably—gets.

"He may get more than he expects this time," said Aldric savagely. He walked to the stable door and looked outside towards the Overlord's tower, which reared its stark outline against the clear and star-shot sky. "Because he must be mad, you know. Quite insane."

"I've seen him, Aldric-*an*. I do know. That's why I daren't refuse. Not openly. Not yet."

*

The apartments set aside for them in the citadel of Seghar were much superior to those just vacated at the Inn of Restful Sleep; but Aldric doubted he would get much sleep here, whether restful or disturbing. There were too many guards—yet, strangely, very few soldiers in the Imperial harness worn by *Kortagor* Jervan. It seemed to Aldric that the sentries he had seen were no more than part-time troops, a militia made up from the fortress's servants and paraded before him to impress by numbers alone. He had been more impressed by their core of mercenaries, the Drusalans and the Tergovans Gueynor had mentioned—and whom he had already met within the chieftain's broken mound. But there were not enough of them. Certainly not enough to justify the amount of money which should be within these walls. Aldric had a vague idea of what stipend Seghar received to foment rebellions against Grand Warlord Etzel; but now that he knew where the Geruath sympathies truly lay, he had expected to see plain traces of the misspent

wealth—rich furnishings, a large, well-equipped retinue . . .
Extravagances of that sort. Yet there was nothing. Unless the gold was sent elsewhere—but he doubted and
dismissed that surmise almost at once; it was too untypi-
cal of what he already knew. Strange . . .

Stranger still was Geruath himself. As had happened
before, the trio had barely unpacked what few belongings they had brought to their respective rooms when
they were commanded—courteously enough, Aldric noted
with a *kailin*'s eye for such niceties, but still commanded
rather than invited—into the presence of the Overlord
of Seghar.

That presence was not overly imposing, as such things
are measured. Geruath was gaunt; indeed he was scrawny
to the point of emaciation, but he endeavoured to counter
his physical insignificance with splendid clothes and all
the trappings of lordship. His robes would have been
magnificent had they been one-half as rich—instead they
were foolish, ridiculous and, even to Aldric's cold single
eye, a little pathetic. He could smell the heavy perfumes
of musk and civet, of lavender and attar of roses. Roses
again . . . ! And beneath it all he could see a man of
middle age, sick in mind and body, terrified of growing
old. Lord Geruath's hair might well have been of a distinguished grey, or with elegant tags of silver at his temples; but it had been dyed a hard, unreal black, sleek as
polished leather, and to match its mock-youthful darkness his face was painted and powdered to the ruddy
tan of a healthy man of thirty.

It should have been laughable. Or perverse. Or simply
decadent. But in truth it was no more than sad.

Yet his weapons were perfection; apart from Isileth
Widowmaker and perhaps two other blades which he
had seen at a distance in Cerdor, Aldric suspected that
the Overlord's matched swords and dagger were quite
possibly the finest in the world. He was begining to realise where King Rynert's gold had gone. And in his secret
heart of hearts, given such an opportunity without risk
of lost honour and its atonement in suicide, he knew
that he would do the same . . .

Kneeling, Aldric pressed brow to crossed hands on the
floor in the Second Obeisance that was due any lord in

his own hall, then sat back neatly on his heels. After a startled glance at the unexpectedly elaborate courtesy—acknowledged with the curtest of nods—Geruath dismissed the Alban as a mere retainer and spoke rapidly to Marek in what sounded like some courtly form of dialect. The choice of language might well have been deliberate, for Geruath's words immediately reverted to a rapid, slightly irritating background noise which made no sense at all to Aldric.

Nor, from her blank expression, to Gueynor. She had copied him: kneeling, bowing and sitting back as he had done not so much to appear a foreigner—although it had given that effect—as for something positive to do. The girl had covered her initial spasm of detestation well; Aldric doubted if, at her age, he could have hidden his true feelings so successfully.

If the guards around the fortress and the outer citadel had been uncomfortably numerous, in here they were unusually few. Given Geruath's propensity for ostentation, a troop in full battle armour would not have been out of place. Instead there were only two soldiers flanking the Overlord's high seat, wearing crested coats like the boy who had come to the inn the previous night; both carried gisarms, and looked as if they knew how to use them.

Seated a little way to one side was an elderly man, balding and harrassed-looking. He wrote in a large, leather-bound book at great speed and with many blots, but seemed always at least two sentences in arrears of what the Lord was saying. The hall scribe, guessed Aldric, giving him his Alban title: *Hanan-Vleihanek,* the Keeper of Years. Certainly he seemed to be making—or trying to make—a record of everything that was said and done here, as any normal Archivist would do, but this was not Alba—it was a border province of the Drusalan Empire, and one could never be entirely sure for whose eyes the information was ultimately destined. Aldric rubbed at his right eye through the cloth which covered it. He had already decided that the organ had merely been "injured" and was "improving" rapidly, because the patch was annoying, uncomfortable and often downright painful. And it was dangerous. He always had a blind side now, had been startled more than once by Gueynor at his elbow when he had not heard the girl approaching, and found distances impossible to judge. Soon he would remove the patch, dab soap into his eye—he flinched from that necessary evil—to make it red and inflamed, and have his full vision restored.

But not yet. The old scribe glanced in his direction, chewed at the frayed end of his pen and scribbled a brief description of the Lord's guests. Soon, thought Aldric. But not just yet . . .

Weapons lined the walls of Geruath's presence-chamber: an excessive quantity of weapons for any room except an armoury. The polished wood and lacquerwork, the semiprecious stones and bronze and leather—and above all else the steel, blued and burnished, etched and plain and razor sharp . . . such an array would have done credit to the Hall of Archives at Dunrath, or Gemmel Snowbeard's arsenal in his labyrinthine home under the Blue Mountains that were Alba's backbone. All were of good quality, fine examples of sword or spear or bow or axe, and a few—a very few, like the blades so ineffectually worn by Geruath—were masterpieces. Someone, somewhere, their name and face elusive, had told Aldric about this: "he searches out old weapons," the forgotten name had said, "and collects them in his tower at Seghar." Those half-remembered words should have given him a warning, should have prepared him . . . They did not.

"Kourgath-*an!*" There was a sharpness in Marek Endain's voice that made Aldric realise it was the demon queller's second time for speaking. Perhaps even the third . . .

"Sir?" he responded, inclining his head to his erstwhile "employer."

"Geruath the Overlord wishes to speak with you." There was worry behind Marek's neutral, bearded features as he leaned closer, slipping momentarily from Jouvaine into Alban. "With you, not to you," he hissed urgently. "He's being pleasant, before Heaven! Try to do likewise, no matter what . . ."

No matter what . . . ? Aldric thought as he nodded, wondering why the Cernuan had felt it necessary to make such a request; and wondering, too, what had disturbed him so much that it showed through his schooled exterior. He soon found out.

"I want," said Geruath brusquely, "to see your sword."

The Overlord might have been pleasant to Marek's ears, but Aldric found both his request and the form it took offensive in the extreme. Of all the elaborate courtesies which governed high-clan Albans, the most elaborate concerned *taikenin.* Any insult to the sword was an insult to its wearer; and any insult to the wearer was answered by his sword. One did not demand to see a *taiken,* any *taiken;* one did not employ the words "I want," at all; and as a collector of weapons Geruath the Overlord most surely was aware of all these things. He might have been testing him, trying his reactions. Or he might merely have been stupid.

"No," Aldric replied, his voice toneless and flat. That was all.

"I want to see it," Geruath repeated.

"No."

"Kourgath, for the love of God . . ." Marek was almost pleading with him, but he could sense Gueynor's silent approval and support. "Kourgath . . . !" the demon queller said again desperately. Aldric looked at him; at the girl; at the Overlord.

"No."

Silence. The exquisitely bundled, painted and perfumed apparition that was Geruath the Overlord rose to his feet, his breathing coming quicker now and an unhealthy flush darkening his powdered cheeks. Bony, veined hands heavy with rings clutched at the carven arms of his chair, working convulsively like a falcon on its perch. Except that falcons had more dignity. The storm brewed, plain in his staring eyes and flexing fingers.

But it did not break. "Leave my presence!" Geruath commanded and his voice was calm, controlled and terrible. "You," he swung on the scribe, "give me your book." The old man sidled forward apprehensively, unsure of what was to come, then cried out as Geruath snatched the Archive from him. Lips moving, the Over-

lord traced what had been written, his finger following
the words and smearing the still-wet ink. "You were able
to write all this down fast enough," he accused and the
scribe cringed back, anticipating a blow. Instead Geruath
gripped the latest page by its outer margin and let the
heavy volume fall. There was a momentary hesitation
and a snapping of threads before the binding gave way
with a sharp rip and the Archive thudded to the floor.
Geruath ignored it. He ignored everyone: the old man,
reaching out with little snatching movements to recover
the book without coming too close to his lord's feet or
fists; the two guards who looked on stoically at a scene
probably familiar to them; he even ignored the cause of
his anger as Aldric stood up, turned and left without a
bow of courtesy, Marek and Gueynor in his wake. Instead Geruath flopped back into his chair and tore the
page apart with manic care and concentration until its
pieces too small for him to grasp . . .

*

Marek Endain had said nothing during the long walk
back to their apartments—his mind, guessed Aldric, was
far too full for words—but Gueynor, out of the demon
queller's sight, had squeezed his hand. Whether she felt
gratitude, or satisfaction, or merely the need for human
contact that he sometimes experienced, Aldric neither
knew nor cared. Nobody apart from another high-clan
Alban could have understood the complex reasoning behind what he had done; but whatever the interpretation
put on his action by these three foreigners—and in affairs of *kailin-eir* honour, Marek was as much a stranger
as the two Jouvaines—it was most likely wrong. It had
not been a demonstration of his independence, nor an
insult to the Overlord for insult's sake, nor a show of
tacit support.

It had been because of his duty. To himself, his
honour . . . his sword. "A man without duty, a man
without honour, this is not a man." So the old saying
went. What, Aldric thought sombrely, would the writer
of that rhyme have made of his own uniquely flexible
form of honour, in which he had shown a steadily increasing lack of compunction about twisting to suit the
needs of the moment . . . ?

Tense and sweaty despite his outward calm, Aldric's present needs were less philosophical. "Some exercise and a bath," he muttered to no one in particular. "There is a proper bath-house in this mausoleum, isn't there?"

Marek neither knew nor cared. There were two unbroached flagons of wine on the table in his room, and after the impromptu interview with Geruath he had an overpowering desire to empty both of them. Even the way in which his door shut and locked behind him managed to sound ill-tempered.

"I shall walk in the gardens for an hour," said Gueynor.

Aldric glanced at her. "Why? You saw what they look like."

"But I remember what they looked like," the girl amended quietly. "And they remind me of things.'

"And after your walk?"

"I want to talk. Privately." She jerked her head briefly towards the demon queller's door. "Alone." Aldric grinned: a quick baring of teeth with much sardonic humour in it but no real amusement.

"He has two bottles in there. I doubt we shall be disturbed."

"Good. I—" She broke off, detecting movement at the end of the corridor. Aldric twisted a little, saw the servant standing idly as if without work to do, realised that the man could have been standing there all day without his knowing it and tore off the eyepatch. Gueynor blinked. "Is that wise?"

"Wisest thing I've done with it so far." He knuckled savagely at the socket, both to make the eye red and justify its being covered up, and to rub away the unfocused blur which filled his vision on that side. The retainer was still there, watching without seeming to, listening likewise. Convenient for me, thought Aldric as he signalled the man with a deliberately peremptory gesture. Yes, you bastard, I want you here . . . And convenient for Geruath or whoever had set him there to spy.

"Enjoy your walk, Aline," he said for the servant's benefit, pitching his voice low enough to sound like an exchange of confidences. Or intimacies. "If I'm bathing when you come back . . ." He let the words trail away throatily and stroked one open hand along Gueynor's neck.

"If you are, Kourgath, then I'll take another stroll." She caught his wrist, turned over the hand and lightly kissed its palm before releasing him and walking away.

"What are you staring at?" Aldric demanded of the servant. He used Drusalan; a local retainer would probably react with blank incomprehension, whereas a mercenary—

"Nothing, lord!"

—would understand what he had said . . . The Alban cleared his throat but passed no comment on his discovery.

In a few minutes he had been conducted to a roofed courtyard near the fortress stables. This was an area plainly set aside for the exclusive use of deadly weapons; the targets ranged along the walls and sunk at irregular intervals into the sand-covered floor showed that much—but their number and various shapes confused Aldric a little until he recalled his impressions of the Overlord. Geruath of Seghar might well be a crazy old man, but he did not seem the kind of weapon collector whose collection was merely ornamental. Every blade and pole-arm which the Alban had seen on the presence-chamber's display racks had been oiled and whetted ready for immediate use. Any missile weapons which the Overlord possessed would almost certainly be in the same hair-raisingly lethal condition.

Doing his best to dismiss both Geruath and his mysteriously as-yet-unseen son, Aldric entered the stable to fetch *taidyin*—wooden practice foils—from his gear and was immediately, forcefully reminded of them once more. For his saddlebags and pack had been searched—thoroughly, efficiently, so neatly that scarcely a garment had been crumpled or moved out of place. But such was the searcher's arrogance that nothing had been closed. Rebuckling the flaps with hands that were surprisingly steady, Aldric breathed a small sigh of relief between his teeth. The intrusion, and the insolence of it, had angered him; but he had expected such an examination of his belongings sooner or later. Remembering the spell-stone, he was heartily glad it had been later . . .

Apparently he was being taken on trust, accepted straight away as no more than he claimed to be—a not unreasonable supposition—because if there had been any doubts at all he would have been scrutinised and spied on and investigated until at last the truth emerged. No disguise could ever withstand hard suspicion; his real trick lay in not provoking it . . .

The stinging crack of *taidyo* against target brought more than one curious observer to the courtyard; some blinked, laughed indulgently and went away, but others stayed, watching. Aldric made no objection to their presence: whatever information they might carry to Lord Geruath would serve only as a none-too-subtle warning that at least one of his guests could take care of himself.

A muscle twinged high in his shoulder. It was stiff from lack of use and Aldric reproved himself silently. His own fault, no one else's. Lack of practice, lack of exercise, lack of too many things. He swung the arm gently, feeling the slide and flexion of joint and sinew work away the pain, and he thought . . . He thought: if only everything was so simple that a sword could solve it. He thought: I hold life and death made manifest in metal, mine to grant or to withhold.

And even as the thoughts flickered through his mind like the turning pages of a book, he knew that they were only thoughts: not desires, not wishes, not even dreams. Death came far too easily already, often with a haste that was almost unseemly. No man who lay with a woman could engender life as quickly as the man who bore a blade could end it. And keeping ebbing life within a ruined body, or death from one determined to embrace it, was impossible. He knew. He had seen too many times: Haranil . . Santon . . . Baiart . . . Evthan . . .

Aldric's fingers flexed around the *taidyo,* both hands on the long hilt that was chequer-cut for gripping. Its carvern patterns bit into his palms. Slowly he raised the length of polished oak above his head and poised it there, immobile in the waiting attitude of high guard left. His tensed arms, his body, his spirit quivered inwardly with passion and a craving for release. He thought, and the thought was cold: what is a sword—a symbol of honour, of rank? Of death. The past cannot be undone. The word, the blade, the arrow—none can be recalled. You can never turn back. You can never go home . . .

The *taidyo* moved. It blurred, a transparent arc sweeping obliquely down. It hissed, ripping through the fabric of the air. It struck—

"Hai!"

And with a crisp, harsh rending the wooden target split asunder, its fibres rupturing along a raw-edged gouge as straight as the stroke of a razor. Slivers pattered against the sand as it twisted, sagged brokenly backwards and flopped like something newly dead.

A small, remote smile crept briefly on to Aldric's face as he heard the murmuring which his demonstration had provoked. All the fury bottled up inside him was gone now, channeled from his body through wood and into wood. And into destruction. So Duergar Vathach had died, burned and blasted by the dark forces of emotion held too long in check. . . "Enough," he breathed softly and laid the notched, chipped *taidyo* aside.

She waited an arm's length from where he stood, patient as the night awaiting dawn; resting on a simple pine rack, stark black and gleaming with lacquer and steel against the grained, blond wood. Isileth Widowmaker.

Aldric bowed fractionally before he lifted the *taiken,* respecting her twenty centuries of age and the purpose for which she had been forged all those long years ago. The killing of men . . . He unwrapped the scabbard's shoulder-strap from where it coiled like a serpent below the longsword's forked, ringed hilt, looped it over his head and made Widowmaker secure on the weapon-belt at his left hip. The touch of his fingers when he settled her weight was a caress such as one might use to stroke a favoured hawk. A man had said once, years past, that Aldric loved his sword as he might love a woman. That had been an insult, answered as such with violence—but in the case of Widowmaker it was true. Almost . . . Not love, perhaps, but trust: complete and absolute, as one must inevitably trust that on which continued life depends.

Conscious of and at the same time ignoring the critical eyes which followed his every move, he drew. First form: *achran-kai,* the inverted cross. Isileth sang from her scabbard and made two cuts that flowed together in a single sweep. Each stroke was precise, controlled and seemingly effortless. Both had taken perhaps half a second.

Taiken-ulleth could be as plain or as elaborate as each swordsman wished his style to be, and that chosen by Aldric—refined like an ink sketch to an elegant, absolute minimum—was perhaps the simplest of all. Which was not to say it was the easiest. Despite their ritual aspect the cuts had real force; graceful they might be, sometimes even beautiful in their austere economy. But they were also, always, deadly.

Aldric knew at once when Geruath the Overlord stepped into the practice yard. He knew before the men on the periphery of his vision stiffened to attention, before they began to bow. The strange and unreliable sixth sense of warning had alerted him before any outward sign was visible, but in this instance the Overlord's presence and his gaze was not so much a mental shadow as a physical pressure between the shoulder-blades. He turned slowly, meeting Geruath unwinking stare for stare. It was Jouvaine who looked away first.

Then, and only then, Aldric slid Widowmaker out of sight with a thin whisper of sound. There was something almost modest in the way he sheathed her blade, as a lover might cloak his lady to preserve her from the lewd gaze of passersby. But his gloved right hand remained around her hilt and it was plain that he could draw and cut within the blinking of an eye. That was an unspoken threat of sorts, but one which Geruath unwisely chose to ignore.

"Good afternoon to you, my lord," the Alban said—his voice a soft, accented purr and his bow, of the least degree, a studied hairsbreadth short of either insult or politeness. Insolent grey-green cat's eyes dared the Overlord to object; even for an Alban, Aldric had no time left for the hypocrisies of false courtesy.

It seemed that Overlord Geruath realised as much, for his own bow was impeccable. Someone had perhaps advised him as to what *eijin* were: high-clan warriors who for reasons of their own had set aside their ranks and titles and with them any need to recognise law, or morality, or honour. Men careless of their own lives as much as those of others. Stories painted them in dark colours, the crimson and vermillion of blood and the black which Aldric wore, and talked of them as though they were remorseless one-man death machines. Such crude descriptions were not entirely true—but neither were they entirely false . . .

"Kourgath-*an*. I would like to speak with you." Geruath spoke in Alban and his voice, suave as a courtier's, was deeper than seemed reasonable from so narrow a chest.

"Then speak. My lord." The honorific came as a careless afterthought, but Geruath ignored its rudeness.

"In private."

"This is private enough for me, my lord. What word in particular had you in mind?"

"*Taiken,*" Geruath said at last. He had more sense than to reach out for the object of his desire, even though the longsword's pommel was close enough to touch. Aldric watched him, deciding how many severed fingers would constitute a reasonable reaction. "That *taiken.*" The finger which he used for pointing was not one of those at risk. Yet. "I offer you a thousand Imperial crowns for it."

Aldric blinked balefully. *How much do you know?* he thought. "The Empire's currency," he said, picking his words with care, "does not have my confidence. It has become a trifle debased of late." *Evthan* . . . "No crowns, my lord."

"Then the same in deniers," Geruath returned without any hesitation.

The blatancy of that admission staggered the Alban, although he concealed it well. Lord Geruath had just confessed—to a total stranger—his possession of a small fortune in Alban gold coins; granted that he might have been lying, but Aldric doubted it. The money was available—somewhere very close, or Geruath would not have mentioned it as an enticement. A thousand deniers . . . ! That was the hire price of a small mercenary army, near enough, and it was being offered for a sword by this petty lord of a backwoods fief. Aldric had been suspicious before, but knew now that the whole business stank of corruption like a month-dead sheep in summertime.

And where did the demon fit into it all . . . ? First a werewolf, now this thing. Another eater of women. Aldric did not like the images which were begining to take shape within his mind, and liked still less the carefully forgotten words accompanying them . . .

> *Issaqua sings the song of desolation*
> *And I know that I am lost*
> *And none can help me now . . .*

What, he wondered, would Geruath's reaction be to hearing those words spoken? Or would Crisen understand their meaning better . . . ? The Alban shook his head, as if dislodging stubborn dreams, and the Overlord took his gesture for refusal.

"Two thousand then," said Geruath. "Or five—or ten if you are prepared to wait!"

Mercies of Heaven . . . The unvoiced oath trickled past dark pictures inside Aldric's brain, half astonishment and half disbelief. "You want this weapon badly, my lord," he murmured. "In the worst possible way. And either you have all this money—or you're the most extravagant liar I have ever met." There now, it's said. So respond to it, you ancient maniac.

Geruath considered the Alban's words impassively. Then he tried to seize Aldric's arm and missed as the younger man snapped one step backwards, his right hand crossing, gripping, drawing . . .

"Hai!"

And not all the swords of all the retainers who now sprang forward could have saved him. As a clean-sliced shred of cloth-of-gold fluttered to the floor, Geruath of Seghar knew he should be dead.

So did Aldric. "Be advised, my lord." His voice had shed its softness, had become instead as harsh as the grating of stones. "Never try to touch me. Call off your vassals." The longsword glittered as he shifted his position. *"Now!"*

Lord Geruath glared down from his full gaunt height

at the Alban's masked, dispassionate face, reading nothing from it and seeing only his own death reflected by the *taiken*. With one hand he gestured to his guards and they fell back. "There is no danger," he told them, though both voice and hand were trembling with fear and rage. "Merely a . . . display of technique. Nothing more."

Aldric relaxed, Widowmaker's point lowering to the sand with a tiny crisp sound he heard quite clearly in the heavy silence. "Thank you, my lord," he said, and bowed.

Breathing heavily, Geruath said nothing for many moments and as he straightened Aldric waited for the inevitable parting shot. It came only after the Overlord had walked away a little—out of reach, but not yet out of earshot. "Kourgath-*eijo*," the Jouvaine hissed, "you may yet give me your blade—freely and of your own will."

There was no expression on the Alban's face as he inclined his head in courteous acknowledgement of the veiled threat, but when he raised it a bleak smile had thinned his lips. "My lord," said Aldric as sardonically as his command of Jouvaine would allow, "I almost did."

8

The Devourer in the Dark

The gardens of Seghar were no more than a memory;
only the scent of flowers remained and that too had
changed—was uncared for, over-rich, nauseously sweet.
But it was the memory of the gardens ten years past
that Gueynor saw as she walked slowly through the confusion of weeds and dying plants, and they were enough.
"I am Gueynor Evenou," she said, "and I am the daughter of Lord Erwan Evenou, and I am the true-born ruler
of this . . . desolation."

There was a belvedere built on top of a small hill,
overlooking what had once been a view. This had been
her realm, her secret place, when she was six years old,
and at first sight it was untouched by the ruin which
surrounded it. Then Gueynor walked closer and saw the
doors hanging from their hinges, the shattered filigree of
the windows, the damp white moulds and fungi that exist
on rottenness crawling slimily across its wooden walls.
Gueynor looked at it, remembering how it had been.
The stink of decay prickled at her nostrils, but despite
that she went inside and, being free for the present from
Aldric Talvalin's well-meant cynicism, allowed herself
to weep.

"Aye, my lady. It was fair—once."

The shock of hearing another voice where none
should have been made her start. *Kortagor* Jervan stood
outlined in the doorway, no longer armoured but
dressed with simple elegance in boots and breeches and
a belted tunic. Something of the surprise she felt must
have shown on her face, for he gestured at the garments
and made a deprecating smile. "Every soldier comes off

duty sometimes, lady Aline—even garrison commanders. My lieutenant has the trey watch this afternoon."

"But why did you come here?"

"Because I like to, sometimes. Because I knew these gardens when they were gardens and not wasteland. I like to remember them as they were." Jervan paused, looked at her. "And because I saw you walking here."

"How would that interest you?"

"Because I have eyes, lady, and the wit to use them properly. And because *you* interest me."

Gueynor stared at him and wished that she had a dagger. "In what way do *I* interest you, garrison commander Jervan?"

"In many ways. Except. . ." deliberately he moved out of the doorway, stepping aside to leave her escape route clear, ". . . the one you fear. I am a married man, lady. Oh, I know that does not render me immune to lust, especially since I am a beast in armour. Or are we called something else nowadays? I ceased listening to the insults long ago. But I have two daughters, and when I look at you I think of them. You are not so old and worldy as your painted face suggests, my lady Aline . . . I see them, and my wife, once a year. Never more. Once a year for the past two years, and then I come back to this . . . dung-heap. A morally and physically reeking pile where"—his eyes searched her face and were evidently satisfied by what they found there—"two mad cockerels compete for the heights to crow from. For all his faults, and his impetuous religious foolishness, your father was quite sane."

To her eternal credit Gueynor did not overreact; she merely raised her brows with curiosity and said, "How could a soldier of the Empire be familiar with a peasant huntsman?"

Jervan grinned hugely at that and clapped his hands. "Very well done, my lady! Masterfully controlled!" Then the ironic humour left his voice and the wolfish amusement drained out of his bearded face. Again the girl wished she was armed . . . "You knew me, that evening at the gate. Did you not?" There was no point in denying it, not now, and Gueynor nodded. "Had it not been for your reaction, I would have given the encounter little thought. You cannot guess how many half-familiar faces trickle in and out during a day, a week, a month; and you recognise your brother's face, your wife's way of wearing her hair, your father's way of walking with a cane he doesn't need . . . And yet not one of them has seen you before, or likely will again. But *you* . . . You knew me and I felt sure that I knew you, but I could not for my life remember where or when. I sat awake most of last night, did you know—of course you didn't, how could you?

"Because you have changed considerably since I let you and your uncle through the Westgate and away, that day ten years ago . . ."

"Who else knows . . . ?" Gueynor's voice was very small.

"Nobody." The *kortagor* laughed shortly, as if length of laughter was laid down in regulations. "The kind of puzzling to which it led me is best done alone—or even the politest of your fellow officers begin to talk." He touched his head significantly. "There is a saying current in Seghar garrison—although not among the lord's-men for obvious reasons—that such-and-such grows lordly. It's an insult. They don't say *crazy* any more; nor *insane;* not even plain and simple *mad.* Just *lordly* . . . They're just ordinary troopers in my garrison, not remarkably intelligent—yet not stupid either, mind you—but what I mean is, they're not witty, not clever with words. But whichever of them coined that description knew exactly what he was trying to say."

"I . . . We saw the Overlord this morning."

"Then you will understand, I think."

"I do." Gueynor took a deep breath and discovered a strange thing: she was no longer afraid. Whatever Jervan was going to do, he would do whether or not she was frightened. And she greatly desired to know what that might be. The best way to find out, as Aldric had taught her, was to ask . . . "Commander Jervan, come to the point. Please . . ."

He saluted and did not grin to dilute it. "You too are growing lordly—and not in the fashion meant by my soldiers. Very well, lady . . . Gainore . . . ?"

"Gueynor."

"Gueynor . . . The records were in some dialect—it's not spelt as it's spoken. I am . . . How much do you know of what has been happening here, lady?"

"Crisen's consort was a witch. There was a mistake in a spell. She was killed. Those are the bare bones of what I've heard; people in Seghar don't talk much to strangers."

"Close enough. Lady Gueynor, what I—" Jervan broke off abruptly and left the summerhouse very fast, without any explanation. She saw for the first time that there was a short sword or long dagger sheathed hilt-downwards in the small of his back, where it had been hidden while he faced her. Even that discovery did not bring back her fear; the weapon was too big, its fittings and furniture too ornate for it to be a concealed blade in the way that Aldric's tiny dirk had been concealed. Dictates of fashion, the girl hazarded.

And then *Kortagor* Jervan was back inside, looking unconcerned. "The advantage of a place like this," he observed, "is that it was built to allow one to see land-scapes, flower-beds—or anyone sneaking through them. Although I doubt that last was an original intention."

"You command this place—why should you worry?"

"Hear me out and then ask again, my lady." He pointed to a seat running round three of the small build-ing's five walls. "That's not so dirty as it looks. Sit down—what I have to say may take time."

"What—briefly—have you to say, *Kortagor?*"

"Briefly . . . Conspiracy, usurpation, treason. Although the words do alter, depending on who hears them. The Overlord would use those I selected; you, or your Alban traveling companion, might have a kinder vocabulary. We shall see . . ."

*

Widowmaker had been stripped bare, right down to the naked blade; she had been cleaned, polished, oiled and even stroked a needless time or two with a whetstone. Now, refurbished and glinting, she lay on her pine wood rack and waited with dreadful patience for the time of killing to come again. The time for which she had been made two thousand years before . . .

Immersed to the neck in fragrant water that was so hot it made the slightest movement painful—but transformed immobility to a blissful languor—Aldric gazed through whorls of steam towards the sword and through it, seeing neither steel nor lacquer as he considered what he had done. Not merely outfaced a provincial Overlord in his own home and before his own men, although— Light of Heaven witness!—that was rash enough. No . . . He had also thrown away whatever chance he might have had through Geruath of introduction to either Goth or Bruda. Whatever his and Gueynor's plans might be for the Overlord, his favour was needed—no, indispensable—for this one enterprise.

Insignificant though he probably was, the half-demented lord of Seghar still carried a thousand times more weight within the Empire than any Alban ever could, be he *eijo, kailin-eir* or *ilauem-arluth,* and without him Aldric's duty to his king had suddenly become more fraught with difficulties and with risks. Lacking the formal modes of ingress that Geruath could have provided, he was as likely to meet an Imperial Prokrator or a Lord General as he was to fly rings around the moon.

The intense heat of the water faded slowly; Aldric had been pleasantly surprised to find such civilised amenities as an Alban bath-house and deep tub in the pest-hole that was Seghar. Most likely it had been installed by Gueynor's father Erwan. Erwan . . . Evthan . . . His mind toyed briefly with the similarities of name, wondering whether there was something more than just coincidence about them . . . Then wondered what had become of Gueynor herself. Despite her refusal of his indelicate hint, she should have joined him by now. Not necessarily in the bath itself, although the notion had momentary attraction; despite the fact that they shared a bed, that they slept together, neither were euphemisms but simply statements. Other than the contacts born of companionship and comfort, Aldric had not touched the Jouvaine girl—much less made love to her—since the night when she had paid him for her uncle's . . . release. Nor had he really wanted to. It would always now, remind him of blood on his hands. Love, lust, idle amusement: none of these would have disturbed him. But the thought that her embraces held the price of a life . . . no matter how noble the sentiment, it was repellent. And there

was always another face over Gueynor's, as if she wore
a mask.

Kyrin . . . Strange how he always seemed to want, to
need, the unattainable. She would be married by now,
maybe already carrying the seed of Seorth's child within
her. Whatever . . . she was lost to him.

"*. . . I know that I am lost . . .*" whispered the distant,
uninvited voice in Aldric's brain. And the scalding water
grew abruptly colder.

"Marek . . . ?" he said, addressing no one but uttering
a thought aloud. What was taking Gueynor so long to
walk through a ruined garden . . . ? A feeling that was
not quite fear but far stronger than mere apprehension
crept over him. Whether it was a sixth-sense stab of
warning or his own mind overheated by the water which
surrounded him, he did not know for certain. But he did
know that the matter had to be resolved if he was to
have peace.

The tub was cooling rapidly now. He surged from the
water and reached for a towel.

*

There was an interval of silence. A breeze began to
blow, chilling the air, and it grew a little darker. Jervan
looked outside, towards the sky, and nodded grimly. "It
will rain soon," he said. Then to Gueynor: "Have you
noticed that? Even the weather here is strange.
Unnatural . . ."

"Commander . . . This is your conspiracy, your
treason—but whose usurpation? And why tell me?"
Gueynor, despite her question, was wary of being told
too much; often the ways of ensuring secrecy were swift
and brutal.

"Have you not already guessed? There was a look
about you, lady. I have been a soldier twenty years—I
know the look of violence held in check as well as any
man. Not delivered by your own hand, maybe, but . . .
The young Alban is a killer."

"He is *not* . . . !" Gueynor's outraged denial cut off
short, for when she considered the little that she knew
of Aldric Talvalin, Jervan's estimation of him was correct. It was strange that she had never thought of him
as such.

"Tell me, lady," said Jervan curiously, "can you be quite sure that he will kill at your command—or, more importantly, that he will not kill when you do not desire it?"

I should tell him nothing, Gueynor thought. It is Aldric's place, not mine, to tell a stranger what he will or will not do.

"Well, my lady . . . can you trust him in the small matter of life and death? Or indeed with anything at all?"

That was enough. She could not, would not allow such imputations to continue. But even in her heat she took care not to betray, by hint or hesitation, that the Alban's name was other than the "Kourgath" he had claimed. "He may be *eijo,* Commander Jervan—but I believe he is a man of honour."

Jervan smiled slightly and it was just a smile, nothing more. No ironies were hidden by his beard. "Of course, lady. I know that. He is an Alban and honour is a part of being such. But the honour of an Alban is not the honour of an ordinary man. Respect is honour; duty is honour; obligation is honour; courage is honour; and obedience is honour. Honour embodies all the virtues.

"But if, when he had a lord whose word he was bound by honour to obey, that lord told your friend to kill, then he would kill. And if he was told to die, then he would die. You have seen the black knife he carries?"

Gueynor nodded. Of all the weapons he possessed, that black dirk was most apparent, for Aldric never let it stray beyond his reach. In any circumstance.

"That is his. For him, and for no one else. So that he may kill himself if honour dictates he must. I have heard this said of Albans, lady, especially *kailinin-eir*—men of the high clans—that they make the best friends in the world. And the worst enemies.

"The old demon queller Endain told me something of your friend's past, lady. Of how he came to be here. There was civil war in Alba this spring—though 'civil war' over-dignifies it—and it seems your friend fought on the wrong side."

"Stop calling him my 'friend' in that tone, Commander."

"What then, lady? Companion? Bodyguard? Lover?"

Jervan's eyes did not leave her face. "I think 'friend' is quite adequate. For as is the way of losers, he lost everything. Holds, and fiefs, and titles—all gone. He is lucky to have his life."

"What trouble was it?" asked Gueynor, intrigued. Aldric, when he mentioned his home—and that was seldom—spoke only in veiled hints as if remembering details hurt him.

"I know little enough, lady. It was small and far away, and the doings of foreigners takes second place to my present duty here. But . . . It seems that one lord stole the lands and fortress of another. There were some killings—but evidently not enough for the thief's security. This first lord's son survived, instead of dying as he should have done by his own hand."

Gueynor's face was incredulous. "By his own . . . ! But why?"

"The Albans see a sole survivor as a coward and a failure. As I told you, a strange people. But four years later he came back at the head of an army: took back his lands, took back his fortress; did some killing on his own account; and then vanished. I think that, having proved conclusively and to his own satisfaction that he was neither a coward nor a man to be taken lightly, he committed suicide at last. Although I have heard it said that he turned religious, that somewhere in the Blue Mountains there lives a monastic hermit who owns a goodly chunk of Alba. But I doubt there's any truth in that tale."

"What was his name, this self-willed lord?"

"Supposedly he was the lord of High Clan Talvalin. The last lord. Aldric."

Gueynor discovered she had developed a sudden uncomfortable tic in her left eyelid, and was only surprised that her whole body did not convulse with shock. Somehow, for some inexplicable reason, she had half anticipated hearing Aldric's name, but despite her expectation Jervan's speaking it aloud appalled her . . . that she had shared her bed, her body, with the young man whom travellers' tales called Deathbringer—for though the *kortagor* had small time for gossip, peasant villagers

gleaned both news and entertainment for such stories . . .
Yet her uncle, entrusted with his true name, had not
made the connection. It was, she thought more calmly,
hardly surprising. He did not look like a Deathbringer.
Nor act like one . . . Not obviously. But Evthan, and
Keel and the other soldiers with him, knew the nickname was well-given.

"You spin out a tale to extraordinary lengths, Commander," Gueynor observed carefully. "I had thought
you were going to tell me something of yourself. And
why I interest you."

"As I said earlier, lady—have you not already
guessed? You interest me because of who you are and
who your father was." He leaned back against the wall
of the summerhouse, carefully choosing an area that was
both dry and reasonably clean, folded arms across chest,
crossed legs at ankles . . . looking indeed the very picture
of a gentleman taking his ease and about to indulge in
inconsequential chat. Except that there was nothing inconsequential about what Jervan had to say.

"There are two powers in this Empire, lady. The
Emperor—and his Grand Warlord. And Lord Geruath,
by lack of diplomacy and tact—and thanks in large part
to the foolishness of his son—has lost the . . .
friendship . . . of both. A deal of money enters this town
each month; Alban money—not gold, but credit scrip
drawn on the merchant guilds. It is intended to finance
unrest, uprisings . . . Anything to keep the Warlord's
attention from Alba. For without war, what realm needs
a Warlord . . . ? Instead it buys Lord Geruath his weapons and Lord Crisen his sorceries, his women and his
wines. There will come a time, and by my judgement
that time is not far off, when either Warlord Etzel or
Ioen the Emperor will send a force to stamp this place
to dust. You see, lady, by lacking the protection granted
by support of one side, our Overlord has no defence
against action taken by the other."

"Get to the point," snapped Gueynor, letting her impatience show at last.

"The point, my lady Gueynor Evenou, is that if you
were to take this citadel and hold it—hold it well—for

one side or the other, then you would almost certainly be regarded with some favour. As a stabilising influence, shall we say . . . ?"

"Say whatever you like. But say it quickly!"

"Certainly you would be permitted to retain your holding here: the support of one side or the other, remember? And . . . and you would have avenged what happened to your father and your mother." Gueynor stared at him but said nothing. "Curious, is it not—the similarity between yourself and the Alban I told you of? Except that you have waited ten years, while he waited only four."

"And what advantage," Gueynor's voice was icy, "do *you* gain from this . . . enterprise?"

"Ah, lady . . . now we do come to the point." Jervan stroked his beard a moment, watching the girl thoughtfully, reading much from her posture and expression that remained unsaid. He nodded once to himself. "I expect advancement, of course," the *kortagor* said in the tone of one stating the obvious.

"And what precisely do you stand to lose if I say *no?*"

Jervan's hooded eyes opened very wide for an instant, reminding Gueynor of a startled hawk; then his right hand moved smoothly to the dagger-hilt at the small of his back. "You would not live long enough to find out. Indeed, you would not live to walk from here, much less betray me." He meant every word.

Gueynor arched an eyebrow at him and smiled in the cool, dismissive fashion she had seen Aldric employ. It was incongruous in such a situation and its very incongruity gave Jervan pause. "I said nothing of betrayal, *Kortagor* Jervan. Only refusal. What will happen to the garrison commander when one or other of the Great Powers stamps this place to—to dust, was it? Will they strike off your head or simply hang you like a common criminal?"

Her shots, though hastily aimed, struck home with considerable force. Jervan did not go so far as to flinch at the girl's words, but something flickered in the depths of his eyes as the pupils dilated slightly. "I think, lady, that you will make an admirable Overlord." It did not sound much like a compliment.

"Overlady you mean, of course, Commander."

Jervan looked at her and smiled wanly, not at this moment inclined to debate the finer points of Drusalan grammar. The title *Overlord* was neutral and did not change its gender to match the holder's sex. "Overlord I said and Overlord I meant. For all the years you spent consorting with your peasant friends"—and he spat the word *peasant*—"you remain aristocratic enough."

"Do you mean . . . lordly?" Suspecting a veiled insult, there was a lethal edge to Gueynor's voice.

"Aristocratic. Not necessarily noble, but arrogant. Arrogant enough for any Princess of the Blood. Even Marevna."

"Commander Jervan, would you speak to me like this if I was your Overlord?"

"No, my lady I would not. But until that time I would. I will. Because you understand the reasons why I do. As you understand the reasons why I do. As you understand them now."

"Very well. So what is your plan?"

"Simple enough. Simple and direct. Use your *eijo*. As I said before, he is a killer. And I fancy he has death in mind for Crisen Geruath. I . . . feel it. And also, if the rumours are true, for the Overlord himself. Geruath Segharlin collects weapons; he has done so for years— yet he remains remarkably ill-informed as to how other men regard their swords."

"Is it, Commander, that you are perceptive—or is it merely that you have a nest of spies throughout this fortress?"

"I guess; and it seems I guess correctly. Remember, Gueynor, I was at the gate. I saw Kourgath-*eijo's* longsword. That is a blade of master quality, and if Geruath has not already made an offer for it he will do so, eventually."

"And then?"

Jervan smiled thinly. "And then . . . ?" he echoed. "I don't think you need me to tell you."

"And what of the guards?" asked Gueynor practically, remembering some of Aldric's muttered observations. "This citadel is over-full of soldiers."

"You need not concern yourself about the guards. All

their wages are months in arrears and only the hope of eventually getting the money they are owed keeps them here. And I know where the treasure-chests are kept."

"Of course . . ."

"Of course! As garrison commander, it is one of my duties to ensure they are paid an adequate—barely adequate—retainer to hold them in Seghar. While a mercenary can smell money in the offing . . . Well, it ensures their loyalty from week to week. Pay them all that they're owed, lady, and they're yours to command."

"And you, Commander? How many months' back pay do you expect to receive from a magnanimous new Overlord?"

The soldier tried, and failed, to suppress a foxy, crafty grin of self-satisfaction. "I am owed no money at all."

"The pay-chests . . ."

He must have caught the look in Gueynor's eye and the unspoken speculation which passed across her face, for the grin turned swiftly to a frown. "Yes, the pay-chests—but not in the way you think. I took only what was my due; not a copper more. Albans don't hold the monopoly on personal honour and I do have some self-respect . . . I was born here, in the Empire. I grew up here; married here, my wife and children live here. I have no desire to leave.

"But I have served the Imperial military for twenty years. Twenty years, lady, sheathed in that damned stinking mail. I should be *hautheisart* by now, or *eldheisart* at least like the others who have lorded it in the citadel; yet I am still merely a *kortagor*." His arm gestured, taking in the ruined gardens, the tumbledown buildings and the grimy towers of the fortress. "Garrison Commander. Of this . . ." Jervan worked his jaws a moment, then spat juicily as a man will who has a filthy taste in his mouth. "I may have access to the money-chests, my lady Gueynor; but what I want is the stuff that money cannot buy—promotion, favour. Power! To be well-placed, to be respected . . . Is that not reasonable for any man to want?"

"That all depends," said a quiet voice behind him, "on whether you want respect during your lifetime or respect for your memory. Which is it, *Kortagor* Jervan?"

*

The feeling had begun as unease, nothing more: a nervousness which had forced him prematurely from his bath. And then it had expanded, bloating to a monstrous *wrongness* that had bordered close to physical nausea.

Aldric had stood naked and dripping in the bathhouse, immobilised by a series of racking shudders which had torn through him like the strokes of a mace, before throwing his unused towel aside and fighting his way into dry garments which had clung to and resisted wet skin every inch of the way. With each moment that passed he grew more sure that something in this fortress had involved Gueynor, would try to involve him—and would probably be something for which he had not planned . . .

Marek Endain might have thrown some light on the matter—except that there was no sign of the demon queller anywhere. It was as if the one man Aldric wanted to talk to, from whom he most needed reassurance, was deliberately avoiding him. Which, given the Cernuan's mood when they had parted, was not overly surprising.

It was then that he began to ask after Gueynor, and consequently it was not coincidence which brought him to the summerhouse: because two servants had given the same answer to his question concerning "Lady Aline's" whereabouts, but the second had added by way of helpfulness that *Kortagor* Jervan had asked a similar question only a short time past . . .

Natural caution had brought Aldric into the sad gardens on soft feet, but the fluttering under his breastbone had made that stealthiness as rapid as was humanly possible. As he approached the tumbledown belvedere he had expected to hear . . . what? The sounds of interrogation, voices raised in threat and protest, something of that sort. Not civilised and almost friendly conversation. No matter that the conversation seemed to be dominated by Jervan's unmistakable tones, what few words he had detected spoken by Gueynor had been casual, relaxed, indeed confident. Certainly more so than he was.

He had waited for an opportune moment, aware that to do so smacked somewhat of melodrama, and then stepped through the door to speak his entrance cue. No more than an actor, Aldric thought sardonically as two heads turned towards him; but in what play? And is it a tragedy or the blackest of comedies . . . ?

"The plotting that goes on in Seghar," he observed aloud, "never fails to astonish me." The Alban spoke as if he had vast and weary experience of Imperial bureaucracy, which indeed had lately become a more blatant exercise in intrigue than at any time in its history. "And I was only curious about a werewolf . . ."

No one had yet employed that word—until now—and Jervan's eyes opened very wide. He had the look of a man who knows more than he is prepared to say, except that with Aldric asking questions and Widowmaker present to ensure answers, the *kortagor* suspected that one way or another he would be prepared to say more than he knew eventually . . . Voord had had that same effect. And yet for someone who could protest that his words were forced from him by the threat of violence, Jervan proved to be surprisingly talkative and even more surprisingly well-informed. Either he was perceptive to a ludicrous degree, or it was as Gueynor had earlier suspected; he had spies everywhere. For his own protection, most likely, gathering the sort of evidence that might save his neck when saving became an urgent matter.

The Jouvaine girl had heard much of his monologue before, but Aldric listened intrigued to what had happened in Seghar and what Jervan thought was going to happen. When he spoke of sorcery, and of the hunter dragged before Lord Crisen for striking a mercenary soldier, Aldric's eyes flicked momentarily to Gueynor's face. The Alban did not like the studied lack of all expression that he saw there—it was unnatural.

"I have my own guesses on this matter, *Kortagor*," he said. "That some spell was used on the forester as a punishment. A cruel and unusual punishment, as the lawyers have it."

"Unusual, yes. But not cruel. Not for the Geruaths. No. The man was available when Crisen took his fancy for shape-changing. A goat would have sufficed otherwise."

Aldric stared at him, his mouth twisting as if he had

drunk vinegar and his mind reeling with the thoughtless savagery Jervan had confirmed. Despite his own suspicions he had tried to believe that what had been done to Evthan was no more than the invention of a sick mind. The truth—that it was instead a studied, ruthless experiment—was far, far worse. *The man was available* . . . Available . . . ! Trying to erase or at least muffle such a line of thought, he asked. "Who was Voord?" and listened without hearing to the reply.

"Voord? An *eldheisart* and a friend of Lord Crisen. He comes from Drakkesborg." Jervan said that as if it had some significance, but the meaning was lost on Aldric. "And he is much more than only that."

"Why . . . ?" The response was dull, incurious, automatic; more because it seemed to be expected of him than because he really wanted to know. But it satisfied Jervan at least.

"If you had met the Lord Commander, Alban, you wouldn't need to ask. Call it a gut-feeling. The same feeling that I get whenever I see a snake."

"I know little of your Imperial ranks, but *eldheisart* seems—"

"High? Voord would be your age or a little more. Too young for such an exalted position!"

There was naked envy in the *kortagor*'s voice and Aldric smiled mechanically at it. "Unless he is something special." *More than he seems—just as Evthan was.* "Don't you think so?"

"It relates to what I told the lady."

Aldric shot another glance at Gueynor, noting that her lack of expression had not changed—indeed, had intensified into something close to vacuity. As if she deliberately tried not to listen—or even think. "Then," said the Alban, "tell me too."

"Independence," Jervan said succinctly. "Neutrality. Protection by—and consequently from—both Powers in this Empire."

"As a city-state? Like those in the West? It would never have been permited . . . ! Are both the Lords of Seghar raving?"

"Not both. Not yet . . . If such a thing could be established it would work!" Aldric disliked the enthusiasm he could hear in Jervan's voice. "I know it would; a neutral go-between has more security than any but the most powerful supporter."

The Alban made a wordless sound as realisation dawned. "Gueynor . . . ?" he breathed.

Jervan nodded. "She would be acceptable. With sensible advisers."

"I don't doubt that for an instant. Your mouth's watering, man. Careful! You aren't lord's-counsel yet."

Aldric's hackles were rising: there had been an idle notion chasing itself around the back of his mind, something to do with restoring Gueynor to what had been her father's place—but now, confronted with the realities of the situation, he shied away. "You seem to have forgotten your uncle easily," he accused.

Gueynor raised her drooping head, turned it a fraction to gaze at him and hooded her eyes with half-lowered, heavy lashes. "One cannot live for revenge alone," she reminded him primly.

"No? I recall a different attitude, not long ago. But no matter. I think Crisen Geruath should pay for what he has done here, and not through"—this for Jervan's benefit— "political altruism. A more intimate recompense . . . for Evthan, and for the thirty others whose names I never knew. But I'm sure you knew them, even if you choose to forget it now. And if you don't consider that sufficient reason by itself, without high-minded talk, then I pity you."

"Keep your pity!" snapped Gueynor. She was beginning to see the Deathbringer in him now—or was it just the high-clan Alban of whom Jervan had spoken. A man who saw blood-vengeance as a necessary expedient, not employed without thought, certainly regretted afterwards—but without hesitation at the instant of its use. That sword . . . Gueynor stared at it and shivered.

Aldric saw the stare, sensed the shiver and smiled crookedly. His observations were coming too close for the Jouvaine woman's comfort, he suspected, and she disliked the experience. "Well, lady, it seems you have chosen. Our paths diverge a little here. I'll leave you to your intrigues. It's a smell I can't grow fond of, because intrigue of one sort or another has robbed me in too

many ways. But your nostrils seem less discriminating.
You may not see me again—and if not, then I think we
both may be the better for it . . ."

His departure was if anything even more dramatic
than his arrival, for as he turned his back on Gueynor
and walked out to the garden a flicker of forked lightning scratched the lowering sky apart, flinging his black,
hard-edged shadow back into the summerhouse with a
vast dry-edged shadow back into the summerhouse with
a vast dry crack of thunder hard on its heels. Had Aldric
been in such a mood, he would have laughed aloud at
the aptness of it all. Instead he merely grimaced and
lengthened his stride to get himself under cover before
the inevitable downpour.

*

Hands clasped behind his back, Aldric stood at a window and watched the rain slant down like arrows. There
was a dry-damp parched smell on the air, a prickling of
electricity on his skin. And a sick anger in his mind that
refused to go away.

"What's troubling you, boy?"

The Alban turned half around, completing the movement with a glance over his shoulder. He had not heard
Marek come into the room, nor his closing of the heavy
door behind him; but the Cernuan was sitting now quite
comfortably at a table on which rested a flagon of wine
and two cups. Aldric did not even object to being called
"boy." Not this time, at least. "Nothing," he responded softly.

Marek was not convinced, and though he did not
speak his face said as much.

"Nothing," Aldric repeated, then amended it to,
"nothing important, that is."

"Why not tell me anyway?" The tone, if not paternal,
was certainly avuncular. "It might make you feel better.
Gemmel told me that you brood too much."

"Gemmel told you . . . Well, well." Aldric's mouth
twisted and if the expression it bore was a smile, then it
was one as mirthless as a shark's. "You know what they
say, don't you? 'Confide in one, never in two; tell three
and the whole world knows.' And I've already told one
too many." He brought both hands round from the small

of his back and clenched the right around his *tsepan,* the
left on Widowmaker's pommel. "Matters were simpler
years ago." The suicide dirk slipped free and he lifted
the blade to study its tapered needle point. "Much simpler. One way or another."

The dirk slapped back into its sheath, handled roughly
the way no *tsepan* ever should be, and he felt shame
that his anger should mistreat an honourable weapon so.
"But I'll have a drink at least."

Towards evening the rain lessened and the sun attempted unsuccessfully to break through. As it mingled
with dusk, the only effect was to fill the sky with the
colours of a bruise. Normally Aldric could have appreciated such subtle shifts of tone and pattern as the clouds
now formed, but tonight the sullen reds seemed ominous. The prickling, tingling sensation had not lessened
with the passing of the storm; instead it had increased
until the skin all over his body seemed acrawl with red-
hot sparks . . . a petty irritation that he feared was an
intimation of pain to come. The Alban took too large a
gulp of wine and tried to put the matter from his mind,
because it filled him with an overpowering desire to
leave the province—and especially the fortress town of
Seghar—far behind him.

The servant whom Marek had sent out for more wine
reappeared in the doorway; he was empty-handed, but
he bore a summons from Geruath the Overlord. Aldric's
stomach lurched. He had anticipated this for hours . . .

They followed the retainer out to the courtyard of
the citadel, under the very shadow of the donjon. An
appropriate place for an execution, thought Aldric, made
more uncomfortable still by the two files of helmeted,
crest-coated guards who flanked their route and fell into
step behind them. But the summons was not that which
he feared—nor was it for the discussion which Marek
had been expecting all day.

Geruath was waiting for them on the steps of his
strange old-new tower. He too was helmeted—this one
fitted with earflaps and a flaring nasal that made his thin
face look thinner still—and he still wore those three su-
perb blades which Aldric had admired at first sight.

Torches ringed him, sending up twisted whorls of smoke into the still-damp air. It was obvious that he meant to start after the demon at once.

His eyes, seeming to squint a little past the nasal bar, burnt into Aldric for an instant and then slid away from him as if the *eijo* did not exist. Or was already dead. Aldric wondered what that meant and guessed he already knew the answer. From now on he would have to guard his back—and not just from whatever was haunting Seghar . . .

Someone offered him a lamp. It was heavy, with a stout metal case around its reservoir of oil, a polished reflector and a lens that bulged like the eye of a fish. Expensive, thought Aldric as he cast its spot of yellow light across the rain-glossed ground and hefted the considerable weight approvingly. Not only did it give better light than a life-flame torch, it probably made a better weapon.

There was an outburst of raised voices from the foot of the wooden tower, and he glanced up to see the cause. A man was arguing with the Overlord—unthinkable enough—and appeared to be getting the best of it—which was so unlikely that it could mean only one thing.

"Crisen!" The name passed Aldric's lips on a released breath, but few shouts carried similar weight. Such was the edge of that single whispered word that Marek's head jerked round to see what had provoked it. There was something more personal here than politics—something, he guessed, to do with the werewolf which had seemed so delicate a matter when the young Alban had first spoken to him.

"Yes, that's Crisen," the demon queller confirmed; then, without much hope of an answer: "Why are you so interested?"

"Purely personal, Marek—"

"And still none of my business. Like the girl . . . ?"

"Leave her out of this!" The command rasped out with such barely restrained venom that the Cernuan was at a loss to know what he had said wrong, only that the subject would be better dropped. At once. "I—I'm sorry." A slight, embarrassed bow gave emphasis to the unexpected apology. "I shouldn't have barked at you like that."

"Mm?" It was an interrogative noise rather than a verbal question. "Forget it. Just idle curiosity, and misplaced at that."

"Why the loud words anyway?" Aldric wondered.

The demon queller jerked towards Crisen Geruath with his fork-bearded chin. "Remember what I said about that . . ." he hesitated briefly, cautiously, and made a sign to avert evil ". . . intruder . . . ?" Aldric understood his reluctance: to name the thing was to call the thing. Evthan had known that rule and yet it had not saved him. Evthan . . . The memory still hurt, for the forester had—almost—been a friend. His fault. He made friends too quickly, too easily, once his doubts and suspicions had been satisfied. Too easily. Especially with women . . .

"That they want it controlled . . . ?"

"Just so. Now the Overlord is having second thoughts about the wisdom of such a course and his loving son"—acid dripped from the syllables—"is endeavouring to strengthen the old man's purpose with well-chosen advice. Hah!"

"So this is Crisen's idea . . ." The Alban was not asking a question this time, merely making an observation—and Marek did not like the tone in which he made it, for it held too many promises . . .

At a word of command the column moved off through darkening streets and reentered the citadel at what seemed its oldest and most crumbling point, clattering down a winding flight of worn stone steps into a place that was familiar to Marek, new to Aldric and equally unpleasant to them both.

There was a cross-corridor at the foot of the stairway with a door halfway along its left branch; a door that had been secured by many bolts, all new, but which Aldric could see had been unlocked—literally and with great violence—at some time in the recent past. Its original fastening had been smashed out of the timber in a great semi-circular bit of wood and metal like the stroke

of a mace, suggesting that something inside had wanted
to get out. And had probably succeeded.

The soldiers detailed to draw the bolts went about
their task in an unmistakably scared manner which suggested that Lord Crisen's great secret was not perhaps
so well-kept as he hoped. Like everyone else, Aldric
backed away when the door opened, even though nothing more than a sickly smell of stale incense came drifting out towards them.

The room had been completely wrecked. What little
furniture it had contained was reduced to rags and
tatters, and their torchlight revealed any parallel triple
gouges in floor, in walls—and even in the ceiling
almost twenty feet above their heads. And the floor
was covered with half-erased magical scribbling which
Marek knelt to inspect. Aldric, from where he stood,
could see how the larger of the two circles had been
broken by ashes and a heavy book, and moved a
little closer; then flinched as his eye picked out a
scattering of blackish-crimson shreds strewn across the
floor. It looked like dried meat. It *was* dried meat . . .
of a sort.

Geruath, moving to the demon queller's side, paid it
little heed. "Does this tell you more than the last time
you looked at it?" he demanded brusquely, speaking in
Jouvaine now as though he no longer cared whether or
not Aldric could understand.

"No," the Cernuan replied. "Yonder circle"—heads
turned to look at it—"was drawn in a hurry. The woman
wasn't expecting that what appeared would be quite so
dangerous. If she was expecting anything at all on that
particular night. I told you why I doubt—"

"What was it?" The Overlord's voice was irritable.
Impatient. As if he no longer had time for theories. As
if he had other things to do before the night was out . . .
"I said, what was it? Can't you tell?"

"No, I can't. My lord." Aldric could hear that the
Cernuan was trying to be patient. "And I refuse to
guess. But I ask again, won't you allow me—"

Geruath barked a refusal and turned away.

Aldric saw his face and knew why Marek had not tried

to argue. "As I said, quite mad," he muttered when the others had moved out of earshot.

Marek looked round, wishing that he had more evidence to study, anything at all which might give him a clue to what was lurking somewhere in the darkness. "Not only mad, but a fool," he said grimly. "The witch had a library somewhere, but he—or Crisen—won't let me into it. If I could see what books she had, I might at least be able to—"

"Guess? You refuse to, surely . . . ?"

"Don't, Aldric. That isn't funny. Not now. But . . ." His voice changed strangely and he stared at the Alban. "But you said something when we first met. When I encharmed you to save my own neck. Say it again."

"I . . ." Now that he had been asked, Aldric felt an overwhelming reluctance to speak the words which had tormented him for so long. As if something was impeding his tongue—something which had no desire to be betrayed. His face went red with effort and Marek could see sweat begin to bead on the younger man's forehead, trickling like great tears across the frown-lines creased into his temples. "No . . . !" he whispered, and there was dread in his voice, "I can't . . . Not here . . . !"

"You *must!*" the demon queller insisted. "Otherwise more people are going to die! Say it, Aldric! You have to say it . . . !"

The Alban's face was like that of a man on the rack: agonised and silent. His lips moved, forming words that Marek could not hear, could not read, could not recognise. There was blood running from between the fingers of Aldric's clenched left hand, where his nails had driven through the skin of his palm. It was as well no one was near, for it seemed to Marek as it would seem to any other observer that his companion was in the throes of a fit.

And then the fit was past. Aldric's eyes, which had squeezed tightly shut, reopened and incredibly he summoned up a smile from somewhere, "M-my mind is my-my own," he faltered. "S-so is my m-mouth." The smile widened fractionally as he took a deep breath. "And no bloody . . . intruder is going to interfere with either."

"Do you know what you have just done?"

"Given myself a headache . . ."

"I told you, don't joke! But you've just thrown off a Binding."

"A what?"

"Binding. Our uninvited guest does not want to be talked about. Your foster-father must have mentioned the charm." If Gemmel had, Aldric could not remember when, but he nodded cautious agreement all the same. "You broke it!"

Aldric could guess how. He still carried the Echainon spellstone inside his jerkin, and was only surprised that its augmenting of his own meagre will had not left him as weak and shaky as it had before . . . "Does this Binding tell you anything about what set it in place?" he asked hopefully.

Two soldiers stalked past, torches raised. They glanced dubiously at the *hlensyarlen* but neither did nor said anything to interfere. Marek watched them a moment before shaking his head, and Aldric's heart sank. "The only thing that will tell me is—"

"What I couldn't tell you. Until now. So . . . I found writing in a burial chamber in the Deep wood. A mound. It had been broken, violated . . . but it was clean inside and there were roses . . . Such roses, Marek. Huge!" The dream that was a nightmare awoke and coiled itself about the inside of his skull like a black viper, but Aldric fought it back to quiescence and continued without even a tremor in his voice. "It—and they—must both have been brought there by someone from Seghar, because I was attacked by lord's-men sent to retrieve it."

Marek thought it prudent not to make inquiries about the fate of the lord's-men. He knew Aldric by reputation and he could guess. Hearing about an opened mound-grave was bad enough; such places had an evil name in the lore that he had learned. But roses . . . ?

"Writing!" the Cernuan prompted. "As in pages from a book?"

"One page." Still unwilling to let his conscious mind dwell on them too much, Aldric nipped his lower lip between his teeth until it hurt, then cleared his throat and let the phrases that had haunted him go free . . .

"It was a rhyme," he said. "A poem, or a prophecy maybe. But it went something like this:

" 'The setting sun grows dim . . .' "

As Marek listened, he felt the hackles slowly rising on the nape of his neck as they had not done in many a long day. The significance of the roses was clear now. All too clear. He wished only that this had not come in his time.

" '. . . Despair and death to all,' "

the Alban finished. He was shivering imperceptibly, as if he was very cold. "Marek, I read that only once, but the memory of it has been with me ever since. I don't know why—I never could remember poetry when I was young. Marek . . ." there was a note of pleading in his voice, "please, what does it *mean* . . . ?"

For the sake of the young *eijo*'s peace of mind, Marek truly did not want to tell him. To put off the inevitable he changed the subject slightly, knowing even as he did so that it would grant him a bare moment's grace. "It has been two nights from full moon," the Cernuan said somberly, as if the thought had just occurred to him. "Two nights since Sedna was . . ."

Aldric stared at the floor. "Eaten," he completed.

"Eaten," Marek echoed. "So although I have no idea of what this . . . thing looks like, I can guess what it *is*."

So could Aldric. His mind had leapfrogged Marek's along that particular unpleasant alleyway and reached the same conclusion before him. "It's hungry. And yet Geruath's soldiers are . . . He's bringing unarmoured men against it!" He hesitated, for the next step was so ugly that he was reluctant to voice it aloud. Then he did: "Or should that be . . . *for* it . . . ?"

*

When they caught up with the Overlord and his retainers, several troopers were beating at the end wall of the corridor while the rest stood back—well back—and watched. A blow rang hollow, the concentration of impact altered slightly and within a minute the outline of a doorway had been forced into the stones. As it moved jerkily backwards, Aldric nudged Marek and both men retired a judicious distance down the corridor. The Alban's right hand was inside his jerkin, gloved fingers tight around the spellband hidden there.

With shocking suddenness the door burst open and gulped three soldiers into the blackness beyond. Aldric's muscles spasmed and the sorcerous weapon sprang free, its spiral-patterned loops of silver and etched steel snug around his wrist and only the thin covering of buckskin preventing an eldritch glow of power from illuminating the corridor from end to end. Then the men reappeared, dusting themselves down and grinning sheepishly. Aldric relaxed, tucked his lethal handful out of sight and bared his teeth a fraction. It was not a smile.

"Why should we be looking here?" he asked the demon queller. "If this thing's a true dem— . . . thing, then it won't need tunnels. Will it?"

"It's become flesh of a sort. It must move as fleshly beings move."

"And can this flesh-of-a-sort be cut?"

"I doubt it."

"So. We'll see . . ."

Once through the hidden doorway, Aldric found himself in a passage. No doubt it was a sound piece of work, but its design gave him the shudders. Unlike some men, even Dewan ar Korentin whom nobody could call a coward, Aldric was quite comfortable below ground. After Gemmel's home far beneath the Blue Mountains, after the Lair of Ykraith and the Dunrath catacombs, he should have been well-used to the subterranean. But all of those places had been well-lit, or familiar, or vaulted and spacious.

This tunnel crouched around him, only an arm's length overhead at the very most. Its walls were neither vertical nor reassuringly pillared, but curved, and their metal supporting props curved with them—giving the whole place an unwholesome air of being halfway through some gross peristaltic closure. Over many years, outlines once hard and artificial had blended with red clay and pallid fungoid growths until the glistening passage resembled something organic. A colossal gullet. It was a fancy given sinister weight by the Alban's recently-voiced suspicions . . .

Geruath had moved his soldiers further down the tunnel and Marek had followed, leaving Aldric alone with his lamp and his imagination. One formed glutinous images just beyond the defined edges of the other's light, furtive half-seen movements that ceased just before his eyes could reach and focus on them. Moisture gathered on a squashy growth above him, then drooled with salivary stealth towards his face.

Aldric was not actually running when he caught up with the others. Not quite . . .

The tunnel had divided. After brief, muttered discussion between the Overlord and his son in which advice was neither asked nor offered, Geruath and Crisen went one way and a six-strong squad was despatched along the other fork. Aldric stayed with the Overlord; in sight or out of it, he distrusted Geruath and he intended keeping a close eye on Crisen. Besides, the Alban thought sourly, hating himself, wherever those two went was probably the safest route. Damn honour for the time being! He wondered if the same notion had prompted Marek, but on reconsideration doubted it. The Cernuan was that rare and often dangerous thing: a truly brave and dedicated man. Dedicated, however, to what . . . ? Duty? Honour? Principle? Or just—cynically—self-preservation like the rest . . .

*

The kneeling trooper gave his boot-straps a final tug, wriggled his toes inside the leather and straightened to find himself alone. His comrades had warned him that they would not wait, but he had thought that they were joking. Until now.

Another division in the passageway told him why the others had disappeared so quickly, and he opened his mouth to call them. Then shut it again for fear of what else might be listening. There were many rumours current in the barracks, all of them different—and all of them variations on a single nasty theme . . . But there were footprints in the russet muck which coated the runnel floor; they at least were more tangible than rumours.

After a moment's hesitation the soldier followed them. And the clinging velvet shadows swallowed him.

A bare ten paces further on he stopped, beginning to shiver with more than the dank cold. He was vulnerable; the whole situation reeked of it. His solitary walk had a horrid inevitability about it, like the fifteen steps from cell to scaffold he had watched other men and women take. It was as if he knew that if he walked on he would die . . . It was also the kind of cheap dramatic cliché that even Imperial playwrights no longer dared to use, the predictable offering-up of a character as a sacrifice on the altar of excitement . . . His vulnerability was like that: so grossly overstated that it was self-defeating. The shivers died away as he was warmed by the new assurance of his own reality: he was a man, he existed, he was not a puppet dancing when another hand tugged strings in a preordained pattern. And he was armed.

The soldier groped at his back for the slung crossbow, taking comfort from the cool weight of its iron-shod stock, and slid it around into the cradle of his left arm. The weapon had a spring-steel prod thicker than his thumb; it would project missiles to and through a target with appalling force. To and through any target, even armoured in proof metal. Any target at all . . .

There was something hanging from the ceiling just ahead of him and he froze in his tracks, all the old fears rushing back. Then breathed a sigh of relief as he played the yellow light of his lantern across its surface. Cave-in, he thought. A rock had slipped free of the all-embracing clay and its enormous weight had buckled the props around itself without being quite heavy enough to break through them and fall onto the ground. He sidestepped the massive boulder warily, staring at it; what he could see of the surface was rounded, smooth and glossy as enamel with the moisture filming it. A thing like that dropping on a man's head would end all his worries . . . The soldier breathed a soft oath and strode on, his curse becoming pale-grey fog as it whispered from his lips into the cold air of the tunnel.

Then he jerked to a halt with sweat popping out all over him. Something just out of his lantern's range had moved. "Bloody wet fungus!" he muttered. "Scared of a bloody reflection!" The words did not reassure him, and the hands which spanned and loaded the heavy crossbow were shaking as he lined the weapon on the lantern's crossbow were shaking as he lined the weapon on the lantern's pool of light.

Whether it was his imagination or a real movement, he saw it again and jerked the trigger. A bolt ripped sparks from stone and sang noisily down the tunnel's oozing throat—loudly enough to drown out any other more furtive movements.

The soldier turned and ran back the way he had come, not daring to reload or even look behind. Not wanting to know what might be at his heels . . .

The hanging boulder, he thought frantically. If he could make it fall, complete the cave-in, it might bring down enough rubble to block the passageway completely. Or make a barricade to hide behind. Or something . . .

As his lamplight swayed across the rock it seemed to move and shudder, but became comfortingly huge and stable when he stopped beside it. It would be big enough to shelter him easily if only he could knock it free. The man swung his crossbow like a hammer, felt the impact slamming up his arms and heard the wooden stock cracking in protest. Part of the weapon's mechanism gave way, but the boulder shifted slightly. Ever so slightly. He hit it again, then a final time with all his strength and jumped sideways out of its path.

Nothing happened.

His lantern showed him: the rock had merely settled a little against its metal props like someone shifting in bed. A trickle of fragments pattered against the ground, but stopped before more than a handful had fallen. The soldier cursed savagely, rage swamping his terror for an instant, and stepped forward with his makeshift bludgeon hefted in both hands.

It was then that he saw the fragments more closely and his gorge rose. They were soft, some pallid and others a rich, sticky crimson like things he might see on a butcher's slab. Except that these chunks of meat were far, far fresher than any butcher's cuts—so fresh and warm that they steamed slightly in the trembling light of his lamp. To recognise the rest of his squad—or what was left of them—had taken two beats of his frantically pumping heart. The wavering lantern slashed shadows and moist reflections from the curving, claustrophobic walls until at last its light reluctantly stroked the curves and angles of the boulder suspended at his shoulder.

Except that it was not a boulder, but something—some *thing*—that had been curled up asleep, or dormant, or . . . digesting . . . cradled in its own long limbs. And he had wakened it! Until then the illusions had been complete. "Shape-shifter," the soldier whimpered with useless understanding, and the creature dropped, falling not as a stone falls but like a cat, unfolding crooked joints and landing lightly for all its spiked and jagged bulk.

The air grew colder and frost formed on the soldier's helmet. That cold air stank of blood and death. Triple-taloned feet grated down through mud on to the stone beneath as Ythek Shri took a single precise, raking step forward. It gurgled softly: a thick, indescribable sound. The soldier's lamp fell with a clatter and in that distorted light the demon's bulk loomed larger still as it leaned gracefully down, head opening like a grotesque blossom in a fanged, horrific yawn . . .

*

Aldric was not the only one to hear it: a low cry more of disbelief than anything else, which reverberated hollowly along the tunnels and faded into disturbing echoes before anyone could do more than guess at its source. But he was the only one apart from Marek to be absolutely sure about its cause, and despite his privately held sardonic view he was the only one at all to make a move towards it.

He had taken barely six jog-trotting strides down the passageway before a shriek of pure animal terror cut through the darkness before him, trailing away to silence like the wavering wolf-song which had mourned at Evthan's funeral. Again the wail throbbed in his ears, more piercing now, impossibly high for any masculine throat—a sound that was fear and agony given voice.

It stopped incomplete with a shocking abruptness and

the Alban began to run. Even though there was the stone of Echainon to explain his foolhardy confidence, he was still gripping Widowmaker when he slithered to a halt, his flaring nostrils filled with a warm slaughterous reek and the incongruous faint scent of roses . . . Pivoting slowly on one heel, he swept the lowering tunnel with lamp and eyes, *taiken* poised to strike at anything that moved. There was nothing but the distant firefly dance of approaching torches. Nothing living.

Aldric braced himself, then turned the light and his accompanying gaze downward to the slimed and stinking floor.

Marek had done well for a fat old man, outrunning all but the few troopers who fidgeted nervously in the background. They were staring at Aldric, who was staring in his turn apparently at nothing. His face was pallid, its skin drawn taut over tightly clamped jaws, and when Marek met his shock-dark agate eyes the demon queller quickly looked away from the horror there. Instead, and most unwisely he glanced down.

"Oh, merciful . . ." he faltered, knowing even as he said it that there had been no mercy here. Marek felt sick—he who was supposedly inured to horrors—because what he was looking at confirmed everything. Even the rose perfume merely underlined it . . . Issaqua. The Bale Flower. But where? And when . . . ?

When Geruath strode up, regardless of the armed retainers flanking him Marek seized the Overlord by one elbow and dragged him towards the pulped obscenity sprawling at their feet. "That, my lord," he hissed in a voice which dripped contempt, "is what your demon does. Will I destroy it—or do you still want it controlled? Well . . . my lord?"

Geruath licked his lips, merely an unconscious aid to thought but in the circumstances hideously inappropriate. Then he shrugged, apparently undisturbed by the atrocity, and even smiled. Staring at him, Aldric's own lips stretched in a snarl of hatred. All the Talvalins hated well, but the last clan-lord of all had had a deal of practice at it. Though he knew that the Overlord's son could see him plainly—and the expression on his face could have been read by a half-blind man—Aldric was past

caring. Past diplomacy, past dissembling; something would
have to die for this. Then he fought down his revulsion
sufficiently to bend over the corpse's shattered head and
very gently close what remained of its eyes.

"I am," he said, straightening up, "going to arm myself. Properly. Then I shall obliterate this demon." Isileth Widowmaker poised significantly at her scabbard's
mouth while he swept them all with a cold glare. "And
anyone—anyone at all—who tries to hinder me . . ."
The blade hissed slowly out of sight.

"What about . . . ?" Crisen nodded towards the
remains.

"Someone give me a helmet," Aldric demanded, ignoring the question. "Now leave me alone." It was not
a request, it certainly was not polite—but it was obeyed
at once by all, even Marek. Only when the others had
gone did Aldric draw out the spellstone. He knew that
this was wrong; he had seen one long-buried body in the
ancient mound, had watched another lowered into the
earth. Jouvaines put their dead into the dirt . . . But
enough foulness had been visited on this poor man already, and Aldric at least had the power to make his
funeral clean.

When he removed its buckskin covering there was no
billowing of blue fire—only a soft shimmer like a luminescent fog, that cast no light, drove back no shadows
and yet was somehow comforting. There was no dishonour and no impropriety in its use. Not for this purpose.
"Abath arhan." The invocation was a whimper, like
prayer and the Echainon stone responded. Pale translucent tongues of lapis lazuli licked at the Alban's hand,
warmed by pity and compassion as once it had blazed
with the white heat of hate. The spellstone's powers
were his now, pulsing with the blood-flow in his veins,
concentrated by the wishes of his mind.

A vast and stooping shape oozed in ponderous silence
from the shadows at his back, and a crooked three-
clawed talon reached smoothly out . . .

"Alh'noen ecchaur i aiyya," Aldric murmured, and all
was sudden brilliance as a clean hot flame poured from
the crystal's heart: engulfing, consuming, purifying in a
single instant. Had the Alban glanced behind him then

he would have seen the demon clearly, revealed by the incandescence of his own making. But he saw nothing, and heard nothing as it fled with long heron-strides back into the friendly darkness.

Aldric knelt, feeling the expected weariness flood over him as he moved, but knowing at the same time that it was less than before. The Echainon stone had taken his emotion, not his energy, and that emotion by its very nature had been directed outward and not in. *"An-diu k'noeth-ei,"* he said, and traced the blessing of farewell above the still-warm ashes on the tunnel floor. Gathering them together—just dust and ashes now, without a trace of moisture—he poured them respectfully into the helmet and inclined his head a little. The spellstone's fires had died to a slow sapphire writhing in the centre of the crystal, and setting the helmet carefully aside he made to take the talisman from his wrist . . . and then hesitated, glancing sharply down the passage in response to a faint tingling in his brain. The sensation was so faint that it was scarcely there at all, and yet . . .

Aldric left the stone where it was, hidden by a glove. That was more comfortable—and more comforting.

*

Back among the Overlord's retainers, Aldric sought out one man and gave him the ash-filled helmet. Taking the makeshift urn with infinite gentleness, the soldier saluted with his free hand and spoke rapidly in that dialect which the Alban had heard so frequently here, but still could not understand.

"He thanks you," Marek Endain translated. "For the way you acted towards one who was a lord's-man and a stranger."

Aldric bowed in response, his face sombre. "Thank him for his courtesy," he said, "and apologise that I do not do so myself." Marek did as he was asked, and as he turned back caught a certain look in Aldric's eye; an instant later he had caught the man's arm for fear that look foreshadowed violence.

Aldric tore his baleful stare—the stare of a cat at an out-of-reach mouse—from the Overlord and his son and glanced instead at Marek, guessing the demon queller's concern. His slow, mirthless grin was cruel in the lamplight as he peeled the other's fingers from his sleeve. "No," he said softly. "Not yet. Not in the midst of their retainers. But soon. I don't have to look for any more reasons . . ."

He had enough and more than enough. And they were no longer the intangibles of a king's command, or a promise made in bed to a faithless woman. They were the same dark, personal justifications which had brought fire and death into the fortress of Dunrath. Revenge for self, revenge for the dead, hatred, loathing, and a knowledge that some men were born to die. Just as he was born to kill them. All he needed now was opportunity . . .

Once through the secret doorway, Aldric waited until two soldiers heaved it shut, then as they left he uncoiled like a sleek black cat from the corner where he had crouched on heels, watching. His lantern was in one hand, the gloved sword-hand, but in the other and almost growing from its surface was a closely fitting thing of steel and silver.

Marek looked at it and then at Aldric's face, unable to decide which he disliked more: the glinting object or the cool familiarity with which the Alban handled it . . .

"Do you realise," Aldric murmured confidentially, "that this door was open?" His voice dropped to hiss of barely-audible impatient menace. "And that the demon— which I will not ask you about again, save once—could have been in front of us . . . ?"

Shadows piled thickly beyond the pool of lamplight and Marek realised with a shiver just how exposed were the cellars after the low, snug tunnels. And even then the monstrosity had killed one man and evaded all the others . . ."

Aldric looked at the Cernuan with grim wisdom in his eyes, knowing the demon queller's thoughts because they so closely matched his own. He took a glove from where it had been tucked into his belt and worked the thin leather on to his left hand until the spellband was hidden once more, then looked around him.

"Though I have seen nothing," he conceded without any comfort. "Yet . . ."

9

Song of Desolation

"**I** regret to say," Lord Geruath muttered half to himself, "that the warlock is correct. This abomination *must* be destroyed . . ." His son watched him stride about, but prudently said nothing. They were alone in the Overlord's private chambers, and Crisen had just watched his father raise a flask of fortified wine and drain it without perceptible effect; even the tremor in Geruath's voice came only from leashed-in fury.

"But surely you must have guessed?" Crisen ventured at last.

"I do not guess!" his father snapped. "Least of all where your convoluted plotting is concerned." Crisen shot a glance from the corner of one eye and felt his stomach lurch. "Oh yes, dear boy. I know all about your plans for Seghar. A city-state independent of all allegiances, was it not . . . ? We must discuss the matter at some time."

"But you know . . ." Crisen burst out, catching himself just in time.

"Nothing?" the Overlord finished, raising his eyebrows. "On the contrary, my secretive son, I know everything. Give me results that I can see, that I can touch, that I can profit by—and I promise you no questions will be asked about how you achieved them. But fail and I will not lift a hand, not a finger to save either you or that reptile you call friend."

"You're mad . . ." It was not an explosive protest but a disbelieving little whimper as the preconceptions of years were overturned. "You *are* . . . Everybody knows it . . ."

Geruath's chuckle was soft, urbane and very sane indeed. "*Lordly* is the current euphemism," he said. "You will learn, Crisen, you will learn. Indeed, you above all should know that things may be other than they appear. Mm?"

"Why, father? In the name of the Fire, why?"

"Your lamented mother did not ask such foolish questions. She accepted that what I did was right—and accepted, too, the profitable proof that it was so. One of the wisest things a man can do is to appear a fool. Fools are not trusted, but neither are they *dis*trusted. They are ignored as harmless. They are tolerated. They are humoured in ways a clever man can never hope to match."

Geruath took another and more controlled sip of wine, then hunted about until he found a cup to drink from. "We could have been in this citadel ten years ago," he said as he played with the silver goblet, turning it over and over in his hands. "Your mother at least could have died an Overlord's lady. But she understood my caution—because your dreams of independence are also mine!"

Crisen started at the revelation. Voord had suggested it to him a year ago, and now it seemed their plan had been pre-empted by a decade—unless Voord had found out about it in Drakkesborg . . . His brain began to spin and a headache started pounding in his temples.

". . . somewhere out of the way," his father was saying softly, almost as if the words were meant for his own ears. "Somewhere to put the crazy man and his whelp where it can seem like a reward for service—but where his ravings and chasings after swords cannot do us any harm . . . Yes . . . and then the Albans cultivated me and I accepted them, and nobody was any the wiser that for once in my life I had enough gold. But listen to the wise words of a madman, Crisen: if your fellow-conspirator, confidant, friend Lord-Commander Voord thinks he can do this without you, then you'll follow the Vreijek girl down something's throat."

"The girl . . . ?"

"It may be wise to play the fool, my son—but this is not the time to start! Of course, the girl! You were besotted with her—"

"I *loved* her, father . . . !"

Geruath ignored him. "Were besotted with her and it affected your efficiency. The Drusalans are most insistent on efficiency . . . so Voord killed her, and so that it would seem an accident he used sorcery. Used the books you bought for Sedna to have her torn apart."

"How—what makes you so sure?"

"Because I have eyes, and I have wits, and I can use them both! You saw, in the library, and yet you chose not to see . . . And now, to vindicate yourself in the eyes of your Imperial friend, to prove that what he thought of you was wrong, you intend to use this obscenity again. And you claim that you loved her . . .

"Voord left with unusual haste, did he not? Without farewells . . . because either he knows exactly what he summoned up—or he does not know and is afraid of finding out. But it is certainly beyond your small capabilities, Crisen my son. This thing is no wolf . . ."

"But—but why not use this opportunity anyway, father? Listen to me! The empire is tearing itself apart; Ioen and Etzel are so busy trying to avoid an outright war that nobody will notice an ambitious man using the chaos to further his own ends. Especially you—you have made no secret of your detestation of sorcery, so who would suspect you of all people as the man who controls a demon—"

"They would be more likely to suspect *you!*"

The criticism did not halt Crisen's flow of words even for an instant. "Kill three other Overlords along the frontier . . ."—he suggested half a dozen in as many breaths—". . . then wait a while before you move, as you did with Seghar, and you would be not a usurper but the man who saved their domains from anarchy. And with the revenue from your new lands it would be easy to bribe someone in Drakkesborg to confirm possession. It's simple—and it would convince the Albans that their money isn't being wasted . . ."

"No! I should never have listened to you in the first place. And when I saw what had been done to Duar, my stomach almost shamed me before the two *hlensyarlen.*"

"You were not so squeamish about Erwan Evenou, ten years past. People always die to further great schemes, father, so why worry needlessly? This demon is no more deadly than a good sharp—*what was that?*" Crisen's head snapped round sharply and cocked on one side to catch the faint sound which had attracted his attention; but to no avail. Frowning, hand on sword-hilt, he walked softly to the chamber door and paused there an instant before reaching out to snatch it open. There was nothing outside save an empty corridor.

"What is the matter with you?" his father demanded.

Crisen looked uncertainly over his shoulder towards the door, then shrugged, and rubbed fingertips to forehead. "Nothing . . . I think."

"And if it was something, what would you think?"

"Music . . . One note."

"A bell? A gong? A flute . . . ?"

"A voice. Many voices . . . Nothing. It must have been inside my head."

"That's an overly elaborate description of what you dismiss as nothing . . ." Geruath's voice was subtly different now and a sneer of contempt underlay what might have been mere bantering. "Forget it! And forget your plans for Seghar—at least, *these* plans. They give our opponents too much leverage—and without support to offset that leverage, either Ioen or Etzel may well spare time from their own squabbles to snuff us out."

"But the demon could—"

"I said, forget it. If I am dealing with Rynert of Alba, then I must have some honour left me . . ."

"Honour is a word that weaklings hide behind—" The words came out without thought and Crisen bit his tongue too late.

Lord Geruath raised flaming eyes towards his son's face, then smashed the back of his hand across that face with all his strength, spinning back the younger man against the wall.

"Never speak to me like that again!" his father hissed. "*Never . . . !* You will rule here only after I am dead— but I assure you that my health is excellent, my son. Remember that: *I* am Overlord of Seghar! I should have known you had no honour in you when you broke into the Kings-mound—"

"You were scarcely backward in plundering it of weapons!"

"Yet I did not enter like a thief!"

"No . . . you just stood by and let me do that for you."

"And why did your friend Voord go creeping to it in the dead of night, eh? Answer me that!"

Crisen shook his pounding head and knuckled, wincing, at the bruises along his jaw. The old man was talking nonsense now, because Voord had never gone near the opened tomb . . .

"Why did he decide to clean it, eh?" the Overlord persisted. "Why . . . ? You haven't got an answer to that, have you?"

"*Eldheisart* Voord did not—"

"He *did!*" Geruath lashed out again and Crisen flinched to avoid the bony knuckles. They missed—but instead a gemstone-heavy ring struck home and split his lower lip wide open . . . "I know—because I had him watched," the Overlord snarled, heedless of what he had just done despite the shreds of his own son's flesh clinging to the jewel on his hand. "He sent a file of my best mercenaries there on some cursed errand—and not a man of them came back! Sorcery, may the Father of Fires burn him black! Eternal shame on the House Segharlin, that my son calls him friend . . ."

Geruath's face was white with fury now, the rouge on his cheekbones a blazing contrast to the ivory skin beneath it, and the saliva clinging to his teeth was growing frothy with the frenzied movements of his mouth. "Get out of my sight!" he shrieked. "Get out and take your filthy plots away with you! I order that the demon is to be destroyed and I will be obeyed! Then . . . then I shall attend to that insolent Alban bastard . . ." His voice dropped to a slavering whisper that was thick with anticipated atrocities. "Have it done. No . . . you do it. *Now!*"

Blood dribbled from Crisen's slack-lipped mouth and dripped unheeded from his chin as he gaped in shock and hate and horror at the mowing, screeching thing which was his father. Geruath had played the madman's part so well and for so long that role and reason and reality had jumbled past the point of separation . . . Collecting his scattered wits, Crisen came to a decision and left the room without a word. Or any indication of respect.

*

The lord's-men were long gone; and with their departure a great stillness filled the dark cellars of the citadel of Seghar. It remained unbroken until at last Marek moved to follow the vanished soldiers.

"Where are you going?" Aldric Talvalin's voice was very quiet, barely carrying to the demon queller's ears, but something about its tone stopped Marek in his tracks.

"Out of here," he said without turning round.

"Away from here," the Alban corrected him, "but not out. Not until you've told me what the hell is going on."

Marek swung his head a little, just enough to see Aldric's face out of the corner of one eye. "Not in this—"

"Yes, in this place. Because there was a man killed in this place: a man who might be alive still if you were not so evasive . . . Or were you simply curious to see what the demon was capable of doing . . . ? Did you sacrifice a life to emphasise your point to Geruath . . . ? Was that the reason, Marek?"

"No!" Outraged by such suggestions, the demon queller twisted to face his accuser. He had expected to see anger, a trace of contempt perhaps; instead he saw only sadness.

"So you say. I hope it's the truth. I wish I could believe it."

"It *is* the truth."

"So. You wanted inside Sedna's library, did you not? Where is it?"

"L-library . . . ?" Marek stammered in surprise. "But I told you: they won't let me see it! The place is locked and guarded—"

"So you've seen the door at least. Good! Lead the way."

"We can't get in!"

Aldric glanced at him and smiled, a contraction of muscles that drew his lips taut for an instant. "Marek Endain, you are a wise, wise man—but still you have much to learn. Especially about me. Walk on; you can tell me about demons as you go . . ."

"But what about the Overlord?"

"What about the Overlord?" Aldric repeated in a flat

voice. Marek looked, and listened, and shrugged expressively. What indeed?

"I know—augmented by guesswork—what has happened here," he began, and flushed angrily as Aldric struck his hands together in soft, ironic applause. "If you're going to—" the Cernuan snapped, then shook his head. "Why bother? You are . . . what Dewan ar Korentin told me to expect. And you are not are not a religious man." Although it was not a question, it seemed to require some kind of answer.

"I respect the Light of Heaven," Aldric said cautiously. "Of course. But I doubt that you could call me holy."

"I greatly doubt it. But you have an education second to none."

The Alban grimaced at that compliment—if such it was—for some of the subjects of his education had caused him to be sent here in the first place. What had Rynert said . . . ? *You are a wizard's fosterling my lord, and his over-apt pupil. You have no compunction about use of the Art Magic . . . You must prove you are a man bound by the Honour-Codes if you are to be trusted . . . The task I set you now will make plain that you are worthy of the title* ilauem-arluth Talvalin *. . ."* Task. A small, neat word for what the king required. *Murder* was more accurate. Murder in cold blood . . . He had killed before, but never like that, and Aldric doubted he could do it even to Crisen Geruath. "I am not an executioner . . ." he muttered, repeating the old litany, then realised that Marek was staring at him.

"I thought," said Marek the demon queller with over-heavy dignity, "you wanted me to tell you what I know of demons . . . ?"

"I do."

"Then grant me the small courtesy of listening . . . !"

Aldric was not in the mood for an argument. "About my education . . . ?" he prompted gently.

"Yes," said Marek, slightly mollified that at least some of his words had been heard. "Then you should know that the gods of one religion are usually the demons of the next. It is their first step down the road from faith through myth into oblivion. When men ceased worship-

ping them, the old gods who were before God"—
Aldric's head jerked round an inch at that, unsettled to
hear dead Evthan's words repeated by someone who had
never heard them—"were cast down, and their shrines
decayed. It is easier by far to call on demons than on
gods: the one hears constant prayer, the other must be
grateful for any small attention to stave off descent into
the forgotten dark. But for all that, they have no love
for the men whose ancestors put them aside in favour
of another. It is common even for ordinary mortals to
brood over a rejection, so how much more—"

"Are you making game of me?" The lethal iciness in
Aldric's voice was like nothing Marek had ever heard
before; it was plainly not provoked by memories of the
Jouvaine girl Gueynor, for what had happened there had
merely made the Alban harsh and irritable. Whereas he
sounded deadly now. Almost too late, Marek recalled
the name of Tehal Kyrin; he had been warned both by
Gemmel Errekren and by ar Korentin to avoid that subject at all costs. And now for the sake of effect, he had
come so close . . .

"The page you found," Marek continued hastily, "was
a warning—"

"As is this: never, ever play with my past again." The
black-clad Alban laid one hand to his longsword's hilt,
but Marek could see that it was not meant as a threat;
more an instinctive reaching-out for something familiar,
for something—if the word could be applied to a
taiken—comforting. "So what did it warn against?"

There was a moment's hesitation while Marek set his
shock-jumbled thoughts in order. He had thought he
knew Aldric now—although the young *eijo* was still full
of disturbing surprises—and thought too that such
knowledge might make his companion easier to understand and less dangerous. It worried him to discover just
how wrong he had been . . .

"It is a chant—a song without music—which has been
a part of demon-lore for centuries. Issaqua"—Marek
blessed himself carefully—"was—is—one of the discarded
gods. The Ancient Ones. He was once Joybringer, Sum-
merlight, a bright being of flowers and growing
things . . ."

"Flowers . . . ?" echoed Aldric, and though there was only cool dryness in the air of the corridor, a faint thread of rose-scented perfume seemed to touch his face with the gossamer lightness of early morning cobweb.

"Issaqua the Bale Flower, Dweller in Shadow, He who sings the Song of Desolation; there are many formal epithets describing him. Or it." He thought a moment. "Or Him, or It," he amended his pronunciation slightly. "Deity or demon, such things must be respected—if only for safety's sake."

"The Song of Desolation . . . *I know that I am lost* . . . so it was Issaqua who tore apart the soldier . . . ?"

"Have you not realised, even now, that you found a single corpse—and yet six men went down that tunnel! Understand me, Aldric—and being what you are, you should take my meaning more readily than any other man in this citadel—Issaqua is a demon lord. He will not answer a direct summons any more than a clan-lord would. The entity which did the killing is an intermediary, a herald, one of those demons with the power to pass beyond the Void with messages of reverence and worship. And with invitations to the Ancient. Half a dozen soldiers died to prove that accepting such an invitation is worthwhile."

"Bait!" spat Aldric in disgust.

"Appetisers," Marek amended bleakly. "A foretaste of the banquet to come."

Aldric's mind veered from the images conjured by those words. "What *is* this herald?" he demanded. "What does it look like . . . ?"

"I don't know."

"You don't . . . !"

"I don't—but get me inside Sedna's library and I might be able—"

"Quiet . . . !" Aldric had snapped to a halt between one step and the next, his head tilting fractionally backwards and his eyes narrowed with concentration. The Cernuan knew a listening posture when he saw it and mouthed *what can you hear?* with sufficient clarity for the Alban to read each word as it was shaped. Then Marek no longer required an answer: instead he heard it too . . .

The sound was almost inaudible: a high, sweet purity in the upper register and a rolling bass sonority in the lower, but both sounds beyond the limits of human hearing. Yet they harmonised, as the howling of wolves will harmonise in still winter dusk across a field of virgin snow, and it was that choral harmony which sent a tingling shudder through every fibre of Aldric's body: not fear, not cold, but a feeling of exaltation that was almost sexual in its intensity. The sensation faded with the note which had brought it into being, dwindling to a caressing vibrato and thence to a forlorn and yearning silence.

Aldric drew in a tremulous breath and wondered if Evthan the wolf had felt so when he threw back his head and wailed into a full-moon-lit sky. He turned to see if Marek felt as he did . . .

The demon queller looked as if he felt sick.

That look washed Aldric's reeling euphoria clear away on a rip-tide of ice-water, and there was no real need for either man to speak. It was Marek who finally said it: *"Issaqua sings the song of desolation . . ."* he quoted softly.

"And fills the world with Darkness . . ." Aldric finished. Then: "Where's the library?"

But Marek was already running.

*

There was one soldier on guard outside the library door, armed with the inevitable gisarm, and he stiffened apprehensively when the two *hlensyarlen* approached him along the gallery. Their smiles did nothing to reassure him, for both men were breathing hard as if they had stopped a headlong dash just out of his sight and the smiles clashed with ill-disguised concern on both their faces. In any case, he was not disposed to be friendly towards anyone right now—his head ached, his relief had not arrived to take over and he was hungry. There was consequently little courtesy in the way he brought the heavy polearm round and down to guard position, and even less in his rasp of: "What do you want?"

Aldric responded in kind; the smile left his face and he jerked one arm toward the door. "We want into that room!" he snapped in Drusalan.

"That's forbidden!" The gisarm's point levelled at Aldric's chest. "By the Overlord's command!"

"But it's by the Overlord's command that we go inside," Marek protested smoothly, lying not in hope of success but to attract the man's attention.

"Where's your confirmation?" The weapon was wavering a little now, its bearer undecided upon whom to concentrate.

"I think you have it," Aldric said to Marek across the guardman's front, and directly the man's eyes shifted to see what the Cernuan's reply might be, he took one step forward and another sideways. Instantly the gisarm's blade snapped out towards him. "Haven't you . . . ?"

"No—I thought you had it." Marek copied the two steps—which had brought them closer to the sentry while at the same time widening the field of view he had to cover—then thrust his right hand inside his robe as a man will when reaching for a hidden dagger. The spearhead jerked round to counter this potential threat. "For a minute there . . ." the hand withdrew, empty, fingers spread. "No. You must have it."

Aldric's left forearm warded the gisarm's haft as it slashed back—far too late, for he was already within the blade's arc—and his right hand was moving too, a lazy sweep across the soldier's midriff that would have been insignificant had the hand not held a knife . . . The guard dropped his own weapon, jerked, began to double over—

—And was slammed back to the vertical against the wall as Aldric held the knife—a small but wickedly sharp affair that seemed almost a part of the Alban's fist—under his nose and prodded persuasively upwards. "Confirmation," Aldric explained. "Not the Overlord's, but mine. Effective all the same. Now, you have a choice: either you open the door or I open your belly." The knife withdrew its bloodied point from the sentry's upper lip, dropped and slotted back into the long clean cut which had laid his crest-coat open from one hip to the other. It felt icy cold against his so-far-unbroken skin, and the man flinched back as far as the wall would allow. Which was not far enough, for the knife followed.

"Have you ever," Aldric asked conversationally, "seen a man stabbed in the stomach?"

Whether the young *eijo* was bluffing, or whether he would have carried out his softly-spoken threat, Marek was not to discover. With a hand that trembled visibly— silent confirmation that he had indeed witnessed the grisly consequence of deep gut-wounds—the trooper withdrew a heavy, complicated key from the pouch at his belt. "Wise man," said the demon queller with an uncertain sidelong glance at Aldric. The key fitted and turned in silence, and the door swung back to reveal the darkness of the unlit room beyond. In the instant of his passage across the threshold there was a meaty impact and he whirled with horror clouding his face.

The soldier was sagging in Aldric's arms, but there was blood neither on the floor, his clothes nor the knife. Only a flaring scarlet blot the size of a silver mark beneath his left ear where the Alban had driven an extended-knuckle punch into a nervespot. With a knife, or an arrow, or a sword, that spot meant death; bare-handed it brought unconsciousness and later probably a splitting headache.

This is the one they call Deathbringer . . . ? Marek thought incredulously. He was certainly behaving out of character . . . Then Aldric dropped the loose-limbed body inside the library and back-heeled the door shut behind him.

*

"Do you really want to see him again?" asked Jervan quietly. "It will only bring you more grief."

"It was my fault, Commander," Gueynor insisted. "I was in the wrong, and I gave him no chance to hear explanations. I tried too much to play the lady; and I have been a peasant these ten years past . . . !"

The two sat on opposite sides of a table in the Garrison Commander's quarters; Jervan had insisted on it after Kourgath's—literally—stormy departure from the summer-house in the ruined gardens. He had felt, but successfully concealed, a pang of jealousy at the way Gueynor had stared after the young mercenary, then had reminded himself with some severity of his wife and

daughters, both the latter being not much younger than
this Jouvaine girl. His interest was material, political—
not, under any circumstances, physical. There was too
much to lose . . .

"In any event, it doesn't matter whether you remain
on friendly terms with this *hlensyarl* or not. What he
intends to do will be not because you want it—but because he wants it. All you need to be is close enough to
take the first advantage of it."

"Like a buzzard—waiting for death."

"If you like." Jervan refused to be ruffled by Gueynor's melancholy. "Everyone who stands to inherit fits
that description, whether they are eager or not. And you
should be very eager, lady. Crisen Geruath owes you
many lives."

"Not me. My uncle. And through him, the Alban.
Kortagor," she raised the blonde head from which Jervan had persuaded her to wash the dye, "I want to leave
Seghar. I want to go home again. I don't want to be
a lady . . ."

That did ruffle the commander, where nothing else
had done. "No! . . ." His hand thumped the table-top
as he half-rose from his chair, then smiled weakly and
subsided again. *Softly, you fool . . . !* "I mean, why not
wait a while and see what happens?"

"Are you afraid of losing privileges that you haven't
yet received, *Kortagor* Jervan?" Gueynor murmured.
There was no scorn in her voice, none of the mockery
which his overreaction justified. Just regret. "If that's so,
then I'm sorry." She seemed to mean it, but sincerity
meant nothing to Jervan at this moment.

"Damn your sorrow," he hissed in a voice so low that
Gueynor barely heard it. "You, my lady," and the title
was a sneer now, "are my means of gaining some
respect—for myself, for my position here, for my family.
And I will not stand to one side and watch while your
overdeveloped integrity robs me of it . . ."

Jervan paused, pushing the heels of one hand into
an eye-socket as if that pressure would relieve the
pounding headache which had filled his skull with pain
within the past ten minutes. He could almost hear the
blood pounding in his temples, and the faint high noise

of the headache ringing deep inside his ears like the cry of innumerable bats. "Understand this: I will not harm you—but neither will I let you go. Not until *I* choose."

As he spoke Jervan backed slowly from the table to the door, withdrawing its key from his tunic pocket. There was only one window to this room, the outermost of his tower apartments, and it opened on an eighty-five-foot drop to the fortress courtyard. "Don't try to get out," he said unnecessarily. "You will be kept quite comfortable, I assure you . . ."

Sidestepping through the door, Jervan snatched it shut behind him as if he feared the slender girl would leap at his throat. Memories, maybe, of her uncle Evthan . . . As he twisted the key and heard the deadbolt shoot across, he also heard her shouting something at him; but the sense was muffled by two thick layers of oak planks set cross-grained to foil assault by axe. Otherwise her words might have interested him considerably.

"When he hears about this, Aldric Talvalin will *kill* you . . . !"

*

Killing was very far from Aldric's mind as he knelt motionless on the balcony outside his room and watched the round, untroubled moon through half-closed eyes. The haunting, gentle music of a rebec drifted through the darkness. Its thin, protracted chords assisted his near-trance and helped him not to think at all.

His battle armour was laid out before him, neat in its proper array, and a thousand tiny moons reflected from the surfaces of helm and war-mask, from mailed and plated sleeves and from the myriad scales of his lamellar cuirass. Except for the Talvalin blue-and-white of silken lacing cords, everything was lacquered to a hard and brilliant black which exuded a faint air of menace even in repose. With the scabbarded length of Isileth Widow-maker resting on his thighs, so did Aldric . . .

He could still hear the demon queller's voice quite clearly, harsh and distinct in a mind rinsed clean by meditation: "Whatever fool performed this summoning is fortunate to be alive . . . !"

*

Marek had snarled the words as he pointed to a chalk-drawn circle on the library floor. There were things within its perimeter that he had no desire to touch, but he approached and knelt and studied them with an air of rising disbelief. A broken flint blade either newly made or a survivor from the Ancient days; spatterings of dried brown blood; and a book. "That is," the Cernuan corrected himself, "if he *is* alive. To be so inadequately prepared, to make a blood-offering in the old way with stone—and then to use this . . ."

He opened his *cymar* at the neck and pulled out a medallion which he wore on a fine chain. It glittered as it turned slowly back and forth, level with his heart. Marek gripped the little metal disc between the finger and thumb of his right hand, then swept his left arm down and across between himself and the book. "I bind you, I secure you, I restrain you," he muttered. "I hold you close with chains of power, I pen you in with bars of force. I am the master of all that you contain. Hear me and obey."

"You are giving orders to a *book?*" Aldric was mildly incredulous, but too wise and far too experienced for blatant disbelief. He stalked warily towards the kneeling Cernuan, placing his feet with care in the uncertain light of the solitary lamp which was all that Marek had risked lighting.

The demon queller glanced up at him. "Your foster-father would do just as I have done," he said, reaching out to lift the heavy volume. "The stories claim that this grimoire can choose what is and is not conjured through it. And I tend to believe everything I hear concerning *Enciervanul Doamnisoar* . . ."

"Avert!" Aldric whispered, touching his mouth and forehead. He knew the name, as Marek plainly suspected: He had heard it spoken in another time, in another place, by another voice. Gemmel-*altrou* Errekren had mentioned this vile text, just once and briefly; the enchanter had blessed himself as ordinary men did when he pronounced its title. *On the Summoning of Demons*— he had called it captured evil; malice trapped within the written word and wrapped in woman's leather . . .

"No man in his right mind would use this foulness

simply to do murder, and not even a madman would overlook Dismissal. But the man who made this pattern has done both. He knew what it was he did, but not whose will he did . . .

"This fortress is pervaded by the influences of Issaqua: cruelties, hatreds, fear and madness. Even you have felt it. Twice you almost killed me. That is the Bale Flower's work: a time for wolves, a time for ravens, when friend turns on friend and the father hates his son . . ."

A time for wolves . . . ? Did Evthan kill his wife and daughter after all? Aldric's mind flinched from the thought. And King Rynert sent me into this potential holocaust to do more killing . . . How much did *he* know?

Marek took in the chalked, bloodied floor with a single weary sweep of his arm. "This place is the focus of the conjuration. It drew down the Warden of Gateways and permitted It to enter. And then the Warden called upon its own Master, Issaqua . . . To fill the world with Darkness. And only we can stop it!"

This was what Aldric had been expecting with a kind of horrid anticipation. He did not protest, did not make excuses about his other duties. All that was past. "The Warden of Gateways?" he wondered aloud in a voice which to his own surprise was free of tremor.

"Ythek'ter auythyu an-shri," Marek said. "The Devourer in the Dark."

*

Ythek Shri . . . Five days ago, he would have laughed. The Devourer was a childhood bogy, the sort of harmless horror that lurked in the shadows cast by bedroom furniture or hid behind sleep-heavy eyelids. It was a dream. A nightmare . . . But too many nightmares had become reality for Aldric Talvalin. He no longer laughed. Perhaps . . . Perhaps that too was a form of madness: to know that one's most secret terrors walked beyond the light and waited patiently for evening.

The melancholy whining of the rebec faltered into silence as something moved. Behind him. In the dark . . .

"Is the demon queller with you?" asked Crisen Geruath.

It was several seconds before Aldric's heart slid back

from his throat and down to his chest where it belonged, and several more before he trusted himself to speak. "He is not." The reply was calm, controlled, remote as if the mind behind the voice was far away; as if he was still deep in meditation. His brain was jangling with alarm both from the fright he had received and from an ominous sense of warning, but only a slight movement of one hand which loosened Widowmaker in her scabbard betrayed that he was aware of anything at all.

With a snap of his fingers to dismiss the musician—who scuttled gratefully from the room as if he too felt something wrong—Crisen sat down on the balcony and tried again. "Will he come here later?"

"I doubt it." As he spoke Aldric's hooded eyes opened, staring at the Overlord's son. Their pupils had expanded hugely in the dim light of moon and stars until mere outlines of greenish iris remained around a dark, infinite depth; and they regarded Crisen with a predatory consideration which would have made him nervous even had his purpose been completely innocent. He shivered violently and began to sweat.

"What do you want?" The Alban's tone was flat and disinterested; when no answer was forthcoming he yawned with the luxurious, studied insolence of a cat. "Then send the player back as you go out." His eyelids drooped once more, declaring the brief conversation to be at an end. It was not.

"Would you kill a man?"

Aldric's black-gloved sword-hand flexed and his eyes snapped wide open. "Who—and why?"

"A-a man whose death would benefit—"

"I want a name and a reason, my Lord Crisen Geruath Segharlin." Although his voice was deceptively gentle Crisen caught his breath at the venom in it. He glanced towards the door as though seized by second thoughts; then back at Aldric as his own words tumbled over one another in their breathless haste to leave his mouth.

"And I want you to kill my father for me . . ." There was a pause while one might count three. "Because I hate him—and I want to see him dead!"

A time for wolves . . . said Aldric's memory. Mastering

his facial muscles with an effort, he set Widowmaker carefully aside and got to his feet, walking indoors with no sound but the faint creak of his arming-leathers. "There is the door." The leathers creaked again as he pointed. "I suggest you leave."

"What?"

"Get out!"

"But you are *eijo*," Crisen protested to his disapproving back. "I saw the way you looked at him. You will kill—"

"I am *eijo*," conceded Aldric flatly. "Not a murderer. I am—" He hesitated, knowing the irrevocable weight of what he was about to say. "I am no man's hired assassin."

And with those words he knew once and for all that everything had been in vain. All the striving and suffering, the blood and fire and pain; all the deaths that could be made worthwhile by one more death—and that so very well-deserved—were wasted by his admission. From where he stood Aldric could see the pulse of life in Crisen's neck; the fragility of eyes and temples; the rise and fall of an unarmoured chest.

Only reach out, *ilauem-arluth;* reach out and snuff out and you are clan-lord indeed. He will not even feel it . . . The melodious enticement of the Song of Desolation whispered in his ears—promising, cajoling, reminding him of other times and other sensations: impact, and the brief jarring resistance as steel entered flesh; the hard crisp noise as bone gave way beneath a perfect stroke; and that breathless moment afterwards when limbs trembled whole and unhurt with the awareness of survival, and the knowledge of another day of life was like rebirth . . .

The *eijo*—for he was truly *eijo* now, landless, lordless, exiled by his own choice—bowed his head in resignation. "Forgive me, father," he murmured. "Once again I break my Word. But I cannot do this thing . . ." Aldric stepped aside to let the Jouvaine go.

Crisen made no excuses, nor attempted any of the suicidal things with which he might have hoped to hide his indiscretion, for though the Alban's longsword lay out on the balcony there was still that ever-present dirk pushed through his belt. But he looked back in desperation with the beginnings of real fear scored into his face. "Please . . . don't tell my father—"

The door opened. "Don't tell me what?" demanded Geruath the Overlord.

Aldric glanced at Crisen and then smiled viciously. "Ask your son!" he snapped. "You will find the answer interesting . . ."

Waving back the guards who would have followed him into the room, Geruath shut and locked the door. He kept the key in his left hand. "Well, Crisen? Interest me."

His son wiped dry lips with the back of one hand and retreated two steps, blanching with terror. "It isn't important, father, I promise you . . ."

"Let me be the judge of that. Tell me—*at once!*"

"A—a task for me—nothing more, I swear . . . !"

"What task?" Geruath moved forward, hunch-shouldered, violence brooding in him like the threat of thunder in still air. "What task, my son . . . answer me before I—"

"No! I—I mean I can't . . ."

"Tell me, Crisen . . ." The words were thick with suspicion, and Aldric could hear the malevolence in them through the half-heard eldritch moaning of a single chord as it awaited . . . something.

The Alban's senses were spinning. A heavy scent of roses swamped his brain with reeling perfume richer than the fumes of wine, sweet and sickly as no natural flower should be. But a Bale Flower . . . ! Dear Light of Heaven, can they not smell it too . . . ! His gaze flicked from son to father and back to son, knowing that something frightful was about to happen. He backed away . . .

And that slight movement registered on Crisen's bulging, panic-stricken eyes. He turned, his arms flung wide as if in supplication, and one hand gripped the *tsepan*-hilt at Aldric's waist. The dirk fitted snugly in its lacquered sheath and always, *always* needed a slight twist to free it—except that this time of all times it drew out eagerly and swiftly. Almost before the Jouvaine's fingers closed . . .

Lord Geruath's expression changed from rage to disbelief the instant a blade gleamed in his son's hand. He began to speak—but the words were lost in a choked gargling as the dirk jabbed underneath his chin to open veins and windpipe. It wrenched free, and a long spurt of vivid crimson followed in its wake. Geruath's head lolled forward, no longer supported by his neck, and he turned slightly to stare at Aldric with a quizzical expression. His mouth opened and a wide ribbon of blood flowed out over its lower lip like a bright red beard; but his question became a surprised cough which misted the air with a fine spray of scarlet and freckled Aldric's face with minute warm droplets.

Then Crisen stabbed him again. In the belly. And ripped the blade out sideways.

Stench . . . There was no smell of roses now. The Overlord staggered, then collapsed, and Aldric felt the dead-weight's sodden heat as his arms supported it a moment before it slithered to the floor in a tangle of slack limbs and open torso. The fingers of one hand clawed at the floor, nails scratching more loudly than the Alban would have believed possible, then trembled once and did not move again. There was bood all over him: on his hands, on his face, smeared vividly across the soft black of his leathers. And Crisen was watching him intently through eyes which seemed far too bright . . .

Horror froze him to the spot for just too long. Not horror at the violence, for he had seen—and done—much worse, but because a father had been knowingly cut down by the hand of his own son. That crime above all others was anathema to Albans. It was unthinkable . . . and beyond belief that he had witnessed it and yet done nothing . . .

Crisen saw the expressions chase each other across a face too deeply shocked to hide them, and drew breath. "It seems," he said, with only the faintest quiver in his voice, "that the task which I required of you is done." The *tsepan* touched his left palm, slicing across it in a dramatically bloody superficial cut before he clutched its blade in sticky fingers—for all the world as if he had just snatched it from Aldric's hand at great risk to himself.

Far too late now, realisation flared within the Alban's shocked and sickened eyes. "So . . ." Crisen whispered, "I no longer need you." He laughed hoarsely; and then screamed: *"Guards!"* until the door burst in.

The soldiers outside had been expecting trouble of some kind since Geruath had first summoned them to attend him; prepared for a disturbance, therefore, they acted instantly on what they saw without waiting for reasons or excuses. The butt of a gisarm slammed into Aldric's stomach, punching the air from his lungs and folding him over the impact; another swept his legs from under him so that he fell with a wet slap into the glistening, still warm morass which once had been Geruath the Overlord.

And yet he made no attempt to resist: that would only compound his apparent guilt. Seghar's magistrate would surely know that an *eijo* would need only that single, obviously mortal thrust to the throat—and any wit at all would tell him that no Alban with a shred of decency would use his *tsepan* to do murder.

Aldric coughed carefully, wincing at the pain thus dealt to his bruised stomach muscles, and raised a head that by now was quite plastered both in blood and the foulness of evisceration. He tried to ignore the stink. But a cold fear began to churn inside him as he saw the soldiers bowing deeply. In respect to their new Overlord, came the tiny rational explanation; the magistrate . . .

Crisen Geruath, Overlord of Seghar, Executor of High and Common Justice, reached out his injured hand with a lordly air and permitted a retainer to bandage it; over the man's shoulder he smiled coldly down at where Aldric crouched in the mire of a dead man's bowels. Any who saw that smile considered it a brave display of stiff-necked courage in the face of pain and grief.

Any except Aldric—but who now would listen to what he might say . . . ? As the Alban was marched out, arms wrenched high up between his shoulder blades by makeshift bonds, Crisen stopped the escort and waved them to one side. Aldric stared dispassionately at him, guessing that this new lord shared the old lord's penchant for a parting shot. And he was right.

Although his voice was already too soft for anyone

else to hear, Crisen leaned so intimately close that Aldric swayed back in disgust. "When I see an opportunity," the Jouvaine purred, with thick self-satisfaction lacing every word, "I take it. With both hands."

10

The Knucklebones
of Sedna

"**I** know the man—and I find what you tell me a hard thing to believe of him." Marek's tone was insistent, and though the opinion he put forward was dangerous, it had to be said aloud before witnesses. Even such unlikely ones as the mailed retainers on either side of the Overlord's great carved chair. Mailed—Marek noted that change. Crested coats had been enough before tonight.

Crisen Geruath gazed at the demon queller and cleared his throat, serene and confident in his own power. "I have a title now, *hlensyarl*," he reminded.

"My Lord," responded Marek, after a pause which was more than long enough to make clear his disapproval.

"Hard to believe or otherwise, Marek Endain," he continued in the same placid voice, "it is true. Your Alban friend slew my poor father with that black knife he carries always."

Had the new Overlord been watching more closely he would have seen real suspicion appear for the first time on Marek's bearded features. As he had said in all honesty, he knew the man—indeed, had experienced unpleasantly close encounters with the blades which Aldric bore concealed about his person—and though a Cernuan who even now had no love for the Horse Lords, he knew that this *Margh-Arluth* above all would not dishonour his *tsepan*. Marek knew of only one use for the black dirk: the death of its owner, either to end the agony of a mortal wound or in *tsepanak'ulleth*, the ritual of formal suicide. It was never, ever used for simple killing. He knew now what he had only suspected before: the Overlord was lying.

"My lord," he asked, respectfully for once, "may I see Kourgath? Before this murder he was my friend . . ."

Crisen nodded and waved dismissal both to Marek and the two soldiers standing with ostentatious nonchalance beside the door. The demon queller glanced at them and kept a frown from his face with difficulty, for he would have much preferred to forego the "honour" of an armed and armoured escort. In Seghar a guard could also be an executioner . . .

As he left the presence chamber with the evidence of Crisen's doubtful courtesy behind him, he heard the Overlord's voice ring out behind him and absently he wondered why it seemed so irritable:

"Bring *Kortagor* Jervan in here at once . . . !"

*

Until they reached a heavily barred door, the two soldiers made no attempt at conversation; and when one, after fumbling with locks and plainly mismatched keys, looked up and asked for Marek's help, the Cernuan came close to outright laughter at such studied clumsiness. Instead, containing himself, he pretended ignorance until the second trooper made his move.

Which took the unsubtle form of a spearpoint lunging at his chest . . .

Marek twisted from the weapon's path, brushing its point aside with one arm and slapped the other open hand against the soldier's chest. It was a heavy blow— yet not heavy enough to explain why the armoured man was flung bodily across the corridor with a hand-print indented deeply in the metal of his breastplate . . .

A sonorous thrumming in the air might have warned the second guard that he had more to deal with than simply the fat man he had been told to kill—but he failed to notice anything amiss until it was far too late. Feinting a jab, the man craftily whirled his spear-butt up from ground level towards the demon queller's head, and was taken off guard by the speed with which the "fat man" ducked.

In his youth Marek had trained with both the straight
spear and the curved; it required no aid from sorcery
for a shift of balance, hands and eyes to signal what was
coming long before the blow itself was launched. As the
stroke wasted its force an inch above his head, Marek's
own fist stabbed out and one extended finger touched
the soldier's midriff with a sharp, high *crack*.

This time with all his inner energies directed through
that single finger, the demon queller folded his opponent
like a broken twig and hurled him up to smash with
stunning force against the ceiling. When the metallic
clatter of the man's descent had faded, Marek listened
for a moment but could hear no other sentries.

"So . . ." He considered the already-blackening fin-
gernail briefly, and guessed that he would likely lose it.
"So two soldiers are enough to kill a fat old man, eh?"
Marek had a sore finger to show for it, but was not even
out of breath. "How very wrong you are, dear Overlord." And then aloud he wondered: "But why kill *me*
at all . . . ?" The Cernuan's subconscious supplied his
answer in a single word.

Ythek . . .

Crisen Geruath had certain plans afoot, and wanted
no outside interference. Marek, the self-proclaimed
queller of demons, personified just such a potential
nuisance—and so the nasty practicality of the Empire's
logic dictated his removal. Yet even nastier to his educated mind were the implications of what had prompted
such a drastic course.

He regretted, now, that he had not given way to his
first impulse and set a cleansing fire to work on the appalling discovery which he had made in Sedna's library
just after Aldric had stalked in silence from the room.
The contents of a locked, blued-steel cabinet. He should
have expected it: books. Such a simple word to describe
them. Accurate, too—until a closer inspection revealed
what books they were . . .

That closer inspection—no more than the reading of
two titles—had set him shaking with revulsion, and he
had pronounced the Charm of Holding with more fer-
vour than he had ever summoned up before, his grip on
the medallion at his neck so tight as to almost buckle

the thin antique metal. The books were old, and they had the mustiness of age about them—a scent as pleasing to any scholar as the bouquet of fine wine. And yet there was another more subtle odour, born of much more than the passage of years. It was—what had the young Alban said?—the reek of written evil.

And yet they were so rare . . . ! *Enciervanul Doamnisoar* he had already seen; and yet not in the original Vlechan which had been so mutilated, expurgated and corrupted down the years. That thought alone had made Marek laugh a mirthless laugh deep in his chest, for how could anything so totally corrupt be corrupted any farther? This was a—*the*—near-legendary Jouvaine translation, and priceless. There was *Hauchttarni*—High Mysteries—and there *The Grey Book of Sanglenn.* The scholar within him had rebelled at any thought of burning such a find: these books and others like them had been forbidden and destroyed by the ignorant for centuries, to such effect that in some instances no wise men could be drawn into an opinion that one or other had ever existed . . .

But he was not a scholar; and it was a grimoire such as those in Sedna's secret library which had caused him to take up the demon queller's mantle ten years earlier, when . . .

Marek had closed his mind to that pain-filled memory, and had closed and locked the cabinet, unable to destroy its contents but equally unwilling to leave them accessible to untutored hands and eyes. Now, standing before another locked and bolted door, he realised with an uncomfortable certainty that he had not done enough. Locks could be unlocked and doors, by their very nature, opened . . .

He half-doubted that he had been brought to Aldric's cell at all; more likely to some deserted part of the citadel where his murder would not be noticed. But having almost made up his mind on that point, Marek did not take time to wonder just exactly what might be behind the door. Still lost in his own thoughts, he reached out and slid back a bolt, deciding that he might as well—another bolt was withdrawn—make sure that there was nothing to be seen inside. Certainly—his fingers closed

around the handle—there was nothing to be heard. The
heavy door swung back. Beyond was darkness.

Marek realised then the depths of his own folly . . .

And in the instant of that realisation something unseen blurred past his head to strike the wall behind him
like a hatchet, and he could hear the rending of a fine-
grained pine wood panel as its fibres split from top to
bottom.

Beyond the gaping doorway, darkness moved . . .

*

"Enough of this, Commander." Crisen's interruption
was lazy and laced with malice. "I already know *where*
she is; the important word was *what*. Quite a different
question—and requiring quite a different answer. So why
the deviation, *Kortagor* Jervan?"

Jervan looked up from his uncomfortable, unaccustomed kneeling position—garrison commanders did not
kneel, they stood up straight like soldiers—and attempted to read something from his new Overlord's face.
The attempt was unsuccessful. He said nothing.

"Come now, Commander." By his tone and his expression Crisen was enjoying himself. "You took her to your
room; therefore you must have found her interesting—in
one way or another. And you the most happily married
man in the entire fortress . . ." Crisen leaned closer and
smiled conspiratorially. "Just between the two of us,
man to man: how was she?" Jervan reddened and the
Overlord's smile stretched wider. "Oh, I see . . . She
was a virgin. Was she . . . ?"

The eagerness with which he asked that final question
came from much more than simple prurience, but such
subtleties were lost on Jervan's burning ears. "Dammit,
I don't know!" the *Kortagor* snapped, then realised uneasily to whom—and to what—he was speaking. ". . . My
lord," he added hastily, before continuing to vindicate
himself. "I swear I did not touch the girl. Sir, she's young
enough to be my daughter . . . !"

Crisen steepled his fingers and studied their interlaced
tips, then rested his chin on them and stared at Jervan,
laughing softly to himself. It was not a pleasant sound.
"So?" he said, and the unfeigned astonishment in the
one word said much about the mind which shaped it.

Then his gaze lifted towards a sound of movement at the back of the hall. "Well?" The question was addressed to someone Jervan could not see unless he turned his head, and he was not prepared to risk such a movement. He wanted both eyes on the Overlord . . .

"It was as you suspected, lord," came the reply. "His door was locked." That sent a premonitory shiver sliding down *Kortagor* Jervan's back.

"And what then?" Crisen prompted with little patience.

"We broke it open, lord." There was a pause, more noise, and then a woman's squeal of frightened outrage. Jervan's stomach turned over. "And we found this inside."

"Why lock the door, Jervan . . . ?" The voice was a caressing murmur for the present, but Jervan had known the last Overlord and knew how quickly softness could turn into rage. Rather than say something wrong, he said nothing at all.

"Oh, come now, Commander." Crisen settled back in his high-backed chair, entirely at ease and certain he controlled the situation. "I asked you a question; you could at least attempt some entertaining lies. Were you, perhaps, hoping to keep this pretty morsel for yourself—despite your protestations of fidelty and chastity? That would be a credible human failing, would it not? Or did you hide her for fear I thought she and Kourgath had conspired together in my poor father's death?"

"So he killed the old swine after all?" shrilled Gueynor delightedly. "A shame that piglets run so fast—*Ow!*" The girl's words were punctuated by the sharp sound of a blow and this time Jervan did turn, half rising to his feet.

"Damn you, let her alone!" His parade-ground bellow shattered the ugly tension in the hall, if only for a moment, and the two retainers standing nearest Gueynor fell back by reflex alone. The red mark of a hand glowed on her pale face.

"Yes, let her alone," came Crisen's voice. "Until I tell you otherwise. Step forward, girl. Let me see what has provoked such uproar . . ."

Gueynor walked with stiff-backed dignity for half a

dozen paces, ignoring the blatant lechery in the soldiers'
eyes—both she and they knew what the Overlord had
meant—but faltered when she came close enough to see
the strange expression on Crisen's face, then broke and
ran to Jervan's arms.

"How touching! But, Commander, I do not recall per-
mitting you to rise, so . . . get down on your knees in
the dust where you belong!"

Jervan tightened his embrace on Gueynor momentarily, reassuring her as he would one of his own children, before turning very slowly to face Crisen. There
was pride on his face now, the haughtiness of a man
who had served in the Imperial military machine for
twenty years and still remained a man. "I will not," he
said flatly. "What you intend to do you will do regardless
of whether I obey or not. So I will not."

"A pretty speech, Commander Jervan," mocked the
Overlord. Only Gueynor and Jervan were close enough
to see that his sarcasm was a veneer; Crisen might seem
confident, but only when that confidence remained unchallenged. His streak of cruelty, however, was much
more than just skin-deep . . . "As you say, I have already
decided what to do. Not so much with you as with
the . . . lady. Are you not even slightly curious about
that . . . ?"

Gueynor's eyes widened and she pressed closer to Jervan as if he could protect her. As if . . . Both were
unarmed, unprotected, and even the oppressive atmosphere was a weapon in Crisen's favour. There was more
quick clattering as another retainer came in, saluted and
marched hurriedly toward the Overlord's high seat. He
carried a book in his arms, cradled there because of its
size, its apparent weight—and also because he plainly
did not want the thing too close to his body.

"My lord," the man said, "two things were not as you
said: the iron casket had been locked and the sentry—"

"Never mind that," Crisen returned dismissively, either not caring about the man or not wanting to hear
what might have happened to him. As if he had no need
to know. "Give that to me." The heavy volume was
handed over, with relief on one side and an unsavory
display of fondness on the other—for Crisen hugged the

book close to his chest as a man might hug a child. Or a lover. He stroked its cover and even that gesture seemed heavy with unpleasantness.

"Do you know what this is, Commander Jervan?" The officer had his suspicions but refused to give Crisen the satisfaction of crowing over him. He shook his head in denial. "I didn't expect you would; although you might have said, 'a book,' or something equally witty. No matter. As you may have heard, thanks to Lord-Commander Voord there is an unexpected guest—yes, guest will suffice. An important guest in Seghar. A guest whose favours I would like to cultivate. So I intend to make this guest a gift . . ."

"No! I will not—"

"How will you not, Commander? She should be honoured." Crisen stared at Gueynor and the tip of his tongue ran once around his lips. "Are you sure she is a virgin . . . ?"

"I told you," Jervan forced his voice to remain low, reasonable, convincing, "I honestly do not know." It seemed important to the Overlord that his answer should be an affirmative, so instead he racked his brains for reasons why the opposite should be true. They were there: good, sound explanations. "But I doubt it. She was married. At last, when I questioned her at the Summergate before she entered Seghar, she told me that she was a widow. And she was keeping company with that Alban mercenary . . ." This he pronounced as if it was conclusive evidence, and to Crisen's mind it probably was so.

Except that he really cared neither one way nor the other. "A pity," he muttered, patting the great book now resting across his knees. "But one detail hardly matters." Gueynor uttered a tiny, piteous whimper without even knowing she had done so, and Crisen favoured her with a wide, benevolent smile. "Because in all other respects, this gift seems most accept—"

It was then that Jervan sprang on him.

The sudden assault for a seemingly cowed inferior took the Overlord totally by surprise, and it was only that surprise which saved his neck from being snapped between the *kortagor*'s outstretched, clawing hands.

Shock made Crisen jump, and that small, violent backward movement was just enough to upset the balance of his great chair . . .

Jervan's impact sent it toppling backwards like a felled tree, breaking his half-formed grip and spilling both men to the floor in a tangle of limbs. Crisen's squeals brought lord's-men running from their places around the hall; one of them bravely seized Gueynor, the rest set about their erstwhile commander with boots and gisarm-butts until his senses swam and one of his wrists was broken.

Only then did they pick Crisen off the floor and dust him down, while he stared fixedly through glittering eyes at Jervan; and the lack of expression on his pallid face, scored now with long red gouges where the *kortagor*'s nails had clawed away long ribbons of skin, was far more frightening than had he raved as his father would have done.

"Stand him on his feet."

The Overlord watched dispassionately as Jervan was dragged upright by main force, the breath of agony hissing through his clenched teeth as his shattered arm was deliberately used to lift him from the ground. Crisen seemed to notice neither the commander's pain nor the way that his retainers eagerly inflicted it in hope of impressing their new master. Instead he walked once round the *kortagor*'s sagging body, studying it with the chilling air of a butcher sizing up a carcass, then glanced straight into Gueynor's terror-clouded eyes and allowed himself a smile. His hand reached out, cupped her chin as she turned her head away and dragged it back to face him, squeezing until her cheeks were puffy and congested with dark blood. "The Devourer will enjoy you, I think," he whispered under his breath so that only the girl could hear. "And He will be grateful for the gift . . ."

Crisen released her, half turned and held out his right hand palm uppermost and empty. "Knife," he said. The chequered wooden hilt of a military dagger was put into his grasp, and he looked down at its chisel point and single razor edge as if he had not seen such a weapon in his life before. One finger stroked the blade, and he gazed incuriously at where it had sliced skin and meat until the ruby beads of blood welled out. Only then did he complete the turn and consider Jervan once again, breathing deeply, drawing a sourceless scent of roses down into his lungs, hearing a soft choral humming in his ears. His eyes were unfocused, seeing nothing—or seeing things denied to other men. Again he smiled.

"Now hold him," Crisen sighed, a disgusting noise. "Hold him firm . . ."

*

Aldric was very different from the elegant figure Marek had last seen, the saturnine and deadly swordsman whose appearance and—increasingly—opinions gave the lie to everything he claimed to be. He was still entirely dressed in black, but where before the sober colour had been contrasted and relieved by polished metals, dazzling white silk and clean skin, here all was the one dingy russet brown. Until he emerged from the darkness of the cell he was one with its shadows, and only the glitter of eyes betrayed that anything beyond the light had any life at all. When he saw Marek—and more importantly, when he saw the slumped unconscious bodies on the floor—his face cracked into a kind of smile. Cracked quite literally, so that a fine web of fractures ran crisscross through the crust of blood which masked his features. Lord Geruath's blood, mostly; but not all. The treatment meted out by Crisen's retainers had not been gentle . . .

"I didn't do it," he said softly after a moment's silence.

"I know," said Marek with equal gentleness. The young man had not expected to see any face again except that of the soldier sent to finish him, and though he had not intended to be slaughtered like a sheep—the metal dish sunk half its diameter in the panelling bore witness to that fact, for its rim had been ground viciously sharp against the stone cell floor—he had certainly resigned himself to dying in one way or another. Marek had given back his life.

"If you had killed the old lord," the demon queller continued, "and God and King Rynert both know that you're capable of doing so, you wouldn't have made such a slaughter-house of it. I saw the body . . . And you would never have dishonoured your *tsepan* like that."

Aldric acknowledged the words with a slight inclination of his head, then eyed the corridor and the two men sprawling in it. He toed one of the retainers on to his back, where the man lay breathing stertorously. There was a little blood around his nostrils, and the unmistakable print of a human hand driven into his armour as if set mere as a decoration. "A form of the High Accelerator," observed Aldric knowledgably, lifting an eyebrow in Marek's direction.

The demon queller gave him a long, hard stare. "When this is over," he said severely, "you and I must have a little talk."

"When this is over," the Alban echoed. "Which it isn't yet. My gear is in one of these other rooms—all of it." Marek knew what that meant. Both of Aldric's hands were bare: without gloves or any other ornament . . . "I heard them carrying it past," Aldric continued "but I don't know which room"—the long corridor was lined with maybe a score of bronze-faced doors—"and I haven't time to search them all."

"No need." Marek Endain grinned a hard, toothy grin that was reminiscent of Aldric's foster-father Gemmel, and gestured with one hand in the air. *"Acchai an-tsalaer h'loeth!"* he said, then clenched his fist and opened it. There was a low droning noise which shot up briefly beyond hearing, and Aldric winced as it stung his ears. One of the many doors burst outward off its hinges and clanged on to the floor. "There you are!"

Armour and weapons had been laid out in orderly fashion, just as they had been lifted from the floor of Aldric's room, and a hasty inspection proved to his own satisfaction that nothing was missing. With the speed born of long practice he scrambled into his battle armour, carefully checking straps and laces as he drew each one tight. Marek watched uncertainly as the young man he thought he now knew by acquaintance as well as by reputation built himself, piece by black steel piece, into an image of war formed of lacquerwork and polished metal. There was a subtle scent which always clung to *an-moyya-tsalaer,* the Great Harness: a harsh odour of metal and oil and leather which was masculine and not unpleasant.

But to the demon queller's sensitive nostrils it reeked of sudden, violent death.

Aldric looped Widowmaker's crossbelt over his shoulder and made her scabbard secure on the weapon-belt about his waist, and then with studied arrogance fitted the steel and silver of the Echainon spellstone around his armoured wrist. Yes indeed, Marek told himself, I look forward to hearing you explain that thing away. If you can. Then he looked at Aldric's face and doubted that such questions would be wise.

"Aldric," he said. The name sounded very loud above the muted scrape of armour being donned and the Alban glanced at him, saying nothing but with curiosity quite clear in his eyes. "Aldric, when you left the library I . . . I went back to the cellar. The room where Sedna died."

"I had not thought you prey to morbid curiosity," Aldric returned, careful that what he said could not be wrongly taken as an insult.

"Not curiosity. Necessity. Once I was certain what . . ."

"Enough ambiguity, Marek. When you found out that this thing was the Devourer . . . !" Aldric ended on a prompting uptone.

"When I knew that it—It was Ythek Shri, I knew what I had to find. And I found them."

"What?" The younger man was plainly becoming impatient.

"Bones." Aldric stared at him so intently that Marek hesitated only briefly before elaborating. "The bones are what anchor the soul to fragile flesh," he intoned as if quoting from a book. The Alban might have questioned that had he been in a pedantic mood, but for now he was content to hear out the demon queller. "So the bones of someone slain by unexpected violence—"

"Violence usually is unexpected," interposed Aldric drily.

"An executioner's sword, after due process of law . . . ?" queried Marek. "No. I think we both understand my precise meaning. And understand that these will have some power."

The small pieces of bone which Marek drew out of his belt-pouch looked insignificant, but he held them with such care—almost reverence—that Aldric moved

close enough to have a better look. "Knucklebones," he
said. "You've cleaned them." There was a pause while
he recalled the other human wreckage on the cellar
floor, and despite his carapace of armour Marek saw him
shudder. "That's just as well . . ."

"The knucklebones of Sedna. They might be of some
use." Marek looked down at the small, ivory-pale fragments and his face clouded with pity. "Some of the people in the fortress told me about her, about how pretty
she was. As dainty as a doll . . ."

"But now she's dust," said Aldric, and the words were
harsher than intended. "Bones and dry dust. Like my
father, my mother, my brothers and sisters . . . We are
all dust, Marek. Soon or late, we return to it."

He had put on silken head-wrap, mesh-mail coif and
peaked, flaring Alban helmet, but it was only when he
laced his war-mask into place that the last vestige of
humanity was extinguished. Marek looked at him and
remembered his first words to this strange old-young
man: *At least you're no demon* . . . Now he wondered,
recalling what he knew of Aldric-*eir* Talvalin. There
were more demons than those described in the books of
Sedna's library . . .

His thoughts were interrupted by a steely singing as
Isileth Widowmaker glided from her scabbard. The
taiken's perfect edges caught and trapped a glitter of
reflected lamplight as Aldric strode past him to the door.

"Come on," the Alban said. "We have business with
Lord Crisen."

Marek stared apprehensively; he was quite sure that
"we" had not included him . . .

*

The most likely place to find any Overlord, even one
so . . . unconventional . . . as Crisen Geruath, was the
great presence chamber at the heart of the inner citadel.
And yet there were none of the guards, none of the
retainers—none of the servants that such an important
hall should have required. There was no movement at
all, and the fortress seemed empty from top to bottom.

"What's the hour?" breathed Aldric. The place was
like a holy house: it discouraged loud voices by its
very atmosphere.

After a heartbeat's pause Marek realised that the question was genuine and not merely noise for its own sake. Aldric had been locked in that lightless cell for long enough to confuse him—as if the beating whose marks showed on his face had not been disturbing enough . . .

"After midnight," the Cernuan returned, honestly regretting he could not be more precise. But he, too, had had more to contend with than simply keeping track of time. "I think, after one in the morning."

"You think . . ." Even so, that would explain the lack of people. Servants had to sleep sometime . . .

Neither man had noticed the stealthy movement of a shadow across the distant corridor junction. It was too dark. Otherwise they might have wondered how so dense a shadow could be cast with no light and only total blackness behind it. For it was blacker even than the darkest darkness . . . But the question went unasked. And consequently unanswered.

Marek turned the next corner a few steps ahead of Aldric—and collided with three lord's-men armed with the inevitable gisarms. They had been moving so furtively that he had not heard them, whether by accident or through fear of what else might be roaming the gloomy corridors of Seghar. Whatever the reason, there was no room on either side for retreat and for an instant no one moved.

That instant was enough for Aldric. In answer to the unexpected, half-heard clattering of armour—and the warning which was screaming in his brain—he darted after Marek, took in the situation at a glance and charged all three men at once. The demon queller flattened himself against a wall and watched with awe that swiftly turned to queasy fascination.

The Alban's wildcat recklessness took the lord's-men totally off guard—after all, it was they who were superior in numbers—and when at last they reacted he was already far too close . . .

Gemmel Errekren had trained his foster-son for four long years; and yet he had been shocked when he had witnessed the training put to use. Marek had not even been warned what to expect, and when the first hot splattering of someone else's blood slapped wetly across his face, his stomach almost turned inside out. *Taiken* drawn and balanced in both hands, Aldric slid between two intersecting spears and ripped a single stroke through the men on either side *Tarannin-kai,* twin thunderbolts: two-sides-at-once. If the Cernuan's stomach was almost everted with nausea, two stomachs were literally everted by sharp steel . . .

Sidestepping the eviscerated bodies as they began to fall, Aldric took an incoming spear-point across the curved peak of his helmet in a burst of vivid yellow sparks, then sliced along the thrust's line and lopped off the spearman's hands above the wrists.

He was armoured, they were not; they hesitated, he did not. That made all the difference and in twelve seconds it was over. Hesitation had already cost him far too much, and at some stage in the darkness of his solitary confinement Aldric had decided he would hesitate, consider, even think no more. He would *act.* The consequences of his darkness-born decision flowed thickly across the floor of Seghar citadel . . . There was no hatred in his mind for any of these men; they were simply doing what they had to do. Dying, mainly, he observed with icy cynicism. But not all of them. One man huddled by the wall, hugging himself with the stumps of bloody arms. Aldric leaned over him, lazily wiping Widowmaker's blade clean with a shred of unsoiled cloth.

"You, man . . . where is your Overlord?" he demanded. Deep in shock, the retainer made no sound. "You still live, after a fashion," Aldric stated bleakly, touching his *taiken*'s point to the man's throat. "That can change. I can change it. So answer me!"

"Aldric! Have you no pity, man?" Dazed by what he had seen, Marek was still unwilling to tolerate the *eijo*'s behaviour. "Remember what you are and not what you pretend to be . . . !"

Aldric straightened, Widowmaker sweeping up to rest against his shoulder, and if he was shamefaced it was lost amid the shadows of his mask and helmet. Nonetheless he bowed and left the soldier in some sort of painful peace. "My conscience," he drawled coldly, and Marek scowled at his tone. "Pity, did you say . . . ?" he continued in the same soft voice. "Of course I have pity."

Then all the softness vanished. "But not here. Not now."

*

The Overlord's apartments were beyond the presence chamber. Aldric knew that much without needing to carve the information out of anyone. Unlatching one side of the great hall's double doors, he swung it open silently and peered inside. A few stubborn sparks glowed and spat in one of the hearths, scenting the air with the resin of burnt pinewood; nothing else moved in the darkness. But there was another smell than that of wood. It was the same sweet tang of incense which had clogged the air in the cellar. Except that this smelled fresh . . .

Sword in hand, Aldric strode towards the dimly outlined door at the far end of the hall, determined to kick it open. Halfway there his feet skidded beneath him, slipping on a wet film which covered the floor and at the same time kicking into lumps of something soft. Beneath the black armour he felt the hair rise on his forearms. "Marek?" His voice was almost inaudible. "Marek—give me some light . . . quickly . . . !" Even as he made the request, and it was a request rather than an order, Aldric was doubting any need for urgency . . . or indeed any need for light.

All that he could recognise was the bearded head. Everything else was simply meat—and meat butchered with more force than skill. "Jervan." The slimy mass might once have been Jervan; might once have been human. Now it was a coagulation of chunks and gobbets glued together by congealing blood.

Aldric stared at it and came very close to retching; not because of what he saw but because of what passed through his mind. Jervan had died like this for a reason—and the only reason which he knew involved Gueynor as well. A concern that came very close to fear uncoiled inside him like a cold black snake, the kind of concern which he had doubted he would ever feel again for Evthan's niece. What in hell would Crisen do to her, if he could do this to his garrison commander? Then the thought solidified and his oath became reality.

What from Hell might Crisen do to her . . . ?

His boot smashed against the door just level with the lock, and he felt timber give beneath the impact. A grey haze of smoke billowed out at him and he coughed sharply as it stung the back of his throat. The light within, whose dim outline he had seen, came from half a dozen fat black candles, each one taller than himself. When Marek saw them, he swore under his breath.

Aldric's curse was louder, harsher and less reverent. Crisen Geruath sat crosslegged on the bare floor of the room with an open book before him, mumbling to himself and tracing the words he spoke with a golden reading-wand. It scraped loudly as it moved back and forth across the roughness of the page's vellum surface, keeping time with the cadences of Crisen's voice. Head bowed forward, intent on what he read, he gave no sign of having seen that death stood in the doorway.

Gueynor lay before him, spreadeagled on her back.

Her outstretched limbs were tied down, wrists and ankles, to four heavy ring-bolts sunk into the wooden floorboards; recently sunk, for the tops were still bright from the denting of the hammer which had driven them home. A pattern drawn in chalk writhed around her body, and that body which Aldric knew so well was covered only by a clinging shift of some fine silky stuff, which followed every contour so that she was both less and more than naked. Skin and silk alike were crisscrossed by lines of drying blood: Jervan's blood, used instead of ink or paint to write the words of consecration on Lord Crisen's offering. The blood had smeared, the chalk-marks had been scruffed—but the effectiveness of both remained unchanged. Marek could see them clearly and he knew: both were—and always had been—useless . . .

Wound between Gueynor's fingers were two bloated black-red roses, their rich fragrance threading sweetly through the smokiness of incense and the stink from corpse-fat candles. A third blossom lay between her breasts, its great hooked thorns made more vicious yet by contrast with the fragile curving flesh; brilliant and baleful against the white shift as heart's-blood spilled on snow. It moved with her breathing and her rapid pulse, petals ablaze with sombre colour and trembling as she trembled. As if they too had life . . .

"Gueynor," said Aldric very softly. The girl's head had turned away when the door burst open; she had not wanted to know the form her death would take, not wanted to watch it stalk across the threshold. But now she looked, unable to reply for her mouth was stuffed obscenely full of cloth that was secured there by a thin cord which had cut deep into dirty, tear-streaked cheeks. Yet she answered the speaking of her name; her fear-wide sapphire eyes glowed from within when she realised that his voice was not a trick played by some hellborn monstrosity; glowed not with happiness, not even with relief, but with simple gratitude. They closed, and a single crystal tear welled from between their lids. And it was as if all the hard words between them had never been . . .

The Alban took a long step forward, staring at the Overlord. Crisen paid him no heed; rings flashed as his hands made elaborate gestures in the bitter air and their hard, gemmed sparkle was mirrored by Aldric's cold slitted eyes.

There were so many things that he could say—that he wanted to say. About the dead: Youenn Sicard; Evthan; Lord Geruath; and now Jervan. Before the Light of Heaven, those were just the faces that he knew . . . ! What about Gueynor's parents Erwan and Sula—or even the witch Sedna, for lover or not, if Crisen had not arranged her killing personally he had certainly connived at it. "Crisen of Seghar," he began with brutal formality, then stopped with a shrug of disgust. Why waste time and breath . . . ? Just do it.

But even when Widowmaker's point reached out to touch the mad lord's face there was no reaction. For he was mad. Marek, kneeling knife in hand to release Gueynor from her bonds, no longer had any doubt about it. Only a madman would sit there with *Enciervanul Doamnisoar* at his knees—Oh, why had he not burned those books . . . !—and mouth the phrases of a major summoning in a room that was completely bare of circles, wards or holding patterns. Yet Crisen had done precisely that. The demon queller looked up and felt a

small tremor of shock rush through him as he saw Aldric's longsword stroke tentatively along the Overlord's
jaw, moving for the great vein underneath his ear. He
did not want to witness yet another death. "Aldric, for
the love of—"

Aldric's armoured head swung round to face him. The
eijo did not speak at first, but the candle-light reached
inside his war-mask and what little of his expression
showed through the trefoil opening was enough for
Marek. He shut his mouth at once, and kept it shut even
when the *taiken* slithered into her scabbard and he knew
what would follow.

"For the love of what?" said Aldric, not asking any
question now. "Honour? Because of Isileth's honour I
will not foul her with this man's blood. Because of my
own honour I will not let him live. So . . ." He spoke
words which brought the spellstone in his hand to life.
"He wants sorcery. He will have it."

The piercing drone which emanated from the stone of
Echainon reached into whatever other world Lord Crisen's mind had strayed to, dragging him back to a sort
of sanity with the knowledge that he too could die. And
would. His glazed eyes flickered, then bulged horribly as
they focused on the blue-white haze of leashed-in force
which danced and flickered around Aldric's mailed fist.
The Overlord's mouth quivered, hanging open so that
saliva drooled unnoticed into his lap.

Aldric's own mouth twisted with distaste and he
wished Rynert the King was here to see the man he
wanted killed. There was nothing to be gained from the
obliteration of such vermin—nothing political, nothing
personal, nothing honourable. And likewise nothing to
be lost. Or any remorse to be felt. Aldric raised his arm
and tongues of flame licked eagerly along its steel-
sheathed surface . . .

Then something rattled at the door.

Aldric spun, clawing out Widowmaker with his free
hand. Nothing burst into the room, but the broken lock
gave way and allowed the heavy door to swing slowly
open on its well-greased hinges. Outside, against the
darkness of the presence chamber, was a man in a crested

coat: a lord's-man, standing casually with both hands clasped behind his back.

"Get out of the way!" said Aldric crisply, although Marek and the still-weak Gueynor were already safe at one side of the room. The retainer's affected nonchalance was too suspicious, too obviously false. It screamed warning of a trap. Yet the man was alone, watching him through dull eyes, his breathing jerky and shallow. Terrified . . . thought Aldric. "What do you want?" he demanded.

The trooper neither moved nor spoke; then one arm swung round . . .

And was just an arm. The hand was gone. Alarm tocsins wailed within the Alban's mind and he threw himself clear of the doorway with the speed of the fear of death.

In that same instant the soldier exploded from neck to crotch in a welter of blood and entrails, his body ripped asunder by what came slashing through it. An enormous talon at the end of an impossibly long, sinewy limb blurred with pile-driver force into the space Aldric had occupied a bare heartbeat earlier, and its three claws slammed shut on nothing. As the mangled decoy was flung aside in a grotesque flail of arms and legs and viscera a black and glinting bulk filled the doorway.

Aldric rolled, rose to one knee and stared aghast as Ythek Shri tried to force a way inside. Wood cracked and plaster crumbled as its massive form squeezed across the threshold, into the place from which the summons and the invitation had originated. Some of the candles had gone out, choked by dust or toppled by falling debris, but there was still sufficient light for him to see the Warden of Gateways—as if he had not already seen far too much for any peace of mind until this thing was dead and he had seen it so . . .

It was vaguely insectlike, slightly reptilian, totally hideous. Slimed and shiny surfaces glistened oozily as the being moved. In an atmosphere where scented smoke had been swamped by the stench of spilled intestines, its unearthly outlines were hellishly at home. And it had laid a trap especially for him . . . Why . . . ? *Why?*

The spellstone throbbed and burned against his hand, yearning, and still he did not realize the answer. Ancient adversaries: Light and darkness, heat and cold . . . The spellstone and the demon . . .

As Ythek advanced through a cloud of dust and fragments its huge head swung from Aldric on one side to Marek on the other. Threats. It considered Gueynor, who had not screamed, not fainted, but who gazed at the Devourer with sick, awestruck fascination. Womanmeat. Hunger spasmed through it momentarily, but was overcome by greater immediacy as its attention turned to Crisen. Summoning. The Overlord's brain almost gave way beneath the weight of icy malice brought to bear on his cowering frame. With a repellent shearing noise the demon's maw gaped wide and it took a long stride forward to the one who would most please its Master. It ignored the others completely.

Gritting his teeth against the pain of power which he had never before experienced—pain which froze with heat and burned with cold—Aldric opened his hand and released the force pent up within the spellstone. Thunder hammered through the small room, blowing out its windows, and the demon's leisurely advance became an impossible leap away from danger. It moved faster than the Alban's eyes could follow; one instant in line with his outstretched arm and the next elsewhere in a blinding bound of speed. Despite the purple-glowing afterflash which blocked his vision, he was upright on unsteady feet with Widowmaker poised before anything else could happen.

Nothing did. Marek, backed into a corner, had one arm protectively round Gueynor's shoulders and the other raised in a gesture of dismissal. Crisen was nowhere in sight, and the only other door out of the room was a mass of shattered timber which still swayed in twisted hinges. Ythek Shri was gone.

"He called it," Marek said shakily. "He called it, and it took him."

Aldric was bent double, hands on knees; he was panting as if he had just run long and hard and his left hand felt as though it had been plunged into boiling water.

All magic has its price . . . But this time the Echainon stone had used *him,* and to maintain the Balance his vigour was returning in great surges, pulsing from the talisman into his palm and thence to every sinew in his body. For a little while he felt as though he could tear Seghar apart with his bare hands; but he knew that this renewed strength would be needed in full measure before the sun rose. If he lived to see it rise at all . . .

"Why did it not want me . . . ?" Gueynor's voice was very small, like that of a child woken in the night by a bad dream. "Crisen was going to—to give me to it. Jervan tried to stop him. So he—he cut. His men held Jervan and he—" She pressed her head against the demon queller's chest and cried as if her heart would break.

"Crisen didn't know what he was doing," Marek explained, more for Aldric's benefit than Gueynor's. "But he thought he did. He thought that the sacrifice of a young woman would enable him to make bargains with Issaqua. Why, I won't even guess. But none of the rituals have been observed—none at all, from the begining of this affair. Ythek has been free all along. Without obligation to anyone. What it does is to please its Master, Issaqua."

"But why take Crisen?" The *eijo* leaned back against the wall, nudging the scorched and tattered remnants of *Enciervanul Doamnisoar* with his boot. The grimoire had been charred to a cinder by the spellstone's flash of fire, and he wondered vaguely whether Crisen Geruath might have suffered the same fate.

"This is a time for wolves and ravens," Marek quoted softly. "Issaqua creates and feeds on darkness. What is darker, Aldric—the soul of this girl, or that of a man who stabbed his own father and cast the blame on someone else . . . ?"

"Then he has escaped me," the Alban grated, and the metallic edge of his voice was not entirely an echo from his war-mask. "Escaped us . . ." Widowmaker glittered as he raised her level with his eyes. "That is unseemly."

"You had your chance. You had many chances. You let each one slip through your fingers." Marek was not disapproving, nor was he taking pleasure in the younger man's mistakes. He was simply stating the facts as he knew them. "And you can put your blade away. Nothing from the world of men can harm the Herald."

"You're wrong!" Aldric's flat assertion surprised the Cernuan.

"Why, and how?"

"Because of Widowmaker."

"Aldric, you have a fine sword—although I'm no judge of *taikenin*. But a sword is just a sword . . ."

"But *this* sword is Isileth."

"Isileth . . . ?" Marek repeated the name, making no secret of his doubts. His gaze focused on the weapon, black steel and braided leather hilt in a lacquered scabbard. "It cannot be," he asserted, then with more confidence: "It isn't old enough."

"She can be, and she is." Both Marek and Gueynor noted the subtle change of pronoun. "The furniture has been renewed, of course. Often: But the blade is unchanged." He unhooked the *taiken* from his weapon belt, bowed very slightly and withdrew a hand's width of steel from the scabbard. "You know the name, so you know the writing. 'Forged was I of iron Heaven-born. Uelan made me. I am Isileth.' Isileth is Widowmaker, Marek; and Widowmaker is mine. You say, nothing in the world of men . . . what do you say concerning iron Heaven-born?"

"I say you are as mad as were the Overlords of this place," Marek retorted quietly. "But you may also be right. I hope so, for all our sakes. Not least your own."

*

Beyond the broken door was a gallery where the Overlord could walk in rainy weather, its walls adorned with tapestries and paintings all of military subjects. It gave Aldric a clue as to where the passage led. "You," he said firmly to Gueynor, "stay here. This thing—"

"Is something I intend to see through," the girl said. "Right to the end."

"You aren't being stubborn—you're being stupid!"

"Why? We'll each know where the other is if I come with you—"

"We had this argument before!"

"And you remember the outcome, I hope?" Gueynor's

voice was entirely reasonable, even though it still trembled slightly. Tonight she had seen and suffered things which would trouble her sleep for months, and only by witnessing the conclusion could she be sure that the world was a safe place after dark. Wisely, she did not appeal to Marek either as arbiter or advocate; the Cernuan stood to·one side with arms folded and said nothing.

Finally Aldric shrugged. "It's your choice. I wash my hands of it. But remember this: don't try to be heroic, or even brave. Trying to stay alive may well prove difficult enough. And I would rather that you lived to be the Overlord of Seghar, Gueynor." He glanced along the gallery, at the light ornamental armours which formed part of its decoration, and then back at the girl's body in its flimsy shift. "Now find something more practical to wear . . ."

*

The gallery ended at the foot of a staircase which spiralled upwards out of sight, and its treads were gashed by the betraying triple gouges of Ythek's claws. "Into Geruath's weapon-tower," muttered Marek. He stared back along the passage. "Why, I wonder? Better wait here for—" There was no one listening. "Dear God and black damnation!" the demon queller swore. "Does he never listen to his own advice . . . ?" With one hand on the medallion at his throat, Marek started up the stairs with all the silent speed that he could muster.

Aldric and Gueynor, already at the top, were slighty disconcerted to find themselves alone before a door which bore all the signs of the demon's passage. "He was behind me, I tell you," the Alban breathed.

"You should have made sure . . ." Gueynor murmured doubtfully.

"No matter now. Wait for him. I'm going through."

"And I'm—"

"Waiting *here!* Gueynor, do it! Please . . . !" There was as much force in his whisper as Aldric dared; he knew that the girl was acting through fear, not false bravado—and he also knew that beyond the door he could protect only himself. With that unpleasant thought pushed to the back of his mind, Aldric eased open the door and slid carefully into the tower.

Inside was the pride of Geruath's weapon collection, lit from outside by stars and by a setting moon three nights past full. It was dark inside the tower, but not completely. There was a strange ruddy luminescence to the air, as if the motes of floating dust were each red-hot and glowing. And then he saw it.

A rose. Of course . . . but such a rose. It hung unsupported on the air, its outlines vague, misty like an image sketched by frost on glass, and it was huge. A monstrous, overblown blossom twice the size of a man's head, its great curving petals pulsed with all the shades of red from incandescent scarlet and vermillion down into crimson and the black of ancient blood. Its perfume was a throbbing intoxication that overwhelmed mere human senses as a spring tide overwhelms sand. And the rose sang. So close to its source, the Song of Desolation was one note in many voices: one note of such sweetness and purity that it burned with the brilliance of a solitary star on a winter's night, but so distant, so inhumanly cold that only the hopeless awareness of his ultimate death remained coherent in Aldric's mind.

Rather than live in despair, it would be better to die now . . .

Aldric's hand closed around his *tsepan*'s hilt . . .

And Gemmel's voice said dryly: "Cheer up, boy—nobody lives forever. Nor would any want to . . . just think of the boredom!" Where the old enchanter's words had come from, the Alban did not know; but they made him smile, and no man can smile while seriously considering his own suicide.

Another light began to fill the tower: the steady radiance of the stone of Echainon. It radiated not heat, but warmth—the warmth of friendship, of comfort, of pity and compassion, of an embrace . . . *Kyrin, O my lady, O my love.* The warmth of humanity, with all its errors and its faults. And the coldness of Issaqua began to fail . . .

Then something moved beyond the rose and he went very, very still. It moved in the darkness beyond the conflicting lights, but it was so much blacker than the deepest shadows that its presence and position were quite plain. *Ythek'ter an-shri* moved to aid its Master.

Aldric felt the scrutiny of an intelligence so inhuman that he could think of no comparison. The demon Herald was aware of him. All the memories of its strength and speed and savagery came flooding back. Yet any predatory beast had those—even the Beast. Even Evthan. But this was Ythek Shri, and it had more powers than any beast.

Talons glittered dully as they lifted towards him, and even twenty feet away their size and power were awesome. But the entity remained immobile, and only flecks of starlight reflecting from its surface sparkled as their sources twinkled so very far away. Then it hissed and closed its claws.

A gale came out of nowhere and rose to a shriek as it wrapped Aldric in a nebulous embrace. Armoured or not, braced legs or not, he was flung backwards against the wall and almost off his feet. With a mocking whistle the witch-wind died away and Aldric regained his balance. He slid Widowmaker out and drew her scabbard up across his back, well clear of both legs. The demon seemed to radiate malevolent amusement at his preparations as he hurriedly assumed a defensive guard, waiting for what was coming next. The wait was short.

Halfway through one breath and the next, his perception of the world went . . . strange. It began as a multi-colored phosphoresence dancing around the outlines of things previously lost in shadow. Then even that weak hold on reality warped out of existence and vertigo hit him like a blow. *Up* was no longer above him, nor *down* beneath his feet.

Instead there was a deep gulf which yawned warm and inviting less than a step from where he stood on nothing. Iridescent light twirled in languorous coils far down in its glowing amber throat; small bright specks of pastel colour rose towards him and glided past his face with a faint hot rush of perfume. The chasm hummed gently cajoling lullaby sounds, sweet tones of half-heard melodies mingled with the distant tinkling of tiny bells. Aldric could hear the double drumbeat of his own heart slow and infinitely deep in his ears, in his bones, in the core of his reeling brain.

All that remained constant and unaffected was a long

silvery glitter which he knew was Widowmaker's blade—
and a twisted black thing which squirmed sluggishly at
the very bottom of the pit. As it began to writhe towards
him, Aldric shut his eyes.

*

Marek forced the wind-jammed door aside and blinked
at what he saw: the beautiful, dreadful Bale Flower of
Issaqua—and Ythek Shri advancing with slow, measured
strides on an armoured figure who seemed not to know
that it was there. Gueynor pushed into the doorway behind him, realised what she was seeing and screamed a
warning at the top of her voice.

Aldric's eyes snapped open and focused on the gleam
of this blade, the one steady thing in a world of flaring
colours and twitching blackness. The giddiness which
had almost claimed him—which had almost spilled him
into the Abyss—was gone now; enough at least for him
to poise the *taiken* double-handed by his head. Secure
in its own invincibility, Ythek the Devourer leaned towards him . . .

Marek Endain raised one hand and began to mutter
the phrases of a spell . . .

Aldric could no longer see the colours, for shifting,
glinting blackness blotted all else out. Widowmaker
trembled slightly. Not with fear, but with tension, for the
muscles of his arms were taut as a full-drawn bowstring
and as eager for release . . .

Something made a slavering sound . . .

And flame scorched the shadow-crowded tower, leaping from Marek's outstretched hand as he pronounced
the Invocation of Fire. Although his spell could do it no
real harm, Ythek's malign concentration wavered. And
Aldric struck with all his strength.

"Hai!" Widowmaker sliced out: there was a chopping
noise as her blade clove . . . *something* . . . and then a
bubbling screech and a clatter of ponderous movement.
Cold flowed down the sword, chilling Aldric's sweaty
hands. Despite his evident success in somehow wounding
the demon, he was terrified; a hackle-raising fear billowed from it, like frigid vapour. Other enemies might
attack his flesh and bone but the *tsalaer* guarded that
with scales and plates and meshed mail; Ythek menaced

his sanity and his frail soul, and against that he had no protection.

And while he subconsciously worried about his soul, the demon Herald's talons almost took him in the chest. Aldric twisted to one side far faster than he could have dreamed and the great hooked claws went screeching across his battle armour's surface instead of punching through—as would have happened had he not rolled with the blow. Even then the impact spun him right around and hurled him effortlessly across the room with all the breath bruised from his lungs. But there was no second attack, no pounce while he was helpless to defend himself.

For this time Ythek Shri had gone for Marek.

A dim flickering of balefire hung about the Cernuan; whether it was the outward sign of attack or of defence, Aldric did not know. Crouched low on spread, well-balanced legs, the demon queller fixed an unwinking stare on the approaching Devourer—and incredibly, the black reptilian bulk faltered, Marek took a long deep breath which seemed to expand his entire body; his eyes blazed and he stretched out his right arm, all his power focused through the extended index finger. There was no noise, no violent display—but Ythek stopped as if it faced an unseen wall, and when Marek took one step forward it retreated that step even though he made no gesture of threat and had drawn no talisman or weapon. There was only that rigid, pointing finger, black-nailed as any peasant's . . .

The knucklebones, thought Aldric through his own whirl of pain and nausea. No . . . not the knucklebones—Gueynor had those now. He was holding back the demon with no more than the force of his own will . . . ! And that will was failing.

"Aldric . . ." The Cernuan's voice was a fragment of its former self, and shook with effort. "Aldric . . . help me Quickly . . . ! Cannot hold . . ."

"Abath arhan!" He shouted the words like a war-cry, like a challenge, and allowed the stone to draw on the power that it had earlier granted him, to reclaim it all and more until his senses swam and his legs grew weak beneath him. In ears and mind the Song of Desolation

grew loud and triumphant, then; louder still, rising to a ululating paean praising darkness and despair. The air was frigid, and white crystals of hoar-frost formed on his harness, blurring the stark outlines of the metal; as he exhaled Aldric could see the fog of his own breath hang before him like the smoke-drift from a firedrake's jaws.

The great armoured triangle of Ythek's head swung to survey him, and as the full weight of its regard pressed down on his cringing brain the Alban understood for one awesome instant just what Marek Endain had faced down . . . The Herald's maw gaped wide, leering at him with an infinity of appalling teeth. Saliva wove a glistening web between them, oozing from their needle points in steaming corrosive threads that splashed and scarred the wooden floor. Pain spiked Aldric's staring eyes, bored into his mind and slowly, slowly the world slid out of focus . . .

Time stopped. Gueynor was beside him, her hand about his wrist—but even through the armour, layers of steel and leather, he could feel that her grip was . . . different. As if her fingers were longer, narrower—as if the hand he saw was not the hand he felt. Aldric's head turned so that he could look her in the face, but that too was changing. Like a painting on thin silk, another face had overlaid the one he knew; delicate as fine porcelain, ivory pale skin framed by dark, dark hair; great sad eyes. And suddenly, though he had never seen the face before, he recognised it—and in the same instant he realised what Gueynor held so tightly in her clenched left hand.

Sedna . . . and the knucklebones of Sedna.

"You have power, Alban." Even the familiar Jouvaine voice was husky with an unmistakably Vreijek accent. "Give it to me. Let me direct it. Trust me . . ." Moving stiffly, like an automaton, Aldric removed the loops of silvered steel from his arms. Without the warm pressure of the spellstone in the centre of his palm he felt at once lighter, younger and yet somehow incomplete. Vulnerable . . .

"Take it," he said to the sorceress who spoke through Gueynor's lips. "Take it, use it and bring it to me." Time began again.

The slight blonde figure which was at the same time tall and dark walked out to the middle of the floor. Beneath the armour which she wore, Gueynor's skin was still marked with the sign of a consecrated sacrifice. She was an unclaimed victim going willingly to face that to which she had been dedicated, and she bore within her and around her the stuff of one who had been neither consecrated nor willing. One whose life had been stolen; whose death had violated the Balance of things . . .

Ythek Shri lowered over her, and Aldric held his breath. Then slowly . . . oh, so very slowly . . . the Devourer backed away. Incredibly, unbelievably, it bowed low and abased itself. Behind and above its Herald, the demonic flower-form of Issaqua throbbed like a beating heart. Its song was very quiet now and the scent of roses barely perceptible . . .

Marek Endain, the queller of demons, let his hands hang down by his sides as he watched. This thing had passed beyond him, leaving his much-vaunted knowledge very far behind. Like Aldric, he could only wait . . .

Until the tower, the citadel, the whole world seemed to explode. A searing lash of energy poured from the stone of Echainon where Sedna held it high in Gueynor's hand. Light met darkness, heat met cold . . . Life met death. The blue fire wrapped Issaqua the Dweller in Shadows with coils of brilliance until no darkness remained even in the crimson heart of the Bale Flower's being. Where there is sufficient light, there can be no shadows; where there is sufficient warmth, cold cannot exist.

Ythek Shri howled its anguish, beating its monstrous talons against the floor as if a self-inflicted pain could cancel one which it could not control. The Warden of Gateways shrieked endlessly as a Gateway not of its own making yawned to draw its substance back into the Void; then the dreadful lost howling shredded to the thin squeals of a pig as Ythek's form wavered and dissolved, dissipating like ink on wet paper. For just one moment more an unclean translucent fog swirled thickly through the withered petals of a crumbling, faded rose . . .

And then there were no more demons.

*

"My lady . . . !" Aldric used the honorific with sincerity for the first time ever, his voice shockingly clear in the vast stillness which no longer thrummed with the Song of Desolation. His ears had grown accustomed to hearing that sound constantly in the background of whatever he heard or said or did, and now that it had been silenced he seemed capable of hearing even the soft beat of Gueynor's heart.

She turned in answer to his voice and she was Gueynor Evenou, Evthan's sister's daughter. Not Sedna ar Gethin the Vreijek witch—not half-and-half—just Gueynor . . . In silence she held out her hands and Aldric took them as they opened. In one the spellstone glowed—and its fires now seemed no more than the gentle fluttering of an alcohol flame—and in the other, there was dust. All that remained of the knucklebones of Sedna. Only dust . . .

Marek, at the Alban's shoulder, looked at it and smiled sadly. "There was little enough for obsequies," he said, and sifted the fine white dust into a leather pouch. "But these poor bones at least received a better and more worthy funeral than I could give."

"You?" said Aldric. "But you didn't even know her . . ."

"She was a sorceress—I am a demon queller. That makes us siblings of a kind. And I do no more than give respect to a sister . . ."

"So it's over," Gueynor said. "At long last." Her relief was undisguised.

"Not yet." Both Marek and the girl looked narrowly at Aldric. He returned their stares without embarrassment and jerked his head toward the darkness of the tower. "Crisen is unaccounted for."

"Crisen is dead," Marek said quietly. "Ythek took him."

"But did you see him dead?" persisted Aldric. "I have my reasons for wanting to be sure . . ."

"No," Marek admitted. "I didn't see him. Because . . ." He hesitated, plainly reluctant to introduce ugliness into the peace of afterwards. "Because if he died as I believe he died, there would be nothing left to see."

"Aldric, please . . ." As he unlaced war-mask and

unbuckled helm and coif, Gueynor touched her fingers gently to the sudden vulnerability of the young *eijo*'s scarred cheek. "Let it go. Dead is dead."

"Maybe so." Aldric remained unconvinced—as unconvinced as Rynert the King also would be. Then he stiffened and his gaze slid past Gueynor to focus on the shadow cast by a rack of weapons. Indrawn breath hissed between his teeth. And the shadow moved.

And he moved. A swift step in front of Gueynor and the Cernuan, and a lifting of his *taiken* to a guard position. "But half dead," he said somberly, "is still alive."

If only just . . . Crisen Geruath had spent only a matter of minutes in the company of demons. Long enough for him to have been obliterated, had that been their intention, yet not long enough for even Ythek Shri to do much which was both delicate and painful. But damage had been done. He lacked an eye, much blood and a deal of living flesh—and it went beyond the merely physical . . . Aldric had seen the expression on Crisen's lacerated face before; then it had been on a hunting dog—but man or dog or any other creature, that vacant blazing of the eyes had just one meaning.

Crisen had gone stark mad.

Gueynor stared in horror and then caught at Aldric's steel-sheathed arm. "Kill him . . ." she whispered.

He glanced sideways, lips skinning from his teeth in a small, appalling smile. "Kill him? Kill that? No . . . If *he* was still Crisen the Overlord then I would kill, and willingly—but *it* is not. That . . . thing is nothing. Less than an animal. Less . . ."—he looked full at the Jouvaine girl—"less even than a wolf."

"What would killing be except a kindness?" Marek said, with a long straight stare at Widowmaker. Aldric caught the look and shook his head just once, turning the *taiken* so that starlight shimmered up and down the blade.

"Pretty . . ." was all he said.

"A kindness," the demon queller repeated with no more attempts at subtlety.

Aldric watched him for a moment, studied Gueynor for the same brief time and nodded. "Just so," he murmured dispassionately. Isileth Widowmaker whispered thinly as she slid into her scabbard. "So show some kindness if you wish. Or not. I am not disposed to it . . ."

They stared at him and then at Crisen; and both huddled unconsciously closer to each other as the sane will do in the presence of insanity and the unremitting hate which is its cousin. The Overlord watched them all. The dull glitter of his one remaining eye did not blink; he scarcely seemed to breathe; even the blood which streaked his lacerated form had long since ceased to flow. About him there was only dreadful immobility.

"God . . ." he said thickly. "My god . . ." It might have been an oath; or a prayer; or a plea for the mercy that was life or maybe death. "My god . . ." Crisen said again. And then his voice rose to a scream: "You killed my god . . . !" He was charging forward now, a reeling, staggering run on flayed and broken feet, and in his ruined hands there gleamed a battle-axe . . .

Aldric did not reply—words were useless here—but his arms thrust out to either side, pitching the demon queller and the girl out of Crisen's way and gaining for himself some space to move.

Barely in time. Sparks and a scraping sound of metal gouging metal came from his shoulder as he flinched aside from underneath the falling axe. Crisen did not shout in triumph, nor utter any war-cry; instead his lips emitted a formless wailing like a dying dog as he stumbled past.

Aldric turned with him, right hand closing on his sword, and Isileth came free in a singing arc of steel. There was scarcely any sound of her point striking home—a slight thud and little more—but the Overlord went down as if his legs were hacked from under him, crashing full-length against the floor and skidding with his own momentum. There was a single cut, less than an inch long, where the base of his skull became the nape of his neck, and this had scarcely bled at all. But it went between the linked bones of his spine and broke the cord within . . .

Crisen lay face downward with his arms, his legs, his body all useless now, and he was dead. But all three had heard his voice in the instant that breath left him. "Oh god . . ." he said. "Oh father . . ." And said no more.

"His father?" wondered Marek.

"Or the Father of Fires, his god?" said Gueynor softly.

Aldric looked down at the corpse as he cleaned and sheathed his sword. "Maybe," he said, and stared out at the pallor in the sky which would become another day. "Maybe . . . But what would make him speak of either—or even think that they would listen . . . ?"

*

Aldric checked his saddle-girth and glanced up towards the sky. It was clear blue: no clouds, no rain, no threat of thunder any more. A summer sky at last. "So," he said in a quiet voice meant for no one's ears but Lyard's and his own, "the sun also rises on this Gate of the Abyss . . ."

"Not so, my lord." Marek, standing beside Gueynor on the steps of the inner citadel, had either heard the words in some strange fashion or had read them from the Alban's lips. "Seghar is not a Gate. Not now. The way is closed."

"Is it?" Patting his courser's neck, Aldric looked towards them across the big Andarran's withers. "Marek Endain, you above all people should know that ways can be reopened. Closed doors can be unlocked." The Alban's right hand touched his crest-collar, and though his voice did not alter he commanded with the full weight of his rank and title in the words: "Stay here; until you are sure that what you claim is true."

Marek did not bow outright—he was a Cernuan and not a man of Alba—but he inclined his head, acknowledging the order as he would one emanating from the king himself.

"Will you not stay, Aldric—even for a little while?" There was an unmistakable note of pleading in Gueynor's eyes. Aldric wavered; *so like Kyrin,* he thought. Then shook his head.

"No. You stay. I have to go . . . in part, to put right what has been set wrong here. Some of my duties remain." Marek gazed at him and nodded, understanding.

"But Aldric . . . !" As he set boot to stirrup and swung into his saddle, Gueynor hurried down the stairs and caught at his leg. "Aldric, what will I do . . . ?"

"Rule," he answered and leaned down to take her hand. "Despite your birth, lady, you are the sole legitimate heir to Seghar. By right of succession and by right of conquest. You are the Overlord, Gueynor." Bending low from the waist, Aldric raised her fingertips and touched them to his forehead in token of respect for her new found rank. "This place is yours, to do with as you will; to hold or to leave. But I ask you one thing only; if you choose to hold Seghar, then give a thought to your dead. Honour them. And hold it well."

*

She stood in the shadow of the Summergate with Marek at her back, and watched as man and horse dwindled slowly towards the forest. Aldric did not look back as he rode away—not even once. That was as she had wished. Yet when the distance-thinned wail of a wolf came drifting down the wind from the Jevaiden, he stiffened in his saddle and made to turn around; but instead recalled his promise and raised one arm instead, as he had at Evthan's funeral. Half in salute, half in farewell.

Then he shook Lyard to a gallop and was swallowed by the trees.

Glossary

-ain. Suffix of friendship or affection. (Alb.)

Altrou. Foster-father; also a title given to priests. (Alb.)

-an. Suffix of courtesy between equals. (Alb.)

Arluth. Lord; master of lands or of a town. (Alb.)

Coyac. Sleeveless jacket of fur, leather or sheepskin. (Jouv.)

Cseirin. Any member of a lord's immediate family. (Alb.)

Cymar. Over-robe for outdoor wear. (Alb.)

Eijo. Wanderer or landless person, especially a lordless warrior. (Alb.)

-eir. Suffix of respect to a superior. (Alb.)

Eldheisart. Imperial military rank next below *hautheisart.* (Drus.)

Elyu-dlas. Formal crested garment in clan colours. (Alb.)

Erhan. Scholar; especially one who travels in order to study. (Alb.)

Exark. Imperial priestly rank; a provincial cleric. (Drus.)

Hlensyarl. Foreigner; a discourteous form. (Drus.)

Ilauem-arluth. Clan-lord. (Alb.)

Kailin. Warrior, man-at-arms. (Alb.)

Kailin-eir. Nobleman of lesser status than *arluth.* (Alb.)

Kortagor. Imperial military rank next below *eldheisart.* (Drus.)

Kourgath. Alban lynx-cat; also a nickname. (Alb.)

an Mergh-Arlethen. Horse-Lords; high-clan Albans living mostly in Prytenon. (Alb.)

Mathern-an arluth. Full title of the King of Alba. (Alb.)

Pesoek. Charm; any lesser spell. (Elth.)

Politark. Imperial priestly rank; a city cleric, superior to *exark*. (Drus.)

Taidyo. Staff-sword; a wooden practice foil. (Alb.)

Taiken. Longsword; the classic *kailin*'s weapon. (Alb.)

Taipan. Shortsword; usually restricted to formal dress *elyu-dlas*. (Alb.)

Taulath. "Shadow-thief"; mercenary spy, saboteur, assassin. (Alb.)

Telek. Spring-gun; close-range personal weapon. (Alb.)

Traugur. Corpse resurrected by necromancy. (Alb.)

Tsalaer. Lamellar cuirass worn without sleeves or leg armour (otherwise *an-moyya-tsalaer* or Great Harness). (Alb.)

Tsepan. Suicide dirk. (Alb.)

Tsepanak'ulleth. Ritual suicide. (Alb.)

Ulleth. Skill, art or "accepted way"; referring to the traditional style. (Alb.)

Ymeth. Dream-smoke; common narcotic drug (Drus.)

CJ Cherryh
Classic Series in New Omnibus Editions

THE DREAMING TREE
Contains the complete duology *The Dreamstone* and *The Tree of Swords and Jewels.*   0-88677-782-8

THE FADED SUN TRILOGY
Contains the complete novels *Kesrith*, *Shon'jir*, and *Kutath.*   0-88677-836-0

THE MORGAINE SAGA
Contains the complete novels *Gate of Ivrel*, *Well of Shiuan*, and *Fires of Azeroth.*   0-88677-877-8

THE CHANUR SAGA
Contains the complete novels *The Pride of Chanur*, *Chanur's Venture* and *The Kif Strike Back.*
0-88677-930-8

ALTERNATE REALITIES
Contains the complete novels *Port Eterntiy*, *Voyager in Night*, and *Wave Without a Shore*   0-88677-946-4

AT THE EDGE OF SPACE
Contains the complete novels *Brothers of Earth* and *Hunter of Worlds.*   0-7564-0160-7

To Order Call: 1-800-788-6262